HIGH CITADEL

LANDSLIDE

Desmond Bagley was born in 1923 in Kendal, Westmorland, and brought up in Blackpool. He began his working life, aged 14, in the printing industry and then did a variety of jobs until going into an aircraft factory at the start of the Second World War.

When the war ended, he decided to travel to southern Africa, going overland through Europe and the Sahara. He worked en route, reaching South Africa in 1951.

Bagley became a freelance journalist in Johannesburg and wrote his first published novel, *The Golden Keel*, in 1962. In 1964 he returned to England and lived in Totnes, Devon, for twelve years. He and his wife Joan then moved to Guernsey in the Channel Islands. Here he found the ideal place for combining his writing and his other interests, which included computers, mathematics, military history, and entertaining friends from all over the world.

Desmond Bagley died in April 1983, having become one of the world's top-selling authors, with his 16 books – two of them published after his death – translated into more than 30 languages.

'I've read all Bagley's books and he's marvellous, the best.'

ALISTAIR MACLEAN

DESMOND BAGLEY

High Citadel

AND

Landslide

HARPER

HARPER
an imprint of HarperCollins*Publishers*
77-85 Fulham Palace Road
Hammersmith, London W6 8JB
www.harpercollins.co.uk

This omnibus edition 2009
1

High Citadel first published in Great Britain by Collins 1965
Landslide first published in Great Britain by Collins 1967
My Old Man's Trumpet first published in *Argosy* magazine 1967

Desmond Bagley asserts the moral right to
be identified as the author of these works

ISBN 978 0 00 730479 0

Printed and bound in Great Britain by
Clays Ltd, St Ives plc

Mixed Sources
Product group from well-managed
forests and other controlled sources
www.fsc.org Cert no. SW-COC-1806
© 1996 Forest Stewardship Council
FSC

FSC is a non-profit international organisation established
to promote the responsible management of the world's forests.
Products carrying the FSC label are independently certified
to assure consumers that they come from forests that are managed
to meet the social, economic and ecological needs
of present and future generations.

Find out more about HarperCollins and the environment at
www.harpercollins.co.uk/green

CONTENTS

High Citadel
1

Landslide
329

My Old Man's Trumpet
635

HIGH CITADEL

To John Donaldson
and Bob Knittel

ONE

The bell shrilled insistently.

O'Hara frowned in his sleep and burrowed deeper into the pillow. He dragged up the thin sheet which covered him, but that left his feet uncovered and there was a sleepy protest from his companion. Without opening his eyes he put his hand out to the bedside table, seized the alarm clock, and hurled it violently across the room. Then he snuggled into the pillow again.

The bell still rang.

At last he opened his eyes, coming to the realization that it was the telephone ringing. He propped himself up on one elbow and stared hatefully into the darkness. Ever since he had been in the hotel he had been asking Ramón to transfer the telephone to the bedside, and every time he had been assured that it would be done tomorrow. It had been nearly a year.

He got out of bed and padded across the room to the dressing-table without bothering to switch on the light. As he picked up the telephone he tweaked aside the window curtain and glanced outside. It was still dark and the moon was setting – he estimated it was about two hours to dawn.

He grunted into the mouthpiece: 'O'Hara.'

'Goddammit, what's the matter with you?' said Filson. 'I've been trying to get you for a quarter of an hour.'

'I was asleep,' said O'Hara. 'I usually sleep at night – I believe most people do, with the exception of Yankee flight managers.'

'Very funny,' said Filson tiredly. 'Well, drag your ass down here – there's a flight scheduled for dawn.'

'What the hell – I just got back six hours ago. I'm tired.'

'You think I'm not?' said Filson. 'This is important – a Samair 727 touched down in an emergency landing and the flight inspector grounded it. The passengers are mad as hornets, so the skipper and the hostess have sorted out priorities and we've got to take passengers to the coast. You know what a connection with Samair means to us; it could be that if we treat 'em nice they'll use us as a regular feeder.'

'In a pig's eye,' said O'Hara. 'They'll use you in an emergency but they'll never put you on their timetables. All you'll get are thanks.'

'It's worth trying,' insisted Filson. 'So get the hell down here.'

O'Hara debated whether to inform Filson that he had already exceeded his month's flying hours and that it was only two-thirds through the month. He sighed, and said, 'All right, I'm coming.' It would cut no ice with Filson to plead regulations; as far as that hard-hearted character was concerned, the I.A.T.A. regulations were meant to be bent, if not broken. If he conformed to every international regulation, his two-cent firm would be permanently in the red.

Besides, O'Hara thought, this was the end of the line for him. If he lost this job survival would be difficult. There were too many broken-down pilots in South America hunting too few jobs and Filson's string-and-sealing-wax outfit was about as low as you could get. Hell, he thought disgustedly, I'm on a bloody escalator going the wrong way – it takes all the running I can do to stay in the same place.

He put down the hand-set abruptly and looked again into the night, scanning the sky. It looked all right here, but what about the mountains? Always he thought about the mountains, those cruel mountains with their jagged white swords stretched skywards to impale him. Filson had better have a good met. report.

He walked to the door and stepped into the corridor, unlit as usual. They turned off all lights in the public rooms at eleven p.m. – it was that kind of hotel. For the millionth time he wondered what he was doing in this godforsaken country, in this tired town, in this sleazy hotel. Unconcernedly naked, he walked down towards the bathroom. In his philosophy if a woman had seen a naked man before then it didn't matter – if she hadn't, it was time she did. Anyway, it was dark.

He showered quickly, washing away the night sweat, and returned to his room and switched on the bedside lamp wondering if it would work. It was always a fifty per cent chance that it wouldn't – the town's electricity supply was very erratic. The filament glowed faintly and in the dim light he dressed – long woollen underwear, jeans, a thick shirt and a leather jacket. By the time he had finished he was sweating again in the warm tropical night. But it would be cold over the mountains.

From the dressing-table he took a metal flask and shook it tentatively. It was only half full and he frowned. He could wake Ramón and get a refill but that was not politic; for one thing Ramón did not like being wakened at night, and for another he would ask cutting questions about when his bill was going to be paid. Perhaps he could get something at the airport.

O'Hara was just leaving when he paused at the door and turned back to look at the sprawling figure in the bed. The sheet had slipped revealing dark breasts tipped a darker colour. He looked at her critically. Her olive skin had an underlying coppery sheen and he thought there was a sizeable admixture of Indian in this one. With a rueful grimace he took a thin wallet from the inside pocket of his leather jacket, extracted two notes and tossed them on the bedside table. Then he went out, closing the door quietly behind him.

II

When he pulled his battered car into the parking bay he looked with interest at the unaccustomed bright lights of the airport. The field was low-grade, classed as an emergency strip by the big operators, although to Filson it was a main base. A Samair Boeing 727 lay sleekly in front of the control tower and O'Hara looked at it enviously for a while, then switched his attention to the hangar beyond.

A Dakota was being loaded and, even at that distance, the lights were bright enough for O'Hara to see the emblem on the tail – two intertwined 'A's, painted artistically to look like mountain peaks. He smiled gently to himself. It was appropriate that he should fly a plane decorated with the Double-A; alcoholics of the world unite – it was a pity Filson didn't see the joke. But Filson was very proud of his Andes Airlift and never joked about it. A humourless man, altogether.

He got out of the car and walked around to the main building to find it was full of people, tired people rudely awakened and set down in the middle of nowhere in the middle of the night. He pushed his way through the crowd towards Filson's office. An American voice with a Western twang complained loudly and bitterly, 'This is a damned disgrace – I'm going to speak to Mr Coulson about it when I get back to Rio.'

O'Hara grinned as he pushed open the door of the office. Filson was sitting at his desk in his shirt-sleeves, his face shiny with sweat. He always sweated, particularly in an emergency and since his life was in a continual state of crisis it was a wonder he didn't melt away altogether. He looked up.

'So you got here at last.'

'I'm always pleased at the welcome I get,' observed O'Hara.

Filson ignored that. 'All right; this is the dope,' he said. 'I've contracted with Samair to take ten of their passengers to Santillana – they're the ones who have to make connections with a ship. You'll take number one – she's being serviced now.' His voice was briskly businesslike and O'Hara could tell by the way he sonorously rolled out the words 'contracted with Samair' that he saw himself as a big-time air operator doing business with his peers instead of what he really was – an ageing ex-pilot making a precarious living off two twenty-five-year-old rattling ex-army surplus planes.

O'Hara merely said, 'Who's coming with me?'

'Grivas.'

'That cocky little bastard.'

'He volunteered – which is more than you did,' snapped Filson.

'Oh?'

'He was here when the 727 touched down,' said Filson. He smiled thinly at O'Hara. 'It was his idea to put it to Samair that we take some of their more urgent passengers, so he phoned me right away. That's the kind of quick thinking we need in this organization.'

'I don't like him in a plane,' said O'Hara.

'So you're a better pilot,' said Filson reluctantly. 'That's why you're skipper and he's going as co-pilot.' He looked at the ceiling reflectively. 'When this deal with Samair comes off maybe I'll promote Grivas to the office. He's too good to be a pilot.'

Filson had delusions of grandeur. O'Hara said deliberately, 'If you think that South American Air is going to give you a feeder contract, you're crazy. You'll get paid for taking their passengers and you'll get their thanks – for what they're worth – and they'll kiss you off fast.'

Filson pointed a pen at O'Hara. 'You're paid to jockey a plane – leave the heavy thinking to me.'

O'Hara gave up. 'What happened to the 727?'

'Something wrong with the fuel feed – they're looking at it now.' Filson picked up a sheaf of papers. 'There's a crate of machinery to go for servicing. Here's the manifest.'

'Christ!' said O'Hara. 'This is an unscheduled flight. Do you have to do this?'

'Unscheduled or not, you're going with a full load. Damned if I send a half empty plane when I can send a full one.'

O'Hara was mournful. 'It's just that I thought I'd have an easy trip for a change. You know you always overload and it's a hell of a job going through the passes. The old bitch wallows like a hippo.'

'You're going at the best time,' said Filson. 'It'll be worse later in the day when the sun has warmed things up. Now get the hell out of here and stop bothering me.'

O'Hara left the office. The main hall was emptying, a stream of disgruntled Samair passengers leaving for the antiquated airport bus. A few people still stood about – those would be the passengers for Santillana. O'Hara ignored them; passengers or freight, it was all one to him. He took them over the Andes and dumped them on the other side and there was no point in getting involved with them. A bus driver doesn't mix with his passengers, he thought; and that's all I am – a bloody vertical bus driver.

He glanced at the manifest. Filson had done it again – there were *two* crates and he was aghast at their weight. One of these days, he thought savagely, I'll get an I.A.T.A. inspector up here at the right time and Filson will go for a loop. He crushed the manifest in his fist and went to inspect the Dakota.

Grivas was by the plane, lounging gracefully against the undercarriage. He straightened when he saw O'Hara and flicked his cigarette across the tarmac but did not step forward to meet him. O'Hara crossed over and said, 'Is the cargo aboard?'

Grivas smiled. 'Yes.'

'Did you check it? Is it secure?'

'Of course, Señor O'Hara. I saw to it myself.'

O'Hara grunted. He did not like Grivas, neither as a man nor as a pilot. He distrusted his smoothness, the slick patina of pseudo good breeding that covered him like a sheen from his patent leather hair and trim toothbrush moustache to his highly polished shoes. Grivas was a slim wiry man, not very tall, who always wore a smile. O'Hara distrusted the smile most of all.

'What's the weather?' he asked.

Grivas looked at the sky. 'It seems all right.'

O'Hara let acid creep into his voice. 'A met. report would be a good thing, don't you think?'

Grivas grinned. 'I'll get it,' he said.

O'Hara watched him go, then turned to the Dakota and walked round to the cargo doors. The Dakota had been one of the most successful planes ever designed, the work-horse of the Allied forces during the war. Over ten thousand of them had fought a good war, flying countless millions of ton-miles of precious freight about the world. It was a good plane in its time, but that was long ago.

This Dakota was twenty-five years old, battered by too many air hours with too little servicing. O'Hara knew the exact amount of play in the rudder cables; he knew how to nurse the worn-out engines so as to get the best out of them – and a poor best it was; he knew the delicate technique of landing so as not to put too much strain on the weakened undercarriage. And he knew that one day the whole sorry fabric would play a murderous trick on him high over the white spears of the Andes.

He climbed into the plane and looked about the cavernous interior. There were ten seats up front, not the luxurious reclining couches of Samair but uncomfortable hard leather chairs each fitted with the safety-belt that even Filson could not skip, although he had grumbled at the added cost. The rest of the fuselage was devoted to cargo space and was at present occupied by two large crates.

O'Hara went round them testing the anchoring straps with his hand. He had a horror that one day the cargo would slide forward if he made a bad landing or hit very bad turbulence. That would be the end of any passengers who had the ill-luck to be flying Andes Airlift. He cursed as he found a loose strap. Grivas and his slipshod ways would be the end of him one day.

Having seen the cargo was secured he went forward into the cockpit and did a routine check of the instruments. A mechanic was working on the port engine so O'Hara leaned out of the side window and asked in Spanish if it was all right. The mechanic spat, then drew his finger across his throat and made a bloodcurdling sound. *'De un momento a otro.'*

He finished the instrument check and went into the hangar to find Fernandez, the chief mechanic, who usually had a bottle or two stored away, strictly against Filson's orders. O'Hara liked Fernandez and he knew that Fernandez liked him; they got on well together and O'Hara made a point of keeping it that way – to be at loggerheads with the chief mechanic would be a passport to eternity in this job.

He chatted for a while with Fernandez, then filled his flask and took a hasty gulp from the bottle before he passed it back. Dawn was breaking as he strode back to the Dakota, and

Grivas was in the cockpit fussing with the disposal of his brief-case. It's a funny thing, thought O'Hara, that the briefcase is just as much a part of an airline pilot as it is of any city gent. His own was under his seat; all it contained was a packet of sandwiches which he had picked up at an all-night café.

'Got the met. report?' he asked Grivas.

Grivas passed over the sheet of paper and O'Hara said, 'You can taxi her down to the apron.'

He studied the report. It wasn't too bad – it wasn't bad at all. No storms, no anomalies, no trouble – just good weather over the mountains. But O'Hara had known the meteorol-ogists to be wrong before and there was no release of the tension within him. It was that tension, never relaxed in the air, that had kept him alive when a lot of better men had died.

As the Dakota came to a halt on the apron outside the main building, he saw Filson leading the small group of pas-sengers. 'See they have their seat-belts properly fastened,' he said to Grivas.

'I'm not a hostess,' said Grivas sulkily.

'When you're sitting on this side of the cockpit you can give orders,' said O'Hara coldly. 'Right now you take them. And I'd like you to do a better job of securing the passen-gers than you did of the cargo.'

The smile left Grivas's face, but he turned and went into the main cabin. Presently Filson came forward and thrust a form at O'Hara. 'Sign this.'

It was the I.A.T.A. certificate of weights and fuel. O'Hara saw that Filson had cheated on the weights as usual, but made no comment and scribbled his signature. Filson said, 'As soon as you land give me a ring. There might be return cargo.'

O'Hara nodded and Filson withdrew. There was the dou-ble slam as the door closed and O'Hara said, 'Take her to the end of the strip.' He switched on the radio, warming it up.

Grivas was still sulky and would not talk. He made no answer as he revved the engines and the Dakota waddled away from the main building into the darkness, ungainly and heavy on the ground. At the end of the runway O'Hara thought for a moment. Filson had not given him a flight number. To hell with it, he thought; control ought to know what's going on. He clicked on the microphone and said, 'A.A. special flight, destination Santillana – A.A. to San Croce control – ready to take off.'

A voice crackled tinnily in his ear. 'San Croce control to Andes Airlift special. Permission given – time 2.33 G.M.T.'

'Roger and out.' He put his hand to the throttles and waggled the stick. There was a stickiness about it. Without looking at Grivas he said, 'Take your hands off the controls.' Then he pushed on the throttle levers and the engines roared. Four minutes later the Dakota was airborne after an excessively long run.

He stayed at the controls for an hour, personally supervising the long climb to the roof of the world. He liked to find out if the old bitch was going to spring a new surprise. Cautiously he carried out gentle, almost imperceptible evolutions, his senses attuned to the feel of the plane. Occasionally he glanced at Grivas who was sitting frozen-faced in the other seat, staring blankly through the windscreen.

At last he was satisfied and engaged the automatic pilot but spent another quarter-hour keeping a wary eye on it. It had behaved badly on the last flight but Fernandez had assured him that it was now all right. He trusted Fernandez, but not that much – it was always better to do the final check personally.

Then he relaxed and looked ahead. It was much lighter in the high air and, although the dawn was behind, the sky ahead was curiously light. O'Hara knew why; it was the snow blink as the first light of the sun caught the high white peaks of the Andes. The mountains themselves were as yet invisible, lost in the early haze rising from the jungle below.

He began to think about his passengers and he wondered if they knew what they had got themselves into. This was no pressurized jet aircraft and they were going to fly pretty high – it would be cold and the air would be thin and he hoped none of the passengers had heart trouble. Presumably Filson had warned them, although he wouldn't put it past that bastard to keep his mouth shut. He was even too stingy to provide decent oxygen masks – there were only mouth tubes in the oxygen bottles to port and starboard.

He scratched his cheek thoughtfully. These weren't the ordinary passengers he was used to carrying – the American mining engineers flying to San Croce and the poorer type of local businessman proud to be flying even by Andes Airlift. These were the Samair type of passengers – wealthy and not over fond of hardship. They were in a hurry, too, or they would have had more sense than to fly Andes Airlift. Perhaps he had better break his rule and go back to talk to them. When they found they weren't going to fly over the Andes but *through* them they might get scared. It would be better to warn them first.

He pushed his uniform cap to the back of his head and said, 'Take over, Grivas. I'm going to talk to the passengers.'

Grivas lifted his eyebrows – so surprised that he forgot to be sulky. He shrugged. 'Why? What is so important about the passengers? Is this Samair?' He laughed noiselessly. 'But, yes, of course – you have seen the girl; you want to see her again, eh?'

'What girl?'

'Just a girl, a woman; very beautiful. I think I will get to know her and take her out when we arrive in – er – Santillana,' said Grivas thoughtfully. He looked at O'Hara out of the corner of his eye.

O'Hara grunted and took the passenger manifest from his breast pocket. As he suspected, the majority were American. He went through the list rapidly. Mr and Mrs Coughlin of Challis, Idaho – tourists; Dr James Armstrong, London, England – no profession stated; Raymond Forester of New York – businessman; Señor and Señorita Montes – Argentinian and no profession stated; Miss Jennifer Ponsky of South Bridge, Connecticut – tourist; Dr Willis of California; Miguel Rohde – no stated nationality, profession – importer; Joseph Peabody of Chicago, Illinois – businessman.

He flicked his finger on the manifest and grinned at Grivas. 'Jennifer's a nice name – but Ponsky? I can't see you going around with anyone called Ponsky.'

Grivas looked startled, then laughed convulsively. 'Ah, my friend, you can have the fair Ponsky – I'll stick to my girl.'

O'Hara looked at the list again. 'Then it must be Señorita Montes – unless it's Mrs Coughlin.'

Grivas chuckled, his good spirits recovered. 'You find out for yourself.'

'I'll do that,' said O'Hara. 'Take over.'

He went back into the main cabin and was confronted by ten uplifted heads. He smiled genially, modelling himself on the Samair pilots to whom public relations was as important as flying ability. Lifting his voice above the roar of the engines, he said, 'I suppose I ought to tell you that we'll be reaching the mountains in about an hour. It will get cold, so I suggest you wear your overcoats. Mr Filson will have told you that this aircraft isn't pressurized, but we don't fly at any great height for more than an hour, so you'll be quite all right.'

A burly man with a whisky complexion interjected, 'No one told me that.'

O'Hara cursed Filson under his breath and broadened his smile. 'Well, not to worry, Mr – er . . .'

'Peabody – Joe Peabody.'

'Mr Peabody. It will be quite all right. There is an oxygen mouthpiece next to every seat which I advise you to use if you feel breathing difficult. Now, it gets a bit wearying shouting like this above the engine noise, so I'll come round and talk to you individually.' He smiled at Peabody, who glowered back at him.

He bent to the first pair of seats on the port side. 'Could I have your names, please?'

The first man said, 'I'm Forester.' The other contributed, 'Willis.'

'Glad to have you aboard, Dr Willis, Mr Forester.'

Forester said, 'I didn't bargain for this, you know. I didn't think kites like this were still flying.'

O'Hara smiled deprecatingly. 'Well, this is an emergency flight and it was laid on in the devil of a hurry. I'm sure it was an oversight that Mr Filson forgot to tell you that this isn't a pressurized plane.' Privately he was not sure of anything of the kind.

Willis said with a smile. 'I came here to study high altitude conditions. I'm certainly starting with a bang. How high do we fly, Captain?'

'Not more than seventeen thousand feet,' said O'Hara. 'We fly through the passes – we don't go over the top. You'll find the oxygen mouthpieces easy to use – all you do is suck.' He smiled and turned away and found himself held. Peabody was clutching his sleeve, leaning forward over the seat behind. 'Hey, Skipper . . .'

'I'll be with you in a moment, Mr Peabody,' said O'Hara, and held Peabody with his eye. Peabody blinked rapidly, released his grip and subsided into his seat, and O'Hara turned to starboard.

The man was elderly, with an aquiline nose and a short grey beard. With him was a young girl of startling beauty, judging by what O'Hara could see of her face, which was not much because she was huddled deep into a fur coat. He said, 'Señor Montes?'

The man inclined his head. 'Don't worry, Captain, we know what to expect.' He waved a gloved hand. 'You see we are well prepared. I know the Andes, señor, and I know these aircraft. I know the Andes well; I have been over them on foot and by mule – in my youth I climbed some of the high peaks – didn't I, Benedetta?'

'*Si, tío,*' she said in a colourless voice. 'But that was long ago. I don't know if your heart . . .'

He patted her on the leg. 'I will be all right if I relax; is that not so, Captain?'

'Do you understand the use of this oxygen tube?' asked O'Hara.

Montes nodded confidently, and O'Hara said, 'Your uncle will be quite all right, Señorita Montes.' He waited for her to reply but she made no answer, so he passed on to the seats behind.

These couldn't be the Coughlins; they were too ill-assorted a pair to be American tourists, although the woman was undoubtedly American. O'Hara said inquiringly, 'Miss Ponsky?'

She lifted a sharp nose and said, 'I declare this is all wrong, Captain. You must turn back at once.'

The fixed smile on O'Hara's face nearly slipped. 'I fly this route regularly, Miss Ponsky,' he said. 'There is nothing to fear.'

But there was naked fear on her face – air fear. Sealed in the air-conditioned quietness of a modern jet-liner she could subdue it, but the primitiveness of the Dakota brought it to the surface. There was no clever decor to deceive her into thinking that she was in a drawing-room, just the stark functionalism of unpainted aluminium, battered and scratched, and with the plumbing showing like a dissected body.

O'Hara said quietly, 'What is your profession, Miss Ponsky?'

'I'm a school teacher back in South Bridge,' she said. 'I've been teaching there for thirty years.'

He judged she was naturally garrulous and perhaps this could be a way of conquering her fear. He glanced at the man, who said, 'Miguel Rohde.'

He was a racial anomaly – a Spanish-German name and Spanish-German features – straw-coloured hair and beady black eyes. There had been German immigration into South America for many years and this was one of the results.

O'Hara said, 'Do you know the Andes, Señor Rohde?'

'Very well,' he replied in a grating voice. He nodded ahead. 'I lived up there for many years – now I am going back.'

O'Hara switched back to Miss Ponsky. 'Do you teach geography, Miss Ponsky?'

She nodded. 'Yes, I do. That's one of the reasons I came to South America on my vacation. It makes such a difference if you can describe things first-hand.'

'Then here you have a marvellous opportunity,' said O'Hara with enthusiasm. 'You'll see the Andes as you never would if you'd flown Samair. And I'm sure that Señor Rohde will point out the interesting sights.'

Rohde nodded understandingly. '*Si*, very interesting; I know it well, the mountain country.'

O'Hara smiled reassuringly at Miss Ponsky, who offered him a glimmering, tremulous smile in return. He caught a twinkle in Rohde's black eyes as he turned to the port side again.

The man sitting next to Peabody was undoubtedly British, so O'Hara said, 'Glad to have you with us, Dr Armstrong – Mr Peabody.'

Armstrong said, 'Nice to hear an English accent, Captain, after all this Spa – '

Peabody broke in. 'I'm damned if I'm glad to be here, Skipper. What in hell kind of an airline is this, for god-sake?'

'One run by an American, Mr Peabody,' said O'Hara calmly. 'As you were saying, Dr Armstrong?'

'Never expected to see an English captain out here,' said Armstrong.

'Well, I'm Irish, and we tend to get about,' said O'Hara. 'I'd put on some warm clothing if I were you. You, too, Mr Peabody.'

Peabody laughed and suddenly burst into song. '"I've got my love to keep me warm".' He produced a hip flask and waved it. 'This is as good as any top-coat.'

For a moment O'Hara saw himself in Peabody and was shocked and afraid. 'As you wish,' he said bleakly, and passed on to the last pair of seats opposite the luggage racks.

The Coughlins were an elderly couple, very Darby and Joanish. He must have been pushing seventy and she was not far behind, but there was a suggestion of youth about their eyes, good-humoured and with a zest for life. O'Hara said, 'Are you all right, Mrs Coughlin?'

'Fine,' she said. 'Aren't we, Harry?'

'Sure,' said Coughlin, and looked up at O'Hara. 'Will we be flying through the Puerto de las Aguilas?'

'That's right,' said O'Hara. 'Do you know these parts?'

Coughlin laughed. 'Last time I was round here was in 1912. I've just come down to show my wife where I spent my misspent youth.' He turned to her. 'That means Eagle Pass, you know; it took me two weeks to get across back in 1910, and here we are doing it in an hour or two. Isn't it wonderful?'

'It sure is,' Mrs Coughlin replied comfortably.

There was nothing wrong with the Coughlins, decided O'Hara, so after a few more words he went back to the cockpit. Grivas still had the plane on automatic pilot and was sitting relaxed, gazing forward at the mountains. O'Hara sat down and looked intently at the oncoming mountain wall. He checked the course and said, 'Keep taking a bearing on Chimitaxl and let me know when it's two hundred and ten degrees true bearing. You know the drill.'

He stared down at the ground looking for landmarks and nodded with satisfaction as he saw the sinuous, twisting course of the Rio Sangre and the railway bridge that crossed it. Flying this route by day and for so long he knew the ground by heart and knew immediately whether he was on time. He judged that the north-west wind predicted by the meteorologists was a little stronger than they had prophesied and altered course accordingly, then he jacked in the auto pilot again and relaxed. All would be quiet until Grivas came up with the required bearing on Chimitaxl. He sat in repose and watched the ground slide away behind – the dun and olive foothills, craggy bare rock, and then the shining snow-covered peaks. Presently he munched on the sandwiches he took from his briefcase. He thought of washing them down with a drink from his flask but then he thought of Peabody's whisky-sodden face. Something inside him seemed to burst and he found that he didn't need a drink after all.

Grivas suddenly put down the bearing compass. 'Thirty seconds,' he said.

O'Hara looked at the wilderness of high peaks before him, a familiar wilderness. Some of these mountains were his friends, like Chimitaxl; they pointed out his route. Others were his deadly enemies – devils and demons lurked among them compounded of down draughts, driving snow and mists. But he was not afraid because it was all familiar and he knew and understood the dangers and how to escape them.

Grivas said, 'Now,' and O'Hara swung the control column gently, experience telling him the correct turn. His feet

automatically moved in conjunction with his hands and the
Dakota swept to port in a wide, easy curve, heading for a
gap in the towering wall ahead.

Grivas said softly, 'Señor O'Hara.'

'Don't bother me now.'

'But I must,' said Grivas, and there was a tiny metallic
click.

O'Hara glanced at him out of the corner of his eye and
stiffened as he saw that Grivas was pointing a gun at him –
a compact automatic pistol.

He jerked his head, his eyes widening in disbelief. 'Have
you gone crazy?'

Grivas's smiled widened. 'Does it matter?' he said indifferently. 'We do not go through the Puerto de las Aguilas
this trip, Señor O'Hara, that is all that matters.' His voice
hardened. 'Now steer course one-eight-four on a true bearing.'

O'Hara took a deep breath and held his course. 'You
must have gone out of your mind,' he said. 'Put down that
gun, Grivas, and maybe we'll forget this. I suppose I have
been bearing down on you a bit too much, but that's no reason to pull a gun. Put it away and we'll straighten things out
when we get to Santillana.'

Grivas's teeth flashed. 'You're a stupid man, O'Hara; do
you think I do this for personal reasons? But since you
mention it, you said not long ago that sitting in the captain's
seat gave you authority.' He lifted the gun slightly. 'You
were wrong – this gives authority; all the authority there is.
Now change course or I'll blow your head off. I can fly this
aircraft too, remember.'

'They'd hear you inside,' said O'Hara.

'I've locked the door, and what could they do? They
wouldn't take the controls from the only pilot. But that
would be of no consequence to you, O'Hara – you'd be
dead.'

O'Hara saw his finger tighten on the trigger and bit his lip before swinging the control column. The Dakota turned to fly south, parallel to the main backbone of the Andes. Grivas was right, damn him; there was no point in getting himself killed. But what the hell was he up to?

He settled on the bearing given by Grivas and reached forward to the auto pilot control. Grivas jerked the gun. 'No, Señor O'Hara; you fly this aircraft – it will give you something to do.'

O'Hara drew back his hand slowly and grasped the wheel. He looked out to starboard past Grivas at the high peaks drifting by. 'Where are we going?' he asked grimly.

'That is of no consequence,' said Grivas. 'But it is not very far. We land at an airstrip in five minutes.'

O'Hara thought about that. There was no airstrip that he knew of on this course. There were no airstrips at all this high in the mountains except for the military strips, and those were on the Pacific side of the Andes chain. He would have to wait and see.

His eyes flickered to the microphone set on its hook close to his left hand. He looked at Grivas and saw he was not wearing his earphones. If the microphone was switched on then any loud conversation would go on the air and Grivas would be unaware of it. It was definitely worth trying.

He said to Grivas, 'There are no airstrips on this course.' His left hand strayed from the wheel.

'You don't know everything, O'Hara.'

His fingers touched the microphone and he leaned over to obstruct Grivas's vision as much as possible, pretending to study the instruments. His fingers found the switch and he snapped it over and then he leaned back and relaxed. In a loud voice he said, 'You'll never get away with this, Grivas; you can't steal a whole aeroplane so easily. When this

Dakota is overdue at Santillana they'll lay on a search – you know that as well as I do.'

Grivas laughed. 'Oh, you're clever, O'Hara – but I was cleverer. The radio is not working, you know. I took out the tubes when you were talking to the passengers.'

O'Hara felt a sudden emptiness in the pit of his stomach. He looked at the jumble of peaks ahead and felt frightened. This was country he did not know and there would be dangers he could not recognize. He felt frightened for himself and for his passengers.

III

It was cold in the passenger cabin, and the air was thin. Señor Montes had blue lips and his face had turned grey. He sucked on the oxygen tube and his niece fumbled in her bag and produced a small bottle of pills. He smiled painfully and put a pill in his mouth, letting it dissolve on his tongue. Slowly some colour came back into his face; not a lot, but he looked better than he had before taking the pill.

In the seat behind, Miss Ponsky's teeth were chattering, not with cold but with conversation. Already Miguel Rohde had learned much of her life history, in which he had not the slightest interest although he did not show it. He let her talk, prompting her occasionally, and all the time he regarded the back of Montes's head with lively black eyes. At a question from Miss Ponsky he looked out of the window and suddenly frowned.

The Coughlins were also looking out of the window. Mr Coughlin said, 'I'd have sworn we were going to head that way – through that pass. But we suddenly changed course south.'

'It all looks the same to me,' said Mrs Coughlin. 'Just a lot of mountains and snow.'

Coughlin said, 'From what I remember, El Puerto de las Aguilas is back there.'

'Oh, Harry, I'm sure you don't really remember. It's nearly fifty years since you were here – and you never saw it from an airplane.'

'Maybe,' he said, unconvinced. 'But it sure is funny.'

'Now, Harry, the pilot knows what he's doing. He looked a nice efficient young man to me.'

Coughlin continued to look from the window. He said nothing more.

James Armstrong of London, England, was becoming very bored with Joe Peabody of Chicago, Illinois. The man was a positive menace. Already he had sunk half the contents of his flask, which seemed an extraordinarily large one, and he was getting combatively drunk. 'Whadya think of the nerve of that goddam fly-boy, chokin' me off like that?' he demanded. 'Actin' high an' mighty jus' like the goddam limey he is.'

Armstrong smiled gently. 'I'm a – er – goddam limey too, you know,' he pointed out.

'Well, jeez, presen' comp'ny excepted,' said Peabody. 'That's always the rule, ain't it? I ain't got anything against you limeys really, excep' you keep draggin' us into your wars.'

'I take it you read the *Chicago Tribune*,' said Armstrong solemnly.

Forester and Willis did not talk much – they had nothing in common. Willis had produced a large book as soon as they exhausted their small talk and to Forester it looked heavy in all senses of the word, being mainly mathematical.

Forester had nothing to do. In front of him was an aluminium bulkhead on which an axe and a first-aid box were mounted. There was no profit in looking at that and consequently his eyes frequently strayed across the aisle to

Señor Montes. His lips tightened as he noted the bad
colour of Montes's face and he looked at the first-aid box
reflectively.

IV

'There it is,' said Grivas. 'You land there.'

O'Hara straightened up and looked over the nose of the
Dakota. Dead ahead amid a jumble of rocks and snow was
a short airstrip, a mere track cut on a ledge of a mountain.
He had time for the merest glimpse before it was gone
behind them.

Grivas waved the gun. 'Circle it,' he said.

O'Hara eased the plane into an orbit round the strip and
looked down at it. There were buildings down there, rough
cabins in a scattered group, and there was a road leading
down the mountain, twisting and turning like a snake.
Someone had thoughtfully cleared the airstrip of snow, but
there was no sign of life.

He judged his distance from the ground and glanced at
the altimeter. 'You're crazy, Grivas,' he said. 'We can't land
on that strip.'

'You can, O'Hara,' said Grivas.

'I'm damned if I'm going to. This plane's overloaded and
that strip's at an altitude of seventeen thousand feet. It
would need to be three times as long for this crate to land
safely. The air's too thin to hold us up at a slow landing
speed – we'll hit the ground at a hell of a lick and we won't
be able to pull up. We'll shoot off the other end of the strip
and crash on the side of the mountain.'

'You can do it.'

'To hell with you,' said O'Hara.

Grivas lifted his gun. 'All right, I'll do it,' he said. 'But I'll
have to kill you first.'

O'Hara looked at the black hole staring at him like an evil eye. He could see the rifling inside the muzzle and it looked as big as a howitzer. In spite of the cold, he was sweating and could feel rivulets of perspiration running down his back. He turned away from Grivas and studied the strip again. 'Why are you doing this?' he asked.

'You would not know if I told you,' said Grivas. 'You would not understand – you are English.'

O'Hara sighed. It was going to be very dicey; *he* might be able to get the Dakota down in approximately one piece, but Grivas wouldn't have a chance – he'd pile it up for sure. He said, 'All right – warn the passengers; get them to the rear of the cabin.'

'Never mind the passengers,' said Grivas flatly. 'You do not think that I am going to leave this cockpit?'

O'Hara said, 'All right, you're calling the shots, but I warn you – don't touch the controls by as much as a finger. You're not a pilot's backside – and you know it. There can be only one man flying a plane.'

'Get on with it,' said Grivas shortly.

'I'll take my own time,' said O'Hara. 'I want a good look before I do a damn thing.'

He orbited the airstrip four more times, watching it as it spun crazily beneath the Dakota. The passengers should know there was something wrong by this time, he thought. No ordinary airliner stood on its wingtip and twitched about like this. Maybe they'd get alarmed and someone would try to do something about it – that might give him a chance to get at Grivas. But what the passengers could do was problematical.

The strip was all too short; it was also very narrow and made for a much smaller aircraft. He would have to land on the extreme edge, his wingtip brushing a rock wall. Then there was the question of wind direction. He looked down at the cabins, hoping to detect a wisp of smoke from the chimneys, but there was nothing.

'I'm going to go in closer – over the strip,' he said. 'But I'm not landing this time.'

He pulled out of orbit and circled widely to come in for a landing approach. He lined up the nose of the Dakota on the strip like a gunsight and the plane came in, fast and level. To starboard there was a blur of rock and snow and O'Hara held his breath. If the wingtip touched the rock wall that would be the end. Ahead, the strip wound under-neath, as though it was being swallowed by the Dakota. There was nothing as the strip ended – just a deep valley and the blue sky. He hauled on the stick and the plane shot skyward.

The passengers will know damn well there's something wrong now, he thought. To Grivas he said, 'We're not going to get this aircraft down in one piece.'

'Just get me down safely,' said Grivas. 'I'm the only one who matters.'

O'Hara grinned tightly. 'You don't matter a damn to me.'

'Then think of your own neck,' said Grivas. 'That will take care of mine, too.'

But O'Hara was thinking of ten lives in the passenger cabin. He circled widely again to make another approach and debated with himself the best way of doing this. He could come in with the undercarriage up or down. A belly-landing would be rough at that speed, but the plane would slow down faster because of the increased friction. The ques-tion was: could he hold her straight? On the other hand if he came in with the undercarriage down he would lose air-speed before he hit the deck – that was an advantage too.

He smiled grimly and decided to do both. For the first time he blessed Filson and his lousy aeroplanes. He knew to a hair how much stress the undercarriage would take; hitherto his problem had been that of putting the Dakota down gently. This time he would come in with under-carriage down, losing speed, and slam her down hard – hard enough to break off the weakened struts like matchsticks. That would give him his belly-landing, too.

He sighted the nose of the Dakota on the strip again. 'Well, here goes nothing,' he said. 'Flaps down; under-carriage down.'

As the plane lost airspeed the controls felt mushy under his hands. He set his teeth and concentrated as never before.

V

As the plane tipped wing down and started to orbit the airstrip Armstrong was thrown violently against Peabody. Peabody was in the act of taking another mouthful of whisky and the neck of the flask suddenly jammed against his teeth. He spluttered and yelled incoherently and thrust hard against Armstrong.

Rohde was thrown out of his seat and found himself sitting in the aisle, together with Coughlin and Montes. He struggled to his feet, shaking his head violently, then he bent to help Montes, speaking quick Spanish. Mrs Coughlin helped her husband back to his seat.

Willis had been making a note in the margin of his book and the point of his pencil snapped as Forester lurched against him. Forester made no attempt to regain his position but looked incredulously out of the window, ignoring Willis's feeble protests at being squashed. Forester was a big man.

The whole cabin was a babel of sound in English and Spanish, dominated by the sharp and scratchy voice of Miss Ponsky as she querulously complained. 'I knew it,' she screamed. 'I knew it was all wrong.' She began to laugh hysterically and Rohde turned from Montes and slapped her with a heavy hand. She looked at him in surprise and suddenly burst into tears.

Peabody shouted, 'What in goddam hell is that limey doing now?' He stared out of the window at the airstrip. 'The bastard's going to land.'

Rohde spoke rapidly to Montes, who seemed so shaken he was apathetic. There was a quick exchange in Spanish between Rohde and the girl, and he pointed to the door leading to the cockpit. She nodded violently and he stood up.

Mrs Coughlin was leaning forward in her seat, comforting Miss Ponsky. 'Nothing's going to happen,' she kept saying. 'Nothing bad is going to happen.'

The aircraft straightened as O'Hara came in for his first approach run. Rohde leaned over Armstrong and looked through the window, but turned as Miss Ponsky screamed in fright, looking at the blur of rock streaming past the starboard window and seeing the wingtip brushing it so closely. Then Rohde lost his balance again as O'Hara pulled the Dakota into a climb.

It was Forester who made the first constructive move. He was nearest the door leading to the cockpit and he grabbed the door handle, turned and pushed. Nothing happened. He put his shoulder to the door but was thrown away as the plane turned rapidly. O'Hara was going into his final landing approach.

Forester grabbed the axe from its clips on the bulkhead and raised it to strike, but his arm was caught by Rohde. 'This is quicker,' said Rohde, and lifted a heavy pistol in his other hand. He stepped in front of Forester and fired three quick shots at the lock of the door.

VI

O'Hara heard the shots a fraction of a second before the Dakota touched down. He not only heard them but saw the altimeter and the turn-and-climb indicator shiver into fragments as the bullets smashed into the instrument panel. But he had not time to see what was happening behind him because just then the heavily overloaded Dakota settled soggily at the extreme end of the strip, moving at high speed.

There was a sickening crunch and the whole air frame shuddered as the undercarriage collapsed and the plane sank on to its belly and slid with a tearing, rending sound towards the far end of the strip. O'Hara fought frantically with the controls as they kicked against his hands and feet and tried to keep the aircraft sliding in a straight line.

Out of the corner of his eye he saw Grivas turn to the door, his pistol raised. O'Hara took a chance, lifted one hand from the stick and struck out blindly at Grivas. He just had time for one blow and luckily it connected somewhere; he felt the edge of his hand strike home and then he was too busy to see if he had incapacitated Grivas.

The Dakota was still moving too fast. Already it was more than halfway down the strip and O'Hara could see the emptiness ahead where the strip stopped at the lip of the valley. In desperation he swung the rudder hard over and the Dakota swerved with a loud grating sound.

He braced himself for the crash.

The starboard wingtip hit the rock wall and the Dakota spun sharply to the right. O'Hara kept the rudder forced right over and saw the rock wall coming right at him. The nose of the plane hit rock and crumpled and the safety glass in the windscreens shivered into opacity. Then something hit him on the head and he lost consciousness.

VII

He came round because someone was slapping his face. His head rocked from side to side and he wanted them to stop because it was so good to be asleep. The slapping went on and on and he moaned and tried to tell them to stop. But the slapping did not stop so he opened his eyes.

It was Forester who was administering the punishment, and, as O'Hara opened his eyes, he turned to Rohde who was standing behind him and said, 'Keep your gun on him.'

Rohde smiled. His gun was in his hand but hanging slackly and pointing to the floor. He made no attempt to bring it up. Forester said, 'What the hell did you think you were doing?'

O'Hara painfully lifted his arm to his head. He had a bump on his skull the size of an egg. He said weakly, 'Where's Grivas?'

'Who is Grivas?'

'My co-pilot.'

'He's here – he's in a bad way.'

'I hope the bastard dies,' said O'Hara bitterly. 'He pulled a gun on me.'

'You were at the controls,' said Forester, giving him a hard look. 'You put this plane down here – and I want to know why.'

'It was Grivas – he forced me to do it.'

'The *señor capitan* is right,' said Rohde. 'This man Grivas was going to shoot me and the *señor capitan* hit him.' He bowed stiffly. *'Muchas gracias.'*

Forester swung round and looked at Rohde, then beyond him to Grivas. 'Is he conscious?'

O'Hara looked across the cockpit. The side of the fuselage was caved in and a blunt spike of rock had hit Grivas in the chest, smashing his rib cage. It looked as though he wasn't going to make it, after all. But he was conscious, all right; his eyes were open and he looked at them with hatred.

O'Hara could hear a woman screaming endlessly in the passenger cabin and someone else was moaning monotonously. 'For Christ's sake, what's happened back there?'

No one answered because Grivas began to speak. He mumbled in a low whisper and blood frothed round his mouth. 'They'll get you,' he said. 'They'll be here any minute now.' His lips parted in a ghastly smile. 'I'll be all right; they'll take me to hospital. But you – you'll . . .' He broke off in a fit of coughing and then continued: '. . . they'll kill the lot of you.' He lifted up his arm, the fingers curling into a fist. *'Vivaca . . .'*

The arm dropped flaccidly and the look of hate in his eyes deepened into surprise – surprise that he was dead.

Rohde grabbed him by the wrist and held it for a moment. 'He's gone,' he said.

'He was a lunatic,' said O'Hara. 'Stark, staring mad.'

The woman was still screaming and Forester said, 'For God's sake, let's get everybody out of here.'

Just then the Dakota lurched sickeningly and the whole cockpit rose in the air. There was a ripping sound as the spike of rock that had killed Grivas tore at the aluminium sheathing of the fuselage. O'Hara had a sudden and horrible intuition of what was happening. 'Nobody move,' he shouted. 'Everyone keep still.'

He turned to Forester. 'Bash in those windows.'

Forester looked in surprise at the axe he was still holding as though he had forgotten it, then he raised it and struck at the opaque windscreen. The plastic filling in the glass sandwich could not withstand his assault and he made a hole big enough for a man to climb through.

O'Hara said, 'I'll go through – I think I know what I'll find. Don't either of you go back there – not yet. And call through and tell anyone who can move to come up front.'

He squeezed through the narrow gap and was astonished to find that the nose of the Dakota was missing. He twisted and crawled out on to the top of the fuselage and looked aft. The tail and one wing were hanging in space over the valley where the runway ended. The whole aircraft was delicately balanced and even as he looked the tail tipped a little and there was a ripping sound from the cockpit.

He twisted on to his stomach and wriggled so that he could look into the cockpit, his head upside-down. 'We're in a jam,' he said to Forester. 'We're hanging over a two-hundred-foot drop, and the only thing that's keeping the whole bloody aeroplane from tipping over is that bit of rock there.' He indicated the rock projection driven into the side of the cockpit.

He said, 'If anyone goes back there the extra weight might send us over because we're balanced just like a see-saw.'

Forester turned his head and bawled, 'Anyone who can move, come up here.'

There was a movement and Willis staggered through the door, his head bloody. Forester shouted, 'Anyone else?'

Señorita Montes called urgently, 'Please help my uncle – oh, please.'

Rohde drew Willis out of the way and stepped through the door. Forester said sharply, 'Don't go in too far.'

Rohde did not even look at him, but bent to pick up Montes who was lying by the door. He half carried, half dragged him into the cockpit and Señorita Montes followed.

Forester looked up at O'Hara. 'It's getting crowded in here; I think we'd better start getting people outside.'

'We'll get them on top first,' said O'Hara. 'The more weight we have at this end, the better. Let the girl come first.'

She shook her head. 'My uncle first.'

'For God's sake, he's unconscious,' said Forester. 'You go out – I'll look after him.'

She shook her head stubbornly and O'Hara broke in impatiently, 'All right, Willis, come on up here; let's not waste time.' His head ached and he was panting in the thin air; he was not inclined to waste time over silly girls.

He helped Willis through the smashed windscreen and saw him settle on top of the fuselage. When he looked into the cockpit again it was evident that the girl had changed her mind. Rohde was talking quietly but emphatically to her and she crossed over and O'Hara helped her out.

Armstrong came next, having made his own way to the cockpit. He said, 'It's a bloody shambles back there. I think the old man in the back seat is dead and his wife is pretty badly hurt. I don't think it's safe to move her.'

'What about Peabody?'

'The luggage was thrown forward on to both of us. He's half buried under it. I tried to get him free but I couldn't.'

O'Hara passed this on to Forester. Rohde was kneeling by Montes, trying to bring him round. Forester hesitated, then said, 'Now we've got some weight at this end it might be safe for me to go back.'

O'Hara said, 'Tread lightly.'

Forester gave a mirthless grin and went back through the door. He looked at Miss Ponsky. She was sitting rigid, her arms clutched tightly about her, her eyes staring unblinkingly at nothing. He ignored her and began to heave suitcases from the top of Peabody, being careful to stow them in the front seats. Peabody stirred and Forester shook him into consciousness, and as soon as he seemed to be able to understand, said, 'Go into the cockpit – the cockpit, you understand,'

Peabody nodded blearily and Forester stepped a little farther aft. 'Christ Almighty!' he whispered, shocked at what he saw.

Coughlin was a bloody pulp. The cargo had shifted in the smash and had come forward, crushing the two back seats. Mrs Coughlin was still alive but both her legs had been cut off just below the knee. It was only because she had been leaning forward to comfort Miss Ponsky that she hadn't been killed like her husband.

Forester felt something touch his back and turned. It was Peabody moving aft. 'I said the cockpit, you damned fool,' shouted Forester.

'I wanna get outa here,' mumbled Peabody. 'I wanna get out. The door's back there.'

Forester wasted no time in argument. Abruptly he jabbed at Peabody's stomach and then brought his clenched fists down at the nape of his neck as he bent over gasping, knocking him cold. He dragged him forward to the door and said to Rohde, 'Take care of this fool. If he causes trouble, knock him on the head.'

He went back and took Miss Ponsky by the arm. 'Come,' he said gently.

She rose and followed him like a somnambulist and he led her right into the cockpit and delivered her to O'Hara. Montes was now conscious and would be ready to move soon.

As soon as O'Hara reappeared Forester said, 'I don't think the old lady back there will make it.'

'Get her out,' said O'Hara tightly. 'For God's sake, get her out.'

So Forester went back. He didn't know whether Mrs Coughlin was alive or dead; her body was still warm, however, so he picked her up in his arms. Blood was still spurting from her shattered shins, and when he stepped into the cockpit Rohde drew in his breath with a hiss. 'On the seat,' he said. 'She needs tourniquets now – immediately.'

He took off his jacket and then his shirt and began to rip the shirt into strips, saying to Forester curtly, 'Get the old man out.'

Forester and O'Hara helped Montes through the windscreen and then Forester turned and regarded Rohde, noting the goose-pimples on his back. 'Clothing,' he said to O'Hara. 'We'll need warm clothing. It'll be bad up here by nightfall.'

'Hell!' said O'Hara. 'That's adding to the risk. I don't – '

'He is right,' said Rohde without turning his head. 'If we do not have clothing we will all be dead by morning.'

'All right,' said O'Hara. 'Are you willing to take the risk?'

'I'll chance it,' said Forester.

'I'll get these people on the ground first,' said O'Hara. 'But while you're at it get the maps. There are some air charts of the area in the pocket next to my seat.'

Rohde grunted. 'I'll get those.'

O'Hara got the people from the top of the fuselage to the ground and Forester began to bring suitcases into the cockpit. Unceremoniously he heaved Peabody through the windscreen and equally carelessly O'Hara dropped him to the ground, where he lay sprawling. Then Rohde handed through the unconscious Mrs Coughlin and O'Hara was surprised at her lightness. Rohde climbed out and, taking her in his arms, jumped to the ground, cushioning the shock for her.

Forester began to hand out suitcases and O'Hara tossed them indiscriminately. Some burst open, but most survived the fall intact.

The Dakota lurched.

'Forester,' yelled O'Hara. 'Come out.'

'There's still some more.'

'Get out, you idiot,' O'Hara bawled. 'She's going.'

He grabbed Forester's arms and hauled him out bodily and let him go thumping to the ground. Then he jumped himself and, as he did so, the nose rose straight into the air and the plane slid over the edge of the cliff with a grinding noise and in a cloud of dust. It crashed down two hundred feet and there was a long dying rumble and then silence.

O'Hara looked at the silent people about him, then turned his eyes to the harsh and savage mountains which surrounded them. He shivered with cold as he felt the keen wind which blew from the snowfields, and then shivered for a different reason as he locked eyes with Forester. They both knew that the odds against survival were heavy and that it was probable that the escape from the Dakota was merely the prelude to a more protracted death.

VIII

'Now, let's hear all this from the beginning,' said Forester.

They had moved into the nearest of the cabins. It proved bare but weatherproof, and there was a fireplace in which Armstrong had made a fire, using wood which Willis had brought from another cabin. Montes was lying in a corner being looked after by his niece, and Peabody was nursing a hangover and looking daggers at Forester.

Miss Ponsky had recovered remarkably from the rigidity of fright. When she had been dropped to the ground she had collapsed, digging her fingers into the frozen gravel in an ecstasy of relief. O'Hara judged she would never have the guts to enter an aeroplane ever again in her life. But now she was showing remarkable aptitude for sick nursing, helping Rohde to care for Mrs Coughlin.

Now there was a character, thought O'Hara; Rohde was a man of unsuspected depths. Although he was not a medical man, he had a good working knowledge of practical medicine which was now invaluable. O'Hara had immediately turned to Willis for help with Mrs Coughlin, but Willis had said, 'Sorry, I'm a physicist – not a physician.'

'Dr Armstrong?' O'Hara had appealed.

Regretfully Armstrong had also shaken his head. 'I'm a historian.'

So Rohde had taken over – the non-doctor with the medical background – and the man with the gun.

O'Hara turned his attention to Forester. 'All right,' he said. 'This is the way it was,'

He told everything that had happened, right back from the take-off in San Croce, dredging from his memory everything Grivas had said. 'I think he went off his head,' he concluded.

Forester frowned. 'No, it was planned,' he contradicted. 'And lunacy isn't planned. Grivas knew this airstrip and he knew the course to take. You say he was at San Croce airfield when the Samair plane was grounded?'

'That's right – I thought it was a bit odd at the time. I mean, it was out of character for Grivas to be haunting the field in the middle of the night – he wasn't that keen on his job.'

'It sounds as though he *knew* the Samair Boeing was going to have engine trouble,' commented Willis.

Forester looked up quickly and Willis said, 'It's the only logical answer – he didn't just steal a plane, he stole the contents; and the contents of the plane were people from the Boeing. O'Hara says those big crates contain ordinary mining machinery and I doubt if Grivas would want that.'

'That implies sabotage of the Boeing,' said Forester. 'If Grivas was expecting the Boeing to land at San Croce, it also implies a sizeable organization behind him.'

'We know that already,' said O'Hara. 'Grivas was expecting a reception committee here. He said, "They'll be here any minute." But where are *they*?'

'And *who* are they?' asked Forester.

O'Hara thought of something else Grivas had said: '. . . they'll kill the lot of you.' He kept quiet about that and asked instead, 'Remember the last thing he said – "*Vivaca*"? It doesn't make sense to me. It sounds vaguely Spanish, but it's no word I know.'

'My Spanish is good,' said Forester deliberately. 'There's no such word.' He slapped the side of his leg irritably. 'I'd give a lot to know what's been going on and who's responsible for all this.'

A weak voice came from across the room. 'I fear, gentlemen, that in a way I am responsible.'

Everyone in the room, with the exception of Mrs Coughlin, turned to look at Señor Montes.

TWO

Montes looked ill. He was worse than he had been in the air. His chest heaved violently as he sucked in the thin air and he had a ghastly pallor. As he opened his mouth to speak again the girl said, 'Hush, *tio*, be quiet. I will tell them,'

She turned and looked across the cabin at O'Hara and Forester. 'My uncle's name is not Montes,' she said levelly. 'It is Aguillar.' She said it as though it was an explanation, entire and complete in itself.

There was a moment of blank silence, then O'Hara snapped his fingers and said softly, 'By God, the old eagle himself.' He stared at the sick man.

'Yes, Señor O'Hara,' whispered Aguillar. 'But a crippled eagle, I am afraid.'

'Say, what the hell is this?' grumbled Peabody. 'What's so special about him?'

Willis gave Peabody a look of dislike and got to his feet. 'I wouldn't have put it that way myself,' he said. 'But I could bear to know more.'

O'Hara said, 'Señor Aguillar was possibly the best president this country ever had until the army took over five years ago. He got out of the country just one jump ahead of a firing squad.'

'General Lopez always was a hasty man,' agreed Aguillar with a weak smile.

41

'You mean the government arranged all this – this jam we're in now – just to get you?' Willis's voice was shrill with incredulity.

Aguillar shook his head and started to speak, but the girl said, 'No, you must be quiet.' She looked at O'Hara appealingly. 'Do not question him now, señor. Can't you see he is ill?'

'Can you speak for your uncle?' asked Forester gently.

She looked at the old man and he nodded. 'What is it you want to know?' she asked.

'What is your uncle doing back in Cordillera?'

'We have come to bring back good government to our country,' she said. 'We have come to throw out Lopez.'

O'Hara gave a short laugh. 'To throw out Lopez,' he said flatly. 'Just like that. An old man and a girl are going to throw out a man with an army at his back.' He shook his head disbelievingly.

The girl flared up. 'What do you know about it; you are a foreigner – you know nothing. Lopez is finished – everyone in Cordillera knows it, even Lopez himself. He has been too greedy, too corrupt, and the country is sick of him.'

Forester rubbed his chin reflectively. 'She could be right,' he said. 'It would take just a puff of wind to blow Lopez over right now. He's run this country right into the ground in the last five years – just about milked it dry and salted enough money away in Swiss banks to last a couple of life-times. I don't think he'd risk losing out now if it came to a showdown – if someone pushed hard enough he'd fold up and get out. I think he'd take wealth and comfort instead of power and the chance of being shot by some gun-happy student with a grievance.'

'Lopez has bankrupted Cordillera,' the girl said. She held up her head proudly. 'But when my uncle appears in Santillana the people will rise, and that will be the end of Lopez.'

'It could work,' agreed Forester. 'Your uncle was well liked. I suppose you've prepared the ground in advance.'

She nodded. 'The Democratic Committee of Action has made all the arrangements. All that remains is for my uncle to appear in Santillana.'

'He may not get there,' said O'Hara. 'Someone is trying to stop him, and if it isn't Lopez, then who the hell is it?'

'The *comunistas*,' the girl spat out with loathing in her voice. 'They cannot afford to let my uncle get into power again. They want Cordillera for their own.'

Forester said, 'It figures. Lopez is a dead duck, come what may; so it's Aguillar versus the communists with Cordillera as the stake.'

'They are not quite ready,' the girl said. 'They do not have enough support among the people. During the last two years they have been infiltrating the government very cleverly and if they had their way the people would wake up one morning to find Lopez gone, leaving a communist government to take his place.'

'Swapping one dictatorship for another,' said Forester. 'Very clever.'

'But they are not yet ready to get rid of Lopez,' she said. 'My uncle would spoil their plans – he would get rid of Lopez and the government, too. He would hold elections for the first time in nine years. So the communists are trying to stop him.'

'And you think Grivas was a communist?' queried O'Hara.

Forester snapped his fingers. 'Of course he was. That explains his last words. He was a communist, all right – Latin-American blend; when he said *"vivaca"* he was trying to say *"Viva* Castro".' His voice hardened. 'And we can expect his buddies along any minute.'

'We must leave here quickly,' said the girl. 'They must not find my uncle.'

O'Hara suddenly swung round and regarded Rohde, who had remained conspicuously silent. He said, 'What do you import, Señor Rohde?'

'It is all right, Señor O'Hara,' said Aguillar weakly. 'Miguel is my secretary.'

Forester looked at Rohde. 'More like your bodyguard.'

Aguillar flapped his hand limply as though the distinction was of no consequence, and Forester said, 'What put you on to him, O'Hara?'

'I don't like men who carry guns,' said O'Hara shortly. 'Especially men who could be communist.' He looked around the cabin. 'All right, are there any more jokers in the pack? What about you, Forester? You seem to know a hell of a lot about local politics for an American businessman.'

'Don't be a damn fool,' said Forester. 'If I didn't take an interest in local politics my corporation would fire me. Having the right kind of government is important to us, and we sure as hell don't want a commie set-up in Cordillera.'

He took out his wallet and extracted a business card which he handed to O'Hara. It informed him that Raymond Forester was the South American sales manager for the Fairfield Machine Tool Corporation.

O'Hara gave it back to him. 'Was Grivas the only communist aboard?' he said. 'That's what I'm getting at. When we were coming in to land, did any of the passengers take any special precautions for their safety?'

Forester thought about it, then shook his head. 'Everyone seemed to be taken by surprise – I don't think any of us knew just what was happening.' He looked at O'Hara with respect. 'In the circumstances that was a good question to ask.'

'Well, I'm not a communist,' said Miss Ponsky sharply. 'The very idea!'

O'Hara smiled. 'My apologies, Miss Ponsky,' he said politely.

Rohde had been tending to Mrs Coughlin; now he stood up. 'This lady is dying,' he said. 'She has lost much blood and she is in shock. And she has the *soroche* – the mountain-sickness. If she does not get oxygen she will surely die.' His black eyes switched to Aguillar, who seemed to have fallen asleep. 'The Señor also must have oxygen – he's in grave danger.' He looked at them. 'We must go down the mountain. To stay at this height is very dangerous.'

O'Hara was conscious of a vicious headache and the fact that his heart was thumping rapidly. He had been long enough in the country to have heard of *soroche* and its effects. The lower air pressure on the mountain heights meant less oxygen, the respiratory rate went up and so did the heart-beat rate, pumping the blood faster. It killed a weak constitution.

He said slowly, 'There were oxygen cylinders in the plane – maybe they're not busted.'

'Good,' said Rohde. 'We will look, you and I. It would be better not to move this lady if possible. But if we do not find the oxygen, then we must go down the mountain.'

Forester said, 'We must keep a fire going – the rest of us will look for wood.' He paused. 'Bring some petrol from the plane – we may need it.'

'All right,' said O'Hara.

'Come on,' said Forester to Peabody. 'Let's move.'

Peabody lay where he was, gasping. 'I'm beat,' he said. 'And my head's killing me.'

'It's just a hangover,' said Forester callously. 'Get on your feet, man.'

Rohde put his hand on Forester's arm. '*Soroche*,' he said warningly. 'He will not be able to do much. Come, señor.'

O'Hara followed Rohde from the cabin and shivered in the biting air. He looked around. The airstrip was built on the only piece of level ground in the vicinity; all else was steeply shelving mountainside, and all around were the pinnacles of the high Andes, clear-cut in the cold and crystal air. They soared skyward, blindingly white against the blue where the snows lay on their flanks, and where the slope was too steep for the snow to stay was the dark grey of the rock.

It was cold, desolate and utterly lifeless. There was no restful green of vegetation, or the flick of a bird's wing – just black, white and the blue of the sky, a hard, dark metallic blue as alien as the landscape.

O'Hara pulled his jacket closer about him and looked at the other huts. 'What is this place?'

'It is a mine,' said Rohde. 'Copper and zinc – the tunnels are over there.' He pointed to a cliff face at the end of the airstrip and O'Hara saw the dark mouths of several tunnels driven into the cliff face. Rohde shook his head. 'But it is too high to work – they should never have tried. No man can work well at this height; not even our mountain *indios.*'

'You know this place then?'

'I know these mountains well,' said Rohde. 'I was born not far from here.'

They trudged along the airstrip and before they had gone a hundred yards O'Hara felt exhausted. His head ached and he felt nauseated. He sucked the thin air into his lungs and his chest heaved.

Rohde stopped and said, 'You must not force your breathing.'

'What else can I do?' said O'Hara, panting. 'I've got to get enough air.'

'Breathe naturally, without effort,' said Rohde. 'You will get enough air. But if you force your breathing you will wash all the carbon dioxide from your lungs, and that will upset the acid base of your blood and you will get muscle cramps. And that is very bad.'

O'Hara moderated his breathing and said, 'You seem to know a lot about it.'

'I studied medicine once,' said Rohde briefly.

They reached the far end of the strip and looked over the edge of the cliff. The Dakota was pretty well smashed up; the port wing had broken off, as had the entire tail section. Rohde studied the terrain. 'We need not climb down the cliff; it will be easier to go round.'

It took them a long time to get to the plane and when they got there they found only one oxygen cylinder intact. It was difficult to get it free and out of the aircraft, but they managed it after chopping away a part of the fuselage with the axe that O'Hara found on the floor of the cockpit.

The gauge showed that the cylinder was only a third full and O'Hara cursed Filson and his cheese-paring, but Rohde seemed satisfied. 'It will be enough,' he said. 'We can stay in the hut tonight.'

'What happens if these communists turn up?' asked O'Hara.

Rohde seemed unperturbed. 'Then we will defend ourselves,' he said equably. 'One thing at a time, Señor O'Hara.'

'Grivas seemed to think they were already here,' said O'Hara. 'I wonder what held them up?'

Rohde shrugged. 'Does it matter?'

They could not manhandle the oxygen cylinder back to the huts without help, so Rohde went back, taking with him some mouthpieces and a bottle of petrol tapped from a wing tank. O'Hara searched the fuselage, looking for anything that might be of value, particularly food. That, he thought, might turn out to be a major problem. All he found was half a slab of milk chocolate in Grivas's seat pocket.

Rohde came back with Forester, Willis and Armstrong and they took it in turns carrying the oxygen cylinder, two by two. It was very hard work and they could only manage to move it twenty yards at a time. O'Hara estimated that back in San Croce he could have picked it up and carried it a mile, but the altitude seemed to have sucked all the strength from their muscles and they could work only a few minutes at a time before they collapsed in exhaustion.

When they got it to the hut they found that Miss Ponsky was feeding the fire with wood from a door of one of the other huts that Willis and Armstrong had torn down and smashed up laboriously with rocks. Willis was particularly glad to see the axe. 'It'll be easier now,' he said.

Rohde administered oxygen to Mrs Coughlin and Aguillar. She remained unconscious, but it made a startling difference to the old man. As the colour came back to his cheeks his niece smiled for the first time since the crash.

O'Hara sat before the fire, feeling the warmth soak into him, and produced his air charts. He spread the relevant chart on the floor and pin-pointed a position with a pencilled cross. 'That's where we were when we changed course,' he said. 'We flew on a true course of one-eighty-four for a shade over five minutes.' He drew a line on the chart. 'We were flying at a little over two hundred knots – say, two hundred and forty miles an hour. That's about twenty miles – so that puts us about – *here*.' He made another cross.

Forester looked over his shoulder. 'The airstrip isn't marked on the map,' he said.

'Rohde said it was abandoned,' said O'Hara.

Rohde came over and looked at the map and nodded. 'You are right,' he said. 'That is where we are. The road down the mountain leads to the refinery. That also is abandoned, but I think some *indios* live there still.'

'How far is that?' asked Forester.

'About forty kilometres,' said Rohde.

'Twenty-five miles,' translated Forester. 'That's a hell of a long way in these conditions.'

'It will not be very bad,' said Rohde. He put his finger on the map. 'When we get to this valley where the river runs we will be nearly five thousand feet lower and we will breathe more easily. That is about sixteen kilometres by the road.'

'We'll start early tomorrow,' said O'Hara.

Rohde agreed. 'If we had no oxygen I would have said go now. But it would be better to stay in the shelter of this hut tonight.'

'What about Mrs Coughlin?' said O'Hara quietly. 'Can we move her?'

'We will have to move her,' said Rohde positively. 'She cannot live at this altitude.'

'We'll rig together some kind of stretcher,' said Forester. 'We can make a sling out of clothing and poles – or maybe use a door.'

O'Hara looked across to where Mrs Coughlin was breathing stertorously, closely watched by Miss Ponsky. His voice was harsh. 'I'd rather that bastard Grivas was still alive if that would give her back her legs,' he said.

II

Mrs Coughlin died during the night without regaining consciousness. They found her in the morning cold and stiff. Miss Ponsky was in tears. 'I should have stayed awake,' she sniffled. 'I *couldn't* sleep most of the night, and then I had to drop off.'

Rohde shook his head gravely. 'She would have died,' he said. 'We could not do anything for her – none of us.'

Forester, O'Hara and Peabody scratched out a shallow grave. Peabody seemed better and O'Hara thought that maybe Forester had been right when he said that Peabody was only suffering from a hangover. However, he had to be prodded into helping to dig the grave.

It seemed that everyone had had a bad night, no one sleeping very well. Rohde said that it was another symptom of *soroche* and the sooner they got to a lower altitude the better. O'Hara still had a splitting headache and heartily concurred.

The oxygen cylinder was empty.

O'Hara tapped the gauge with his finger but the needle stubbornly remained at zero. He opened the cock and bent his head to listen but there was no sound from the valve. He had heard the gentle hiss of oxygen several times during the night and had assumed that Rohde had been tending to Mrs Coughlin or Aguillar.

He beckoned to Rohde. 'Did you use all the oxygen last night?'

Rohde looked incredulously at the gauge. 'I was saving some for today,' he said. 'Señor Aguillar needs it.'

O'Hara bit his lip and looked across to where Peabody sat. 'I thought he looked pretty chipper this morning.'

Rohde growled something under his breath and took a step forward, but O'Hara caught his arm. 'It can't be proved,' he said. 'I could be wrong. And anyway, we don't want any rows right here. Let's get down this mountain.' He kicked the cylinder and it clanged emptily. 'At least we won't have to carry this.'

He remembered the chocolate and brought it out. There were eight small squares to be divided between ten of them, so he, Rohde and Forester did without and Aguillar had two pieces. O'Hara thought that he must have had three because the girl did not appear to eat her ration.

Armstrong and Willis appeared to work well as a team. Using the axe, they had ripped some timber from one of the huts and made a rough stretcher by pushing lengths of wood through the sleeves of two overcoats. That was for Aguillar, who could not walk.

They put on all the clothes they could and left the rest in suitcases. Forester gave O'Hara a bulky overcoat. 'Don't mess it about if you can help it,' he said. 'That's vicuna – it cost a lot of dough.' He grinned. 'The boss's wife asked me to get it this trip; it's the old man's birthday soon.'

Peabody grumbled when he had to leave his luggage and grumbled more when O'Hara assigned him to a stretcher-carrying stint. O'Hara resisted taking a poke at him; for one thing he did not want open trouble, and for another he did not know whether he had the strength to do any damage. At the moment it was all he could do to put one foot in front of the other.

So they left the huts and went down the road, turning their backs on the high peaks. The road was merely a rough track cut out of the mountainside. It wound down in a series of hairpin bends and Willis pointed out where blasting had been done on the corners. It was just wide enough to take a single vehicle but, from time to time, they came across a wide part where two trucks could pass.

O'Hara asked Rohde, 'Did they intend to truck all the ore from the mine?'

'They would have built a telfer,' said Rohde. 'An endless rope with buckets. But they were still proving the mine. Petrol engines do not work well up here – they need superchargers.' He stopped suddenly and stared at the ground.

In a patch of snow was the track of a tyre.

'Someone's been up here lately,' observed O'Hara. 'Supercharged or not. But I knew that.'

'How?' Rohde demanded.

'The airstrip had been cleared of snow.'

Rohde patted his breast and moved away without saying anything. O'Hara remembered the pistol and wondered what would happen if they came up against opposition.

Although the path was downhill and the going comparatively good, it was only possible to carry the stretcher a hundred yards at a time. Forester organized relays, and as one set of carriers collapsed exhaustedly another took over. Aguillar was in a comatose condition and the girl walked next to the stretcher, anxiously watching him. After a mile they stopped for a rest and O'Hara said to Rohde, 'I've got a flask of spirits. 'I've been saving it for when things really get tough. Do you think it would help the old man?'

'Let me have it,' said Rohde.

O'Hara took the flask from his hip and gave it to Rohde, who took off the cap and sniffed the contents. *'Aguardiente,'* he said. 'Not the best drink but it will do.' He looked at O'Hara curiously. 'Do you drink this?'

'I'm a poor man,' said O'Hara defensively.

Rohde smiled. 'When I was a student I also was poor. I also drank *aguardiente*. But I do not recommend too much,' He looked across at Aguillar. 'I think we save this for later.' He recapped the flask and handed it back to O'Hara. As O'Hara was replacing it in his pocket he saw Peabody staring at him. He smiled back pleasantly.

After a rest of half an hour they started off again. O'Hara, in the lead, looked back and thought they looked like a bunch of war refugees. Willis and Armstrong were stumbling along with the stretcher, the girl keeping pace alongside; Miss Ponsky was sticking close to Rohde, chatting as though on a Sunday afternoon walk, despite her shortness of breath, and Forester was in the rear with Peabody shambling beside him.

After the third stop O'Hara found that things were going better. His step felt lighter and his breathing eased, although the headache stayed with him. The stretcher-bearers found that they could carry for longer periods, and Aguillar had come round and was taking notice.

O'Hara mentioned this to Rohde, who pointed at the steep slopes about them. 'We are losing a lot of height,' he said. 'It will get better now.'

After the fourth halt O'Hara and Forester were carrying the stretcher. Aguillar apologized in a weak voice for the inconvenience he was causing, but O'Hara forbore to answer – he needed all his breath for the job. Things weren't that much better.

Forester suddenly stopped and O'Hara thankfully laid down the stretcher. His legs felt rubbery and the breath rasped in his throat. He grinned at Forester, who was beating his hands against his chest. 'Never mind,' he said. 'It should be warmer down in the valley.'

Forester blew on his fingers. 'I hope so.' He looked up at O'Hara. 'You're a pretty good pilot,' he said. 'I've done some flying in my time, but I don't think I could do what you did yesterday.'

'You might if you had a pistol at your head,' said O'Hara with a grimace. 'Anyway, I couldn't leave it to Grivas – he'd have killed the lot of us, starting with me first.'

He looked past Forester and saw Rohde coming back up the road at a stumbling run, his gun in his hand. 'Something's happening.'

He went forward to meet Rohde, who gasped, his chest heaving. 'There are huts here – I had forgotten them.'

O'Hara looked at the gun. 'Do you need that?'

Rohde gave a stark smile. 'It is possible, señor.' He waved casually down the road with the pistol. 'I think we should be careful. I think we should look first before doing anything. You, me, and Señor Forester.'

'I think so too,' said Forester. 'Grivas said his pals would be around and this seems a likely place to meet them.'

'All right,' said O'Hara, and looked about. There was no cover on the road but there was a jumble of rocks a little way back. 'I think everyone else had better stick behind that lot,' he said. 'If anything does break, there's no point in being caught in the open.'

They went back to shelter behind the rocks and O'Hara told everyone what was happening. He ended by saying, 'If there's shooting you don't do a damned thing – you freeze and stay put. Now I know we're not an army but we're likely to come under fire all the same – so I'm naming Doctor Willis as second-in-command. If anything happens to us you take your orders from him.' Willis nodded.

Aguillar's niece was talking to Rohde, and as O'Hara went to join Forester she touched him on the arm. 'Señor.'

He looked down at her. 'Yes, señorita.'

'Please be careful, you and Señor Forester. I would not want anything to happen to you because of us.'

'I'll be careful,' said O'Hara. 'Tell me, is your name the same as your uncle's?'

'I am Benedetta Aguillar,' she said.

He nodded. 'I'm Tim O'Hara. I'll be careful.'

He joined the other two and they walked down the road to the bend. Rohde said, 'These huts were where the miners lived. This is just about as high as a man can live permanently – a man who is acclimatized such as our mountain *indios*. I think we should leave the road here and approach from the side. If Grivas did have friends, here is where we will find them.'

They took to the mountainside and came upon the camp from the top. A level place had been roughly bull-dozed out of the side of the mountain and there were about a dozen timber-built huts, very much like the huts by the airstrip.

'This is no good,' said Forester. 'We'll have to go over this miniature cliff before we can get at them.'

'There's no smoke,' O'Hara pointed out.

'Maybe that means something – maybe it doesn't,' said Forester. 'I think that Rohde and I will go round and come up from the bottom. If anything happens, maybe you can cause a diversion from up here.'

'What do I do?' asked O'Hara. 'Throw stones?'

Forester shook with silent laughter. He pointed down the slope to beyond the camp. 'We'll come out about there. You can see us from here but we'll be out of sight of anyone in the camp. If all's clear you can give us the signal to come up.' He looked at Rohde, who nodded.

Forester and Rohde left quietly and O'Hara lay on his belly, looking down at the camp. He did not think there was anyone there. It was less than five miles up to the airstrip by the road and there was nothing to stop anybody going up there. If Grivas's confederates were anywhere, it was not likely that they would be at this camp – but it was as well to make sure. He scanned the huts but saw no sign of movement.

Presently he saw Forester wave from the side of the rock he had indicated and he waved back. Rohde went up first, in a wide arc to come upon the camp at an angle. Then Forester moved forward in the peculiar scuttling, zigzagging run of the experienced soldier who expects to be shot at. O'Hara wondered about Forester; the man had said he could fly an aeroplane and now he was behaving like a trained infantryman. He had an eye for ground, too, and was obviously accustomed to command.

Forester disappeared behind one of the huts and then Rohde came into sight at the far end of the camp, moving warily with his gun in his hand. He too disappeared, and O'Hara felt tension. He waited for what seemed a very long time, then Forester walked out from behind the nearest hut, moving quite unconcernedly. 'You can come down,' he called. 'There's no one here.'

O'Hara let out his breath with a rush and stood up. 'I'll go back and get the rest of the people down here,' he shouted, and Forester waved in assent.

O'Hara went back up the road, collected the party and took them down to the camp. Forester and Rohde were waiting in the main 'street' and Forester called out, 'We've struck it lucky; there's a lot of food here.'

Suddenly O'Hara realized that he hadn't eaten for a day and a half. He did not feel particularly hungry, but he knew that if he did not eat he could not last out much longer – and neither could any of the others. To have food would make a lot of difference on the next leg of the journey.

Forester said, 'Most of the huts are empty, but three of them are fitted out as living quarters complete with kerosene heaters.'

O'Hara looked down at the ground which was criss-crossed with tyre tracks. 'There's something funny going on,' he said. 'Rohde told me that the mine has been abandoned for a long time, yet there's all these signs of life and no one around. What the hell's going on?'

Forester shrugged. 'Maybe the commie organization is slipping,' he said. 'The Latins have never been noted for good planning. Maybe someone's put a spoke in their wheel.'

'Maybe,' said O'Hara. 'We might as well take advantage of it. What do you think we should do now – how long should we stay here?'

Forester looked at the group entering one of the huts, then up at the sky. 'We're pretty beat,' he said. 'Maybe we ought to stay here until tomorrow. It'll take us a while to get fed and it'll be late before we can move out. We ought to stay here tonight and keep warm.'

'We'll consult Rohde,' said O'Hara. 'He's the expert on mountains and altitude.'

The huts were well fitted. There were paraffin stoves, bunks, plenty of blankets and a large assortment of canned foods. On the table in one of the huts there were the remnants of a meal, the plates dirty and unwashed and frozen dregs of coffee in the bottom of tin mugs. O'Hara felt the thickness of the ice and it cracked beneath the pressure of his finger.

'They haven't been gone long,' he said. 'If the hut was unheated this stuff would have frozen to the bottom.' He passed the mug to Rohde. 'What do you think?'

Rohde looked at the ice closely. 'If they turned off the heaters when they left, the hut would stay warm for a while,' he said. He tested the ice and thought deeply. 'I would say two days,' he said finally.

'Say yesterday morning,' suggested O'Hara. 'That would be about the time we took off from San Croce.'

Forester groaned in exasperation. 'It doesn't make sense. Why did they go to all this trouble, make all these preparations, and then clear out? One thing's sure: Grivas expected a reception committee – and where the hell is it?'

O'Hara said to Rohde, 'We are thinking of staying here tonight. What do you think?'

'It is better here than at the mine,' said Rohde. 'We have lost a lot of height. I would say that we are at an altitude of about four thousand metres here – or maybe a little more. That will not harm us for one night; it will be better to stay here in shelter than to stay in the open tonight, even if it is lower down the mountain.' He contracted his brows. 'But I suggest we keep a watch.'

Forester nodded. 'We'll take it in turns.'

Miss Ponsky and Benedetta were busy on the pressure stoves making hot soup. Armstrong had already got the heater going and Willis was sorting out cans of food. He called O'Hara over. 'I thought we'd better take something with us when we leave,' he said. 'It might come in useful.'

'A good idea,' said O'Hara.

Willis grinned. 'That's all very well, but I can't read Spanish. I have to go by the pictures on the labels. Someone had better check on these when I've got them sorted out.'

Forester and Rohde went on down the road to pick a good spot for a sentry, and when Forester came back he said, 'Rohde's taking the first watch. We've got a good place where we can see bits of road a good two miles away. And if they come up at night they're sure to have their lights on.'

He looked at his watch. 'We've got six able-bodied men, so if we leave here early tomorrow, that means two-hour watches. That's not too bad – it gives us all enough sleep.'

After they had eaten Benedetta took some food down to Rohde and O'Hara found himself next to Armstrong. 'You said you were a historian. I suppose you're over here to check up on the Incas,' he said.

'Oh, no,' said Armstrong. 'They're not my line of country at all. My line is medieval history.'

'Oh,' said O'Hara blankly.

'I don't know anything about the Incas and I don't particularly want to,' said Armstrong frankly. He smiled gently. 'For the past ten years I've never had a real holiday. I'd go on holiday like a normal man – perhaps to France or Italy – and then I'd see something interesting. I'd do a bit of investigating – and before I'd know it I'd be hard at work.'

He produced a pipe and peered dubiously into his tobacco pouch. 'This year I decided to come to South America for a holiday. All there is here is pre-European and modern history – no medieval history at all. Clever of me, wasn't it?'

O'Hara smiled, suspecting that Armstrong was indulging in a bit of gentle leg-pulling. 'And what's your line, Doctor Willis?' he asked.

'I'm a physicist,' said Willis. 'I'm interested in cosmic rays at high altitudes. I'm not getting very far with it, though.'

They were certainly a mixed lot, thought O'Hara, looking across at Miss Ponsky as she talked animatedly to Aguillar. Now there was a sight – a New England spinster schoolmarm lecturing a statesman. She would certainly have plenty to tell her pupils when she arrived back at the little schoolhouse.

'What was this place, anyway?' asked Willis.

'Living quarters for the mine up on top,' said O'Hara. 'That's what Rohde tells me.'

Willis nodded. 'They had their workshops down here, too,' he said. 'All the machinery has gone, of course, but there are still a few bits and pieces left.' He shivered. 'I can't say I'd like to work in a place like this.'

O'Hara looked about the hut. 'Neither would I.' He caught sight of an electric conduit tube running down a wall. 'Where did their electricity supply come from, I wonder?'

'They had their own plant; there's the remains of it out back. The generator has gone – they must have salvaged it when the mine closed down. They scavenged most everything, I guess; there's precious little left.'

Armstrong drew the last of the smoke from his failing pipe with a disconsolate gurgle. 'Well, that's the last of the tobacco until we get back to civilization,' he said as he knocked out the dottle. 'Tell me, Captain; what are you doing in this part of the world?'

'Oh, I fly aeroplanes from anywhere to anywhere,' said O'Hara. Not any more I don't, he thought. As far as Filson was concerned, he was finished. Filson would never forgive a pilot who wrote off one of his aircraft, no matter what the reason. I've lost my job, he thought. It was a lousy job but it had kept him going, and now he'd lost it.

The girl came back and he crossed over to her. 'Anything doing down the road?' he asked.

She shook her head. 'Nothing. Miguel says everything is quiet.'

'He's quite a character,' said O'Hara. 'He certainly knows a lot about these mountains – and he knows a bit about medicine too.'

'He was born near here,' Benedetta said. 'And he was a medical student until – ' She stopped.

'Until what?' prompted O'Hara.

'Until the revolution.' She looked at her hands. 'All his family were killed – that is why he hates Lopez. That is why he works with my uncle – he knows that my uncle will ruin Lopez.'

'I thought he had a chip on his shoulder,' said O'Hara.

She sighed. 'It is a great pity about Miguel; he was going to do so much. He was very interested in the *soroche*, you know; he intended to study it as soon as he had taken his degree. But when the revolution came he had to leave the country and he had no money so he could not continue his studies. He worked in the Argentine for a while, and then he met my uncle. He saved my uncle's life.'

'Oh?' O'Hara raised his eyebrows.

'In the beginning Lopez knew that he was not safe while my uncle was alive. He knew that my uncle would organize an opposition – underground, you know. So wherever my uncle went he was in danger from the murderers hired by Lopez – even in the Argentine. There were several attempts to kill him, and it was one of these times that Miguel saved his life.'

O'Hara said, 'Your uncle must have felt like another Trotsky. Joe Stalin had him bumped off in Mexico.'

'That is right,' she said with a grimace of distaste. 'But they were communists, both of them. Anyway, Miguel stayed with us after that. He said that all he wanted was food to eat and a bed to sleep in, and he would help my uncle come back to Cordillera. And here we are.'

Yes, thought O'Hara; marooned up a bloody mountain with God knows what waiting at the bottom.

Presently Armstrong went out to relieve Rohde. Miss Ponsky came across to talk to O'Hara. 'I'm sorry I behaved so stupidly in the airplane,' she said crossly. 'I don't know what came over me.'

O'Hara thought there was no need to apologize for being half frightened to death; he had been bloody scared himself. But he couldn't say that – he couldn't even mention the word *fear* to her. That would be unforgivable; no one likes to be reminded of a lapse of that nature – not even a maiden lady getting on in years. He smiled and said diplomatically, 'Not everyone would have come through an experience like that as well as you have, Miss Ponsky.'

She was mollified and he knew that she had been in fear of a rebuff. She was the kind of person who would bite on a sore tooth, not letting it alone. She smiled and said, 'Well now, Captain O'Hara – what do you think of all this talk about communists?'

'I think they're capable of anything,' said O'Hara grimly.

'I'm going to put in a report to the State Department when I get back,' she said. 'You ought to hear what Señor Aguillar has been telling me about General Lopez. I think the State Department should help Señor Aguillar against General Lopez *and* the communists.'

'I'm inclined to agree with you,' said O'Hara. 'But perhaps your State Department doesn't believe in interfering in Cordilleran affairs.'

'Stuff and nonsense,' said Miss Ponsky with acerbity. 'We're supposed to be fighting the communists, aren't we? Besides, Señor Aguillar assures me that he'll hold elections as soon as General Lopez is kicked out. He's a *real* democrat just like you and me.'

O'Hara wondered what would happen if another South American state did go communist. Cuban agents were filtering all through Latin America like woodworms in a piece of furniture. He tried to think of the strategic importance of Cordillera – it was on the Pacific coast and it straddled the Andes, a gun pointing to the heart of the continent. He thought the Americans would be very upset if Cordillera went communist.

Rohde came back and talked for a few minutes with Aguillar, then he crossed to O'Hara and said in a low voice, 'Señor Aguillar would like to speak to you.' He gestured to

Forester and the three of them went to where Aguillar was resting in a bunk.

He had brightened considerably and was looking quite spry. His eyes were lively and no longer filmed with weariness, and there was a strength and authority in his voice that O'Hara had not heard before. He realized that this was a strong man; maybe not too strong in the body because he was becoming old and his body was wearing out, but he had a strong mind. O'Hara suspected that if the old man had not had a strong will, the body would have crumpled under the strain it had undergone.

Aguillar said, 'First I must thank you gentlemen for all you have done, and I am truly sorry that I have brought this calamity upon you.' He shook his head sadly. 'It is the innocent bystander who always suffers in the clash of our Latin politics. I am sorry that this should have happened and that you should see my country in this sad light.'

'What else could we do?' asked Forester. 'We're all in the same boat.'

'I'm glad you see it that way,' said Aguillar. 'Because of what may come next. What happens if we meet up with the communists who should be here and are not?'

'Before we come to that there's something I'd like to query,' said O'Hara. Aguillar raised his eyebrows and motioned him to continue, so O'Hara said deliberately, 'How do we know they are communists? Señorita Aguillar tells me that Lopez has tried to liquidate you several times. How do you know he hasn't got wind of your return and is having another crack at you?'

Aguillar shook his head. 'Lopez has – in your English idiom – shot his bolt. I *know*. Do not forget that I am a practical politician and give me credit for knowing my own work. Lopez forgot about me several years ago and is only interested in how he can safely relinquish the reins of power and retire. As for the communists – for years I have watched them work in my country, undermining the government and wooing the people. They have not got far with the people, or they would have disposed of Lopez by now. I am their only danger and I am sure that our situation is their work.'

Forester said casually, 'Grivas was trying to make a clenched fist salute when he died.'

'All right,' said O'Hara. 'But why all this rigmarole of Grivas in the first place? Why not just put a time bomb in the Dakota – that would have done the job very easily.'

Aguillar smiled. 'Señor O'Hara, in my life as a politician I have had four bombs thrown at me and every one was defective. Our politics out here are emotional and emotion does not make for careful workmanship, even of bombs. And I am sure that even communism cannot make any difference to the native characteristics of my people. They wanted to make very sure of me and so they chose the unfortunate Grivas as their instrument. Would you have called Grivas an emotional man?'

'I should think he was,' said O'Hara, thinking of Grivas's exultation even in death. 'And he was pretty slipshod too.'

Aguillar spread his hands, certain he had made his point. But he drove it home. 'Grivas would be happy to be given such work; it would appeal to his sense of drama – and my people have a great sense of drama. As for being – er – slipshod, Grivas bungled the first part of the operation by stupidly killing himself, and the others have bungled the rest of it by not being here to meet us.'

O'Hara rubbed his chin. As Aguillar drew the picture it made a weird kind of sense.

Aguillar said, 'Now, my friends, we come to the next point. Supposing, on the way down this mountain, we meet these men – these communists? What happens then?' He regarded O'Hara and Forester with bright eyes. 'It is not your fight – you are not Cordillerans – and I am interested to know what you would do. Would you give this dago politician into the hands of his enemies or . . .'

'Would we fight?' finished Forester.

'It is my fight,' said O'Hara bluntly. 'I'm not a Cordilleran, but Grivas pulled a gun on me and made me crash my plane. I didn't like that, and I didn't like the sight of the Coughlins. Anyway, I don't like the sight of communists, and I think that, all in all, this is my fight.'

'I concur,' said Forester.

Aguillar raised his hand. 'But it is not as easy as that, is it? There are others to take into account. Would it be fair on Miss – er – Ponsky, for instance? Now what I propose is this. Miguel, my niece and I will withdraw into another cabin while you talk it over – and I will abide by your joint decision.'

Forester looked speculatively at Peabody, who was just leaving the hut. He glanced at O'Hara, then said, 'I think we should leave the question of fighting until there's something to fight. It's possible that we might just walk out of here.'

Aguillar had seen Forester's look at Peabody. He smiled sardonically. 'I see that you are a politician yourself, Señor Forester.' He made a gesture of resignation. 'Very well, we will leave the problem for the moment – but I think we will have to return to it.'

'It's a pity we had to come down the mountain,' said Forester. 'There's sure to be an air search, and it might have been better to stay by the Dakota.'

'We could not have lived up there,' said Rohde.

'I know, but it's a pity all the same.'

'I don't think it makes much difference,' said O'Hara. 'The wreck will be difficult to spot from the air – it's right at the foot of a cliff.' He hesitated. 'And I don't know about an air search – not yet, anyway.'

Forester jerked his head. 'What the hell do you mean by that?'

'Andes Airlift isn't noted for its efficiency and Filson, my boss, isn't good at paperwork. This flight didn't even have a number – I remember wondering about it just before we took off. It's on the cards that San Croce control haven't bothered to notify Santillana to expect us.' As he saw Forester's expression he added, The whole set-up is shoe-string and sealing-wax – it's only a small field.'

'But surely your boss will get worried when he doesn't hear from you?'

'He'll worry,' agreed O'Hara. 'He told me to phone him from Santillana – but he won't worry too much at first. There have been times when I haven't phoned through on his say-so and had a rocket for losing cargo. But I don't think he'll worry about losing the plane for a couple of days at least.'

Forester blew out his cheeks. 'Wow – what a Rube Goldberg organization. Now I really feel lost.'

Rohde said, 'We must depend on our own efforts. I think we can be sure of that.'

'We flew off course too,' said O'Hara. 'They'll start the search north of here – when they start.'

Rohde looked at Aguillar whose eyes were closed. 'There is nothing we can do now,' he said. 'But we must sleep. It will be a hard day tomorrow.'

III

Again O'Hara did not sleep very well, but at least he was resting on a mattress instead of a hard floor, with a full belly. Peabody was on watch and O'Hara was due to relieve him at two o'clock; he was glad when the time came.

He donned his leather jacket and took the vicuna coat that Forester had given him. He suspected that he would be glad of it during the next two hours. Forester was awake and waved lazily as he went out, although he did not speak.

The night air was thin and cold and O'Hara shivered as he set off down the road. As Rohde had said, the conditions for survival were better here than up by the airstrip, but it was still pretty dicey. He was aware that his heart was thumping and that his respiration rate was up. It would be much better when they got down to the *quebrada*, as Rohde called the lateral valley to which they were heading.

He reached the corner where he had to leave the road and headed towards the looming outcrop of rock which Rohde had picked as a vantage point. Peabody should have been perched on top of the rock and should have heard him coming, but there was no sign of his presence.

O'Hara called softly, 'Peabody!'

There was silence.

Cautiously he circled the outcrop to get it silhouetted against the night sky. There was a lump on top of the rock which he could not quite make out. He began to climb the rock and as he reached the top he heard a muffled snore. He shook Peabody and his foot clinked on a bottle – Peabody was drunk.

'You bloody fool,' he said and started to slap Peabody's face, but without appreciable result. Peabody muttered in his drunken stupor but did not recover consciousness. 'I ought to let you die of exposure,' whispered O'Hara viciously, but he knew he could not do that. He also knew that he could not hope to carry Peabody back to the camp by himself. He would have to get help.

He stared down the mountainside but all was quiet, so he climbed down the rock and headed back up the road. Forester was still awake and looked up inquiringly as O'Hara entered the hut. 'What's the matter?' he asked, suddenly alert.

'Peabody's passed out,' said O'Hara. 'I'll need help to bring him up.'

'Damn this altitude,' said Forester, putting on his shoes.

'It wasn't the altitude,' O'Hara said coldly. 'The bastard's dead drunk.'

Forester muffled an imprecation. 'Where did he get the stuff?'

'I suppose he found it in one of the huts,' said O'Hara. 'I've still got my flask – I was saving it for Aguillar.'

'All right,' said Forester. 'Let's lug the damn fool up here.'

It wasn't an easy thing to do. Peabody was a big, flabby man and his body lolled uncooperatively, but they managed it at last and dumped him unceremoniously in a bunk. Forester gasped and said, 'This idiot will be the death of us all if we don't watch him.' He paused. 'I'll come down with you – it might be better to have two pairs of eyes down there right now.'

They went back and climbed up on to the rock, lying side by side and scanning the dark mountainside. For fifteen minutes they were silent, but saw and heard nothing. 'I think it's okay,' said Forester at last. He shifted his position to ease his bones. 'What do you think of the old man?'

'He seems all right to me,' said O'Hara.

'He's a good joe – a good liberal politician. If he lasts long enough he might end up by being a good liberal statesman – but liberals don't last long in this part of the world, and I think he's a shade too soft.' Forester chuckled. 'Even when it's a matter of life and death – *his* life and death, not to mention his niece's – he still sticks to democratic procedure. He wants us to vote on whether we shall hand him over to the commies. Imagine that!'

'I wouldn't hand anyone over to the communists,' said O'Hara. He glanced sideways at the dark bulk of Forester. 'You said you could fly a plane – I suppose you do it as a matter of business; company plane and all that.'

'Hell, no,' said Forester. 'My outfit's not big enough or advanced enough for that. I was in the Air Force – I flew in Korea.'

'So did I,' said O'Hara. 'I was in the R.A.F.'

'Well, what do you know.' Forester was delighted. 'Where were you based?'

O'Hara told him and he said, 'Then you were flying Sabres like I was. We went on joint operations – hell, we must have flown together.'

'Probably.'

They lay in companionable silence for a while, then Forester said, 'Did you knock down any of those Migs? I got four, then they pulled me out. I was mad about that – I wanted to be a war hero; an ace, you know.'

'You've got to get five in the American Air Force, haven't you?'

'That's right,' said Forester. 'Did you get any?'

'A couple,' said O'Hara. He had shot down eight Migs but it was a part of his life he preferred to forget, so he didn't elaborate. Forester sensed his reserve and was quiet. After a few minutes he said, 'I think I'll go back and get some sleep – if I can. We'll be on our way early.'

When he had gone O'Hara stared into the darkness and thought about Korea. That had been the turning point of his life: before Korea he had been on his way up; after Korea there was just the endless slide, down to Filson and now beyond. He wondered where he would end up.

Thinking of Korea brought back Margaret and the letter. He had read the letter while on ready call on a frozen air-field. The Americans had a name for that kind of letter – they called them 'Dear Johns'. She was quite matter-of-fact about it and said that they were adult and must be sensible about this thing – all the usual rationalizations which covered plain infidelity. Looking back on it afterwards O'Hara could see a little humour in it – not much, but some. He was one of the inglorious ten per cent of any army fighting away from home, and he had lost his wife to a civilian. But it wasn't funny at all reading that letter on the cold airfield in Korea.

Five minutes later there was a scramble and he was in the air and thirty minutes later he was fighting. He went into battle with cold ferocity and a total lack of judgment. In three minutes he shot down two Migs, surprising them by sheer recklessness. Then a Chinese pilot with a cooler mind shot *him* down and he spent the rest of the war in a prison cage.

He did not like to think of that period and what had happened to him. He had come out of it with honour, but the psychiatrists had a field day with him when he got back to England. They did what they could but they could not break down the shell he had built about himself – and neither, by that time, could he break out.

And so it went – invalided out of the Air Force with a pension which he promptly commuted; the good jobs – at first – and then the poorer jobs, until he got down to Filson. And always the drink – more and more booze which had less and less effect as he tried to fill and smother the aching emptiness inside him.

He moved restlessly on the rock and heard the bottle clink. He put out his hand, picked it up and held it to the sky. It was a quarter full. He smiled. He could not get drunk on that but it would be very welcome. Yet as the fiery fluid spread and warmed his gut he felt guilty.

IV

Peabody was blearily belligerent when he woke up and found O'Hara looking at him. At first he looked defensive, then his instinct for attack took over. 'I'm not gonna take anything from you,' he said shakily. 'Not from any goddam limey.'

O'Hara just looked at him. He had no wish to tax Peabody with anything. Weren't they members of the same club? he thought sardonically. Fellow drunks. Why, we even drink from the same bottle. He felt miserable.

Rohde took a step forward and Peabody screamed, 'And I'm not gonna take anything from a dago either.'

'Then perhaps you'll take it from me,' snapped Forester. He took one stride and slapped Peabody hard on the side of the face. Peabody sagged back on the bed and looked into Forester's cold eyes with an expression of fear and bewilderment on his face. His hand came up to touch the red blotch on his cheek. He was just going to speak when Forester pushed a finger at him. 'Shut up! One cheep out of you and I'll mash you into a pulp. Now get your big fat butt off that bed and get to work – and if you step out of line again I swear to God I'll kill you.'

The ferocity in Forester's voice had a chilling effect on Peabody. All the belligerence drained out of him. 'I didn't mean to – ' he began.

'Shut up!' said Forester and turned his back on him. 'Let's get this show on the road,' he announced generally.

They took food and a pressure stove and fuel, carrying it in awkwardly contrived packs cobbled from their overcoats. O'Hara did not think that Forester's boss would thank him for the vicuna coat, already showing signs of hard use.

Aguillar said he could walk, provided he was not asked to go too fast, so Forester took the stretcher poles and lashed them together in what he called a *travois*. 'The Plains Indians used this for transport,' he said. 'They got along without wheels – so can we.' He grinned. 'They pulled with horses and we have only manpower, but it's downhill all the way.'

The *travois* held a lot, much more than a man could carry, and Forester and O'Hara took first turn at pulling the triangular contraption, the apex bumping and bouncing on the stony ground. The others fell into line behind them and once more they wound their way down the mountain.

O'Hara looked at his watch – it was six a.m. He began to calculate – they had not come very far the previous day, not more than four or five miles, but they had been rested, warmed and fed, and that was all to the good. He doubted if they could make more than ten miles a day, so that meant another two days to the refinery, but they had enough food for at least four days, so they would be all right even if Aguillar slowed them down. Things seemed immeasurably brighter.

The terrain around them began to change. There were tufts of grass scattered sparsely and an occasional wild flower, and as they went on these signs of life became more frequent. They were able to move faster, too, and O'Hara said to Rohde, 'The low altitude seems to be doing us good.'

'That – and acclimatization,' said Rohde. He smiled grimly. 'If it does not kill you, you can get used to it – eventually.'

They came to one of the inevitable curves in the road and Rohde stopped and pointed to a silvery thread. 'That is the *quebrada* – where the river is. We cross the river and turn north. The refinery is about twenty-four kilometres from the bridge.'

'What's the height above sea-level?' asked O'Hara. He was beginning to take a great interest in the air he breathed – more interest than he had ever taken in his life.

'About three thousand five hundred metres,' said Rohde.

Twelve thousand feet, O'Hara thought. That's much better.

They made good time and decided they would be able to have their midday rest and some hot food on the other side of the bridge. 'A little over five miles in half a day,' said Forester, chewing on a piece of jerked beef. 'That won't be bad going. But I hope to God that Rohde is right when he says that the refinery is still inhabited.'

'We will be all right,' said Rohde. 'There is a village ten miles the other side of the refinery. Some of us can go on and bring back help if necessary.'

They pushed on and found that suddenly they were in the valley. There was no more snow and the ground was rocky, with more clumps of tough grass. The road ceased to twist and they went past many small ponds. It was appreciably warmer too, and O'Hara found that he could stride out without losing his breath.

We've got it made, he thought exultantly.

Soon they heard the roar of the river which carried the meltwater from the snowfields behind them and suddenly they were all gay. Miss Ponsky chattered unceasingly, exclaiming once in her high-pitched voice as she saw a bird, the first living, moving thing they had seen in two days. O'Hara heard Aguillar's deep chuckle and even Peabody cheered up, recovering from Forester's tongue-lashing.

O'Hara found himself next to Benedetta. She smiled at him and said, 'Who has the pressure stove? We are going to need it soon.'

He pointed back to where Willis and Armstrong were pulling the *travois*. 'I packed it in there,' he said.

They were very near the river now and he estimated that the road would have one last turn before they came to the bridge. 'Come on,' he said. 'Let's see what's round the corner.'

They stepped out and round the curve and O'Hara suddenly stopped. There were men and vehicles on the other side of the swollen river and the bridge was down.

A faint babble of voices arose above the river's roar as they were seen and some of the men on the other side started to run. O'Hara saw a man reach into the back of a truck and lift out a rifle and there was a popping noise as others opened up with pistols.

He lurched violently into Benedetta, sending her flying just as the rifle cracked, and she stumbled into cover, dropping some cans in the middle of the road. As O'Hara fell after her one of the cans suddenly leaped into the air as a bullet hit it, and leaked a tomato bloodiness.

THREE

O'Hara, Forester and Rohde looked down on the bridge from the cover of a group of large boulders near the edge of the river gorge. Below, the river rumbled, a green torrent of ice-water smoothly slipping past the walls it had cut over the aeons. The gorge was about fifty yards wide.

O'Hara was still shaking from the shock of being unexpectedly fired upon. He had thrown himself into the side of the road, winding himself by falling on to a can in the pocket of his overcoat. When he recovered his breath he had looked with stupefaction at the punctured can in the middle of the road, bleeding a red tomato and meat gravy. That could have been me, he thought – or Benedetta.

It was then that he started to shake.

They had crept back round the corner, keeping in cover, while rifle bullets flicked chips of granite from the road surface. Rohde was waiting for them, his gun drawn and his face anxious. He looked at Benedetta's face and his lips drew back over his teeth in a snarl as he took a step forward.

'Hold it,' said Forester quietly from behind him. 'Let's not be too hasty.' He put his hand on O'Hara's arm. 'What's happening back there?'

O'Hara took a grip on himself. 'I didn't have time to see much. I think the bridge is down; there are some trucks on the other side and there seemed to be a hell of a lot of men.'

Forester scanned the ground with a practised eye. 'There's plenty of cover by the river – we should be able to get a good view from among those rocks without being spotted. Let's go.'

So here they were, looking at the ant-like activity on the other side of the river. There seemed to be about twenty men; some were busy unloading thick planks from a truck, others were cutting rope into lengths. Three men had apparently been detailed off as sentries; they were standing with rifles in their hands, scanning the bank of the gorge. As they watched, one of the men must have thought he saw something move, because he raised his rifle and fired a shot.

Forester said, 'Nervous, aren't they? They're firing at shadows.'

O'Hara studied the gorge. The river was deep and ran fast – it was obviously impossible to swim. One would be swept away helplessly in the grip of that rush of water and be frozen to death in ten minutes. Apart from that, there were the problems of climbing down the edge of the gorge to the water's edge and getting up the other side, not to mention the likelihood of being shot.

He crossed the river off his mental list of possibilities and turned his attention to the bridge. It was a primitive suspension contraption with two rope catenaries strung from massive stone buttresses on each side of the gorge. From the catenaries other ropes, graded in length, supported the main roadway of the bridge which was made of planks. But there was a gap in the middle where a lot of planks were missing and the ropes dangled in the breeze.

Forester said softly, 'That's why they didn't meet us at the airstrip. See the truck in the river – downstream, slapped up against the side of the gorge?'

O'Hara looked and saw the truck in the water, almost totally submerged, with a standing wave of water swirling over the top of the cab. He looked back at the bridge. 'It seems as though it was crossing from this side when it went over.'

'That figures,' said Forester. 'I reckon they'd have a couple of men to make the preliminary arrangements – stocking up the camp and so on – in readiness for the main party. When the main party was due they came down to the bridge to cross – God knows for what reason. But they didn't make it – and they buggered the bridge, with the main party still on the other side.'

'They're repairing it now,' said O'Hara. 'Look.'

Two men crawled on to the swaying bridge pushing a plank before them. They lashed it into place with the aid of a barrage of shouted advice from terra firma and then retreated. O'Hara looked at his watch; it had taken them half an hour.

'How many planks to go?' he asked.

Rohde grunted. 'About thirty.'

'That gives us fifteen hours before they're across,' said O'Hara.

'More than that,' said Forester. 'They're not likely to do that trapeze act in the dark.'

Rohde took out his pistol and carefully sighted on the bridge, using his forearm as a rest. Forester said, 'That's no damned use – you won't hit anything at fifty yards with a pistol.'

'I can try,' said Rohde.

Forester sighed. 'All right,' he conceded. 'But just one shot to see how it goes. How many slugs have you got?'

'I had two magazines with seven bullets in each,' said Rohde. 'I have fired three shots.'

'You pop off another and that leaves ten. That's not too many.'

Rohde tightened his lips stubbornly and kept the pistol where it was. Forester winked at O'Hara and said, 'If you don't mind I'm going to retire now. As soon as you start shooting they're going to shoot right back.'

He withdrew slowly, then turned and lay on his back and looked at the sky, gesturing for O'Hara to join him. 'It looks as though the time is ripe to hold our council of war,' he said. 'Surrender or fight. But there may be a way out of it – have you got that air chart of yours?'

O'Hara produced it. 'We can't cross the river – not here, at least,' he said.

Forester spread out the chart and studied it. He put his finger down. 'Here's the river – and this is where we are. This bridge isn't shown. What's this shading by the river?'

'That's the gorge.'

Forester whistled. 'Hell, it starts pretty high in the mountains, so we can't get around it upstream. What about the other way?'

O'Hara measured off the distance roughly. 'The gorge stretches for about eighty miles down stream, but there's a bridge marked here – fifty miles away, as near as dammit.'

'That's a hell of a long way,' commented Forester. 'I doubt if the old man could make it – not over mountain country.'

O'Hara said, 'And if that crowd over there have any sense they'll have another truckload of men waiting for us if we do try it. They have the advantage of being able to travel fast on the lower roads.'

'The bastards have got us boxed in,' said Forester. 'So it's surrender or fight.'

'I surrender to no communists,' said O'Hara.

There was a flat report as Rohde fired his pistol and, almost immediately, an answering fusillade of rifle shots, the sound redoubled by echoes from the high ground behind. A bullet ricocheted from close by and whined over O'Hara's head.

Rohde came slithering down. 'I missed,' he said.

Forester refrained from saying, 'I told you so,' but his expression showed it. Rohde grinned. 'But it stopped them working on the bridge – they went back fast and the plank dropped in the river.'

'That's something,' said O'Hara. 'Maybe we can hold them off that way.'

'For how long?' asked Forester. 'We can't hold them off for ever – not with ten slugs. We'd better hold our council of war. You stay here, Miguel; but choose a different observation point – they might have spotted this one.'

O'Hara and Forester went back to the group on the road. As they approached O'Hara said in a low voice, 'We'd better do something to ginger this lot up; they look too bloody nervous.'

There was a feeling of tension in the air. Peabody was muttering in a low voice to Miss Ponsky, who for once was silent herself. Willis was sitting on a rock, nervously tapping his foot on the ground, and Aguillar was speaking rapidly to Benedetta some little way removed from the group. The only one at ease seemed to be Armstrong, who was placidly sucking on an empty pipe, idly engaged in drawing patterns on the ground with a stick.

O'Hara crossed to Aguillar. 'We're going to decide what to do,' he said. 'As you suggested.'

Aguillar nodded gravely. 'I said that it must happen.'

O'Hara said, 'You're going to be all right.' He looked at Benedetta; her face was pale and her eyes were dark smudges in her head. He said, 'I don't know how long this is going to take, but why don't you begin preparing a meal for us. We'll all feel better when we've eaten.'

'Yes, child,' said Aguillar. 'I will help you. I am a good cook, Señor O'Hara.'

O'Hara smiled at Benedetta. 'I'll leave you to it, then.'

He walked over to where Forester was giving a pep talk. 'And that's the position,' he was saying. 'We're boxed in and there doesn't seem to be any way out of it – but there is always a way out of anything, using brains and determination. Anyway, it's a case of surrender or fight. I'm going to fight – and so is Tim O'Hara here; aren't you, Tim?'

'I am,' said O'Hara grimly.

'I'm going to go round and ask your views, and you must each make your own decision,' continued Forester. 'What about you, Doctor Willis?'

Willis looked up and his face was strained. 'It's difficult, isn't it? You see, I'm not much of a fighter. Then again, it's a question of the odds – can we win? I don't see much reason in putting up a fight if we're certain of losing – and I don't see any chance at all of our winning out.' He paused, then said hesitantly, 'But I'll go with the majority vote.'

Willis, you bastard, you're a fine example of a fence-sitter, thought O'Hara.

'Peabody?' Forester's voice cut like a lash.

'What the hell has this got to do with us?' exploded Peabody. 'I'm damned if I'm going to risk my life for any wop politician. I say hand the bastard over and let's get the hell out of here.'

'What do you say, Miss Ponsky?'

She gave Peabody a look of scorn, then hesitated. All the talk seemed to be knocked out of her, leaving her curiously deflated. At last she said in a small voice, 'I know I'm only a woman and I can't do much in the way of fighting, and I'm scared to death – but I think we ought to fight.' She ended in a rush and looked defiantly at Peabody. 'And that's my vote.'

Good for you, Miss Ponsky, cheered O'Hara silently. That's three to fight. It's now up to Armstrong – he can tip it for fighting or make a deadlock, depending on his vote.

'Doctor Armstrong, what do you have to say?' queried Forester.

Armstrong sucked on his pipe and it made an obscene noise. 'I suppose I'm more an authority on this kind of situation than anyone present,' he observed. 'With the possible exception of Señor Aguillar, who at present is cooking our lunch, I see. Give me a couple of hours and I could quote a hundred parallel examples drawn from history.'

Peabody muttered in exasperation, 'What the hell!'

'The question at issue is whether to hand Señor Aguillar to the gentlemen on the other side of the river. The important point, as I see it affecting us, is what would they do with him? And I can't really see that there is anything they can do with him other than kill him. Keeping high-standing politicians as prisoners went out of fashion a long time ago. Now, if they kill him they will automatically be forced to kill us. They would not dare take the risk of letting this story loose upon the world. They would be most painfully criticized, perhaps to the point of losing what they have set out to gain. In short, the people of Cordillera would not stand for it. So you see, we are not fighting for the life of Señor Aguillar; we are fighting for our own lives.'

He put his pipe back into his mouth and made another rude noise.

'Does that mean that you are in favour of fighting?' asked Forester.

'Of course,' said Armstrong in surprise. 'Haven't you been listening to what I've been saying?'

Peabody looked at him in horror. 'Jesus!' he said. 'What have I got myself into?' He buried his head in his hands.

Forester grinned at O'Hara, and said, 'Well, Doctor Willis?'

'I fight,' said Willis briefly.

O'Hara chuckled. One academic man had convinced another.

Forester said, 'Ready to change your mind, Peabody?'

Peabody looked up. 'You really think they're going to rub us all out?'

'If they kill Aguillar I don't see what else they can do,' said Armstrong reasonably. 'And they will kill Aguillar, you know.'

'Oh, hell,' said Peabody in an anguish of indecision.

'Come on,' Forester ordered harshly. 'Put up or shut up.'

'I guess I'll have to throw in with you,' Peabody said morosely.

'That's it, then,' said Forester. 'A unanimous vote. I'll tell Aguillar and we'll discuss how to fight over some food.' Miss Ponsky went to help the Aguillars with their cooking and O'Hara went back to the river to see what Rohde was doing. He looked back and saw that Armstrong was talking to Willis and again drawing on the ground with a stick. Willis looked interested.

Rohde had chosen a better place for observation and at first O'Hara could not find him. At last he saw the sole of a boot protruding from behind a rock and joined Rohde, who seemed pleased. 'They have not yet come out of their holes,' he said. 'It has been an hour. One bullet that missed has held them up for an hour.'

'That's great,' said O'Hara sardonically. 'Ten bullets – ten hours.'

'It is better than that,' protested Rohde. 'They have thirty planks to put in – that would take them fifteen hours without my bullets. With the shooting it will take them twenty-five hours. They will not work at night – so that is two full days.'

O'Hara nodded. 'It gives us time to decide what to do next,' he admitted. But when the bullets were finished and the bridge completed a score of armed and ruthless men would come boiling over the river. It would be a slaughter.

'I will stay here,' said Rohde. 'Send some food when it is ready.' He nodded towards the bridge. 'It takes a brave man to walk on that, knowing that someone will shoot at him. I do not think these men are very brave – maybe it will be more than one hour to a bullet.'

O'Hara went back and told Forester what was happening and Forester grimaced. 'Two days – maybe – two days to come up with something. But with what?'

O'Hara said, 'I think a Committee of Ways and Means is indicated.'

They all sat in a circle on the sparse grass and Benedetta and Miss Ponsky served the food on the aluminium plates they had found at the camp. Forester said, 'This is a war council, so please stick to the point and let's have no idle chit-chat – we've no time to waste. Any sensible suggestions will be welcome.'

There was a dead silence, then Miss Ponsky said, 'I suppose the main problem is to stop them repairing the bridge. Well, couldn't we do something at this end – cut the ropes or something?'

'That's good in principle,' said Forester. 'Any objections to it?' He glanced at O'Hara, knowing what he would say.

O'Hara looked at Forester sourly; it seemed as though he was being cast as the cold-water expert and he did not fancy the role. He said deliberately, 'The approaches to the bridge from this side are wide open; there's no cover for at least a hundred yards – you saw what happened to Benedetta and me this morning. Anyone who tried to get to the bridge along the road would be cut down before he'd got halfway. It's point blank range, you know – they don't have to be crack shots.' He paused. 'Now I know it's the only way we *can* get at the bridge, but it seems impossible to me.'

'What about a night attack?' asked Willis.

'That sounds good,' said Forester.

O'Hara hated to do it, but he spoke up. 'I don't want to sound pessimistic, but I don't think those chaps over there are entirely stupid. They've got two trucks and four jeeps, maybe more, and those vehicles have at least two headlights apiece. They'll keep the bridge well lit during the dark hours.'

There was silence again.

Armstrong cleared his throat. 'Willis and I have been doing a little thinking and maybe we have something that will help. Again I find myself in the position of being something of an expert. You know that my work is the study of medieval history, but it so happens that I'm a specialist, and my speciality is medieval warfare. The position as I see it is that we are in a castle with a moat and a drawbridge. The drawbridge is fortuitously pulled up, but our enemies are trying to rectify that state of affairs. Our job is to stop them.'

'With what?' asked O'Hara. 'A push of a pike?'

'I wouldn't despise medieval weapons too much, O'Hara,' said Armstrong mildly. 'I admit that the people of those days weren't as adept in the art of slaughter as we are, but still, they managed to kill each other off at a satisfactory rate. Now, Rohde's pistol is highly inaccurate at the range he is forced to use. What we want is a more efficient missile weapon than Rohde's pistol.'

'So we all make like Robin Hood,' said Peabody derisively. 'With the jolly old longbow, what? For Christ's sake, Professor!'

'Oh, no,' said Armstrong. 'A longbow is very chancy in the hands of a novice. It takes five years at least to train a good bowman.'

'I can use the bow,' said Miss Ponsky unexpectedly. Everyone looked at her and she coloured. 'I'm president of the South Bridge Ladies' Greenwood Club. Last year I won our own little championship in the Hereford Round.'

'That's interesting,' said Armstrong.

O'Hara said, 'Can you use a longbow lying down, Miss Ponsky?'

'It would be difficult,' she said. 'Perhaps impossible.'

O'Hara jerked his head at the gorge. 'You stand up there with a longbow and you'll get filled full of holes.'

She bridled. 'I think you'd do better helping than pouring cold water on all our ideas, Mr O'Hara.'

'I've got to do it,' said O'Hara evenly. 'I don't want anyone killed uselessly.'

'For God's sake,' exclaimed Willis. 'How did a longbow come into this? That's out – we can't make one; we haven't the material. Now, will you listen to Armstrong; he has a point to make.' His voice was unexpectedly firm.

The flat crack of Rohde's pistol echoed on the afternoon air and there was the answering fire of shots from the other side of the gorge. Peabody ducked and O'Hara looked at his watch. It had been an hour and twenty minutes – and they had nine bullets left.

Forester said, 'That's one good thing – we're safe here. Their rifles won't shoot round corners. Make your point, Doctor Armstrong.'

'I was thinking of something more on the lines of a prodd or crossbow,' said Armstrong. 'Anyone who can use a rifle can use a crossbow and it has an effective range of over a hundred yards.' He smiled at O'Hara. 'You can shoot it lying down, too.'

O'Hara's mind jumped at it. They could cover the bridge and also the road on the other side where it turned north and followed the edge of the gorge and where the enemy trucks were. He said, 'Does it have any penetrative power?'

'A bolt will go through mail if it hits squarely,' said Armstrong.

'What about a petrol tank?'

'Oh, it would penetrate a petrol tank quite easily.'

'Now, take it easy,' said Forester. 'How in hell can we make a crossbow?'

'You must understand that I'm merely a theoretician where this is concerned,' explained Armstrong. 'I'm no mechanic or engineer. But I described what I want to Willis and he thinks we can make it.'

'Armstrong and I were rooting round up at the camp,' said Willis. 'One of the huts had been a workshop and there was a lot of junk lying about – you know, the usual bits and pieces that you find in a metal-working shop. I reckon they didn't think it worthwhile carting the stuff away when they abandoned the place. There are some flat springs and odd bits of metal rod; and there's some of that concrete reinforcing steel that we can cut up to make arrows.'

'Bolts,' Armstrong corrected mildly. 'Or quarrels, if you prefer. I thought first of making a prodd, you know; that's a type of crossbow which fires bullets, but Willis has convinced me that we can manufacture bolts more easily.'

'What about tools?' asked O'Hara. 'Have you anything that will cut metal?'

'There are some old hacksaw blades,' Willis said. 'And I saw a couple of worn-out files. And there's a hand-powered grindstone that looks as though it came out of the Ark. I'll make out; I'm good with my hands and I can adapt Armstrong's designs with the material available.'

O'Hara looked at Forester, who said slowly, 'A weapon accurate to a hundred yards built out of junk seems too good to be true. Are you certain about this, Doctor Armstrong?'

'Oh, yes,' said Armstrong cheerfully. 'The crossbow has killed thousands of men in its time – I see no reason why it shouldn't kill a few more. And Willis seems to think he can make it.' He smiled. 'I've drawn the blueprints there.' He pointed to a few lines scratched in the dust.

'If we're going to do this, we'd better do it quickly,' said O'Hara.

'Right.' Forester looked up at the sun. 'You've got time to make it up to the camp by nightfall. It's uphill, but you'll be travelling light. You go too, Peabody; Willis can use another pair of hands.'

Peabody nodded quickly. He had no taste for staying too near the bridge.

'One moment,' said Aguillar, speaking for the first time. 'The bridge is made of rope and wood – very combustible materials. Have you considered the use of fire? Señor O'Hara gave me the idea when he spoke of petrol tanks.'

'Um,' said O'Hara. 'But how to get the fire to the bridge?'

'Everyone think of that,' said Forester. 'Now let's get things moving.'

Armstrong, Willis and Peabody left immediately on the long trudge up to the camp. Forester said, 'I didn't know what to make of Willis – he's not very forthcoming – but I've got him tagged now. He's the practical type; give him something to do and he'll get it done, come hell or high water. He'll do.'

Aguillar smiled. 'Armstrong is surprising, too.'

'My God!' said Forester. 'Crossbows in this day and age!'

O'Hara said, 'We've got to think about making camp. There's no water here, and besides, our main force is too close to the enemy. There's a pond about half a mile back – I think that's a good spot.'

'Benedetta, you see to that,' Aguillar commanded. 'Miss Ponsky will help you.' He watched the two women go, then turned with a grave face. 'There is something we must discuss, together with Miguel. Let us go over there.'

Rohde was happy. 'They have not put a plank in the bridge yet. They ran again like the rabbits they are.'

Aguillar told him what was happening and he said uncertainly, 'A crossbow?'

'I think it's crazy, too,' said Forester. 'But Armstrong reckons it'll work.'

'Armstrong is a good man,' said Aguillar. 'He is thinking of immediate necessities – but I think of the future. Suppose we hold off these men; suppose we destroy the bridge – what then?'

'We're not really any better off,' said O'Hara reflectively. 'They've got us pinned down anyway.'

'Exactly,' said Aguillar. 'True, we have plenty of food, but that means nothing. Time is very valuable to these men, just as it is to me. They gain everything by keeping me inactive.'

'By keeping you here they've removed you from the game,' agreed Forester. 'How long do you think it will be before they make their *coup d'état*?'

Aguillar shrugged. 'One month – maybe two. Certainly not longer. We advanced our own preparations because the communists showed signs of moving. It is a race between us with the destiny of Cordillera as the prize – maybe the destiny of the whole of Latin America is at stake. And the time is short.'

'Your map, Señor O'Hara,' said Rohde suddenly.

O'Hara took out the chart and spread it on a rock, and Rohde traced the course of the river north and south, shaking his head. 'This river – this gorge – is a trap, pinning us against the mountains,' he said.

'We've agreed it's no use going for the bridge downstream,' said Forester. 'It's a hell of a long way and it's sure to be guarded.'

'What's to stop *them* crossing that bridge and pushing up on this side of the river to outflank us?' asked O'Hara.

'As long as they think they can repair this bridge they won't do that,' Aguillar said. 'Communists are not supermen; they are as lazy as other people and they would not relish crossing eighty kilometres of mountain country – that would take at least four days. I think they will be content to stop the bolt hole.'

Rohde's fingers swept across the map to the west. 'That leaves the mountains.'

Forester turned and looked at the mountain wall, at the icy peaks. 'I don't like the sound of that. I don't think Señor Aguillar could make it.'

'I know,' said Rohde. 'He must stay here. But someone must cross the mountains for help.'

'Let's see if it's practicable,' said O'Hara. 'I was going to fly through the Puerto de las Aguilas. That means that anyone going back would have to go twenty miles north before striking west through the pass. And he'd have to go pretty high to get round this bloody gorge. The pass isn't so bad – it's only about fourteen thousand feet.'

'A total of about thirty miles before he got into the Santos Valley,' said Forester. 'That's on straight line courses. It would probably be fifty over the ground.'

There is another way,' said Rohde quietly. He pointed to the mountains. 'This range is high, but not very wide. On the other side lies the Santos Valley. If you draw a line on the map from here to Altemiros in the Santos Valley you will find that it is not more than twenty-five kilometres.'

O'Hara bent over the map and measured the distance. 'You're right; about fifteen miles – but it's all peaks.'

'There is a pass about two miles north-west of the mine,' said Rohde. 'It has no name because no one is so foolish as to use it. It is about five thousand eight hundred metres.'

Forester rapidly translated. 'Wow! Nineteen thousand feet.'

'What about lack of oxygen?' asked O'Hara. 'We've had enough trouble with that already. Could a man go over that pass without oxygen?'

'I have done so,' said Rohde. 'Under more favourable conditions. It is a matter of acclimatization. Mountaineers know this; they stay for days at one level and then move up the mountain to another camp and stay a few days there also before moving to a higher level. It is to attune their bodies to the changing conditions.' He looked up at the mountains. 'If I went up to the camp tomorrow and spent a day there then went to the mine and stayed a day there – I think I could cross that pass.'

Forester said, 'You couldn't go alone.'

'I'll go with you,' said O'Hara promptly.

'Hold on there,' said Forester. 'Are you a mountaineer?'

'No,' said O'Hara.

'Well, I am. I mean, I've scrambled about in the Rockies – that should count for something.' He appealed to Rohde. 'Shouldn't it?'

Aguillar said, 'You should not go alone, Miguel.'

'Very well,' said Rohde. 'I will take one man – you.' He nodded to Forester and smiled grimly. 'But I promise you – you will be sorry.'

Forester grinned cheerfully and said, 'Well, Tim, that leaves you as garrison commander. You'll have your hands full.'

'*Si*,' said Rohde. 'You must hold them off.'

A new sound was added to the noise of the river and Rohde immediately wriggled up to his observation post, then beckoned to O'Hara. 'They are starting their engines,' he said. 'I think they are going away.'

But the vehicles did not move. 'What are they doing?' asked Rohde in perplexity.

'They're charging their batteries,' said O'Hara. 'They're making sure that they'll have plenty of light tonight.'

II

O'Hara and Aguillar went back to help the women make camp, leaving Rohde and Forester watching the bridge. There was no immediate danger of the enemy forcing the crossing and any unusual move could soon be reported.

Forester's attitude had changed as soon as the decision to cross the mountains had been made. He no longer drove hard for action, seemingly being content to leave it to O'Hara. It was as though he had tacitly decided that there could be only one commander and the man was O'Hara.

O'Hara's lips quirked as he mentally reviewed his garrison: An old man and a young girl; two sedentary academic types; a drunk and someone's maiden aunt; and himself – a broken-down pilot. On the other side of the river were at least twenty ruthless men – with God knows how many more to back them up. His muscles tensed at the thought that they were communists; sloppy South American communists, no doubt – but still communists.

Whatever happens, they're not going to get me again, he thought.

Benedetta was very quiet and O'Hara knew why. To be shot at for the first time took the pith out of a person – one came to the abrupt realization that one was a soft bag of wind and liquids, vulnerable and defenceless against steel-jacketed bullets which could rend and tear. He remembered the first time he had been in action, and felt very sorry for Benedetta; at least he had been prepared, however inadequately, for the bullets – the bullets and the cannon shells.

He looked across at the scattered rocks on the bleak hillside. 'I wonder if there's a cave over there?' he suggested. 'That would come in handy right now.' He glanced at Benedetta. 'Let's explore a little.'

She looked at her uncle who was helping Miss Ponsky check the cans of food. 'All right,' she said.

They crossed the road and struck off at right angles, making their way diagonally up the slope. The ground was covered with boulders and small pebbles and the going was difficult, their feet slipping as the stones shifted. O'Hara thought that one could break an ankle quite easily and a faint idea stirred at the back of his mind.

After a while they separated, O'Hara to the left and the girl to the right. For an hour they toiled among the rocks, searching for something that would give shelter against the night wind, however small. O'Hara found nothing, but he heard a faint shout from Benedetta and crossed the hillside to see what she had found.

It was not a cave, merely a fortuitous tumbling of the rocks. A large boulder had rolled from above and wedged itself between two others, forming a roof. It reminded O'Hara of a dolmen he had seen on Dartmoor, although the whole thing was very much bigger. He regarded it appreciatively. At least it would be shelter from snow and rain and it gave a little protection from the wind.

He went inside and found a hollow at the back. 'This is good,' he said. 'This will hold a lot of water – maybe twenty gallons.'

He turned and looked at Benedetta. The exercise had brought some colour into her cheeks and she looked better. He produced his cigarettes. 'Smoke?'

She shook her head. 'I don't.'

'Good!' he said with satisfaction. 'I was hoping you didn't.' He looked into the packet – there were eleven left. 'I'm a selfish type, you know; I want these for myself.'

He sat down on a rock and lit his cigarette, voluptuously inhaling the smoke. Benedetta sat beside him and said, 'I'm glad you decided to help my uncle.'

O'Hara grinned. 'Some of us weren't too sure. It needed a little tough reasoning to bring them round. But it was finally unanimous.'

She said in a low voice, 'Do you think there's any chance of our coming out of this?'

O'Hara bit his lip and was silent for a time. Then he said, 'There's no point in hiding the truth – I don't think we've got a cat in hell's chance. If they bust across the bridge and we're as defenceless as we are now, we won't have a hope.'

He waved his hand at the terrain. 'There's just one chance – if we split up, every man for himself heading in a different direction, then they'll have to split up, too. This is rough country and one of us might get away to tell what happened to the rest. But that's pretty poor consolation.'

'Then why did you decide to fight?' she said in wonder.

O'Hara chuckled. 'Armstrong put up some pretty cogent arguments,' he said, and told her about it. Then he added, 'But I'd have fought anyway. I don't like those boys across the river; I don't like what they do to people. It makes no difference if their skins are yellow, white or brown – they're all of the same stripe.'

'Señor Forester was telling me that you fought together in Korea,' Benedetta said.

'We might have – we probably did. He was in an American squadron which we flew with sometimes. But I never met him.'

'It must have been terrible,' she said. 'All that fighting.'

'It wasn't too bad,' said O'Hara. 'The fighting part of it.' He smiled. 'You *do* get used to being shot at, you know. I think that people can get used to anything if it goes on long enough – most things, anyway. That's the only way wars can be fought – because people can adapt and treat the craziest things as normal. Otherwise they couldn't go through with it.'

She nodded. 'I know. Look at us here. Those men shoot at us and Miguel shoots back – he regards it as the normal thing to do.'

'It *is* the normal thing to do,' said O'Hara harshly. 'The human being is a fighting animal; it's that quality which has put him where he is – the king of this planet.' His lips twisted. 'It's also the thing that's maybe holding him back from bigger things.' He laughed abruptly. 'Christ, this is no time for the philosophy of war – I'd better leave that to Armstrong.'

'You said something strange,' said Benedetta. 'You said that Korea wasn't too bad – the fighting part of it. What *was* bad, if it wasn't the fighting?'

O'Hara looked into the distance. 'It was when the fighting stopped – when *I* stopped fighting – when I couldn't fight any more. Then it was bad.'

'You were a prisoner? In the hands of the Chinese? Forester said something of that.'

O'Hara said slowly, 'I've killed men in combat – in hot blood – and I'll probably do it again, and soon, at that. But what those communist bastards can do intellectually and with cold purpose is beyond . . .' He shook his head irritably. 'I prefer not to talk about it.'

He had a sudden vision of the bland, expressionless features of the Chinese lieutenant, Feng. It was something that had haunted his dreams and woken him screaming ever since Korea. It was the reason he preferred to go to sleep in a sodden, dreamless and mindless coma. He said, 'Let's talk about you. You speak good English – where did you learn it?'

She was aware that she had trodden on forbidden and shaky ground. 'I'm sorry if I disturbed you, Señor O'Hara,' she said contritely.

'That's all right. But less of the Señor O'Hara; my name is Tim.'

She smiled quickly. 'I was educated in the United States, Tim. My uncle sent me there after Lopez made the revolution.' She laughed. 'I was taught English by a teacher very like Miss Ponsky.'

'Now there's a game old trout,' said O'Hara. 'Your uncle sent you? What about your parents?'

'My mother died when I was a child. My father – Lopez had him shot.'

O'Hara sighed. 'We both seem to be scraping on raw nerves, Benedetta. I'm sorry.'

She said sadly, 'It's the way the world is, Tim.'

He agreed sombrely. 'Anyone who expects fair play in this world is a damn fool. That's why we're in this jam. Come on, let's get back; this isn't getting us anywhere.' He pinched off his cigarette and carefully put the stub back in the packet.

As Benedetta rose she said, 'Do you think that Señor Armstrong's idea of a crossbow will work?'

'I don't,' said O'Hara flatly. 'I think that Armstrong is a romantic. He's specialized as a theoretician in wars a thousand years gone, and I can't think of anything more futile than that. He's an ivory-tower man – an academician – bloodthirsty in a theoretical way, but the sight of blood will turn his stomach. And I think he's a little bit nuts.'

III

Armstrong's pipe gurgled as he watched Willis rooting about in the rubbish of the workshop. His heart was beating rapidly and he felt breathless, although the altitude did not seem to affect him as much as the previous time he had been at the hutted camp. His mind was turning over the minutiae of his profession – the science of killing without gunpowder. He thought coldly and clearly about the ranges, trajectories and penetrations that could be obtained from pieces of bent steel and twisted gut, and he sought to adapt the ingenious mechanisms so clearly diagrammed in his mind to the materials and needs of the moment. He looked up at the roof beams of the hut and a new idea dawned on him. But he put it aside – the crossbow came first.

Willis straightened, holding a flat spring. 'This came from an auto – will it do for the bow?'

Armstrong tried to flex it and found it very stiff. 'It's very strong,' he said. 'Probably stronger than anything they had in the Middle Ages. This will be a very powerful weapon. Perhaps this is too strong – we must be able to bend it.'

'Let's go over that problem again,' Willis said.

Armstrong drew on the back of an envelope. 'For the light sporting bows they had a goat's-foot lever, but that is not strong enough for the weapon we are considering. For the heavier military bows they had two methods of bending – the cranequin, a ratchet arranged like this, which was demounted for firing, and the other was a windlass built into the bow which worked a series of pulleys.'

Willis looked at the rough sketches and nodded. 'The windlass is our best bet,' he said. 'That ratchet thing would be difficult to make. And if necessary we can weaken the spring by grinding it down.' He looked around. 'Where's Peabody?'

'I don't know,' said Armstrong. 'Let's get on with this.'

'You'd better find him,' Willis said. 'We'll put him on to making arrows – that should be an easy job.'

'Bolts or quarrels,' said Armstrong patiently.

'Whatever they're called, let's get on with it,' Willis said.

They found Peabody taking it easy in one of the huts, heating a can of beans. Reluctantly he went along to the workshop and they got to work. Armstrong marvelled at the dexterity of Willis's fingers as he contrived effective parts from impossible materials and worse tools. They found the old grindstone to be their most efficient cutting tool, although it tended to waste material. Armstrong sweated in turning the crank and could not keep it up for long, so they took it in turns, he and Willis silently, Peabody with much cursing.

They ripped out electric wiring from a hut and tore down conduit tubing. They cut up reinforcing steel into lengths and slotted the ends to take flights. It was cold and their hands were numb and the blood oozed from the cuts made when their makeshift tools slipped.

They worked all night and dawn was brightening the sky as Armstrong took the completed weapon in his hands and looked at it dubiously. 'It's a bit different from how I imagined it, but I think it will do.' He rubbed his eyes wearily. 'I'll take it down now – they might need it.'

Willis slumped against the side of the hut. 'I've got an idea for a better one,' he said. 'That thing will be a bastard to cock. But I must get some sleep first – and food.' His voice trailed to a mumble and he blinked his eyes rapidly.

All that night the bridge had been illuminated by the headlamps of the enemy vehicles and it was obviously hopeless to make a sortie in an attempt to cut the cables. The enemy did not work on the bridge at night, not relishing being in a spotlight when a shot could come out of the darkness.

Forester was contemptuous of them. 'The goddam fools,' he said. 'If we can't hit them in daylight then it's sure we can't at night – but if they'd any sense they'd see that they could spot our shooting at night and they'd send a man on to the bridge to draw our fire – then they'd fill our man full of holes.'

But during the daylight hours the enemy *had* worked on the bridge, and had been less frightened of the shots fired at them. No one had been hit and it had become obvious that there was little danger other than that from a freakishly lucky shot. By morning there were but six bullets left for Rohde's pistol and there were nine more planks in the bridge.

By nine o'clock Rohde had expended two more bullets and it was then that Armstrong stumbled down the road carrying a contraption. 'Here it is,' he said. 'Here's your crossbow.' He rubbed his eyes which were red-rimmed and tired. 'Professionally speaking, I'd call it an arbalest.'

'My God, that was quick,' said O'Hara.

'We worked all night,' Armstrong said tiredly. 'We thought you'd need it in a hurry.'

'How does it work?' asked O'Hara, eyeing it curiously.

'The metal loop on the business end is a stirrup,' said Armstrong. 'You put it on the ground and put your foot in it. Then you take this cord and clip the hook on to the bowstring and start winding on this handle. That draws back the bowstring until it engages on this sear. You drop a bolt in this trough and you're ready to shoot. Press the trigger and the sear drops to release the bowstring.'

The crossbow was heavy in O'Hara's hands. The bow itself was made from a car spring and the bowstring was a length of electric wire woven into a six-strand cord to give it strength. The cord which drew it back was also electric wire woven from three strands. The sear and trigger were carved from wood, and the trough where the bolt went was made from a piece of electric conduit piping.

It was a triumph of improvisation.

'We had to weaken the spring,' said Armstrong. 'But it's still got a lot of bounce. Here's a bolt – we made a dozen.'

The bolt was merely a length of round steel, three-eighths of an inch in diameter and fifteen inches long. It was very rusty. One end was slotted to hold metal flights cut from a dried-milk can and the other end was sharpened to a point. O'Hara hefted it thoughtfully; it was quite heavy. 'If this thing doesn't kill immediately, anyone hit will surely die of blood-poisoning. Does it give the range you expected?'

'A little more,' said Armstrong. 'These bolts are heavier than the medieval originals because they're steel throughout instead of having a wooden shaft – but the bow is very powerful and that makes up for it. Why don't you try it out?'

O'Hara put his foot in the stirrup and cranked the windlass handle. He found it more difficult than he had anticipated – the bow was very strong. As he slipped a bolt into the trough he said, 'What should I shoot at?'

'What about the earth bank over there?'

The bank was about sixty yards away. He raised the crossbow and Armstrong said quickly, 'Try it lying down, the way we'll use it in action. The trajectory is very flat so you won't have much trouble with sighting. I thought we'd wait until we got down here before sighting in.' He produced a couple of gadgets made of wire. 'We'll use a ring-and-pin sight.'

O'Hara lay down and fitted the rough wooden butt awkwardly into his shoulder. He peered along the trough and sighted as best he could upon a brown patch of earth on the bank. Then he squeezed the trigger and the crossbow bucked hard against his shoulder as the string was released.

There was a puff of dust frum the extreme right of the target at which he had aimed. He got up and rubbed his shoulder. 'My God!' he said with astonishment. 'She's got a hell of a kick.'

Armstrong smiled faintly. 'Let's retrieve the bolt.'

They walked over to the bank but O'Hara could not see it. 'It went in about here,' he said. 'I saw the dust distinctly – but where is it?'

Armstrong grinned. 'I told you this weapon was powerful. There's the bolt.'

O'Hara grunted with amazement as he saw what Armstrong meant. The bolt had penetrated more than its own length into the earth and had buried itself completely. As Armstrong dug it out, O'Hara said, 'We'd better all practise with this thing and find out who's the best shot.' He looked at Armstrong. 'You'd better get some sleep; you look pooped.'

'I'll wait until I see the bow in action,' said Armstrong. 'Maybe it'll need some modification. Willis is making another – he has some ideas for improvements – and we put Peabody to making more bolts.' He stood upright with the bolt in his hands. 'And I've got to fix the sights.'

All of them, excepting Aguillar and Rohde, practised with the crossbow, and – perhaps not surprisingly – Miss

Ponsky turned out to be the best shot, with Forester coming next and O'Hara third. Shooting the bow was rough on Miss Ponsky's shoulder, but she made a soft shoulder-pad and eight times out of ten she put a bolt into a twelve-inch circle, clucking deprecatingly when she missed.

'She's not got the strength to crank it,' said Forester. 'But she's damned good with the trigger.'

'That settles it,' said O'Hara. 'She gets first crack at the enemy – if she'll do it.' He crossed over to her and said with a smile, 'It looks as though you're elected to go into action first. Will you give it a go?'

Her face paled and her nose seemed even sharper. 'Oh, my!' she said, flustered. 'Do you think I can do it?'

'They've put in another four planks,' said O'Hara quietly. 'And Rohde's saving his last four bullets until he's reasonably certain of making a hit. This is the only other chance we've got – and you're the best shot.'

Visibly she pulled herself together and her chin rose in determination. 'All right,' she said. 'I'll do my best.'

'Good! You'd better come and have a look at the bridge to get your range right – and maybe you'd better take a few practice shots at the same range.'

He took her up to where Rohde was lying. 'Miss Ponsky's going to have a go with the crossbow,' he said.

Rohde looked at it with interest. 'Does it work?'

'It's got the range and velocity,' O'Hara told him. 'It should work all right.' He turned his attention to the bridge. Two men had just put in another plank and were retreating. The gap in the bridge was getting very small – soon it would be narrow enough for a determined man to leap. 'You'd better take the nearest man the next time they come out,' he said. 'What would you say the range is?'

Miss Ponsky considered. 'A little less than the range I've been practising at,' she said. 'I don't think I need to practise any more.' There was a tremor in her voice.

O'Hara regarded her. 'This has got to be done, Miss Ponsky. Remember what they did to Mrs Coughlin – and what they'll do to us if they get across the bridge.'

'I'll be all right,' she said in a low voice.

O'Hara nodded in satisfaction. 'You take Rohde's place. I'll be a little way along. Take your time – you needn't hurry. Regard it as the target practice you've just been doing.'

Forester had already cocked the bow and handed it up to Miss Ponsky. She put a bolt in the trough and slid forward on her stomach until she got a good view of the bridge. O'Hara waited until she was settled, then moved a little way farther along the edge of the gorge. He looked back and saw Forester talking to Armstrong, who was lying full-length on the ground, his eyes closed.

He found a good observation post and lay waiting. Presently the same two men appeared again, carrying a plank. They crawled the length of the bridge, pushing the plank before them until they reached the gap – even though none of them had been hit, they weren't taking unnecessary chances. Once at the gap they got busy, lashing the plank to the two main ropes.

O'Hara found his heart thumping and the wait seemed intolerably long. The nearest man was wearing a leather jacket similar to his own and O'Hara could see quite clearly the flicker of his eyes as he gazed apprehensively at the opposite bank from time to time. O'Hara clenched his fist. 'Now!' he whispered. 'For God's sake – now!'

He did not hear the twang as the crossbow fired, but he saw the spurt of dust from the man's jacket as the bolt hit him, and suddenly a shaft of steel sprouted from the man's back just between the shoulder blades. There was a faint cry above the roar of the river and the man jerked his legs convulsively. He thrust his arms forward, almost in an imploring gesture, then he toppled sideways and rolled off the edge of the bridge, to fall in a spinning tangle of arms and legs into the raging river.

The other man paused uncertainly, then ran back across the bridge to the other side of the gorge. The bridge swayed under his pounding feet and as he ran he looked back fearfully. He joined the group at the end of the bridge and O'Hara saw him indicate his own back and another man shaking his head in disbelief.

Gently he withdrew and ran back to the place from which Miss Ponsky had fired the shot. She was lying on the ground, her body racked with sobs, and Forester was bending over her. 'It's all right, Miss Ponsky,' he was saying. 'It had to be done.'

'But I've killed a man,' she wailed. 'I've taken a life.'

Forester got her to her feet and led her away, talking softly to her all the time. O'Hara bent and picked up the crossbow. 'What a secret weapon!' he said in admiration. 'No noise, no flash – just *zing*.' He laughed. 'They still don't know what happened – not for certain. Armstrong, you're a bloody genius.'

But Armstrong was asleep.

IV

The enemy made no further attempts to repair the bridge that morning. Instead, they kept up a steady, if slow, light barrage of rifle fire, probing the tumble of rocks at the edge of the gorge in the hope of making hits. O'Hara withdrew everyone to safety, including Rohde. Then he borrowed a small mirror from Benedetta and contrived a makeshift periscope, being careful to keep the glass in the shadow of a rock so that it would not reflect direct sunlight. He fixed it so that an observer could lie on his back in perfect cover, but could still keep an eye on the bridge. Forester took first watch.

O'Hara said, 'If they come on the bridge again use the gun – just one shot. We've got them off-balance now and a bit nervous. They don't know if that chap fell off the bridge by accident, whether he was shot and they didn't hear the report, or whether it was something else. *We* know it was something else and so does the other man who was on the bridge, but I don't think they believe him. There was a hell of an argument going on the last I saw of it. At any rate, I think they'll be leery of coming out now, and a shot ought to put them off.'

Forester checked the pistol and looked glumly at the four remaining bullets. 'I feel a hell of a soldier – firing off twenty-five per cent of the available ammunition at one bang.'

'It's best this way,' said O'Hara. 'They don't know the state of our ammunition, the crossbow is our secret weapon, and by God we must make the best use of it. I have ideas about that, but I want to wait for the second crossbow.' He paused. 'Have you any idea how many of the bastards are across there?'

'I tried a rough count,' said Forester. 'I made it twenty-three. The leader seems to be a big guy with a Castro beard. He's wearing some kind of uniform – jungle-green pants and a bush-jacket.' He rubbed his chin and said thoughtfully, 'It's my guess that he's a Cuban specialist.'

'I'll look out for him,' said O'Hara. 'Maybe if we can nail him the rest will pack up.'

'Maybe,' said Forester non-committally.

O'Hara trudged back to the camp which had now been transferred to the rock shelter on the hillside. That was a better defensive position and could not be so easily rushed, the attackers having to move over broken ground. But O'Hara had no great faith in it; if the enemy crossed the bridge they could move up the road fast, outflanking the rock shelter to move in behind and surround them. He had cudgelled his brain to find a way of blocking the road but had not come up with anything.

But there it was – a better place than the camp by the pond and the roadside. The trouble was water, but the rock hollow at the rear of the shelter had been filled with twenty-five gallons of water, transported laboriously a canful at a time, much of it spilling on the way. And it was a good place to sleep, too.

Miss Ponsky had recovered from her hysteria but not from her remorse. She was unaccustomedly quiet and withdrawn, speaking to no one. She had helped to transport the water and the food but had done so mechanically, as if she did not care. Aguillar was grave. 'It is not right that this should be,' he said. 'It is not right that a lady like Miss Ponsky should have to do these things.'

O'Hara felt exasperated. 'Dammit, we didn't start this fight,' he said. 'The Coughlins are dead, and Benedetta was nearly killed – not to mention me. I'll try not to let it happen again, but she *is* the best shot and we *are* fighting for our lives.'

'You are a soldier,' said Aguillar. 'Almost I seem to hear you say, with Napoleon, that one cannot make an omelette without breaking eggs.' His voice was gently sardonic.

O'Hara disregarded that. 'We must all practise with the bow – we must learn to use it while we have time.'

Aguillar tapped him on the arm. 'Señor O'Hara, perhaps if I gave myself to these people they would be satisfied.'

O'Hara stared at him. 'You know they wouldn't; they can't let us go – knowing what we know.'

Aguillar nodded. 'I know that; I was wondering if you did.' He shrugged half-humorously. 'I wanted you to convince me there is nothing to gain by it – and you have. I am sorry to have brought this upon all these innocent people.'

O'Hara made an impatient noise and Aguillar continued, 'There comes a time when the soldier takes affairs out of the hands of the politician – all ways seem to lead to violence. So I must cease to be a politician and become a soldier. I will learn how to shoot this bow well, señor.'

'I wouldn't do too much, Señor Aguillar,' said O'Hara. 'You must conserve your strength in case we must move suddenly and quickly. You're not in good physical shape, you know.'

Aguillar's voice was sharp. 'Señor, I will do what I must.'

O'Hara said no more, guessing he had touched on Spanish-American pride. He went to talk to Miss Ponsky.

She was kneeling in front of the pressure stove, apparently intent on watching a can of water boil, but her eyes were unfocused and staring far beyond. He knew what she was looking at – the steel bolt that had sprouted like a monstrous growth in the middle of a man's back.

He said, 'Killing another human being is a terrible thing, Miss Ponsky. I know – I've done it, and I was sickened for days afterwards. The first time I shot down an enemy fighter in Korea I followed him down – it was a dangerous thing to do, but I was young and inexperienced then. The Mig went down in flames, and his ejector seat didn't work, so he opened the canopy manually and jumped out against the slipstream.

'It was brave or desperate of that man to do that. But he had the Chinese sort of courage – or maybe the Russian courage, for all I know. You see, I didn't know the nationality or even the colour of the man I had killed. He fell to earth, a spinning black speck. His parachute didn't open. I knew he was a dead man.'

O'Hara moistened his lips. 'I felt bad about that, Miss Ponsky; it sickened me. But then I thought that the same man had been trying to kill me – he nearly succeeded, too. He had pumped my plane full of holes before I got him and I crash-landed on the airstrip. I was lucky to get away with it – I spent three weeks in hospital. I finally worked it out that it was a case of him or me, and I was the lucky one.

I don't know if he would have had regrets if he had killed me – I think probably not. Those people aren't trained to have much respect for life.'

He regarded her closely. 'These people across the river are the same that I fought in Korea, no matter that their skins are a different colour. We have no fight with them if they will let us go in peace – but they won't do that, Miss Ponsky. So it's back to basics; kill or be killed and the devil take the loser. You did all right, Miss Ponsky; what you did may have saved all our lives and maybe the lives of a lot of people in this country. Who knows?'

As he lapsed into silence she turned to him and said in a husky, broken voice, 'I'm a silly old woman, Mr O'Hara. For years I've been talking big, like everyone else in America, about fighting the communists; but I didn't have to do it myself, and when it comes to doing it yourself it's a different matter. Oh, we women cheered our American boys when they went to fight – there's no one more bloodthirsty than one who doesn't have to do the fighting. But when you do your own killing, it's a dreadful thing, Mr O'Hara.'

'I know,' he said. 'The only thing that makes it bearable is that if you don't kill, then you are killed. It reduces to a simple choice in the end.'

'I realize that now, Mr O'Hara,' she said. 'I'll be all right now.'

'My name is Tim,' he said. 'The English are pretty stuffy about getting on to first-name terms, but not we Irish.'

She gave him a tremulous smile. 'I'm Jennifer.'

'All right, Jenny,' said O'Hara. 'I'll try not to put you in a spot like that again.'

She turned her head away and said in a muffled voice, 'I think I'm going to cry.' Hastily she scrambled to her feet and ran out of the shelter.

Benedetta said from behind O'Hara, 'That was well done, Tim.'

He turned and looked at her stonily. 'Was it? It was something that had to be done.' He got up and stretched his legs. 'Let's practise with that crossbow.'

V

For the rest of the day they practised, learning to allow for wind and the effect of a change of range. Miss Ponsky tightened still further her wire-drawn nerves and became instructress, and the general level of performance improved enormously.

O'Hara went down to the gorge and, by triangulation, carefully measured the distance to the enemy vehicles and was satisfied that he had the range measured to a foot. Then he went back and measured the same distance on the ground and told everyone to practise with the bow at that range. It was one hundred and eight yards.

He said to Benedetta, 'I'm making you my chief-of-staff – that's a sort of glorified secretary that a general has. Have you got pencil and paper?'

She smiled and nodded, whereupon he reeled off a dozen things that had to be done. 'You pass on that stuff to the right people in case I forget – I've got a hell of a lot of things on my mind right now and I might slip up on something important when the action starts.'

He set Aguillar to tying bunches of rags around half a dozen bolts, then shot them at the target to see if the rags made any difference to the accuracy of the flight. There was no appreciable difference, so he soaked one of them in paraffin and lit it before firing, but the flame was extinguished before it reached the target.

He swore and experimented further, letting the paraffin burn fiercely before he pulled the trigger. At the expense of a scorched face he finally landed three fiercely burning bolts squarely in the target and observed happily that they continued to burn.

'We'll have to do this in the day-time,' he said. 'It'll be bloody dangerous in the dark – they'd spot the flame before we shot.' He looked up at the sun. 'Tomorrow,' he said. 'We've got to drag this thing out as long as we can.'

It was late afternoon before the enemy ventured on to the bridge again and they scattered at a shot from Rohde who, after a long sleep, had taken over again from Forester. Rohde fired another shot before sunset and then stopped on instructions from O'Hara. 'Keep the last two bullets,' he said. 'We'll need them.'

So the enemy put in three more planks and stepped up their illumination that night, although they dared not move on the bridge.

FOUR

Forester awoke at dawn. He felt refreshed after having had a night's unbroken sleep. O'Hara had insisted that he and Rohde should not stand night watches but should get as much sleep as they could. This was the day that he and Rohde were to go up to the hutted camp to get acclimatized and the next day to go on up to the mine.

He looked up at the white mountains and felt a sudden chill in his bones. He had lied to O'Hara when he said he had mountaineered in the Rockies – the highest he had climbed was to the top of the Empire State Building in an elevator. The high peaks were blindingly bright as the sun touched them and he wrinkled his eyes to see the pass that Rohde had pointed out. Rohde had said he would be sorry and Forester judged he was right; Rohde was a tough cookie and not given to exaggeration.

After cleaning up he went down to the bridge. Armstrong was on watch, lying on his back beneath the mirror. He was busy sketching on a scrap of paper with a pencil stub, glancing up at the mirror every few minutes. He waved as he saw Forester crawling up and said, 'All quiet. They've just switched off the lights.'

Forester looked at the piece of paper. Armstrong had drawn what looked like a chemist's balance. 'What's that?' he asked. 'The scales of justice?'

Armstrong looked startled and then pleased. 'Why, sir, you have identified it correctly,' he said.

Forester did not press it further. He thought Armstrong was a nut – clever, but still a nut. That crossbow of his had turned out to be some weapon – but it took a nut to think it up. He smiled at Armstrong and crawled away to where he could get a good look at the bridge.

His mouth tightened when he saw how narrow the gap was. Maybe he wouldn't have to climb the pass after all; maybe he'd have to fight and die right where he was. He judged that by the afternoon the gap would be narrow enough for a man to jump and that O'Hara had better prepare himself for a shock. But O'Hara had seemed untroubled and talked of a plan, and Forester hoped to God that he knew what he was doing.

When he got back to the rock shelter he found that Willis had come down from the hutted camp. He had hauled a *travois* the whole way and it was now being unpacked. He had brought more food, some blankets and another crossbow which he was demonstrating to O'Hara.

'This will be faster loading,' he said. 'I found some small gears, so I built them into the windlass – they make the cranking a lot easier. How did the other bow work?'

'Bloody good,' said O'Hara. 'It killed a man.'

Willis paled a little and the unshaven bristles stood out against his white skin. Forester smiled grimly. The backroom boys always felt squeamish when they heard the results of their tinkering.

O'Hara turned to Forester. 'As soon as they start work on the bridge we'll give them a surprise,' he said. 'It's time we put a bloody crimp in their style. We'll have breakfast and then go down to the bridge – you'd better stick around and see the fun; you can leave immediately afterwards.'

He swung around. 'Jenny, don't bother about helping with the breakfast. You're our star turn. Take a crossbow and have a few practice shots at the same range as yester-day.' As she paled, he smiled and said gently, 'We'll be going down to the bridge and you'll be firing at a stationary, inanimate target.'

Forester said to Willis, 'Where's Peabody?'

'Back at the camp – making more arrows.'

'Have any trouble with him?'

Willis grinned briefly. 'He's a lazy swine but a couple of kicks up the butt soon cured that,' he said, unexpectedly coarsely. 'Where's Armstrong?'

'On watch down by the bridge.'

Willis rubbed his chin with a rasping noise. 'That man's got ideas,' he said. 'He's a whole Manhattan Project by him-self. I want to talk to him.'

He headed down the hill and Forester turned to Rohde, who had been talking to Aguillar and Benedetta in Spanish. 'What do we take with us?'

'Nothing from here,' Rohde said. 'We can get what we want at the camp; but we must take little from there – we travel light.'

O'Hara looked up from the can of stew he was opening. 'You'd better take warm clothing – you can have my leather jacket,' he offered.

'Thanks,' Forester said.

O'Hara grinned. 'And you'd better take your boss's vicuna coat – he may need it. I hear it gets cold in New York.'

Forester smiled and took the can of hot stew. 'I doubt if he'll appreciate it,' he said drily.

They had just finished breakfast when Willis came run-ning back. 'They've started work on the bridge,' he shouted. 'Armstrong wants to know if he should shoot.'

'Hell no,' said O'Hara. 'We've only got two bullets.' He swung on Rohde. 'Go down there, get the gun from Armstrong and find yourself a good spot for shooting – but don't shoot until I tell you.'

Rohde plunged down the hill and O'Hara turned to the others. 'Everyone gather round,' he ordered. 'Where's Jenny?'

'I'm here,' called Miss Ponsky from inside the shelter.

'Come to the front, Jenny; you'll play a big part in all this.' O'Hara squatted down and drew two parallel lines in the dust with a sharp stone. 'That's the gorge and this is the bridge. Here is the road; it crosses the bridge, turns sharply on the other side and runs on the edge of the gorge, parallel to the river.'

He placed a small stone on his rough diagram. 'Just by the bridge there's a jeep, and behind it another jeep. Both are turned so that their lights illuminate the bridge. Behind the second jeep there's a big truck half full of timber.' O'Hara placed a larger stone. 'Behind the truck there's another jeep. There are some other vehicles farther down, but we're not concerned with those now.'

He shifted his position. 'Now for our side of the gorge. Miguel will be here, upstream of the bridge. He'll take one shot at the men on the bridge. He won't hit anyone – he hasn't yet, anyway – but that doesn't matter. It'll scare them and divert their attention, which is what I want.

'Jenny will be *here*, downstream of the bridge and immediately opposite the truck. The range is one hundred and eight yards, and we know the crossbow will do it because Jenny was shooting consistently well at that range all yesterday afternoon. As soon as she hears the shot she lets fly at the petrol tank of the truck.'

He looked up at Forester. 'You'll be right behind Jenny. As soon as she has fired she'll hand you the bow and tell you if she's hit the tank. If she hasn't, you crank the bow, reload it and hand it back to her for another shot. If she *has* hit it, then you crank it, run up to where Benedetta will be waiting and give it to her cocked but unloaded.'

He placed another small stone. 'I'll be there with Benedetta right behind me. She'll have the other crossbow ready cocked and with a fire-bolt in it.' He looked up at her. 'When I give you the signal you'll light the paraffin rags on the bolt and hand the crossbow to me, and I'll take a crack at the truck. We might need a bit of rapid fire at this point, so crank up the bows. You stick to seeing that the bolts are properly ignited before the bows are handed to me, just like we did yesterday in practice.'

He stood up and stretched. 'Is that clear to everyone?'

Willis said, 'What do I do?'

'Anyone not directly concerned with this operation will keep his head down and stay out of the way.' O'Hara paused. 'But stand by in case anything goes wrong with the bows.'

'I've got some spare bowstrings,' said Willis. 'I'll have a look at that first bow to see if it's okay.'

'Do that,' said O'Hara. 'Any more questions?'

There were no questions. Miss Ponsky held up her chin in a grimly determined manner; Benedetta turned immediately to collect the fire-bolts which were her care; Forester merely said, 'Okay with me.'

As they were going down the hill, though, he said to O'Hara, 'It's a good plan, but your part is goddam risky. They'll see those fire-bolts before you shoot. You stand a good chance of being knocked off.'

'You can't fight a war without risk,' said O'Hara. 'And that's what this is, you know; it's as much a war as any bigger conflict.'

'Yeah,' said Forester thoughtfully. He glanced at O'Hara sideways. 'What about me doing this fire-bolt bit?'

O'Hara laughed. 'You're going with Rohde – you picked it, you do it. You said I was garrison commander, so while you're here you'll bloody well obey orders.'

Forester laughed too. 'It was worth a try,' he said.

Close to the gorge they met Armstrong. 'What's going on?' he asked plaintively.

'Willis will tell you all about it,' said O'Hara. 'Where's Rohde?'

Armstrong pointed. 'Over there.'

O'Hara said to Forester, 'See that Jenny has a good seat for the performance,' and went to find Rohde.

As always, Rohde had picked a good spot. O'Hara wormed his way next to him and asked, 'How much longer do you think they'll be fixing that plank?'

'About five minutes.' Rohde lifted the pistol, obviously itching to take a shot.

'Hold it,' O'Hara said sharply. 'When they come with the next plank give them five minutes and then take a crack. We've got a surprise cooking for them.'

Rohde raised his eyebrows but said nothing. O'Hara looked at the massive stone buttresses which carried the cables of the bridge. 'It's a pity those abutments aren't made of timber – they'd have burnt nicely. What the hell did they want to build them so big for?'

'The Incas always built well,' said Rohde.

'You mean this is Inca work?' said O'Hara, astonished.

Rohde nodded. 'It was here before the Spaniards came. The bridge needs constant renewal, but the buttresses will last for ever.'

'Well, I'm damned,' said O'Hara. 'I wonder why the Incas wanted a bridge here – in the middle of nowhere.'

'The Incas did many strange things.' Rohde paused. 'I seem to remember that the ore deposit of this mine was found by tracing the surface workings of the Incas. They would need the bridge if they worked metals up here.'

O'Hara watched the men on the other side of the gorge. He spotted the big man with the beard whom Forester thought was the leader, wearing a quasi-uniform and with a pistol at his waist. He walked about bellowing orders and when he shouted men certainly jumped to it. O'Hara smiled grimly as he saw that they did not bother to take cover at all. No one had been shot at while on the other side – only when on the bridge – and that policy was now going to pay off.

He said to Rohde, 'You know what to do. I'm going to see to the rest of it.' He slid back cautiously until it was safe to stand, then ran to where the rest were waiting, skirting the dangerous open ground at the approach to the bridge.

He said to Benedetta, 'I'll be posted there; you'd better get your stuff ready. Have you got matches?'

'I have Señor Forester's cigarette lighter.'

'Good. You'd better keep it burning all the time, once the action starts. I'm just going along to see Jenny, then I'll be back.'

Miss Ponsky was waiting with Forester a little farther along. She was bright-eyed and a little excited and O'Hara knew that she'd be all right if she didn't have to kill anyone. Well, that was all right, too; she would prepare the way and he'd do the killing. He said, 'Have you had a look?'

She nodded quickly. 'The gas tank is that big cylinder fastened under the truck.'

'That's right; it's a big target. But try to hit it squarely – a bolt might glance off unless you hit it in the middle.'

'I'll hit it,' she said confidently.

He said, 'They've just about finished putting a plank in. When they start to fasten the next one Rohde is going to give them five minutes and then pop off. That's your signal.'

She smiled at him. 'Don't worry, Tim, I'll do it.'

Forester said, 'I'll keep watch. When they bring up the plank Jenny can take over.'

'Right,' said O'Hara and went back to Benedetta. Armstrong was cocking the crossbow and Benedetta had arranged the fire-bolts in an arc, their points stuck in the earth. She lifted a can. 'This is the last of the kerosene; we'll need more for cooking.'

O'Hara smiled at this incongruous domestic note, and Willis said, 'There's plenty up at the camp; we found two forty-gallon drums.'

'Did you, by God?' said O'Hara. 'That opens up possibilities.' He climbed up among the rocks to the place he had chosen and tried to figure what could be done with a forty-gallon drum of paraffin. But then two men walked on to the bridge carrying a plank and he froze in concentration. One thing at a time, Tim, my boy, he thought.

He turned his head and said to Benedetta who was standing below, 'Five minutes.'

He heard the click as she tested the cigarette lighter and turned his attention to the other side of the gorge. The minutes ticked by and he found the palms of his hands sweating. He wiped them on his shirt and cursed suddenly. A man had walked by the truck and was standing negligently in front of it – dead in front of the petrol tank.

'For Christ's sake, move on,' muttered O'Hara. He knew that Miss Ponsky must have the man in her sights – but would she have the nerve to pull the trigger? He doubted it.

Hell's teeth, I should have told Rohde what was going on, he thought. Rohde wouldn't know about the crossbow and would fire his shot on time, regardless of the man covering the petrol tank. O'Hara ground his teeth as the man, a short, thick-set Indian type, produced a cigarette and carelessly struck a match on the side of the truck.

Rohde fired his shot and there was a yell from the bridge. The man by the truck stood frozen for a long moment and then started to run. O'Hara ignored him from then on – the man disappeared, that was all he knew – and his attention was riveted on the petrol tank. He heard a dull *thunk* even at that distance, and saw a dark shadow suddenly appear in the side of the tank, and saw the tank itself shiver abruptly.

Miss Ponsky had done it!

O'Hara wiped the sweat from his eyes and wished he had binoculars. Was that petrol dropping on to the road? Was that dark patch in the dust beneath the truck the spreading stain of leaking petrol, or was it just imagination? The trigger-happy bandits on the other side were letting go with all they had in their usual futile barrage, but he ignored the racket and strained his aching eyes.

The Indian came back and looked with an air of puzzlement at the truck. He sniffed the air suspiciously and then bent down to look underneath the vehicle. Then he let out a yell and waved violently.

By God, thought O'Hara exultantly, it *is* petrol!

He turned and snapped his fingers at Benedetta who immediately lit the fire-bolt waiting ready in the crossbow. O'Hara thumped the rock impatiently with his fist while she waited until it got well alight. But he knew this was the right way – if the rags were not burning well the flame would be extinguished in flight.

She thrust the bow at him suddenly and he twisted with it in his hands, the flame scorching his face. Another man had run up and was looking incredulously under the truck. O'Hara peered through the crude wire sight and through the flames of the burning bolt and willed himself to take his time. Gently he squeezed the trigger.

The butt lurched against his shoulder and he quickly twisted over to pass the bow back into Benedetta's waiting hands, but he had time to see the flaming bolt arch well over the truck to bury itself in the earth on the other side of the road.

This new bow was shooting too high.

He grabbed the second bow and tried again, burning his fingers as he incautiously put his hand in the flame. He could feel his eyebrows shrivelling as he aimed and again the butt slammed his shoulder as he pulled the trigger. The shot went too far to the right and the bolt skidded on the road surface, sending up a shower of sparks.

The two men by the truck had looked up in alarm when the first bolt had gone over their heads. At the sight of the second bolt they both shouted and pointed across the gorge.

Let this one be it, prayed O'Hara, as he seized the bow from Benedetta. This is the one that shoots high, he thought, as he deliberately aimed for the lip of the gorge. As he squeezed the trigger a bullet clipped the rock by his head and a granite splinter scored a bloody line across his forehead. But the bolt went true, a flaming line drawn across the gorge which passed between the two men and beneath the truck.

With a soft thud the dripping petrol caught alight and the truck was suddenly enveloped in flames. The Indian staggered out of the inferno, his clothing on fire, and ran screaming down the road, his hands clawing at his eyes. O'Hara did not see the other man; he had turned and was grabbing for the second bow.

But he didn't get off another shot. He had barely lined up the sights on one of the jeeps when the bow slammed into him before he touched the trigger. He was thrown back violently and the bow must have sprung of its own volition, for he saw a fire-bolt arch into the sky. Then his head struck a rock and he was knocked unconscious.

II

He came round to find Benedetta bathing his head, looking worried. Beyond, he saw Forester talking animatedly to Willis and beyond them the sky, disfigured by a coil of black, greasy smoke. He put his hand to his head and winced. 'What the hell hit me?'

'Hush,' said Benedetta. 'Don't move.'

He grinned weakly and lifted himself up on his elbow. Forester saw that he was moving. 'Are you all right, Tim?'

'I don't know,' said O'Hara. 'I don't think so.' His head ached abominably. 'What happened?'

Willis lifted the crossbow. 'A rifle bullet hit this,' he said. 'It smashed the stirrup – you were lucky it didn't hit you. You batted your head against a rock and passed out.'

O'Hara smiled painfully at Benedetta. 'I'm all right,' he said and sat up. 'Did we do the job?'

Forester laughed delightedly. 'Did we do the job? Oh, boy!' He knelt down next to O'Hara. 'To begin with, Rohde actually hit his man on the bridge when he shot – plugged him neatly through the shoulder. That caused all the commotion we needed. Jenny Ponsky had a goddam tricky time with that guy in front of the gas tank, but she did her job in the end. She was shaking like a leaf when she gave me the bow.'

'What about the truck?' asked O'Hara. 'I saw it catch fire – that's about the last thing I did see.'

'The truck's gone,' said Forester. 'It's still burning – and the jeep next to it caught fire when the second gas tank on the other side of the truck blew up. Hell, they were running about like ants across there.' He lowered his voice. 'Both the men who were by the truck were killed. The Indian ran plumb over the edge of the gorge – I reckon he was blinded – and the other guy was burned to a crisp. Jenny didn't see it and I didn't tell her.'

O'Hara nodded; it would be a nasty thing for her to live with.

'That's about it,' said Forester. 'They've lost all their timber – it burned with the truck. They've lost the truck and a jeep and they've abandoned the jeep by the bridge – they couldn't get it back past the burning truck. All the other vehicles they've withdrawn a hell of a long way down the road where it turns away from the gorge. I'd say it's a good half-mile. They were hopping mad, judging by the way they opened up on us. They set up the damnedest barrage of rifle fire – they must have all the ammunition in the world.'

'Anybody hurt?' demanded O'Hara.

'You're our most serious casualty – no one else got a scratch.'

'I must bandage your head, Tim,' said Benedetta.

'We'll go up to the pond,' said O'Hara.

As he got to his feet Aguillar approached. 'You did well, Señor O'Hara,' he said.

O'Hara swayed and leaned on Forester for support. 'Well enough, but they won't fall for that trick again. All we've bought is time.' His voice was sober.

'Time is what we need,' said Forester. 'Earlier this morning I wouldn't have given two cents for our scheme to cross the mountains. But now Rohde and I can leave with an easy conscience.' He looked at his watch. 'We'd better get on the road.'

Miss Ponsky came up. 'Are you all right, Mr O'Hara – Tim?'

'I'm fine,' he said. 'You did all right, Jenny.'

She blushed. 'Why – thank you, Tim. But I had a dreadful moment. I really thought I'd have to shoot that man by the truck.'

O'Hara looked at Forester and grinned weakly and Forester suppressed a macabre laugh. 'You did just what you were supposed to do,' said O'Hara, 'and you did it very well.' He looked around. 'Willis, you stay down here – get the gun from Rohde and if anything happens fire the last bullet. But I don't think anything will happen – not yet a while. The rest of us will have a war council up by the pond. I'd like to do that before Ray goes off.'

'Okay,' said Forester.

They went up to the pond and O'Hara walked over to the water's edge. Before he took a cupped handful of water he caught sight of his own reflection and grimaced distastefully.

He was unshaven and very dirty, his face blackened by smoke and dried blood and his eyes red-rimmed and sore from the heat of the fire-bolts. My God, I look like a tramp, he thought.

He dashed cold water at his face and shivered violently, then turned to find Benedetta behind him, a strip of cloth in her hands. 'Your head,' she said. 'The skin was broken.'

He put a hand to the back of his head and felt the stickiness of drying blood. 'Hell, I must have hit hard,' he said.

'You're lucky you weren't killed. Let me see to it.'

Her fingers were cool on his temples as she washed the wound and bandaged his head. He rubbed his hand raspingly over his cheek; Armstrong is always clean-shaven, he thought; I must find out how he does it.

Benedetta tied a neat little knot and said, 'You must take it easy today, Tim. I think you are concussed a little.'

He nodded, then winced as a sharp pain stabbed through his head. 'I think you're right. But as for taking it easy – that isn't up to me; that's up to the boys on the other side of the river. Let's get back to the others.'

Forester rose up as they approached. 'Miguel thinks we should get going,' he said.

'In a moment,' said O'Hara. 'There are a few things I want to find out.' He turned to Rohde. 'You'll be spending a day at the camp and a day at the mine. That's two days used up. Is this lost time necessary?'

'It is necessary and barely enough,' said Rohde. 'It should be longer.'

'You're the expert on mountains,' said O'Hara. 'I'll take your word for it. How long to get across?'

'Two days,' said Rohde positively. 'If we have to take longer we will not do it at all.'

'That's four days,' said O'Hara. 'Add another day to convince someone that we're in trouble and another for that someone to do something about it. We've got to hold out for six days at least – maybe longer.'

Forester looked grave. 'Can you do it?'

'We've got to do it,' said O'Hara. 'I think we've gained one day. They've got to find some timber from somewhere, and that means going back at least fifty miles to a town. They might have to get another truck as well – and it all takes time. I don't think we'll be troubled until tomorrow – maybe not until the next day. But I'm thinking about your troubles – how are you going to handle things on the other side of the mountain?'

Miss Ponsky said, 'I've been wondering about that, too. You can't go to the government of this man Lopez. He would not help Señor Aguillar, would he?'

Forester smiled mirthlessly. 'He wouldn't lift a finger. Are there any of your people in Altemiros, Señor Aguillar?'

'I will give you an address,' said Aguillar. 'And Miguel will know. But you may not have to go as far as Altemiros.'

Forester looked interested and Aguillar said to Rohde, 'The airfield.'

'Ah,' said Rohde. 'But we must be careful.'

'What's this about an airfield?' Forester asked.

'There is a high-level airfield in the mountains this side of Altemiros,' said Aguillar. 'It is a military installation which the fighter squadrons use in rotation. Cordillera has four squadrons of fighter aircraft – the eighth, the tenth, the fourteenth and the twenty-first squadrons. We – like the communists – have been infiltrating the armed forces. The fourteenth squadron is ours; the eighth is communist; and the other two still belong to Lopez.'

'So the odds are three to one that any squadron at the airfield will be a rotten egg,' commented Forester.

'That is right,' said Aguillar. 'But the airfield is directly on your way to Altemiros. You must tread carefully and act discreetly, and perhaps you can save much time. The commandant of the fourteenth squadron, Colonel Rodriguez, is an old friend of mine – he is safe.'

'If he's there,' said Forester. 'But it's worth the chance. We'll make for this airfield as soon as we've crossed the mountains.'

'That's settled,' said O'Hara with finality. 'Doctor Armstrong, have you any more tricks up your medieval sleeve?'

Armstrong removed his pipe from his mouth. 'I think I have. I had an idea and I've been talking to Willis about it and he thinks he can make it work.' He nodded towards the gorge. 'Those people are going to be more prepared when they come back with their timber. They're not going to stand up and be shot at like tin ducks in a shooting gallery – they're going to have their defences against our cross-bows. So what we need now is a trench mortar.'

'For Christ's sake,' exploded O'Hara. 'Where the devil are we going to get a trench mortar?'

'Willis is going to make it,' Armstrong said equably. 'With the help of Señor Rohde, Mr Forester and myself – and Mr Peabody, of course, although he isn't much help, really.'

'So I'm going to make a trench mortar,' said Forester helplessly. He looked baffled. 'What do we use for explosives? Something cleverly cooked up out of match-heads?'

'Oh, you misunderstand me,' said Armstrong. 'I mean the medieval equivalent of a trench mortar. We need a machine that will throw a missile in a high trajectory to lob *behind* the defences which our enemies will undoubtedly have when they make their next move. There are no really new principles in modern warfare, you know; merely new methods of applying the old principles. Medieval man knew all the principles.'

He looked glumly at his empty pipe. 'They had a variety of weapons. The onager is no use for our purpose, of course. I did think of the mangonel and the ballista, but I discarded those too, and finally settled on the trebuchet. Powered by gravity, you know, and very effective.'

If the crossbows had not been such a great success O'Hara would have jeered at Armstrong, but now he held his peace, contenting himself with looking across at Forester ironically. Forester still looked baffled and shrugged his shoulders. 'What sort of missile would the thing throw?' he asked.

'I was thinking of rocks,' said Armstrong. 'I explained the principle of the trebuchet to Willis and he has worked it all out. It's merely the application of simple mechanics, you know, and Willis has got all that at his fingertips. We'll probably make a better trebuchet than they could in the Middle Ages – we can apply the scientific principles with more understanding. Willis thinks we can throw a twenty-pound rock over a couple of hundred yards with no trouble at all.'

'Wow!' said O'Hara. He visualized a twenty-pound boulder arching in a high trajectory – it would come out of the sky almost vertically at that range. 'We can do the bridge a bit of no good with a thing like that.'

'How long will it take to make?' asked Forester.

'Not long,' said Armstrong. 'Not more than twelve hours, Willis thinks. It's a very simple machine, really.'

O'Hara felt in his pocket and found his cigarette packet. He took one of his last cigarettes and gave it to Armstrong. 'Put that in your pipe and smoke it. You deserve it.'

Armstrong smiled delightedly and began to shred the cigarette. 'Thanks,' he said. 'I can think much better when I smoke.'

O'Hara grinned. 'I'll give you all my cigarettes if you can come up with the medieval version of the atom bomb.'

'That was gunpowder,' said Armstrong seriously. 'I think that's beyond us at the moment.'

'There's just one thing wrong with your idea,' O'Hara commented. 'We can't have too many people up at the camp. We must have somebody down at the bridge in case the enemy does anything unexpected. We've got to keep a fighting force down here.'

'I'll stay,' said Armstrong, puffing at his pipe contentedly. 'I'm not very good with my hands – my fingers are all thumbs. Willis knows what to do; he doesn't need me.'

'That's it, then,' said O'Hara to Forester. 'You and Miguel go up to the camp, help Willis and Peabody build this contraption, then push on to the mine tomorrow. I'll go down and relieve Willis at the bridge.'

III

Forester found the going hard as they climbed up to the camp. His breath wheezed in his throat and he developed slight chest pains. Rohde was not so much affected and Willis apparently not at all. During the fifteen-minute rest at the halfway point he commented on it. 'That is acclimatization,' Rohde explained. 'Señor Willis has spent much time at the camp – to come down means nothing to him. For us going up it is different.'

'That's right,' said Willis. 'Going down to the bridge was like going down to sea-level, although the bridge must be about twelve thousand feet up.'

'How high is the camp?' asked Forester.

'I'd say about fourteen and a half thousand feet,' said Willis. 'I'd put the mine at a couple of thousand feet higher.'

Forester looked up at the peaks. 'And the pass is nineteen thousand. Too close to heaven for my liking, Miguel.'

Rohde's lips twisted. 'Not heaven – it is a cold hell.'

When they arrived at the camp Forester was feeling bad and said so. 'You will be better tomorrow,' said Rohde.

'But tomorrow we're going higher,' said Forester morosely.

'One day at each level is not enough to acclimatize,' Rohde admitted. 'But it is all the time we can afford.'

Willis looked around the camp. 'Where the hell is Peabody? I'll go and root him out.'

He wandered off and Rohde said, 'I think we should search this camp thoroughly. There may be many things that would be of use to O'Hara.'

'There's the kerosene,' said Forester. 'Maybe Armstrong's gadget can throw fire bombs. That would be one way of getting at the bridge to burn it.'

They began to search the huts. Most of them were empty and disused, but three of them had been fitted out for habitation and there was much equipment. In one of the huts they found Willis shaking a recumbent Peabody, who was stretched out on a bunk.

'Five arrows,' said Willis bitterly. 'That's all this bastard has done – made five arrows before he drank himself stupid.'

'Where's he getting the booze?' asked Forester.

'There's a case of the stuff in one of the other huts.'

'Lock it up if you can,' said Forester. 'If you can't, pour it away – I ought to have warned you about this, but I forgot. We can't do much about him now – he's too far gone.'

Rohde who had been exploring the hut grunted suddenly as he took a small leather bag from a shelf. 'This is good.'

Forester looked with interest at the pale green leaves which Rohde shook out into the palm of his hand. 'What's that?'

'Coca leaves,' said Rohde. 'They will help us when we cross the mountain.'

'Coca?' said Forester blankly.

'The curse of the Andes,' said Rohde. 'This is where cocaine comes from. It has been the ruin of the *indios* – this and *aguardiente*. Señor Aguillar intends to restrict the growing of coca when he comes into power.' He smiled slowly. 'It would be asking too much to stop it altogether.'

'How is it going to help us?' asked Forester.

'Look around for another bag like this one containing a white powder,' said Rohde. As they rummaged among the shelves, he continued, 'In the great days of the Incas the use of coca was restricted to the nobles. Then the royal messengers were permitted to use it because it increased their running power and stamina. Now all the *indios* chew coca – it is cheaper than food.'

'It isn't a substitute for food, is it?'

'It anaesthetises the stomach lining,' said Rohde. 'A starving man will do anything to avoid the pangs of hunger. It is also a narcotic, bringing calmness and tranquillity – at a price.'

'Is this what you're looking for?' asked Forester. He opened a small bag he had found and tipped out some of the powder. 'What is it?'

'Lime,' said Rohde. 'Cocaine is an alkaloid and needs a base for it to precipitate. While we are waiting for Señor Willis to tell us what to do, I will prepare this for us.'

He poured the coca leaves into a saucer and began to grind them, using the back of a spoon as a pestle. The leaves were brittle and dry and broke up easily. When he had ground them to a powder he added lime and continued to grind until the two substances were thoroughly mixed. Then he put the mixture into an empty tin and added water, stirring until he had a light green paste. He took another tin and punched holes in the bottom, and, using it as a strainer, he forced the paste through.

He said, 'In any of the villages round here you can see the old women doing this. Will you get me some small, smooth stones?'

Forester went out and got the stones and Rohde used them to roll and squeeze the paste like a pastrycook. Finally the paste was rolled out for the last time and Rohde cut it into rectangles with his pocket-knife. 'These must dry in the sun,' he said. 'Then we put them back in the bags.'

Forester looked dubiously at the small green squares. 'Is this stuff habit-forming?'

'Indeed it is,' said Rohde. 'But do not worry; this amount will do us no harm. And it will give us the endurance to climb the mountains.'

Willis came back. 'We can swing it,' he said. 'We've got the material to make this – what did Armstrong call it?'

'A trebuchet,' Forester said.

'Well, we can do it,' said Willis. He stopped and looked down at the table. 'What's that stuff?'

Forester grinned. 'A substitute for prime steak; Miguel just cooked it up.' He shook his head. 'Medieval artillery and pep pills – what a hell of a mixture.'

'Talking about steak reminds me that I'm hungry,' said Willis. 'We'll eat before we get started.'

They opened some cans of stew and prepared a meal. As Forester took the first mouthful, he said, 'Now tell me – what the hell is a trebuchet?'

Willis smiled and produced a stub of pencil. 'Just an application of the lever,' he said. 'Imagine a thing like an out-of-balance seesaw – like this.' Rapidly he sketched on the soft pine top of the table. 'The pivot is here and one arm is, say, four times as long as the other. On the short arm you sling a weight, of, say, five hundred pounds, and on the other end you have your missile – a twenty-pound rock.'

He began to jot down calculations. 'Those medieval fellows worked empirically – they didn't have the concepts of energy that we have. We can do the whole thing precisely from scratch. Assuming your five-hundred-pound weight drops ten feet. The acceleration of gravity is such that, taking into account frictional losses at the pivot, it will take half a second to fall. That's five thousand foot-pounds in a half-second, six hundred thousand foot-pounds to the minute, eighteen horse-power of energy applied instantaneously to a twenty-pound rock on the end of the long arm.'

'That should make it move,' said Forester.

'I can tell you the speed,' said Willis. 'Assuming the ratio between the two arms is four to one, then the . . . the . . .' He stopped, tapped on the table for a moment, then grinned. 'Let's call it the muzzle velocity, although this thing hasn't a muzzle. The muzzle velocity will be eighty feet per second.'

'Is there any way of altering the range?'

'Sure,' said Willis. 'Heavy stones won't go as far as light stones. You want to decrease the range, you use a heavier rock. I must tell O'Hara that – he'd better get busy collecting and grading ammunition.'

He began to sketch on the table in more detail. 'For the pivot we have the back axle of a wrecked truck that's back of the huts. The arms we make from the roof beams of a hut. There'll have to be a cup of some kind to hold the missile – we'll use a hub-cap bolted on to the end of the long arm. The whole thing will need a mounting but we'll figure that out when we come to it.'

Forester looked at the sketch critically. 'It's going to be damned big and heavy. How are we going to get it down the mountain?'

Willis grinned. 'I've figured that out too. The whole thing will pull apart and we'll use the axle to carry the rest of it. We'll wheel the damn thing down the mountain and assemble it again at the bridge.'

'You've done well,' said Forester.

'It was Armstrong who thought it up,' said Willis. 'For a scholar, he has the most murderous tendencies. He knows more ways of killing people – say, have you ever heard of Greek fire?'

'In a vague sort of way.'

'Armstrong says it was as good as napalm, and that the ancients used to have flame-throwers mounted on the prows of their warships. We've done a bit of thinking along those lines and got nowhere.' He looked broodingly at his sketch. 'He says this thing is nothing to the siege weapons they had. They used to throw dead horses over city walls to start a plague. How heavy is a horse?'

'Maybe horses weren't as big in those days,' said Forester.

'Any horse that could carry a man in full armour was no midget,' Willis pointed out. He spooned the last of the gravy from his plate. 'We'd better get started – I don't want to work all night again.'

Rohde nodded briefly and Forester looked over at Peabody, snoring on the bunk. 'I think we'll start with a bucket of the coldest water we can get,' he said.

IV

O'Hara looked across the gorge.

Tendrils of smoke still curled from the burnt-out vehicles and he caught the stench of burning rubber. He looked speculatively at the intact jeep at the bridgehead and debated whether to do something about it, but discarded the idea almost as soon as it came to him. It would be useless to destroy a single vehicle – the enemy had plenty more – and he must husband his resources for more vital targets. It was not his intention to wage a war of attrition; the enemy could beat him hands down at that game.

He had been along the edge of the gorge downstream to where the road turned away, half a mile from the bridge, and had picked out spots from which crossbowmen could keep up a harassing fire. Glumly, he thought that Armstrong was right – the enemy would not be content to be docile targets; they would certainly take steps to protect themselves against further attack. The only reason for the present success was the unexpectedness of it all, as though a rabbit had taken a weasel by the throat.

The enemy was still vigilant by the bridge. Once, when O'Hara had incautiously exposed himself, he drew a concentrated fire that was unpleasantly accurate and it was only his quick reflexes and the fact that he was in sight for so short a time that saved him from a bullet in the head. We can take no chances, he thought; no chances at all.

Now he looked at the bridge with the twelve-foot gap yawning in the middle and thought of ways of getting at it. Fire still seemed the best bet and Willis had said that there were two drums of paraffin up at the camp. He measured with his eye the hundred-yard approach to the bridge; there was a slight incline and he thought that, given a good push, a drum would roll as far as the bridge. It was worth trying.

Presently Armstrong came down to relieve him. 'Grub's up,' he said.

O'Hara regarded Armstrong's smooth cheeks. 'I didn't bring my shaving-kit,' he said. 'Apparently you did.'

'I've got one of those Swiss wind-up dry shavers,' said Armstrong. 'You can borrow it if you like. It's up at the shelter in my coat pocket.'

O'Hara thanked him and pointed out the enemy observation posts he had spotted. 'I don't think they'll make an attempt on the bridge today,' he said, 'so I'm going up to the camp this afternoon. I want those drums of paraffin. But if anything happens while I'm gone and the bastards get across, then you scatter. Aguillar, Benedetta and Jenny rendezvous at the mine – not the camp – and they go up the mountain the hard way, steering clear of the road. You get up to the camp by the road as fast as you can – you'd better move fast because they'll be right on your tail.'

Armstrong nodded. 'I have the idea. We stall them off at the camp, giving the others time to get to the mine.'

'That's right,' said O'Hara. 'But you're the boss in my absence and you'll have to use your own judgment.'

He left Armstrong and went back to the shelter, where he found the professor's coat and rummaged in the pockets. Benedetta smiled at him and said, 'Lunch is ready.'

'I'll be back in a few minutes,' he said, and went down the hill towards the pond, carrying the dry shaver.

Aguillar pulled his overcoat tighter about him and looked at O'Hara's retreating figure with curious eyes. 'That one is strange,' he said. 'He is a fighter but he is too cold – too objective. There is no hot blood in him, and that is not good for a young man.'

Benedetta bent her head and concentrated on the stew. 'Perhaps he has suffered,' she said.

Aguillar smiled slightly as he regarded Benedetta's averted face. 'You say he was a prisoner in Korea?' he asked.

She nodded.

'Then he must have suffered,' agreed Aguillar. 'Perhaps not in the body, but certainly in the spirit. Have you asked him about it?'

'He will not talk about it.'

Aguillar wagged his head. That is also very bad. It is not good for a man to be so self-contained – to have his violence pent-up. It is like screwing down the safety-valve on a boiler – one can expect an explosion.' He grimaced. 'I hope I am not near when that young man explodes.'

Benedetta's head jerked up. 'You talk nonsense, Uncle. His anger is directed against those others across the river. He would do us no harm.'

Aguillar looked at her sadly. 'You think so, child? His anger is directed against himself as the power of a bomb is directed against its casing – but when the casing shatters everyone around is hurt. O'Hara is a dangerous man.'

Benedetta's lips tightened and she was going to reply when Miss Ponsky approached, lugging a crossbow. She seemed unaccountably flurried and the red stain of a blush was ebbing from her cheeks. Her protection was volubility.

'I've got both bows sighted in,' she said rapidly. 'They're both shooting the same now, and very accurately. They're very strong too – I was hitting a target at one hundred and twenty yards. I left the other with Doctor Armstrong; I thought he might need it.'

'Have you seen Señor O'Hara?' asked Benedetta.

Miss Ponsky turned pink again. 'I saw him at the pond,' she said in a subdued voice. 'What are we having for lunch?' she continued brightly.

Benedetta laughed. 'As always – stew.'

Miss Ponsky shuddered delicately. Benedetta said, 'It is all that Señor Willis brought from the camp – cans of stew. Perhaps it is his favourite food.'

'He ought to have thought of the rest of us,' complained Miss Ponsky.

Aguillar stirred. 'What do you think of Señor Forester, madam?'

'I think he is a very brave man,' she said simply. 'He and Señor Rohde.'

'I think so too,' said Aguillar. 'But also I think there is something strange about him. He is too much the man of action to be a simple businessman.'

'Oh, I don't know,' Miss Ponsky demurred. 'A good businessman must be a man of action, at least in the States.'

'Somehow I don't think Forester's idea is the pursuit of the dollar,' Aguillar said reflectively. 'He is not like Peabody.'

Miss Ponsky flared. 'I could spit when I think of that man. He makes me ashamed to be an American.'

'Do not be ashamed,' Aguillar said gently. 'He is not a coward because he is an American; there are cowards among all people.'

O'Hara came back. He looked better now that he had shaved the stubble from his cheeks. It had not been easy; the clockwork rotary shaver had protested when asked to attack the thicket of his beard, but he had persisted and was now smooth-cheeked and clean. The water in the pond had been too cold for bathing, but he had stripped and taken a sponge-bath and felt the better for it. Out of the corner of his eye he had seen Miss Ponsky toiling up the hill towards the shelter and hoped she had not seen him – he did not want to offend the susceptibilities of maiden ladies.

'What have we got?' he asked.

'More stew,' said Aguillar wryly.

O'Hara groaned and Benedetta laughed. He accepted the aluminium plate and said, 'Maybe I can bring something else when I go up to the camp this afternoon. But I won't have room for much – I'm more interested in the paraffin.'

Miss Ponsky asked, 'What is it like by the river?'

'Quiet,' said O'Hara. 'They can't do much today so they're contenting themselves with keeping the bridge covered. I think it's safe enough for me to go up to the camp.'

'I'll come with you,' said Benedetta quickly.

O'Hara paused, his fork in mid-air. 'I don't know if . . .'

'We need food,' she said. 'And if you cannot carry it, somebody must.'

O'Hara glanced at Aguillar, who nodded tranquilly. 'I will be all right,' he said.

O'Hara shrugged. 'It will be a help,' he admitted.

Benedetta sketched a curtsy at him, but there was a flash of something in her eyes that warned O'Hara he must tread gently. 'Thank you,' she said, a shade too sweetly. 'I'll try not to get in the way.'

He grinned at her. 'I'll tell you when you are.'

V

Like Forester, O'Hara found the going hard on the way up to the camp. When he and Benedetta took a rest halfway, he sucked in the thin, cold air greedily, and gasped, 'My God, this is getting tough.'

Benedetta's eyes went to the high peaks. 'What about Miguel and Señor Forester? They will have it worse.'

O'Hara nodded, then said, 'I think your uncle ought to come up to the camp tomorrow. It is better that he should do it when he can do it in his own time, instead of being chased. And it will acclimatize him in case we have to retreat to the mine.'

'I think that is good,' she said. 'I will go with him to help, and I can bring more food when I return.'

'He might be able to help Willis with his bits and pieces,' said O'Hara. 'After all, he can't do much down at the bridge anyway, and Willis wouldn't mind another pair of hands.'

Benedetta pulled her coat about her. 'Was it as cold as this in Korea?'

'Sometimes,' O'Hara said. He thought of the stone-walled cell in which he had been imprisoned. Water ran down the walls and froze into ice at night – and then the weather got worse and the walls were iced day and night. It was then that Lieutenant Feng had taken away all his clothing. 'Sometimes,' he repeated bleakly.

'I suppose you had warmer clothing than we have,' said Benedetta. 'I am worried about Forester and Miguel. It will be very cold up in the pass.'

O'Hara felt suddenly ashamed of himself and his self-pity. He looked away quickly from Benedetta and stared at the snows above. 'We must see if we can improvise a tent for them. They'll spend at least one night in the open up there.' He stood up. 'We'd better get on.'

The camp was busy with the noise of hammering and the trebuchet was taking shape in the central clearing between the huts. O'Hara stood unnoticed for a moment and looked at it. It reminded him very much of something he had once seen in an avant-garde art magazine; a modern sculptor had assembled a lot of junk into a crazy structure and had given it some high-falutin' name, and the trebuchet had the same appearance of wild improbability.

Forester paused and leaned on the length of steel he was using as a crude hammer. As he wiped the sweat from his eyes he caught sight of the newcomers and hailed them. 'What the hell are you doing here? Is anything wrong?'

'All's quiet,' said O'Hara reassuringly. 'I've come for one of the drums of paraffin – and some grub.' He walked round the trebuchet. 'Will this contraption work?'

'Willis is confident,' said Forester. 'That's good enough for me.'

'You won't be here,' O'Hara said stonily. 'But I suppose I'll have to trust the boffins. By the way – it's going to be bloody cold up there – have you made any preparations?'

'Not yet. We've been too busy on this thing.'

'That's not good enough,' said O'Hara sternly. 'We're depending on you to bring the good old U.S. cavalry to the rescue. You've got to get across that pass – if you don't, then this piece of silly artillery will be wasted. Is there anything out of which you can improvise a tent?'

'I suppose you're right,' said Forester. 'I'll have a look around.'

'Do that. Where's the paraffin?'

'Paraffin? Oh, you mean the kerosene. It's in that hut there. Willis locked it up; he put all the booze in there – we had to keep Peabody sober somehow.'

'Um,' said O'Hara. 'How's he doing?'

'He's not much good. He's out of condition and his disposition doesn't help. We've got to drive him.'

'Doesn't the bloody fool realize that if the bridge is forced he'll get his throat cut?'

Forester sighed. 'It doesn't seem to make any difference – logic isn't his strong point. He goofs off at the slightest opportunity.'

O'Hara saw Benedetta going into one of the huts. 'I'd better get that paraffin. We must have it at the bridge before it gets dark.'

He got the key of the hut from Willis and opened the door. Just inside was a crate, half-filled with bottles. There was a stir of longing in his guts as he looked at them, but he suppressed it firmly and switched his attention to the two drums of paraffin. He tested the weight of one of them, and thought, this is going to be a bastard to get down the mountain.

He heaved the drum on to its side and rolled it out of the hut. Across the clearing he saw Forester helping Benedetta to make a *travois*, and crossed over to them. 'Is there any rope up here?'

'Rope we've got,' replied Forester. 'But Rohde was worried about that – he said we'll need it in the mountains, rotten though it is; and Willis needs it for the trebuchet, too. But there's plenty of electric wire that Willis ripped out to make crossbow-strings with.'

'I'll need some to help me get that drum down the mountain – I suppose the electric wire will have to do.'

Peabody wandered over. His face had a flabby, unhealthy look about it and he exuded the scent of fear. 'Say, what is this?' he demanded. 'Willis tells me that you and the spic are making a getaway over the mountains.'

Forester's eyes were cold. 'If you want to put it that way – yes.'

'Well, I wanna come,' said Peabody. 'I'm not staying here to be shot by a bunch of commies.'

'Are you crazy?' said Forester.

'What's so crazy about it? Willis says it's only fifteen miles to this place Altemiros.'

Forester looked at O'Hara speechlessly. O'Hara said quietly, 'Do you think it's going to be like a stroll in Central Park, Peabody?'

'Hell, I'd rather take my chance in the mountains than with the commies,' said Peabody. 'I think you're crazy if you think you can hold them off. What have you got? You've got an old man, a silly bitch of a school-marm, two nutty scientists and a girl. And you're fighting with bows and arrows, for God's sake.' He tapped Forester on the chest. 'If you're making a getaway, I'm coming along.'

Forester slapped his hand away. 'Now get this, Peabody, you'll do as you're damn well told.'

'Who the hell are you to give orders?' said Peabody with venom. 'To begin with I take no orders from a limey – and I don't see why you should be so high and mighty, either. I'll do as I damn well please.'

O'Hara caught Forester's eye. 'Let's see Rohde,' he said hastily. He had seen Forester balling his fist and wanted to prevent trouble, for an idea was crystallizing in his mind.

Rohde was positively against it. 'This man is in no condition to cross the mountains,' he said. 'He will hold us back, and if he holds us back none of us will get across. We cannot spend more than one night in the open.'

'What do you think?' Forester asked O'Hara.

'I don't like the man,' said O'Hara. 'He's weak and he'll break under pressure. If he breaks it might be the end of the lot of us. I can't trust him.'

'That's fair enough,' Forester agreed. 'He's a weak sister, all right. I'm going to overrule you, Miguel; he comes with us. We can't afford to leave him with O'Hara.'

Rohde opened his mouth to protest but stopped when he saw the expression on Forester's face. Forester grinned wolfishly and there was a hard edge to his voice when he said, 'If he hold us up, we'll drop the bastard into the nearest crevasse. Peabody will have to put up or shut up.'

He called Peabody over. 'All right, you come with us. But let's get this straight right from the start. You take orders.'

Peabody nodded. 'All right,' he mumbled. 'I'll take orders from you.'

Forester was merciless. 'You'll take orders from anyone who damn well gives them from now on. Miguel is the expert round here and when he gives an order – you jump fast.'

Peabody's eyes flickered, but he gave in. He had no option if he wanted to go with them. He shot a look of dislike at Rohde and said, 'Okay, but when I get back Stateside the State Department is going to get an earful from me. What kind of place is this where good Americans can be pushed around by spics and commies?'

O'Hara looked at Rohde quickly. His face was as placid as though he had not heard. O'Hara admired his self-control – but he pitied Peabody when he got into the mountains.

Half an hour later he and Benedetta left. She was pulling the *travois* and he was clumsily steering the drum of paraffin. There were two loops of wire round the drum in a sling so that he could have a measure of control. They had wasted little time in saying goodbye to Rohde and Forester, and still less on Peabody. Willis had said, 'We'll need you up here tomorrow; the trebuchet will be ready then.'

'I'll be here,' promised O'Hara. 'If I haven't any other engagements.'

It was difficult going down the mountain, even though they were on the road. Benedetta hauled on the *travois* and had to stop frequently to rest, and more often to help O'Hara with the drum. It weighed nearly four hundred pounds and seemed to have a malevolent mind of its own. His idea of being able to steer it by pulling on the wires did not work well. The drum would take charge and go careering at an angle to wedge itself in the ditch at the side of the road. Then it would be a matter of sweat and strain to get it out, whereupon it would charge into the opposite ditch.

By the time they got down to the bottom O'Hara felt as though he had been wrestling with a malign and evil adversary. His muscles ached and it seemed as though someone had pounded him with a hammer all over his body. Worse, in order to get the drum down the mountain at all he had been obliged to lighten the load by jettisoning a quarter of the contents and had helplessly watched ten gallons of invaluable paraffin drain away into the thirsty dust.

When they reached the valley Benedetta abandoned the *travois* and went for help. O'Hara had looked at the sky and said, 'I want this drum at the bridge before nightfall.'

Night swoops early on the eastern slopes of the Andes. The mountain wall catches the setting sun, casting long shadows across the hot jungles of the interior. At five in the afternoon the sun was just touching the topmost peaks and O'Hara knew that in an hour it would be dark.

Armstrong came up to help and O'Hara immediately asked, 'Who's on watch?'

'Jenny. She's all right. Besides, there's nothing doing at all.'

With two men to control the erratic drum it went more easily and they manoeuvred it to the bridgehead within half an hour. Miss Ponsky came running up. 'They switched on their lights just now and I think I heard an auto engine from way back along there.' She pointed downstream.

'I would have liked to try and put out the headlamps on this jeep,' she said. 'But I didn't want to waste an arrow – a quarrel – and in any case there's something in front of the glass.'

'They have stone guards in front of the lights,' said Armstrong. 'Heavy mesh wire.'

'Go easy on the bolts, anyway,' said O'Hara. 'Peabody was supposed to be making some but he's been loafing on the job.' He carefully crept up and surveyed the bridgehead. The jeep's headlights illuminated the whole bridge and its

approaches and he knew that at least a dozen sharp pairs
of eyes were watching. It would be suicidal to go out there.

He dropped back and looked at the drum in the fading
light. It was much dented by its careering trip down the
mountain road but he thought it would roll a little farther.
He said, 'This is the plan. We're going to burn the bridge.
We're going to play the same trick that we played this
morning but we'll apply it on this side of the bridge.'

He put his foot on top of the drum and rocked it gently. 'If
Armstrong gives this one good heave it should roll right
down to the bridge – if we're lucky. Jenny will be standing up
there with her crossbow and when it gets into the right position she'll puncture it. I'll be in position too, with Benedetta
to hand me the other crossbow with a fire-bolt. If the drum
is placed right then we'll burn through the ropes on this side
and the whole bloody bridge will drop into the water.'

'That sounds all right,' said Armstrong.

'Get the bows, Jenny,' said O'Hara and took Armstrong to
one side, out of hearing of the others. 'It's a bit more tricky
than that,' he said. 'In order to get the drum in the right
place you'll have to come into the open.' He held his head
on one side; the noise of the vehicle had stopped. 'So I want
to do it before they get any more lights on the job.'

Armstrong smiled gently. 'I think your little bit is more
dangerous than mine. Shooting those fire-bolts in the dark
will make you a perfect target – it won't be as easy as this
morning, and then you nearly got shot.'

'Maybe,' said O'Hara. 'But this has got to be done. This is
how we do it. When that other jeep – or whatever it is –
comes up, maybe the chaps on the other side won't be so
vigilant. My guess is that they'll tend to watch the vehicle
manoeuvre into position; I don't think they're a very
disciplined crowd. Now, while that's happening is the time
to do your stuff. I'll give you the signal.'

'All right, my boy,' said Armstrong. 'You can rely on me.'

O'Hara helped him to push the drum into the position easiest for him, and then Miss Ponsky and Benedetta came up with the crossbows. He said to Benedetta, 'When I give Armstrong the signal to push off the drum, you light the first fire-bolt. This has got to be done quickly if it's going to be done at all.'

'All right, Tim,' she said.

Miss Ponsky went to her post without a word.

He heard the engine again, this time louder. He saw nothing on the road downstream and guessed that the vehicle was coming slowly and without lights. He thought they'd be scared of being fired on during that half-mile journey. By God, he thought, if I had a dozen men with a dozen bows I'd make life difficult for them. He smiled sourly. Might as well wish for a machine-gun section – it was just as unlikely a possibility.

Suddenly the vehicle switched its lights on. It was quite near the bridge and O'Hara got ready to give Armstrong the signal. He held his hand until the vehicle – a jeep – drew level with the burnt-out truck, then he said in a whispered shout, 'Now!'

He heard the rattle as the drum rolled over the rocks and out of the corner of his eye saw the flame as Benedetta ignited the fire-bolt. The drum came into sight on his left, bumping down the slight incline which led towards the bridge. It hit a larger stone which threw it off course. Christ, he whispered, we've bungled it.

Then he saw Armstrong run into the open, chasing after the drum. A few faint shouts came from across the river and there was a shot. 'You damned fool,' yelled O'Hara. 'Get back.' But Armstrong kept running forward until he had caught up with the drum and, straightening it on course again, he gave it another boost.

There was a *rafale* of rifle-fire and spurts of dust flew about Armstrong's feet as he ran back at full speed, then a

metallic *thunk* as a bullet hit the drum and, as it turned,
O'Hara saw a silver spurt of liquid rise in the air. The enemy
were divided in their intentions – they did not know which
was more dangerous, Armstrong or the drum. And so
Armstrong got safely into cover.

Miss Ponsky raised the bow. 'Forget it, Jenny,' roared
O'Hara. 'They've done it for us.'

Again and again the drum was hit as it rolled towards the
bridge and the paraffin spurted out of more holes, rising in
gleaming jets into the air until the drum looked like some
strange kind of liquid Catherine wheel. But the repeated
impact of bullets was slowing it down and there must have
been a slight and unnoticed rise in the ground before the
bridge because the drum rolled to a halt just short of the
abutments.

O'Hara swore and turned to grasp the crossbow which
Benedetta was holding. Firing in the dark with a fire-bolt
was difficult; the flame obscured his vision and he had to
will himself consciously to take aim slowly. There was
another babble of shouts from over the river and a bullet
ricocheted from a rock nearby and screamed over his head.

He pressed the trigger gently and the scorching heat was
abruptly released from his face as the bolt shot away into
the opposing glare of headlamps. He ducked as another
bullet clipped the rock by the side of his head and thrust
the bow at Benedetta for reloading.

It was not necessary. There was a dull explosion and a
violent flare of light as the paraffin around the drum caught
fire. O'Hara, breathing heavily, moved to another place
where he could see what was happening. It would have
been very foolish to pop his head up in the same place from
which he had fired his bolt.

It was with dejection that he saw a raging fire arising
from a great pool of paraffin just short of the bridge. The
drum had stopped too soon and although the fire was

spectacular it would do the bridge no damage at all. He watched for a long time, hoping the drum would explode and scatter burning paraffin on the bridge, but nothing happened and slowly the fire went out.

He dropped back to join the others. 'Well, we messed that one up,' he said bitterly.

'I should have pushed it harder,' Armstrong said.

O'Hara flared up in anger. 'You damned fool, if you hadn't run out and given it another shove it wouldn't have gone as far as it did. Don't do an idiotic thing like that again – you nearly got killed!'

Armstrong said quietly, 'We're all of us on the verge of getting killed. Someone has to risk something besides you.'

'I should have surveyed the ground more carefully,' said O'Hara self-accusingly.

Benedetta put a hand on his arm. 'Don't worry, Tim; you did the best you could.'

'Sure you did,' said Miss Ponsky militantly. 'And we've shown them we're still here and fighting. I bet they're scared to come across now for fear of being burned alive.'

'Come,' said Benedetta. 'Come and eat.' There was a flash of humour in her voice. 'I didn't bring the *travois* all the way down, so it will be stew again.'

Wearily O'Hara turned his back on the bridge. It was the third night since the plane crash – and six more to go!

FIVE

Forester attacked his baked beans with gusto. The dawn light was breaking, dimming the bright glare of the Coleman lamp and smoothing out the harsh shadows on his face. He said, 'One day at the mine – two days crossing the pass – another two days getting help. We must cut that down somehow. When we get to the other side we'll have to act quickly.'

Peabody looked at the table morosely, ignoring Forester. He was wondering if he had made the right decision, done the right thing by Joe Peabody. The way these guys talked, crossing the mountains wasn't going to be so easy. Aw, to hell with it – he could do anything any other guy could do – especially any spic.

Rohde said, 'I thought I heard rifle-fire last night – just at sunset.' His face was haunted by the knowledge of his helplessness.

'They should be all right. I don't see how the commies could have repaired the bridge and got across so quickly,' said Forester reasonably. 'That O'Hara's a smart cookie. He must have been doing something with that drum of kerosene he took down the hill yesterday. He's probably cooked the bridge to a turn.'

Rohde's face cracked into a faint smile. 'I hope so.'

Forester finished his beans. 'Okay, let's get the show on the road.' He turned round in his chair and looked at the huddle of blankets on the bunk. 'What about Willis?'

'Let him sleep,' said Rohde. 'He worked harder and longer than any of us.'

Forester got up and examined the packs they had made up the previous night. Their equipment was pitifully inadequate for the job they had to do. He remembered the books he had read about mountaineering expeditions – the special rations they had, the lightweight nylon ropes and tents, the wind-proof clothing and the specialized gear – climbing-boots, ice-axes, pitons. He smiled grimly – yes, and porters to help hump it.

There was none of that here. Their packs were roughly cobbled together from blankets; they had an ice-axe which Willis had made – a roughly shaped metal blade mounted on the end of an old broom handle; their ropes were rotten and none too plentiful, scavenged from the rubbish heap of the camp and with too many knots and splices for safety; their climbing-boots were clumsy miners' boots made of thick, unpliant leather, heavy and graceless. Willis had discovered the boots and Rohde had practically gone into raptures over them.

He lifted his pack and wished it was heavier – heavier with the equipment they needed. They had worked far into the night improvising, with Willis and Rohde being the most inventive. Rohde had torn blankets into long strips to make puttees, and Willis had practically torn down one of the huts single-handed in his search for extra long nails to use as pitons. Rohde shook his head wryly when he saw them. 'The metal is too soft, but they will have to do.'

Forester heaved the pack on to his back and fastened the crude electric wiring fastenings. Perhaps it's as well we're staying a day at the mine, he thought; maybe we can do better than this. There are suitcases up there with proper straps, there is the plane – surely we can find something in there we can use. He zipped up the front of the leather jacket and was grateful to O'Hara for the loan of it. He suspected it would be windy higher up, and the jacket was windproof.

As he stepped out of the hut he heard Peabody cursing at the weight of his pack. He took no notice but strode on through the camp, past the trebuchet which crouched like a prehistoric monster, and so to the road which led up the mountain. In two strides Rohde caught up and came abreast of him. He indicated Peabody trailing behind. 'This one will make trouble,' he said.

Forester's face was suddenly bleak. 'I meant what I said, Miguel. If he makes trouble, we get rid of him.'

It took them a long time to get up to the mine. The air became very thin and Forester could feel that his heartbeat had accelerated and his heart thumped in his chest like a swinging stone. He breathed faster and was cautioned by Rohde against forced breathing. My God, he thought; what to is it going to be like in the pass?

They reached the airstrip and the mine at midday. Forester felt dizzy and a little nauseated and was glad to reach the first of the deserted huts and to collapse on the floor. Peabody had been left behind long ago; they had ignored his pleas for them to stop and he had straggled farther and farther behind on the trail until he had disappeared from sight. 'He'll catch up,' Forester said. 'He's more scared of the commies than he is of me.' He grinned with savage satisfaction. 'But I'll change that before we're through.'

Rohde was in nearly as bad shape as Forester, although he was more used to the mountains. He sat on the floor of the hut, gasping for breath, too weary to shrug off his pack. They both relaxed for over half an hour before Rohde made any constructive move. At last he fumbled with numb fingers at the fastenings of his pack, and said, 'We must have warmth; get out the kerosene.'

As Forester undid his pack Rohde took the small axe which had been brought from the Dakota and left the hut. Presently Forester heard him chopping at something in one of the other huts and guessed he had gone for the makings of a fire. He got out the bottle of kerosene and put it aside, ready for when Rohde came back.

An hour later they had a small fire going in the middle of the hut. Rohde had used the minimum of kerosene to start it and small chips of wood built up in a pyramid. Forester chuckled. 'You must have been a boy scout.'

'I was,' said Rohde seriously. 'That is a fine organization.' He stretched. 'Now we must eat.'

'I don't feel hungry,' objected Forester.

'I know – neither do I. Nevertheless, we must eat.' Rohde looked out of the window towards the pass. 'We must fuel ourselves for tomorrow.'

They warmed a can of beans and Forester choked down his share. He had not the slightest desire for food, nor for anything except quietness. His limbs felt flaccid and heavy and he felt incapable of the slightest exertion. His mind was affected, too, and he found it difficult to think clearly and to stick to a single line of thought. He just sat there in a corner of the hut, listlessly munching his lukewarm beans and hating every mouthful.

He said, 'Christ, I feel terrible.'

'It is the *soroche*,' said Rohde with a shrug. 'We must expect to feel like this.' He shook his head regretfully. 'We are not allowing enough time for acclimatization.'

'It wasn't as bad as this when we came out of the plane,' said Forester.

'We had oxygen,' Rohde pointed out. 'And we went down the mountain quickly. You understand that this is dangerous?'

'Dangerous? I know I feel goddam sick.'

'There was an American expedition here a few years ago, climbing mountains to the north of here. They went quickly to a level of five thousand metres – about as high as we are now. One of the Americans lost consciousness because of the *soroche*, and although they had a doctor, he died while being taken down the mountain. Yes, it is dangerous, Señor Forester.'

Forester grinned weakly. 'In a moment of danger we ought to be on a first-name basis, Miguel. My name is Ray.'

After a while they heard Peabody moving outside. Rohde heaved himself to his feet and went to the door. 'We are here, señor.'

Peabody stumbled into the hut and collapsed on the floor. 'You lousy bastards,' he gasped. 'Why didn't you wait?'

Forester grinned at him. 'We'll be moving really fast when we leave here,' he said. 'Coming up from the camp was like a Sunday morning stroll compared to what's coming next. We'll not wait for you then, Peabody.'

'You son of a bitch. I'll get even with you,' Peabody threatened.

Forester laughed. 'I'll ram those words down your throat – but not now. There'll be time enough later.'

Rohde put out a can of beans. 'You must eat, and we must work. Come, Ray.'

'I don't wanna eat,' moaned Peabody.

'Suit yourself,' said Forester. 'I don't care if you starve to death.' He got up and went out of the hut, following Rohde. 'This loss of appetite – is that *soroche*, too?'

Rohde nodded. 'We will eat little from now on – we must live on the reserves of our bodies. A fit man can do it – but that man . . .? I don't know if he can do it.'

They walked slowly down the airstrip towards the crashed Dakota. To Forester it seemed incredible that O'Hara had found it too short on which to land because to him it now appeared to be several miles long. He plodded on, mechanically putting one foot in front of the other,

while the cold air rasped in his throat and his chest heaved
with the drudging effort he was making.

They left the airstrip and skirted the cliff over which the
plane had plunged. There had been a fresh fall of snow
which mantled the broken wings and softened the jagged
outlines of the holes torn in the fuselage. Forester looked
down over the cliff, and said, 'I don't think this can be seen
from the air – the snow makes perfect camouflage. If there
is an air search I don't think they'll find us.'

Walking with difficulty over the broken ground, they
climbed to the wreck and got inside through the hole
O'Hara had chopped when he and Rohde had retrieved the
oxygen cylinder. It was dim and bleak inside the Dakota and
Forester shivered, not from the cold which was becoming
intense, but from the odd idea that this was the corpse of a
once living and vibrant thing. He shook the idea from him,
and said, 'There were some straps on the luggage rack –
complete with buckles. We could use those, and O'Hara says
there are gloves in the cockpit.'

'That is good,' agreed Rohde. 'I will look towards the
front for what I can find.'

Forester went aft and his breath hissed when he saw the
body of old Coughlin, a shattered smear of frozen flesh and
broken bones on the rear seat. He averted his eyes and
turned to the luggage-rack and began to unbuckle the
straps. His fingers were numb with the cold and his movements clumsy, but at last he managed to get them free – four
broad canvas straps which could be used on the packs. That
gave him an idea and he turned his attention to the seat
belts, but they were anchored firmly and it was hopeless to
try to remove them without tools.

Rohde came aft carrying the first-aid box which he had
taken from the bulkhead. He placed it on a seat and opened
it, carefully moving his fingers among the jumbled contents.
He grunted. 'Morphine.'

'Damn,' said Forester. 'We could have used that on Mrs Coughlin.'

Rhode held up the shattered end of an ampoule. 'It would have been no use; they are all broken.'

He put some bandages away in his pocket, then said, 'This will be useful – aspirin.' The bottle was cracked, but it still held together and contained a hundred tablets. They both took two tablets and Rohde put the bottle in his pocket. There was nothing more in the first-aid box that was usable.

Forester went into the cockpit. The body of Grivas was there, tumbled into an obscene attitude, and still with the look of deep surprise frozen into the open eyes which were gazing at the shattered instrument panel. Forester moved forward, thinking that there must be something in the wreck of an aircraft that could be salvaged, when he kicked something hard that slid down the inclined floor of the cockpit.

He looked down and saw an automatic pistol.

My God, he thought; we'd forgotten that. It was Grivas's gun, left behind in the scramble to get out of the Dakota. It would have been of use down by the bridge, he thought, picking it up. But it was too late for that now. The metal was cold in his hand and he stood for a moment, undecided, then he slipped it into his pocket, thinking of Peabody and of what lay on the other side of the pass.

Equipment for well-dressed mountaineers, he thought sardonically; one automatic pistol.

They found nothing more that was of use in the Dakota, so they retraced their steps along the airstrip and back to the hut. Forester took the straps and a small suitcase belonging to Miss Ponsky which had been left behind. From these unlikely ingredients he contrived a serviceable pack which sat on his shoulders more comfortably than the one he had.

Rohde went to look at the mine and Peabody sat slackly in a corner of the hut watching Forester work with lacklustre eyes. He had not eaten his beans, nor had he attempted to keep the fire going. Forester, when he came into the hut, had looked at him with contempt but said nothing. He took the axe and chipped a few shavings from the baulk of wood that Rohde had brought in, and rebuilt the fire.

Rohde came in, stamping the snow from his boots. 'I have selected a tunnel for O'Hara,' he said. 'If the enemy force the bridge then O'Hara must come up here; I think the camp is indefensible.'

Forester nodded, 'I didn't think much of it myself,' he said, remembering how they had 'assaulted' the empty camp on the way down the mountain.

'Most of the tunnels drive straight into the mountain,' said Rohde. 'But there is one which has a sharp bend about fifty metres from the entrance. It will give protection against rifle fire.'

'Let's have a look at it,' said Forester.

Rohde led the way to the cliff face behind the huts and pointed out the tunnels. There were six of them driven into the base of the cliff. 'That is the one,' he said.

Forester investigated. It was a little over ten feet high and not much wider, just a hole blasted into the hard rock of the mountainside. He walked inside, finding it deepening from gloom to darkness the farther he went. He put his hands before him and found the side wall. As Rohde had said, it bent to the left sharply and, looking back, he saw that the welcome blue sky at the entrance was out of sight.

He went no farther, but turned around and walked back until he saw the bulk of Rohde outlined against the entrance. He was surprised at the relief he felt on coming out into the daylight, and said, 'Not much of a home from home – it gives me the creeps.'

'Perhaps that is because men have died there.'

'Died?'

'Too many men,' said Rohde. 'The government closed the mine – that was when Señor Aguillar was President.'

'I'm surprised that Lopez didn't try to coin some money out of it,' commented Forester.

Rohde shrugged. 'It would have cost a lot of money to put back into operation. It was uneconomical when it ran – just an experiment in high-altitude mining. I think it would have closed anyway.'

Forester looked around. 'When O'Hara comes up here he'll be in a hell of a hurry. What about building him a wall at the entrance here? We can leave a note in the hut telling him which tunnel to take.'

'That is well thought,' said Rohde. 'There are many rocks about.'

'Three will do better than two,' said Forester. 'I'll roust out Peabody.' He went back to the hut and found Peabody still in the same corner gazing blankly at the wall. 'Come on, buster,' Forester commanded. 'Rise and shine; we've got a job of work on hand.'

Peabody's eyelids twitched. 'Leave me alone,' he said thickly.

Forester stooped, grasped Peabody by the lapels and hauled him to his feet. 'Now, listen, you crummy bastard; I told you that you'd have to take orders and that you'd have to jump to it. I've got a lower boiling-point than Rohde, so you'd better watch it.'

Peabody began to beat at him ineffectually and Forester shoved and slammed him against the wall. 'I'm sick,' gasped Peabody. 'I can't breathe.'

'You can walk and you can carry rocks,' said Forester callously. 'Whether you breathe or not while you do it is immaterial. Personally, I'll be goddam glad when you do stop breathing. Now, are you going to leave this hut on your own two feet or do I kick you out?'

Muttering obscenities Peabody staggered to the door. Forester followed him to the tunnel and told him to start gathering rocks and then he pitched to with a will. It was hard physical labour and he had to stop and rest frequently, but he made sure that Peabody kept at it, driving him unmercifully.

They carried the rocks to the tunnel entrance, where Rohde built a rough wall. When they had to stop because of encroaching darkness, they had built little more than a breast-work. Forester sagged to the ground and looked at it through swimming eyes. 'It's not much, but it will have to do.' He beat his arms against his body. 'God, but it's cold.'

'We will go back to the hut,' said Rohde. 'There is nothing more we can do here.'

So they went back to the hut, relit the fire and prepared a meal of canned stew. Again, Peabody would not eat, but Rohde and Forester forced themselves, choking over the succulent meat and the rich gravy. Then they turned in for the night.

II

Oddly enough, Forester was not very tired when he got up at dawn and his breathing was much easier. He thought – if we could spend another day here it would be much better. I could look forward to the pass with confidence. Then he rejected the thought – there was no more time.

In the dim light he saw Rohde wrapping strips of blanket puttee-fashion around his legs and silently he began to do the same. Neither of them felt like talking. Once that was done he went across to the huddle in the corner and stirred Peabody gently with his foot.

'Lemme alone,' mumbled Peabody indistinctly.

Forester sighed and dropped the tip of his boot into Peabody's ribs. That did the trick. Peabody sat up cursing and Forester turned away without saying anything.

'It seems all right,' said Rohde from the doorway. He was staring up at the mountains.

Forester caught a note of doubt in his voice and went to join him. It was a clear crystal dawn and the peaks, caught by the rising sun, stood out brilliantly against the dark sky behind. Forester said, 'Anything wrong?'

'It is very clear,' said Rohde. Again there was a shadow of doubt in his voice. 'Perhaps too clear.'

'Which way do we go?' asked Forester.

Rohde pointed. 'Beyond that mountain is the pass. We go round the base of the peak and then over the pass and down the other side. It is this side which will be difficult – the other side is nothing.'

The mountain Rohde had indicated seemed so close in the clear morning air that Forester felt that he could put out his hand and touch it. He sighed with relief. 'It doesn't look too bad.'

Rohde snorted. 'It will be worse than you ever dreamed,' he said and turned away. 'We must eat again.'

Peabody refused food again and Forester, after a significant glance from Rohde, said, 'You'll eat even if I have to cram the stuff down your gullet. I've stood enough nonsense from you, Peabody; you're not going to louse this up by passing out through lack of food. But I warn you, if you do – if you hold us up for as little as one minute – we'll leave you.'

Peabody looked at him with venom but took the warmed-up can and began to eat with difficulty. Forester said, 'How are your boots?'

'Okay, I guess,' said Peabody ungraciously.

'Don't guess,' said Forester sharply. 'I don't care if they pinch your toes off and cut your feet to pieces – I don't care if they raise blisters as big as golf balls – I don't care as far as you're concerned. But I am concerned about you holding us up. If those boots don't fit properly, say so now.'

'They're all right,' said Peabody. 'They fit all right.'

Rohde said, 'We must go. Get your packs on.'

Forester picked up the suitcase and fastened the straps about his body. He padded the side of the case with the blanket material of his old pack so that it fitted snugly against his back, and he felt very pleased with his ingenuity.

Rohde took the primitive ice-axe and stuck the short axe from the Dakota into his belt. He eased the pack on his back so that it rested comfortably and looked pointedly at Peabody, who scrambled over to the corner where his pack lay. As he did so, something dropped with a clatter to the floor.

It was O'Hara's flask.

Forester stooped and picked it up, then fixed Peabody with a cold stare. 'So you're a goddam thief, too.'

'I'm not,' yelled Peabody. 'O'Hara gave it to me.'

'O'Hara wouldn't give you the time of day,' snarled Forester. He shook the flask and found it empty. 'You little shit,' he shouted, and hurled the flask at Peabody. Peabody ducked, but was too late and the flask hit him over the right eye.

Rohde thumped the butt of the ice-axe on the floor. 'Enough,' he commanded. 'This man cannot come with us – we cannot trust him.'

Peabody looked at him in horror, his hand dabbing at his forehead. 'But you gotta take me,' he whispered. 'You gotta. You can't leave me to those bastards down the mountain.'

Rohde's lips tightened implacably and Peabody whimpered. Forester took a deep breath and said, 'If we leave him here he'll only go back to O'Hara; and he's sure to balls things up down there.'

'I don't like it,' said Rohde. 'He is likely to kill us on the mountain.'

Forester felt the weight of the gun in his pocket and came to a decision. 'You're coming with us, Peabody,' he said harshly. 'But one more fast move and you're a dead duck.' He turned to Rohde. 'He won't hold us up – not for one minute, I promise you.' He looked Rohde in the eye and Rohde nodded with understanding.

'Get your pack on, Peabody,' said Forester. 'And get out of that door on the double.'

Peabody lurched away from the wall and seemed to cringe as he picked up his pack. He scuttled across the hut, running wide of Forester, and bolted through the door. Forester pulled a scrap of paper and a pencil from his pocket. 'I'll leave a note for Tim, telling him of the right tunnel. Then we'll go.'

III

It was comparatively easy at first, at least to Forester's later recollection. Although they had left the road and were striking across the mountainside, they made good time. Rohde was in the lead with Peabody following and Forester at the rear, ready to flail Peabody if he lagged. But to begin with there was no need for that; Peabody walked as though he had the devil at his heels.

At first the snow was shallow, dry and powdery, but then it began to get deeper, with a hard crust on top. It was then that Rohde stopped. 'We must use the ropes.'

They got out their pitiful lengths of rotten rope and Rohde carefully tested every knot. Then they tied themselves together, still in the same order, and carried on. Forester looked up at the steep white slope which seemed to stretch unendingly to the sky and thought that Rohde had been right – this wasn't going to be easy.

They plodded on, Rohde as trailbreaker and the other two thankful that he had broken a path for them in the thickening snow. The slope they were crossing was steep and swept dizzyingly below them and Forester found himself wondering what would happen if one of them fell. It was likely that he would drag down the other two and they would all slide, a tangled string of men and ropes, down the thousands of feet to the sharp rocks below.

Then he shook himself irritably. It wouldn't be like that at all. That was the reason for the ropes, so that a man's fall could be arrested.

From ahead he heard a rumble like thunder and Rohde paused. 'What is it?' shouted Forester.

'Avalanche,' replied Rohde. He said no more and resumed his even pace.

My God, thought Forester; I hadn't thought of avalanches. This could be goddam dangerous. Then he laughed to himself. He was in no more danger than O'Hara and the others down by the bridge – possibly less. His mind played about with the relativity of things and presently he was not thinking at all, just putting one foot in front of the other with mindless precision, an automaton toiling across the vast white expanse of snow like an ant crawling across a bed sheet.

He was jolted into consciousness by stumbling over Peabody, who lay sprawled in the snow, panting stertorously, his mouth opening and closing like a goldfish. 'Get up, Peabody,' he mumbled. 'I told you what would happen if you held us up. Get up, damn you.'

'Rohde's . . . Rohde's stopped,' panted Peabody.

Forester looked up and squinted against a vast dazzle. Specks danced in front of his eyes and coalesced into a vague shape moving towards him. 'I am sorry,' said Rohde, unexpectedly closely. 'I am a fool. I forgot this.'

Forester rubbed his eyes. I'm going blind, he thought in an access of terror; I'm losing my sight.

'Relax,' said Rohde. 'Close your eyes; rest them.'

Forester sank into the snow and closed his eyes. It felt as though there were hundreds of grains of sand beneath the lids and he felt the cold touch of tears on his cheeks. 'What is it?' he asked.

'Ice glare,' said Rohde. 'Don't worry; it will be all right. Just keep your eyes closed for a few minutes.'

He kept his eyes closed and gradually felt his muscles lose tension and he was grateful for this pause. He felt tired – more tired than he had ever felt in his life – and he wondered how far they had come. 'How far have we come?' he asked.

'Not far,' said Rohde.

'What time is it?'

There was a pause, then Rohde said, 'Nine o'clock.'

Forester was shocked. 'Is that all?' He felt as though he had been walking all day.

'I'm going to rub something on your eyes,' said Rohde, and Forester felt cold fingers massaging his eyelids with a substance at once soft and gritty.

'What is it, Miguel?'

'Wood ash. It is black – it will cut the glare, I think. I have heard it is an old Eskimo practice; I hope it will work.'

After a while Forester ventured to open his eyes. To his relief he could see, not as well as he could normally, but he was not as blind as during that first shocking moment when he thought he had lost his sight. He looked over to where Rohde was ministering to Peabody and thought – yes, that's another thing mountaineers have – dark glasses. He blinked painfully.

Rohde turned and Forester burst out laughing at the sight of him. He had a broad, black streak across his eyes and looked like a Red Indian painted to go on the warpath. Rohde smiled. 'You too look funny, Ray,' he said. Then more soberly, 'Wrap a blanket round your head like a hood, so that it cuts out some of the glare from the side.' Forester unfastened his pack and regretfully tore out the blanket from the side of the case. His pack would not be so comfortable from now on. The blanket provided enough material to make hoods for the three of them, and then Rohde said, 'We must go on.'

Forester looked back. He could still see the huts and estimated that they had not gained more than five hundred feet of altitude although they had come a considerable distance. Then the rope tugged at his waist and he stepped out, following the stumbling figure of Peabody.

It was midday when they rounded the shoulder of the mountain and were able to see their way to the pass. Forester sank to his knees and sobbed with exhaustion and Peabody dropped in his tracks as though knocked on the head. Only Rohde remained on his feet, staring up towards the pass, squinting with sore eyes. 'It is as I remembered it,' he said. 'We will rest here.'

Ignoring Peabody, he squatted beside Forester. 'Are you all right?'

'I'm a bit bushed,' said Forester, 'but a rest will make a lot of difference.'

Rohde took off his pack and unfastened it. 'We will eat now.'

'My God, I couldn't,' said Forester.

'You will be able to stomach this,' said Rohde, and produced a can of fruit. 'It is sweet for energy.'

There was a cold wind sweeping across the mountainside and Forester pulled the jacket round him as he watched Rohde dig into the snow. 'What are you doing?'

'Making a windbreak.' He took a Primus stove and put it into the hole he had dug where it was sheltered from the wind. He lit it, then handed an empty bean can to Forester. 'Fill that with snow and melt it; we must drink something hot. I will see to Peabody.'

At the low atmospheric pressure the snow took a long time to melt and the resulting water was merely tepid. Rohde dropped a bouillon cube into it, and said, 'You first.'

Forester gagged as he drank it, and then filled the can with snow again. Peabody had revived and took the next canful, then Forester melted more snow for Rohde. 'I haven't looked up the pass,' he said. 'What's it like?'

Rohde looked up from the can of fruit he was opening. 'Bad,' he said. 'But I expected that.' He paused. 'There is a glacier with many crevasses.'

Forester took the proffered can silently and began to eat. He found the fruit acceptable to his taste and his stomach – it was the first food he had enjoyed since the plane crash and it put new life into him. He looked back; the mine was out of sight, but far away he could see the river gorge, many thousands of feet below. He could not see the bridge.

He got to his feet and trudged forward to where he could see the pass. Immediately below was the glacier, a jumble of ice blocks and a maze of crevasses. It ended perhaps three thousand feet lower and he could see the blue waters of a mountain lake. As he looked he heard a whip-crack as of a stroke of lightning and the mutter of distant thunder and saw a plume of white leap up from the blue of the lake.

Rohde spoke from behind him. 'That is a *laguna*,' he said. 'The glaciers are slowly retreating here and there is always a lake between the glacier and the moraine. But that is of no interest to us; we must go there.' He pointed across the glacier and swept his arm upwards.

Across the valley of the pass white smoke appeared suddenly on the mountainside and a good ten seconds afterwards came a low rumble. 'There is always movement in the mountains,' said Rohde. 'The ice works on the rock and there are many avalanches.'

Forester looked up. 'How much higher do we have to climb?'

'About five hundred metres – but first we must go down a little to cross the glacier.'

'I don't suppose we could go round it,' said Forester.

Rohde pointed downwards towards the lake. 'We would lose a thousand metres of altitude and that would mean another night on the mountain. Two nights up here would kill us.'

Forester regarded the glacier with distaste; he did not like what he saw and for the first time a cold knot of fear formed in his belly. So far there had been nothing but exhausting work, the labour of pushing through thick snow in bad and unaccustomed conditions. But here he was confronted with danger itself – the danger of the toppling ice block warmed to the point of insecurity by the sun, the trap of the snow-covered crevasse. Even as he watched he saw a movement on the glacier, a sudden alteration of the scene, and he heard a dull rumble.

Rohde said, 'We will go now.'

They went back to get their packs. Peabody was sitting in the snow, gazing apathetically at his hands folded in his lap. Forester said, 'Come on, man; get your pack on,' but Peabody did not stir. Forester sighed regretfully and kicked him in the side, not too violently. Peabody seemed to react only to physical stimuli, to threats of violence.

Obediently he got up and put on his pack and Rohde refastened the rope about him, careful to see that all was secure. Then they went on in the same order. First the more experienced Rohde, then Peabody, and finally Forester.

The climb down to the glacier – a matter of about two hundred feet – was a nightmare to Forester, although it did not seem to trouble Rohde and Peabody was lost in the daze of his own devising and was oblivious of the danger. Here the rock was bare of snow, blown clean by the strong wind which swept down the pass. But it was rotten and covered with a slick layer of ice, so that any movement at all was dangerous. Forester cursed as his feet slithered on the ice; we should have spikes, he thought; this is madness.

It took an hour to descend to the glacier, the last forty feet by what Rohde called an *abseil*. There was a vertical ice-covered cliff and Rohde showed them what to do. He hammered four of their makeshift pitons into the rotten rock and looped the rope through them. They went down in reverse order, Forester first, with Rohde belaying the rope. He showed Forester how to loop the rope round his body so that he was almost sitting in it, and how to check his descent if he went too fast.

'Try to keep facing the cliff,' he said. 'Then you can use your feet to keep clear – and try not to get into a spin.'

Forester was heartily glad when he reached the bottom – this was not his idea of fun. He made up his mind that he would spend his next vacation as far from mountains as he could, preferably in the middle of Kansas.

Then Peabody came down, mechanically following Rohde's instructions. He had no trace of fear about him – his face was as blank as his mind and all fear had been drained out of him long before, together with everything else. He was an automaton who did precisely what he was told.

Rohde came last with no one to guard the rope above him. He dropped heavily the last ten feet as the pitons gave way one after the other in rapid succession and the rope dropped in coils about his prostrate body. Forester helped him to his feet. 'Are you okay?'

Rohde swayed. 'I'm all right,' he gasped. 'The pitons – find the pitons.'

Forester searched about in the snow and found three of the pitons; he could not find the fourth. Rohde smiled grimly. 'It is as well I fell,' he said. 'Otherwise we would have had to leave the pitons up there, and I think we will need them later. But we must keep clear of rock; the *verglas* – the ice on the rock – is too much for us without crampons.'

Forester agreed with him from the bottom of his heart, although he did not say so aloud. He recoiled the rope and made one end fast about his waist while Rohde attended to Peabody. Then he looked at the glacier.

It was as fantastic as a lunar landscape – and as dead and removed from humanity. The pressures from below had squeezed up great masses of ice which the wind and the sun had carved into grotesque shapes, all now mantled with thick snow. There were great cliffs with dangerous over-hanging columns which threatened to topple, and there were crevasses, some open to the sky and some, as Forester knew, treacherously covered with snow. Through this wilderness, this maze of ice, they had to find their way.

Forester said, 'How far to the other side?'

Rohde reflected. 'Three-quarters of one of your North American miles.' He took the ice-axe firmly in his hand. 'Let us move – time is going fast.'

He led the way, testing every foot with the butt of the ice-axe. Forester noticed that he had shortened the intervals between the members of the party and had doubled the ropes, and he did not like the implication. The three of them were now quite close together and Rohde kept urging Peabody to move faster as he felt the drag on the rope when Peabody lagged. Forester stooped and picked up some snow; it was powdery and did not make a good snowball, but every time Peabody dragged on Rohde's rope he pelted him with snow.

The way was tortuous and more than once Rohde led them into a dead end, the way blocked by vertical ice walls or wide crevasses, and they would have to retrace their steps and hunt for a better way. Once, when they were seemingly entrapped in a maze of ice passages, Forester totally lost his sense of direction and wondered hopelessly if they would be condemned to wander for ever in this cold hell.

His feet were numb and he had no feeling in his toes. He mentioned this to Rohde, who stopped immediately. 'Sit down,' he said. 'Take off your boots.'

Forester stripped the puttees from his legs and tried to untie his bootlaces with stiff fingers. It took him nearly fifteen minutes to complete this simple task. The laces were stiffened with ice, his fingers were cold, and his mind did not seem able to control the actions of his body. At last he got his boots off and stripped off the two pairs of socks he wore.

Rohde closely examined his toes and said, 'You have the beginning of frostbite. Rub your left foot – I'll rub the right.'

Forester rubbed away violently. His big toe was bone-white at the tip and had a complete lack of sensation. Rohde was merciless in his rubbing; he ignored Forester's yelp of anguish as the circulation returned to his foot and continued to massage with vigorous movements.

Forester's feet seemed to be on fire as the blood forced its way into the frozen flesh and he moaned with the pain. Rohde said sternly, 'You must not let this happen. You must work your toes all the time – imagine you are playing a piano with your feet – your toes. Let me see your fingers.'

Forester held out his hands and Rohde inspected them. 'All right,' he said. 'But you must watch for this. Your toes, your fingers and the tips of your ears and the nose. Keep rubbing them.' He turned to where Peabody was sitting slackly. 'And what about him?'

With difficulty Forester thrust his feet into his frozen boots, retied the laces and wrapped the puttees round his legs. Then he helped Rohde to take off Peabody's boots. Handling him was like handling a dummy – he neither hindered nor helped, letting his limbs be moved flaccidly.

His toes were badly frostbitten and they began to massage his feet. After working on him for ten minutes he suddenly moaned and Forester looked up to see a glimmer of intelligence steal into the dead eyes. 'Hell!' Peabody protested. 'You're hurting me.'

They took no notice of him and continued to work away. Suddenly Peabody screamed and began to thrash about, and Forester grabbed his arms. 'Be sensible, man,' he shouted. He looked up at Peabody. 'Keep moving your toes. Move them all the time in your boots.'

Peabody was moaning with pain but it seemed to have the effect of bringing him out of his private dream. He was able to put on his own socks and boots and wrap the puttees round his legs, and all the time he swore in a dull monotone, uttering a string of obscenities directed against the mountains, against Rohde and Forester for being un-caring brutes, and against the fates in general for having got him into this mess.

Forester looked across at Rohde and grinned faintly, and Rohde picked up the ice-axe and said, 'We must move – we must get out of here.'

Somewhere in the middle of the glacier Rohde, after casting fruitlessly in several directions, led them to a cre-vasse and said, 'Here we must cross – there is no other way.'

There was a snow bridge across the crevasse, a frail span connecting the two sides. Forester went to the edge and looked down into the dim green depths. He could not see the bottom.

Rohde said, 'The snow will bear our weight if we go over lying flat so that the weight is spread.' He tapped Forester on the shoulder. 'You go first.'

Peabody said suddenly, 'I'm not going across there. You think I'm crazy?'

Forester had intended to say the same but the fact that a man like Peabody had said it put some spirit into him. He said harshly – and the harshness was directed at himself for his moment of weakness – 'Do as you're damn well told.'

Rohde re-roped them so that the line would be long enough to stretch across the crevasse, which was about fifteen feet wide, and Forester approached cautiously. 'Not on hands and knees,' said Rohde. 'Lie flat and wriggle across with your arms and legs spread out.'

With trepidation Forester lay down by the edge of the crevasse and wriggled forward on to the bridge. It was only six feet wide and, as he went forward on his belly in the way he had been taught during his army training, he saw the snow crumble from the edge of the bridge to fall with a soft sigh into the abyss.

He was very thankful for the rope which trailed behind him, even though he knew it was probably not strong enough to withstand a sudden jerk, and it was with deep thankfulness that he gained the other side to lie gasping in the snow, beads of sweat trickling into his eyes.

After a long moment he stood up and turned. 'Are you all right?' asked Rohde.

'I'm fine,' he said, and wiped the sweat from his forehead before it froze.

'To hell with this,' shouted Peabody. 'You're not going to get me on that thing.'

'You'll be roped from both sides,' said Forester. 'You can't possibly fall – isn't that right, Miguel?'

'That is so,' said Rohde.

Peabody had a hunted look about him. Forester said, 'Oh, to hell with him. Come across, Miguel, and leave the stupid bastard.'

Peabody's voice cracked. 'You can't leave me *here*,' he screamed.

'Can't we?' asked Forester callously. 'I told you what would happen if you held us up.'

'Oh, Jesus!' said Peabody tearfully, and approached the snow bridge slowly.

'Get down,' said Rohde abruptly.

'On your belly,' called Forester.

Peabody lay down and began to inch his way across. He was shaking violently and twice he stopped as he heard snow swish into the crevasse from the crumbling edge of the bridge. As he approached Forester he began to wriggle along faster and Forester became intent on keeping the rope taut, as did Rohde, paying out as Peabody moved away from him.

Suddenly Peabody lost his nerve and got up on to his hands and knees and scrambled towards the end of the bridge. 'Get down, you goddam fool,' Forester yelled.

Suddenly he was enveloped in a cloud of snow dust and Peabody cannoned into him, knocking him flat. There was a roar as the bridge collapsed into the crevasse in a series of diminishing echoes, and when Forester got to his feet he looked across through the swirling fog of powdery snow and saw Rohde standing helplessly on the other side.

He turned and grabbed Peabody, who was clutching at the snow in an ecstasy of delight at being on firm ground. Hauling him to his feet, Forester hit him with his open palm in a vicious double slap across the face. 'You selfish bastard,' he shouted. 'Can't you ever do anything right?'

Peabody's head lolled on his shoulders and there was a vacant look in his eyes. When Forester let him go he dropped to the ground, muttering incomprehensibly, and grovelled at Forester's feet. Forester kicked him for good measure and turned to Rohde. 'What the hell do we do now?'

Rohde seemed unperturbed. He hefted the ice-axe like a spear and said, 'Stand aside.' Then he threw it and it stuck into the snow in front of Forester. 'I think I can swing across,' he said. 'Hammer the axe into the snow as deep as you can.'

Forester felt the rope at his waist. 'This stuff isn't too strong, you know. It won't bear much weight.'

Rohde measured the gap with his eye. 'I think there is enough to make a triple strand,' he said. 'That should take my weight.'

'It's your neck,' said Forester, and began to beat the ice-axe into the snow. But he knew that *all* their lives were at stake. He did not have the experience to make the rest of the trip alone – his chances were still less if he was hampered by Peabody. He doubted if he could find his way out of the glacier safely.

He hammered the axe into the snow and ice for three-quarters of its length and tugged at it to make sure it was firm. Then he turned to Peabody, who was sobbing and drooling into the snow and stripped the rope from him. He tossed the ends across to Rohde who tied them round his waist and sat on the edge of the crevasse, looking into the depths between his knees and appearing as unconcerned as though he was sitting in an armchair.

Forester fastened the triple rope to the ice-axe and belayed a loop around his body, kicking grooves in the snow for his heels. 'I've taken as much of the strain as I can,' he called.

Rohde tugged on the taut rope experimentally, and seemed satisfied. He paused. 'Put something between the rope and the edge to stop any chafing.' So Forester stripped off his hood and wadded it into a pad, jamming it between the rope and the icy edge of the crevasse.

Rohde tugged again and measured his probable point of impact fifteen feet down on the farther wall of the crevasse.

Then he launched himself into space.

Forester saw him disappear and felt the sudden strain on the rope, then heard the clash of Rohde's boots on the ice wall beneath. Thankfully he saw that there was no sudden easing of the tension on the rope and knew that Rohde had made it. All that remained now was for him to climb up.

It seemed an age before Rohde's head appeared above the edge and Forester went forward to haul him up. This is one hell of a man, he thought; this is one hell of a good joe. Rohde sat down not far from the edge and wiped the sweat from his face. 'That was not a good thing to do,' he said.

Forester cocked his head at Peabody. 'What do we do about him? He'll kill us all yet.' He took the gun from his pocket and Rohde's eyes widened. 'I think this is the end of the trail for Peabody.'

Peabody lay in the snow muttering to himself and Forester spoke as though he were not there, and it is doubtful if Peabody heard what was being said about him.

Rohde looked Forester in the eye. 'Can you shoot a defenceless man – even him?'

'You're damned right I can,' snapped Forester. 'We don't have only our own lives to think of – there are the others down at the bridge depending on us; this crazy fool will let us all down.'

He lifted the pistol and aimed at the back of Peabody's head. He was just taking up the slack on the trigger when his wrist was caught by Rohde. 'No, Ray; you are not a murderer.'

Forester tensed the muscles of his arm and fought Rohde's grip for a moment, then relaxed, and said, 'Okay, Miguel; but you'll see I'm right. He's selfish and he'll never do anything right – but I guess we're stuck with him.'

IV

Altogether it took them three hours to cross the glacier and by then Forester was exhausted, but Rohde would allow no rest. 'We must get as high as we can while there is still light,' he said. 'Tonight will weaken us very much – it is not good to spend a night in the open without a tent or the right kind of clothing.'

Forester managed a grin. Everything to Rohde was either good or not good; black and white with no shades of grey. He kicked Peabody to his feet and said tiredly, 'Okay; lead on, MacDuff.'

Rohde looked up at the pass. 'We lost height in crossing the glacier; we still have to ascend between five and six hundred metres to get to the top.'

Sixteen hundred to two thousand feet, Forester translated silently. He followed Rohde's gaze. To their left was the glacier, oozing imperceptibly down the mountain and scraping itself by a rock wall. Above, the clean sweep of snow was broken by a line of cliffs halfway up to the top of the pass. 'Do we have to climb *that*?' he demanded.

Rohde scrutinized the terrain carefully, then shook his head. 'I think we can go by the cliffs there – on the extreme right. That will bring us on top of the cliffs. We will bivouac there tonight.'

He put his hand in his pocket and produced the small leather bag of coca quids he had compounded back in the camp. 'Hold out your hand,' he said. 'You will need these now.'

He shook a dozen of the green squares into Forester's palm and Forester put one into his mouth and chewed it. It had an acrid and pungent taste which pleasantly warmed the inside of his mouth. 'Not too many,' warned Rohde. 'Or your mouth will become inflamed.'

It was useless giving them to Peabody. He had relapsed into his state of automatism and followed Rohde like a dog on a lead, obedient to the tugs on the rope. As Rohde set out on the long climb up to the cliffs he followed, mechanically going through the proper climbing movements as though guided by something outside himself. Forester, watching him from behind, hoped there would be no crisis; as long as things went well Peabody would be all right, but in an emergency he would certainly break, as O'Hara had prophesied.

He did not remember much of that long and toilsome climb. Perhaps the coca contributed to that, for he found himself in much the same state as he imagined Peabody to be in. Rhythmically chewing the quid, he climbed automatically, following the trail broken by the indefatigable Rohde.

At first the snow was thick and crusted, and then, as they approached the extreme right of the line of cliffs, the slope steepened and the snow cover became thinner and they found that under it was a sheet of ice. Climbing in these conditions without crampons was difficult, and, as Rohde confessed a little time afterwards, would have been considered impossible by anyone who knew the mountains.

It took them two hours to get above the rock cliffs and to meet a great disappointment. Above the cliffs and set a few feet back was a continuous ice wall over twenty feet high, surmounted by an overhanging snow cornice. The wall stretched across the width of the pass in an unbroken line.

Forester, gasping for breath in the thin air, looked at it in dismay. We've had it, he thought; how can we get over this? But Rohde, gazing across the pass, did not lose hope. He pointed. 'I think the ice wall is lower there in the middle. Come, but stay away from the edge of the cliff.'

They started out along the ledge between the ice wall and the edge of the cliff. At first the ledge was narrow, only a matter of feet, but as they went on it became broader and Rohde advanced more confidently and faster. But he seemed worried. 'We cannot stay here,' he said. 'It is very dangerous. We must get above this wall before nightfall.'

'What's the hurry?' asked Forester. 'If we stay here, the wall will shelter us from the wind – it's from the west and I think it's rising.'

'It is,' replied Rohde. He pointed upwards. 'That is what I worry about – the cornice. We cannot stay below it – it might break away – and the wind in the west will build it to breaking-point. It is going to snow – look down.'

Forester looked into the dizzying depths below the cliffs and saw a gathering greyness of mist. He shivered and retreated to safety, then followed the shambling figure of Peabody.

It was not five minutes later when he felt his feet suddenly slide on the ice. Frantically he tried to recover his balance but to no effect, and he found himself on his back, swooping towards the edge of the cliff. He tried to brake himself with his hands and momentarily saw the smear of blood on the ice as, with a despairing cry, he went over the edge.

Rohde, hearing the cry and feeling the tug of Peabody on the rope, automatically dug the ice-axe firmly into the ice and took the strain. When he turned his head he saw only Peabody scrabbling at the edge of the cliff, desperately trying to prevent himself from being pulled off. He was screaming incoherently, and of Forester there was no sign.

Forester found the world wheeling crazily before his eyes, first a vast expanse of sky and a sudden vista of valleys and mountains half obscured by wreaths of mist, then the grey rock close by as he spun and dangled on the end of the rope, suspended over a sheer drop of three hundred feet on to the steep snow slopes beneath. His chest hurt and he found that the rope had worked itself under his armpits and was constricting his ribs. From above he heard the terrified yammerings of Peabody.

With a heave Rohde cracked the muscles of his back and hoped the rotten rope would not break. He yelled to Peabody, 'Pull on the rope – get him up.' Instead he saw the flash of steel and saw that Peabody had a clasp-knife and was sawing at the rope where it went over the edge of the cliff.

Rohde did not hesitate. His hand went to his side and found the small axe they had taken from the Dakota. He drew it from his belt, reversing it quickly so that he held it by the handle. He lifted it, poised, for a second, judging his aim, and then hurled it at Peabody's head.

It struck Peabody squarely on the nape of the neck, splitting his skull. The terrified yelping stopped and from below Forester was aware of the startling silence and looked up. A knife dropped over the edge of the cliff and the blade cut a gash in his cheek before it went spinning into the abyss below, and a steady drip of blood rained on him from above.

SIX

O'Hara had lost his flask.

He thought that perhaps he had left it in the pocket of the leather jacket he had given Forester, but then he remembered going through the pockets first. He looked about the shelter, trying not to draw attention to himself, but still could not find it and decided that it must be up at the camp.

The loss worried him unreasonably. To have a full flask at his side had comforted him; he knew that whenever he wanted a drink then it was there ready to hand, and because it was there he had been able, in some odd way, to resist the temptation. But now he felt an aching longing in the centre of his being for a drink, for the blessed relief of alcohol and the oblivion it would bring.

It made him very short-tempered.

The night had been quiet. Since the abortive attempt to burn the bridge the previous evening, nothing had happened. Now, in the dawn light, he was wondering whether it would be safe to bring down the trebuchet. His resources in manpower were slender and to bring the trebuchet from the camp would leave the bridge virtually defenceless. True, the enemy was quiet, but that was no guarantee of future inactivity. He had no means of telling how long it would take them to obtain more timber and to transport it.

It was the common dilemma of the military man – trying to guess what the enemy was doing on the other side of the hill and balancing guesses against resources.

He heard the clatter of a stone and turned his head to find Benedetta coming towards him. He waved her back and slid down from his observation post. 'Jenny has made coffee,' she said. 'I will keep watch. Has anything happened?'

He shook his head. 'Everything's quiet. They're still there, of course; if you stick your neck out you'll get your head blown off – so be careful.' He paused; he badly needed to discuss his problems with someone else, not to shrug off responsibility but to clarify the situation in his own mind. He missed Forester.

He told Benedetta what he was thinking and she said immediately, 'But, of course, I will come up to the camp.'

'I might have known,' he said unreasonably. 'You won't be separated from your precious uncle.'

'It is not like that,' she said sharply. 'All you men are needed to bring down this machine, but what good can Jenny *and* I do down here? If we are attacked we can only run; and it does not take two to watch. Four can bring the machine from the camp quicker than three – even though one of them *is* a woman. If the enemy attacks in force Jenny will warn us.'

He said slowly, 'We'll have to take the risk, of course; we've got no choice. And the sooner we move the better.'

'Send Jenny down quickly,' said Benedetta. 'I'll wait for you at the pond.'

O'Hara went up to the shelter and was glad of the mug of steaming coffee that was thrust into his hands. In between gulps he rapidly detailed his plan and ended by saying, 'It puts a great deal on your shoulders, Jenny. I'm sorry about that.'

'I'll be all right,' she said quietly.

'You can have two shots – no more,' he said. 'We'll leave both bows cocked for you. If they start to work on the bridge, fire two bolts and then get up to the camp as fast as you can. With luck, the shots will slow them down enough for us to get back in time to fight them off. And for God's sake don't fire them both from the same place. They're getting smart over there and they have all our favourite posts spotted.'

He surveyed the small group. 'Any questions?'

Aguillar stirred. 'So I am to return to the camp. I feel I am a drag on you; so far I have done nothing – nothing.'

'God in heaven!' exclaimed O'Hara. 'You're our kingpin – you're the reason for all this. If we let them get you we'll have fought for nothing.'

Aguillar smiled slowly. 'You know as well as I do that I do not matter any more. True, it is me they want, but they cannot let you live as well. Did not Doctor Armstrong point out that very fact?'

Armstrong removed his pipe from his mouth. 'That might be so, but you're in no condition to fight,' he said bluntly. 'And while you're down here you are taking O'Hara's mind off his job. You'd be better out of the way up at the camp where you can do something constructive, like making new bolts.'

Aguillar bent his head. 'I stand corrected and rightly so. I am sorry, Señor O'Hara, for making more trouble than I need.'

'That's all right,' said O'Hara awkwardly. He felt sorry for Aguillar; the man had courage, but courage was not enough – or perhaps it was not the right kind of courage. Intellectual bravery was all very well in its place.

It was nearer three hours than two before they arrived at the camp, the slowness being caused by Aguillar's physical weakness, and O'Hara was fretting about what could have happened at the bridge. At least he had heard no rifle fire, but the wind was blowing away from the mountains and he doubted if he would have heard it anyway. This added to his tension.

Willis met them. 'Did Forester and Rohde get away all right – and our good friend Peabody?' asked O'Hara.

'They left before I awoke,' said Willis. He looked up at the mountains. 'They should be at the mine by now.'

Armstrong circled the trebuchet, making pleasurable noises. 'I say, you've done a good job here, Willis.'

Willis coloured a little. 'I did the best I could in the time we had – and with what we had.'

'I can't see how it can possibly work,' said O'Hara.

Willis smiled. 'Well, it's stripped down for transport. It's more or less upside-down now; we can wheel it down the road on the axle.'

Armstrong said, 'I was thinking of the Russo-Finnish war; a bit out of my field, I know, but the Finns were in very much the same case as we are – dreadfully under-equipped and using their ingenuity to the utmost. I seem to remember they invented the Molotov Cocktail.'

O'Hara's mind leapt immediately to the remaining drum of paraffin and to the empty bottles he had seen lying round the camp. 'My God, you've done it again,' he said. 'Gather together all the bottles you can find.'

He strode across to the hut where the paraffin was stored, and Willis called after him, 'It's open – I was in there this morning.'

He pushed open the door and paused as he saw the crate of liquor. Slowly he bent down and pulled out a bottle. He cradled it in his hand, then held it up to the light; the clear liquid could have been water; but he knew the deception. This was the water of Lethe which brought blessed forgetfulness, which untied the knots in his soul. His tongue crept out to lick his lips.

He heard someone approaching the hut and quickly put the bottle on a shelf, pushing it behind a box and out of

sight. When Benedetta came in he was bending over the
paraffin drum, unscrewing the cap.

She was laden with empty bottles. 'Willis said you wanted
these. What are they for?'

'We're making bombs of a sort. We'll need some strips of
cloth to make wicks and stoppers; see if you can find something.'

He began to fill the bottles and presently Benedetta came
back with the cloth and he showed her how to stuff the
necks of the bottles, leaving an easily ignitable wick. 'Where
are the others?' he asked.

'Willis had an idea,' she said. 'Armstrong and my uncle
are helping him.'

He filled another bottle. 'Do you mind leaving your uncle
up here alone?'

'What else can we do?' she asked. She bent her head. 'He
has always been alone. He never married, you know. And
then he has known a different kind of loneliness – the loneliness of power.'

'And have *you* been lonely – since . . .'

'Since my family were killed?' She looked up and there
was something in her dark eyes that he could not fathom.
'Yes, I have. I joined my uncle and we were two lonely
people together in foreign countries.' Her lips curved. 'I
think you are also a lonely man, Tim.'

'I get along,' he said shortly, and wiped his hands on a
piece of rag.

She stood up. 'What will you do when we leave here?'

'Don't you mean, *if* we leave here?' He stood too and
looked down at her upraised face. 'I think I'll move on;
there's nothing for me in Cordillera now. Filson will never
forgive me for bending one of his aeroplanes.'

'Is there nothing you want to stay for?'

Her lips were parted and on impulse he bent his head
and kissed her. She clung to him and after a long moment

he sighed. A sudden wonder had burst upon him and he said in surprise, 'Yes, I think there is something to stay for.'

They stood together quietly for a few minutes, not speaking. It is in the nature of lovers to make plans, but what could they plan for? So there was nothing to say.

At last Benedetta said, 'We must go, Tim. There is work to do.'

He released her. 'I'll see what the others are doing. You'd better throw the booze out of the liquor crate and put the paraffin bottles in it; we can strap it on to the trebuchet.'

He walked out of the hut and up to the other end of the camp to see what was happening. Halfway there he stopped in deep thought and cursed quietly. He had at last recognized the strange look in Benedetta's eyes. It had been compassion.

He took a deep breath, then straightened his shoulders and walked forward again, viciously kicking at a stone. He heard voices to his left and tramped over to the hillside, where he saw Willis, Armstrong and Aguillar grouped round an old cable drum.

'What's all this?' he asked abruptly.

'Insurance,' said Armstrong cheerfully. 'In case the enemy gets across the bridge.'

Willis gave another bang with the rock he was holding and O'Hara saw he had hammered a wedge to hold the drum in position. 'You know what this is,' he said. 'It's one of those wooden drums used to transport heavy cable – looks like a big cotton reel, doesn't it?'

It did indeed look like a cotton reel, eight feet in diameter. 'Well?' said O'Hara.

'The wood is rotten, of course – it must have been standing in the open for years,' said Willis. 'But it's heavy and it will roll. Take a few steps down the hill and tell me what you see.'

O'Hara walked down the hill and came to a steep drop, and found he was overlooking a cutting, blasted when the road was being made. Willis said from behind him, 'The drum is out of sight of the road. We wait until a jeep or a truck is coming up, then we pull away the chocks and with a bit of luck we cause a smash and block the road.'

O'Hara looked back at Aguillar, whose grey face told of the exertions he had made. He felt anger welling up inside him and jerked his head curtly to Willis and Armstrong. He walked out of earshot of Aguillar, then said evenly, suppressing his anger, 'I think it would be a good idea if we didn't go off half-cocked on independent tracks.'

Willis looked surprised and his face flushed. 'But – '

O'Hara cut him short. 'It's a bloody good idea, but you might have had some consultation about it. I could have helped to get the drum down into position and the old man could have filled paraffin bottles. You know he's got a heart condition, and if he drops dead on us those swine on the other side of the river have won.' He tapped Willis on the chest. 'And I don't intend to let that happen if I have to kill you, me and every other member of this party to get Aguillar away to safety.'

Willis looked shocked. 'Speak for yourself, O'Hara,' he said angrily. 'I'm fighting for my own life.'

'Not while I'm in command, you're not. You'll bloody well obey orders and you'll consult me on everything you do.'

Willis flared up. 'And who put you in command?'

'I did,' said O'Hara briefly. He stared at Willis. 'Want to make an issue of it?'

'I might,' said Willis tightly.

O'Hara stared him down. 'You won't,' he said with finality.

Willis's eyes flickered away. Armstrong said quietly, 'It would be a good idea if we didn't fight among ourselves.' He turned to Willis. 'O'Hara is right, though; we shouldn't have let Aguillar push the drum.'

'Okay, okay,' said Willis impatiently. 'But I don't go for this death-or-glory stuff.'

'Look,' said O'Hara. 'You know what I think? I think I'm a dead man as I stand here right now. I don't think we've a hope in hell of stopping those communist bastards crossing the bridge; we might slow them down but we can't stop them. And once they get across they'll hunt us down and slaughter us like pigs – that's why I think I'm a dead man. It's not that I particularly like Aguillar, but the communists want him and I'm out to stop them – that's why I'm so tender of him.'

Willis had gone pale. 'But what about Forester and Rohde?'

'I think they're dead too,' said O'Hara coldly. 'Have you any idea what it's like up there? Look, Willis; I flew men and equipment for two Yankee mountaineering expeditions and one German. And with all their modern gadgets they failed in their objectives three-quarters of the time.' He waved his arm at the mountains. 'Hell, half these mountains don't even have names, they're so inaccessible.'

Armstrong said, 'You paint a black picture, O'Hara.'

'Is it a true picture?'

'I fear it is,' said Armstrong ruefully.

O'Hara shook his head irritably. 'This isn't doing any good. Let's get that contraption down to the bridge.'

II

It was not as difficult as O'Hara anticipated getting the trebuchet down the mountain road. Willis had done a good job in mounting it for ease of transportation and it took only three hours to get back, the main difficulty being to manoeuvre the clumsy machine round the hairpin bends. At every bend he half expected to see Miss Ponsky running up to tell them that the communists had made their attack, but all was quiet and he did not even hear the crack of a rifle. Things were too quiet, he thought; maybe they were running out of ammunition – there was none of the desultory firing that had gone on the previous day.

They pushed the trebuchet off the road to the place indicated by Willis, and O'Hara said expressionlessly, 'Benedetta, relieve Jenny; tell her to come up and see me.'

She looked at him curiously, but he had turned away to help Willis and Armstrong dismantle the trebuchet preparatory to erecting it as a weapon. They were going to mount it on a small knoll in order to get the height, so that the heavy weight on the shorter arm could have a good fall.

Miss Ponsky came up to him and told him that everything had been quiet. He thought for a moment and then said, 'Did you hear any trucks?'

'Not since they took away the jeep this morning.'

He rubbed his chin. 'Maybe we hit them harder than we thought. You're sure they're still there?'

'Oh, yes,' she said brightly. 'I had that thought myself some hours ago so I waggled something in full view.' She blushed. 'I put my hat on a stick – I've seen it done in old movies on TV.'

He smiled. 'Did they hit it?'

'No – but they came close.'

'You're doing all right, Jenny.'

'You must be hungry – I'll make a meal.' Her lips twitched. 'I think this is fun, you know.' She turned and hurried up the road, leaving him standing dumbfounded. Fun!

Assembling the trebuchet took two hours and when it was completed Armstrong, begrimed but happy, said with satisfaction, 'There, now; I never expected to see one of these in action.' He turned to O'Hara. 'Forester came upon me sketching a trebuchet for Willis; he asked if I were drawing the scales of justice and I said that I was. He must have thought me mad, but it was perceptive of him.'

He closed his eyes and recited as though quoting a dictionary entry. 'From the medieval Latin *trebuchetum*; old French, *trébuchet*; a pair of scales, an assay balance.' He opened his eyes and pointed. 'You see the resemblance?'

O'Hara did see. The trebuchet looked like a warped balance, very much out of proportion, with one arm much longer than the other. He said, 'Does this thing have much of a kick – much recoil?'

'Nothing detectable; the impact is absorbed by the ground.'

O'Hara looked at the crazy system of ropes and pulleys. 'The question is now – will the beast work?'

There was an edge of irritability to Willis's voice. 'Of course it will work. Let's chuck this thing.' He pointed to a round boulder about the size of a man's head.

'All right,' said O'Hara. 'Let's give it a bang. What do we do?'

'First we haul like hell on this rope,' said Willis.

The rope was connected, through a three-part pulley arrangement, to the end of the long arm. As O'Hara and Willis pulled, the arm came down and the shorter arm with the weight rose into the air. The weight was a big, rusty iron bucket which Willis had found and filled with stones. As the long arm came to the ground, Armstrong stepped forward and threw over a lever and a wooden block dropped over the arm, holding it down. Willis picked up the boulder and placed it in the hub-cap which served as a cup.

'We're ready,' he said. 'I've already aligned the thing in the general direction of the bridge; we need someone down there to call the fall of the shot.'

'I'll go,' said O'Hara. He walked across to where Benedetta was keeping watch and slid down beside her, being careful to keep his head down. 'They're going to let fly,' he said.

She turned her head to look at the trebuchet. 'Do you think this will work?'

'I don't know.' He grimaced. 'All I know is that it's a hell of a way to fight a war.'

'We're ready,' shouted Armstrong.

O'Hara waved and Armstrong pulled the firing lever sharply. The weight dropped and the long arm bearing the missile flipped up into the air. There was an almighty crash as the iron bucket hit the ground, but O'Hara's attention was on the rock as it arched over his head. It was in the air a long time and went very high; then it reached the top of its trajectory and started to fall to earth, gaining speed appreciably as it plummeted. It fell far on the other side of the bridge, beyond the road and the burned vehicles, into the mountainside. A plume of dust fountained from the side of the hill to mark its fall.

'Jesus!' whispered O'Hara. 'The thing has range.' He slipped from his place and ran back. 'Thirty yards over – fifteen to the right. How heavy was that rock?'

'About thirty pounds,' said Willis offhandedly. 'We need a bigger one.' He heaved on the trebuchet. 'We'll swing her a bit to the left.'

O'Hara could hear a babble of voices from across the river and there was a brief rattle of rifle fire. Or should I call it musketry? he thought, just to keep it in period. He laughed and smote Armstrong on the back. 'You've done it again,' he roared. 'We'll pound that bridge to matchwood.'

But it was not to prove as easy as he thought. It took an hour to fire the next six shots – and not one of them hit the bridge. They had two near misses and one that grazed the catenary rope on the left, making the bridge shiver from end to end. But there were no direct hits.

Curiously, too, there was no marked reaction from the enemy. A lot of running about and random shooting followed each attempt, but there was no coherent action. What could they do after all, O'Hara thought; nothing could stop the rocks once they were in flight.

'Why can't we get the range right – what the hell's the matter with this thing?' he demanded at last.

Armstrong said mildly, 'I knew a trebuchet wasn't a precision weapon, in a general way, of course; but this brings it home. It does tend to scatter a bit, doesn't it?'

Willis looked worried. 'There's a bit of a whip in the arm,' he said. 'It isn't stiff enough. Then again, we haven't a standard shot; there are variations in weight and that causes the overs and unders. It's the whip that's responsible for the variations from side to side.'

'Can you do anything about the whip in the arm?'

Willis shook his head. 'A steel girder would help,' he said ironically.

'There must be some way of getting a standard weight of shot.'

So the ingenious Willis made a rough balance which, he said, would match one rock against another to the nearest half-pound. And they started again. Four shots later, they made the best one of the afternoon.

The trebuchet crashed again and a cloud of dust rose from where the bucket smashed into the ground. The long arm came over, just like a fast bowler at cricket, thought O'Hara, and the rock soared into the sky, higher and higher. Over O'Hara's head it reached its highest point and began to fall, seeming to go true to its target. 'This is it,' said O'Hara urgently. 'This is going to be a smash hit.'

The rock dropped faster and faster under the tug of gravity and O'Hara held his breath. It dropped right between the catenary ropes of the bridge and, to O'Hara's disgust, fell plumb through the gap in the middle, sending a plume of white spray leaping from the boiling river to splash on the underside of the planking.

'God Almighty!' he howled. 'A perfect shot – and in the wrong bloody place.'

But he had a sudden hope that what he had said to Willis up at the camp would prove to be wrong; that he was not a dead man – that the enemy would *not* get over the bridge – that they all had a fighting chance. As hope surged in him a knot of tension tightened in his stomach. When he had no hope his nerves had been taut enough, but the offer of continued life made life itself seem more precious and not to be lost or thrown away – and so the tension was redoubled. A man who considers himself dead has no fear of dying, but with hope came a trace of fear.

He went back to the trebuchet. 'You're a bloody fine artilleryman,' he said to Willis in mock-bitter tones.

Willis bristled. 'What do you mean?'

'I mean what I say – you're a bloody fine artilleryman. That last shot was perfect – but the bridge wasn't there at that point. The rock went through the gap.'

Willis grinned self-consciously and seemed pleased. 'It looks as though we've got the range.'

'Let's get at it,' said O'Hara.

For the rest of the afternoon the trebuchet thumped and crashed at irregular intervals. They worked like slaves hauling on the ropes and bringing rocks to the balance. O'Hara put Miss Ponsky in charge of the balance and as the afternoon wore on they became expert at judging the weight – it was no fun to carry a forty-pound rock a matter of a couple of hundred yards, only to have it rejected by Miss Ponsky.

O'Hara kept an eye on his watch and recorded the number of shots, finding that the rate of fire had speeded up to above twelve an hour. In two and a half hours they fired twenty-six rocks and scored about seven hits; about one in four. O'Hara had seen only two of them land but what he saw convinced him that the bridge could not take that kind of pounding for long. It was a pity that the hits were scattered on the bridge – a concentration would have been better – but they had opened a new gap of two planks and several more were badly bent. It was not enough to worry a man crossing the bridge – not yet – but no one would take a chance with a vehicle.

He was delighted – as much by the fact that the enemy was helpless as by anything else. There was nothing they could do to stop the bridge being slowly pounded into fragments, short of bringing up a mortar to bombard the trebuchet. At first there had been the usual futile rifle-fire, but that soon ceased. Now there was merely a chorus of jeers from the opposite bank when a shot missed and a groan when a hit was scored.

It was half an hour from nightfall when Willis came to him and said, 'We can't keep this up. The beast is taking a hell of a battering – she's shaking herself to pieces. Another two or three shots and she'll collapse.'

O'Hara swore and looked at the grey man – Willis was covered in dust from head to foot. He said slowly, 'I had hoped to carry on through the night – I wanted to ruin the bridge beyond repair.'

'We can't,' said Willis flatly. 'She's loosened up a lot and there's a split in the arm – it'll break off if we don't bind it up with something. If that happens the trebuchet is the pile of junk it started out as.'

O'Hara felt impotent fury welling up inside him. He turned away without speaking and walked several paces before he said over his shoulder, 'Can you fix it?'

'I can try,' said Willis. 'I think I can.'

'Don't try – don't think. Fix it,' said O'Hara harshly, as he walked away. He did not look back.

III

Night.

A sheath of thin mist filmed the moon, but O'Hara could still see as he picked his way among the rocks. He found a comfortable place in which to sit, his back resting against a vertical slab. In front of him was a rock shelf on which he carefully placed the bottle he carried. It reflected the misted moon deep in its white depths as though enclosing a nacreous pearl.

He looked at it for a long time.

He was tired; the strain of the last few days had told heavily on him and his sleep had been a matter of a few hours snatched here and there. But Miss Ponsky and Benedetta were now taking night watches and that eased the burden. Over by the bridge Willis and Armstrong were tinkering with the trebuchet, and O'Hara thought he should go and help them but he did not. To hell with it, he thought; let me have an hour to myself.

The enemy – the peculiarly faceless enemy – had once more brought up another jeep and the bridge was again well illuminated. They weren't taking any chances of losing the bridge by a sudden fire-burning sortie. For two days they had not made a single offensive move apart from their futile barrages of rifle-fire. They're cooking something up, he thought; and when it comes, it's going to surprise us.

He looked at the bottle thoughtfully.

Forester and Rohde would be leaving the mine for the pass at dawn and he wondered if they would make it. He had been quite honest with Willis up at the camp – he honestly did not think they had a hope. It would be cold up there and they had no tent and, by the look of the sky, there was going to be a change in the weather. If they did not cross the pass – maybe even if they did – the enemy had won; the God of Battles was on their side because they had the bigger battalions.

With a deep sigh he picked up the bottle and unscrewed the cap, giving way to the lurking devils within him.

IV

Miss Ponsky said, 'You know, I'm enjoying this – really I am.'

Benedetta looked up, startled. 'Enjoying it!'

'Yes, I am,' said Miss Ponsky comfortably, 'I never thought I'd have such an adventure.'

Benedetta said carefully, 'You know we might all be killed?'

'Oh, yes, child; I know that. But I know now why men go to war. It's the same reason that makes them gamble, but in war they play for the highest stake of all – their own lives. It adds a certain edge to living.'

She pulled her coat closer about her and smiled. 'I've been a school teacher for thirty years,' she said. 'And you know how folk think of spinster schoolmarms – they're supposed to be prissy and sexless and unromantic, but I was never like that. If anything I was too romantic, surely too much so for my own good. I saw life in terms of old legends and historical novels, and of course life isn't like that at all. There was a man, you know, once . . .'

Benedetta was silent, not wishing to break the thread of this curious revelation.

Miss Ponsky visibly pulled herself together. 'Anyway, there I was – a very romantic young girl growing into middle age and rising a little in her profession. I became a headmistress – a sort of dragon to a lot of children. I suppose my romanticism showed a little by what I did in my spare time; I was quite a good fencer when I was younger, and of course, later there was the archery. But I wished I could have been a man and gone away and had adventures – men are so much *freer*, you know. I had almost given up hope when this happened.'

She chuckled happily. 'And now here I am rising fifty-five and engaged in a desperate adventure. Of course I know I might be killed but it's all worth it, every bit of it; it makes up for such a lot.'

Benedetta looked at her sadly. What was happening threatened to destroy her uncle's hopes for their country and Miss Ponsky saw it in the light of dream-like romanticism, something from Robert Louis Stevenson to relieve the sterility of her life. She had jibbed at killing a man, but now she was blooded and would never look upon human life in the same light again. And when – or if – she went back home again, dear safe old South Bridge, Connecticut, would always seem a little unreal to her – reality would be a bleak mountainside with death coming over a bridge and a sense of quickened life as her blood coursed faster through parched veins.

Miss Ponsky said briskly, 'But I mustn't run on like this. I must go down to the bridge; I promised Mr O'Hara I would. He's such a handsome young man, isn't he? But he looks so sad sometimes.'

Benedetta said in a low voice, 'I think he is unhappy.'

Miss Ponsky nodded wisely. 'There has been a great grief in his life,' she said, and Benedetta knew that she was casting

O'Hara as a dark Byronic hero in the legend she was living. But he's not like that, she cried to herself; he's a man of flesh and blood, and a stupid man too, who will not allow others to help him, to share his troubles. She thought of what had happened up at the camp, of O'Hara's kisses and the way she had been stirred by them – and then of his inexplicable coldness towards her soon afterwards. If he would not share himself, she thought, perhaps such a man was not for her – but she found herself wishing she was wrong.

Miss Ponsky went out of the shelter. 'It's becoming a little misty,' she said. 'We must watch all the more carefully.'

Benedetta said, 'I'll come down in two hours.'

'Good,' said Miss Ponsky gaily, and clattered her way down to the bridge.

Benedetta sat for a while repairing a rent in her coat with threads drawn out of the hem and using the needle which she always carried stuck in the lining of her handbag. The small domestic task finished, she thought, Tim's shirt is torn – perhaps I can mend that.

He had been glumly morose during the evening meal and had gone away immediately afterwards to the right along the mountainside, away from the bridge. She had recognized that he had something on his mind and had not interrupted, but had marked the way he had gone. Now she got up and stepped out of the shelter.

She came upon him suddenly from behind after being guided by the clink of glass against stone. He was sitting gazing at the moon, the bottle in his hand, and was quietly humming a tune she did not know. The bottle was half-empty.

He turned as she stepped forward out of the shadows and held out the bottle. 'Have a drink; it's good for what ails you.' His voice was slurred and furry.

'No, thank you, Tim.' She stepped down and sat beside him. 'You have a tear in your shirt – I'll mend it if you come back to the shelter.'

'Ah, the little woman. Domesticity in a cave.' He laughed humourlessly.

She indicated the bottle. 'Do you think this is good – at this time?'

'It's good at this or any other time – but especially at this time.' He waved the bottle. 'Eat, drink and be merry – for tomorrow we certainly die.' He thrust it at her. 'Come on, have a snort.'

She took the proffered bottle and quickly smashed it against a rock. He made a movement as though to save it, and said, 'What the hell did you do that for?' in an aggrieved voice.

'Your name is not Peabody,' she said cuttingly.

'What do you know about it? Peabody and I are old pals – bottle-babies, both of us.' He stooped and groped. 'Maybe it's not all gone – there might be some to be saved.' He jerked suddenly. 'Damn, I've cut my bloody finger,' he said and laughed hysterically. 'Look, I've got a bloody finger.'

She saw the blood dripping from his hand, black in the moonlight. 'You're irresponsible,' she said. 'Give me your hand.' She lifted her skirt and ripped at her slip, tearing off a strip of cloth for a bandage.

O'Hara laughed uproariously. 'The classic situation,' he said. 'The heroine bandages the wounded hero and does all the usual things that Hollywood invented. I suppose I should turn away like the gent I'm supposed to be, but you've got nice legs and I like looking at them.'

She was silent as she bandaged his finger. He looked down at her dark head and said, 'Irresponsible? I suppose I am. So what? What is there to be responsible for? The world can go to hell in a hand-basket for all I care.' He crooned. 'Naked came I into the world and naked I shall go out of it – and what lies between is just a lot of crap.'

'That's a sad philosophy of life,' she said, not raising her head.

He put his hand under her chin to lift her head and stared at her. 'Life? What do you know about life? Here you are – fighting the good fight in this crummy country – and for what? So that a lot of stupid Indians can have something that, if they had any guts at all, they'd get for themselves. But there's a big world outside which is always interfering – and you'll kowtow to Russia or America in the long run; you can't escape that fate. If you think that you'll be masters in your own country, you're even more stupid than I thought you were.'

She met his eyes steadily. In a quiet and tranquil voice she said, 'We can try.'

'You'll never do it,' he answered, and dropped his hand. 'This is a world of dog eat dog and this country is one of the scraps that the big dogs fight over. It's a world of eat or be eaten – kill or be killed.'

'I don't believe that,' she said.

He gave a short laugh. 'Don't you? Then what the hell are we doing here? Why don't we pack up our things and just go home? Let's pretend there's no one on the other side of the river who wants to kill us on sight.'

She had no answer to that. He put his arm round her and she felt his hand on her knee, moving up her thigh under her skirt. She struggled loose and hit him with her open palm as hard as she could. He looked at her and there was a shocked expression in his eyes as he rubbed his cheek.

She cried, 'You are one of the weak ones, Tim O'Hara, you are one of those who are killed and eaten. You have no courage and you always seek refuge – in the bottom of a bottle, in the arms of a woman, what does it matter? You're a pitiful, twisted man.'

'Christ, what do you know about me?' he said, stung by the contempt in her voice but knowing that he liked her contempt better than her compassion.

'Not much. And I don't particularly like what I know. But I do know that you're worse than Peabody – he's a weak man who can't help it; you're a strong man who refuses to be strong. You spend all your time staring at your own navel in the belief that it's the centre of the universe, and you have no human compassion at all.'

'Compassion?' he shouted. 'I have no need of your compassion – I've no time for people who are sorry for me. I don't need it.'

'Everyone needs it,' she retorted. 'We're all afraid – that's the human predicament, to be afraid, and any man who says he isn't is a liar.' In a quieter voice she went on, 'You weren't always like this, Tim – what caused it?'

He dropped his head into his hands. He could feel something breaking within him; there was a shattering and a crumbling of his defences, the walls he had hidden behind for so long. He had just realized the truth of what Benedetta said; that his fear was not an abnormality but the normal situation of mankind and that it was not weakness to admit it.

He said in a muffled voice, 'Good Christ, Benedetta, I'm frightened – I'm scared of falling into their hands again.'

'The communists?'

He nodded.

'What did they do to you?'

So he told her and in the telling her face went white. He told her of the weeks of lying naked in his own filth in that icy cell; of the enforced sleeplessness, the interminable interrogations; of the blinding lamps and the electric shocks; of Lieutenant Feng. 'They wanted me to confess to spreading plague germs,' he said. He raised his head and she saw the streaks of tears in the moonlight. 'But I didn't; it wasn't true, so I didn't.' He gulped. 'But I nearly did.'

In her innermost being she felt a scalding contempt for herself – she had called *this* man weak. She cradled his head to her breast and felt the deep shudders which racked him. 'It's all right now, Tim,' she said. 'It's all right.'

He felt a draining of himself, a purging of the soul in the catharsis of telling to another human being that which had been locked within him for so long. And in a strange way, he felt strengthened and uplifted as he got rid of all the psychic pus that had festered in his spirit. Benedetta took the brunt of this verbal torrent calmly, comforting him with disconnected, almost incoherent endearments. She felt at once older and younger than he, which confused her and made her uncertain of what to do.

At last the violence of his speech ebbed and gradually he fell silent, leaning back against the rock as though physically exhausted. She held both his hands and said, 'I'm sorry, Tim – for what I said.'

He managed a smile. 'You were right – I have been a thorough bastard, haven't I?'

'With reason.'

'I must apologize to the others,' he said. 'I've been riding everybody too hard.'

She said carefully, 'We aren't chess pieces, Tim, to be moved as though we had no feelings. And that's what you have been doing, you know; moving my uncle, Willis and Armstrong – Jenny, too – as though they were just there to solve the problem. You see, it isn't only your problem – it belongs to all of us. Willis has worked harder than any of us; there was no need to behave towards him as you did when the trebuchet broke down.'

O'Hara sighed. 'I know,' he said. 'But it seemed the last straw. I was feeling bloody-minded about everything just then. But I'll apologize to him.'

'A better thing would be to help him.'

He nodded. 'I'll go now.' He looked at her and wondered if he had alienated her for ever. It seemed to him that no woman could love him who knew about him what this woman knew. But then Benedetta smiled brilliantly at him, and he knew with relief that everything was going to be all right.

'Come,' she said. 'I'll walk with you as far as the shelter.' She felt an almost physical swelling pain in her bosom, a surge of wild, unreasonable happiness, and she knew that she had been wrong when she had felt that Tim was not for her. This was the man with whom she would share her life – for as long as her life lasted.

He left her at the shelter and she kissed him before he went on. As she saw the dark shadow going away down the mountain she suddenly remembered and called, 'What about the tear in your shirt?'

His answer came back almost gaily. 'Tomorrow,' he shouted, and went on to the glimmer of light where Willis was working against time.

V

The morning dawned mistily but the rising sun soon burned away the haze. They held a dawn conference by the tre-buchet to decide what was to be done next. 'What do you think?' O'Hara asked Willis. 'How much longer will it take?'

Armstrong clenched his teeth round the stem of his pipe and observed O'Hara with interest. Something of note had happened to this young man; something good. He looked over to where Benedetta was keeping watch on the bridge – her radiance this morning had been unbelievable, a shining effulgence that cast an almost visible glow about her. Armstrong smiled – it was almost indecent how happy these two were.

Willis said, 'It'll be better now we can see what we're doing. I give us another couple of hours.' His face was drawn and tired.

'We'll get to it,' said O'Hara. He was going to continue but he paused suddenly, his head on one side. After a few seconds Armstrong also caught what O'Hara was listening to – the banshee whine of a jet plane approaching fast.

It was on them suddenly, coming low up-river. There was a howl and a wink of shadow as the aircraft swept over them to pull up into a steep climb and a sharp turn. Willis yelled, 'They've found us – they've found us.' He began to jump up and down in a frenzy of excitement, waving his arms.

'It's a Sabre,' O'Hara shouted. 'And it's coming back.'

They watched the plane reach the top of its turning climb and come back at them in a shallow dive. Miss Ponsky screamed at the top of her voice, her arms going like a semaphore, but O'Hara said suddenly, 'I don't like this – everyone scatter – take cover.'

He had seen aircraft behave like that in Korea, and he had done it himself; it had all the hallmarks of the beginning of a strafing attack.

They scattered like chickens at the sudden onset of a hawk and again the Sabre roared over, but there was no chatter of guns – just the diminishing whine of the engine as it went away down river. Twice more it came over them and the tough grass standing in clumps trembled stiff stems in the wake of its passage. And then it was gone in a long, almost vertical climb heading west over the mountains.

They came out of cover and stood in a group looking towards the peaks. Willis was the first to speak. 'Damn you,' he shouted at O'Hara. 'Why did you make us hide? That plane must have been searching for us.'

'Was it?' asked O'Hara. 'Benedetta, does Cordillera have Sabres in the Air Force?'

'That was an Air Force fighter,' she said. 'I don't know which squadron.'

'I missed the markings,' said O'Hara. 'Did anyone get them?'

No one had.

'I'd like to know which squadron that was,' mused O'Hara. 'It could make a difference.'

'I tell you it was part of the search,' insisted Willis.

'Nothing doing,' said O'Hara. 'The pilot of that plane knew exactly where to come – he wasn't searching. Someone had given him a pinpoint map position. There was nothing uncertain about his passes over us. We didn't tell him; Forester didn't tell him – they're only just leaving the mine now – so who did?'

Armstrong used his pipe as a pointer. They did,' he said, and pointed across the river. 'We must assume that it means nothing good.'

O'Hara was galvanized into activity. 'Let's get this bloody beast working again. I want that bridge ruined as soon as possible. Jenny, take a bow and go downriver to where you can get a good view of the road where it bends away. If anyone comes through, take a crack at them and then get back here as fast as you can. Benedetta, you watch the bridge – the rest of us will get cracking here.'

Willis had been too optimistic, because two hours went by and the trebuchet was still in pieces and far from being in working order. He wiped a grimy hand across his face. 'It's not so bad now – another hour will see it right.'

But they did not get another hour. Benedetta called out, 'I can hear trucks.' Following immediately upon her words came the rattle of rifle shots from downriver and another sound that chilled O'Hara – the unmistakable rat-a-tat of a machine-gun. He ran over to Benedetta and said breathlessly, 'Can you see anything?'

'No,' she answered; then, 'Wait – yes, three trucks – big ones.'

'Come down,' said O'Hara. 'I want to see this.'

She climbed down from among the rocks and he took her place. Coming up the road at a fast clip and trailing a cloud of dust was a big American truck and behind it another, and another. The first one was full of men, at least twenty of them, all armed with rifles. There was something odd about it that O'Hara could not at first place, then he saw the deep skirting of steel plate below the truck body which covered the petrol tank. The enemy was taking precautions.

The truck pulled to a halt by the bridge and the men piled out, being careful to keep the truck between themselves and the river. The second truck stopped behind; this was empty of men apart from two in the cab, and O'Hara could not see what the covered body contained. The third truck also contained men, though not as many, and O'Hara felt cold as he saw the light machine-gun being unloaded and taken hurriedly to cover.

He turned and said to Benedetta, 'Give me that bow, and get the others over here.' But when he turned back there was no target for him; the road and mountainside opposite seemed deserted of life, and the three trucks held no profit for him.

Armstrong and Willis came up and he told them what was happening. Willis said, 'The machine-gun sounds bad, I know, but what can they do with it that they can't do with the rifles they've got? It doesn't make us much worse off.'

'They can use it like a hose-pipe,' said O'Hara. 'They can squirt a steam of bullets and systematically hose down the side of the gorge. It's going to be bloody dangerous using the crossbow from now on.'

'You say the second truck was empty,' observed Armstrong thoughtfully.

'I didn't say that; I said it had no men. There must be something in there but the top of the body is swathed in canvas and I couldn't see.' He smiled sourly. 'They've probably got a demountable mountain howitzer or a mortar in there – and if they have anything like that we've had our chips.'

Armstrong absently knocked his pipe against a rock, forgetting it was empty. 'The thing to do now is have a parley,' he said unexpectedly. 'There never was a siege I studied where there wasn't a parley somewhere along the line.'

'For God's sake, talk sense,' said O'Hara. 'You can only parley when you've got something to offer. These boys are on top and they know it; why should they parley? Come to that – why should *we*? We know they'll offer us the earth, and we know damned well they'll not keep their promises – so what's the use?'

'We have something to offer,' said Armstrong calmly. 'We have Aguillar – they want him, so we'll offer him.' He held up his hands to silence the others' protests. 'We know what they'll offer us – our lives, and we know what their promises are worth, but that doesn't matter. Oh, we don't give them Aguillar, but with a bit of luck we can stretch the parley out into a few hours, and who knows what a few hours may mean later on?'

O'Hara thought about it. 'What do you think, Willis?'

Willis shrugged. 'We don't stand to lose anything,' he said, 'and we stand to gain time. Everything we've done so far has been to gain time.'

'We could get the trebuchet into working order again,' mused O'Hara. 'That alone would be worth it. All right, let's try it out.'

'Just a minute,' said Armstrong. 'Is anything happening across there yet?'

O'Hara looked across the gorge; everything was still and quiet. 'Nothing.'

'I think we'd better wait until they start to do something,' counselled Armstrong. 'It's my guess that the new arrivals and the old guard are in conference; they may take a while and there's no point in breaking it up. *Any* time we gain is to our advantage, so let's wait awhile.'

Benedetta, who was standing by quietly, now spoke. 'Jenny hasn't come back yet.'

O'Hara whirled. 'Hasn't she?'

Willis said, 'Perhaps she'll have been hit; that machine-gun . . .' His voice tailed away.

'I'll go and see,' said Benedetta.

'No,' said O'Hara sharply. 'I'll go – she may need to be carried and you can't do that. You'd better stay here on watch and the others can get on with repairing the tre-buchet.'

He plunged away and ran across the level ground, skirt-ing the bridgehead where there was no cover and began to clamber among the rocks on the other side, making his way downriver. He had a fair idea of the place Miss Ponsky would have taken and he made straight for it. As he went he swore and cursed under his breath; if she had been killed he would never forgive himself.

It took him over twenty minutes to make the journey – good time considering the ground was rough – but when he arrived at the most likely spot she was not there. But there were three bolts stuck point first in the ground and a small pool of sticky blood staining the rock.

He bent down and saw another blood-spot and then another. He followed this bloody spoor and back-tracked a hundred yards before he heard a weak groan and saw Miss Ponsky lying in the shadow of a boulder, her hand clutch-ing her left shoulder. He dropped to his knee beside her and lifted her head. 'Where were you hit, Jenny? In the shoulder?'

Her eyes flickered open and she nodded weakly.

'Anywhere else?'

She shook her head and whispered, 'Oh, Tim, I'm sorry. I lost the bow.'

'Never mind that,' he said, and ripped the blouse from her shoulder, careful not to jerk her. He sighed in relief; the wound was not too bad, being through the flesh part of the shoulder and not having broken the bone so far as he could judge. But she had lost a lot of blood and that had weakened her, as had the physical shock.

She said in a stronger voice, 'But I shouldn't have lost it – I should have held on tight. It fell into the river, Tim; I'm so sorry.'

'Damn the bow,' he said. 'You're more important.' He plugged the wound on both sides with pieces torn from his shirt, and made a rough bandage. 'Can you walk?'

She tried to walk and could not, so he said cheerfully, 'Then I'll have to carry you – fireman's lift. Up you come.' He slung her over his shoulder and slowly made his way back to the bridge. By the time he got to the shelter and delivered her to Benedetta she was unconscious again.

'All the more need for a parley,' he said grimly to Armstrong. 'We must get Jenny on her feet again and capable of making a run for it. Has anything happened across there?'

'Nothing. But we've nearly finished the trebuchet.'

It was not much later that two men began to strip the canvas from the second truck and O'Hara said, 'Now we give it a go.' He filled his lungs and shouted in Spanish, 'Señors – Señors! I wish to speak to your leader. Let him step forward – we will not shoot.'

The two men stopped dead and looked at each other. Then they stared across the gorge, undecided. O'Hara said, in a sardonic aside to Armstrong, 'Not that we've got much to shoot with.'

The men appeared to make up their minds. One of them ran off and presently the big man with the beard appeared from among the rocks, climbed down and walked to the abutments of the bridge. He shouted, 'Is that Señor Aguillar?'

'No,' shouted O'Hara, changing into English. 'It is O'Hara.'

'Ah, the pilot.' The big man responded in English, rather startling O'Hara with his obvious knowledge of their identities. 'What do you want, Señor O'Hara?'

Benedetta had returned to join them and now said quickly, 'This man is not a Cordilleran; his accent is Cuban.'

O'Hara winked at her. 'Señor Cuban, why do you shoot at us?'

The big man laughed jovially. 'Have you not asked Señor Aguillar? Or does he still call himself Montes?'

'Aguillar is nothing to do with me,' called O'Hara. 'His fight is not mine – and I'm tired of being shot at.'

The Cuban threw back his head and laughed again, slapping his thigh. 'So?'

'I want to get out of here.'

'And Aguillar?'

'You can have him. That's what you're here for, isn't it?'

The Cuban paused as though thinking deeply, and O'Hara said to Benedetta, 'When I pinch you, scream your head off.' She looked at him in astonishment, then nodded.

'Bring Aguillar to the bridge and you can go free, Señor O'Hara.'

'What about the girl?' asked O'Hara.

'The girl we want too, of course.'

O'Hara pinched Benedetta in the arm and she uttered a blood-curdling scream, artistically chopping it off as though a hand had been clapped to her mouth. O'Hara grinned at her and waited a few moments before he raised his voice. 'Sorry, Señor Cuban; we had some trouble.' He let caution appear in his tone. 'I'm not the only one here – there are others.'

'You will all go free,' said the big man with an air of largesse. 'I myself will escort you to San Croce. Bring Aguillar to the bridge now; let us have him and you can all go.'

'That is impossible,' O'Hara protested. 'Aguillar is at the upper camp. He went there when he saw what was happening here at the bridge. It will take time to bring him down.'

The Cuban lifted his head suspiciously. 'Aguillar ran away?' he asked incredulously.

O'Hara swore silently; he had not thought that Aguillar would be held in such respect by his enemies. He quickly improvised. 'He was sent away by Rohde, his friend. But Rohde has been killed by your machine-gun.'

'Ah, the man who shot at us on the road just now.' The Cuban looked down at his tapping foot, apparently undecided. Then he lifted his head. 'Wait, Señor O'Hara.'

'How long?'

'A few minutes, that is all.' He walked up the road and disappeared among the rocks.

Armstrong said, 'He's gone to consult with his second-in-command.'

'Do you think he'll fall for it?'

'He might,' said Willis. 'It's an attractive proposition. You baited it well – he thinks that Rohde has been keeping us in line and that now he's dead we're about to collapse. It was very well done.'

The Cuban was away for ten minutes, then he came back to the bridge accompanied by another man, a slight swarthy Indian type. 'Very well,' he called. 'As the *norteamericanos* say, you have made a deal. How long to bring Aguillar?'

'It's a long way,' shouted O'Hara. 'It will take some time – say, five hours.'

The two men conferred and then the Cuban shouted, 'All right, five hours.'

'And we have an armistice?' shouted O'Hara. 'No shooting from either side?'

'No shooting,' promised the Cuban.

O'Hara sighed. 'That's it. We must get the trebuchet finished. We've got five hours' grace. How's Jenny, Benedetta?'

'She will be all right. I gave her some hot soup and wrapped her in a blanket. She must be kept warm.'

'Five hours isn't a long time,' said Armstrong. 'I know we were lucky to get it, but it still isn't long. Maybe we can string it out a little longer.'

'We can try,' said O'Hara. 'But not for much longer. They'll get bloody suspicious when the five hours have gone and we haven't produced Aguillar.'

Armstrong shrugged. 'What can they do that they haven't been trying to do for the last three days?'

VI

The day wore on.

The trebuchet was repaired and O'Hara made plans for the rage that was to come. He said, 'We have one crossbow and a pistol with one bullet – that limits us if it comes to infighting. Benedetta, you take Jenny up to the camp as soon as she can walk. She won't be able to move fast, so you'd better get a head start in case things blow up here. I still don't know what they've got in the second truck, but it certainly isn't intended to do us any good.'

So Benedetta and Miss Ponsky went off, taking a load of Molotov cocktails with them. Armstrong and O'Hara watched the bridge, while Willis tinkered with the trebuchet, doing unnecessary jobs. On the other side of the river men had popped out from among the rocks, and the hillside seemed alive with them as they unconcernedly smoked and chatted. It reminded O'Hara of the stories he had heard of the first Christmas of the First World War.

He counted the men carefully and compared notes with Armstrong. 'I make it thirty-three,' he said.

'I get thirty-five,' said Armstrong. 'But I don't suppose the difference matters.' He looked at the bowl of his pipe. 'I wish I had some tobacco,' he said irritably.

'Sorry, I'm out of cigarettes.'

'You're a modern soldier,' said Armstrong. 'What would you do in their position? I mean, how would you handle the next stage of the operation?'

O'Hara considered. 'We've done the bridge a bit of no good with the trebuchet, but not enough. Once they've got that main gap repaired they can start rushing men across, but not vehicles. I'd make a rush and form a bridgehead at this end, spreading out along this side of the gorge where we are now. Once they've got us away from here it won't be much trouble to repair the rest of the bridge to the point where they can bring a couple of jeeps over. Then I'd use the jeeps as tanks, ram them up to the mine as fast as possible – they'd be there before we could arrive on foot. Once they hold both ends of the road where can we retreat to? There's not a lot we can do about it – that's the hell of it.'

'Um,' said Armstrong glumly. 'That's the appreciation I made.' He rolled over on his back. 'Look, it's clouding over.'

O'Hara turned and looked up at the mountains. A dirty grey cloud was forming and had already blotted out the higher peaks and now swirled in misty coils just above the mine. 'That looks like snow,' he said. 'If there was ever a chance of a real air-search looking for and finding us, it's completely shot now. And it must have caught Ray flat-footed.' He shivered. 'I wouldn't like to be in their boots.'

They watched the cloud for some time and suddenly Armstrong said, 'It may be all right for us, though; I believe it's coming low. We could do with a good, thick mist.'

When the truce had but one hour to go the first grey tendrils of mist began to curl about the bridge and O'Hara sat up as he heard a motor engine. A new arrival pulled up behind the trucks, a big Mercedes saloon car out of which got a man in trim civilian clothes. O'Hara stared across the gorge as the man walked to the bridge and noted the short square build and the broad features. He nudged Armstrong. 'The commissar has arrived,' he said.

'A Russian?'

'I'd bet you a pound to a pinch of snuff,' said O'Hara.

The Russian – if such he was – conferred with the Cuban and an argument seemed to develop, the Cuban waving his arms violently and the Russian stolidly stonewalling with his hands thrust deep into his coat pockets. He won the argument for the Cuban suddenly turned away and issued a string of rapid orders and the hillside on the other side of the gorge became a sudden ants' nest of activity.

The idling men disappeared behind the rocks again and it was as though the mountain had swallowed them. With frantic speed four men finished stripping the canvas from the second truck and the Cuban shouted to the Russian and waved his arms. The Russian, after one long look over the gorge, nonchalantly turned his back and strolled towards his car.

'By God, they're going to break the truce,' said O'Hara tightly. He grabbed the loaded crossbow as the machine-gun suddenly ripped out and stitched the air with bullets. 'Get back to the trebuchet.' He aimed the bow carefully at the Russian's back, squeezed the trigger and was mortified to miss. He ducked to reload and heard the crash of the trebuchet behind him as Willis pulled the firing lever.

When he raised his head again he found that the trebuchet shot had missed and he paled as he saw what had been pulled out of the truck. It was a prefabricated length of bridging carried by six men who had already set foot on the bridge itself. Following them was a squad of men running at full speed. There was nothing that a single crossbow bolt could do to stop them and there was no time to reload the trebuchet – they would be across the bridge in a matter of seconds.

He yelled at Willis and Armstrong. 'Retreat! Get back up the road – to the camp!' and ran towards the bridgehead, bow at the ready.

The first man was already across, scuttling from side to side, a sub-machine-gun at the ready. O'Hara crouched behind a rock and took aim, waiting until the man came closer. The mist was thickening rapidly and it was difficult to judge distances, so he waited until he thought the man was twenty yards away before he pulled the trigger.

The bolt took the man full in the chest, driving home right to the fletching. He shouted in a bubbling voice and threw his hands up as he collapsed, and the tightening death grip on the gun pulled the trigger. O'Hara saw the rest of the squad coming up behind him and the last thing he saw before he turned and ran was the prone figure on the ground quivering as the sub-machine-gun fired its magazine at random.

SEVEN

Rohde hacked vigorously at the ice wall with the small axe. He had retrieved it – a grisly job – and now it was coming in very useful, returning to its designed function as an instrument for survival. Forester was lying, a huddled heap of old clothing, next to the ice wall, well away from the edge of the cliff. Rohde had stripped the outer clothing from Peabody's corpse and used it to wrap up Forester as warmly as possible before he pushed the body into the oblivion of the gathering mists below.

They needed warmth because it was going to be a bad night. The ledge was now enveloped in mist and it had started to snow in brief flurries. A shelter was imperative. Rohde stopped for a moment to bend over Forester who was still conscious, and adjusted the hood which had fallen away from his face. Then he resumed his chopping at the ice wall.

Forester had never felt so cold in his life. His hands and feet were numb and his teeth chattered uncontrollably. He was so cold that he welcomed the waves of pain which rose from his chest; they seemed to warm him and they prevented him from slipping into unconsciousness. He knew he must not let that happen because Rohde had warned him about it, slapping his face to drive the point home.

It had been a damned near thing, he thought. Another couple of slashes from Peabody's knife and the rope would have parted to send him plunging to his death on the snow slopes far below. Rohde had been quick enough to kill Peabody when the need for it arose, even though he had been squeamish earlier. Or perhaps it wasn't that; perhaps he believed in expending just the necessary energy and effort that the job required. Forester, watching Rohde's easy strokes and the flakes of ice falling one by one, suddenly chuckled – a time-and-motion-study killer; that was one for the books. His weak chuckle died away as another wave of pain hit him; he clenched his teeth and waited for it to leave.

When Rohde had killed Peabody he had waited rigidly for a long time, holding the rope taut for fear that Peabody's body would slide over the edge, taking Forester with it. Then he began to dig the ice-axe deeper into the snow, hoping to use it to belay the rope; but he encountered ice beneath the thin layer of snow and, using only one hand, he could not force the axe down.

He changed his tactics. He pulled up the axe and, frightened of being pulled forward on the slippery ice, first chipped two deep steps into which he could put his feet. That gave him the leverage to haul himself upright by the rope and he felt Peabody's body shift under the strain. He stopped because he did not know how far Peabody had succeeded in damaging the rope and he was afraid it might part and let Forester go.

He took the axe and began to chip at the ice, making a large circular groove about two feet in diameter. He found it a difficult task because the head of the axe, improvised by Willis, was set at an awkward angle on the shaft and it was not easy to use. After nearly an hour of chipping he deepened the groove enough to take the rope, and carefully unfastening it from round his waist he belayed it round the ice mushroom he had created.

That left him free to walk to the edge of the cliff. He did not go forward immediately but stood for a while, stamping his feet and flexing his muscles to get the blood going again. He had been lying in a very cramped position. When he looked over the edge he saw that Forester was unconscious, dangling limply on the end of the rope, his head lolling.

The rope was badly frayed where Peabody had attacked it, so Rohde took a short length from round his waist and carefully knotted it above and below the potential break. That done, he began to haul up the sagging and heavy body of Forester. It was hopeless to think of going farther that day. Forester was in no condition to move; the fall had tightened the rope cruelly about his chest and Rohde, probing carefully, thought that some ribs were cracked, if not broken. So he rolled Forester up in warm clothing and relaxed on the ledge between the rock cliff and the ice wall, wondering what to do next.

It was a bad place to spend a night – even a good night – and this was going to be a bad one. He was afraid that if the wind rose to the battering strength that it did during a blizzard, then the overhanging cornice on the ice wall would topple – and if it did they would be buried without benefit of gravediggers. Again, they must have shelter from the wind and the snow, so he took the small axe, wiped the blood and the viscous grey matter from the blade, and began to chip a shallow cave in the ice wall.

II

The wind rose just after nightfall and Rohde was still working. As the first fierce gusts came he stopped and looked around wearily; he had been working for nearly three hours, chipping away at the hard ice with a blunt and inadequate instrument more suited to chopping household firewood. The small cleft he had made in the ice would barely hold the two of them but it would have to do.

He dragged Forester into the ice cave and propped him up against the rear wall, then he went out and brought in the three packs, arranging them at the front of the cave to form a low and totally inadequate wall which, however, served as some sort of bulwark against the drifting snow. He fumbled in his pocket and turned to Forester. 'Here,' he said urgently. 'Chew these.'

Forester mumbled and Rohde slapped him. 'You must not sleep – not yet,' he said. 'You must chew coca.' He forced open Forester's mouth and thrust a coca quid into it.

It took him over half an hour to open a pack and assemble the Primus stove. His fingers were cold and he was suffering from the effects of high altitude – the loss of energy and the mental haziness which dragged the time of each task to many times its normal length. Finally, he got the stove working. It provided little heat and less light, but it was a definite improvement.

He improvised a windshield from some pitons and pieces of blanket. Fortunately the wind came from behind, from the top of the pass and over the ice wall, so that they were in a relatively sheltered position. But vicious side gusts occasionally swept into the cave, bringing a flurry of snow-flakes and making the Primus flare and roar. Rohde was glum when he thought of the direction of the wind. It was good as far as their present shelter went, but the snow cornice on top of the wall would begin to build up and as it grew heavier it would be more likely to break off. And, in the morning when they set off again, they would be climbing in the teeth of a gale.

He prayed the wind would change direction before then.

Presently he had melted enough snow to make a warm drink, but Forester found the taste of the bouillon nauseating and could not drink it, so he heated some more water and they drank that; at least it put some warmth into their bellies.

Then he got to work on Forester, examining his hands and feet and pummelling him violently over many protests. After this Forester was wide awake and in full possession of his senses and did the same for Rohde, rubbing hands and feet to bring back the circulation. 'Do you think we'll make it, Miguel?' he asked.

'Yes,' said Rohde shortly; but he was having his first doubts. Forester was not in good condition for the final assault on the pass and the descent of the other side. It was not a good thing for a man with cracked ribs. He said, 'You must keep moving – your fingers and toes, move them all the time. You must rub your face, your nose and ears. You must not sleep.'

'We'd better talk,' suggested Forester. 'Keep each other awake.' He raised his head and listened to the howls of the wind. 'It'll be more like shouting, though, if this racket keeps up. What shall we talk about?'

Rohde grunted and pulled the hood about his ears. 'O'Hara told me you were an airman.'

'Right,' said Forester. 'I flew towards the end of the war – in Italy mostly. I was flying Lightnings. Then when Korea came I was dragged in again – I was in the Air Force Reserve, you see. I did a conversion on to jets and then I flew Sabres all during the Korean war, or at least until I was pulled out to go back Stateside as an instructor. I think I must have flown some missions with O'Hara in Korea.'

'So he said. And after Korea?'

Forester shrugged. 'I was still bitten with the airplane bug; the company I work for specializes in airplane maintenance.' He grinned. 'When all this happened I was on my way to Santillana to complete a deal with your Air Force for maintenance equipment. You still have Sabres, you know; I sometimes get to flying them if the squadron commandant is a good guy.' He paused. 'If Aguillar pulls off his *coup d'état* the deal may go sour – I don't know why the hell I'm taking all this trouble.'

Rohde smiled, and said, 'If Señor Aguillar comes into power your business will be all right – he will remember. And you will not have to pay the bribes you have already figured into your costing.' His voice was a little bitter.

'Hell,' said Forester. 'You know what it's like in this part of the world – especially under Lopez. Make no mistake, I'm for Aguillar; we businessmen like an honest government – it makes things easier all round.' He beat his hands together. 'Why are you for Aguillar?'

'Cordillera is my country,' said Rohde simply, as though that explained everything, and Forester thought that meeting an honest patriot in Cordillera was a little odd, like finding a hippopotamus in the Arctic.

They were silent for a while, then Forester said, 'What time is it?'

Rohde fumbled at his wristwatch. 'A little after nine.'

Forester shivered. 'Another nine hours before sunrise.' The cold was biting deep into his bones and the wind gusts which flailed into their narrow shelter struck right through his clothing, even through O'Hara's leather jacket. He wondered if they would be alive in the morning; he had heard and read too many tales of men dying of exposure, even back home and closer to civilization, to have any illusions about the precariousness of their position.

Rohde stirred and began to empty two of the packs. Carefully he arranged the contents where they would not roll out of the cave, then gave an empty pack to Forester. Put your feet in this,' he said. 'It will be some protection against the cold.'

Forester took the pack and flexed the blanket material, breaking off the encrusted ice. He put his feet into it and pulled the drawstring about the calves of his legs. 'Didn't you say you'd been up here before?' he asked.

'Under better conditions,' answered Rohde. 'It was when I was a student many years ago. There was a mountaineering expedition to climb this peak – the one to our right here.'

'Did they make it?'

Rohde shook his head. 'They tried three times – they were brave, those Frenchmen. Then one of them was killed and they gave up.'

'Why did you join them?' asked Forester curiously.

Rohde shrugged. 'I needed the money – students always need money – and they paid well for porters. And, as a medical student, I was interested in the *soroche*. Oh, the equipment those men had! Fleece-lined under-boots and thick leather over-boots with crampons for the ice; quilted jackets filled with down; strong tents of nylon and long lengths of nylon rope – and good steel pitons that did not bend when you hammered them into the rock.' He was like a starving man voluptuously remembering a banquet he had once attended.

'And you came over the pass?'

'From the other side – it was easier that way. I looked down over this side from the top and was glad we did not have to climb it. We had a camp – camp three – on top of the pass; and we came up slowly, staying some days at each camp to avoid the *soroche*.'

'I don't know why men climb mountains,' said Forester, and there was a note of annoyance in his voice. 'God knows I'm not doing it because I want to; it beats me that men do it for pleasure.'

'Those Frenchmen were geologists,' said Rohde. 'They were not climbing for the sake of climbing. They took many rock samples from the mountains around here. I saw a map they had made – published in Paris – and I read they had found many rich minerals.'

'What's the use?' queried Forester. 'No one can work up here.'

'Not now,' agreed Rohde. 'But later – who knows?' His voice was serenely confident.

They talked together for a long time, each endeavouring to urge along the lagging clock. After a time Rohde began to sing – folk-songs of Cordillera and later the half-forgotten German songs that his father had taught him. Forester contributed some American songs, avoiding the modern pop tunes and sticking to the songs of his youth. He was halfway through 'I've Been Working on the Railroad' when there was a thunderous crash from the left which momentarily drowned even the howls of the gale.

'What's that?' he asked, startled.

'The snow cornice is falling,' said Rohde. 'It has built up because of the wind; now it is too heavy and not strong enough to bear its own weight.' He raised his eyes to the roof of the ice cave. 'Let us pray that it does not fall in this place; we would be buried.'

'What time is it?'

'Midnight. How do you feel?'

Forester had his arms crossed over his chest. 'Goddam cold.'

'And your ribs – how are they?'

'Can't feel a thing.'

Rohde was concerned. 'That is bad. Move, my friend; move yourself. You must not allow yourself to freeze.' He began to slap and pummel Forester until he howled for mercy and could feel the pain in his chest again.

Just after two in the morning the snow cornice over the cave collapsed. Both Rohde and Forester had become dangerously moribund, relapsing into a half-world of cold and numbness. Rohde heard the preliminary creaking and stirred feebly, then sagged back weakly. There was a noise as of a bomb exploding as the cornice broke and a cloud of dry, powdery snow was driven into the shelter, choking and cold.

Rohde struggled against it, waving his arms in swimming motions as the tide of snow covered his legs and crept up to his chest. He yelled to Forester, 'Keep a space clear for yourself.'

Forester moaned in protest and waved his hands ineffectually, and luckily the snow stopped its advance, leaving them buried to their shoulders. After a long, dying rumble which seemed to come from an immense distance they became aware that it was unnaturally quiet; the noise of the blizzard which had battered at their ears for so long that they had ceased to be aware of it had gone, and the silence was loud and ear-splitting.

'What's happened?' mumbled Forester. Something was holding his arms imprisoned and he could not get them free. In a panic he began to struggle wildly until Rohde shouted, 'Keep still.' His voice was very loud in the confined space.

For a while they lay still, then Rohde began to move cautiously, feeling for his ice-axe. The snow in which he was embedded was fluffy and uncompacted, and he found he could move his arms upwards. When he freed them he began to push the snow away from his face and to plaster and compress it against the wall of the cave. He told Forester to do the same and it was not long before they had scooped out enough space in which to move. Rohde groped in his pocket for matches and tried to strike one, but they were all wet, the soggy ends crumbling against the box.

Forester said painfully, 'I've got a lighter,' and Rohde heard a click and saw a bright point of blinding light. He averted his eyes from the flame and looked about him. The flame burned quite still without flickering and he knew that they were buried. In front, where the opening to the cave had been, was an unbroken wall of compacted snow.

He said, 'We must make a hole or suffocate,' and groped in the snow for the small axe. It took him a long time to find it and his fingers encountered several other items of their inadequate equipment before he succeeded. These he put carefully to one side – everything would be important from now on.

He took the axe and, sitting up with his legs weighed down with snow, he began to hew at the wall before him. Although it was compacted it was not as hard to cut as the ice from which he had chopped the cave and he made good progress. But he did not know how much snow he had to go through before he broke through to the other side. Perhaps the fall extended right across the ledge between the ice wall and the cliff edge and he would come out upon a dizzying drop.

He put the thought out of his mind and diligently worked with the axe, cutting a hole only of such size as he needed to work in. Forester took the snow as it was scooped out of the hole and packed it to one side, observing after a while, 'We're not going to have much room if this goes on much longer.'

Rohde kept silent, cutting away in the dark, for he had blown out the small flame. He worked by sense of touch and at last he had penetrated as far as he could with the small axe, thrusting his arm right up to the shoulder into the hole he had made. He had still not come to the other side of the snow fall, and said abruptly, 'The ice-axe.'

Forester handed it to him and Rohde thrust it into the hole, driving vigorously. There was no room to cut with this long axe, so he pushed, forcing it through by sheer muscle power. To his relief, something suddenly gave and there was a welcome draught of cold air. It was only then he realized how foetid the atmosphere had become. He collapsed, half on top of Forester, panting with his exertions and taking deep breaths of air.

Forester pushed him and he rolled away. After a while he said, 'The fall is about two metres thick – we should have no trouble in getting through.'

'We'd better get at it, then,' said Forester.

Rohde considered the proposition and decided against it. 'This might be the best thing for us. It is warmer in here now, the snow is shielding us from the wind. All we have to do is to keep that hole clear. And there will not be another fall.'

'Okay,' said Forester. 'You're the boss.'

Warmth was a relative term. Cutting the hole had made Rohde sweat freely and now he could feel the sweat freezing to ice on his body under his clothing. Awkwardly he began to strip and had Forester rub his body all over. Forester gave a low chuckle as he massaged, and said, 'A low-temperature Turkish bath – I'll have to introduce it to New York. We'll make a mint of money.'

Rohde dressed again and asked, 'How are you feeling?'

'Goddam cold,' said Forester. 'But otherwise okay.'

'That shock did us good,' said Rohde. 'We were sinking fast – we must not let that happen again. We have another three hours to go before dawn – let us talk and sing.'

So they sang lustily, the sound reverberating from the hard and narrow confines of the ice cave, making them sound, as Forester put it, 'like a pair of goddam bathroom Carusos.'

III

Half an hour before dawn Rohde began to cut their way out and he emerged into a grey world of blustery wind and driving snow. Forester was shocked at the conditions outside the cave. Although it was daylight, visibility was restricted to less than ten yards and the wind seemed to pierce right through him. He put his lips to Rohde's ear and shouted, 'Draughty, isn't it?'

Rohde turned, his lips curled back in a fierce grin. 'How is your chest?'

Forester's chest hurt abominably, but his smile was ami-
able. 'Okay. I'll follow where you go.' He knew they could
not survive another night on the mountain – they had to
get over the pass this day or they would die.

Rohde pointed upward with the ice-axe. 'The cornice is
forming again, but it is not too bad; we can go up here. Get
the packs together.' He stepped to the ice wall and began to
cut steps skilfully, while Forester repacked their equipment.
There was not much – some had been lost, buried under the
snow fall, and some Rohde had discarded as being unnecessary deadweight to carry on this last desperate dash. They
were stripped down to essentials.

Rohde cut steps in the fifteen-foot ice wall as high as he
could reach while standing on reasonably firm ground, then
climbed up and roped himself to pitons and stood in the
steps he had already cut, chopping vigorously. He cut the
steps very deep, having Forester in mind, and it took him
nearly an hour before he was satisfied that Forester could
climb the wall safely.

The packs were hauled up on a rope and then Forester
began the climb, roped to Rohde. It was the most difficult
task he had faced in his life. Normally he could have almost
run up the broad and deep steps that Rohde had cut but
now the bare ice burned his hands, even through the
gloves, his chest ached and stabbing pains pierced him as he
lifted his arms above his head, and he felt weak and tired as
though the very breath of life had been drained from him.
But he made it and collapsed at Rohde's feet.

Here the wind was a howling devil driving down the pass
and bearing with it great clouds of powdery snow and ice
particles which stung the face and hands. The din was indescribable, a freezing pandemonium from an icy hell, deafening in its loudness. Rohde bent over Forester, shielding him
from the worst of the blast, and made him sit up. 'You can't
stay here,' he shouted. 'We must keep moving. There is no

more hard climbing – just the slope to the top and down the other side.'

Forester flinched as the ice particles drove like splinters into his face and he looked up into Rohde's hard and indomitable eyes. 'Okay, buster,' he croaked harshly. 'Where you go, so can I.'

Rohde thrust some coca quids into his hand. 'You will need these.' He checked the rope round Forester's waist and then picked up both packs, tentatively feeling their weight. He ripped them open and consolidated the contents into one pack, which he slung on his back despite Forester's protests. The empty pack was snatched by the wind and disappeared into the grey reaches of the blizzard behind them.

Forester stumbled to his feet and followed in the tracks that Rohde broke. He hunched his shoulders and held his head down, staring at his feet in order to keep the painful wind from his face. He wrapped the blanket hood about the lower part of his face but could do nothing to protect his eyes, which became red and sore. Once he looked up and the wind caught him right in the mouth, knocking the breath out of him as effectively as if he had been punched in the solar plexus. Quickly he bent his head again and trudged on.

The slope was not very steep, much less so than below the cliffs, but it meant that to gain altitude they had that much farther to go. He tried to work it out; they had to gain a thousand feet of height and the slope was, say, thirty degrees – but then his bemused mind bogged down in the intricacies of trigonometry and he gave up the calculation.

Rohde plodded on, breaking the deep snow and always testing the ground ahead with the ice-axe, while the wind shrieked and plucked at him with icy fingers. He could not see more than ten yards ahead but he trusted to the slope of the mountainside as being sufficient guide to the top of the pass. He had never climbed this side of the pass but had looked down from the top, and he hoped his memory of it was true and that what he had told Forester was correct – that there would be no serious climbing – just this steady plod.

Had he been alone he could have moved much faster, but he deliberately reduced his pace to help Forester. Besides, it helped conserve his own energy, which was not inexhaustible, although he was in better condition than Forester. But then, he had not fallen over a cliff. Like Forester, he went forward bent almost double, the wind tearing at his clothing and the snow coating his hood with a thickening film of ice.

After an hour they came to a slight dip where the slope eased and found that the ground became almost level. Here the snow had drifted and was very deep, getting deeper the farther they went up. Rohde raised his head and stared upwards, shielding his eyes with his hand and looking through the slits made by his fingers. There was nothing to be seen beyond the grey whirling world in which they were enclosed. He waited until Forester came abreast of him and shouted, 'Wait here; I will go ahead a little way.'

Forester nodded wearily and sank to the snow, turning his back to the gale and hunching himself into a foetus-like attitude. Rohde unfastened the rope around his waist and dropped it by Forester's side, then went on. He had gone a few paces when he turned to look back and saw the dim huddle of Forester and, between them, the broken crust of the snow. He was satisfied that he could find his way back by following his own trail, so he pressed on into the blizzard.

Forester put another coca quid into his mouth and chewed it slowly. His gloved hand was clumsy and he pulled off the glove to pick up the quid from the palm of his hand. He was cold, numb to the bone, and his mouth was the only part of him that was pleasantly warm, a synthetic warmth induced by the coca. He had lost all sense of time; his watch had stopped long ago and he had no way of knowing how long they had been trudging up the mountain since scaling the ice wall. The cold seemed to have frozen his mind as well as his body, and he had the distinct impression that they had been going for several hours – or perhaps it was only several minutes; he did not know. All he knew was that he did not care much. He felt he was condemned to walk and climb for ever in this cold and bleak mountain world.

He lay apathetically in the snow for a long time and then, as the coca took effect, he roused himself and turned to look in the direction Rohde had gone. The wind flailed his face and he jerked and held up his hand, noticing absently that his knuckles had turned a scaly lizard-blue and that his fingers were cut in a myriad places by the wind-driven ice.

There was no sign of Rohde and Forester turned away, feeling a little surge of panic in his belly. What if Rohde could not find him again? But his mind was too torpid, too drugged by the cold and the coca, to drive his body into any kind of constructive action, and he slumped down to the snow again, where Rohde found him when he came back.

He was aroused by Rohde shaking him violently by the shoulder. 'Move, man. You must not sit there and freeze. Rub your face and put on your glove.'

Mechanically he brought up his hand and dabbed ineffectually at his face. He could feel no contact at all, both hand and face were anaesthetized by the cold. Rohde struck his face twice with vigorous open-hand slaps and Forester was annoyed. 'All right,' he croaked. 'No need to hit me.' He slapped his hands together until the circulation came back and then began to massage his face.

Rohde shouted, 'I went about two hundred metres – the snow was waist-deep and getting deeper. We cannot go that way; we must go round.'

Forester felt a moment of despair. Would this never end? He staggered to his feet and waited while Rohde tied the rope, then followed him in a direction at right-angles to the course they had previously pursued. The wind was now striking at them from the side and, walking as they were across the slope, the buffeting gusts threatened to knock them off their feet and they had to lean into the wind to maintain a precarious balance.

The route chosen by Rohde skirted the deep drifts, but he did not like the way they tended to lose altitude. Every so often he would move up again towards the pass, and every time was forced down again by deepening snow. At last he found a way upwards where the slope steepened and the snow cover was thinner, and once more they gained altitude in the teeth of the gale.

Forester followed in a half-conscious stupor, mechanically putting one foot in front of the other in an endless lurching progression. From time to time as he cautiously raised his eyes he saw the dim snow-shrouded figure of Rohde ahead, and after a time his mind was wiped clean of all other considerations but that of keeping Rohde in sight and the rope slack. Occasionally he stumbled and fell forward and the rope would tighten and Rohde would wait patiently until he recovered his feet, and then they would go on again, and upwards – always upwards.

Suddenly Rohde halted and Forester shuffled to his side. There was a hint of desperation in Rohde's voice as he pointed forward with the ice-axe. 'Rock,' he said slowly. 'We have come upon rock again.' He struck the ice-glazed outcrop with the axe and the ice shattered. He struck again at the bare rock and it crumbled flakes falling away to dirty the white purity of the snow. The rock is rotten,' said Rohde. 'It is most dangerous. And there is the *verglas*.'

Forester forced his lagging brain into action. 'How far up do you think it extends?'

'Who knows?' said Rohde. He turned and squatted with his back to the wind and Forester followed his example. 'We cannot climb this. It was bad enough on the other side of the glacier yesterday when we were fresh and there was no wind. To attempt this now would be madness.' He beat his hands together.

'Maybe it's just an isolated outcrop,' suggested Forester. 'We can't see very far, you know.'

Rohde grasped the ice-axe. 'Wait here. I will find out.'

Once again he left Forester and scrambled upwards. Forester heard the steady chipping of the axe above the noise of the wind and pieces of ice and flakes of rock fell down out of the grey obscurity. He paid out rope as Rohde tugged and the hood about his head flapped loose and the wind stung his cheeks smartly.

He had just lifted his hand to wrap the hood about his face when Rohde fell. Forester heard the faint shout and saw the shapeless figure hurtling towards him from above out of the screaming turmoil. He grabbed the rope, turned and dug his heels into the snow ready to take the shock. Rohde tumbled past him in an uncontrollable fall and slid down the slope until he was brought up sharply on the end of the rope by a jerk which almost pulled Forester off his feet.

Forester hung on until he was sure that Rohde would go no farther down the slope. He saw him stir and then roll over to sit up and rub his leg. He shouted, 'Miguel, are you okay?' then began to descend.

Rohde turned his face upwards and Forester saw that each hair of his beard stubble was coated with rime. 'My leg,' he said. 'I've hurt my leg.'

Forester bent over him and straightened the leg, probing with his fingers. The trouser-leg was torn and, as Forester put his hand inside, he felt the sticky wetness of blood. After a while he said, 'It's not broken, but you've scraped it badly.'

'It is impossible up there,' said Rohde, his face twisted in pain. 'No man could climb that – even in good weather.'

'How far does the rock go?'

'As far as I could see, but that was not far.' He paused. 'We must go back and try the other side.'

Forester was appalled. 'But the glacier is on the other side; we can't cross the glacier in this weather.'

'Perhaps there is a good way up this side of the glacier,' said Rohde. He turned his head and looked up towards the rocks from which he had fallen. 'One thing is certain – that way is impossible.'

'We want something to bind this trouser-leg together,' said Forester. 'I don't know much about it, but I don't think it would be a good thing if this torn flesh became frostbitten.'

'The pack,' said Rohde. 'Help me with the pack.'

Forester helped him take off the pack and he emptied the contents into the snow and tore up the blanket material into strips which he bound tightly round Rohde's leg. He said wryly, 'Our equipment gets less and less. I can put some of this stuff into my pocket, but not much.'

'Take the Primus,' said Rohde. 'And some kerosene. If we have to go as far as the glacier perhaps we can find a place beneath an ice fall that is sheltered from the wind, where we can make a hot drink.'

Forester put the bottle of kerosene and a handful of bouillon cubes into his pocket and slung the pressure stove over his shoulder suspended by a length of electric wire. As he did so, Rohde sat up suddenly and winced as he put unexpected pressure on his leg. He groped in the snow with scrabbling fingers. 'The ice-axe,' he said frantically. 'The ice-axe – where is it?'

'I didn't see it,' said Forester.

They both looked into the whirling grey darkness down the slope and Rohde felt an empty sensation in the pit of his stomach. The ice-axe had been invaluable; without it they could not have come as far as they had, and without it he doubted if they could get to the top of the pass. He looked down and saw that his hands were shaking uncontrollably and he knew he was coming to the end of his strength – physical and mental.

But Forester felt a renewed access of spirit. He said, 'Well, what of it? This goddam mountain has done its best to kill us and it hasn't succeeded yet – and my guess is that it won't. If we've come this far we can go the rest of the way. It's only another five hundred feet to the top – five hundred lousy feet – do you hear that, Miguel?'

Rohde smiled wearily. 'But we have to go down again.'

'So what? It's just another way of getting up speed. I'll lead off this time. I can follow our tracks back to where we turned off.'

And it was in this spirit of unreasonable and unreasoning optimism that Forester led the way down with Rohde limping behind. He found it fairly easy to follow their tracks and followed them faithfully, even when they wavered where Rohde had diverged. He had not the same faith in his own wilderness pathfinding that he had in Rohde's, and he knew that if he got off track in this blizzard he would never find it again. As it was, when they reached where they had turned off to the right and struck across the slope, the track was so faint as to be almost indistinguishable, the wind having nearly obliterated it with drifting snow.

He stopped and let Rohde catch up. 'How's the leg?'

Rohde's grin was a snarl. 'The pain has stopped. It is numb with the cold – and very stiff.'

I'll break trail then,' said Forester. 'You'd better take it easy for a while.' He smiled and felt the stiffness of his cheeks. 'You can use the rope like a rein to guide me – one tug to go left, two tugs to go right.'

Rohde nodded without speaking, and they pressed on again. Forester found the going harder in the unbroken snow, especially as he did not have the ice-axe to test the way ahead. It's not so bad here, he thought; there are no crevasses – but it'll be goddam tricky if we have to cross the glacier. In spite of the hard going, he was better mentally than he had been; the task of leadership kept him alert and forced his creaking brain to work.

It seemed to him that the wind was not as strong and he hoped it was dropping. From time to time he swerved to the right under instruction from Rohde, but each time came to deep drifts and had to return to the general line of march. They came to the jumbled ice columns of the glacier without finding a good route up to the pass.

Forester dropped to his knees in the snow and felt tears of frustration squeeze out on to his cheeks. 'What now?' he asked – not that he expected a good answer.

Rohde fell beside him, half-sitting, half-lying, his stiff leg jutting out before him. 'We go into the glacier a little way to find shelter. The wind will not be as bad in there.' He looked at his watch then held it to his ear. 'It is two o'clock – four hours to nightfall; we cannot spare the time but we must drink something hot, even if it is only hot water.'

'Two o'clock,' said Forester bitterly. 'I feel as though I've been wandering round this mountain for a hundred years, and made personal acquaintance with every goddam snowflake.'

They pushed on into the tangled ice maze of the glacier and Forester was deathly afraid of hidden crevasses. Twice he plunged to his armpits in deep snow and was hauled out with difficulty by Rohde. At last they found what they were looking for – a small cranny in the ice sheltered from the wind – and they sank into the snow with relief, glad to be out of the cutting blast.

Rohde assembled the Primus and lit it and then melted some snow. As before, they found the rich meaty taste of the bouillon nauseating and had to content themselves with hot water. Forester felt the heat radiating from his belly and was curiously content. He said, 'How far to the top from here?'

'Seven hundred feet, maybe,' said Rohde.

'Yes, we slipped about two hundred feet by coming back.' Forester yawned. 'Christ, it's good to be out of the wind; I feel a good hundred per cent warmer – which brings me up to freezing-point.' He pulled the jacket closer about him and regarded Rohde through half-closed eyes. Rohde was looking vacantly at the flaring Primus, his eyes glazed with fatigue.

Thus they lay in their ice shelter while the wind howled about them and flurries of driven snow eddied in small whirlpools in that haven of quiet.

IV

Rohde dreamed.

He dreamed, curiously enough, that he was asleep – asleep in a vast feather bed into which he sank with voluptuous enjoyment. The bed enfolded him in soft comfort, seeming to support his tired body and to let him sink at the same time. Both he and the bed were falling slowly into a great chasm, drifting down and down and down, and suddenly he knew to his horror that this was the comfort of death and that when he reached the bottom of the pit he would die.

Frantically he struggled to get up, but the bed would not let him go and held him back in cloying folds and he heard a quiet maniacal tittering of high-pitched voices laughing at him. He discovered that his hand held a long, sharp knife and he stabbed at the bed with repeated plunges of his arm, ripping the fabric and releasing a fountain of feathers which whirled in the air before his eyes.

He started and screamed and opened his eyes. The scream came out as a dismal croak and he saw that the feathers were snowflakes dancing in the wind and beyond was the wilderness of the glacier. He was benumbed with the cold and he knew that if he slept he would not wake again.

There was something strange about the scene that he could not place and he forced himself to analyse what it was, and suddenly he knew – the wind had dropped. He got up stiffly and with difficulty and looked at the sky; the mist was clearing rapidly and through the dissipating wreaths he saw a faint patch of blue sky.

He turned to Forester who was lying prostrate, his head on one side and his cheek touching the ice, and wondered if he was dead. He leaned over him and shook him and Forester's head flopped down on to his chest. 'Wake up,' said Rohde, the words coming rustily to his throat. 'Wake up – come on, wake up.'

He took Forester by the shoulder and shook him and Forester's head lolled about, almost as though his neck was broken. Rohde seized his wrist and felt for the pulse; there was a faint fluttering beneath the cold skin and he knew that Forester was still alive – but only just.

The Primus stove was empty – he had fallen asleep with it still burning – but there was a drain of kerosene left in the bottle. He poured it into the Primus and heated some water with which he bathed Forester's head, hoping that the warmth would penetrate somehow and unfreeze his brain. After a while Forester stirred weakly and mumbled something incoherently.

Rohde slapped his face. 'Wake up; you cannot give in now.' He dragged Forester to his feet and he promptly collapsed. Again Rohde hauled him up and supported him. 'You must walk,' he said. 'You must not sleep.' He felt in his pocket and found one last coca quid which he forced into Forester's mouth. 'Chew,' he shouted. 'Chew and walk.'

Gradually Forester came round – never fully conscious but able to use his legs in an automatic manner, and Rohde walked him to and fro in an effort to get the blood circulating again. He talked all the time, not because he thought Forester could understand him, but to break the deathly silence that held the mountain now that the wind had gone. 'Two hours to nightfall,' he said. 'It will be dark in two hours. We must get to the top before then – long before then. Here, stand still while I fasten the rope.'

Forester obediently stood still, swaying slightly on his feet, and Rohde fastened the rope around his waist. 'Can you follow me? Can you?'

Forester nodded slowly, his eyes half open.

'Good,' said Rohde. 'Then come on.'

He led the way out of the glacier and on to the mountain slopes. The mist had now gone and he could see right to the top of the pass, and it seemed but a step away – a long step. Below, there was an unbroken sea of white cloud, illumined by the late afternoon sun into a blinding glare. It seemed solid and firm enough to walk on.

He looked at the snow slopes ahead and immediately saw what they had missed in the darkness of the blizzard – a definite ridge running right to the top of the pass. The snow cover would be thin there and would make for easy travel. He twitched on the rope and plunged forward, then glanced back at Forester to see how he was doing.

Forester was in the middle of a cold nightmare. He had been so warm, so cosily and beautiful warm, until Rohde had so rudely brought him back to the mountains. What the devil was the matter with the guy? Why couldn't he let a man sleep when he wanted to instead of pulling him up a mountain? But Rohde was a good joe, so he'd do what he said – but why was he doing it? Why was he on this mountain?

He tried to think but the reason eluded him. He dimly remembered a fall over a cliff and that this guy Rohde had saved his life. Hell, that was enough, wasn't it? If a guy saves your life he was entitled to push you around a little afterwards. He didn't know what he wanted, but he was with him all the way.

And so Forester shambled on, not knowing where or why, but content to follow where Rohde led. He kept falling because his legs were rubbery and he could not make them do precisely what he wanted, and every time he fell Rohde would return the length of the rope and help him to his feet. Once he started to slide and Rohde almost lost his balance and they both nearly tumbled down the slope, but Rohde managed to dig his heels into the snow and so stopped them.

Although Rohde's stiff leg impeded him, Forester impeded him more. But even so they made good time and the top of the pass came nearer and nearer. There was only two hundred feet of altitude to make when Forester collapsed for the last time. Rohde went back along the rope but Forester could not stand. Cold and exhaustion had done their work in sapping the life energy from a strong man, and he lay in the snow unable to move.

A glimmer of intelligence returned to him and he peered at Rohde through red-rimmed eyes. He swallowed painfully and whispered, 'Leave me, Miguel; I can't make it. You've *got* to get over the pass.'

Rohde stared down at him in silence.

Forester croaked, 'Goddam it – get the hell out of here.' Although his voice was almost inaudible it was as loud as he could shout and the violence of the effort was too much for him and he relapsed into unconsciousness.

Still in silence Rohde bent down and gathered Forester into his arms. It was very difficult to lift him on to his shoulder in a fireman's lift – there was the steepness of the slope, his stiff leg and his general weakness – but he managed it and, staggering a little under the weight, he put one foot in front of the other.

And then the other.

And so on up the mountain. The thin air wheezed in his throat and the muscles of his thighs cracked under the strain. His stiff leg did not hurt but it was a hindrance because he had to swing it awkwardly sideways in an arc in order to take a step. But it was beautifully firm when he took the weight on it. Forester's arms swung limply, tapping against the backs of his legs with every movement and this irritated him for a while until he no longer felt the tapping. Until he no longer felt anything at all.

His body was dead and it was only a bright hot spark of will burning in his mind that kept him going. He looked dispassionately at this flame of will, urging it to burn brighter when it flickered and screening out all else that would quench it. He did not see the snow or the sky or the crags and peaks which flanked him. He saw nothing at all, just a haze of darkness shot with tiny sparks of light flaring inside his eyeballs.

One foot forward easily – that was his good foot. The next foot brought round in a stiff semi-circle to grope for a footing. This was harder because the foot was dead and he could not feel the ground. Slowly, very slowly, take the weight. Right – that was good. Now the other foot – easy again.

He began to count, got up to eleven and lost count. He started again and this time got up to eight. After that he did not bother to count but just went forward, content to know that one foot was moving in front of the other.

Pace . . . halt . . . swing . . . grope . . . halt . . . pace . . . halt . . . swing . . . grope . . . halt . . . pace . . . halt . . . swing . . . grope . . . halt . . . swing . . . something glared against his closed eyes and he opened them to stare full into the sun.

He stopped and then closed his eyes painfully, but not before he had seen the silver streak on the horizon and knew it was the sea. He opened his eyes again and looked down on the green valley and the white scattering of houses that was Altemiros lying snugly between the mountains and the lesser foothills beyond.

His tongue came out to lick ice-cracked lips stiffly. 'Forester,' he whispered. 'Forester, we are on top.'

But Forester was past caring, hanging limply unconscious across Rohde's broad shoulder.

EIGHT

Aguillar looked dispassionately at a small cut on his hand –
one of many – from which the blood was oozing. I will
never be a mechanic, he thought; I can guide people, but
not machines. He laid down the broken piece of hacksaw
blade and wiped away the blood, then sucked the wound.
When the blood ceased to flow he picked up the blade and
got to work on the slot he was cutting in the length of steel
reinforcing rod.

He had made ten bolts for the crossbows, or at least he
had slotted them and put in the metal flights. To sharpen
them was beyond his powers; he could not turn the old
grindstone and sharpen a bolt at the same time, but he was
confident that, given another pair of hands, the ten bolts
would be usable within the hour.

He had also made an inventory of the contents of the
camp, checked the food supplies and the water, and in
general had behaved like any army quartermaster. He had
a bitter-sweet feeling about being sent to the camp. He recognized that he was no use in a fight; he was old and weak
and had heart trouble – but there was more to it than that.
He knew that he was a man of ideas and not a man of
action, and the fact irked him, making him feel inadequate.

His sphere of action lay in the making of decisions and in
administration; in order to get into a position to make valid

decisions and to have something to administer he had schemed and plotted and manipulated the minds of men, but he had never fought physically. He did not believe in fighting, but hitherto he had thought about it in the abstract and in terms of large-scale conflicts. This sudden plunge into the realities of death by battle had led him out of his depth.

So here he was, the eternal politician, with others, as always, doing the fighting and dying and suffering – even his own niece. As he thought of Benedetta the blade slipped and he cut his hand again. He muttered a brief imprecation and sucked the blood, then looked at the slot he had cut and decided it was deep enough. There would be no more bolts; the teeth of the hacksaw blade were worn smooth and would hardly cut cheese, let alone steel.

He fitted the flight into the slot, wedging it as Willis had shown him, and then put the unsharpened bolt with the others. It was strange, he thought, that night was falling so suddenly, and went out of the hut to be surprised by the deepening mist. He looked up towards the mountains, now hidden from sight, and felt deep sorrow as he thought of Rohde. And of Forester, yes – he must not forget Forester and the other *norteamericano,* Peabody.

Faintly from the river he head the sound of small-arms fire and his ears pricked. Was that a machine-gun? He had heard that sound when Lopez and the army had ruthlessly tightened their grip on Cordillera five years earlier, and he did not think he was mistaken. He listened again but it was only some freak of the mountain winds that had brought the sound to his ears and he heard nothing more. He hoped that it was not a machine-gun – the dice were already loaded enough.

He sighed and went back into the hut and selected a can of soup from the shelf for his belated midday meal. He had just finished eating the hot soup half an hour later when he heard his niece calling him. He went out of the hut, tightening his coat against the cold air, and found that the mist was very much thicker. He shouted to Benedetta to let her know where he was and soon a dim figure loomed through the fog, a strange figure, misshapen and humped, and for a moment he felt fear.

Then he saw that it was Benedetta supporting someone and he ran forward to help her. She was breathing painfully and gasped, 'It's Jenny, she's hurt.'

'Hurt? How?'

'She was shot,' said Benedetta briefly.

He was outraged. 'This American lady – shot! This is criminal.'

'Help me take her inside,' said Benedetta. They got Miss Ponsky into the hut and laid her in a bunk. She was conscious and smiled weakly as Benedetta tucked in a blanket, then closed her eyes in relief. Benedetta looked at her uncle. 'She killed a man and helped to kill others – why shouldn't she be shot at? I wish I were like her.'

Aguillar looked at her with pain in his eyes. He said slowly, 'I find all this difficult to believe. I feel as though I am in a dream. Why should these people shoot a woman?'

'They didn't know she was a woman,' said Benedetta impatiently. 'And I don't suppose they cared. She was shooting at them when it happened, anyway. I wish I could kill some of them.' She looked up at Aguillar. 'Oh, I know you always preach the peaceful way, but how can you be peaceful when someone is coming at you with a gun? Do you bare your breast and say, "Kill me and take all I have"?'

Aguillar did not answer. He looked down at Miss Ponsky and said, 'Is she badly hurt?'

'Not dangerously,' said Benedetta. 'But she has lost a lot of blood.' She paused. 'As we were coming up the road I heard a machine-gun.'

He nodded. 'I thought I heard it – but I was not sure.' He held her eyes. 'Do you think they are across the bridge?'

'They might be,' said Benedetta steadily. 'We must prepare. Have you made bolts? Tim has the crossbow and he will need them.'

'Tim? Ah – O'Hara.' He raised his eyebrows slightly, then said, 'The bolts need sharpening.'

'I will help you.'

She turned the crank on the grindstone while Aguillar sharpened the steel rods to a point. As he worked he said, 'O'Hara is a strange man – a complicated man. I do not think I fully understand him.' He smiled slightly. 'That is an admission from me.'

'I understand him – now,' she said. Despite the cold, a film of sweat formed on her forehead as she turned the heavy crank.

'So? You have talked with him?'

While the showers of sparks flew and the acrid stink of burning metal filled the air she told Aguillar about O'Hara and his face grew pinched as he heard the story. 'That is the enemy,' she said at length. 'The same who are on the other side of the river.'

Aguillar said in a low voice, 'There is so much evil in the world – so much evil in the hearts of men.'

They said nothing more until all the bolts were sharpened and then Benedetta said, 'I am going out on the road. Will you watch Jenny?'

He nodded silently and she walked along the street between the two rows of huts. The mist was getting even thicker so that she could not see very far ahead, and tiny droplets of moisture condensed on the fabric of her coat. If it gets colder it will snow, she thought.

It was very quiet on the road, and very lonely. She did not hear a sound except for the occasional splash of a drop of water falling from a rock. It was as though being in the middle of a cloud was like being wrapped in cotton-wool; this was very dirty cotton-wool, but she had done enough flying to know that from above the cloud bank would be clean and shining.

After some time she walked off the road and crossed the rocky hillside until the gigantic cable drum loomed through the mist. She paused by the enormous reel, then went forward to the road cutting and looked down. The road surface was barely visible in the pervading greyness and she stood there uncertainly, wondering what to do. Surely there was something she could be doing.

Fire, she thought suddenly, we can fight them with fire. The drum was already poised to crash into a vehicle coming up the road, and fire would add to the confusion. She hurried back to the camp and collected the bottles of paraffin she had brought back from the bridge, stopping briefly to see how Miss Ponsky was.

Aguillar looked up as she came in. 'There is soup,' he said. 'It will be good in this cold, my dear.'

Benedetta spread her hands gratefully to the warmth of the paraffin heater, and was aware that she was colder than she had thought. 'I would like some soup,' she said. She looked over to Miss Ponsky. 'How are you, Jenny?'

Miss Ponsky, now sitting up, said briskly, 'Much better, thank you. Wasn't it silly of me to get shot? I shouldn't have leaned out so far – and then I missed. And I lost the bow.'

'I would not worry,' said Benedetta with a quick smile. 'Does your shoulder hurt?'

'Not much,' said Miss Ponsky. 'It will be all right if I keep my arm in a sling. Señor Aguillar helped me to make one.'

Benedetta finished her soup quickly and mentioned the bottles, which she had left outside. 'I must take them up to the road,' she said.

'Let me help you,' said Aguillar.

'It is too cold out there, *tio*,' she said. 'Stay with Jenny.'

She took the bottles down to the cable drum and then sat on the edge of the cutting, listening. A wind was rising and the mist swirled in wreaths and coils, thinning and thickening in the vagaries of the breeze. Sometimes she could see as far as the bend in the road, and at other times she could not see the road at all although it was only a few feet below her. And everything was quiet.

She was about to leave, sure that nothing was going to happen, when she heard the faint clatter of a rock from far down the mountain. She felt a moment of apprehension and scrambled to her feet. The others would not be coming unless they were in retreat, and in that case it could just as well be an enemy as a friend. She turned and picked up one of the bottles and felt for matches in her pocket.

It was a long time before she heard anything else and then it was the thud of running feet on the road. The mist had thinned momentarily and she saw a dim figure come round the bend and up the road at a stumbling run. As the figure came closer she saw that it was Willis.

'What is happening?' she called.

He looked up, startled to hear a voice from above his head and in a slight panic until he recognized it. He stopped, his chest heaving, and went into a fit of coughing. 'They've come across,' he gasped. 'They broke across.' He coughed again, rackingly. 'The others are just behind me,' he said. 'I heard them running – unless . . .'

'You'd better come up here,' she said.

He looked up at Benedetta, vaguely outlined at the top of the fifteen-foot cutting. 'I'll come round by the road,' he said, and began to move away at a fast walk.

By the time he joined her she had already heard someone else coming up the road, and remembering Willis's *unless*, she lay down by the edge and grasped the bottle. It was Armstrong, coming up at a fast clip. 'Up here,' she called. 'To the drum.'

He cast a brief glance upwards but wasted no time in greeting, nor did he slacken his pace. She watched him go until he was lost in the mist and waited for him to join them.

They were both exhausted, having made the five-mile journey uphill in a little over an hour and a half. She let them rest a while and get their breath before she asked them, 'What happened?'

'I don't know,' said Willis. 'We were on the trebuchet; we'd let fly when O'Hara told us to – it was ready loaded – and then he yelled for us to clear out, so we took it on the run. There was a devil of a lot of noise going on – a lot of shooting, I mean.'

She looked at Armstrong. He said, 'That's about it. I think O'Hara got one of them – I heard a man scream in a choked sort of way. But they came across the bridge; I saw them as I looked back – and I saw O'Hara run into the rocks. He should be along any minute now.'

She sighed with relief.

Willis said, 'And he'll have the whole pack of them on his heels. What the hell are we going to do?' There was a hysterical note in his voice.

Armstrong was calmer. 'I don't think so. O'Hara and I talked about this and we came to the conclusion that they'll play it safe and repair the bridge while they can, and then run jeeps up to the mine before we can get there.' He looked up at the cable drum. 'This is all we've got to stop them.'

Benedetta held up the bottle. 'And some of these.'

'Oh, good,' said Armstrong approvingly. 'Those should help.' He thought a little. 'There's not much your uncle can do – or Miss Ponsky. I suggest that they get started for the mine right now – and if they hear anyone or anything coming up the road behind them to duck into the rocks until they're sure it's safe. Thank God for this mist.'

Benedetta did not stir and he said, 'Will you go and tell them?'

She said, 'I'm staying here. I want to fight.'

'I'll go,' said Willis. He got up and faded into the mist.

Armstrong caught the desperate edge in Benedetta's voice and patted her hand in a kindly, fatherly manner. 'We all have to do the best we can,' he said. 'Willis is frightened, just as I am, and you are, I'm sure.' His voice was grimly humorous. 'O'Hara was talking to me about the situation back at the bridge and I gathered he didn't think much of Willis. He said he wasn't a leader – in fact, his exact words were, "He couldn't lead a troop of boy scouts across a street." I think he was being a bit hard on poor Willis – but, come to that, I gathered that he didn't think much of me either, from the tone of his voice.' He laughed.

'I'm sure he didn't mean it,' said Benedetta. 'He has been under a strain.'

'Oh, he was right,' said Armstrong. 'I'm no man of action. I'm a man of ideas, just like Willis.'

'And my uncle,' said Benedetta. She sat up suddenly. 'Where *is* Tim? He should have been here by now.' She clutched Armstrong's arm. *'Where is he?'*

II

O'Hara was lying in a crack in the rocks watching a pair of stout boots that stamped not more than two feet from his head, and trying not to cough. Events had been confused just after the rush across the bridge, he had not been able to get to the road – he would have been cut down before going ten yards in the open – so he had taken to the rocks, scuttling like a rabbit for cover.

It was then that he had slipped on a mist-wetted stone and turned his ankle, to come crashing to the ground. He had lain there with all the wind knocked out of him, expecting to feel the thud of bullets that would mean his death, but nothing like that happened. He heard a lot of shouting and knew his analysis of the enemy intentions had proved correct; they were spreading out along the edge of the gorge and covering the approaches to the bridge.

The mist helped, of course. He still had the crossbow and was within hearing distance of the noisy crowd which surrounded the man he had shot through the chest. He judged that they did not relish the task of winkling out a man with a silent killing weapon from the hillside, especially when death could come from the mist. There was a nervous snapping edge to the voices out there and he smiled grimly; knives they knew and guns they understood, but this was something different, something they regarded with awe.

He felt his ankle. It was swollen and painful and he wondered if it would bear his weight, but this was neither the time nor the place to stand. He took his small pocket-knife and slit his trousers, cutting a long strip. He did not take off his shoe because he knew he would not be able to get it on again, so he tied the strip of cloth tightly around the swelling and under the instep of his shoe, supporting his ankle.

He was so intent on this that he did not see the man approach. The first indication was the slither of a kicked pebble and he froze rigid. From the corner of his eye he saw the man standing sideways to him, looking back towards the bridge. O'Hara kept very still, except for his arm which groped for a handy-sized rock. The man scratched his ribs in a reflective sort of way, moved on and was lost in the mist.

O'Hara let loose his pent-up breath in a silent sigh and prepared to move. He had the crossbow and three bolts which had a confounded tendency to clink together unless he was careful. He slid forward on his belly, worming his way among the rocks, trying to go upwards, away from the bridge. Again he was warned of imminent peril by the rattle of a rock and he rolled into a crack between two boulders and then he saw the boots appear before his face and struggled with a tickle in his throat, fighting to suppress the cough.

The man stamped his feet noisily and beat his hands together, breathing heavily. Suddenly he turned with a clatter of boots and O'Hara heard the metallic snap as a safety-catch went off. *'Quien?'*

'Santos.'

O'Hara recognized the voice of the Cuban. So his name was Santos – he'd remember that and look him up if he ever got out of this mess.

The man put the rifle back on safety and Santos said in Spanish, 'See anything?'

'Nothing.'

Santos grunted in his throat. 'Keep moving; go up the hill – they won't hang about here.'

The other man said, 'The Russian said we must stay down here.'

'To hell with him,' growled Santos. 'If he had not interfered we would have old Aguillar in our hands right now. Move up the hill – and get the others going too.'

The other did not reply but obediently moved off, and O'Hara heard him climbing higher. Santos stayed only a moment and then clattered away noisily in his steel-shod boots, and again O'Hara let out his breath softly.

He waited a while and thought of what to do next. If Santos was moving the men away up the hill, then his obvious course was to go down. But the enemy seemed to be divided into two factions and the Russian might still have kept some men below. Still, he would have to take that chance.

He slid out of the crack and began to crawl back the way he had come, inching his way along on his belly and being careful of his injured ankle. He was pleased to see that the mist was thickening and through it he heard shouts from the bridge and the knocking of steel on wood. They were getting on with their repairs and traffic in the vicinity of the bridge would be heavy, so it was a good place to stay away from. He wanted to find a lone man far away from his fellows and preferably armed to the teeth. A crossbow was all very well, but he could do with something that had a faster rate of fire.

He altered course and headed for the trebuchet, stopping every few yards to listen and to peer through the mist. As he approached he heard laughter and a few derogatory comments shouted in Spanish. There was a crowd round the trebuchet and apparently they found it a humorous piece of machinery. He stopped and cocked the crossbow awkwardly, using the noise of the crowd as cover for any clinkings he might make. Then he crawled closer and took cover behind a boulder.

Presently he heard the bull-roar of Santos. 'Up the hill, you lot. In the name of Jesus, what are you doing wasting time here? Juan, you stay here; the rest of you get moving.'

O'Hara flattened behind the boulder as the men moved off to the accompaniment of many grumbles. None of them came close to him, but he waited a few minutes before he began to crawl in a wide circle round the trebuchet, looking for the man left on guard. The bridge was illuminated by headlights and their glow lit the mist with a ghostly radiance, and at last he crept up on the guard who was just in the right position – silhouetted against the light.

Juan, the guard, was very young – not more than twenty – and O'Hara hesitated. Then he steeled himself because there was more at stake here than the life of a misguided youth. He lifted the crossbow and aimed carefully, then hesitated again, his finger on the trigger. His hesitation this time was for a different reason; Juan was playing soldiers, strutting about with his sub-machine-gun at the ready, and, O'Hara suspected, with the safety-catch off. He remembered the man he had shot by the bridge and how a full magazine had emptied in a dead hand, so he waited, not wanting any noise when he pulled the trigger.

At last Juan got tired of standing sentry and became more interested in the trebuchet. He leaned over to look at the mechanism which held down the long arm, found his gun in his way and let it fall to be held by the shoulder-sling. He never knew what hit him as the heavy bolt struck him between the shoulders at a range of ten yards. It knocked him forward against the long arm, the bolt protruding through his chest and skewering him to the baulk of timber. He was quite dead when O'Hara reached him.

Ten minutes later O'Hara was again esconced among the rocks, examining his booty. He had the sub-machine-gun, three full magazines of ammunition, a loaded pistol and a heavy broad-bladed knife. He grinned in satisfaction – now he was becoming dangerous, he had got himself some sharp teeth.

III

Benedetta, Armstrong and Willis waited in the cold mist by the cable drum. Willis fidgeted, examining the wedge-shaped chock that prevented the drum from rolling on to the road and estimated the amount of force needed to free it when the time came. But Benedetta and Armstrong were quite still, listening intently for any sound that might come up the hill.

Armstrong was thinking that they would have to be careful; any person coming up might be O'Hara and they would have to make absolutely sure before jumping him, something that would be difficult in this mist. Benedetta's mind was emptied of everything except a deep sorrow. Why else was O'Hara not at the camp unless he were dead, or worse, captured? She knew his feelings about being captured again and she knew he would resist that, come what may. That made the likelihood of his being dead even more certain, and something within her died at the thought.

Aguillar had been difficult about retreating to the mine. He had wanted to stay and fight, old and unfit as he was, but Benedetta had overruled him. His eyes had widened in surprise as he heard the incisive tone of command in her voice. 'There are only three of us fit to fight,' she said. 'We can't spare one to help Jenny up to the mine. Someone must help her and you are the one. Besides, it is even higher up there than here, remember – you will have to go slowly so you must get away right now.'

Aguillar glanced at the other two men. Willis was morosely kicking at the ground and Armstrong smiled slightly, and Aguillar saw that they were content to let Benedetta take the lead and give the orders in the absence of O'Hara. She has turned into a young Amazon, he thought; a raging young lioness. He went up to the mine road with Miss Ponsky without further argument.

Willis stopped fiddling with the chock. 'Where are they?' he demanded in a high voice. 'Why don't they come and get it over with?'

Benedetta glanced at Armstrong who said, 'Quiet! Not so loud.'

'All right,' said Willis, whispering. 'But what's keeping them from attacking us?'

'We have already discussed that,' said Benedetta. She turned to Armstrong. 'Do you think we can defend the camp?'

He shook his head. 'It's indefensible. We haven't a hope. If we can block the road, our next step is to retreat to the mine.'

'Then the camp must be burned,' said Benedetta decisively. 'We must not leave it to give comfort and shelter to them.' She looked at Willis. 'Go back and splash kerosene in the huts – all of them. And when you hear noise and shoot-ing from here, set everything on fire.'

'And then what?' he asked.

'Then you make your way up to the mine as best you can.' She smiled slightly. 'I would not come up this way again – go straight up and find the road at a higher level. We will be coming up too – as fast as we can.'

Willis withdrew and she said to Armstrong, 'That one is frightened. He tries to hide it, but it shows. I cannot trust him here.'

'I'm frightened too. Aren't you?' asked Armstrong curiously.

'I was,' she said. 'I was afraid when the airplane crashed and for a long time afterwards. My bones were jelly – my legs were weak at the thought of fighting and dying. Then I had a talk with Tim and he taught me not to be that way.' She paused. 'That was when he told me how frightened he was.'

'What a damned silly situation this is,' said Armstrong in wonder. 'Here we are waiting to kill men whom we don't know and who don't know us. But that's always the way in a war, of course.' He grinned. 'But it is damned silly all the same; a middle-aged professor and a young woman lurking on a mountain with murderous intent. I think – '

She put her hand on his arm. 'Hush!'

He listened. 'What is it?'

'I thought I heard something.'

They lay quietly, their ears straining and hearing nothing but the sough of the wind on the mist-shrouded mountain. Then Benedetta's hand tightened on his arm as she heard, far away, the characteristic sound of a gear change. 'Tim was right,' she whispered. 'They're coming up in a truck or a jeep. We must get ready.'

'I'll release the drum,' Armstrong said. 'You stay on the edge here, and give a shout when you want it to go.' He scrambled to his feet and ran back to the drum.

Benedetta ran along the edge of the cutting where she had placed the Molotov cocktails. She lit the wicks of three of them and each flamed with a halo in the mist. The rags, slightly damp with exposure, took a long time to catch alight well. She did not think their light could be seen from the road below; nevertheless, she put them well back from the edge.

The vehicle was labouring heavily, the engine coughing in the thin air. Twice it stopped and she heard the revving of the self-starter. This was no supercharged engine designed for high-altitude operation and the vehicle could not be making more than six or seven miles an hour up the steep slopes of the road. But it was moving much faster than a man could climb under the same conditions.

Benedetta lay on the edge of the cutting and looked down the road towards the bend. The mist was too thick to see that far and she hoped the vehicle had lights strong enough to give her an indication of its position. The growlings of the engine increased and then faded as the vehicle twisted and turned round the hairpin bends, and she thought she heard a double note as of two engines. One or two, she thought; it does not matter.

Armstrong crouched by the cable drum, grasping the short length of electric wire which was fastened to the chock. He peered towards the cutting but saw nothing but a blank wall of grey mist. His face was strained as he waited.

Down the road Benedetta saw a faint glow at the corner of the road and knew that the first vehicle was coming up on the other side of the bend. She glanced back to see if the paraffin wicks were still burning, then turned back and saw two misty eyes of headlamps as the first vehicle made the turn. She had already decided when to shout to Armstrong – a rock was her mark and when the headlights drew level with it, that was the time.

She drew her breath as the engine coughed and died away and the jeep – for through the mist she could now see what it was – drew to a halt. There was a whine from the starter and the jeep began to move again. Behind it two more headlights came into view as a second vehicle pulled round the bend.

Then the headlights of the jeep were level with the rock, and she jumped up, shouting, 'Now! Now! Now!'

There was a startled shout from below as she turned and grabbed the paraffin bottles, easy to see as they flamed close at hand. There was a rumble as the drum plunged forward and she looked up to see it charging down the slope like a juggernaut to crash over the side of the cutting.

She heard the smash and rending of metal and a man screamed. Then she ran back to the edge and hurled a bottle into the confusion below.

The heavy drum had dropped fifteen feet on to the front of the jeep, crushing the forepart entirely and killing the driver. The bottle broke beside the dazed passenger in the wrecked front seat and the paraffin ignited in a great flare and he screamed again, beating at the flames that enveloped him and trying to release his trapped legs. The two men in the back tumbled out and ran off down the road towards the truck coming up behind.

Armstrong ran up to Benedetta just as she threw the second bottle. He had two more in his hand which he lit from the flaming wick of the remaining one and ran along the edge of the cutting towards the truck, which had drawn to a halt. There was a babble of shouts from below and a couple of wild shots which came nowhere near him as he stood on the rim and looked into the truck full of men.

Deliberately he threw one bottle hard at the top of the cab. It smashed and flaming paraffin spread and dripped down past the open window and there came an alarmed cry from the driver. The other bottle he tossed into the body of the truck and in the flickering light he saw the mad scramble to get clear. No one had the time or inclination to shoot at him.

He ran back to Benedetta who was attempting to light another bottle, her hand shaking and her breath coming in harsh gasps. Exertion and the reaction of shock were taking equal toll of her fortitude. 'Enough,' he panted. 'Let's get out of here.' As he spoke, there was an explosion and a great flaring light from the jeep and he grinned tightly. 'That wasn't paraffin – that was petrol. Come on.'

As they ran they saw a glow from the direction of the camp – and then another and another. Willis was doing his job of arson.

IV

O'Hara's ankle was very painful. Before making his move up the hill he had rebound it, trying to give it some support, but it still could not bear his full weight. It made clambering among the rocks difficult and he made more noise than he liked.

He was following the line of beaters that Santos had organized and luckily they were making more noise than he as they stumbled and fell about in the mist, and he thought they weren't making too good a job of it. He had his own troubles; the crossbow and the sub-machine-gun together were hard to handle and he thought of discarding the bow, but then thought better of it. It was a good, silent weapon and he still had two bolts.

He had a shock when he heard the roar of Santos ordering his men to return to the road and he shrank behind a boulder in case any of the men came his way. None did, and he smiled as he thought of the note of exasperation in Santos's voice. Apparently the Russian was getting his own

way after all, and he was certain of it when he heard the
engines start up from the direction of the bridge.

That was what they should have done in the first place –
this searching of the mountain in the mist was futile. The
Russian was definitely a better tactician than Santos; he had
not fallen for their trick of promising to give up Aguillar,
and now he was preparing to ram his force home to the
mine.

O'Hara grimaced as he wondered what would happen at
the camp.

Now that the mountainside ahead of him was clear of the
enemy he made better time, and deliberately stayed as close
as he could to the road. Soon he heard the groan of engines
again and knew that the communist mechanized division
was on its way. He saw the headlights as a jeep and a truck
went past and he paused, listening for what was coming
next. Apparently that was all, so he boldly stepped out on to
the road and started to hobble along on the smooth surface.

He thought it was safe enough; he could hear if another
truck came up behind and there was plenty of time to take
cover. Still, as he walked he kept close to the edge of the
road, the sub-machine-gun at the ready and his eyes carefully scanning the greyness ahead.

It took him a very long time to get anywhere near the
camp and long before that he heard a few scattered shots
and what sounded like an explosion, and he thought he
could detect a glow up the mountain but was not sure
whether his eyes were playing tricks. He redoubled his
caution, which was fortunate, because presently he heard
the thud of boots ahead of him and he slipped in among
the rocks on the roadside sweating with exertion.

A man clattered past at a dead run, and O'Hara heard the
wheezing of his breath. He stayed hidden until there was
nothing more to be heard, then came on to the road again
and resumed his hobbling climb. Half an hour later he heard

the sound of an engine from behind him and took cover again and watched a jeep go by at a crawl. He thought he could see the Russian but was not sure, and the jeep had gone by before he thought to raise the gun.

He cursed himself at the missed opportunity. He knew there was no point in killing the rank-and-file indiscriminately – there were too many of them – but if he could knock out the king-pins, then the whole enemy attack would collapse. The Russian and the Cuban would be his targets in future, and all else would be subordinated to the task of getting them in his sights.

He knew that something must have happened up ahead and tried to quicken his pace. The Russian had been sent for and that meant the enemy had run into trouble. He wondered if Benedetta was safe and felt a quick anger at these ruthless men who were harrying them like animals.

As he climbed higher he found that his eyes had not deceived him – there was a definite glow of fire from up ahead, reflected and subdued by the surrounding mist. He stopped and considered. The fire seemed to be localized in two patches; one small patch which seemed to be on the road and another, which was so large that he could not believe it. Then he smiled – of course, that was the camp; the whole bloody place was going up in flames.

He had better give both localities a wide berth, he thought; so he left the road again, intending to cast a wide circle and come upon the road again above the camp. But curiosity drew him back to where the smaller fire was and where he suspected the Russian had gone.

The mist was too thick to see exactly what had happened but from the shouts he gathered that the road was blocked. Hell, he thought; that's the cutting where Willis was going to dump the cable drum. It looks as though it's worked. But he could not explain the fire which was now guttering out, so he tried to get closer.

His ankle gave way suddenly and he fell heavily, the crossbow falling from his grasp with a terrifying loud noise as it hit a rock, and he came down hard on his elbow and gasped with pain. He lay there, just by the side of the road and close by the Russian's jeep, his lips drawn back from his teeth in agony as he tried to suppress the groan which he felt was coming, and waited for the surprised shout of discovery.

But the enemy were making too much noise themselves as they tried to clear the road and O'Hara heard the jeep start up and drive a little way forward. Slowly the pain ebbed away and cautiously he tried to get up, but to his horror he found that his arm seemed to be trapped in a crevice between the rocks. Carefully he pulled and heard the clink as the sub-machine-gun he was holding came up against stone, and he stopped. Then he pushed his arm down and felt nothing.

At any other time he would have found it funny. He was like a monkey that had put its hand in the narrow neck of a bottle to grasp an apple and could not withdraw it without releasing the apple. He could not withdraw his arm without letting go of the gun, and he dared not let it go in case it made a noise. He wriggled cautiously, then stopped as he heard voices from close by.

'I say my way was best.' It was the Cuban.

The other voice was flat and hard, speaking in badly-accented Spanish. 'What did it get you? Two sprained ankles and a broken leg. You were losing men faster than Aguillar could possibly kill them for you. It was futile to think of searching the mountain in this weather. You've bungled this right from the start.'

'Was your way any better?' demanded Santos in an aggrieved voice. 'Look at what has happened here – a jeep and a truck destroyed, two men killed and the road blocked. I still say that men on foot are better.'

The other man – the Russian – said coldly, 'It happened because you are stupid – you came up here as though you were driving through Havana. Aguillar is making you look like a fool, and I think he is right. Look, Santos, here is a pack of defenceless airline passengers and they have held you up four days; they have killed six of your men and you have a lot more wounded and out of action because of your own stupidity. Right from the start you should have made certain of the bridge – you should have been at the mine when Grivas landed the plane – but you bungled even there. Well, I am taking over from now, and when I come to write my report you are not going to look very good in Havana – not to mention Moscow.'

O'Hara heard him walk away and sweated as he tried to free his arm. Here he had the two of them together and he could not do a damn' thing about it. With one burst he could have killed them both and chanced getting away afterwards, but he was trapped. He heard Santos shuffle his feet indecisively and then walk quickly after the Russian, mumbling as he went.

O'Hara lay there while they hooked up the Russian's jeep to the burned-out truck and withdrew it, to push it off the road and send it plunging down the mountain. Then they dragged out the jeep and did the same with it, and finally got to work on the cable drum. It took them two hours and, to O'Hara, sweating it out not more than six yards from where they were working, it seemed like two days.

V

Willis struggled to get back his breath as he looked down at the burning camp, thankful for the long hours he had put in at that high altitude previously. He had left Benedetta and Armstrong, glad to get away from the certainty of a hand-to-hand fight, defenceless against the ruthless armed men who were coming to butcher them. He could see no prospect of any success; they had fought for days against tremendous odds and the outlook seemed blacker than ever. He did not relish the fact of his imminent death.

With difficulty he had rolled out the drum of paraffin and went from hut to hut, soaking the interior woodwork as thoroughly as possible. While in the last hut he thought he heard an engine and stepped outside to listen, catching the sound of the grinding of gears.

He struck a match, then paused. Benedetta had told him to wait for the shooting or noise and that had not come yet. But it might take some time for the huts to catch alight properly and, from the expression he had seen on Benedetta's face, the shooting was bound to come.

He tossed the match near a pool of paraffin and it caught fire in a flare of creeping flame which ran quickly up the woodwork. Hastily he lit the bundle of paraffin-soaked rags he held and ran along the line of huts, tossing them inside. As he reached the end of the first line he heard a distant crash from the road and a couple of shots. Better make this quick, he thought; now's the time to get out of here.

By the time he left the first line of huts was well aflame, great gouts of fire leaping from the windows. He scrambled up among the rocks above the camp and headed for the road, and when he reached it looked back to see the volcano of the burning camp erupting below. He felt satisfaction at that – he always liked to see a job well done. The mist was too thick to see more than the violent red and yellow glow, but he could make out enough to know that all the huts were well alight and there were no significant gaps. They won't sleep in there tonight, he thought, and turned to run up the road.

He went on for a long time, stopping occasionally to catch his labouring breath and to listen. He heard nothing once he was out of earshot of the camp. At first he had heard a faint shouting, but now everything was silent on the mountainside apart from the eerie keening of the wind. He did not know whether Armstrong and Benedetta were ahead of him or behind, but he listened carefully for any sound coming from the road below. Hearing nothing, he turned and pushed on again, feeling the first faint intimation of lack of oxygen as he went higher.

He was nearing the mine when he caught up with the others, Armstrong turning on his heels with alarm as he heard Willis's footsteps. Aguillar and Miss Ponsky were there also, having made very slow progress up the road. Armstrong said, falsely cheerful, 'Bloody spectacular, wasn't it?'

Willis stopped, his chest heaving. 'They'll be cold tonight – maybe they'll call off the final attack until tomorrow.'

Armstrong shook his head in the gathering darkness. 'I doubt it. Their blood is up – they're close to the kill.' He looked at Willis, who was panting like a dog. 'You'd better take it easy and help Jenny here – she's pretty bad. Benedetta and I can push up to the mine and see what we can do up there.'

Willis stared back. 'Do you think they're far behind?'

'Does it matter?' asked Benedetta. 'We fight here or we fight at the mine.' She absently kissed Aguillar and said something to him in Spanish, then gestured to Armstrong and they went off fairly quickly.

It did not take them long to get to the mine, and as Armstrong surveyed the three huts he said bleakly, 'These are as indefensible as the camp. However, let's see what we can do.'

He entered one of the huts and looked about in the gloom despairingly. He touched the wooden wall and thought, bullets will go through these like paper – we'd be better off scattered on the hillside facing death by exposure. He was roused by a cry from Benedetta, so he went outside.

She was holding a piece of paper in her hand and peering at it in the light of a burning wooden torch. She said excitedly, 'From Forester – they prepared one of the mine tunnels for us.'

Armstrong jerked up his head. 'Where?' He took the piece of paper and examined the sketch on it, then looked about. 'Over there,' he said pointing.

He found the tunnel and the low wall of rocks which Forester and Rohde had built. 'Not much, but it's home,' he said, looking into the blackness. 'You'd better go back and bring the others, and I'll see what it's like inside.'

By the time they all assembled in the tunnel mouth he had explored it pretty thoroughly with the aid of a smoky torch. 'A dead end,' he said. 'This is where we make our last stand.' He pulled a pistol from his belt. 'I've still got Rohde's gun – with one bullet; can anyone shoot better than me?' He offered the gun to Willis. 'What about you, General Custer?'

Willis looked at the pistol. 'I've never fired a gun in my life.'

Armstrong sighed. 'Neither have I, but it looks as though this is my chance.' He thrust the pistol back in his belt and said to Benedetta, 'What's that you've got?'

'Miguel left us some food,' she said. 'Enough for a cold meal.'

'Well, we won't die hungry,' said Armstrong sardonically.

Willis made a sudden movement. 'For God's sake, don't talk that way.'

'I'm sorry,' said Armstrong. 'How are Miss Ponsky and Señor Aguillar?'

'As well as might be expected,' said Benedetta bitterly. 'For a man with a heart condition and an elderly lady with a hole in her shoulder, trying to breathe air that is not there.' She looked up at Armstrong. 'You think there is any chance for Tim?'

He averted his head. 'No,' he said shortly, and went to the mouth of the tunnel, where he lay down behind the low breastwork of rocks and put the gun beside him. If I wait I might kill someone, he thought; but I must wait until they're very close.

It was beginning to snow.

VI

It was very quiet by the cutting, although O'Hara could hear voices from farther up the road by the burning camp. There was not much of a glow through the mist now, and he judged that the huts must just about have burned down to their foundations. Slowly he relaxed his hand and let the sub-machine-gun fall. It clattered to the rocks and he pulled up his arm and massaged it.

He felt very damp and cold and wished he had been able to strip the llama-skin coat from the sentry by the trebuchet – young Juan would not have needed it. But it would have taken too long, apart from being a gruesome job, and he had not wanted to waste the time. Now he wished he had taken the chance.

He stayed there, sitting quietly for some time, wondering if anyone had noticed the noise of metal on stone. Then he set himself to retrieve the gun. It took him ten minutes to fish it from the crevice with the aid of the crossbow, and then he set off up the mountain again, steering clear of the road. At least the enforced halt had rested him.

Three more trucks had come up. They had not gone straight up to the mine – not yet; the enemy had indulged in a futile attempt to quench the fires of the flaming camp and that had taken some time. Knowing that the trucks were parked above the camp, he circled so as to come out upon them. His ankle was bad, the flesh soft and puffy, and

he knew he could not walk very much farther – certainly
not up to the mine. It was in his mind to get himself a truck
the same way he got himself a gun – by killing for it.

A crowd of men were climbing into the trucks when he
got back to the road and he felt depressed but brightened a
little when he saw that only two trucks were being used.
The jeep was drawn up alongside and O'Hara heard the
Russian giving orders in his pedantic Spanish and fretted
because he was not within range. Then the jeep set off up
the road and the trucks rolled after it with a crashing of
gears, leaving the third parked.

He could not see whether a guard had been left so he
began to prowl forward very cautiously. He did not think
that there was a guard – the enemy would not think of taking such a precaution, as everyone was supposed to have
been driven up to the mine. So he was very shocked when
he literally fell over a sentry, who had left his post by the
truck and was relieving himself among the rocks by the
roadside.

The man grunted in surprise as O'Hara cannoned into
him. *'Cuidado!'* he said, and then looked up. O'Hara
dropped both his weapons as the man opened his mouth
and clamped the palm of his hand over the other's jaw
before he could shout. They strained against each other
silently, O'Hara forcing back the man's head, his fingers
clawing for the vulnerable eyes. His other arm was wrapped
around the man's chest, clutching him tight.

His opponent flailed frantically with both arms and
O'Hara knew that he was in no condition for a real knock-
down-drag-out fight, with this man. He remembered the
knife in his belt and decided to take a chance, depending on
swiftness of action to kill the man before he made a noise.
He released him suddenly, pushing him away, and his hand
went swiftly to his waist. The man staggered and opened his
mouth again and O'Hara stepped forward and drove the

knife in a straight stab into his chest just below the breast-bone, giving it an upward turn as it went in.

The man coughed in a surprised hiccuping fashion and leaned forward, toppling straight into O'Hara's arms. As O'Hara lowered him to the ground he gave a deep sigh and died. Breathing heavily, O'Hara plucked out the knife and a gush of hot blood spurted over his hand. He stood for a moment, listening, and then picked up the sub-machine-gun from where he had dropped it. He felt a sudden shock as his finger brushed the safety-catch – it was in the off position; the sudden jar could well have fired a warning shot.

But that was past and he was beyond caring. He knew he was living from minute to minute and past possibilities and actions meant nothing to him. All that mattered was to get up to the mine as quickly as possible – to nail the Cuban and the Russian – and to find Benedetta.

He looked into the cab of the truck and opened the door. It was a big truck and from where he sat when he pulled himself into the cab he could see the dying embers of the camp. He did not see any movement there, apart from a few low flames and a curl of black smoke which was lost immediately in the mist. He turned back, looked ahead and pressed the starter.

The engine fired and he put it into gear and drove up the road, feeling a little light-headed. In a very short space of time he had killed three men, the first he had ever killed face to face, and he was preparing to go on killing for as long as was necessary. His mind had returned to the tautness he remembered from Korea before he had been shot down; all his senses were razor-sharp and his mind emptied of every-thing but the task ahead.

After a while he switched off the lights. It was risky, but he had to take the chance. There was the possibility that in the mist he could lose the road on one of the bends and go down the mountain out of control; but far worse was the risk that the enemy in the trucks ahead would see him and lay an ambush.

The truck ground on and on and the wheel bucked against his hand as the jolts were transmitted from the road surface. He went as fast as he thought safe, which was really not fast at all, but at last, rounding a particularly hair-raising corner, he saw a red tail-light disappearing round the next bend. At once he slowed down, content to follow at a discreet distance. There was nothing he could do on the road – his time would come at the mine.

He put out his hand to the sub-machine-gun resting on the seat next to him and drew it closer. It felt very comforting.

He reached a bend he remembered, the final corner before the level ground at the mine. He drew into the side of the road and put on the brake, but left the engine running. Taking the gun, he dropped to the ground, wincing as he felt the weight on his bad ankle, and hobbled up the road. From ahead he could hear the roar of engines stopping one by one, and when he found a place from where he could see, he discovered the other trucks parked by the huts and in the glare of headlights he saw the movement of men.

The jeep revved up and started to move, the beams of its lights stabbing through the mist and searching along the base of the cliff where the mine tunnels had been driven. First one black cavern was illuminated and then another, and then there was a raised shout of triumph, a howl of fierce joy, as the beams swept past the third tunnel and returned almost immediately to show a low rock wall at the entrance and the white face of a man who quickly dodged back out of sight.

O'Hara wasted no time in wondering who it was. He hobbled back to his truck and put it in gear. Now was the time to enter that bleak arena.

NINE

Forester felt warm and at ease, and to him the two were synonymous. Strange that the snow is so warm and soft, he thought; and opened his eyes to see a glare of white before him. He sighed and closed his eyes again, feeling a sense of disappointment. It *was* snow, after all. He supposed he should make an effort to move and get out of this deliciously warm snow or he would die, but he decided it was not worth the effort. He just let the warmth lap him in comfort and for a second before he relapsed into unconsciousness he wondered vaguely where Rohde had got to.

The next time he opened his eyes the glare of white was still there but now he had recovered enough to see it for what it was – the brilliance of sunlight falling on the crisply laundered white counterpane that covered him. He blinked and looked again, but the glare hurt his eyes, so he closed them. He knew he should do something but what it was he could not remember, and he passed out again while struggling to keep awake long enough to remember what it was.

Vaguely, in his sleep, he was aware of the passage of time and he knew he must fight against this, that he must stop the clock, hold the moving fingers, because he had something to do that was of prime urgency. He stirred and moaned, and a nurse in a trim white uniform gently sponged the sweat from his brow.

But she did not wake him.

At last he woke fully and stared at the ceiling. That was also white, plainly whitewashed with thick wooden beams. He turned his head and found himself looking into kindly eyes. He licked dry lips and whispered, 'What happened?'

'*No comprendo,*' said the nurse. 'No talk – I bring doctor.'

She got up and his eyes moved as she went out of the room. He desperately wanted her to come back, to tell him where he was and what had happened and where to find Rohde. As he thought of Rohde it all came back to him – the night on the mountain and the frustrating attempts to find a way over the pass. Most of it he remembered, although the end bits were hazy – and he also remembered why that impossible thing had been attempted.

He tried to sit up but his muscles had no strength in them and he just lay there, breathing hard. He felt as though his body weighed a thousand pounds and as though he had been beaten all over with a rubber hose. Every muscle was loose and flabby, even the muscles of his neck, as he found when he tried to raise his head. And he felt very, very tired.

It was a long time before anyone came into the room, and then it was the nurse bearing a bowl of hot soup. She would not let him talk and he was too weak to insist, and every time he opened his mouth she ladled a spoonful of soup into it. The broth gave him new strength and he felt better, and when he had finished the bowl he said, 'Where is the other man – *el otro hombre?*'

'Your friend will be all right,' she said in Spanish, and whisked out of the room before he could ask anything else.

Again it was a long time before anyone came to see him. He had no watch, but by the position of the sun he judged it was about midday. But which day? How long had he been there? He put up his hand to scratch an intolerable itching in his chest and discovered why he felt so heavy and uncomfortable; he seemed to be wrapped in a couple of miles of adhesive tape.

A man entered the room and closed the door. He said in an American accent, 'Well, Mr Forester, I hear you're better.' He was dressed in hospital white and could have been a doctor. He was elderly but still powerfully built, with a shock of white hair and the crowsfeet of frequent laughter around his eyes.

Forester relaxed. 'Thank God – an American,' he said. His voice was much stronger.

'I'm McGruder – Doctor McGruder.'

'How did you know my name?' asked Forester.

'The papers in your pocket,' said McGruder. 'You carry an American passport.'

'Look,' said Forester urgently. 'You've got to let me out of here. I've got things to do. I've got to – '

'You're not leaving here for a long time,' said McGruder abruptly. 'And you couldn't stand if you tried.'

Forester sagged back in bed. 'Where is this place?'

'San Antonio Mission,' said McGruder,' 'I'm the Big White Chief here. Presbyterian, you know.'

'Anywhere near Altemiros?'

'Sure. Altemiros village is just down the road – almost two miles away.'

'I want a message sent,' said Forester rapidly. 'Two messages – one to Ramón Sueguerra in Altemiros and one to Santillana to the – '

McGruder held up his hand. 'Whoa up, there; you'll have a relapse if you're not careful. Take it easy.'

'For God's sake,' said Forester bitterly. 'This is urgent.'

'For God's sake nothing is urgent,' said McGruder equably. 'He has all the time there is. What I'm interested in right now is why one man should come over an impossible pass in a blizzard carrying another man.'

'Did Rohde carry me? How is he?'

'As well as can be expected,' said McGruder. 'I'd be interested to know why he carried you.'

'Because I was dying,' said Forester. He looked at McGruder speculatively, sizing him up. He did not want to make a blunder – the communists had some very unexpected friends in the strangest places – but he did not think he could go wrong with a Presbyterian doctor, and McGruder *looked* all right. 'All right,' he said at last. 'I suppose I'll have to tell you. You look okay to me.'

McGruder raised his eyebrows but said nothing, and Forester told him what was happening on the other side of the mountains, beginning with the air crash but leaving out such irrelevancies as the killing of Peabody, which, he thought, might harm his case. As he spoke McGruder's eyebrows crawled up his scalp until they were almost lost in his hair.

When Forester finished he said, 'Now that's as improbable a story as I've ever heard. You see, Mr Forester, I don't entirely trust you. I had a phone call from the Air Force base – there's one quite close – and they were looking for you. Moreover, you were carrying this.' He put his hand in his pocket and pulled out a pistol. 'I don't like people who carry guns – it's against my religion.'

Forester watched as McGruder skilfully worked the action and the cartridges flipped out. He said, 'For a man who doesn't like guns you know a bit too much about their workings.'

'I was a Marine at Iwo Jima,' said McGruder. 'Now why would the Cordilleran military be interested in you?'

'Because they've gone communist.'

'Tchah!' said McGruder disgustedly. 'You talk like an old maid who sees burglars under every bed. Colonel Rodriguez is as communist as I am.'

Forester felt a sudden hope. Rodriguez was the commandant of Fourteenth Squadron and the friend of Aguillar. 'Did you speak to Rodriguez?' he asked.

'No,' said McGruder. 'It was some junior officer.' He paused. 'Look, Forester, the military want you and I'd like you to tell me why.'

'Is Fourteenth Squadron still at the airfield?' countered Forester.

'I don't know. Rodriguez did say something about moving – but I haven't seen him for nearly a month.'

So it was a toss-up, thought Forester disgustedly. The military were friend or foe and he had no immediate means of finding out – and it looked as though McGruder was quite prepared to hand him over. He said speculatively, 'I suppose you try to keep your nose clean. I suppose you work in with the local authorities and you don't interfere in local politics.'

'Indeed I don't,' said McGruder. 'I don't want this mission closed. We have enough trouble as it is.'

'You *think* you have trouble with Lopez, but that's nothing to the trouble you'll have when the commies move in,' snapped Forester. 'Tell me, is it against your religion to stand by and wait while your fellow human beings – some of them fellow countrymen, not that that matters – are slaughtered not fifteen miles from where you are standing?'

McGruder whitened about the nostrils and the lines deepened about his mouth. 'I almost think you are telling the truth,' he said slowly.

'You're damn right I am.'

Ignoring the profanity McGruder said, 'You mentioned a name – Sueguerra. I know Señor Sueguerra very well. I play chess with him whenever I get into the village. He is a good man, so that is a point for you. What was the other message – to Santillana?'

'The same message to a different man,' said Forester patiently. 'Bob Addison of the United States Embassy. Tell them both what I've told you – and tell Addison to get the lead out of his breeches fast.'

McGruder wrinkled his brow. 'Addison? I believe I know all the Embassy staff, but I don't recall an Addison.'

'You wouldn't,' said Forester. 'He's an officer of the Central Intelligence Agency of the United States. We don't advertise.'

McGruder's eyebrows crawled up again. 'We?'

Forester grinned weakly. 'I'm a C.I.A. officer, too. But you'll have to take it on trust – I don't carry the information tattooed on my chest.'

II

Forester was shocked to hear that Rohde was likely to lose his leg. 'Frostbite in a very bad open wound is not conducive to the best of health,' said McGruder dryly. 'I'm very sorry about this; I'll try to save the leg, of course – it's a pity that this should happen to so brave a man.'

McGruder now appeared to have accepted Forester's story, although he had taken a lot of convincing and had doubts about the wisdom of the State Department. 'They're stupid,' he said. 'We don't want open American interference down here – that's certain to stir up anti-Americanism. It's giving the communists a perfect opening.'

'For God's sake, I'm not interfering actively,' protested Forester. 'We knew that Aguillar was going to make his move and my job was to keep a friendly eye on him, to see that he got through safely.' He looked at the ceiling and said bitterly, 'I seem to have balled it up, don't I?'

'I don't see that you could have done anything different,' observed McGruder. He got up from the bedside. 'I'll check up on which squadron is at the airfield, and I'll go to see Sueguerra myself.'

'Don't forget the Embassy.'

'I'll put a phone call through right away.'

But that proved to be difficult because the line was not open. McGruder sat at his desk and fumed at the unresponsive telephone. This was something that happened about once a week and always at a critical moment. At last he put down the hand-set and turned to take off his white coat, but hesitated as he heard the squeal of brakes from the courtyard. He looked through his office window and saw a military staff car pull up followed by a truck and a military ambulance. A squad of uniformed and armed men debussed from the truck under the barked orders of an N.C.O., and an officer climbed casually out of the staff car.

McGruder hastily put on the white coat again and when the officer strode into the room he was busy writing at his desk. He looked up and said, 'Good day – er – Major. To what do I owe this honour?'

The officer clicked his heels punctiliously. 'Major Garcia, at your service.'

The doctor leaned back in his chair and put both his hands flat on the desk. 'I'm McGruder. What can I do for you, Major?'

Garcia flicked his glove against the side of his well-cut breeches. 'We – the Cordilleran Air Force, that is – thought we might be of service,' he said easily. 'We understand that you have two badly injured men here – the men who came down from the mountain. We offer the use of our medical staff and the base hospital at the airfield.' He waved. 'The ambulance is waiting outside.'

McGruder swivelled his eyes to the window and saw the soldiers taking up position outside. They looked stripped for action. He flicked his gaze back to Garcia. 'And the escort!'

Garcia smiled. *'No es nada,'* he said casually. 'I was conducting a small exercise when I got my orders, and it was as easy to bring the men along as to dismiss them and let them idle.'

McGruder did not believe a word of it. He said pleasantly, 'Well, Major, I don't think we need trouble the military. I haven't been in your hospital at the airfield, but this place of mine is well enough equipped to take care of these men. I don't think they need to be moved.'

Garcia lost his smile. 'But we insist,' he said icily.

McGruder's mobile eyebrows shot up. 'Insist, Major Garcia? I don't think you're in a position to insist.'

Garcia looked meaningly at the squad of soldiers in the courtyard. 'No?' he asked silkily.

'No,' said McGruder flatly. 'As a doctor, I say that these men are too sick to be moved. If you don't believe me, then trot out your own doctor from that ambulance and let *him* have a look at them. I am sure he will tell you the same.'

For the first time Garcia seemed to lose his self-possession. 'Doctor?' he said uncertainly. 'Er. . . we have brought no doctor.'

'No doctor?' said McGruder in surprise. He wiggled his eyebrows at Garcia. 'I am sure you have misinterpreted your orders, Major Garcia. I don't think your commanding officer would approve of these men leaving here unless under qualified supervision; and I certainly don't have the time to go with you to the airfield – I am a busy man.'

Garcia hesitated and then said sullenly, 'Your telephone – may I use it?'

'Help yourself,' said McGruder. 'But it isn't working – as usual.'

Garcia smiled thinly and spoke into the mouthpiece. He got an answer, too, which really surprised McGruder and told him of the seriousness of the position. This was not an ordinary breakdown of the telephone system – it was planned; and he guessed that the exchange was under military control.

When next Garcia spoke he came to attention and McGruder smiled humourlessly; that would be his commanding officer and it certainly wouldn't be Rodriguez – he didn't go in for that kind of spit-and-polish. Garcia explained McGruder's attitude concisely and then listened to the spate of words which followed. There was a grim smile on his face as he put down the telephone. 'I regret to tell you, Doctor McGruder, that I must take those men.'

He stepped to the window and called his sergeant as McGruder came to his feet in anger. 'And I say the men are too ill to be moved. One of those men is an American, Major Garcia. Are you trying to cause an international incident?'

'I am obeying orders,' said Garcia stiffly. His sergeant came to the window and he gave a rapid stream of instructions, then turned to McGruder. 'I have to inform you that these men stand accused of plotting against the safety of the State. I am under instructions to arrest them.'

'You're nuts,' said McGruder. 'You take these men and you'll be up to your neck in diplomats.' He moved over to the door.

Garcia stood in front of him. 'I must ask you to move away from the door, Doctor McGruder, or I will be forced to arrest you, too.' He spoke over McGruder's shoulder to a corporal standing outside. 'Escort the doctor into the court-yard.'

'Well, if you're going to feel like that about it, there's nothing I can do,' said McGruder. 'But that commanding officer of yours – what's his name . . . ?'

'Colonel Coello.'

'Colonel Coello is going to find himself in a sticky posi-tion.' He stood aside and let Garcia precede him into the corridor.

Garcia waited for him, slapping the side of his leg impatiently. 'Where are the men?'

McGruder led the way down the corridor at a rapid pace. Outside Forester's room he paused and deliberately raised his voice. 'You realize I am letting these men go under protest. The military have no jurisdiction here and I intend to protest to the Cordilleran government through the United States Embassy. And I further protest upon medical grounds – neither of these men is fit to be moved.'

'Where are the men?' repeated Garcia.

'I have just operated on one of them – he is recovering from an anaesthetic. The other is also very ill and I insist on giving him a sedative before he is moved.'

Garcia hesitated and McGruder pressed him. 'Come, Major; military ambulances have never been noted for smooth running – you would not begrudge a man a painkiller.' He tapped Garcia on the chest. 'This is going to make headlines in every paper across the United States. Do you want to make matters worse by appearing anti-humanitarian?'

'Very well,' said Garcia unwillingly.

'I'll get the morphine from the surgery,' said McGruder and went back, leaving Garcia standing in the corridor.

Forester heard the raised voices as he was polishing the plate of the best meal he had ever enjoyed in his life. He realized that something was amiss and that McGruder was making him appear sicker than he was. He was willing to play along with that, so he hastily pushed the tray under the bed and when the door opened he was lying flat on his back with his eyes closed. As McGruder touched him he groaned.

McGruder said, 'Mr Forester, Major Garcia thinks you will be better looked after in another hospital, so you are being moved.' As Forester opened his eyes McGruder frowned at him heavily. 'I do not agree with this move, which is being done under *force majeure*, and I am going to consult the appropriate authorities. I am going to give you a sedative so that the journey will not harm you, although it is not far – merely to the airfield.'

He rolled up the sleeve of Forester's pyjamas and dabbed at his arm with cotton-wool, then produced a hypodermic syringe which he filled from an ampoule. He spoke casually. 'The tape round your chest will support your ribs but I wouldn't move around much – not unless you have to.' There was a subtle emphasis on the last few words and he winked at Forester.

As he pushed home the needle in Forester's arm he leaned over and whispered, 'It's a stimulant.'

'What was that?' said Garcia sharply.

'What was what?' asked McGruder, turning and skewering Garcia with an icy glare. 'I'll trouble you not to interfere with a doctor in his duties. Mr Forester is a very sick man, and on behalf of the United States government I am holding you and Colonel Coello responsible for what happens to him. Now, where are your stretcher-bearers?'

Garcia snapped to the sergeant at the door, *'Una camilla.'* The sergeant bawled down the corridor and presently a stretcher was brought in. McGruder fussed about while Forester was transferred from the bed, and when he was settled said, 'There, you can take him.'

He stepped back and knocked a kidney basin on the floor with a clatter. The noise was startling in that quiet room, and while everyone's attention was diverted McGruder hastily thrust something hard under Forester's pillow.

Then Forester was borne down the corridor and into the open courtyard and he winced as the sun struck his eyes. Once in the ambulance he had to wait a long time before anything else happened and he closed his eyes, feigning sleep, because the soldier on guard kept peering at him. Slowly he brought his hand up under the coverlet towards the pillow and eventually touched the butt of a gun.

Good old McGruder, he thought; the Marines to the rescue. He hooked his finger in the trigger guard and gradually brought the gun down to his side, where he thrust it into the waistband of his pyjamas at the small of his back where it could not be seen when he was transferred to another bed. He smiled to himself; at other times lying on a hard piece of metal might be thought extremely uncomfortable, but he found the touch of the gun very comforting.

And what McGruder had said was comforting, too. The tape would hold him together and the stimulant would give him strength to move. Not that he thought he needed it; his strength had returned rapidly once he had eaten, but no doubt the doctor knew best.

Rohde was pushed into the ambulance and Forester looked across at the stretcher. He was unconscious and there was a hump under the coverlet where his legs were. His face was pale and covered with small beads of sweat and he breathed stertorously.

Two soldiers climbed into the ambulance and the doors were slammed, and after a few minutes it moved off. Forester kept his eyes closed at first – he wanted the soldiers to believe that the hypothetical sedative was taking effect. But after a while he decided that these rank and file would probably not know anything about a sedative being given to him, so he risked opening his eyes and turned his head to look out of the window.

He could not see much because of the restricted angle of view, but presently the ambulance stopped and he saw a wrought-iron gate and through the bars a large board. It depicted an eagle flying over a snow-capped mountain, and round this emblem in a scroll and written in ornate letters were the words: ESQUADRON OCTAVO.

He closed his eyes in pain. They had drawn the wrong straw; this was the communist squadron.

III

McGruder watched the ambulance leave the courtyard followed by the staff car. Then he went into his office, stripped off his white coat and put on his jacket. He took his car keys from a drawer and went round to the hospital garage, where he got a shock. Lounging outside the big doors was a soldier in a sloppy uniform – but there was nothing sloppy about the rifle he was holding, nor about the gleaming bayonet.

He walked over and barked authoritatively, 'Let me pass.'

The soldier looked at him through half-closed eyes and shook his head, then spat on the ground. McGruder got mad and tried to push his way past but found the tip of the bayonet pricking his throat. The soldier said, 'You see the sergeant – if he says you can take a car, then you take a car.'

McGruder backed away, rubbing his throat. He turned on his heel and went to look for the sergeant, but got nowhere with him. The sergeant was a sympathetic man when away from his officers and his broad Indian face was sorrowful. 'I'm sorry, Doctor,' he said. 'I just obey orders – and my orders are that no one leaves the mission until I get contrary orders.'

'And when will that be?' demanded McGruder.

The sergeant shrugged. 'Who knows?' he said with the fatalism of one to whom officers were a race apart and their doings incomprehensible.

McGruder snorted and withdrew to his office, where he picked up the telephone. Apparently it was still dead, but when he snapped, 'Get me Colonel Coello at the military airfield,' it suddenly came to life and he was put through – not to Coello, but to some underling.

It took him over fifteen minutes before he got through to Coello and by then he was breathing hard with ill-suppressed rage. He said aggressively, 'McGruder here. What's all this about closing down San Antonio Mission?'

Coello was suave. 'But the mission is not closed, Doctor; anyone can enter.'

'But I can't leave,' said McGruder. 'I have work to do.'

'Then do it,' said Coello. 'Your work is in the mission, Doctor; stick to your job – like the cobbler. Do not interfere in things which do not concern you.'

'I don't know what the hell you mean,' snarled McGruder with a profanity he had not used since his Marine days. 'I have to pick up a consignment of drugs at the railroad depot in Altemiros. I need them and the Cordilleran Air Force is stopping me getting them – that's how I see it. You're not going to look very good when this comes out, Colonel.'

'But you should have said this earlier,' said Coello soothingly. 'I will send one of the airfield vehicles to pick them up for you. As you know, the Cordilleran Air Force is always ready to help your mission. I hear you run a very good hospital, Doctor McGruder. We are short of good hospitals in this country.'

McGruder heard the cynical amusement in the voice. He said irascibly, 'All right,' and banged the phone down. Mopping his brow he thought that it was indeed fortunate there *was* a consignment of drugs waiting in Altemiros. He paused, wondering what to do next, then he drew a sheet of blank paper from a drawer and began writing.

Half an hour later he had the gist of Forester's story on paper. He folded the sheets, sealed them in an envelope and put the envelope into his pocket. All the while he was conscious of the soldier posted just outside the window who was keeping direct surveillance of him. He went out into the corridor to find another soldier lounging outside the office door whom he ignored, carrying on down towards the wards and the operating theatre. The soldier stared after him with incurious eyes and drifted down the corridor after him.

McGruder looked for Sánchez, his second-in-command, and found him in one of the wards. Sánchez looked at his face and raised his eyebrows. 'What is happening, Doctor?'

'The local military have gone berserk,' said McGruder unhappily. 'And I seem to be mixed up in it – they won't let me leave the mission.'

'They won't let *anyone* leave the mission,' said Sánchez. 'I tried.'

'I must get to Altemiros,' said McGruder. 'Will you help me? I know I'm usually non-political, but this is different. There's murder going on across the mountains.'

'Eight Squadron came to the airfield two days ago – I have heard strange stories about Eight Squadron,' said Sánchez reflectively. 'You may be non-political, Doctor McGruder, but I am not. Of course I will help you.'

McGruder turned and saw the soldier gazing blankly at him from the entrance of the ward. 'Let's go into your office,' he said.

They went to the office and McGruder switched on an X-ray viewer and pointed out the salient features of an X-ray plate to Sánchez. He left the door open and the soldier leaned on the opposite wall of the corridor, solemnly picking his teeth. 'This is what I want you to do,' said McGruder in a low voice.

Fifteen minutes later he went to find the sergeant and spoke to him forthrightly. 'What are your orders concerning the mission?' he demanded.

The sergeant said, 'Not to let anyone leave – and to watch you, Doctor McGruder.' He paused. 'I'm sorry.'

'I seem to have noticed that I've been watched,' said McGruder with heavy irony. 'Now, I'm going to do an operation. Old Pedro must have his kidneys seen to or he will die. I can't have any of your men in the operating theatre, spitting all over the floor; we have enough trouble attaining asepsis as it is.'

'We all know you *norteamericanos* are very clean,' acknowledged the sergeant. He frowned. 'This room – how many doors?'

'One door – no windows,' said McGruder. 'You can come and look at it if you like; but don't spit on the floor.'

He took the sergeant into the operating theatre and satisfied him that there was only one entrance. 'Very well,' said the sergeant. 'I will put two men outside the door – that will be all right.'

McGruder went into the sluice room and prepared for the operation, putting on his gown and cap and fastening the mask loosely about his neck. Old Pedro was brought up on a stretcher and McGruder stood outside the door while he was pushed into the theatre. The sergeant said, 'How long will this take?'

McGruder considered. 'About two hours – maybe longer. It is a serious operation, Sergeant.'

He went into the theatre and closed the door. Five minutes later the empty stretcher was pushed out and the sergeant looked through the open door and saw the doctor masked and bending over the operating table, a scalpel in his hand. The door closed, the sergeant nodded to the sentries and wandered towards the courtyard to find a sunny spot. He quite ignored the empty stretcher being pushed by two chattering nurses down the corridor.

In the safety of the bottom ward McGruder dropped from under the stretcher where he had been clinging and flexed the muscles of his arms. Getting too old for these acrobatics, he thought, and nodded to the nurses who had pushed in the stretcher. They giggled and went out, and he changed his clothes quickly.

He knew of a place where the tide of prickly pear which covered the hillside overflowed into the mission grounds. For weeks he had intended to cut down the growth and tidy it up, but now he was glad that he had let it be. No sentry in his right mind would deliberately patrol in the middle of a grove of sharp-spined cactus, no matter what his orders, and McGruder thought he had a chance of getting through.

He was right. Twenty minutes later he was on the other side of a low rise, the mission out of sight behind him and the houses of Altemiros spread in front. His clothes were torn and so was his flesh – the cactus had not been kind.

He began to run.

IV

Forester was still on his stretcher. He had expected to be taken into a hospital ward and transferred to a bed, but instead the stretcher was taken into an office and laid across two chairs. Then he was left alone, but he could hear the shuffling feet of a sentry outside the door and knew he was well guarded.

It was a large office overlooking the airfield, and he guessed it belonged to the commanding officer. There were many maps on the walls and some aerial photographs, mainly of mountain country. He looked at the décor without interest; he had been in many offices like this when he was in the American Air Force and it was all very familiar, from the group photographs of the squadron to the clock let into the boss of an old wooden propeller.

What interested him was the scene outside. One complete wall of the office was a window and through it he could see the apron outside the control tower and, farther away, a group of hangars. He clicked his tongue as he recognized the aircraft standing on the apron – they were Sabres.

Good old Uncle Sam, he thought in disgust; always willing to give handouts, even military handouts, to potential enemies. He looked at the fighter planes with intense curiosity. They were early model Sabres, now obsolete in the major air forces, but quite adequate for the defence of a country like Cordillera which had no conceivable military

enemies of any strength. As far as he could see, they were
the identical model he had flown in Korea. I could fly one
of those, he thought, if I could just get into the cockpit.

There were four of them standing in a neat line and he
saw they were being serviced. Suddenly he sat up – no, not
serviced – those were rockets going under the wings. And
those men standing on the wings were not mechanics, they
were armourers loading cannon shells. He did not have to
be close enough to see the shells; he had seen this operation
performed many times in Korea and he knew automatically
that these planes were being readied for instant action.

Christ! he thought bitterly; it's like using a steam hammer to crack a nut. O'Hara and the others won't have a
chance against this lot. But then he became aware of something else – this must mean that O'Hara was still holding
out; that the communists across the bridge were still baffled.
He felt exhilarated and depressed at the same time as he
watched the planes being readied.

He lay back again and felt the gun pressing into the small
of his back. This was the time to prepare for action, he realized, so he pulled out the gun, keeping a wary eye on the
door, and examined it. It was the pistol he had brought over
the mountain – Grivas's pistol. Cold and exposure to the
elements had not done it any good – the oil had dried out
and the action was stiff – but he thought it would work. He
snapped the action several times, catching the rounds as
they flipped from the breech, then he reloaded the magazine and worked the action again, putting a round in the
breech ready for instant shooting.

He stowed the pistol by his side under the coverlet and
laid his hand on the butt. Now he was ready – as ready as
he could be.

He waited a long time and began to get edgy. He felt
little tics all over his body as small muscles jumped and
twitched, and he had never been so wide-awake in his life.

That's McGruder's stimulant he thought: I wonder what it was and if it'll mix with all the coca I've taken.

He kept an eye on the Sabres outside. The ground crews had completed their work long before someone opened the door of the office, and Forester looked up to see a man with a long, saturnine face looking down at him. The man smiled. '*Colonel Coello, a sus ordenes.*' He clicked his heels.

Forester blinked his eyes, endeavouring to simulate sleepiness. 'Colonel who?' he mumbled.

The colonel sat behind the desk. 'Coello,' he said pleasantly. 'I am the commandant of this fighter squadron.'

'It's the damnedest thing,' said Forester with a baffled look. 'One minute I was in hospital, and the next minute I'm in this office. Familiar surroundings, too; I woke up and became interested in those Sabres.'

'You have flown?' asked Coello politely.

'I sure have,' said Forester. 'I was in Korea – I flew Sabres there.'

'Then we can talk together as comrades,' said Coello heartily. 'You remember Doctor McGruder?'

'Not much,' said Forester. 'I woke up and he pumped me full of stuff to put me to sleep again – then I found myself here. Say, shouldn't I be in hospital or something?'

'Then you did not talk to McGruder about anything – anything at all?'

'I didn't have the chance,' said Forester. He did not want to implicate McGruder in this. 'Say, Colonel, am I glad to see you. All hell is breaking loose on the other side of the mountains. There's a bunch of bandits trying to murder some stranded airline passengers. We were on our way here to tell you.'

'On your way *here?*'

That's right; there was a South American guy told us to come here – now, what was his name?' Forester wrinkled his brow.

'Aguillar – perhaps?'

'Never heard that name before,' said Forester. 'No, this guy was called Montes.'

'And Montes told you to come *here?*' said Coello incredulously. 'He must have thought that fool Rodriguez was here. You were two days too late, Mr Forester.' He began to laugh.

Forester felt a cold chill run through him but pressed on with his act of innocence. 'What's so funny?' he asked plaintively. 'Why the hell are you sitting there laughing instead of doing something about it?'

Coello wiped the tears of laughter from his eyes. 'Do not worry, Señor Forester; we know all about it already. We are making preparations for . . . er . . . a rescue attempt.'

I'll bet you are, thought Forester bitterly, looking at the Sabres drawn up on the apron. He said, 'What the hell! Then I nearly killed myself on the mountain for nothing. What a damned fool I am.'

Coello opened a folder on his desk. 'Your name is Raymond Forester; you are South American Sales Manager for the Fairfield Machine Tool Corporation, and you were on your way to Santillana.' He smiled as he looked down at the folder. 'We have checked, of course; there is a Raymond Forester who works for this company, and he *is* sales manager in South America. The C.I.A. can be efficient in small matters, Mr Forester.'

'Huh!' said Forester. 'C.I.A.? What the devil are you talking about?'

Coello waved his hand airily. 'Espionage! Sabotage! Corruption of public officials! Undermining the will of the people! Name anything bad and you name the C.I.A. – and also yourself, Mr Forester.'

'You're nuts,' said Forester disgustedly.

'You are a meddling American,' said Coello sharply. 'You are a plutocratic, capitalistic lackey. One could forgive you if you were but a tool; but you do your filthy work in full awareness of its evil. You came to Cordillera to foment an imperialistic revolution, putting up that scoundrel Aguillar as a figurehead for your machinations.'

'Who?' said Forester. 'You're still nuts.'

'Give up, Forester; stop this pretence. We know all about the Fairfield Machine Tool Corporation. It is a cover that capitalistic Wall Street has erected to hide your imperialistic American secret service. We know all about you and we know all about Addison in Santillana. He has been removed from the game – and so have you, Forester.'

Forester smiled crookedly. 'The voice is Spanish-American, but the words come from Moscow – or is it Peking this time?' He nodded towards the armed aircraft. 'Who is really doing the meddling round here?'

Coello smiled. 'I am a servant of the present government of General Lopez. I am sure he would be happy to know that Aguillar will soon be dead.'

'But I bet you won't tell him,' said Forester. 'Not if I know how you boys operate. You'll use the threat of Aguillar to drive Lopez out as soon as it suits you.' He tried to scratch his itching chest but was unsuccessful. 'You jumped me and Rohde pretty fast – how did you know we were at McGruder's hospital?'

'I am sure you are trying to sound more stupid than you really are,' said Coello. 'My dear Forester, we are in radio communication with our forces on the other side of the mountains.' He sounded suddenly bitter. 'Inefficient though they are, they have at least kept their radio working. You were seen by the bridge. And when men come over that pass, do you think the news can be kept quiet? The whole of Altemiros knows of the mad American who has done the impossible.'

But they don't know why I did it, thought Forester savagely; and they'll never find out if this bastard has his way.

Coello held up a photograph. 'We suspected that the C.I.A. might have someone with Aguillar. It was only a suspicion then, but now we know it to be a fact. This photograph was taken in Washington six months ago.'

He skimmed it over and Forester looked at it. It was a glossy picture of himself and his immediate superior talking together on the steps of a building. He flicked the photograph with his fingernail. 'Processed in Moscow?'

Coello smiled and asked silkily, 'Can you give me any sound reasons why you should not be shot?'

'Not many,' said Forester off-handedly. 'But enough.' He propped himself up on one elbow and tried to make it sound good. 'You're killing Americans on the other side of those mountains, Coello. The American government is going to demand an explanation – an investigation.'

'So? There is an air crash – there have been many such crashes even in North America. Especially can they occur on such ill-run air lines as Andes Airlift, which, incidentally, is owned by one of your own countrymen. An obsolete aircraft with a drunken pilot – what more natural? There will be no bodies to send back to the United States, I assure you. Regrettable, isn't it?'

'You don't know the facts of life,' said Forester. 'My government is going to be very interested. Now, don't get me wrong; they're not interested in air crashes as such. But *I* was in that airplane and they're going to be goddam suspicious. There'll be an official investigation – Uncle Sam will goose the I.A.T.A. into making one – and there'll be a concurrent undercover investigation. This country will be full of operatives within a week – you can't stop them all and you can't hide all the evidence. The truth is going to come out and the U.S. government will be delighted to blow the lid off. Nothing would please them more.'

He coughed, sweating a little – now it had to sound really good. 'Now, there's a way round all that.' He sat up on the stretcher. 'Have you a cigarette?'

Coello's eyes narrowed as he picked up a cigarette-box from the desk and walked round to the stretcher. He offered the open box and said, 'Am I to understand that you're trying to bargain for your life?'

'You're dead right,' said Forester. He put a whine in his voice. 'I've no hankering to wear a wooden overcoat, and I know how you boys operate on captured prisoners.'

Thoughtfully Coello flicked his lighter and lit Forester's cigarette. 'Well?'

Forester said, 'Look, Colonel; supposing I was the only survivor of that crash – thrown clear by some miraculous chance. Then I could say that the crash was okay; that it was on the up-and-up. Why wouldn't they believe me? I'm one of their bright boys.'

Coello nodded. 'You are bright.' He smiled. 'What guarantee have we that you will do this for us?'

'Guarantee? You know damn well I can't give you one. But I tell you this, buddy-boy; you're not the boss round here – not by a long shot. And I'm stuffed full of information about the C.I.A. – operation areas, names, faces, addresses, covers – you ask for it, I've got it. And if your boss ever finds out that you've turned down a chance like this you're going to be in trouble. What have you got to lose? All you have to do is to put it to your boss and let him say "yes" or "no". If anything goes wrong he'll have to take the rap from higher up, but you'll be in the clear.'

Coello tapped his teeth with a fingernail. 'I think you're playing for time, Forester.' He thought deeply. 'If you can give me a sensible answer to the next question I might believe you. You say you are afraid of dying. If you are so afraid, why did you risk your life in coming over the pass?'

Forester thought of Peabody and laughed outright. 'Use your brains. I was being shot at over there by that god-dam bridge. Have you ever tried to talk reasonably with

someone who shoots at you if you bat an eyelid? But
you're not shooting at me, Colonel; I can talk to you.
Anyway, I reckoned it was a sight safer on the mountain
than down by the bridge – and I've proved it, haven't I?
I'm here and I'm still alive.'

'Yes,' said Coello pensively. 'You are still alive.' He
went to his desk. 'You might as well begin by proving
your goodwill immediately. We sent a reconnaissance
plane over to see what was happening and the pilot took
these photographs. What do you make of them?'

He tossed a sheaf of glossy photographs on to the foot
of the stretcher. Forester leaned over and gasped. 'Have a
heart, Colonel; I'm all bust up inside – I can't reach.'

Coello leaned over with a ruler and flicked them within his reach, and Forester fanned them out. They were
good; a little blurred because of the speed of the aircraft,
but still sharp enough to make out details. He saw the
bridge and a scattering of upturned faces, white blobs
against a grey background. And he saw the trebuchet. So
they'd got it down from the camp all right. 'Interesting,' he
said.

Coello leaned over. 'What is that?' he asked. 'Our experts
have been able to make nothing of it.' His finger was pointing at the trebuchet.

Forester smiled. 'I'm not surprised,' he said. 'There's a
nutcase over there; a guy called Armstrong. He conned the
others into building that gadget; it's called a trebuchet and
it's for throwing stones. He said the last time it was used was
when Cortes besieged Mexico City and then it didn't work
properly. It's nothing to worry about.'

'No?' said Coello. 'They nearly broke down the bridge
with it.'

Forester gave a silent cheer, but said nothing. He was
itching to pull out his gun and let Coello have it right where
it hurt most, but he would gain nothing by that – just a

bullet in the brain from the guard and no chance of doing anything more damaging.

Coello gathered the photographs together and tapped them on his hand. 'Very well,' he said. 'We will not shoot you – yet. You have possibly gained yourself another hour of life – perhaps much longer. I will consult my superior and let him decide what to do with you.'

He went to the door, then turned. 'I would not do anything foolish; you realize you are well guarded.'

'What the hell can I do?' growled Forester. 'I'm bust up inside and all strapped up; I'm as weak as a kitten and full of dope. I'm safe enough.'

When Coello closed the door behind him Forester broke out into a sweat. During the last half-hour Coello had nearly been relieved of the responsibility of him, for he had almost had a heart attack on three separate occasions. He hoped he had established the points he had tried to make; that he could be bought – something which might gain precious time; that he was too ill to move – Coello might get a shock on that one; and that Coello himself had nothing to lose by waiting a little – nothing but his life, Forester hoped.

He touched the butt of the gun and gazed out of the window. There was action about the Sabres on the apron; a truck had pulled up and a group of men in flying kit were getting out – three of them. They stood about talking for some time and then went to their aircraft and got settled in the cockpits with the assistance of the ground crew. Forester heard the whine of the engines as the starter truck rolled from one plane to another and, one by one, the planes slowly taxied forward until they went out of his sight.

He looked at the remaining Sabre. He knew nothing about the Cordilleran Air Force insignia, but the three stripes on the tail looked important. Perhaps the good

colonel was going to lead this strike himself; it would be just
his mark, thought Forester with animosity.

V

Ramón Sueguerra was the last person he would have
expected to be involved in a desperate enterprise involving
the overthrow of governments, thought McGruder, as he
made his devious way through the back streets of Altemiros
towards Sueguerra's office. What had a plump and comfortable merchant to do with revolution? Yet perhaps the Lopez
régime was hurting him more than most – his profits were
eaten up by bribes; his markets were increasingly more
restricted; and the fibre of his business slackened as the general economic level of the country sagged under the misrule
of Lopez. Not all revolutions were made by the starving pro-
letariat.

He came upon the building which housed the multitudinous activities of Sueguerra from the rear and entered by
the back door. The front door was, of course, impossible;
directly across the street was the post and telegraph office,
and McGruder suspected that the building would be occupied by men of Eighth Squadron. He went into Sueguerra's
office as he had always done – with a cheery wave to his
secretary – and found Sueguerra looking out of the window
which faced the street.

He was surprised to see McGruder. 'What brings you
here?' he asked. 'It's too early for chess, my friend.' A truck
roared in the street outside and his eyes flickered back to
the window and McGruder saw that he was uneasy and
worried.

'I won't waste your time,' said McGruder, pulling the
envelope from his pocket. 'Read this – it will be quicker
than my explanations.'

As Sueguerra read he sank into his chair and his face whitened. 'But this is incredible,' he said. 'Are you sure of this?'

'They took Forester and Rohde from the mission,' said McGruder. 'It was done by force.'

'The man Forester I do not know – but Miguel Rohde should have been here two days ago,' said Sueguerra. 'He is supposed to take charge in the mountains when . . .'

'When the revolution begins?'

Sueguerra looked up. 'All right – call it revolution if you will. How else can we get rid of Lopez?' He cocked his head to the street. 'This explains what is happening over there; I was wondering about that.'

He picked up a white telephone. 'Send in Juan.'

'What are you going to do?' asked McGruder.

Sueguerra stabbed his finger at the black telephone. 'That is useless, my friend, as long as the post office is occupied. And this local telephone exchange controls all the communications in our mountain area. I will send Juan, my son, over the mountains, but he has a long way to go and it will take time – you know what our roads are like.'

'It will take him four hours or more,' agreed McGruder.

'Still, I will send him. But we will take more direct action.' Sueguerra walked over to the window and looked across the street to the post office. 'We must take the post office.'

McGruder's head jerked up. 'You will fight Eighth Squadron?'

Sueguerra swung round. 'We must – there is more than telephones involved here.' He walked over to his desk and sat down. 'Doctor McGruder, we always knew that when the revolution came and if Eighth Squadron was stationed here, then Eighth Squadron would have to be removed from the game. But how to do it – that was the problem.'

He smiled slightly. 'The solution proved to be ridiculously easy. Colonel Rodriguez has mined all important installations on the airfield. The mines can be exploded electrically – and the wires lead from the airfield to Altemiros; they were installed under the guise of telephone cables. It just needs one touch on a plunger and Eighth Squadron is out of action.'

Then he thumped the desk and said savagely, 'An extra lead was supposed to be installed in my office this morning – as it is, the only way we can do it is to take the post office by force, because that is where the electrical connection is.'

McGruder shook his head. 'I'm no electrical engineer, but surely you can tap the wire *outside* the post office.'

'It was done by Fourteenth Squadron engineers in a hurry,' said Sueguerra. 'And they were pulled out when Eighth Squadron so unexpectedly moved in. There are hundreds of wires in the civil and military networks and no one knows which is the right one. But I know the right connection *inside* the post office – Rodriguez showed it to me.'

They heard the high scream of a jet as it flew over Altemiros from the airfield, and Sueguerra said, 'We must act quickly – Eighth Squadron must not be allowed to fly.'

He burst into activity and McGruder paled when he saw the extent of his preparations. Men assembled in his warehouses as though by magic and innocent tea-chests and bales of hides disgorged an incredible number of arms – both rifles and automatic weapons. The lines deepened in McGruder's face and he said to Sueguerra, 'I will not fight, you know.'

Sueguerra clapped him on the back. 'We do not need you – what is one extra man? And in any case we do not want a *norteamericano* involved. This is a home-grown revolution. But there may be some patching-up for you to do when this is over.'

But there was little fighting at the post office. The attack was so unexpected and in such overwhelming strength that the Eighth Squadron detachment put up almost no resistance at all, and the only casualty was a corporal who got a bullet in his leg because an inexperienced and enthusiastic amateur rifleman had left off his safety-catch.

Sueguerra strode into the post office. 'Jaime! Jaime! Where is that fool of an electrician? Jaime!'

'I'm here,' said Jaime, and came forward carrying a large box under his arm. Sueguerra took him into the main switch-room and McGruder followed.

'It's the third bank of switches – fifteenth from the right and nineteenth from the bottom,' said Sueguerra, consulting a scrap of paper.

Jaime counted carefully. 'That's it,' he said. 'Those two screw connections there.' He produced a screwdriver. 'I'll be about two minutes.'

As he worked a plane screamed over the town and then another and another. 'I hope we're not too late,' whispered Sueguerra.

McGruder put his hand on his arm. 'What about Forester and Rohde?' he said in alarm. 'They are at the airfield.'

'We do not destroy hospitals,' said Sueguerra. 'Only the important installations are mined – the fuel and ammunition dumps, the hangars, the runways, the control tower. We only want to immobilize them – they are Cordillerans, you know.'

Jaime said, 'Ready,' and Sueguerra lifted the plunger.

'It must be done,' he said, and abruptly pushed down hard.

VI

It seemed that Coello *was* leading the strike because the next time he entered the office he was in full flying kit, parachute pack and all. He looked sour. 'You have gained yourself more time, Forester. The decision on you will have to wait. I have other, more urgent, matters to attend to. However, I have something to show you – an educative demonstration.' He snapped his fingers and two soldiers entered and picked up the stretcher.

'What sort of a demonstration?' asked Forester as he was carried out.

'A demonstration of the dangers of lacking patriotism,' answered Coello, smiling. 'Something you may be accused of by *your* government one day, Mr Forester.'

Forester lay limply on the stretcher as it was carried out of the building and wondered what the hell was going on. The bearers veered across the apron in front of the control tower, past the single Sabre fighter, and Coello called to a mechanic, *'Diez momentos'.* The man saluted, and Forester thought, Ten minutes? Whatever it is, it won't take long.

He turned his head as he heard the whine of an aircraft taking off and saw a Sabre clearing the ground, its wheels retracting. Then there was another, and then the third. They disappeared over the horizon and he wondered where they were going – certainly in the wrong direction if they intended to strafe O'Hara.

The small party approached one of the hangars. The big sliding doors were closed and Coello opened the wicket door and went inside, the stretcher-bearers following. There were no aircraft in the hangar and their footfalls echoed hollowly in dull clangour from the metal walls. Coello went into a side room, waddling awkwardly in his flying gear, and motioned for the stretcher to be brought in. He saw the stretcher placed across two chairs, then told the soldiers to wait outside.

Forester looked up at him. 'What the hell is this?' he demanded.

'You will see,' said Coello calmly, and switched on the light. He went to the window and drew a cord and the curtains came across. 'Now then,' he said, and crossed the room to draw another cord and curtains parted on an internal window looking into the hangar. 'The demonstration will begin almost immediately,' he said, and cocked his head on one side as though listening for something.

Forester heard it too, and looked up. It was the banshee howl of a diving jet plane, growing louder and louder until it threatened to shatter the eardrums. With a shriek the plane passed over the hangar and Forester reckoned with professional interest that it could not have cleared the hangar roof by many feet.

'We begin,' said Coello, and indicated the hangar.

Almost as though the diving plane had been a signal, a file of soldiers marched into the hangar and stood in a line, an officer barking at them until they trimmed the rank. Each man carried a rifle at the slope and Forester began to have a prickly foreknowledge of what was to come.

He looked at Coello coldly and began to speak but the howling racket of another diving plane drowned his words. When the plane had gone he turned and saw with rage in his heart that Rohde was being dragged in.

He could not walk and two soldiers were half dragging, half carrying him, his feet trailing on the concrete floor. Coello tapped on the window with a pencil and the soldiers brought Rohde forward. His face was dreadfully battered, both eyes were turning black and he had bruised cheeks. But his eyes were open and he regarded Forester with a lacklustre expression and opened his mouth and said a few words which Forester could not hear. He had some teeth missing.

'You've beaten him up, you bastard,' exploded Forester.

Coello laughed. 'The man is a Cordilleran national, a traitor to his country, a conspirator against his lawful government. What do you do with traitors in the United States, Forester?'

'You hypocritical son-of-a-bitch,' said Forester with heat. 'What else are *you* doing but subverting the government?'

Coello grinned. 'That is different; *I* have not been caught. Besides, I regard myself as being on the right side – the stronger side is always right, is it not? We will crush all these puling, whining liberals like Miguel Rohde and Aguillar.' He bared his teeth. 'In fact, we will crush Rohde now – and Aguillar in not more than forty-five minutes.'

He waved to the officer in the hangar and the soldiers began to drag Rohde away. Forester began to curse Coello, but his words were destroyed in the quivering air as another plane dived on the hangar. He looked after the pitiful figure of Rohde and waited until it was quiet, then he said, 'Why are you doing this?'

'Perhaps to teach you a lesson,' said Coello lightly. 'Let this be a warning – if you cross us, this can happen to you.'

'But you're not too certain of your squadron, are you?' said Forester. 'You're going to shoot Rohde and your military vanity makes you relish a firing-squad, but you can't afford a public execution – the men of the squadron might not stand for it. I'm right, aren't I?'

Coello gestured irritably. 'Leave these mental probings to your bourgeois psychoanalysts.'

'And you've laid on a lot of noise to drown the shots,' persisted Forester as he heard another plane begin its dive.

Coello said something which was lost in the roar and Forester looked at him in horror. He did not know what to do. He could shoot Coello, but that would not help Rohde; there were more than a dozen armed men outside, and some were watching through the window. Coello laughed silently and pointed. When Forester could hear what he was saying, he shuddered. 'The poor fool cannot stand, he will be shot sitting down.'

'God damn you,' groaned out Forester. 'God damn your lousy soul to hell.'

A soldier had brought up an ordinary kitchen chair which he placed against the wall, and Rohde was dragged to it and seated, his stiff leg sticking out grotesquely in front of him. A noose of rope was tossed over his head and he was bound to the chair. The soldiers left him and the officer barked out a command. The firing-squad lifted their rifles as one man and aimed, and the officer lifted his arm in the air.

Forester looked on helplessly but with horrified fascination, unable to drag his eyes away. He talked loudly, directing a stream of vicious obscenities at Coello in English and Spanish, each one viler than the last.

Another Sabre started its dive, the hand of the officer twitched and, as the noise grew to its height, he dropped his arm sharply and there was a rippling flash along the line of men. Rohde jerked convulsively in the chair as the bullets slammed into him and his body toppled on one side, taking the chair with it. The officer drew his pistol and walked over to examine the body.

Coello pulled the drawstring and the curtains closed, shutting off the hideous sight. Forester snarled, *'Hijo de puta!'*

'It will do you no good calling me names,' said Coello. 'Although as a man of honour I resent them and will take the appropriate steps.' He smiled. 'Now I will tell you the reason for this demonstration. From your rather crude observations I gather you are in sympathy with the unfortunate Rohde – the late Rohde, I should say. I was instructed to give you this test by my superior and I regret to inform you that you have failed. I think you have proved that you were not entirely sincere in the offer you made earlier, so I am afraid that you must go the same way as Rohde.' His hand went to the pistol at his belt. 'And after you – Aguillar. He will come to his reckoning not long from now.' He began to draw the pistol. 'Really, Forester, you should have known better than to – '

His words were lost in the uproar of another diving Sabre and it was then that Forester shot him, very coldly and precisely, twice in the stomach. He did not pull out the gun, but fired through the coverlet.

Coello shouted in pain and surprise and put his hands to his belly, but nothing could be heard over the tremendous racket above. Forester shot him again, this time to kill, right through the heart, and Coello rocked back as the bullet hit him and fell against the desk, dragging the blotter and the inkwell to the floor with him. He stared up with blank eyes at the ceiling, seeming to listen to the departing aircraft.

Forester slid from the stretcher and went to the door, gun in hand. Softly he turned the key, locking himself in, then he cautiously parted the curtain and looked into the hangar. The file of men – the firing-squad – were marching out, followed by the officer, and two soldiers were throwing a piece of canvas over the body of Rohde.

Forester waited until they had gone, then went to the door again and heard a shuffling of feet outside. His personal guard was still there, waiting to take him to Coello's office or wherever Coello should direct. Something would have to be done about that.

He began to strip Coello's body, bending awkwardly in the mummy-like wrappings of tape which constricted him. His ribs hurt, but not very much, and his body seemed to glory in the prospect of action. The twitchiness had gone now that he was moving about and he blessed McGruder for that enlivening injection.

He and Coello were much of a size and the flying overalls and boots fitted well enough. He strapped on the parachute and then lifted Coello on to the stretcher, covering him with the sheet carefully so that the face could not be seen. Then he put on the heavy plastic flying helmet with the dangling oxygen mask, and picked up the pistol.

When he opened the door he appeared to be having some trouble with the fastenings of the mask, for he was fumbling with the straps, his hand and the mask obscuring his face. He gestured casually with the pistol he held in his other hand and said to the sentries, *'Vaya usted por allí,'* pointing to the other end of the hangar. His voice was very indistinct.

He was prepared to shoot it out if either of the soldiers showed any sign of suspicion and his finger was nervous on the trigger. The eyes of one of the men flicked momentarily to the room behind Forester, and he must have seen the shrouded body on the stretcher. Forester was counting on military obedience and the natural fear these men had for their officers. They had already witnessed one execution and if that mad dog, Coello, had held another, more private, killing, what was it to them?

The soldier clicked to attention. *'Si, mio Colonel,'* he said, and they both marched stiffly down to the end of the hangar. Forester watched them go out by the bottom door, then locked the office, thrust the pistol into the thigh pocket of the overalls and strode out of the hangar, fastening the oxygen mask as he went.

He heard the whistle of jet planes overhead and looked up to see three Sabres circling in tight formation. As he watched they broke off into a straight course, climbing eastward over the mountains. They're not waiting for Coello, he thought; and broke into a clumsy run.

The ground crew waiting by the Sabre saw him coming and were galvanized into action. As he approached he pointed to the departing aircraft and shouted, *'Rapidemente! Dése prisa!'* He ran up to the Sabre with averted face and scrambled up to the cockpit, being surprised when one of the ground crew gave him a boost from behind.

He settled himself before the controls and looked at them; they were familiar but at the same time strange through long absence. The starter truck was already plugged in, its crew looking up at him with expectant faces. Damn, he thought; I don't know the command routine in Spanish.

He closed his eyes and his hands went to the proper switches and then he waved.

Apparently that was good enough; the engine burst into noisy song and the ground crew ran to uncouple the starter cable. Another man tapped him on the helmet and closed the canopy and Forester waved again, indicating that the wheels should be unchocked. Then he was rolling, and he turned to taxi up the runway, coupling up the oxygen as he went.

At the end of the runway he switched on the radio, hoping that it was already netted in to the control tower; not that he wanted to obey any damned instructions they gave, but he wanted to know what was going on. A voice crackled in the headphones. 'Colonel Coello?'

'*Si*,' he mumbled.

'You are cleared for take-off.'

Forester grinned, and rammed the Sabre straight down the runway. His wheels were just off the ground when all hell broke loose. The runway seemed to erupt before him for its entire length and the Sabre staggered in the air. He went into a steep, climbing turn and looked down at the airfield in astonishment. The ground was alive with the deep red flashes of violent explosions and even as he watched, he saw the control tower shiver and disintegrate into a pile of rubble and a pillar of smoke coiled up to reach him.

He fought with the controls as a particularly violent eruption shivered the air, making the plane swerve drunkenly. 'Who's started the goddam war?' he demanded of no one in particular. There was just a nervous crackle in the earphones to answer him – the control tower had cut out.

He gave up the futile questioning. Whatever it was certainly did him no harm and Eighth Squadron looked as though it was hamstrung for a long time. With one last look at the amazing spectacle on the ground, he set the Sabre in a long climb to the westward and clicked switches on the radio, searching for the other three Sabres. Two channels were apparently not in use, but he got them on the third, carrying on an idle conversation and in total ignorance of the destruction of their base, having already travelled too far to have seen the debacle.

A sloppy, undisciplined lot, he thought; but useful. He looked down as he eavesdropped and saw the pass drifting below him, the place where he had nearly died, and decided that flying beat walking. Then he scanned the sky ahead, looking for the rest of the flight. From their talk he gathered that they were orbiting a pre-selected point while waiting for Coello and he wondered if they were already briefed on the operation or whether Coello had intended to brief them in flight. That might make a difference to his tactics.

At last he saw them orbiting the mountain by the side of the pass, but very high. He pulled gently on the control column and went to meet them. These were going to be three very surprised communists.

TEN

Armstrong heard trucks grinding up the mountain road. 'They're coming,' he said, and looked out over the breast-work of rock, his fingers curling round the butt of the gun.

The mist seemed to be thinning and he could see as far as the huts quite clearly and to where the road debouched on to the level ground; but there was still enough mist to halo the headlights even before the trucks came into view.

Benedetta ran up the tunnel and lay beside him. He said, 'You'd better get back; there's nothing you can do here.' He lifted the pistol. 'One bullet. That's all the fighting we can do.'

'They don't know that,' she retorted.

'How is your uncle?' he asked.

'Better, but the altitude is not good for him.' She hesitat-ed. 'I am not happy about Jenny; she is in a fever.'

He said nothing; what was a fever or altitude sickness when the chances were that they would all be dead within the hour? Benedetta said, 'We delayed them about three hours at the camp.'

She was not really speaking sense, just making inconse-quential noises to drown her own thoughts – and all her thoughts were of O'Hara. Armstrong looked at her sideways.

'I'm sorry to be pessimistic,' he said. 'But I think this is the last act. We've done very well considering what we had to fight with, but it couldn't go on for ever. Napoleon was right – God is on the side of the big battalions.'

Her voice was savage. 'We can still take some of them with us.' She grasped his arm. 'Look, they're coming.'

The first vehicle was breasting the top of the rise. It was quite small and Armstrong judged it was a jeep. It came forward, its headlights probing the mist, and behind it came a big truck, and then another. He heard shouted commands and the trucks rolled as far as the huts and stopped, and he saw men climbing out and heard the clatter of boots on rock.

The jeep curved in a great arc, its lights cutting a swathe like a scythe, and Armstrong suddenly realized that it was searching the base of the cliffs where the tunnels were. Before he knew it he was fully illuminated, and as he dodged back into cover, he heard the animal roar of triumph from the enemy as he was seen.

'Damn!' he said. 'I was stupid.'

'It does not matter,' Benedetta said. 'They would have found us soon.' She lay down and cautiously pulled a rock from the pile. 'I think I can see through here,' she whispered. 'There is no need to put your head up.'

Armstrong heard steps from behind as Willis came up. 'Keep down,' he said quietly. 'Flat on your stomach.'

Willis wriggled alongside him. 'What's going on?'

'They've spotted us,' said Armstrong. 'They're deploying out there; getting ready to attack.' He laughed humourlessly. 'If they knew what we had to defend ourselves with, they'd just walk in.'

'There's another truck coming,' said Benedetta bitterly. 'I suppose it's bringing more men; they need an army to crush us.'

'Let me see,' said Armstrong. Benedetta rolled away from the spy-hole and Armstrong looked through. 'It's got no lights – that's odd; and it's moving fast. Now it's changing direction and going towards the huts. It doesn't seem to be slowing down.'

They could hear the roar of the engine, and Armstrong yelled, 'It's going faster – it's going to smash into them.' His voice cracked on a scream. 'Do you think it could be O'Hara?'

O'Hara held tight to the jolting wheel and rammed the accelerator to the floorboards. He had been making for the jeep but then he had seen something much more important; in the light of the truck headlights a group of men were assembling a light machine-gun. He swung the wheel and the truck swerved, two wheels coming off the ground and then bouncing back with a spine-jolting crash. The truck swayed alarmingly, but he held it on its new course and switched on his lights and saw the white faces of men turn towards him and their hands go up to shield their eyes from the glare.

Then they were running aside but two of them were too late and he heard the squashy thumps as the front of the truck hit them. But he was not concerned with men – he wanted the gun – and the truck lifted a little as he drove the off-side wheels over the machine-gun, grinding it into the rock. Then he had gone past and there was a belated and thin scattering of shots from behind.

He looked for the jeep, hauled the wheel round again, and the careering truck swung and went forward like a projectile. The driver of the jeep saw him coming and tried to run for it; the jeep shot forward, but O'Hara swerved again and the jeep was fully illuminated as he made for a head-on crash. He saw the Russian point a pistol and there was a flash and the truck windscreen starred in front of his face. He ducked involuntarily.

The driver of the jeep swung his wheel desperately, but turned the wrong way and came up against the base of the cliff. The jeep spun again, but the mistake had given O'Hara his chance and he charged forward to ram the jeep broadside on. He saw the Russian throw up his arms and disappear from sight as the light vehicle was hurled on its side with a tearing and rending sound, and then O'Hara had slammed into reverse and was backing away.

He looked back towards the trucks and saw a mob of men running towards him, so he picked up the sub-machine-gun from the floor of the cab and he steadied it on the edge of the window. He squeezed the trigger three times, altering his aim slightly between bursts, and the mob broke up into fragments, individual men rolling on the open ground and desperately seeking cover.

As O'Hara engaged in bottom gear, a bullet tore through the body of the truck, and then another, but he took no notice. The front of the truck slammed into the overturned jeep again, catching it on the underside of the chassis. Remorselessly O'Hara pushed forward using the truck as a bulldozer and mashed the jeep against the cliff face with a dull crunching noise. When he had finished no human sounds came from the crushed vehicle.

But that act of anger and revenge was nearly the end of him. By the time he had reversed the truck and swung clear again he was under heavy fire. He rolled forward and tried to zigzag, but the truck was slow in picking up speed and a barrage of fire came from the semi-circle of men surrounding him. The windscreen shattered into opacity and he could not see where he was heading.

Benedetta, Armstrong and Willis were on their feet yelling, but no bullets came their way – they were not as dangerous as O'Hara. They watched the truck weaving drunkenly and saw sparks fly as steel-jacketed bullets ricocheted from the metal armour Santos had installed. Willis shouted, 'He's in trouble,' and before they could stop him he had vaulted the rock wall and was running for the truck.

O'Hara was steering with one hand and using the butt of the sub-machine-gun as a hammer in an attempt to smash the useless windscreen before him. Willis leaped on the running-board and just as his fingers grasped the edge of the door O'Hara was hit. A rifle bullet flew the width of the cab and smashed his shoulder, slamming him into the door and nearly upsetting Willis's balance. He gave a great cry and slumped down in his seat.

Willis grabbed the wheel with one hand, turned it awk-wardly. He shouted, 'Keep your foot on the accelerator,' and O'Hara heard him through a dark mist of pain and pushed down with his foot. Willis turned the truck towards the cliff and tried to head for the tunnel. He saw the rear view mir-ror disintegrate and he knew that the bullet that had hit it had passed between his body and the truck. That did not seem to matter – all that mattered was to get the truck into cover.

Armstrong saw the truck turn and head towards him. 'Run,' he shouted to Benedetta, and took to his heels, drag-ging her by the hand and making down the tunnel.

Willis saw the mouth of the tunnel yawn darkly before him and pressed closer to the body of the truck. As the nose of the truck hit the low wall, rocks exploded into the interior, splintering against the tunnel sides.

Then Willis was hit. The bullet took him in the small of the back and he let go of the wheel and the edge of the door. In the next instant, as the truck roared into the tunnel to crash at the bend, Willis was wiped off the running-board by the rock face and was flung in a crumpled heap to the ground just by the entrance.

He stirred slightly as a bullet clipped the rock just above his head and his hands groped forward helplessly, the fingers scrabbling at the cold rock. Then two bullets hit him almost simultaneously and he jerked once and was still.

II

It seemed enormously quiet as Armstrong and Benedetta dragged O'Hara from the cab of the truck. The shooting had stopped and there was no sound at all apart from the creakings of the cooling engine and the clatter as Armstrong kicked something loose on the floor of the cab. They were working in darkness because a well-directed shot straight down the tunnel would be dangerous.

At last they got O'Hara into safety round the corner and Benedetta lit the wick of the last paraffin bottle. O'Hara was unconscious and badly injured; his right arm hung limp and his shoulder was a ghastly mess of torn flesh and splintered bone. His face was badly cut too, because he had been thrown forward when the truck had crashed at the bend of the tunnel and Benedetta looked at him with tears in her eyes and wondered where to start.

Aguillar tottered forward, the breath wheezing in his chest, and said with difficulty, 'In the name of God, what has happened?'

'You cannot help, *tío*,' she said. 'Lie down again.' Aguillar looked down at O'Hara with shocked eyes – it was brought home to him that war is a bloody business. Then he said, 'Where is Señor Willis?'

'I think he's dead,' said Armstrong quietly. 'He didn't come back.'

Aguillar sank down silently next to O'Hara, his face grey. 'Let me help,' he said.

'I'll go back on watch,' said Armstrong. 'Though what use that will be I don't know. It'll be dark soon. I suppose that's what they're waiting for.'

He went away into the darkness towards the truck, and Benedetta examined O'Hara's shattered shoulder. She looked up at Aguillar helplessly. 'What can I do? This needs a doctor – a hospital; we cannot do anything here.'

'We must do what we can,' said Aguillar. 'Before he recovers consciousness. Bring the light closer.'

He began to pick out fragments of bone from the bloody flesh and by the time he had finished and Benedetta had bandaged the wound and put the arm in a sling O'Hara was wide awake, suppressing his groans. He looked up at Benedetta and whispered, 'Where's Willis?'

She shook her head slowly and O'Hara turned his face away. He felt a growing rage within him at the unfairness of things; just when he had found life again he must leave it – and what a way to leave; cooped up in a cold, dank tunnel at the mercy of human wolves. From nearby he could hear a woman babbling incoherently. 'Who is that?'

'Jenny,' said Benedetta. 'She is delirious.'

They made O'Hara as comfortable as possible and then Benedetta stood up. 'I must help Armstrong.' Aguillar looked up and saw that her face was taut with anger and fatigue, the skin drawn tightly over her cheekbones and dark smudges below her eyes. He sighed softly and nipped the guttering wick into darkness.

Armstrong was crouched by the truck. 'I was waiting for someone,' he said.

'Who were you expecting?' she said sarcastically. 'We two are the only able-bodied left.' Then she said in a low voice, 'I'm sorry.'

'That's all right,' said Armstrong. 'How's Tim?'

Her voice was bitter. 'He'll live – if he's allowed to.'

Armstrong said nothing for a long time, allowing the anger and frustration to seep from her, then he said, 'Everything's quiet; they haven't made a move and I don't understand it. I'd like to go up there and have a look when it gets really dark outside.'

'Don't be an idiot,' said Benedetta in alarm. 'What can a defenceless man do?'

'Oh, I wouldn't start anything,' said Armstrong. 'And I wouldn't be exactly defenceless. Tim had one of those little machine-guns with him, and I think there are some full magazines. I haven't been able to find out how it works in the dark; I think I'll go back and examine it in the light of our lamp. The crossbow is here, too; and a couple of bolts – I'll leave those here with you.'

She took his arm. 'Don't leave yet.'

He caught the loneliness and desolation in her voice and subsided. Presently he said, 'Who would have thought that Willis would do a thing like that? It was the act of a really brave man and I never thought he was that.'

'Who knows what lies inside a man?' said Benedetta softly, and Armstrong knew she was thinking of O'Hara.

He stayed with her a while and talked the tension out of her, then went back and lit the lamp. O'Hara looked across at him with pain-filled eyes. 'Has the truck had it?'

'I don't know,' said Armstrong. 'I haven't looked yet.'

'I thought we might make a getaway in it,' said O'Hara.

'I'll have a look at it. I don't think it took much damage from the knocks it had – those chaps had it pretty well armoured against our crossbow bolts. But I don't think the bullets did it any good; the armour wouldn't be proof against those.'

Aguillar came closer. 'Perhaps we might try in the darkness – to get away, I mean.'

'Where to?' asked Armstrong practically. 'They'll have the bridge covered – and I wouldn't like to take a truck across that at night – it would be suicidal. And they'll have plenty of light up here, too; they'll keep the entrance to the tunnel well covered.' He rubbed the top of his head. 'I don't know why they don't just come in and take us right now.'

'I think I killed the top man,' said O'Hara. 'I hope I did. And I don't think Santos has the stomach to push in here – he's scared of what he might meet.'

'Who is Santos?' asked Aguillar.

'The Cuban.' O'Hara smiled weakly. 'I got pretty close to him down below.'

'You did a lot of damage when you came up in the truck,' observed Armstrong. 'I don't wonder they're scared. Maybe they'll give up.'

'Not now,' said O'Hara with conviction. 'They're too close to success to give up now. Anyway, all they have to do now is to camp outside and starve us out.'

They were silent for a long time thinking about that, then Armstrong said, 'I'd rather go down in glory.' He pulled forward the sub-machine-gun. 'Do you know how this thing works?'

O'Hara showed him how to work the simple mechanism, and when he had gone back to his post Aguillar said, 'I am sorry about your shoulder, señor.'

O'Hara bared his teeth in a brief grin. 'Not as sorry as I am – it hurts like the devil. But it doesn't matter, you know; I'm not likely to feel pain for long.'

Aguillar's asthmatical wheezing stopped momentarily as he caught his breath. 'Then you think this is the end?'

'I do.'

'A pity, señor. I could have made much use of you in the new Cordillera. A man in my position needs good men – they are as hard to find as the teeth of a hen.'

'What use would a broken-down pilot be to you? Men like me come ten a penny.'

'I do not think so,' said Aguillar seriously. 'You have shown much initiative in this engagement and that is a commodity which is scarce. As you know, the military forces of Cordillera are rotten with politics and I need men to lift them out of the political arena – especially the fighter squadrons. If you wish to stay in Cordillera, I think I can promise you a position in the Air Force.'

For a moment O'Hara forgot that the hours – and perhaps minutes – of his life were measured. He said simply, 'I'd like that.'

'I'm glad,' said Aguillar. 'Your first task would be to straighten out Eighth Squadron. But you must not think that because you are marrying into the President's family that the way will be made easy for you.' He chuckled as he felt O'Hara start. 'I know my niece very well, Tim. Never has she felt about a man as she feels about you. I hope you will be very happy together.'

'We will be,' said O'Hara, then fell silent as reality flooded upon him once more – the realization that all this talk of marriage and future plans was futile. After a while, he said wistfully, 'These are pipe dreams, Señor Aguillar; reality is much more frightening. But I do wish . . .'

'We are still alive,' said Aguillar. 'And while the blood runs in a man nothing is impossible for him.'

He said nothing more and O'Hara heard only the rasping of his breath in the darkness.

III

When Armstrong joined Benedetta he looked towards the entrance of the tunnel and saw that night had fallen and there was a bright glare of headlamps flooding the opening. He strained his eyes and said, 'The mist seems to be thickening, don't you think?'

'I think so,' said Benedetta listlessly.

'Now's the time to scout around,' he said.

'Don't,' Benedetta implored him. 'They'll see you.'

'I don't think they can; the mist is throwing the light back at them. They'd see me if I went outside, but I don't intend to do that. I don't think they can see a damned thing in the tunnel.'

'All right, then. But be careful.'

He smiled as he crawled forward. In their circumstances the word 'careful' seemed ridiculous. It was like telling a man who had jumped from an aeroplane without a parachute to be careful. All the same, he was most careful to make no noise as he inched his way towards the entrance, hampered by the shattered remnants of the rock wall.

He stopped some ten yards short of the opening, knowing that to go farther would be too risky, and peered into the misty brightness. At first he could see nothing, but by shielding his eyes from the worst of the glare he managed to pick out some details. Two trucks were parked at an angle to the cliff, one on each side of the tunnel, and when the light from the left truck flickered he knew someone had walked in front of it.

He stayed there for some time and twice he made deliberate movements, but it was as he thought – he could not be seen. After a while he began to crawl about gathering rocks, which he built up into a low wall, barely eighteen inches high. It was not much but it would give solid protection against rifle fire to anyone lying behind it. This took him a long time and there was no action from outside; occasionally he heard a man coughing, and sometimes the sound of voices, but apart from that there was nothing.

Eventually he picked up the sub-machine-gun and went back to the truck. Benedetta whispered from the darkness, 'What are they doing?'

'Damned if I know,' he said, and looked back. 'It's too quiet out there. Keep a good watch; I'm going to have a look at the truck.'

He squeezed her hand and then groped his way to the cab of the truck and climbed inside. Everything seemed to be all right, as far as he could judge, barring the windscreen which could not be seen through. He sat in the driving-seat and thought about what would happen if they had to make a break for it.

To begin with, he would be driving – there was no one else who could handle the truck – and he would have to reverse out of the tunnel. There would be one man in the passenger seat beside him and the others in the back.

He examined the rest of the truck, more by feel than sight. Two of the tyres had been badly scored by bullets but miraculously the inner tubes had not been penetrated. The petrol tanks, too, were intact, protected by the deep skirts of mild steel, added to guard against crossbow bolts.

He had fears about the radiator, but a groping journey under the truck revealed no fatal drip of water and he was reassured about that. His only worries were that the final crash might have damaged the steering or the engine, but those could not be tested until the time came to go. He did not want to start the engine now – let sleeping dogs lie, he thought.

He rejoined Benedetta. 'That's that,' he said with satisfaction. 'She seems to be in good fettle. I'll take over here. You'd better see how the others are.'

She turned immediately, and he knew she was eager to get back to O'Hara.

'Wait a minute,' he said. 'You'd better know the drill if we have to make a sudden move.' He lifted the gun. 'Can you use this?'

'I don't know.'

Armstrong chuckled. 'I don't know if I can, either – it's too modern for me. But O'Hara reckons it's easy enough; you just pull the trigger and let her go. He says it takes a bit of holding down and you must be careful to slip off the safety-catch. Now, I'll be driving, with your uncle sitting next to me on the floor of the cab. Tim and Jenny will be in the back, flat on the floor. And there'll be you in the back, too – with this gun. It'll be a bit dangerous – you'll have to show yourself if you shoot.'

Her voice was stony. 'I'll shoot.'

'Good girl,' he said, and patted her on the shoulder. 'Give Tim my love when you give him yours.' He heard her go, then moved up the tunnel to the wall he had built and lay behind it, the sub-machine-gun ready to hand. He put his hand in his pocket and felt for his pipe, then uttered a muffled 'Damn!' It was broken, the two pieces separate in his hand. He put the stem in his mouth and chewed on the mouthpiece, never taking his eyes from the entrance.

IV

The day dawned mistily, a dazzling whiteness at the mouth of the tunnel, and Armstrong shifted his position for the hundredth time, trying to find a place to ease his aching bones. He glanced across at O'Hara on the other side of the tunnel and thought, it's worse for him than for me.

When O'Hara had heard of the rebuilt wall he had insisted on moving there. 'I haven't a hope of sleep,' he said. 'Not with this shoulder. And I've got a fully loaded pistol. I might as well stand – or lie – sentry out there as just lie here. I should be of some use, even if only to allow everyone else to get some sleep.'

But in spite of that Armstrong had not slept. He ached too much to sleep, even though he felt more exhausted than ever before in his life, but he smiled cheerily at O'Hara in the growing light and lifted his head above the low barricade.

There was nothing to be seen except the white swirling mist, an impenetrable curtain. He said softly, 'Tim, why didn't they jump us in the night?'

'They know we have this gun,' said O'Hara. 'I wouldn't like to come running into this tunnel knowing that – especially at night.'

'Um,' said Armstrong in an unconvinced tone. 'But why haven't they tried to soften us up with rifle fire? They must know that any fire directed into this tunnel will ricochet from the walls – they don't have to be too accurate.'

O'Hara was silent, and Armstrong continued reflectively: 'I wonder if there *is* anyone out there?'

'Don't be a damn' fool,' said O'Hara. 'That's something we can't take a chance on – not yet. Besides, there was someone to turn the lights off not very long ago.'

'True,' said Armstrong, and turned as he heard a movement in the tunnel, and Benedetta crawled up holding a bundle in her arms.

'The last of the food,' she said. 'There's not much – and we have no water at all.'

Armstrong's mouth turned down. 'That's bad.'

As he and O'Hara shared the food they heard a stirring outside and the murmur of voices. 'Changing the guard,' said O'Hara. 'I heard it before about four hours ago when you were asleep. They're still there, all right.'

'Me! Asleep!' said Armstrong in an aggrieved voice. 'I didn't sleep a wink all night.'

O'Hara smiled. 'You got three or four winks out of the forty.' He became serious. 'If we really need water we can drain some from the truck radiator, but I wouldn't do that unless absolutely necessary.'

Benedetta regarded O'Hara with worry in her eyes. He had a hectic flush and looked too animated for a man who had nearly been shot to death. Miss Ponsky had had the same reaction, and now she was off her head with delirium, unable to eat and crying for water. She said, 'I think we ought to have water now; Jenny needs it.'

'In that case we'll tap the radiator,' said Armstrong. 'I hope the anti-freeze compound isn't poisonous; I think it's just alcohol, so it should be all right.'

He crawled back with Benedetta and squeezed underneath the truck to unscrew the drain-cock. He tapped out half a can of rusty-looking water and passed it to her. 'That will have to do,' he said. 'We can't take too much – we might need the truck.'

The day wore on and nothing happened. Gradually the mist cleared under the strengthening sun and then they could see out of the tunnel, and Armstrong's hopes were shattered as he saw a group of men standing by the huts. Even from their restricted view they could see that the enemy was in full strength.

'But can they see us?' mused O'Hara. 'I don't think they can. This cavern must look as dark as the Black Hole of Calcutta from outside.'

'What the devil are they doing?' asked Armstrong, his eyes level with the top of a rock.

O'Hara watched for a long time, then he said in wonder, 'They're piling rocks on the ground – apart from that they're doing nothing.'

They watched for a long time and all the enemy did was to pile stones in a long line stretching away from the tunnel. After a while they appeared to tire of that and congregated into small groups, chatting and smoking. They seemed to have the appearance of men waiting for something, but why they were waiting or what the rocks were for neither O'Hara nor Armstrong could imagine.

It was midday when Armstrong, his nerves cracking under the strain, said, 'For God's sake, let's do something – something constructive.'

O'Hara's voice was flat and tired. 'What?'

'If we're going to make a break in the truck we might have to do it quickly. I suggest we put Jenny in the back of the truck right away, and get the old man settled in the front seat. Come to think of it, he'll be a damn sight more comfortable on a soft seat.'

O'Hara nodded. 'All right. Leave that sub-machine-gun with me. I might need it.'

Armstrong went back to the truck, walking upright. To hell with crawling on my belly like a snake, he thought; let me walk like a man for once. The enemy either did not see or saw and did not care. No shots were fired.

He saw Miss Ponsky safely into the back of the truck and then he escorted Aguillar to the cab. Aguilar was in a bad way, much worse than he had been. His speech was incoherent and his breathing was bad; he was in a daze and did not appear to know where he was. Benedetta was pale and worried and stayed to look after him.

When Armstrong dropped behind the rock wall, he said, 'If we don't get out of here soon that bloody crowd will have won.'

O'Hara jerked his head in surprise. 'Why?'

'Aguillar – he looks on the verge of a heart attack; if he doesn't get down to where he can breathe more easily he'll peg out.'

O'Hara looked outside and gestured with his good arm. 'There are nearly two dozen men within sight; they'd shoot hell out of us if we tried to break out now. Look at what happened to me yesterday when they were hampered by mist – there's no mist now and we wouldn't stand a chance. We'll have to wait.'

So they waited – and so did the enemy. And the day went on, the sun sloping back overhead into mid-afternoon. It was three o'clock when O'Hara stirred and then relaxed and shook his head. 'I thought. . . but no.'

He settled himself down, but a moment later his head jerked up again. 'It *is* – can't you hear it?'

'Hear what?' asked Armstrong.

'A plane – or planes,' said O'Hara excitedly.

Armstrong listened and caught the shrill whine of a jet plane passing overhead, the noise muffled and distorted. 'By God, you're right,' he said. He looked at O'Hara in sudden consternation. 'Ours or theirs?'

But O'Hara had already seen their doom. He leaned up and looked, horrified, to the mouth of the tunnel. Framed in the opening against the sky was a diving plane coming head on and, as he watched, he saw something drop from each wing, and a spurt of vapour.

'Rockets!' he screamed. 'For Christ's sake, get down!'

V

Forester had climbed to meet the three Sabres and as he approached they saw him and fell into a loose formation and awaited him. He came in from behind and increased speed, getting the leader in his sights. He flicked off the safety switches and his thumb caressed the firing-button. This boy would never know what hit him.

All the time there was a continual jabber in his earphones as the leader called Coello. At last, assuming that Coello's radio was at fault, he said, 'Since you are silent, *mio Colonel*, I will lead the attack.' It was then that Forester knew that these men had been briefed on the ground – and he pressed the firing-button.

Once again he felt the familiar jolt in the air, almost a halt, and saw the tracer shells streaking and corkscrewing towards their target. The leading Sabre was a-dance with coruscations of light as the shells burst, and suddenly it blew up in a gout of black smoke with a red heart at the centre.

Forester weaved to avoid wreckage and then went into a sharp turn and climbed rapidly, listening to the horrified exclamations from the other pilots. They babbled for a few moments then one of them said, 'Silence. I will take him.'

Forester searched the skies and thought – he's quick off the mark. He felt chilled; these boys would be young and have fast reflexes and they would be trained to a hair. He had not flown for nearly ten years, beyond the few annual hours necessary to keep up his rating, and he wondered grimly how long he would last.

He found his enemies. One was swooping in a graceful dive towards the ground and the other was climbing in a wide circle to get behind him. As he watched, the pilot fired his rockets aimlessly. 'Oh, no, you don't, you bastard,' said Forester. 'You don't catch me like that.' He knew his opponent had jettisoned his rockets in order to reduce weight and drag and to gain speed. For a moment he was tempted to do the same and to fight it out up there in the clean sky, but he knew he could not take the chance. Besides he had a better use for his rockets.

Instead, he pushed the control column forward and went into a screaming dive. This was dangerous – his opponent would be faster in the dive and it had been drilled into Forester never, *never* to lose height while in combat. He kept his eyes on the mirror and soon the Sabre came into view behind, catching up fast. He waited until the very last moment, until he was sure he was about to be fired on, then pushed the stick forward again and went into a suicidal vertical dive.

His opponent overshot him, taken unaware by the craziness of this manoeuvre performed so near the ground. Forester ignored him, confident that he had lost him for the time being; he was more concerned with preventing his plane from splattering itself all over the mountainside. He felt juddering begin as the Sabre approached the sound barrier; the whole fabric of the plane groaned as he dragged it out of the dive and he hoped the wings would not come off.

By the time he was flying level the ground was a scant two hundred feet below, snow and rock merging together in a grey blur. He lifted the Sabre up a few hundred feet and circled widely away from the mountains, looking for the gorge and the bridge. He spotted the gorge immediately – it was too unmistakable to be missed, and a minute later he saw the bridge. He turned over it, scanning the ground, but saw no one, and then it was gone behind and he lifted up to the slope of the mountain, flying over the winding road he had laboriously tramped so often.

Abruptly he changed course, wanting to approach the mine parallel to the mountainside, and as he did so he looked up and saw a Sabre a thousand feet higher, launching two rockets. That's the second one, he thought. I was too late.

He turned again and screamed over the mine, the airstrip unwinding close below. Ahead were the huts and some trucks and a great arrow made of piled rocks pointing to the cliff face. And at the head of the arrow a boiling cloud of smoke and dust where the rockets had driven home into the cliff. 'Jesus!' he said involuntarily, 'I hope they survived that.'

Then he had flashed over and went into a turn to come back. Come back he did with an enemy hammering on his heels. The Sabre he had eluded high in the sky had found him again and its guns were already crackling. But the range was too great and he knew that the other pilot, tricked before, was now waiting for him to play some other trick. This sign of inexperience gave him hope, but the other Sabre was faster and he must drop his rockets.

He had seen a good, unsuspecting target, yet to hit it he would have to come in on a smooth dive and stood a good chance of being hit by his pursuer. His lips curled back over his teeth and he held his course, sighting on the trucks and the huts and the group of men standing in their shelter. With one hand he flicked the rocket-arming switches and then fired, almost in the same instant.

The salvo of rockets streaked from under his wings, spearing down towards the trucks and the men who were looking up and waving. At the last moment, when they saw death coming from the sky, they broke and ran – but it was too late. Eight rockets exploded among them and as Forester roared overhead he saw a three-ton truck heave bodily into the air to fall on its side. He laughed out loud; a rocket that would stop a tank dead in its tracks would certainly shatter a truck.

The Sabre felt more handy immediately the rockets were gone and he felt the increase in speed. He put the nose down and screamed along the airstrip at zero feet, not looking back to see the damage he had done and striving to elude his pursuer by flying as low as he dared. At the end of the runway he dipped even lower over the wreckage of the Dakota and skidded in a frantic sideslip round the mountainside.

He looked in the mirror and saw his opponent take the corner more widely and much higher. Forester grinned; the bastard hadn't dared to come down on the deck and so he couldn't bring his guns to bear and he'd lost distance by his wide turn. Now to do him.

He fled up the mountainside parallel with the slope and barely twenty feet from the ground. It was risky, for there were jutting outcrops of rock which stretched out black fangs to tear out the belly of the Sabre if he made the slightest miscalculation. During the brief half-minute it took to reach clear sky, sweat formed on his forehead.

Then he was free of the mountain, and his enemy stooped to make his kill, but Forester was expecting it and went into a soaring vertical climb with a quick roll on top of the loop and was heading away in the opposite direction. He glanced back and grinned in satisfaction; he had tested the enemy and found him wanting – that young man would not take risks and Forester knew he could take him, so he went in for the kill.

It was brief and brutal. He turned to meet the oncoming plane and made as though to ram deliberately. At the closing speed of nearly fifteen hundred miles an hour the other pilot flinched as Forester knew he would, and swerved aside. By the time he had recovered Forester was on his tail and the end was mercifully quick – a sharp burst from the cannons at minimum range and the inevitable explosion in mid-air. Again Forester swerved to avoid wreckage. As he climbed to get his bearings, he reflected that battle experience still counted for a lot and the assessment of personality for still more.

VI

Armstrong was deaf; the echoes of that vast explosion still rumbled in the innermost recesses of the tunnel but he did not hear them. Nor could he see much because of the coils of dust which thickened the air. His hands were vainly clutching the hard rock of the tunnel floor as he pressed himself to the ground and his mind felt shattered.

It was O'Hara who recovered first. Finding himself still alive and able to move, he raised his head to look at the tunnel entrance. Light showed dimly through the dust. He missed, he thought vacantly; the rockets missed – but not by much. Then he shook his head to clear it and stumbled across to Armstrong who was still grovelling on the ground. He shook him by the shoulder. 'Back to the truck,' he shouted. 'We've got to get out. He won't miss the second time round.'

Armstrong lifted his head and gazed at O'Hara dumbly, and O'Hara pointed back to the truck and made a dumb show of driving. He got to his feet shakily and followed O'Hara, still feeling his head ringing from the violence of the explosion.

O'Hara yelled, 'Benedetta – into the truck.' He saw her in and handed her the sub-machine-gun, then climbed in himself with her aid and lay down next to Miss Ponsky. Outside he heard the scream of a jet going by and a series of explosions in the distance. He hoped that Armstrong was in a condition to drive.

Armstrong climbed into the cab and felt the presence of Aguillar in the next seat. 'On the floor,' he said, pushing him down, and then his attention was wholly absorbed by the task before him. He pressed the starter-button and the starter whined and groaned. He stabbed it again and again until, just as he was giving up hope, the engine fired with a coughing roar.

Putting the gears into reverse, he leaned out of the cab and gazed back towards the entrance and let out the clutch. The truck bumped backwards clumsily and scraped the side wall. He hauled on the wheel and tried to steer a straight course for the entrance – as far as he could tell the steering had not been damaged and it did not take long to do the fifty yards. Then he stopped just short of the mouth of the tunnel in preparation for the dash into the open.

Benedetta gripped the unfamiliar weapon in her hands and held it ready, crouching down in the back of the truck. O'Hara was sitting up, a pistol in his good hand; he knew that if he lay down he would have difficulty in getting up again – he could only use one arm for leverage. Miss Ponsky was mercifully unaware of what was going on; she babbled a little in her stupor and then fell silent as the truck backed jerkily into the open and turned.

O'Hara heard Armstrong battering at the useless wind-screen and prepared himself for a fusillade of rifle fire.

Nothing came and he looked round and what he saw made him blink incredulously. It was a sight he had seen before but he had not expected to see it here. The huts and trucks were shattered and wrecked and bodies lay about them. From a wounded man there came a mournful keening and there were only two men left on their feet, staggering about blindly and in a daze. He looked the awful scene over with a professional eye and knew that an aircraft had fired a ripple of eight rockets at this target, blasting it thoroughly.

He yelled, 'Armstrong – get the hell out of here while we can,' then sagged back and grinned at Benedetta. 'One of those fighter boys made a mistake and hammered the wrong target; he's going to get a strip torn off him when he gets back to base.'

Armstrong smashed enough of the windscreen away so that he could see ahead, then put the truck into gear and went forward, turning to go past the huts and down the road. He looked in fascinated horror at the wreckage until it was past and then applied himself to the task of driving an unfamiliar and awkward vehicle down a rough mountain road with its multitude of hairpin bends. As he went, he heard a jet plane whine overhead very low and he tensed, waiting for the slam of more explosions, but nothing happened and the plane went out of hearing.

Above, Forester saw the truck move off. One of them still left, he thought; and dived, his thumb ready on the firing-button. At the last moment he saw the streaming hair of a woman standing in the back and hastily removed his thumb as he screamed over the truck. My God, that was Benedetta – they've got themselves a truck.

He pulled the Sabre into a climb and looked about. He had not forgotten the third plane and hoped it had been scared off because a strange lassitude was creeping over him and he knew that the effects of McGruder's stimulant were wearing off. He tried to ease the ache in his chest while circling to keep an eye on the truck as it bounced down the mountain road.

O'Hara looked up at the circling Sabre. 'I don't know what to make of that chap,' he said. 'He must know we're here, but he's doing nothing about it.'

'He must think we're on his side,' said Benedetta. 'He must think that of anyone in a truck.'

'That sounds logical,' O'Hara agreed. 'But someone did a good job of working over our friends up on top and it wasn't a mistake an experienced pilot would make.' He winced as the truck jolted his shoulder. 'We'd better prepare to pile out if he shows signs of coming in to strafe us. Can you arrange signals with Armstrong?'

Benedetta turned and hung over the side, craning her neck to see Armstrong at the wheel. 'We might be attacked from the air,' she shouted. 'How can we stop you?'

Armstrong slowed for a nasty corner. 'Thump like hell on top of the cab – I'll stop quick enough. I'm going to stop before we get to the camp, anyway; there might be someone laying for us down there.'

Benedetta relayed this to O'Hara and he nodded. 'A pity I can't use that thing,' he said, indicating the sub-machine-gun. 'If you have to shoot, hold it down; it kicks like the devil and you'll find yourself spraying the sky if you aren't careful.'

He looked up at her. The wind was streaming her black hair and moulding the tattered dress to her body. She was cradling the sub-machine-gun in her hands and looking up at the plane and he thought in sudden astonishment, My God, a bloody Amazon – she looks like a recruiting poster for partisans. He thought of Aguillar's offer of an Air Force commission and had a sudden and irrational conviction that they would come through this nightmare safely.

Benedetta threw up her hand and cried in a voice of despair, 'Another one – another plane.'

O'Hara jerked his head and saw another Sabre curving overhead much higher and the first Sabre going to join it. Benedetta said bitterly, 'Always they must hunt in packs – even when they know we are defenceless.'

But O'Hara, studying the manoeuvring of the two aircraft with a war-experienced eye, was not sure about that. 'They're going to fight,' he said with wonder. 'They're jockeying for position. By God, they're going to fight each other.' His raised and incredulous voice was sharply punctuated by the distant clatter of automatic cannon.

Forester had almost been caught napping. He had only seen the third enemy Sabre when it was much too close for comfort and he desperately climbed to get the advantage of height. As it was, the enemy fired first and there was a thump and a large, ragged hole magically appeared in his wing as a cannon shell exploded. He side-slipped evasively, then drove his plane into a sharp, climbing turn.

Below, O'Hara yelled excitedly and thumped with his free hand on the side of the cab. 'Forester and Rohde – they've got across the mountain – they must have.'

The truck jolted to a sudden stop and Armstrong shot out of the cab like a startled jack-rabbit and dived into the side of the road. From the other side Aguillar stepped down painfully into the road and was walking away slowly when he heard the excited shouts from the truck. He turned and then looked upwards to the embattled Sabres.

The fight was drifting westward and presently the two aircraft disappeared from sight over the mountain, leaving only the white inscription of vapour trails in the blue sky. Armstrong came up to the side of the truck. 'What the devil's happening?' he asked with annoyance. 'I got the fright of my life when you thumped on the cab.'

'I'm damned if I know,' said O'Hara helplessly. 'But some of these planes seem to be on our side; a couple are having a dogfight now.' He threw out his arm. 'Look, here they come again.'

The two Sabres were much lower as they came in sight round the mountain, one in hot pursuit of the other. There was a flickering on the wings of the rear plane as the cannon hammered and suddenly a stream of oily smoke burst from the leading craft. It dropped lower and a black speck shot upwards. 'He's bailed out,' said O'Hara. 'He's had it.'

The pursuing Sabre pulled up in a climb, but the crippled plane settled into a steepening dive to crash on the mountainside. A pillar of black, greasy smoke marked the wreck and a parachute, suddenly opened, drifted across the sky like a blown dandelion seed.

Armstrong looked up and watched the departing victor which was easing into a long turn, obviously intent on coming back. 'That's all very well,' he said worriedly. 'But who won – us or them?'

'Everyone out,' said O'Hara decisively. 'Armstrong, give Benedetta a hand with Jenny.'

But they had no time, for suddenly the Sabre was upon them, roaring overhead in a slow roll. O'Hara, who was cradling Miss Ponsky's head with his free arm, blew out his breath expressively. 'Our side seems to have won that one,' he said. 'But I'd like to know who the hell our side is.' He watched the Sabre coming back, dipping its wings from side to side. 'Of course, it *couldn't* be Forester – that's impossible. A pity. He always wanted to become an ace, to make his fifth kill.'

The plane dipped and turned as it came over again and headed down the mountain and presently they heard cannon-fire again. 'Everyone in the truck,' commanded O'Hara. 'He's shooting up the camp – we'll have no trouble there. Armstrong, you get going and don't stop for a damned thing until we're on the other side of the bridge.' He laughed delightedly. 'We've got air cover now.'

They pressed on and passed the camp. There was a fiercely burning truck by the side of the road, but no sign of anyone living. Half an hour later they approached the bridge and Armstrong drew to a slow halt by the abutments, looking about him anxiously. He heard the Sabre going over again and was reassured, so he put the truck into gear and slowly inched his way on to the frail and unsubstantial structure.

Overhead, Forester watched the slow progress of the truck as it crossed the bridge. He thought there was a wind blowing down there because the bridge seemed to sway and shiver, but perhaps it was only his tired eyes playing tricks. He cast an anxious eye on his fuel gauges and decided it was time to put the plane down – and he hoped he could put it down in one piece. He felt desperately tired and his whole body ached.

Making one last pass at the bridge to make sure that all was well, he headed away following the road, and had gone only a few miles when he saw a convoy of vehicles coming up, some of them conspicuously marked with the RedCross. So that's that, he thought; McGruder got through and someone got on the phone to this side of the mountains and stirred things up. It couldn't possibly be another batch of communists – what would they want with ambulances?

He lifted his eyes and looked ahead for flat ground and a place to land.

Aguillar watched Armstrong's face lighten as the wheels of the truck rolled off the bridge and they were at last on the other side of the river. So many good people, he thought; and so many good ones dead – the Coughlins, Señor Willis – Miss Ponsky so dreadfully wounded and O'Hara also. But O'Hara would be all right; Benedetta would see to that. He smiled as he thought of them, of all the years of their future happiness. And then there were the others, too – Miguel and the two Americans, Forester and Peabody. The State of Cordillera would honour them all – yes, even Peabody, and especially Miguel Rohde.

It would be much later that he heard of what had happened to Peabody – and to Rohde.

O'Hara looked at Miss Ponsky. 'Will she be all right?'

'The wound is clean – not as bad as yours, Tim. A hospital will do you both a lot of good.' Benedetta fell silent.

'What will you do now?'

'I suppose I should go back to San Croce to hand my resignation to Filson – and to punch him on the nose, too – but I don't think I will. He's not worth it, so I won't bother.'

'You are returning to England, then?' She seemed despondent.

O'Hara smiled. 'A future President of a South American country has offered me an interesting job. I think I might stick around if the pay is good enough.'

He gasped as Benedetta rushed into his one-armed embrace. 'Ouch! Careful on this shoulder! And for God's sake, drop that damned gun – you might cause an accident.'

Armstrong was muttering to himself in a low chant and Aguillar turned his head. 'What did you say, señor?'

Armstrong stopped and laughed. 'Oh, it's something about a medieval battle; rather a famous one where the odds were against winning. Shakespeare said something about it which I've been trying to remember – he's not my line, really; he's weak on detail but he gets the spirit all right. It goes something like this.' He lifted his voice and declaimed:

'"He that shall live this day, and see old age,
Will yearly on the vigil feast his neighbours,
And say, To-morrow is Saint Crispin's.
Then will he strip his sleeve and show his scars,
And say, These wounds I had on Crispin's day.
Old men forget; yet all shall be forgot,
But he'll remember with advantages
What feats he did that day . . .
We few, we happy few."'

He fell silent and after a few minutes gave a low chuckle. 'I think Jenny Ponsky will be able to teach that very well when she returns to her school. Do you think *she'll* "strip her sleeve and show her scars"?'

The truck lurched down the road towards freedom.

LANDSLIDE

ONE

I was tired when I got off the bus at Fort Farrell. No matter how soft the suspension of the bus and how comfortable the seat you still feel as though you've been sitting on a sack of rocks for a few hours, so I was tired and not very impressed by my first view of Fort Farrell – *The Biggest Little City in the North-Eastern Interior* – or so the sign said at the city limits. Someone must have forgotten Dawson Creek.

This was the end of the line for the bus and it didn't stay long. I got off, nobody got on, and it turned and wheeled away back towards the Peace River and Fort St John, back towards civilization. The population of Fort Farrell had been increased by one – temporarily.

It was mid-afternoon and I had time to do the one bit of business that would decide if I stayed in this backwoods metropolis, so instead of looking for a hotel I checked my bag at the depot and asked where I could find the Matterson Building. The little fat guy who appeared to be the factotum around the depot looked at me with a twinkle in his eye and tittered. 'You must be a stranger round here.'

'Seeing I just got off the bus it may be possible,' I conceded. I wanted to get information, not to give it.

He grunted and the twinkle disappeared. 'It's on King Street; you can't miss it unless you're blind,' he said curtly.

He was another of those cracker-barrel characters who think they've got the franchise on wisecracks – small towns are full of them. To hell with him! I was in no mood for making friends, although I would have to try to influence people pretty soon.

High Street was the main drag, running as straight as though it had been drawn by a rule. Not only was it the main street but it was practically the only street of Fort Farrell – pop. 1,806 plus one. There was the usual line of false-fronted buildings trying to look bigger than they were and holding the commercial enterprises by which the locals tried to make an honest dollar – the gas stations and auto dealers, a grocery that called itself a supermarket, a barber's shop, 'Paris Modes' selling women's fripperies, a store selling fishing tackle and hunting gear. I noticed that the name of Matterson came up with monotonous regularity and concluded that Matterson was a big pumpkin in Fort Farrell.

Ahead was surely the only real, honest-to-God building in the town: an eight-storeyed giant which, I was sure, must be the Matterson Building. Feeling hopeful for the first time, I quickened my pace, but slowed again as High Street widened into a small square, green with cropped lawns and shady with trees. In the middle of the square was a bronze statue of a man in uniform, which at first I thought was the war memorial; but it turned out to be the founding father of the city – one William J. Farrell, a lieutenant of the Royal Corps of Engineers. *Pioneers, O Pioneers* – the guy was long since dead and the sightless eyes of his effigy stared blindly down false-fronted High Street while the irreverent birds made messes in his uniform cap.

Then I stared unbelievingly at the name of the square while an icy shudder crawled down my spine. Trinavant Park stood on the intersection of High Street and Farrell Street and the name, dredged out from a forgotten past, hit me like a blow in the belly. I was still shaken when I reached the Matterson Building.

Howard Matterson was a hard man to see. I smoked three cigarettes in his outer office while I studied the pneumatic charms of his secretary and thought about the name of Trinavant. It was not so common a name that it cropped up in my life with any regularity; in fact, I had come across it only once before and in circumstances I preferred not to remember. You might say that a Trinavant had changed my life, but whether he had changed it for better or worse there was no means of knowing. Once again I debated the advisability of staying in Fort Farrell, but a thin wallet and an empty belly can put up a powerful argument so I decided to stick around and see what Matterson had to offer.

Suddenly and without warning Matterson's secretary said, 'Mr Matterson will see you now.' There had been no telephone call or ring of bell and I smiled sourly. So he was one of those, was he? One of the guys who exercised his power by saying, 'Keep Boyd waiting for half an hour, Miss So-and-so, then send him in,' with the private thought – 'That'll show the guy who is boss around here.' But maybe I was misjudging him – maybe he really was busy.

He was a big, fleshy man with a florid face and, to my surprise, not any older than me – say, about thirty-three. Going by the extensive use of his name in Fort Farrell, I had expected an older man; a young man doesn't usually have time to build an empire, even a small one. He was broad and beefy but tending to run to fat, judging by the heaviness of his jowls and the folds about his neck, yet big as he was I topped him by a couple of inches. I'm not exactly a midget.

He stood up behind his desk and extended his hand. 'Glad to meet you, Mr Boyd. Don Halsbach has said a lot of nice things about you.'

So he ought, I thought; *considering I found him a fortune.*
Then I was busy coping with Matterson's knuckle-cracking
grip. I mashed his fingers together hard to prove I was as big
a he-man as he was and he grinned at me. 'Okay, take a
seat,' he said, releasing my hand. 'I'll fill you in on the deal.
It's pretty routine.'

I sat down and accepted a cigarette from the box he
pushed across the desk. 'There's just one thing,' I said. 'I
wouldn't want to fool you, Mr Matterson. This hasn't got to
be a long job. I want to get clear of it by the spring thaw.'

He nodded. 'I know. Don told me about that – he said
you want to get back to the North-West Territories for the
summer. Do you think you'll make any money at that kind
of geology?'

'Other people have,' I said. 'There have been lots of good
strikes made. I think there's more metal in the ground up
there than we dream of and all we have to do is to find it.'

He grinned at me. '*We* meaning you.' Then he shook his
head. 'You're in advance of your time, Boyd. The North-
West isn't ready for development yet. What's the use of
making a big strike in the middle of a wilderness when it
would cost millions in development?'

I shrugged. 'If the strike is big enough the money will be
there.'

'Maybe,' Matterson said noncommittally. 'Anyway, from
what Don told me, you want a short-term job so you can get
a grubstake together in order to go back. Is that it?'

'Just about.'

'All right, we're your boys. This is the situation. The
Matterson Corporation has a lot of faith in the potentialities
of this section of British Columbia and we're in development
up to our necks. We run a lot of interlinked operations –
logging-centred mostly – like pulp for paper, plywood, manufactured lumber and so on. We're going to build a newsprint
plant and we're making extensions to our plywood plants.

But there's one thing we're short of and that's power – specifically electrical power.'

He leaned back in his chair. 'Now we could run a pipeline to the natural gas fields around Dawson Creek, pipe in the gas and use it to fuel a power station, but it would cost a lot of money and we'd be paying for the gas for evermore. If we did that the gas suppliers would have a hammerlock on us and would want to muscle in with their surplus money to buy a slice of what we've got – and they'd be able to do it, too, because they'd control our power.' He stared at me. 'We don't want to give away slices – we want the whole goddam pie – and this is how we do it.'

He waved at a map on the wall. 'British Columbia is rich in water power but for the most part it's undeveloped – we get 1,500,000 kilowatts out of a possible 22,000,000. Up here in the North-East there are a possible 5,000,000 kilowatts without a single generating set to make the juice. That's a hell of a lot of power going to waste.'

I said, 'They're building the Portage Mountain Dam on the Peace River.'

Matterson snorted. 'That'll take years and we can't wait for the Government to build a billion-dollar dam – we need the power now. So that is what we do. We're going to build our own dam – not a big one but big enough for us and for any likely expansion in the foreseeable future. We have a site staked out and we have Government blessing. What we want you to do is to see we don't make one of those mistakes for which we'll kick ourselves afterwards. We don't want to flood twenty square miles of valley only to find we've buried the richest copper strike in Canada under a hundred feet of water. This area has never been really checked over by a geologist and we want you to give it a thorough going-over before we build the dam. Can you do it?'

'Seems easy enough from where I'm sitting,' I said. 'I'd like to see it on a map.'

Matterson gave a satisfied nod and picked up the telephone. 'Bring in the maps of the Kinoxi area, Fred.' He turned to me. 'We're not in the mining business but we'd hate to pass up a chance.' He rubbed his chin reflectively. 'I've been thinking for some time we ought to do a geological survey of our holdings – it could pay off. If you do a good job here you might be in line for the contract.'

'I'll think about it,' I said coolly. I never liked to be tied down.

A man came in carrying a roll of maps. He looked more like a banker than J. P. Morgan – correctly dressed and natty in a conservative business suit. His face was thin and expressionless and his eyes were a cold, pale blue. Matterson said, 'Thanks, Fred,' as he took the maps. 'This is Mr Boyd, the geologist we're thinking of hiring. Fred Donner, one of our executives.'

'Pleased to meet you,' I said. Donner nodded curtly and turned to Matterson who was unrolling the maps. 'National Concrete want to talk turkey about a contract.'

'Stall them,' said Matterson. 'We don't sign a thing until Boyd has done his job.' He looked up at me. 'Here it is. The Kinoxi is a tributary of the Kwadacha which flows into the Finlay and so into the Peace River. Here, there's an escarpment and the Kinoxi goes over in a series of rapids and riffles, and just behind the escarpment is a valley.' His hand chopped down on the map. 'We put the dam here to flood the valley and get a good and permanent head of water and we put the powerhouse at the bottom of the escarpment – that gives us a good fall. The survey teams tells us that the water will back up the valley for about ten miles, with an average width of two miles. That'll be a new lake – Lake Matterson.'

'That's a lot of water,' I observed.

'It won't be very deep,' said Matterson. 'So we figure we can get away with a low cost dam.' He stabbed his finger

down. 'It's up to you to tell us if we're losing out on anything in those twenty square miles.'

I examined the map for a while, then said, 'I can do that.
Where exactly is this valley?'

'About forty miles from here. We'll be driving a road in
when we begin to build the dam, but that won't help you.
It's pretty isolated.'

'Not so much as the North-West Territories,' I said. 'I'll
make out.'

'I guess you will at that,' said Matterson with a grin. 'But
it won't be as bad as all that. We'll fly you in and out in the
Corporation helicopter.'

I was pleased about that; it would save me a bit of shoe-
leather. I said, 'I might want to sink some trial boreholes –
depending on what I find. You can hire a drilling rig and I
might want two of your men to do the donkey work.'

Donner said, 'That's going to an extreme length, isn't it?
I doubt if it's justified. And I think your contract should
specify that you do any necessary work yourself.'

I said evenly, 'Mr Donner, I don't get paid for drilling
holes in the ground. I'm paid for using my brains in interpreting the cores that come out of those holes. Now, if you
want me to do the whole job single-handed that's all right
with me, but it will take six times as long and you'll be
charged *my* rate for the job – and I don't come cheap. I'm
just trying to save you money.'

Matterson waved his hand. 'Cut it out, Fred; it may
never happen. You'll only want to drill if you come across
anything definite – isn't that right, Boyd?'

'That's it.'

Donner looked down at Matterson with his cold eyes.
'Another thing,' he said. 'You'd better not have Boyd survey
the northern end. It's not . . .'

'I know what it's not, Fred,' cut in Matterson irritably.
'I'll get Clare straightened out on that.'

'You'd better,' said Donner. 'Or the whole scheme might collapse.'

That exchange meant nothing to me but it was enough to give me the definite idea that these two were having a private fight and I'd better not get in the way. That wanted clearing up, so I butted in and said, 'I'd like to know who my boss is on this survey. Who do I take my orders from – you, Mr Matterson? Or Mr Donner here?'

Matterson stared at me. 'You take them from me,' he said flatly. 'My name is Matterson and this is the Matterson Corporation.' He flicked his gaze up at Donner as though defying him to make an issue of it, but Donner backed down after a long moment by giving a sharp nod.

'Just as long as I know,' I said easily.

Afterwards we got down to dickering about the terms of my contract. Donner was a penny-pincher and, as he had made me mad by trying to skinflint on the possible boring operations, I set my price higher than I would have done normally. Although it seemed to be a straightforward job and I did need the money, there were undercurrents that I didn't like. There was also the name of Trinavant that had come up, although that seemed to have no particular relevance. But the terms I finally screwed out of Donner were so good that I knew I would have to take the job – the money would set me up in business for a year in the North-West.

Matterson was no help to Donner. He just sat on the sidelines and grinned while I gouged him. It was certainly a hell of a way to run a corporation! After the business details had been settled Matterson said, 'I'll reserve a room for you at the Matterson House. It doesn't compare with the Hilton, but I think you'll be comfortable enough. When can you start on the job?'

'As soon as I get my equipment from Edmonton.'

'Fly it in,' said Matterson. 'We'll pay the freight.'

Donner snorted and walked out of the room like a man who knows when he isn't wanted.

II

The Matterson House Hotel proved to be incorporated into the Matterson Building so I hadn't far to go when I left Matterson's office. I also noticed a string of company offices all bearing the name of Matterson and there was the Matterson Bank on the corner of the block. It seemed that Fort Farrell was a real old-fashioned company town, and when Matterson built his dam there would be the Matterson Power Company to add to his list. He was getting a real stranglehold on this neck of the woods.

I arranged with the desk clerk to have my bag brought up from the bus depot, then said, 'Do you have a newspaper here?'

'Comes out Friday.'

'Where's the office?'

'Trinavant Park – north side.'

I walked out into the fading afternoon light and back down High Street until I came to the square. Lieutenant Farrell was staring sightlessly into the low sun which illuminated his verdigris-green face blotched with white where the birds had made free with him. I wondered what he would have thought if he knew how his settlement had turned out. Judging by the expression on his face he *did* know – and he didn't think much of it.

The office of the *Fort Farrell Recorder* seemed to be more concerned with jobbing printing than with the production of a newspaper, but my first question was answered satisfactorily by the young girl who was the whole of the staff – at least, all of it that was in sight.

'Sure we keep back copies. How far do you want to go back?'

'About ten years.'

She grimaced. 'You'll want the bound copies, then. You'll have to come into the back office.' I followed her into a dusty room. 'What was the exact date?'

I had no trouble in remembering that – everyone knows his own birthday. 'Tuesday, September 4th, 1956.'

She looked up at a shelf and said helplessly, 'That's the one up there. I don't think I can reach it.'

'Allow me,' I said, and reached for it. It was a volume the size and weight of a dozen Bibles and it gave me a lot less trouble than it would have given her! I supposed it weighed pretty near as much as she did.

She said, 'You'll have to read it in here; and you mustn't cut the pages – that's our record copy.'

'I won't,' I promised, and put it on a deal table. 'Can I have a light, please?'

'Sure.' She switched on the light as she went out.

I pulled up a chair and opened the heavy cover of the book. It contained two years' issues of the *Fort Farrell Recorder* – one hundred and four reports on the health and sickness of a community; a record of births and deaths, joys and sorrows, much crime and yet not a lot, all things considered, and a little goodness – there should have been more but goodness doesn't make the headlines. A typical country newspaper.

I turned to the issue of September 7th – the week-end after the accident – half afraid of what I would find, half afraid I wouldn't find anything. But it was there and it had made the front page headlines, too. It screamed at me in heavy black letters splashed across the yellowing sheet: JOHN TRINAVANT DIES IN AUTO SMASH.

Although I knew the story by heart, I read the newspaper account with care and it did tell me a couple of things I hadn't known before. It was a simple story, regrettably not

uncommon, but one which did not normally make headlines as it had done here. As I remembered, it rated a quarter-
column at the bottom of the second page of the Vancouver
Sun and a paragraph filler in Toronto.

The difference was that John Trinavant had been a
power in Fort Farrell as being senior partner in the firm of
Trinavant and Matterson. God the Father had suddenly
died and Fort Farrell had mourned. Mourned publicly and
profusely in black print on white paper.

John Trinavant (aged 56) had been travelling from
Dawson Creek to Edmonton with his wife, Anne (no age
given), and his son, Frank (aged 22). They had been travelling in Mr Trinavant's new car, a Cadillac, but the shiny new
toy had never reached Edmonton. Instead, it had been
found at the bottom of a two-hundred-foot cliff not far off
the road. Skid marks and slashes in the bark of trees had
shown how the accident happened. 'Perhaps,' said the coro-
ner, 'it may be that the car was moving too fast for the driver
to be in proper control. That, however, is something no one
will know for certain.'

The Cadillac was a burnt-out hulk, smashed beyond
repair. Smashed beyond repair were also the three
Trinavants, all found dead. A curious aspect of the accident,
however, was the presence of a fourth passenger, a young
man now identified as Robert Grant, who had been found
alive, but only just so, and who was now in the City
Hospital suffering from third-degree burns, a badly fractured skull and several other assorted broken bones. Mr
Grant, it was tentatively agreed, must have been a hitch-
hiker whom Mr Trinavant, in his benevolence, had picked
up somewhere on the way between Dawson Creek and the
scene of the accident. Mr Grant was not expected to live.
Too bad for Mr Grant.

All Fort Farrell and, indeed, all Canada (said the leader
writer) should mourn the era which had ended with the

passing of John Trinavant. The Trinavants had been connected with the city since the heroic days of Lieutenant Farrell and it was a grief (to the leader writer personally) that the name of Trinavant was now extinguished in the male line. There was, however, a niece, Miss C. T. Trinavant, at present at school in Lausanne, Switzerland. It was to be hoped that this tragedy, the death of her beloved uncle, would not be permitted to interrupt the education he had so earnestly desired to give her.

I sat back and looked at the paper before me. So Trinavant had been a partner of Matterson – but not the Matterson I had met that day because he was too young. At the time of the smash he would have been in his early twenties – say about the age of young Frank Trinavant who was killed, or about my age at that time. So there must be another Matterson – Howard Matterson's father, presumably – which made Howard the Crown Prince of the Matterson empire. Unless, of course, he had already succeeded.

I sighed as I wondered what devil of coincidence had brought me to Fort Farrell; then I turned to the next issue and found – nothing! There was no follow on to the story in that issue or the next. I searched further and found that for the next year the name of Trinavant was not mentioned once – no follow-up, no obituary, no reminiscences from readers – nothing at all. As far as the *Fort Farrell Recorder* was concerned, it was as though John Trinavant had never existed – he had been *unpersonned*.

I checked again. It was very odd that in Trinavant's home town – the town where he was virtually king – the local newspaper had not coined a few extra cents out of his death. That was a hell of a way to run a newspaper!

I paused. That was the second time in one day that I had made the same observation – the first time in relation to Howard Matterson and the way he ran the Matterson

Corporation. I wondered about that and that led me to something else – who owned the *Fort Farrell Recorder?*

The little office girl popped her head round the door. 'You'll have to go now; we're closing up.'

I grinned at her. 'I thought newspaper offices never closed.'

'This isn't the Vancouver *Sun,*' she said. 'Or the Montreal *Star.*'

It sure as hell isn't, I thought.

'Did you find what you were looking for?' she asked.

I followed her into the front office. 'I found some answers, yes; and a lot of questions.' She looked at me uncomprehendingly. I said, 'Is there anywhere a man can get a cup of coffee round here?'

'There's the Greek place right across the square.'

'What about joining me?' I thought that maybe I could get some answers out of her.

She smiled. 'My mother told me not to go out with strange men. Besides, I'm meeting my boy.'

I looked at all the alive eighteen years of her and wished I were young again – as before the accident. 'Some other time, perhaps,' I said.

'Perhaps.'

I left her inexpertly dabbing powder on her nose and headed across the square with the thought that I'd get picked up for kidnapping if I wasn't careful. I don't know why it is, but in any place that can support a cheap eatery – and a lot that can't – you'll find a Greek running the local coffee-and-doughnut joint. He expands with the community and brings in his cousins from the old country and pretty soon, in an average-size town, the Greeks are running the catering racket, splitting it with the Italians who tend to operate on a more sophisticated level. This wasn't the first Greek place I'd eaten in and it certainly wouldn't be the last – not while I was a poverty-stricken geologist chancing his luck.

I ordered coffee and pie and took it over to a vacant table intending to settle down to do some hard thinking, but I didn't get much chance of that because someone came up to the table and said, 'Mind if I join you?'

He was old, maybe as much as seventy, with a walnut-brown face and a scrawny neck where age had dried the juices out of him. His hair, though white, was plentiful and inquisitive blue eyes peered from beneath shaggy brows. I regarded him speculatively for a long time, and at last he said, 'I'm McDougall – chief reporter for the local scandal sheet.'

I waved him to a chair. 'Be my guest.'

He put down the cup of coffee he was holding and grunted softly as he sat down. 'I'm also the chief compositor,' he said. 'And the only copy-boy. I'm the rewrite man, too. The whole works.'

'Editor, too?'

He snorted derisively. 'Do I look like a newspaper editor?'

'Not much.'

He sipped his coffee and looked at me from beneath the tangle of his brows. 'Did you find what you were looking for, Mr Boyd?'

'You're well-informed,' I commented. 'I've not been in town two hours and already I can see I'm going to be reported in the *Recorder*. How do you do it?'

He smiled. 'This is a small town and I know every man, woman and child in it. I've just come from the Matterson Building and I know all about you, Mr Boyd.'

This McDougall looked like a sharp old devil. I said, 'I'll bet you know the terms of my contract, too.'

'I might.' He grinned at me and his face took on the look of a mischievous small boy. 'Donner wasn't too pleased.' He put down his cup. 'Did you find out what you wanted to know about John Trinavant?'

I stubbed out my cigarette. 'You have a funny way of running a newspaper, Mr McDougall. I've never seen such a silence in print in my life.'

The smile left his face and he looked exactly what he was – a tired old man. He was silent for a moment, then he said unexpectedly, 'Do you like good whisky, Mr Boyd?'

'I've never been known to refuse.'

He jerked his head in the direction of the newspaper office. 'I have an apartment over the shop and a bottle in the apartment. Will you join me? I suddenly feel like getting drunk.'

For an answer I rose from the table and paid the tab for both of us. While walking across the park McDougall said, 'I get the apartment free. In return I'm on call twenty-four hours a day. I don't know who gets the better of the bargain.'

'Maybe you ought to negotiate a new deal with your editor.'

'With Jimson? That's a laugh – he's just a rubber stamp used by the owner.'

'And the owner is Matterson,' I said, risking a shaft at random.

McDougall looked at me out of the corner of his eye. 'So you've got that far, have you? You interest me, Mr Boyd; you really do.'

'You are beginning to interest me,' I said.

We climbed the stairs to his apartment, which was sparsely but comfortably furnished. McDougall opened a cupboard and produced a bottle. 'There are two sorts of Scotch,' he said. 'There's the kind which is produced by the million gallons: a straight-run neutral grain spirit blended with good malt whisky to give it flavour, burnt caramel added to give it colour, and kept for seven years to protect the sacred name of Scotch whisky.' He held up the bottle. 'And then there's the real stuff – fifteen-year-old unblended malt lovingly made and lovingly drunk. This is from Islay – the best there is.'

He poured two hefty snorts of the light straw-coloured liquid and passed one to me. I said, 'Here's to you, Mr McDougall. What brand of McDougall are you, anyway?'

I would swear he blushed. 'I've a good Scots name and you'd think that would be enough for any man, but my father had to compound it and call me Hamish. You'd better call me Mac like everyone else and that way we'll avoid a fight.' He chuckled. 'Lord, the fights I got into when I was a kid.'

I said, 'I'm Bob Boyd.'

He nodded. 'And what interests you in the Trinavants?'

'Am I interested in them?'

He sighed. 'Bob, I'm an old-time newspaperman so give me credit for knowing how to do my job. I do a run-down on everyone who checks the back files; you'd be surprised how often it pays off in a story. I've been waiting for someone to consult that particular issue for ten years.'

'Why should the *Recorder* be interested in the Trinavants now?' I asked. 'The Trinivants are dead and the *Recorder* killed them deader. You wouldn't think it possible to assassinate a memory, would you?'

'The Russians are good at it; they can kill a man and still leave him alive – the walking dead,' said McDougall. 'Look at what they did to Khrushchev. It's just that Matterson hit on the idea, too.'

'You haven't answered my question,' I said tartly. 'Quit fencing around, Mac.'

'The *Recorder* isn't interested in the Trinavants,' he said. 'If I put in a story about any of them – if I even mentioned the name – I'd be out on my can. This is a *personal* interest, and if Bull Matterson knew I was even talking about the Trinavants I'd be in big trouble.' He stabbed his finger at me. 'So keep your mouth shut, you understand.' He poured out another drink and I could see his hand shaking. 'Now, what's your story?'

I said, 'Mac, until you tell me more about the Trinavants I'm not going to tell *you* anything. And don't ask me why because you won't get an answer.'

He looked at me thoughtfully for a long time, then said, 'But you'll tell me eventually?'

'I might.'

That stuck in his gullet but he swallowed it. 'All right; it looks as though I've no option. I'll tell you about the Trinavants.' He pushed the bottle across. 'Fill up, son.'

The Trinavants were an old Canadian family founded by a Jacques Trinavant who came from Brittany to settle in Quebec back in the seventeen-hundreds. But the Trinavants were not natural settlers nor were they merchants – not in those days. Their feet were itchy and they headed west. John Trinavant's great-great-grandfather was a *voyageur* of note; other Trinavants were trappers and there was an unsubstantiated story that a Trinavant crossed the continent and saw the Pacific before Alexander Mackenzie.

John Trinavant's grandfather was a scout for Lieutenant Farrell, and when Farrell built the fort he decided to stay and put down roots in British Columbia. It was good country, he liked the look of it and saw the great possibilities. But just because the Trinavants ceased to be on the move did not mean they had lost their steam. Three generations of Trinavants in Fort Farrell built a logging and lumber empire, small but sound.

'It was John Trinavant who really made it go,' said McDougall. 'He was a man of the twentieth century – born in 1900 – and he took over the business young. He was only twenty-three when his father died. British Columbia in those days was pretty undeveloped still, and it's men like John Trinavant who have made it what it is today.'

He looked at his glass reflectively. 'I suppose that, from a purely business point of view, one of the best things that Trinavant ever did was to join up with Bull Matterson.'

'That's the second time you've mentioned him,' I said. 'He can't be the man I met at the Matterson Building.'

'Hell, no; that's Howard – he's just a punk kid,' said McDougall contemptuously. 'I'm talking about the old man – Howard's father. He was a few years older than Trinavant and they hooked on to each other in 1925. John Trinavant had the brains and directed the policy of the combination while Matterson supplied the energy and drive, and things really started to hum around here. One or the other of them had a finger in every goddam pie; they consolidated the logging industry and they were the first to see that raw logs are no damn' use unless you can do something with them, preferably on the spot. They built pulping plants and ply-wood plants and they made a lot of money, especially during the war. By the end of the war the folks around here used to get a lot of fun out of sitting around of an evening just trying to figure out how much Trinavant and Matterson were worth.'

He leaned over and took the bottle. 'Of course, it wasn't all logging – they diversified early. They owned gas stations, ran a bus service until they sold out to Greyhound, owned grocery stores and dry goods stores – everyone in this area paid them tribute in one way or another.' He paused, then said broodingly, 'I don't know if that's a good thing for a community. I don't like paternalism, even with the best intentions. But that's the way it worked out.'

I said, 'They also owned a newspaper.'

McDougall's face took on a wry look. 'It's the only one of Matterson's operations that doesn't give him a cash return. It doesn't pay. This town isn't really big enough to support a newspaper, but John Trinavant started it as a public service, as a sideline to the print shop. He said the townsfolk

had a right to know what was going on, and he never interfered with editorial policy. Matterson runs it for a different
reason.'

'What's that?'

'To control public opinion. He daren't close it down
because Fort Farrell is growing and someone else might start
an *honest* newspaper which he doesn't control. As long as he
holds on to the *Recorder* he's safe because as sure as hell
there's not room for two newspapers.'

I nodded. 'So Trinavant and Matterson each made a
fortune. What then?'

'Then nothing,' said McDougall. 'Trinavant was killed
and Matterson took over the whole shooting-match – lock,
stock and barrel. You see, there weren't any Trinavants left.'

I thought about that. 'Wasn't there one left? The editorial
in the *Recorder* mentioned a Miss Trinavant, a niece of
John.'

'You mean Clare,' said McDougall. 'She wasn't really a
niece, just a vague connection from the East. The Trinavants
were a strong stock a couple of hundred years ago but the
Eastern branch withered on the vine. As far as I know Clare
Trinavant is the last Trinavant in Canada. John came across
her by accident when he was on a trip to Montreal. She was
an orphan. He reckoned she must be related to the family
somehow, so he took her in and treated her like his own
daughter.'

'Then she wasn't his heir?'

McDougall shook his head. 'Not his natural heir. He didn't
adopt her legally and it seems there's never been any way
to prove the family connection, so she lost out as far as that
goes.'

'Then who *did* get Trinavant's money? And how did
Matterson grab Trinavant's share of the business?'

McDougall gave me a twisted grin. 'The answers to those
two questions are interlocked. John's will established a trust

fund for his wife and son, the whole of the capital to revert
to young Frank at the age of thirty. All the proper safeguards
were built in and it was a good will. Of course, provision had
to be made in case John outlived everybody concerned and
in that case the proceeds of the trust were to be devoted to
the establishment of a department of lumber technology at a
Canadian university.'

'Was that done?'

'It was. The trust is doing good work – but not as well as
it might, and for the answer to that one you have to go back
to 1929. It was then that Trinavant and Matterson realized
they were in the empire-building business. Neither of them
wanted the death of the other to put a stop to it, so they
drew up an agreement that on the death of either of them
the survivor would have the option of buying the other's
share at book value. And that's what Matterson did.'

'So the trust was left with Trinavant's holdings but the
trustees were legally obliged to sell to Matterson if he
chose to exercise his option. I don't see much wrong with
that.'

McDougall clicked his tongue in annoyance. 'Don't be
naïve, Boyd.' He ticked off points on his fingers. 'The option
was to be exercised at book value and by the time Donner
had finished juggling the books my guess is that the book
value had slumped in some weird way. That's one angle.
Secondly, the Chairman of the Board of Trustees is William
Justus Sloane, and W.J. practically lives in Bull Matterson's
pocket these days. The Board of Trustees promptly reinvested
what little they got from Matterson right back into the
newly organized Matterson Corporation, and if anyone *controls* that dough now it's old Bull. Thirdly, it took the Board
of Trustees an awful long time to get off its collective fanny
to do anything about ratifying the terms of the trust. It took
no less than four years to get that Department of Lumber
Technology going, and it was a pretty half-hearted effort at

that. From what I hear the department is awfully short of funds. Fourthly, the terms of the sale of Trinavant's holdings to Bull were never made public. I reckon he should have cut up for something between seven and ten million dollars but the Board of Trustees only invested two million in the Matterson Corporation and in *non-voting* stock, by God, which was just ducky for Bull Matterson. Fifthly . . . aaah . . . what am I wasting my time for?'

'So you reckon Bull Matterson practically stole the Trinavant money.'

'There's no *practically* about it,' McDougall snapped.

'Bad luck for Miss Clare,' I said.

'Oh, she did all right. There was a special codicil in the will that took care of her. John left her half a million dollars and a big slice of land. That's something Bull hasn't been able to get his hooks on – not that he hasn't tried.'

I thought of the tone of the leader in which the recommendation had been made that Miss Trinavant's education should not be interrupted. 'How old was she when Trinavant was killed?'

'She was a kid of seventeen. Old John had sent her to Switzerland to complete her education.'

'And who wrote the leader on September 7th, 1956?'

McDougall smiled tightly. 'So you caught that? You're a smart boy, after all. The leader was written by Jimson but I bet Matterson dictated it. It's a debatable point whether or not that option agreement could have been broken, especially since Clare wasn't legally of John's family, but he wasn't taking any chances. He flew out to Switzerland himself and persuaded her to stay, and he put that leader under her nose as an indication that the people of Fort Farrell thought likewise. She knew the *Recorder* was an honest newspaper; what she didn't know was that Matterson corrupted it the week Trinavant died. She was a girl of seventeen who knew nothing about business.'

'So who looked after her half million bucks until she came of age?'

'The Public Trustee,' said McDougall. 'It's pretty automatic in cases like hers. Bull tried to horn in on it, of course, but he never got anywhere.'

I went over the whole unsavoury story in my mind, then shook my head. 'What I don't understand is why Matterson clamped down on the name of Trinavant. What did he have to hide?'

'I don't know,' confessed McDougall. 'I was hoping that the man who consulted that issue of the *Recorder* after ten years would be able to tell *me*. But from that day to this the name of Trinavant has been blotted out in this town. The Trinavant Bank was renamed the Matterson Bank, and every company that held the name was rebaptized. He even tried to change the name of Trinavant Square but he couldn't get it past Mrs Davenant – she's the old battle-axe who runs the Fort Farrell Historical Society.'

I said, 'Yes, if it hadn't been for that I wouldn't have known this was Trinavant's town.'

'Would it have made any difference?' When I made no answer McDougall said, 'He couldn't rename Clare Trinavant either. It's my guess he's been praying to God she gets married. She lives in the district, you know – and she hates his guts.'

'So the old man's still alive.'

'He sure is. Must be seventy-five now, and he wears his age well – he's still full of piss and vinegar, but he always was a rumbustious old stallion. John Trinavant was the brake on him, but when John went then old Bull really broke loose. He organized the Matterson Corporation as a holding company and really went to town on money-making, and he wasn't particular how he made it – he still isn't, for that matter. And the amount of forest land he owns . . .'

I broke in. 'I thought all forest land was Crown land.'

'In British Columbia ninety-five per cent *is* Crown land, but five per cent – say, seven million acres – is under private ownership. Bull owns no less than one million acres, and he has felling franchises on another two million acres of Crown land. He cuts sixty million cubic feet of lumber a year. He's always on the edge of getting into trouble because of over-cutting – the Government doesn't like that – but he's always weaselled his way out. Now he's starting his own hydro-electric plant, and when he has that he'll really have this part of the country by the throat.'

I said, 'Young Matterson told me the hydro plant was to supply power to the Matterson Corporation's own opera-tions.'

McDougall's lip quirked satirically. 'And what do you think Fort Farrell is but a Matterson operation? We have a two-bit generating plant here that's never up to voltage and always breaking down, so now the Matterson Electricity Company moves in. And Matterson operations have a way of spreading wider. I believe old Bull has a vision of the Matterson Corporation controlling a slice of British Columbia from Fort St John to Kispiox, from Prince George clear to the Yukon – a private kingdom to run as he likes.'

'Where does Donner come into all this?' I asked curiously.

'He's a money man – an accountant. He thinks in nothing but dollars and cents and he'll squeeze a dollar until it cries uncle. Now there's a really ruthless, conniving bastard for you. He figures out the schemes and Bull Matterson makes them work. But Bull has put himself upstairs as Chairman of the Board – he leaves the day-to-day running of things to young Howard – and Donner is now riding herd on Howard to prevent him running hog-wild.'

'He's not doing too good a job,' I said, and told him of the episode in Howard's office.

McDougall snorted. 'Donner can handle that young
punk with one hand tied behind his back. He'll give way on
things that don't matter much, but on anything important
Howard definitely comes last. Young Howard puts up a good
front and may look like a man, but he's soft inside. He's not
a tenth of the man his father is.'

I sat and digested all that for a long time, and finally said,
'All right, Mac; you said you had a personal interest in all
this. What is it?'

He stared me straight in the eye and said, 'It may come
as a surprise to you to find that even newspapermen have a
sense of honour. John Trinavant was my friend; he used to
come up here quite often and drink my whisky and have a
yarn. I was sick to my stomach at what the *Recorder* did to
him and his family when they died, but I stood by and let it
happen. Jimson is an incompetent fool and I could have put
such a story on the front page of this newspaper that John
Trinavant would never have been forgotten in Fort Farrell.
But I didn't, and you know why? Because I was a coward;
because I was scared of Bull Matterson; because I was frightened of losing my job.'

His voice broke a little. 'Son, when John Trinavant was
killed I was rising sixty, already an elderly man. I've always
been a free-spender and I had no money, and it's always
been in my mind that I come from a long-lived family. I
reckoned I had many years ahead of me, but what can an old
man of sixty do when he loses his job?' His voice strengthened. 'Now I'm seventy-one and still working for Matterson.
I do a good job for him – that's why he keeps me on here.
It's not charity because Matterson doesn't even know the
meaning of the word. But in the last ten years I've saved a
bit and now that I don't have so many years ahead of me I'd
like to do something for my friend, John Trinavant. I'm not
running scared any more.'

I said, 'What would you propose to do?'

He took a deep breath. 'You can tell *me*. A man doesn't walk in off the street and read a ten-year-old issue of a newspaper without a reason. I want to know that reason.'

'No, Mac,' I said. 'Not yet. I don't know if I have a reason or not. I don't know if I have a right to interfere. I came to Fort Farrell purely by chance and I don't know if this is any of my business.'

He puffed out his cheeks and blew out his breath explosively. 'I don't get it,' he said. 'I just don't get it.' He wore a baffled look. 'Are you telling me that you read that ten-year-old issue just for kicks – or just because you like browsing through crummy country newspapers? Maybe you wanted to check which good housewife won the pumpkin pie baking competition that week. Is that it?'

'No dice, Mac,' I said. 'You won't get it out of me until I'm ready, and I'm a long way off yet.'

'All right,' he said quietly. 'I've told you a lot – enough to get my head chopped off if Matterson hears about it. I've put my neck right on the block.'

'You're safe with me, Mac.'

He grunted. 'I sure as hell hope so. I'd hate to be fired now with no good coming of it.' He got up and took a file from a shelf. 'I might as well give you a bit more. It struck me that if Matterson wanted to erase the name of Trinavant the reason might be connected with the way Trinavant died.' He took a photograph from the file and passed it to me. 'Know who that is?'

I looked at the fresh young face and nodded. I had seen a copy of the same photograph before but I didn't tell McDougall. 'Yes, it's Robert Grant.' I laid it on the table.

'The fourth passenger in the car,' said McDougall, tapping the photograph with his fingernail. 'That young man lived. Nobody expected him to live, but he did. Six months after Trinavant died I had a vacation coming, so I used it to do some quiet checking out of reach of old Bull.

I went over to Edmonton and visited the hospital. Robert Grant had been transferred to Quebec; he was in a private clinic and he was incommunicado. From then on I lost track of him – and it's a hard task to hide from an old newspaperman with a bee in his bonnet. I sent copies of this photograph to a few of my friends – newspapermen scattered all over Canada – and not a thing has come up in ten years. Robert Grant has disappeared off the face of the earth.'

'So?'

'Son, have you seen this man?'

I looked down at the photograph again. Grant looked to be only a boy, barely in his twenties and with a fine full life ahead of him. I said slowly, 'To my best knowledge I've never seen that face.'

'Well, it was a try,' said McDougall. 'I had thought you might be a friend of his come to see how the land lies.'

'I'm sorry, Mac,' I said. 'I've never met this man. But why would he want to come here, anyway? Isn't Grant an irrelevancy?'

'Maybe,' said McDougall thoughtfully. 'And maybe not. I just wanted to talk to him, that's all.' He shrugged. 'Let's have another drink, for God's sake!'

That night I had the Dream. It was at least five years since I had had it last and, as usual, it frightened hell out of me. There was a mountain covered with snow and with jagged black rocks sticking out of the snow like snaggle teeth. I wasn't climbing the mountain or descending – I was merely standing there as though rooted. When I tried to move my feet it was as though the snow was sticky like an adhesive and I felt like a fly trapped on flypaper.

The snow was falling all the time; drifts were building up and presently the snow was knee-high and then at mid-thigh. I knew that if I didn't move I would be buried so I struggled again and bent down and pushed at the snow with my bare hands.

It was then that I found that the snow was not cold, but red hot in temperature, even though it was perfectly white in my dreams. I cried in agony and jerked my hands away and waited helplessly as the snow imperceptibly built up around my body. It touched my hands and then my face and I screamed as the hot, hot snow closed about me burning, burning, burning . . .

I woke up covered in sweat in that anonymous hotel room and wished I could have a jolt of Mac's fine Islay whisky.

TWO

The first thing I can ever remember in my life is pain. It is not given to many men to experience their birth-pangs and I don't recommend it. Not that any commendation of mine, for or against, can have any effect – none of us chooses to be born and the manner of our birth is beyond our control.

I felt the pain as a deep-seated agony all over my body. It became worse as time passed by, a red-hot fire consuming me. I fought against it with all my heart and seemed to prevail, though they tell me that the damping of the pain was due to the use of drugs. The pain went away and I became unconscious.

At the time of my birth I was twenty-three years old, or so I am reliably informed.

I am also told that I spent the next few weeks in a coma, hovering on that thin marginal line between life and death. I am inclined to think of this as a mercy because if I had been conscious enough to undergo the pain I doubt if I would have lived and my life would indeed have been short.

When I recovered consciousness again the pain, though still crouched in my body, had eased considerably and I found it bearable. Less bearable was the predicament in which I found myself. I was spreadeagled – tied by ankles and wrists – lying on my back and apparently immersed in liquid.

I had very little to go on because when I tried to open my eyes I found that I couldn't. There was a tightness about my face and I became very much afraid and began to struggle.

A voice said urgently, 'You must be quiet. You must not move. You must *not* move.'

It was a good voice, soft and kind, so I relaxed and descended into that merciful coma again.

A number of weeks passed during which time I was conscious more frequently. I don't remember much of this period except that the pain became less obtrusive and I became stronger. They began to feed me through a tube pushed between my lips, and I sucked in the soups and the fruit juices and became even stronger. Three times I was aware that I had been taken to an operating theatre; I learned this not from my own knowledge but by listening to the chatter of nurses. But for the most part I was in a happy state of thoughtlessness. It never occurred to me to wonder what I was doing there or how I had got there, any more than a newborn baby in a cot thinks of those things. As a baby, I was content to let things go their own way so long as I was comfortable and comforted.

The time came when they cut the bandage from my face and eyes. A voice, a man's voice I had heard before, said, 'Now, take it easy. Keep your eyes closed until I tell you to open them.'

Obediently I closed my eyes tightly and heard the snip of the scissors as they clipped through the gauze. Fingers touched my eyelids and there was a whispered, '*Seems* to be all right.' Someone was breathing into my face. The voice said, 'All right; you can open them now.'

I opened my eyes to a darkened room. In front of me was the dim outline of a man. He said, 'How many fingers am I holding up?'

A white object swam into vision. I said, 'Two.'

'And how many now?'

'Four.'

He gave a long, gusty sigh. 'It looks as though you are going to have unimpaired vision after all. You're a very lucky young man, Mr Grant.'

'Grant?'

The man paused. 'Your name is Grant, isn't it?'

I thought about it for a long time and the man assumed I wasn't going to answer him. He said, 'Come now; if you are not Grant, then who are you?'

It is then they tell me that I screamed and they had to administer more drugs. I don't remember screaming. All I remember is the awful blank feeling when I realized that I didn't know who I was.

I have given the story of my rebirth in some detail. It is really astonishing that I lived those many weeks, conscious for a large part of the time, without ever worrying about my personal identity. But all that was explained afterwards by Susskind.

Dr Matthews, the skin specialist, was one of the team which was cobbling me together, and he was the first to realize that there was something more wrong with me than mere physical disability, so Susskind was added to the team. I never called him anything other than Susskind – that's how he introduced himself – and he was never anything else than a good friend. I guess that's what makes a good psychiatrist. When I was on my feet and moving around outside hospitals we used to go out and drink beer together. I don't know if that's a normal form of psychiatric treatment – I thought head-shrinkers stuck pretty firmly to the little padded seat at the head of the couch – but Susskind had his own ways and he turned out to be a good friend.

He came into the darkened room and looked at me. 'I'm Susskind,' he said abruptly. He looked about the room. 'Dr Matthews says you can have more light. I think it's a good idea.' He walked to the window and drew the curtains. 'Darkness is bad for the soul.'

He came back to the bed and stood looking down at me. He had a strong face with a firm jaw and a beak of a nose, but his eyes were incongruously soft and brown, like those of an intelligent ape. He made a curiously disarming gesture, and said, 'Mind if I sit down?'

I shook my head so he hooked his foot on a chair and drew it closer. He sat down in a casual manner, his left ankle resting on his right knee, showing a large expanse of sock patterned jazzily and two inches of hairy leg. 'How are you feeling?'

I shook my head.

'What's the matter? Cat got your tongue?' When I made no answer he said, 'Look, boy, you seem to be in trouble. Now, I can't help you if you don't talk to me.'

I'd had a bad night, the worst in my life. For hours I had struggled with the problem – *who am I?* – and I was no nearer to finding out than when I started. I was worn out and frightened and in no mood to talk to anyone.

Susskind began to talk in a soft voice. I don't remember everything he said that first time but he returned to the theme many times afterwards. It went something like this:

'Everyone comes up against this problem some time in his life; he asks himself the fundamentally awkward question: 'Who am I?' There are many related questions, too, such as, 'Why am I?' and 'Why am I *here*?' To the uncaring the questioning comes late, perhaps only on the death-bed. To the thinking man this self-questioning comes sooner and has to be resolved in the agony of personal mental sweat.

'Out of such self-questioning have come a lot of good things – and some not so good. Some of the people who have asked these questions of themselves have gone mad, others have become saints, but most of us come to a compromise. Out of these questions have arisen great religions. Philosophers have written too many books about them, books containing a lot of undiluted crap and a few grains of sense. Scientists have looked for the answers in the movement of atoms and the working of drugs. This is the problem which exercises all of us, every member of the human race, and if it doesn't happen to an individual then that individual cannot be considered to be human.

'Now, you've bumped up against this problem of personal identity head-on and in an acute form. You think that just because you can't remember your name you're a nothing. You're wrong. The self does not exist in a name. A name is just a word, a form of description which we give ourselves – a mere matter of convenience. The self – that awareness in the midst of your being which you call *I* – is still there. If it weren't, you'd be dead.

'You also think that just because you can't remember incidents in your past life your personal world has come to an end. Why should it? You're still breathing; you're still alive. Pretty soon you'll be out of this hospital – a thinking, questioning man, eager to get on with what he has to do. Maybe we can do some reconstructions; the odds are that you'll have all your memories back within days or weeks. Maybe it will take a bit longer. But I'm here to help you do it. Will you let me?'

I looked up at that stern face with the absurdly gentle eyes and whispered, 'Thanks.' Then, because I was very tired, I fell asleep and when I woke up again Susskind had gone.

But he came back next day. 'Feeling better?'

'Some.'

He sat down. 'Mind if I smoke?' He lit a cigarette, then looked at it distastefully. 'I smoke too many of these damn' things.' He extended the pack. 'Have one?'

'I don't use them.'

'How do you know?'

I thought about that for fully five minutes while Susskind waited patiently without saying a word. 'No,' I said. 'No, I don't smoke. I *know* it.'

'Well, that's a good start,' he said with fierce satisfaction. 'You know *something* about yourself. Now, what's the first thing you remember?'

I said immediately, 'Pain. Pain and floating. I was tied up, too.'

Susskind went into that in detail and when he had finished I thought I caught a hint of doubt in his expression, but I could have been wrong. He said, 'Have you any idea how you got into this hospital?'

'No,' I said. 'I was *born* here.'

He smiled. 'At your age?'

'I don't know how old I am.'

'To the best of our knowledge you're twenty-three. You were involved in an auto accident. Have you any ideas about that?'

'No.'

'You know what an automobile is, though.'

'Of course.' I paused. 'Where was the accident?'

'On the road between Dawson Creek and Edmonton. You know where those places are?'

'I know.'

Susskind stubbed out his cigarette. 'These ash-trays are too damn' small,' he grumbled. He lit another cigarette. 'Would you like to know a little more about yourself? It will be hearsay, not of your own personal knowledge, but it might help. Your name, for instance.'

I said, 'Dr Matthews called me by the name of Grant.'

Susskind said carefully, 'To the best of our knowledge that is your name. More fully, it is Robert Boyd Grant. Want to know anything else?'

'Yes,' I said. 'What was I doing? What was my job?'

'You were a college student studying at the University of British Columbia in Vancouver. Remember anything about that?'

I shook my head.

He said suddenly, 'What's a mofette?'

'It's an opening in the ground from which carbon dioxide is emitted – volcanic in origin.' I stared at him. 'How did I know that?'

'You were majoring in geology,' he said drily. 'What was your father's given name?'

'I don't know,' I said blankly. 'You said "was". Is he dead?'

'Yes,' said Susskind quickly. 'Supposing you went to Irving House, New Westminster – what would you expect to find?'

'A museum.'

'Have you any brothers or sisters?'

'I don't know.'

'Which – if any – political party do you favour?'

I thought about it, then shrugged. 'I don't know – but I don't know if I took any interest in politics at all.'

There were dozens of questions and Susskind shot them at me fast, expecting fast answers. At last he stopped and lit another cigarette. 'I'll give it to you straight, Bob, because I don't believe in hiding unpleasant facts from my customers and because I think you can take it. Your loss of memory is entirely personal, relating solely to yourself. Any knowledge which does not directly impinge on the ego, things like the facts of geology, geographical locations, car driving know-how – all that knowledge has been retained whole and entire.'

He flicked ash carelessly in the direction of the ash-tray. 'The more personal things concerning yourself and your relationships with others are gone. Not only has your family been blotted out but you can't remember another single person – not your geology tutor or even your best buddy at college. It's as though something inside you decided to wipe the slate clean.'

I felt hopelessly lost. What was there left for a man of my age with no personal contacts – no family, no friends? My God, I didn't even have any enemies, and it's a poor man who can say that.

Susskind poked me gently with a thick forefinger. 'Don't give up now, bud; we haven't even started. Look at it this way – there's many a man who would give his soul to be able to start again with a clean slate. Let me explain a few things to you. The unconscious mind is a funny animal with its own operating logic. This logic may appear to be very odd to the conscious mind but it's still a valid logic working strictly in accordance within certain rules, and what we have to do is to figure out the rules. I'm going to give you some psychological tests and then maybe I'll know better what makes you tick. I'm also going to do some digging into your background and maybe we can come up with something there.'

I said, 'Susskind, what chance is there?'

'I won't fool you,' he said. 'Due to various circumstances which I won't go into right now, yours is not entirely a straightforward case of loss of memory. Your case is one for the books – and I'll probably write the book. Look, Bob; a guy gets a knock on the head and he loses his memory – but not for long; within a couple of days, a couple of weeks at the most, he's normal again. That's the common course of events. Sometimes it's worse than that. I've just had a case of an old man of eighty who was knocked down in the street. He came round in hospital the next day and found he'd lost a year of his life – he couldn't remember a damn' thing of the year previous to the accident and, in my opinion, he never will.'

He waved his cigarette under my nose. 'That's general loss of memory. A *selective* loss of memory like yours isn't common at all. Sure, it's happened before and it'll happen again, but not often. And, like the general loss, recovery is variable. The trouble is that selective loss happens so infrequently that we don't have much on it. I could give you a line that you'll have your memory back next week, but I won't because I don't know. The only thing we can do is to work on it. Now, my advice to you is to quit worrying about it and to concentrate on other things. As soon as you can use your eyes for reading I'll bring in some textbooks and you can get back to work. By then the bandages will be off your hands and you can do some writing, too. You have an examination to pass, bud, in twelve months' time.'

II

Susskind drove me to work and ripped into me when I lagged. His tongue could get a vicious edge to it when he thought it would do me good, and as soon as the bandages were off he pushed my nose down to the textbooks. He gave me a lot of tests – intelligence, personality, vocational – and seemed pleased at the results.

'You're no dope,' he announced, waving a sheaf of papers. 'You scored a hundred and thirty-three on the Wechsler-Bellevue – you have intelligence, so use it.'

My body was dreadfully scarred, especially on the chest. My hands were unnaturally pink with new skin and when I touched my face I could feel crinkled scar tissue. And that led to something else. One day Matthews came to see me with Susskind in attendance. 'We've got something to talk about, Bob,' he said.

Susskind chuckled and jerked his head at Matthews. 'A serious guy, this – very portentous.'

'It is serious,' said Matthews. 'Bob, there's a decision you have to make. I've done all I can do for you in this

hospital. Your eyes are as good as new but the rest of you
is a bit battered and that's something I can't improve on.
I'm no genius – I'm just an ordinary hospital surgeon spe-
cializing in skin.' He paused and I could see he was selecting his words. 'Have you ever wondered why you've never
seen a mirror?'

I shook my head, and Susskind chipped in, 'Our Robert
Boyd Grant is a very undemanding guy. Would you like to
see yourself, Bob?'

I put my fingers to my cheeks and felt the roughness. 'I
don't know that I would,' I said, and found myself shaking.

'You'd better,' Susskind advised. 'It'll be brutal, but it'll
help you make up your mind in the next big decision.'

'Okay,' I said.

Susskind snapped his fingers and the nurse left the room
to return almost immediately with a large mirror which she
laid face down on the table. Then she went out again and
closed the door behind her. I looked at the mirror but made
no attempt to pick it up. 'Go ahead,' said Susskind, so I
picked it up reluctantly and turned it over.

'My God!' I said, and quickly closed my eyes, feeling the
sour taste of vomit in my throat. After a while I looked
again. It was a monstrously ugly face, pink and seamed with
white lines in arbitrary places. It looked like a child's first
clumsy attempt to depict the human face in wax. There was
no character there, no imprint of dawning maturity as there
should have been in someone of my age – there was just a
blankness.

Matthews said quietly, 'That's why you have a private
room here.'

I began to laugh. 'It's funny; it's really damn' funny. Not
only have I lost myself, but I've lost my face.'

Susskind put his hand on my arm. 'A face is just a face.
No man can choose his own face – it's something that's
given to him. Just listen to Dr Matthews for a minute.'

Matthews said, 'I'm no plastic surgeon.' He gestured at the mirror which I still held. 'You can see that. You weren't in any shape for the extensive surgery you needed when you came in here – you'd have died if we had tried to pull any tricks like that. But now you're in good enough shape for the next step – if you want to take it.'

'And that is?'

'More surgery – by a good man in Montreal. The top man in the field in Canada, and maybe in the Western Hemisphere. You can have a face again, and new hands, too.'

'More surgery!' I didn't like that; I'd had enough of it.

'You have a few days to make up your mind,' said Matthews.

'Do you mind, Matt?' said Susskind. 'I'll take over from here.'

'Of course,' said Matthews. 'I'll leave you to it. I'll be seeing you, Bob.'

He left the room, closing the door gently. Susskind lit a cigarette and threw the pack on the table. He said quietly, 'You'd better do it, bud. You can't walk round with a face like that – not unless you intend taking up a career in the horror movies.'

'Right!' I said tightly. I knew it was something that had to be done. I swung on Susskind. 'Now tell me something – who is paying for all this? Who is paying for this private room? Who is paying for the best plastic surgeon in Canada?'

Susskind clicked his tongue. 'That's a mystery. Someone loves you for sure. Every month an envelope comes addressed to Dr Matthews. It contains a thousand dollars in hundred-dollar bills and one of these.' He fished in his pocket and threw a scrap of paper across the table.

I smoothed it out. There was but one line of typescript on it: FOR THE CARE OF ROBERT BOYD GRANT.

I looked at him suspiciously. 'You're not doing this, are you?'

'Good Christ!' he said. 'Show me a hospital head-shrinker who can afford to give away twelve thousand bucks a year. I couldn't afford to give you twelve thousand cents.' He grinned. 'But thanks for the compliment.'

I pushed the paper with my finger. 'Perhaps this is a clue to who I am.'

'No, it's not,' said Susskind flatly. He looked unhappy. 'Maybe you've noticed I've not told you much about yourself. I did promise to dig into your background.'

'I was going to ask you about that.'

'I did some digging,' he said. 'And what I've been debating is not what I should tell you, but if I should tell you at all. You know, Bob, people get my profession all wrong. In a case like yours they think I should help you to get back your memory come hell or high water. I take a different view. I'm like the psychiatrist who said that his job was to help men of genius keep their neuroses. I'm not interested in keeping a man normal – I want to keep him happy. It's a symptom of the sick world we live in that the two terms are not synonymous.'

'And where do I come in on this?'

He said solemnly, 'My advice to you is to let it go. Don't dig into your past. Make a new life for yourself and forget everything that happened before you came here. I'm not going to help you recover your memory.'

I stared at him. 'Susskind, you can't say that and expect me just to leave it there.'

'Won't you take my word for it?' he asked gently.

'No!' I said. 'Would you if you were in my place?'

'I guess not,' he said, and sighed. 'I suppose I'll be bending a few professional ethics, but here goes. I'm going to make it short and sharp. Now, take a hold of yourself, listen to me and shut up until I've finished.'

He took a deep breath. 'Your father deserted your mother soon after you were born, and no one knows if he's alive or dead. Your mother died when you were ten and, from what I can gather, she was no great loss. She was, to put it frankly, nothing but a cheap chippy and, incidentally, she wasn't married to your father. That left you an orphan and you went into an institution. It seems you were a young hellion and quite uncontrollable so you soon achieved the official status of delinquent. Had enough?'

'Go on,' I whispered.

'You started your police record by the theft of a car, so you wound up in reform school for that episode. It seems it wasn't a good reform school; all you learned there was how to make crime pay. You ran away and for six months you existed by petty crime until you were caught. Fortunately you weren't sent back to the same reform school and you found a warden who knew how to handle you and you began to straighten out. On leaving reform school you were put in a hostel under the care of a probation officer and you did pretty well at high school. Your good intelligence earned you good marks so you went to college. Right then it looked as though you were all right.'

Susskind's voice took on a savage edge. 'But you slipped. You couldn't seem to do anything the straight way. The cops pulled you in for smoking marijuana – another bad mark on the police blotter. Then there was an episode when a girl died in the hands of a quack abortionist – a name was named but nothing could be proved, so maybe we ought to leave that one off the tab. Want any more?'

'There's more?'

Susskind nodded sadly. 'There's more.'

'Let me have it,' I said flatly.

'Okay. Again you were pulled in for drug addiction; this time you were mainlining on heroin. You just about hit the bottom there. There was some evidence that you were pushing drugs to get the dough to feed the habit, but not enough to nail you. However, now the cops were laying for you. Then came the clincher. You knew the Dean of Men was considering throwing you out of college and, God knows, he had enough reason. Your only hope was to promise to reform but you had to back it up with something – such as brilliant work. But drugs and brilliant work don't go hand in hand so you were stupid enough to break into an office and try to doctor your examination marks.'

'And I was caught at it,' I said dully.

'It would have been better if you were,' said Susskind. 'No, you weren't caught red-handed but it was done in such a ham-fisted way that the Principal sent a senior student to find you. He found you all right. He found you hopped up on dope. You beat this guy half to death and lit out for places unknown. God knows where you thought you were going to take refuge – the North Pole, maybe. Anyway, a nice guy called Trinavant gave you a lift and the next thing was – Bingo! – Trinavant was dead, his wife was dead, his son was dead, and you were seven-eighths dead.' He rubbed his eyes. 'That just about wraps it up,' he said tiredly.

I was cold all over. 'You think I killed this man, Trinavant, and his family?'

'I think it was an accident, nothing more,' said Susskind. 'Now listen carefully, Bob; I told you the unconscious mind has its own brand of peculiar logic. I found something very peculiar going on. When you were pulled in on the heroin charge you were given a psychiatric examination, and I've seen the documents. One of the tests was a Bernreuter Personality Inventory and you may remember that I also gave you that test.'

'I remember.'

Susskind leaned back in his chair. 'I compared the two profiles and they didn't check out at all; they could have been two different guys. And I'll tell you something, Bob:

the guy that was tested by the police psychiatrist I wouldn't trust with a bent nickel, but I'd trust *you* with my life.'

'Someone's made a mistake,' I said.

He shook his head vigorously. 'No mistake. Do you remember the man I brought in here who sat in on some of your tests? He's an authority on an uncommon condition of the human psyche – multiple personality. Did you ever read a book called *The Three Faces of Eve*?'

'I saw the movie – Joanne Woodward was in it.'

'That's it. Then perhaps you can see what I'm getting at. Not that you have anything like she had. Tell me, what do you think of the past life of this guy called Robert Boyd Grant?'

'It made me sick to my stomach,' I said. 'I can't believe I did that.'

'*You* didn't,' said Susskind sharply. 'This is what happened, to the best of my professional belief. This man, Robert Boyd Grant, was a pretty crummy character, and he knew it himself. My guess is that he was tired of living with himself and he wanted to escape from himself – hence the drugs. But marijuana and heroin are only temporary forms of escape, and like everyone else he was locked in the prison of his own body. Perhaps he sickened himself but there was nothing he could do about it – a conscious and voluntary change of basic personality is practically an impossibility.

'But as I said, the unconscious has its own logic and we, in this hospital, accidentally gave it the data it needed. You had third-degree burns over sixty per cent of your body when you were brought in here. We couldn't put you in a bed in that condition, so you were suspended in a bath of saline solution which, to your unconscious, was a pretty good substitute for amniotic fluid. Do you know what that is?'

'A return to the womb?'

Susskind snapped his fingers. 'You're with it. Now I'm speaking in impossibly untechnical terms, so don't go quoting me, especially to other psychiatrists. I think this condition was tailor-made for your unconscious mind. Here was a chance for rebirth which was grabbed at. Whether the second personality was lying there, ready to be used, or whether it was constructed during the time you were in that bath, we shall never know – and it doesn't matter. That there is a second personality – a better personality – is a fact, and it's something I'd swear to in a court of law, which I might have to do yet. You're one of the few people who can really call yourself a new man.'

It was a lot to take in at once – too much. I said, 'God! You've handed me something to think about.'

'I had to do it,' said Susskind. 'I had to explain why you mustn't probe into the past. When I told you what a man called Robert Grant had done it was like listening to an account of the actions of someone else, wasn't it? Let me give you an analogy: when you go to the movies and see a lion jumping at you, well – that's just the movies and there's no harm done; but if you go to Africa and a lion jumps at you, that's hard reality and you're dead. If you insist on digging into the past and succeed in *remembering as personal memories* the experiences of this other guy, then you'll split yourself down the middle. So leave it alone. You're someone with no past and a great future.'

I said, 'What chance is there that this other – bad – personality might take over again spontaneously?'

'I'd say there's very little chance of that,' said Susskind slowly. 'You rate as a strong-willed individual; the other guy had a weak will – strong-willed people generally don't go for drugs, you know. We all of us have a devil lurking inside us; we all have to suppress the old Adam. You're no different from anyone else.'

I picked up the mirror and studied the reflected carica-ture. 'What did I . . . what did *he* look like?'

Susskind took out his wallet and extracted a photograph. 'I don't see the point in showing you this, but if you want to see it, here it is.'

Robert Boyd Grant was a fresh-faced youngster with a smooth, unlined face. There was no trace of dissipation such as one might have expected – he could have been any college student attending any college on the North American continent. He wasn't bad-looking, either, in an immature way, and I doubted if he'd had any trouble finding a girl-friend to put in the family way.

'I'd forget about that face,' advised Susskind. 'Don't go back into the past. Roberts, the plastic surgeon, is a sculptor in flesh; he'll fix you up with a face good enough to play romantic lead with Elizabeth Taylor.'

I said, 'I'll miss you, Susskind.'

He chuckled fatly. 'Miss me? You're not going to miss me, bud; I'm not going to let you get away – I'm going to write the book on you, remember.' He blew out a plume of smoke. 'I'm getting out of hospital work and going into private practice. I've been offered a partnership – guess where? Right – Montreal!'

Suddenly I felt much better now I knew Susskind was still going to be around. I looked at the photograph again and said, 'Perhaps I'd better go the whole way. New man . . . new face . . . why not new name?'

'A sound idea,' agreed Susskind. 'Any ideas on that?'

I gave him the photograph. 'That's Robert Grant,' I said. 'I'm Bob Boyd. It's not too bad a name.'

III

I had three operations in Montreal covering the space of a year. I spent many weeks with my left arm strapped up against my right cheek in a skin grafting operation and, no sooner was that done, than my right arm was up against my left cheek.

Roberts was a genius. He measured my head meticulously and then made a plaster model which he brought to my room. 'What kind of a face would you like, Bob?' he asked.

It took a lot of figuring out because this was playing for keeps – I'd be stuck with this face for the rest of my life. We took a long time working on it with Roberts shaping modelling clay on to the plaster base. There were limitations, of course; some of my suggestions were impossible. 'We have only a limited amount of flesh to work with,' said Roberts. 'Most plastic surgery deals mainly with the removal of flesh; nose-bobbing, for instance. This is a more ticklish job and all we can do is a limited amount of redistribution.'

I guess it was fun in a macabre sort of way. It isn't everyone who gets the chance to choose his own face even if the options are limited. The operations weren't so funny but I sweated it out, and what gradually emerged was a somewhat tough and battered face, the face of a man much older than twenty-four. It was lined and seamed as though by much experience, and it was a face that looked much wiser than I really was.

'Don't worry,' said Roberts. 'It's a face you'll grow into. No matter how carefully one does this there are the inevitable scars, so I've hidden those in folds of flesh, folds which usually come only with age.' He smiled. 'With a face like this I don't think you'll have much competition from people your own age; they'll walk stiff-legged around you without even knowing why. You'd better take some advice from Susskind on how to handle situations like that.'

Matthews had handed over to Susskind the administration of the thousand dollars a month from my unknown benefactor. Susskind interpreted FOR THE CARE OF ROBERT

BOYD GRANT in a wide sense; he kept me hard at my studies and, since I could not go to college, he brought in private tutors. 'You haven't much time,' he warned. 'You were born not a year ago and if you flub your education now you'll wind up washing dishes for the rest of your life.'

I worked hard – it kept my mind off my troubles. I found I liked geology and, since I had a skull apparently stuffed full of geological facts it wasn't too difficult to carry on. Susskind made arrangements with a college and I wrote my examinations between the second and third operations with my head and arm still in bandages. I don't know what I would have done without him.

After the examinations I took the opportunity of visiting a public library and, in spite of what Susskind had said, I dug out the newspaper reports of the auto smash. There wasn't much to read apart from the fact that Trinavant was a big wheel in some jerkwater town in British Columbia. It was just another auto accident that didn't make much of a splash. Just after that I started to have bad dreams and that scared me, so I didn't do any more investigations.

Then suddenly it was over. The last operation had been done and the bandages were off. In the same week the examination results came out and I found myself a B.Sc. and a newly fledged geologist with no job. Susskind invited me to his apartment to celebrate. We settled down with some beer, and he asked, 'What are you going to do now? Go for your doctorate – '

I shook my head. 'I don't think so – not just yet. I want to get some field experience.'

He nodded approvingly. 'Got any ideas about that?'

I said, 'I don't think I want to be a company man; I'd rather work for myself. I reckon the North-West Territories are bursting with opportunities for a freelance geologist.'

Susskind was doubtful. 'I don't know if that's a good thing.' He looked across at me and smiled. 'A mite self-conscious about your face, are you? And you want to get away from people – go into the desert – is that it?'

'There's a little of that in it,' I said unwillingly. 'But I meant what I said. I think I'll make out in the north.'

'You've been in hospitals for a year and a half,' said Susskind. 'And you don't know many people. What you should do is to go out, get drunk, make friends – maybe get yourself a wife.'

'Good God!' I said. 'I couldn't get married.'

He waved his tankard. 'Why not? You find yourself a really good girl and tell her the whole story. It won't make any difference to her if she loves you.'

'So you're turning into a marriage counsellor,' I said. 'Why have you never got married?'

'Who'd marry a cantankerous bastard like me?' He moved restlessly and spilled ash down his shirt-front. 'I've been holding out on you, bud. You've been a pretty expensive proposition, you know. You don't think a thousand bucks a month has paid for what you've had? Roberts doesn't come cheap and there were the tutors, too – not to mention my own ludicrously expensive services.'

I said, 'What are you getting at, Susskind?'

'When the *first* envelope came with its cargo of a thousand dollars, this was in it.'

He handed me a slip of paper. There was the line of typing: FOR THE CARE OF ROBERT BOYD GRANT. Underneath was another sentence: IN THE EVENT OF THESE FUNDS BEING INSUFFICIENT, PLEASE INSERT THE FOLLOWING AD IN THE PERSONAL COLUMN OF THE VANCOUVER SUN – R.B.G. WANTS MORE.

Susskind said, 'When you came up to Montreal I decided it was time for more money so I put the ad. in the paper. Whoever is printing this money doubled the ante. In the last year and a half you've had thirty-six thousand dollars; there are nearly four thousand bucks left in the kitty – what do you want to do with it?'

'Give it to some charity,' I said.

'Don't be a fool,' said Susskind. 'You'll need a stake if you're setting off into the wide blue yonder. Pocket your pride and take it.'

'I'll think about it,' I said.

'I don't see what else you can do but take it,' he observed; 'You haven't a cent otherwise.'

I fingered the note. 'Who do you think this is? And why is he doing it?'

'It's no one out of your past, that's for sure,' said Susskind. 'The gang that Grant was running with could hardly scratch up ten dollars between them. All hospitals get these anonymous donations. They're not usually as big as this nor so specific, but the money comes in. It's probably some eccentric millionaire who read about you in the paper and decided to do something about it.' He shrugged. 'There are two thousand bucks a month still coming in. What do we do about that?'

I scribbled on the note and tossed it back to him. He read it and laughed. '"R.B.G. SAYS STOP." I'll put it in the personal column and see what happens.' He poured us more beer. 'When are you taking off for the icy wastes?'

I said, 'I guess I will use the balance of the money. I'll leave as soon as I can get some equipment together.'

Susskind said, 'It's been nice having you around, Bob. You're quite a nice guy. Remember to keep it that way, do you hear? No poking and prying – keep your face to the future and forget the past and you'll make out all right. If you don't you're liable to explode like a bomb. And I'd like to hear how you're getting on from time to time.'

Two weeks later I left Montreal and headed north-west. I suppose if anyone was my father it was Susskind, the man with the tough, ruthless, kindly mind. He gave me a taste for tobacco in the form of cigarettes, although I never got around to smoking as many as he did. He also gave me my life and sanity.

His full name was Abraham Isaac Susskind.

I always called him Susskind.

THREE

The helicopter hovered just above treetop height and I shouted to the pilot, 'That'll do it; just over there in the clearing by the lake.'

He nodded, and the machine moved sideways slowly and settled by the lakeside, the downdraught sending ripples bouncing over the quiet water. There was the usual soggy feeling on touchdown as the weight came on to the hydraulic suspension and then all was still save for the engine vibrations as the rotor slowly flapped around.

The pilot didn't switch off. I slammed the door open and began to pitch out my gear – the unbreakable stuff that would survive the slight fall. Then I climbed down and began to take out the cases of instruments. The pilot didn't help at all; he just sat in the driving seat and watched me work. I suppose it was against his union rules to lug baggage.

When I had got everything out I shouted to him, 'You'll be back a week tomorrow?'

'Okay,' he said. 'About eleven in the morning.'

I stood back and watched him take off and the helicopter disappeared over the trees like a big ungainly grasshopper. Then I set about making camp. I wasn't going to do anything more that day except make camp and, maybe, do a little fishing. That might sound as though I was cheating the Matterson Corporation out of the best part of a day's work, but I've always found that it pays not to run headlong into a job.

A lot of men – especially city men – live like pigs when they're camping. They stop shaving, they don't dig a proper latrine, and they live exclusively on a diet of beans. I like to make myself comfortable, and that takes time. Another thing is that you can do an awful lot of work when just loafing around camp. When you're waiting for the fish to bite your eye is taking in the lie of the land and that can tell an experienced field geologist a hell of a lot. You don't have to eat all of an egg to know it's rotten and you don't have to pound every foot of land to know what you'll find in it and what you won't find.

So I made camp. I dug the latrine and used it because I needed to. I got some dry driftwood from the shore and built a fire, then dug out the coffee-pot and set some water to boil. By the time I'd gathered enough spruce boughs to make a bed it was time to have coffee, so I sat with my back against a rock and looked over the lake speculatively.

From what I could see the lake lay slap-bang on a discontinuity. This side of the lake was almost certainly mesozoic, a mixture of sedimentary and volcanic rocks – good prospecting country. The other side, by the lie of the land and what I'd seen from the air, was probably palaeozoic, mostly sedimentary. I doubted if I'd find much over there, but I had to go and look.

I took a sip of the scalding coffee and scooped up a handful of pebbles to examine them. Idly I let them fall from my hand one at a time, then threw the last one into the lake where it made a small 'plop' and sent out a widening circle of ripples. The lake itself was a product of the last ice age. The ice had pushed its way all over the land, the tongues of glaciers carving valleys through solid rock. It lay on the land for a long time and then, as quickly as it had come, so it departed.

Speed is a relative term. To a watching man a glacier moves slowly but it's the equivalent of a hundred yards' sprint when compared to other geological processes. Anyway, the glaciers retreated, dropping the rock fragments they had fractured and splintered from the bedrock. When that happened a rock wall was formed called a moraine, a natural dam behind which a lake or pond can form. Canada is full of them, and a large part of Canadian geology is trying to think like a piece of ice, trying to figure which way the ice moved so many thousands of years ago so that you can account for the rocks which are otherwise unaccountably out of place.

This lake was more of a large pond. It wasn't more than a mile long and was fed by a biggish stream which came in from the north. I'd seen the moraine from the air and traced the stream flowing south from the lake to where it tumbled over the escarpment and where the Matterson Corporation was going to build a dam.

I threw out the dregs of coffee and washed the pot and the enamel cup, then set to and built a windbreak. I don't like tents – they're no warmer inside than out and they tend to leak if you don't coddle them. In good weather all a man needs is a windbreak, which is easily assembled from materials at hand which don't have to be back-packed like a tent, and in bad weather you can make a waterproof roof if you have the know-how. But it took me quite a long time in the North-West Territories to get that know-how.

By mid-afternoon I had the camp ship-shape. Everything was where I wanted it and where I could get at it quickly if I needed it. It was a standard set-up I'd worked out over the years. The Polar Eskimos have carried *that* principle to a fine art; a stranger can drop into an unknown igloo, put out his hand in the dark and be certain of finding the oil-lamp or the bone fish-hooks. Armies use it, too; a man transferred to a strange camp still knows where to find the paymaster without half trying. I suppose it can be defined as good housekeeping.

The plop of a fish in the lake made me realize I was hungry, so I decided to find out how good the trout were. Fish is no good for a sustained diet in a cold climate – for that you need good fat meat – but I'd had all the meat I needed in Fort Farrell and the idea of lake trout sizzling in a skillet felt good. But next day I'd see if I could get me some venison, if I didn't have to go too far out of my way for it.

That evening, lying on the springy spruce and looking up at a sky full of diamonds, I thought about the Trinavants. I'd deliberately put the thing out of my mind because I was a little scared of monkeying around with it in view of what Susskind had said, but I found I couldn't leave it alone. It was like when you accidentally bite the inside of your cheek and you find you can't stop tongueing the sore place.

It certainly was a strange story. Why in hell should Matterson want to erase the name and memory of John Trinavant? I drew on a cigarette thoughtfully and watched the dull red eye of the dying embers on the fire. I was more and more certain that whatever was going on was centred on that auto accident. But three of the participants were dead, and the fourth couldn't remember anything about it, and what's more, didn't want to. So that seemed a dead end.

Who profited from the Trinavants' death? Certainly Bull Matterson had profited. With that option agreement he had the whole commercial empire in his fist – and all to himself. A motive for murder? Certainly Bull Matterson ran his business hard on cruel lines if McDougall was to be believed. But not every tight-fisted businessman was a murderer.

Item: Where was Bull Matterson at the time of the accident?

Who else profited? Obviously Clare Trinavant. And where was she at the time of the accident? In Switzerland, you damn' fool, and she was a chit of a schoolgirl at that. Delete Clare Trinavant.

Who else?

Apparently no one else profited – not in money, anyway. Could there be a way to profit other than in money? I didn't know enough about the personalities involved even to speculate, so that was another dead end – for the time being.

I jerked myself from the doze. What the hell was I thinking of? I wasn't going to get mixed up in this thing. It was too dangerous for me personally.

I was even more sure of that when I woke up at two o'clock in the morning drenched with sweat and quivering with nerves. I had had the Dream again.

II

Things seemed brighter in the light of the dawn, but then they always do. I cooked breakfast – beans, bacon and fried eggs – and wolfed it down hungrily, then picked up the pack I had assembled the night before. A backwoods geologist on the move resembles a perambulating Christmas tree more than anything else, but I'm a bigger man than most and it doesn't show much on me. However, it still makes a sizeable load to tote, so you can see why I don't like tents.

I made certain that the big yellow circle on the back of the pack was clearly visible. That's something I consider really important. Anywhere you walk in the woods on the North American continent you're likely to find fool hunters who'll let loose a 30.30 at anything that moves. That big yellow circle was just to make them pause before they squeezed the trigger, just time enough for them to figure that there are no yellow-spotted animals haunting the woods. For the same reason I wore a yellow-and-red checkered mackinaw that a drunken Indian wouldn't be seen dead in, and a woollen cap with a big red bobble on the top. I was a real colourful character.

I checked the breech of my rifle to make sure there wasn't one up the spout, slipped on the safety-catch and set off, heading south along the lake shore. I had established my base and I was ready to do the southern end of the survey. In one week the helicopter would pick me up and take me north, ready to cover the northern end. This valley was going to get a thorough going-over.

At the end of the first day I checked my findings against the Government geological map which was, to say the best of it, sketchy; in fact, in parts it was downright blank. People sometimes ask me: 'Why doesn't the Government do a *real* geological survey and get the job done once and for all?' All I can say is that those people don't understand anything about the problems. It would take an army of geologists a hundred years to check every square mile of Canada, and then they'd have to do it again because some joker would have invented a gadget to see metals five hundred feet underground; or, maybe, someone else would find a need for some esoteric metal hitherto useless. Alumina ores were pretty useless in 1900 and you couldn't give away uranium in the 1930s. There'll still be jobs for a guy like me for many years to come.

What little was on the Government map checked with what I had, but I had it in more detail. A few traces of molybdenum and a little zinc and lead, but nothing to get the Matterson Corporation in an uproar about. When a geologist speaks of a trace, he means just that.

I carried on the next day, and the day after that, and by the end of the week I'd made pretty certain that the Matterson Corporation wasn't going to get rich mining the southern end of the Kinoxi Valley. I had everything packed back at the camp and was sitting twiddling my thumbs when the helicopter arrived, and I must say he was dead on time.

This time he dropped me in the northern area by a stream, and again I spent the day making camp. The next day I was off once more in the usual routine, just putting one foot in front of the other and keeping my eyes open.

On the third day I realized I was being watched. There wasn't much to show that this was so, but there was enough; a scrap of wool caught on a twig near the camp which hadn't been there twelve hours earlier, a fresh scrape on the bark of a tree which I hadn't made and, once only, a wink of light from a distant hillside to show that someone had incautiously exposed binoculars to direct sunlight.

Now, in the north woods it's downright discourteous to come within spitting distance of a man's camp and not make yourself known, and anyone who hadn't secrecy on his mind wouldn't do it. I don't particularly mind a man having his secrets – I've got some of my own – but if a man's secrets involve me then I don't like it and I'm apt to go off pop. Still, there wasn't much I could do about it except carry on and hope to surprise this snoopy character somehow.

On the fifth day I had just the far northern part of the valley to inspect, so I decided to go right as far as I had to and make an overnight camp at the top of the valley. I was walking by the stream, trudging along, when a voice behind me said, 'Where do you think you're going?'

I froze, then turned round carefully. A tall man in a red mackinaw was standing just off the trail casually holding a hunting rifle. The rifle wasn't pointing right at me; on the other hand, it wasn't pointing very far away. In fact, it was a moot point whether I was being held up at gun-point or not. Since this guy had just stepped out from behind a tree he had deliberately ambushed me, so I didn't care to make an issue of it right then – it wouldn't have been the right time. I just said, 'Hi! Where did you spring from?'

His jaw tightened and I saw he wasn't very old, maybe in his early twenties. He said, 'You haven't answered my question.'

I didn't like that tightening jaw and I hoped his trigger finger wasn't tightening too. Young fellows his age can go off at half-cock awfully easily. I shifted the pack on my back. 'Just going up to the head of the valley.'

'Doing what?'

I said evenly, 'I don't know what business it is of yours, buster, but I'm doing a survey for the Matterson Corporation.'

'No, you're not,' he said. 'Not on this land.' He jerked his head down the valley. 'See that marker?'

I looked in the direction he indicated and saw a small cairn of stones, much overgrown, which is why I hadn't spotted it before. It would have been pretty invisible from the other side. I looked at my young friend. 'So?'

'So that's where Matterson land stops.' He grinned, but there was no humour in him. 'I was hoping you'd come this way – the marker makes explanations easier.'

I walked back and looked at the cairn, then glanced at him to find he had followed me with the rifle still held easily in his hands. We had the cairn between us, so I said, 'It's all right if I stand here?'

'Sure,' he said airily. 'You can stand there. No law against it.'

'And you don't mind me taking off my pack?'

'Not so long as you don't put it this side of the marker.' He grinned and I could see he was enjoying himself. I was prepared to let him – for the moment – so I said nothing, swung the pack to the ground and flexed my shoulders. He didn't like that – he could see how big I was, and the rifle swung towards me, so there was no question now about being held up.

I pulled the maps out of a side pocket of the pack and consulted them. 'There's nothing here about this,' I said mildly.

'There wouldn't be,' he said. 'Not on Matterson maps. But this is Trinavant land.'

'Oh! Would that be Clare Trinavant?'

'Yeah, that's right.' He shifted the rifle impatiently.

I said, 'Is she available? I'd like to see her.'

'She's around, but you won't see her – not unless she wants to see *you*.' He laughed abruptly. 'I wouldn't stick around waiting for her; you might take root.'

I jerked my head down the valley. 'I'll be camped in that clearing. You push off, sonny, and tell Miss Trinavant that I know where the bodies are buried.' I don't know why I said it but it seemed a good thing to say at the time.

His head came up. 'Huh?'

'Run away and tell Miss Trinavant just that,' I said. 'You're just an errand boy, you know.' I stooped, picked up the pack, and turned away, leaving him standing there with his mouth open. By the time I reached the clearing and looked back he had gone.

The fire was going and the coffee was bubbling when I heard voices from up the valley. My friend, the young gunman, came into sight but he'd left his artillery home this time. Behind him came a woman, trimly dressed in jeans, an open-necked shirt and a mackinaw. Some women can wear jeans but not many; Ogden Nash once observed that before a woman wears pants she should see herself walking away. Miss Trinavant definitely had the kind of figure that would look well in anything, even an old burlap sack.

And she looked beautiful even when she was as mad as a hornet. She came striding over to me in a determined sort of way, and demanded, 'What is all this? Who are you?'

'My name's Boyd,' I said. 'I'm a geologist working on contract for the Matterson Corporation. I'm . . .'

She held up her hand and looked at me with frosty eyes. I'd never seen green frost before. 'That's enough. This is as far up valley as you go, Mr Boyd. See to it, Jimmy.'

'That's what I told him, Miss Trinavant, but he didn't want to believe me.'

I turned my head and looked at him. 'Stay out of this, Jimmy boy: Miss Trinavant is on Matterson land by invitation – you're not, so buzz off. And don't point a gun at me again or I'll wrap it round your neck.'

'Miss Trinavant, that's a lie,' he yelled. 'I never——'

I whirled and hit him. It's a neat trick if you can get in the right position – you straighten your arm out stiff and pivot from the hips – your hand picks up a hell of a velocity by the time it makes contact. The back of my hand caught him under the jaw and damn' near lifted him a foot off the ground. He landed flat on his back, flopped around a couple of times like a newly landed trout, and then lay still.

Miss Trinavant was looking at me open-mouthed – I could see her lovely tonsils quite plainly. I rubbed the back of my hand and said mildly, 'I don't like liars.'

'He wasn't lying,' she said passionately. 'He had no gun.'

'I know when I'm being looked at by a 30.30,' I said, and stabbed my finger at the prostrate figure in the pine needles. 'That character has been snooping after me for the last three days: I don't like that, either. He just got what was coming to him.'

By the way she bared her teeth she was getting set to bite me. 'You didn't give him a chance, you big barbarian.'

I let that one go. I've been in too many brawls to be witless enough to give the other guy a chance – I leave that to the sporting fighters who earn a living by having their brains beaten out.

She knelt down, and said, 'Jimmy, Jimmy, are you all right?' Then she looked up. 'You must have broken his jaw.'

'No,' I said. 'I didn't hit him hard enough. He'll just be sore in body and spirit for the next few days.' I took a pannikin and filled it with water from the stream and dumped it on Jimmy's face. He stirred and groaned. 'He'll be fit to walk in a few minutes. You'd better get him back to wherever you have your camp. And you can tell him that if he comes after me with a gun again I'll kill him.'

She breathed hard but said nothing, concentrating on arousing Jimmy. Presently he was conscious enough to stand up on groggy feet and he looked at me with undisguised hatred. I said, 'When you've got him bedded down I'll be glad to see you again, Miss Trinavant. I'll still be camped here.'

She turned a startled face towards me. 'What makes you think I ever want to see you again?' she flared.

'Because I know where the bodies are buried,' I said pleasantly. 'And don't be afraid; I've never been known to hit a woman yet.'

I would have sworn she used some words I'd heard only in logging camps, but I couldn't be certain because she muttered them under her breath. Then she turned to give Jimmy a hand and I watched them go past the marker and out of sight. The coffee was pretty nigh ruined by this time so I tossed it out and set about making more, and a glance at the sun decided me to think about bedding down for the night.

It was dusk when I saw her coming back, a glimmering figure among the trees. I had made myself comfortable and was sitting with my back to a tree tending the fat duck which was roasting on a spit before the fire. She came up and stood over me. 'What do you *really* want?' she asked abruptly.

I looked up. 'You hungry?' She stirred impatiently, so I said, 'Roast duck, fresh bread, wild celery, hot coffee – how does that sound?'

She dropped down to my level. 'I told Jimmy to watch out for you,' she said. 'I knew you were coming. But I didn't tell him to go on Matterson land – and I didn't say anything about a gun.'

'Perhaps you should have,' I observed. 'Perhaps you should have said, "No gun".'

'I know Jimmy's a bit wild,' she said. 'But that's no excuse for what you did.'

I took a flat cake of bread out of the clay oven and slapped it on a platter. 'Have you ever looked down the muzzle of a gun?' I asked. 'It's a mighty unsettling sensation, and I tend to get violent when I'm nervous.' I handed her the platter. 'What about some duck?'

Her nostrils quivered as the fragrance rose from the spitted bird and she laughed. 'You've sold me. It smells so good.'

I began to carve the duck. 'Jimmy's not much hurt except in what he considers to be his pride. If he goes around pointing guns at people, one of these days there's going to be a bang and he'll hang as high as Haman. Maybe I've saved his life. Who is he?'

'One of my men.'

'So you knew I was coming,' I said thoughtfully. 'News gets around these parts fast, considering it's so under-populated.'

She selected a slice of breast from her platter and popped it into her mouth. 'Anything that concerns me I get to know about. Say, this is good!'

'I'm not such a good cook,' I said. 'It's the open air that does it. How do I concern you?'

'You work for Matterson; you were on my land. That concerns me.'

I said, 'When I contracted to do this job Howard Matterson had a bit of an argument with a man called Donner. Matterson said he'd straighten out the matter with someone called Clare – presumably you. Did he?'

'I haven't seen Howard Matterson in a month – and I don't care if I never see him again.'

'You can't blame me for not knowing the score,' I said. 'I thought the job was above board. Matterson has a strange way of running his business.'

She picked up a drumstick and gnawed on it delicately. 'Not strange – just crooked. Of course, it all depends on which Matterson you're talking about. Bull Matterson is the crooked one; Howard is just plain sloppy.'

'You mean he *forgot* to talk to you about it?' I said unbelievingly.

'Something like that.' She pointed the drumstick at me. 'What's all this about bodies?'

I grinned. 'Oh, I just wanted to talk to you. I knew that would bring you running.'

She stared at me. 'Why should it?'

'It did – didn't it?' I pointed out. 'It's a variation of the old story of the practical joker who sent a cable to a dozen of his friends: FLY – ALL IS DISCOVERED. Nine of them hastily left town. Everyone has a skeleton in some cupboard of their lives.'

'You were just pining for company,' she said sardonically.

'Would I pass up the chance of dining with a beautiful woman in the backwoods?'

'I don't believe you,' she said flatly. 'You can cut out the flattery. For all you knew I might have been an old hag of ninety, unless, of course, you'd been asking questions around beforehand. Which you obviously have. What are you up to, Boyd?'

'Okay,' I said. 'How's this for a starter? Did you ever get around to investigating that Trinavant-Matterson partnership agreement, together with the deal Matterson made with the trustees of the estate? It seems to me that particular business transaction could bear looking into. Why doesn't someone do something about it?'

She stared at me wide-eyed. 'Wow! If you've been asking questions like that around Fort Farrell you're going to be in trouble as soon as old Bull finds out.'

'Yes,' I said. 'I understand he'd rather forget the Trinavants ever existed. But don't worry; he won't get to hear of it. My source of information is strictly private.'

'I wasn't worrying,' she said coldly. 'But perhaps you think you can handle the Mattersons the same way you handled Jimmy. I wouldn't bank on it.'

'I didn't think you cared – and I was right,' I said with a grin. 'But why doesn't someone investigate that smelly deal? You, for instance.'

'Why should I?' she said offhandedly. 'It has nothing to do with me how much Bull Matterson gyps the trustees. Tangling with the Mattersons wouldn't put money in my pocket.'

'You mean you don't care that John Trinavant's intentions have been warped and twisted to put money in Matterson's pocket?' I asked softly.

I thought she was going to throw the platter at me. Her face whitened and pink spots appeared in her cheeks. 'Damn you!' she said hotly. Slowly she simmered down. 'I did try once,' she admitted. 'And I got nowhere. Donner has the books of the Matterson Corporation in such a goddam tangle it would take a team of high-priced lawyers ten years to unsnarl everything. Even I couldn't afford that and my attorney advised me not to try. Why are you so interested anyway?'

I watched her sop up gravy with a piece of bread; I like a girl with a healthy appetite. 'I don't know that I am interested. It's just another point to wonder about. Like why does Matterson want to bury the Trinavants – permanently?'

'You stick your neck out, you'll get it chopped off,' she warned. 'Matterson doesn't like questions like that.' She put down her platter, stood up and went down to the stream to wash her hands. When she came back she was wiping them on a man-sized handkerchief.

I poured her a cup of coffee. 'I'm not asking Matterson – I'm asking a Trinavant. Isn't it something a Trinavant wonders about from time to time?'

'Sure! And like everyone else we get no answers.' She looked at me closely. 'What are you after, Boyd? And who the hell are you?'

'Just a beat-up freelance geologist. Doesn't Matterson ever worry you?'

She sipped the hot coffee. 'Not much. I spend very little time here. I come back for a few months every year to annoy him, that's all.'

'And you still don't know what he has against the Trinavants?'

'No.'

I looked into the fire and said pensively, 'Someone was saying that he wished you'd get married. The implication was that there'd be no one around with the name of Trinavant any more.'

She flared hotly. 'Has Howard been – ?' Then she stopped and bit her lip.

'Has Howard been . . . what?'

She rose to her feet and dusted herself down. 'I don't think I like you, Mr Boyd. *You* ask too many questions, and *I* get no answers. I don't know who you are or what you want. If you want to tangle with Matterson that's your affair; my disinterested advice would be "Don't!" because he'll chop you up into little pieces. Still, why should I care? But let me tell you one thing – don't interfere with me.'

'What would you do to me that Matterson wouldn't?'

'The name of Trinavant isn't quite forgotten,' she said. 'I have some good friends.'

'They'd better be better than Jimmy,' I said caustically. Then I wondered why I was fighting with her; it didn't make sense. I scrambled to my feet. 'Look, I have no fight with you and I've no cause to interfere in your life, either. I'm a pretty harmless guy except when someone pokes a gun in my direction. I'll just go back and report to Howard Matterson that you wouldn't let me on your land. There's no grief in it for me.'

'You do that,' she said. There was puzzlement in her voice as she added, 'You're a funny one, Boyd. You come here as a stranger and you dig up a ten-year-old mystery everyone has forgotten. Where did you get it from?'

'I don't think my informant would care to be named.'

'I bet he wouldn't,' she said with contempt. 'I thought everyone in Fort Farrell had developed a conveniently bad memory as well as a yellow streak.'

'Maybe you have friends in Fort Farrell, too,' I said softly.

She zipped up her mackinaw against the chill of the night air. 'I'm not going to stick around here bandying mysteries with you, Boyd,' she said. 'Just remember one thing. Don't come on my land – ever.'

She turned to go away, and I said, 'Wait! There are ghosties and ghoulies and beasties, and things that go bump in the night; I wouldn't want you to walk into a bear. I'll escort you back to your camp.'

'My God, a backwoods cavalier!' she said in disgust, but she stayed around to watch me kick earth over the embers of the fire. While I checked my rifle she looked around at my gear, dimly illuminated in the moonlight. 'You make a neat camp.'

'Comes of experience,' I said. 'Shall we go?' She fell into step beside me and, as we passed the marker, I said, 'Thanks for letting me on your land, Miss Trinavant.'

'I'm a sucker for sweet talk,' she said, and pointed. 'We go that way.'

III

Her 'camp' was quite a surprise. After we had walked for over half an hour up a slope that tested the calf muscles there came the unexpected dark loom of a building. The hunting beam of the flashlamp she produced disclosed walls of fieldstone and logs and the gleam of large windows. She pushed open an unlocked door, then said a little irritably, 'Well, aren't you coming in?'

The interior was even more of a surprise. It was warm with central heating and it was *big*. She flicked a switch and a small pool of light appeared, and the room was so large that it retreated away into shadows. One entire wall was windowed and there was a magnificent view down the valley. Away in the distance I could see the moonglow on the lake I had prospected around.

She flicked more switches and more lights came on, revealing the polished wooden floor carpeted with skins, the modern furniture, the wall brightly lined with books and a scattering of phonograph records on the floor grouped around a built-in hi-fi outfit as though someone had been interrupted.

This was a millionaire's version of a log cabin. I looked about, probably with my mouth hanging open, then said, 'If this were in the States, a guy could get to be President just by being born here.'

'I don't need any wisecracks,' she said. 'If you want a drink, help yourself; it's over there. And you might do something about the fire; it isn't really necessary but I like to see flames.'

She disappeared, closing a door behind her, and I laid down my rifle. There was a massive fieldstone chimney with a fireplace big enough to roast a moose in which a few red embers glowed faintly, so I replenished it from the pile of logs stacked handily and waited until the flames came and I was sure the fire had caught hold. Then I did a tour of the room, hoping she wouldn't be back too soon. You can find out a lot about a person just by looking at a room as it's lived in.

The books were an eclectic lot; many modern novels but very little of the avant-garde, way-out stuff; a solid wedge of English and French classics, a shelf of biographies and a sprinkling of histories, mostly of Canada and, what was surprising, a scad of books on archaeology, mostly Middle-Eastern. It looked as though Clare Trinavant had a mind of her own.

I left the books and drifted around the room, noting the odd pieces of pottery and statuary, most of which looked older than Methuselah; the animal photographs on the walls, mainly of Canadian animals, and the rack of rifles and shotguns in a glassed-in case. I peered at these curiously through the glass and saw that, although the guns appeared to be well kept, there was a film of dust on them. Then I looked at a photograph of a big brute of a brown bear and decided that, even with a telephoto lens, whoever had taken that shot had been too damn' close.

She said from close behind me, 'Looks a bit like you, don't you think?'

I turned. 'I'm not that big. He'd make six of me.'

She had changed her shirt and was wearing a well-cut pair of slacks that certainly hadn't been bought off any shelf. She said, 'I've just been in to see Jimmy. I think he'll be all right.'

'I didn't hit him harder than necessary,' I said. 'Just enough to teach him manners.' I waved my arm about the room. 'Some shack!'

'Boyd, you make me sick,' she said coldly. 'And you can get the hell out of here. You have a dirty mind if you think I'm shacked up with Jimmy Waystrand.'

'Hey!' I said. 'You jump to an awful fast conclusion, Trinavant. All I meant was that this is a hell of a place you have here. I didn't expect to find *this* in the woods, that's all.'

Slowly the pink spots in her cheeks died away, and she said, 'I'm sorry if I took you the wrong way. Maybe I'm a little jumpy right now, and if I am, you're responsible, Boyd.'

'No apology necessary, Trinavant.'

She began to giggle and it developed into a full-throated laugh. I joined in and we had an hysterical thirty seconds. At last she controlled herself. 'No,' she said, shaking her head. 'That won't do. You can't call me Trinavant – you'd better make it Clare.'

'I'm Bob,' I said. 'Hello, Clare.'

'Hello, Bob.'

'You know, I didn't really mean to imply that Jimmy was anything to you,' I said. 'He isn't man enough for you.'

She stopped smiling and, folding her arms, she regarded me for a long time. 'Bob Boyd, I've never known another man who makes my hackles rise the way you do. If you think I judge a man by the way he behaves in a fight you're dead wrong. The trouble with you is that you've got logopaedia – every time you open your mouth you put your foot in it. Now, for God's sake, keep your mouth shut and get me a drink.'

I moved towards what looked like the drinks cabinet. 'You shouldn't steal your wisecracks from the Duke of Edinburgh,' I said. 'That's verging on *lèse majesté*. What will you have?'

'Scotch and water – fifty-fifty. You'll find a good Scotch in there.'

Indeed it was a good Scotch! I lifted out the bottle of *Islay Mist* reverently and wondered how long ago it was since Hamish McDougall had seen Clare Trinavant. But I said nothing about that. Instead, I kept my big mouth shut as she had advised and poured the drinks.

As I handed her the glass she said, 'How long have you been in the woods this trip?'

'Nearly two weeks.'

'How would you like a hot bath?'

'Clare, for that you can have my soul,' I said fervently. Lake water is damned cold and a man doesn't bathe as often as he should when in the field.

She pointed. 'Through that door – second door on the left. I've put towels out for you.'

I picked up my glass. 'Mind if I take my drink?'

'Not at all.'

The bathroom was a wonder to behold. Tiled in white and dark blue, you could have held a convention in there – if that was the kind of convention you had in mind. The bath was sunk into the floor and seemed as big as a swimming-pool, and the water poured steaming out of the faucet. And there was a plenitude of bath towels, each about an acre in extent.

As I lay soaking I thought about a number of things. I thought of the possible reason why Clare Trinavant should bring up the name of Howard Matterson when I brought up the subject of her marriage. I thought of the design of the labels of Scotch, especially on those from the island of Islay. I thought of the curve of Clare Trinavant's neck as it rose from the collar of her shirt. I thought of a man I had never seen – Bull Matterson – and wondered what he was like in appearance. I thought of the tendril of hair behind Clare Trinavant's ear.

None of these thoughts got me anywhere in particular, so I got out of the bath and finished the Scotch while I dried myself. As I dressed I became aware of music drifting through the cabin – some cabin! – which drowned out the distant throbbing of a diesel generator, and when I got back to Clare I found her sitting on the floor listening to the last movement of Sibelius's First Symphony.

She waved me to the drinks cabinet and held up an empty glass, so I gave us both a refill and we sat quietly until the music came to an end. She shivered slightly and pointed to the moonlit view down the valley. 'I always think the music is describing this.'

'Finland has pretty much the same scenery as Canada,' I said. 'Woods and lakes.'

One eyebrow lifted. 'Not only a backwoods cavalier, but an educated one.'

I grinned at her. 'I've had a college education, too.'

She coloured a little and said quietly, 'I'm sorry. I shouldn't have said that. It was bitchy, wasn't it?'

'That's all right.' I waved my hand. 'What made you build here?'

'As your mysterious informant has probably told you, I was brought up around here. Uncle John left me this land. I love it, so I built here.' She paused. 'And, since you're so well informed, you probably know that he wasn't really my uncle.'

'Yes,' I said. 'I have only one criticism. Your rifles and shotguns need cleaning more often.'

'I don't use them now,' she said. 'I've lost the taste for killing animals just for fun. I do my shooting with a camera now.'

I indicated the close-up of the snapping jaws of the brown bear. 'Such as that?' She nodded, and I said, 'I hope you had your rifle handy when you took that shot.'

'I was in no danger,' she said. We fell into a companionable silence, looking into the fire. After a few minutes, she said, 'How long will you be working for Matterson, Bob?'

'Not long. I've just about got the job cleaned up now – with the exception of the Trinavant land.' I smiled. 'I think I'll give that a miss – the owner is a shade tetchy.'

'And then?' Clare questioned.

'And then back to the North-West Territories.'

'Who do you work for up there?'

'Myself.' I told her a little of what I was doing. 'I hadn't been going for more than eighteen months when I made a strike. It brought me in enough to keep me going for the next five years and in that time I didn't find a thing that was worth anything. That's why I'm here working for Matterson – getting a stake together again.'

She was thoughtful. 'Looking for the pot of gold at the end of the rainbow?'

'Something like that,' I admitted. 'And you? What do you do?'

'I'm an archaeologist,' she said unexpectedly.

'Oh!' I said, rather inadequately.

She roused herself and turned to look at me. 'I'm not a dilettante, Bob. I'm not a rich bitch playing around with a hobby until I can find a husband. I really work at it – you should read the papers I've written.'

'Don't be so damned defensive,' I said. 'I believe you. Where do you do your prospecting?'

She laughed at that. 'Mostly in the Middle East, although I've done one dig in Crete.' She pointed to a small statuette of a woman bare to the waist and in a flounced skirt. 'That came from Crete – the Greek government let me bring it out.'

I picked it up. 'I wonder if this is Ariadne?'

'I've had that thought.' She looked across at the window. 'Every year I try to come back here. The Mediterranean lands are so bare and treeless – I have to come back to my own place.'

'I know what you mean.'

We talked for a long time while the fire died. I don't remember now exactly what we talked about – it was just about the trivialities that went to make up our respective lives. At last, she said, 'My God, but I'm suddenly sleepy. What time is it?'

'Two a.m.'

She laughed. 'No wonder, then.' She paused. 'There's a spare bed if you'd like to stay. It's pretty late to be going back to your camp.' She looked at me sternly. 'But remember – no passes. One pass and you're out on your ear.'

'All right, Clare. No passes,' I promised.

I was back in Fort Farrell two days later and, as soon as I got to my room at the Matterson House Hotel, I filled the bath-tub and got down to my favourite pastime of soaking, drinking and thinking deep thoughts.

I had left Clare early on the morning following our encounter and was surprised to find her reserved and some-what distant. True, she cooked a good man-sized breakfast, but that was something a good housewife would do for her worst enemy by reflex action. I thought that perhaps she was regretting her fraternization with the enemy – after all, I *was* working for Matterson – or maybe she was miffed because I *hadn't* made a pass at her. You never know with women.

Anyway, she was pretty curt in her leave-taking. When I commented that her cabin would be on the edge of a new lake as soon as Matterson had built the dam, she said vio-lently, 'Matterson isn't going to drown *my* land. You can tell him from me that I'm going to fight him.'

'Okay, I'll tell him.'

'You'd better go, Boyd. I'm sure you have a lot to do.'

'Yes, I have,' I said. 'But I won't do it on your land.' I picked up my rifle. 'Keep smiling, Trinavant.'

So I went, and halfway down the trail I turned to look back at the house, but all I could see was the figure of Jimmy Waystrand standing straddle-legged like a Hollywood cow-boy at the top of the rise, making sure I left.

It didn't take long to check the rest of the Matterson patch and I was back at my main camp early and loafed about for a day until the helicopter came for me. An hour later I was back in Fort Farrell and wallowing in the bathtub.

Languidly I splashed hot water and figured out my schedule. The telephone in the bedroom rang but I ignored it and pretty soon it got tired and stopped. I had to see Howard Matterson, then I wanted to check with McDougall to confirm a suspicion. All that remained after that was to write a report, collect my dough and catch the next bus out of town. There was nothing for me in Fort Farrell beyond a lot of personal grief.

The telephone began to ring again so I splashed out of the tub and walked into the bedroom. It was Howard Matterson and he seemed to be impatient at being kept waiting. 'I heard you were back,' he said. 'I've been expecting you up here.'

'I'm ironing out the kinks in a bathtub,' I said. 'I'll be up to see you when I'm ready.'

There was a silence while he digested that – I guess he wasn't used to waiting on other people. Finally, he said, 'Okay, make it quick. Have a good trip?'

'Moderately so,' I said. 'I'll tell you about it when I come up. I'll pack in a nutshell what you want to know – there's no sound geological reason for any mining operations in the Kinoxi Valley. I'll fill in the details later.'

'Ah! That's what I wanted to know.' He rang off.

I dressed leisurely, then went up to his office. I was kept waiting even longer this time – forty minutes. Maybe Howard figured I rated a wait for the way I answered telephones. But he was pleasant enough when I finally got past his secretary. 'Glad to see you,' he said. 'Have any trouble?'

I lifted an eyebrow. 'Was I expected to have any trouble?'

The smile hovered on his face as though uncertain whether to depart or not, but it finally settled back into place again. 'Not at all,' he said heartily. 'I knew I'd picked a competent man.'

'Thanks,' I said drily. 'I had to put a crimp in someone's style, though. You'd better know about it because you might be getting a complaint. Know a man called Jimmy Waystrand?'

Matterson busied himself in lighting a cigar. 'At the north end?' he asked, not looking at me.

'That's right. It came to fisticuffs, but I managed all right,' I said modestly.

Matterson looked pleased. 'Then you did the *whole* survey.'

'No, I didn't.'

He tried to look stern. 'Oh! Why not?'

'Because I don't slug women,' I said urgently. 'Miss Trinavant was most insistent that I did not survey her land on behalf of the Matterson Corporation.' I leaned forward. 'I believe you told Mr Donner that you would straighten out that little matter with Miss Trinavant. Apparently you didn't.'

'I tried to get hold of her, but she must have been away,' he said. He drummed his fingers on the desk. 'A pity about that, but it can't be helped, I suppose.'

I thought he was lying, but it wouldn't help to say so. I said, 'As far as the rest of the area goes, there's nothing worth digging up as far as I can see.'

'No trace of oil or gas?'

'Nothing like that. I'll give you a full report. Maybe I can borrow a girl from your typing pool; you'll get it quicker that way.' And I'd get out of town quicker, too.

'Sure,' he said. 'I'll arrange that. Let me have it as soon as you can.'

'Right,' I said, and got up to go. At the door I paused. 'Oh, there's just one thing. By the lake in the valley I found traces of quick clay – it's not uncommon in sedimentary deposits in these parts. It's worth doing a further check; it could cause you trouble.'

'Sure, sure,' he said. 'Put it in your report.'

As I went down to the street I wondered if Matterson knew what I was talking about. Still, he'd get a full explanation in the report.

I walked down to Trinavant Park and saw that Lieutenant Farrell was still on guard duty policing the pigeons, then I went into the Greek joint and ordered a cup of coffee substitute and sat at a table. If McDougall was half the newspaperman he said he was, I could expect him any moment. Sure enough, he walked in stiffly within fifteen minutes and sat down next to me wordlessly.

I watched him stir his coffee. 'What's the matter, Mac? Lost your tongue?'

He smiled. 'I was waiting for you to tell me something. I'm a good listener.'

I said deliberately, 'There's nothing to stop Matterson building his dam – except Clare Trinavant. Why didn't you tell me she was up there?'

'I thought you'd do better making the discovery for yourself. Did you run into trouble, son?'

'Not much! Who is this character, Jimmy Waystrand?'

McDougall laughed. 'Son of the caretaker at Clare's place – a spunky young pup.'

'He's seen too many Hollywood westerns,' I said, and described what had happened.

McDougall looked grave. 'The boy wants talking to. He had no right trailing people on Matterson land – and as for the rifle . . .' He shook his head. 'His father ought to rip the hide off him.'

'I think I put him on the right way.' I glanced at him. 'When did you last see Clare Trinavant?'

'When she came through town, about a month ago.'

'And she's been up at the cabin ever since?'

'So far as I know. She never moves far from it.'

I thought it wouldn't be too much trouble for Howard Matterson to climb into that helicopter of his for the fifty-mile flight from Fort Farrell. Then why hadn't he done so? Perhaps it was as Clare had said, that he was a sloppy businessman. I said, 'What's between Clare and Howard Matterson?'

McDougall smiled grimly. 'He wants to marry her.'

I gaped, then burst out laughing. 'He hasn't a snowball's hope. You ought to hear the things she says about the Mattersons – father and son.'

'Howard has a pretty thick skin,' said McDougall. 'He hopes to wear her down.'

'He won't do that by keeping away from her,' I said. 'Or by flooding her land. By the way, what's her legal position on that?'

'Tricky. You know that most of the hydro-electric resources of British Columbia are government-controlled through B.C. Electric. There are exceptions – the Aluminium Company of Canada built its own plant at Kitimat and that's the precedent that governs Matterson's project here. He's been lobbying the Government and has things pretty well lined up. If a land resources tribunal decides this is in the public interest, then Clare loses out.'

He smiled sadly, 'Jimson and the *Fort Farrell Recorder* are working on that angle right now, but he knows better than to ask me to write any of that crap, so he keeps me on nice safe topics like weddings and funerals. According to the editorial he was writing when I left the office, the Matterson Corporation is the pure knight guarding the public interest.'

'He must have got the word from Howard,' I said. 'I gave him the results not long ago. I'm sorry about that, Mac.'

'It isn't your fault; you were just doing your job.' He looked at me out of the corner of his eye. 'Have you decided what you are going to do?'

'About what?'

'About this whole stinking set-up. I thought you'd taken time off to decide when you were out in the woods.'

'Mac, I'm no shining knight, either. There isn't anything I could do that would be any use, and I don't know anything that could help.'

'I don't believe you,' McDougall said bluntly.

'You can believe what you damn' well like,' I said. I was getting tired of his prodding and pushing, and maybe I was feeling a mite guilty – although why I should feel guilty I wouldn't know. 'I'm going to write a report, collect my pay and climb on to a bus heading out of here. Any mess you have in Fort Farrell is none of my business.'

He stood up. 'I should have known,' he said wearily. 'I thought you were the man. I thought you'd have had the guts to put the Mattersons back where they belong, but I guess I was wrong.' He pointed a shaky finger at me. 'You know something. I *know* you know something. Whatever your lousy reasons for keeping it to yourself, I hope you choke on them. You're a gutless, spineless imitation of a man and I'm glad you're leaving Fort Farrell because I'd hate to vomit in the street every time I saw you.'

He turned and walked into the street shakily and I watched him aim blindly across the square. I felt very sorry for him but I could do nothing for him. The man who had the information he needed was not Bob Boyd but Robert Grant, and Robert Grant was ten years dead.

I had one last brush with Howard Matterson when I turned in the report. He took the papers and maps and tossed them on to his desk. 'I hear you had a cosy chat with Clare Trinavant.'

'I stood her a dinner,' I said. 'Who wouldn't?'

'And you went up to her cabin.'

'That's right,' I said easily. 'I thought it was in your interest. I thought that perhaps I could talk her round to a more reasonable frame of mind.'

His voice was like ice. 'And was it in my interest that you stayed all night?'

That gave me pause. By God, the man was jealous! But where could he have got his information? Clare certainly wouldn't have told him, so I was pretty certain it must have been young Jimmy Waystrand. The young punk was hitting back at me by tattling to Matterson. It must have been pretty common knowledge in Fort Farrell that Howard was hot for Clare and getting nowhere.

I smiled pleasantly at Matterson. 'No, that was in *my* interest.'

His face went a dull red and he lumbered to his feet. 'That's not funny,' he said in a voice like gravel. 'We think a lot of Miss Trinavant round here – and a lot about her reputation.' He started to move around the desk, flexing his shoulders, and I knew he was getting ready to take me.

It was unbelievable – the guy hadn't grown up. He was behaving like any callow teenager whose brains are still in his fists, or like a deer in the rutting season ready to take on all comers in defence of his harem. A clear case of retarded development.

I said, 'Matterson, Clare Trinavant is quite capable of taking care of herself *and* her reputation. And you won't do her reputation any good by brawling – I happen to know her views on that subject. And she'd certainly get to know about it because if you lay a finger on me I'll toss you out of the nearest window and it'll be a matter for public concern.'

He kept on coming, then thought better of it, and stopped. I said, 'Clare Trinavant offered me a bath and a bed for the night – and it wasn't her bed. And if that's what you think of her, no wonder you're not making the grade. Now, I'd like my pay.'

In a low, suppressed voice he said, 'There's an envelope on the desk. Take it and get out.'

I stretched out my hand and took the envelope, ripped it open and took out the slip of paper. It was a cheque drawn on the Matterson Bank for the full and exact amount agreed on. I turned and walked out of his office boiling with rage, but not so blindly that I didn't go immediately to the Matterson Bank to turn the cheque into money before Howard stopped it.

With a wad of bills in my wallet I felt better. I went to my room, packed my bag and checked out within half an hour. Going down King Street, I paid my last respects to Lieutenant Farrell, the hollow man of Trinavant Park, and walked on past the Greek place towards the bus depot. There was a bus leaving and I was glad to be on it and rid of Fort Farrell.

It wasn't much of a town.

FOUR

I did another freelance job during the winter down in the Okanagan valley near the U.S. border and before the spring thaw I was all set to go back to the North-West Territories as soon as the snows melted. There's not a great deal of joy for a geologist in a snow-covered landscape – he has to be able to see what he's looking for. It was only during the brief summer that I had a chance, and so I had to wait a while.

During this time, in my correspondence with Susskind, I told him of what had happened in Fort Farrell. His answer reassured me that I had done the right thing.

'I think you were well advised to cut loose from Fort Farrell; that kind of prying would not do you any good at all. If you stay away your bad dreams should tail off in a few weeks providing you don't deliberately think about the episode.

'Speaking as a psychiatrist, I find the ambivalent behaviour of Howard Matterson to be an almost classic example of what, to use the only expression conveniently available, is called a "love-hate" relationship. I don't like this phrase because it has been chewed to death by the *littérateurs* (why must writers seize on our specialized vocabulary and twist meanings out of all recognition?) but it describes the symptoms, if only inadequately. He wants her, he hates her; he must destroy her and have her simultaneously. In other words, Mr Matterson wants to eat his cake and have it, too. Taken all in all, Matterson seems to be a classic case of emotional immaturity – at least, he has all the symptoms. You're well away from him; such men are dangerous. You have only to look at Hitler to see what I mean.

'But I must say that your Trinavant sounds quite a dish!

'I've just remembered something I should have told you about years ago. Just about the time you left Montreal a private enquiry agent was snooping about asking questions about you, or rather, about Robert Grant. I gave him no joy and sent him away with a flea in his ear and my boot up his rump. I didn't tell you about it at the time because, in my opinion, you were then in no fit state to be the recipient of news of that sort; and subsequently I forgot about it.

'At the time I wondered what it was about and I still have not come to any firm conclusion. It certainly was nothing to do with the Vancouver police because, as you know, I straightened them out about you, and a hell of a task it was. Most laymen are thick-headed about psychiatry, but police and legal laymen have heads of almost impenetrable oak. They seem to think that the McNaughten Rules are a psychiatric dictum and not a mere legal formalism, and it was no mean feat getting them to see sense and getting Bob Boyd off the hook for what Robert Grant had done. But I did it.

'So who could have employed this private eye? I did a check and I came up with nothing – it is not my field. Anyway, it is many years ago and probably means nothing now, but I thought I might as well tell you that someone, other than your mysterious benefactor, was interested in you.'

That was interesting news but many years out of date. I chewed it over for some time, but, like Susskind, I could come to no conclusion, so I let it lie.

In the spring I headed north to the MacKenzie District where I fossicked about all summer somewhere between the Great Slave Lake and Coronation Gulf. It's a lonely life – there are not many people up there – but one meets the occasional trapper and there are always the wandering Eskimos in the far north. Again, it was a bad year and I thought briefly of giving it up as a bad job and settling for a salaried existence as a company wage slave. But I knew I wouldn't do that; I'd tasted too much freedom to be nailed down and I'd make a bad company man. But if I were to continue I'd have to go south again to assemble a stake for the next summer, so I humped my pack for civilization.

I suppose I was all sorts of a fool to go back to British Columbia. I wanted to follow Susskind's advice and forget all about Fort Farrell, but the mind is not as easily controlled as all that. During the lonely days, and more especially the lonelier nights, I had thought about the odd fate of the Trinavants. I felt a certain responsibility because I had certainly been in that Cadillac when it crashed, and I felt an odd guilt about what might have caused it. I also felt guilty about running away from Fort Farrell – McDougall's last words still stuck in my craw – even though I had Susskind's assurance that I had done the right thing.

I thought a lot about Clare Trinavant, too – more than was good for a lone man in the middle of the wilderness.

Anyway, I went back and did a winter job around Kamloops in British Columbia, working for an academic team investigating earth tremors. I say 'academic' but the tab was picked up by the United States Government because this work could lead to a better means of detecting underground atomic tests, so perhaps it was not so academic, after all. The pay wasn't too good and the work and general atmosphere a bit too long-haired for me, but I worked through the winter and saved as much as I could.

As spring approached I began to get restless, but I knew I had not saved up enough to go back north for another summer's exploration. It really began to look as though this was the end of the line and I would have to settle down to the company grind. As it turned out I got the money in another way, but I would rather have worked twenty years for a company than gain the money the way I did.

I received a letter from Susskind's partner, a man called Jarvis. He wrote to tell me that Susskind had unexpectedly died of a heart attack and, as executor of the estate, he informed me that Susskind had left me $5,000.

'I know that you and Dr Susskind had a very special relationship, deeper than that normal to doctor and patient,' wrote Jarvis. 'Please accept my deepest regrets, and you will know, of course, that I stand ready to help you in my professional capacity at any time you may need me.'

I felt a deep sense of loss. Susskind was the only father I ever had or knew; he had been my only anchor in a world that had unexpectedly taken away three-quarters of my life. Even though we met but infrequently, our letters kept us close, and now there would be no more letters, no more gruff, irreverent, shrewd Susskind.

I suppose the news knocked me off my bearings for a while. At any rate, I began to think of the geological structure of the North-East Interior of British Columbia, and to wonder if it was at all necessary to go back to the far north that summer. I decided to go back to Fort Farrell.

Thinking of it in hindsight, I now know the reason. While I had Susskind I had a line back to my beginnings. Without Susskind there was no line and again I had to fight for my personal identity; and the only way to do it was to find my past, harrowing though the experience might be. And the way to the past lay through Fort Farrell, in the death of the Trinavant family and the birth of the Matterson logging empire.

At the time, of course, I didn't think that way. I just did things without thinking at all. I turned in the job, packed my bags and was on my way to Fort Farrell within the month.

The place hadn't changed any.

I got off the bus at the depot and there was the same fat little guy who looked me up and down. 'Welcome back,' he said.

I grinned at him. 'I don't need to know where the Matterson Building is this time. But you can tell me one thing – is McDougall still around?'

'He was up to last week – I haven't seen him since.'

'You'd be good in a witness-box,' I said. 'You know how to make a careful statement.'

I went up King Street and into Trinavant Park and saw that there had been a change, after all. The Greek place now had a name – a garish neon sign proclaimed it to be the Hellenic Café. Lieutenant Farrell was still the same, though; he hadn't moved a muscle. I checked into the Matterson House Hotel and wondered how long I'd be staying there. Once I started lifting stones to see what nasty things lay underneath I could see that innkeeper Matterson might not want to have me around as part of his clientele. But this was for the future; now I might as well see how the land lay with Howard.

I took the elevator up to his office. He had a new secretary and I asked her to tell the boss that Mr Boyd wanted to see him. I got into Howard's office in the record-breaking time of two minutes. Howard must have been very curious to know why I was back in Fort Farrell.

He hadn't changed, either, although there was no real reason why he should. He was still the same bull-necked, beefy guy, running to fat, but I thought I detected a shade more fat this time. 'Well, well,' he said. 'I'm certainly surprised to see you again.'

'I don't know why you should be,' I said innocently. 'Considering that you offered me a job.'

He goggled at me incredulously. '*What?*'

'You offered me a job. You said you wanted a geological survey of all the Matterson holdings, and you offered the job to me. Don't you remember?'

He remembered that his mouth was open after a while and snapped it shut. 'By Christ, but you've got a nerve! Do you think that . . .' He stopped and chuckled fatly. 'No, Mr Boyd. I'm afraid we've changed our minds about that project.'

'That's a pity,' I said. 'I find myself unable to go north this year.'

He grinned maliciously. 'What's the matter? Couldn't you find anyone to stake you?'

'Something like that,' I said, and let a worried look appear on my face.

'It's tough all round,' he said, enjoying himself, 'but I'm sorry to tell you that I don't think there's a job going anywhere in this territory for a man in your line. In fact, I'll go further: I don't think there's *any* job around here that you could hold down. The employment situation is terrible in Fort Farrell this year.' A thought struck him. 'Of course, I might be able to find you a job as a bell-hop in the hotel. I have influence there, you understand. I hope you're strong enough to carry bags?'

I wasn't worried about letting him have his fun. 'I don't think I'm down to that yet,' I said, and stood up.

That didn't suit Howard; he wasn't through with grinding my face in the mud. 'Sit down,' he said genially. 'Let's talk about old times.'

'Okay,' I said, and sat down again. 'Seen anything of Clare Trinavant lately?'

That one really harpooned him. 'We'll keep her name out of this,' he snapped.

'I only wanted to know if she was around,' I said reasonably. 'She's a real nice woman – I'd like to meet her again some time.'

He looked like someone who'd just swallowed his gum. The idea had just sunk in that I was really interested in Clare Trinavant – and he wasn't far wrong, at that. It looked as though my tenure of the hotel room would be even shorter than I thought. He recovered. 'She's out of town,' he said with satisfaction. 'She's out of the country. In fact, she's even out of the hemisphere, and she won't be back for a long time. I'm sorry about that – really I am.'

That was a pity; I'd been looking forward to exchanging insults with her again. Still, she wasn't the main reason I was back in Fort Farrell, even though she was a possibly ally I had lost.

I stood up again. 'You're right,' I said regretfully. 'It's tough all round.' This time he didn't try to stop me; perhaps he didn't like my brand of chatty conversation. I made for the door, and said, 'I'll be seeing you.'

'Are you going to stick around here?' he demanded.

I laughed at him. 'That depends if the employment situation is as bad as you say.' I closed the door on him and grinned at his secretary. 'A mighty fine boss you've got there. Yes, sir!' She looked at me as though I were mad, so I winked at her and carried on.

Baiting Howard Matterson was childish and pretty pointless, but I felt the better for it; it gave a boost to my flagging morale. I hadn't had much to do with him personally, and beyond the comments of Clare Trinavant and McDougall, I knew nothing about him. But now I knew he was a brave boy indeed; nothing suited Howard better than to put the boot to a man who was down. His little exhibition of sadism made me feel better and gave added enjoyment to the task of cutting him down to size.

* * *

As I walked along King Street I glanced at my watch and quickened my pace. If McDougall still kept to his usual schedule he'd be having his afternoon coffee at the Greek place – the Hellenic Café. Sure enough, there he was, brooding over an empty cup. I went to the counter and bought two cups of coffee which came to me via a chromium-plated monster which squirted steam from every joint and sounded like the first stage of an Atlas missile taking off.

I took the coffee over to the table and dumped a cup in front of Mac. If he was surprised to see me he didn't show it. His eyelids just flickered and he said, 'What do *you* want?'

I sat down next to him. 'I had a change of heart, Mac.'

He said nothing, but the droop of his shoulders altered to a new erectness. I indicated the Espresso machine. 'When did that sign of prosperity come in?'

'A couple of months ago – and the coffee's godawful,' he said sourly. 'Glad to see you, son.'

I said, 'I'll make this quick because I have an idea that it would be better all round if we aren't seen together too often. Howard Matterson knows I'm in town and I suspect he's mad at me.'

'Why should he be?'

'I had a barney with him just before I left – eighteen months ago.' I told Mac what had happened between us and of my suspicions of young Jimmy Waystrand.

Mac clicked his tongue. 'The bastard!' he exclaimed. 'You know what Howard did? He told Clare you'd boasted to him about spending the night in her cabin. She went flaming wild and cursed you up hill and down dale. You're not her favourite house guest any more.'

'And she believed him?'

'Why wouldn't she? Who else could have told Howard? No one thought of Jimmy.' He grunted suddenly. 'So that's how he got a good job up at the dam. He's working for the Matterson Corporation now.'

'So they're constructing the dam,' I said.

'Yeah. Public opinion was well moulded and Matterson rammed it through over Clare's objections. They began building last summer and they're working as though Matterson ordered it finished for yesterday. They couldn't pour concrete in winter, of course, but they're pouring it now in a round-the-clock operation. In three months there'll be a ten-mile lake in that valley. They've already started to rip out the trees – but not Clare's trees, though. She says she'd rather see her trees drowned than go to a Matterson mill.'

'I've got something to tell you,' I said. 'But it's too long and complicated to go into here. I'll come up to your apartment tonight.'

His face crinkled into a smile. 'Clare left some *Islay Mist* for me when she went. You know she's not here?'

'Howard took great pleasure in informing me,' I said drily.

'Um,' he said, and suddenly drained his cup of coffee. 'I've just remembered there's something I have to do. I'll see you to-night – about seven.' He rose stiffly. 'My bones are getting older,' he said wryly, and headed for the street.

I finished my coffee more leisurely and then went back to the hotel. My pace was quicker than that of McDougall and I'd almost caught up with him on High Street when he turned off and disappeared into the telegraph office. I carried on. There wasn't any more I wanted to say to him that couldn't wait until evening and, as I had told him, the less we were seen together the better. In a few days I wouldn't be too popular around Fort Farrell and any Matterson employee who was seen to be too friendly with me wouldn't be too safe in his job. I'd hate to get McDougall fired.

I had not been evicted from my room yet – but that was a problem I had to bring up with Mac. Probably Howard didn't think I'd have the brazen nerve to stay at the Matterson House and it wouldn't have entered his mind to check – but as soon as I started to make a nuisance of myself he'd find out and I'd be out on my ear. I would ask Mac about alternative accommodation.

I lounged about until just before seven and then went over to Mac's apartment and found him taking his ease before a log fire. He pointed wordlessly to the bottle on the table and I poured myself a drink and joined him.

For a while I looked at the dancing flames, then said, 'What I'm going to tell you I'm not sure you're going to believe, Mac.'

'You can't surprise a newspaperman my age,' he said. 'We're like priests and doctors – we hear a lot of stories that we don't tell. You'd be surprised at the amount of news that's not fit to print, one way or another.'

'Okay,' I said. 'But I still think it's going to surprise you – and it's something I haven't told another living soul – the only other people who know about it are a few doctors.'

I launched forth on the story and told him everything – the waking up in hospital, Susskind's treatment, the plastic surgery – everything, including the mysterious $36,000 and the investigation by the private detective. I finished up by saying, 'That's why I told you that I didn't *know* anything that could help. I wasn't lying, Mac.'

'God, I feel sorry about that now,' he mumbled. 'I said things to you that no man should say to another.'

'You weren't to know,' I said. 'No apologies needed.'

He got up and found the file he had shown me before and dug out the photograph of Robert Grant. He looked at me closely and then his eyes switched to the photograph and then back to me again. 'It's incredible,' he breathed. 'It's goddam incredible. There's no resemblance at all.'

'I took Susskind's advice,' I said. 'Roberts, the surgeon, had a copy of that and used it as an example of what *not* to do.'

'Robert Grant – Robert *B*. Grant,' he murmured. 'Why in hell didn't I have the sense to find out what that initial stood for? A fine reporter I am!' He put the photograph back in the file. 'I don't know, Bob. You've put a lot of doubt in my mind. I don't know whether we should go through with this thing now.'

'Why not? Nothing has changed. The Trinavants are still dead and Matterson is still screwing the lid down. Why shouldn't you want to go ahead?'

'From what you've told me, you stand in some personal risk,' he said slowly. 'Once you start monkeying about with your mind anything could happen. You could go nuts.' He shook his head. 'I don't like it.'

I stood up and paced the floor. 'I've *got* to find out, Mac – no matter what Susskind said. While he was alive I was all right; I leaned on him a lot. But now I have to find out *who I am*. It's killing me not to know.' I halted behind his chair. 'I'm not doing this for you, Mac; I'm doing it for me. I was in that car when it crashed, and it seems to me that this whole mystery stems from that crash.'

'But what can you do?' asked Mac helplessly. 'You don't *remember* anything.'

I sat down again. 'I'm going to stir things up. Matterson doesn't want the Trinavants talked about. Well, I'm going to do a lot of talking in the next few days. Something will break sooner or later. But first I want to get some ammunition, and you can supply that.'

'You're really intent on going through with this?' asked Mac.

'I am.'

He sighed. 'All right, Bob. What do you want to know?'

'One thing I'd give a lot to know is where old man Matterson was when the crash happened.'

Mac grimaced wryly. 'I got there ahead of you. I had that nasty suspicion, too. But there's no joy there. Guess who's his alibi?'

'I wouldn't know.'

'Me, goddam it!' said Mac disgustedly. 'He was in the office of the *Recorder* for most of that day. I wish I couldn't vouch for it, but I can.'

'What time of day did the crash happen?'

'It's no good,' said Mac. 'I thought of that, too. I've juggled the time factors and there's absolutely no way in which Bull Matterson can be placed at the scene of the accident.'

'He stood to gain a lot,' I said. 'He was the only gainer – everyone else lost. I'm convinced he had something to do with it.'

'For God's sake, when did you hear of one millionaire killing another?' Mac suddenly went very still. 'Personally, that is,' he said softly.

'You mean he could have hired someone to do it?'

Mac looked tired and old. 'He could – and if he did we haven't a hope in hell of proving it. The killer is probably living it up in Australia on a fat bank-roll. It's nearly twelve years ago, Bob; how in hell can we prove anything now?'

'We'll find a way,' I said stubbornly. 'That partnership agreement – was it really on the level?'

He nodded. 'Seemed so. John Trinavant was a damn' fool not to have revoked it when he got married and started a family.'

'No possibility of forgery?'

'There's a thought,' said Mac, but shook his head. 'Not a chance. Old Bull dug up a living witness to the signatures.' He got up to put another log on the fire, then turned and said despondently, 'I don't see a single thing we can do.'

'Matterson has a weak point,' I said. 'He's tried to lose the name of Trinavant and he must have had a good reason for it. Well, I'm going to get the name of Trinavant talked about in Fort Farrell. He must react to that in some way.'

'Then what?'

'Then we play it as the chips fall.' I hesitated. 'If necessary, I'll come right into the open. I'll announce that I'm Robert Grant, the guy who was in the Trinavants' car. That should cause a tremor.'

'*If* there was any jiggery-pokery about that car crash, and *if* Matterson had anything to do with it, the roof will fall in on your head,' warned Mac. 'If Matterson did kill the Trinavants you'll be in trouble. A three-time murderer won't hesitate at another.'

'I can look after myself,' I said – and hoped it was true. 'That's another thing. I won't be able to stay at the Matterson House once I start stirring the mud. Can you recommend alternative accommodation?'

'I've built a cabin on a piece of land just outside town,' said Mac. 'You can move in there.'

'Hell, I can't do that. Matterson will tie you in with me and *your* head will be on the block.'

'It's about time I retired,' said Mac equably. 'I was going to quit at the end of summer, anyway; and it doesn't matter if it's a mite sooner. I'm an old man, Bob – rising seventy-two; it's about time I rested the old bones. I'll be able to get in the fishing I've been promising myself.'

'All right,' I said. 'But batten down the hurricane hatches. Matterson will raise a big wind.'

'I'm not scared of Matterson,' he said. 'I never have been and he knows it. He'll just fire me and that will be that. Hell, I'm keeping a future Pulitzer prizewinner out of a job, anyway. It's time I packed up. There's just one story I want to write and it'll hit headlines all over Canada. I'm depending on you to give it to me.'

'I'll do my best,' I said.

Lying in bed that evening, I had a thought that made my blood run cold. McDougall had suggested that Matterson could have hired someone to do his dirty work and the terrifying possibility came to me that the someone could have been an unscrupulous bastard called Robert Grant.

Supposing Grant had boobed on the job and become involved in the accident himself by mischance. Supposing that Robert Boyd Grant was a triple murderer – what did that make me, Bob Boyd?

I broke into a cold sweat. Maybe Susskind had been right. Perhaps I'd discover in my past enough to drive me out of my mind.

I tossed and turned for most of the night and tried to get a grip on myself. I thought about every angle in an attempt to prove Grant's innocence. From what Susskind had told me, Grant had been on the run when the accident happened; the police were after him for an assault on a college student. Was it likely, then, that he would deliberately murder just because someone asked him?

He might – if his total getaway could thereby be financed.

But how would Bull Matterson know that Grant was the man he wanted? You don't walk up to the average college student and say, 'I've got a family of three I want knocked off – what about it?' That would be ridiculous.

I began to think that the whole structure McDougall and I had built up was nonsensical, plausible though it might appear. How could one accuse a respectable, if ruthless, millionaire of murder? It was laughable.

Then I thought of my mysterious benefactor and the $36,000. Was this the pay-off to Grant? And what about that damned private detective? Where did he fit into the picture?

I dropped into an uneasy sleep and had the Dream, slipping into the hot snow and watching my flesh blister and blacken. And there was something else this time. I heard noises – the sharp crackle of flames from somewhere, and there was a dancing red light on the snow which sizzled and melted into rivulets of blood.

II

I was in no good mood when I went down to the street next morning. I was tired and depressed and I ached all over as though I had been beaten. The bright sunshine didn't help, either, because my eyes were gritty, and I felt as though there were many grains of sand under my eyelids. Altogether I wasn't in any good shape.

Over a cup of strong black coffee I began to feel better. *You knew you were going to have a tough time,* I argued with myself. *Are you going to chicken out now? Hell, you haven't even started yet – it's going to get tougher than this.*

That's what I'm afraid of, I told myself.

Think what a wallop you're going to give Matterson, I answered back. *Forget yourself and think of that bastard.*

By the time I finished the coffee I had argued myself back into condition and felt hungry, so I ordered breakfast, which helped a lot more. It's surprising how many psychological problems can be traced to an empty gut. I went out into King Street and looked up and down. There was a new car dealer a little way down the street and a used car lot up the street. The big place was owned by Matterson and, since I didn't want to put any money in his pocket, I strolled up to the used car lot.

I looked at the junk that was lying round and a thin-faced man popped out of a hut at the front of the lot. 'Anything I can do for you? Got some good stuff here going cheap. Best autos in town.'

'I'm looking for a small truck – four by four.'

'Like a jeep?'

'If you have one.'

He shook his head. 'Got a Land-Rover, though. How about that? Better than the jeep, I think.'

'Where is it?'

He pointed to a tired piece of scrap iron on four wheels. 'There she is. You won't do better than that. British made, you know. Better than any Detroit iron.'

'Don't push so hard, bud,' I said, and walked over to have a look at the Land-Rover. Someone had used it hard; the paint had worn and there were dents in every conceivable place and in some which weren't so conceivable. The interior of the cab was well worn, too, and looked pretty rough, but a Land-Rover isn't a luxury limousine in the first place. The tyres were good.

I stepped back. 'Can I look under the hood?'

'Sure.' He released the catch and lifted the hood, chattering as he did so. 'This is a good buy – only had one owner.'

'Sure,' I said. 'A little old lady who only used it to go to church every Sunday.'

'Don't get me wrong,' he said. 'I really mean that. It belonged to Jim Cooper; he runs a truck farm just outside town. He turned this in and got himself a new one. But this crate still runs real good.'

I looked at the engine and halfway began to believe him. It was spotless and there were no telltale oil drips. But what the transmission was like was another story, so I said, 'Can I take her out for half an hour?'

'Help yourself,' he said. 'You'll find the key in the lock.'

I wheeled out the Land-Rover and headed north to where I knew I could find a bad road. It was also in the direction of where McDougall had his cabin and I thought I might as well check on its exact position in case I had to find it in a hurry. I found a nice corrugated stretch of road and accelerated to find out what the springing was like. It seemed to be all right, although there were some nasty sounds coming from the battered body that I didn't care for.

I found the turn-off for Mac's place without much trouble and found a really bad road, a hummocky trail rising and dipping with the fall of the land and with several bad patches of mud. Here I experimented with the variety of gears which constitute the charm of the Land-Rover, and I also tried out the front-wheel drive and found everything in reasonable condition.

Mac's cabin was small but beautifully positioned on a rise overlooking a stretch of woodland, and just behind it was a stream which looked as though it might hold some good fish. I spent five minutes looking the place over, then I headed back to town to do a deal with the friendly small-town car dealer.

We dickered a bit and then finally settled on a price – a shade more than I had intended to pay and a shade less than he had intended to get, which made both of us moderately unhappy. I paid him the money and decided I might as well start here as anywhere else. 'Do you remember a man called Trinavant – John Trinavant?'

He scratched his head. 'Say, yes; of *course* I remember old John. Funny – I haven't thought of him in years. Was he a friend of yours?'

'Can't say I remember meeting him,' I said. 'Did he live round here?'

'Live round here? Mister, he *was* Fort Farrell!'

'I thought that was Matterson.'

A gobbet of spit just missed my foot. 'Matterson!' The tone of voice told me what he thought of that.

I said, 'I hear he was killed in an auto accident. Is that right?'

'Yeah. And his son and wife both. On the road to Edmonton. Must be over ten years ago now. A mighty nasty thing, that was.'

'What kind of a car was he driving?'

He looked at me with speculative eyes. 'You got any special interest, Mister . . .?'

'The name's Boyd,' I said. 'Bob Boyd. Someone asked me to check if I was in these parts. It seems as though Trinavant did my friend a good turn years ago – there was some money involved, I believe.'

'I can believe that of John Trinavant; he was a pretty good guy. My name's Summerskill.'

I grinned at him. 'Glad to meet you, Mr Summerskill. Did Trinavant buy his car from you?'

Summerskill laughed uproariously, 'Hell, no! I don't have that class. Old John was a Cadillac man, and, anyway, he owned his own place up the road a piece – Fort Farrell Motors. It belongs to Matterson now.'

I looked up the street. 'Must make pretty tough competition for you,' I said.

'Some,' he agreed. 'But I do all right, Mr Boyd.'

'Come to think of it,' I said, 'I've seen nothing else but the name of Matterson since I've been here, Mr Summerskill. The Matterson Bank, Matterson House Hotel – and I believe there's a Matterson Corporation. What did he do – buy out Trinavant?'

Summerskill grimaced. 'What you've seen is the tip of the iceberg. Matterson pretty near owns this part of the country – logging operations, sawmills, pulp mills. He's bigger than old John ever was – in power, that is. But not in heart, no, sir! No one had a bigger heart than John Trinavant. As for Matterson buying out Mr Trinavant – well, I could tell you a thing or two about that. But it's an old story and better forgotten.'

'Looks as though I came too late.'

'Yeah, you tell your friend he was ten years too late. If he owed old John any dough it's too late to pay it back now.'

'I don't think it was the money,' I said. 'My friend just wanted to make contact again.'

Summerskill nodded. 'Yeah, it's like that. I was born in Hazelton and I went away just as soon as I could, but of course I had a hankering to go back, so I did after five years. And you know what? The first two guys I went to see had died – the first two guys on my list. Things change around a place, they certainly do.'

I stuck my hand out. 'Well, it's been nice doing business with you, Mr Summerskill.'

'Any time, Mr Boyd.' We shook hands. 'You want any spares, you come right back.'

I climbed up into the cab and leaned out of the window. 'If the engine drops out of this heap in the next couple of days you'll be seeing me soon enough,' I promised, softening it with a grin.

He laughed and waved me away, and as I drove down King Street I thought that the memory of John Trinavant had been replanted in at least one mind. With a bit of luck Summerskill would mention it to his wife and a couple of his buddies. *You know what? Me and a stranger had a chat about a guy I haven't thought of in years.* You *must remember old John Trinavant. Remember when he started the* Recorder *and everyone thought it would go bust?*

So it would go, I hoped; and the ripples would go wider and wider, especially if I dropped some more rocks into this stagnant pool. Sooner or later the ripples would reach the ferocious old pike who ruled the pool, and I hoped he would take action.

I pulled up in front of the Forestry Service office and went inside. The Forestry Officer was called Tanner and he was cordial if not hopeful. I told him I was passing through and that I was interested in tree-farm licences.

'Not a chance, Mr Boyd,' he said. 'The Matterson Corporation has licensed nearly all the Crown lands round here. There are one or two pockets left but they're so small you could spit across them.'

I scratched my jaw. 'Perhaps if I could see a map?' I suggested.

'Sure,' he said promptly, and quickly produced a large-scale map of the area which he spread on his desk. 'There you have it in a nutshell.' His finger traced a wide sweep. 'All this is the holding of the Matterson Corporation – privately owned. And this here . . .' a much larger sweep this time . . . 'is Crown land franchised to the Matterson Corporation under tree-farm licences.'

I looked closely at the map, which made very interesting viewing. To divert Tanner from what I was really after, I said, 'What about public sustained-yield units?' Those were areas where the Forestry Service did all the work but let the felling franchises out on short-term contracts.

'None of those round here, Mr Boyd. We're too far off the beaten track for the Forestry Service to run tree farms. Most of the sustained-yield units are down south.'

'It certainly looks like a closed shop,' I commented. 'Any truth in what I hear that the Matterson Corporation got into trouble for over-felling?'

Tanner looked at me warily. Over-felling is the most heinous crime in the Forestry Service book. 'I couldn't say about that,' he said stiffly.

I wondered if he had been bought by Matterson, but on second thoughts I didn't think so. Buying a forestry officer in British Columbia would be like buying a Cardinal of the Church – just about impossible. Fifty per cent of the province's revenue comes from timber and conservation is the great god. To come out against conservation is like coming out against motherhood.

I checked the map again. 'Thanks for your trouble, Mr Tanner,' I said. 'You've been very obliging, but there seems precious little for me here. Any of these tree-farm licences likely to fall vacant?'

'Not for a long time, Mr Boyd. The Matterson Corporation has put in a lot of capital in sawmills and pulp mills; they insisted on long-term licences.'

I nodded. 'Very wise; I'd want the same. Well, thanks again, Mr Tanner.'

I left him without satisfying the wondering look in his eye and drove down to the depot where I picked up a lot of geological gear that I had sent in advance. The fat depot superintendent helped me load the Land-Rover, and said, 'You figuring on staying?'

'For a while,' I said. 'Just for a while. You can call me Trinavant's last hope.'

A salacious leer spread over his face. 'Clare Trinavant? You want to watch out for Howard Matterson.'

I suppressed the desire to push his face in. 'Not Clare Trinavant,' I said gently. 'John Trinavant. And I can take care of Howard Matterson, too, if he interferes. Have you got a phone anywhere?'

He still wore the surprised look as he said abstractedly, 'In the hall.'

I strode past him and he came pattering after me. 'Hey, mister, John Trinavant is dead – he's been dead for over ten years.'

I stopped. 'I know he's dead. That's the point. Don't you get it? Now beat it. This is a private telephone call.'

He turned away with a baffled shrug and a muttered, 'Aw, nuts!' I smiled because another rock had been thrown into the pool and another set of ripples started to affright the hungry pike.

Did you hear about that crazy man that just blew into town? Said he was Trinavant's last hope. I thought he meant Clare; you know, Clare Trinavant, but he said he meant John. Can you beat that, with old John been dead for ten – no, twelve – years! This guy was here a couple of years back and had words with Howard Matterson about Clare Trinavant. How do I know? Because Maggie Hope told me – she was Howard's secretary then. I warned her not to shoot her mouth off but it was no good. Howard fired her. But this guy is crazy, for sure. I mean, John Trinavant – he's dead.

I phoned the *Recorder* office and got hold of Mac. 'Do you know of a good lawyer?' I asked.

'I might,' he said cautiously. 'What do you want a lawyer for?'

'I want a lawyer who isn't afraid of bucking Matterson. I know the land laws but I want a lawyer who can give legal punch to what I know – dress the stuff up in that scary legal language.'

'There's old Fraser – he's retired now but he's a friend of mine and he doesn't like Matterson one little bit. Would he do?'

'He'll do,' I said. 'As long as he's not too old to go into court if necessary.'

'Oh, Fraser can go into court. What are you up to, Bob?'

I grinned. 'I'm going prospecting on Matterson land. My guess is that Matterson isn't going to like it.'

There was a muffled noise in the receiver and I put the phone down gently.

FIVE

They had driven a new road up to the Kinoxi Valley to take care of the stream of construction trucks carrying materials for the dam and the logging trucks bringing the lumber from the valley. It was a rough road, not too well graded and being chewed to pieces by the heavy traffic. Where there was mud they had corduroyed it with ten-inch logs which made your teeth rattle, and in places they had cut through the soil down to bedrock to provide a firmer footing.

No one took any notice of me; I was merely another man driving a battered truck which looked as though it had a right to be there. The road led to the bottom of the low escarpment where they were building the generator house, a squat structure rafted on a sea of churned-up mud in which a gang of construction workers sweated and swore. Up the escarpment, by the side of the brown-running stream, ran the flume, a 36-inch pipe to bring the water to the powerhouse. The road took off on the other side of the stream and clung to a hillside, zig-zagging its way to the top and towards the dam.

I was surprised to see how far they had got with the construction. McDougall was right: the Kinoxi Valley would be under water in three months. I pulled off the road and watched them pour concrete for a few minutes and noted the smooth way in which the sand and gravel trucks were handled. This was an efficient operation.

A big logging truck passed, going downhill like a juggernaut, and the Land-Rover rocked on its springs in the wind of its passing. There was not likely to be another close behind it so I pressed on up the road, past the dam and into the valley where I ran the Land-Rover off the road and behind trees where it was not likely to be seen. Then I went on foot away from the road, taking a slanting, climbing course across the hillside until I was high enough to get a good view of the valley.

It was a scene of desolation. The quiet valley I had known, where the fish jumped in the stream and the deer browsed in the woodlands, had been destroyed. In its place was a wilderness of jagged stumps and a tangle of felled brushwood on a ground of mud criss-crossed by the track marks of the trucks. Away up the valley, near the little lake, there was still the green of trees, but I could hear, even at that distance, the harsh scream of the power saws biting into living wood.

British Columbia is very conservation-minded where its lumber resources are concerned. Out of every dollar earned in the province fifty cents comes ultimately from the logging industry and the Government wants that happy state of affairs to continue. So the Forestry Service polices the woodlands and controls the cutting. There are an awful lot of men who get a kick out of murdering a big tree and there are a few money-greedy bastards who are willing to let them get their kicks because of the number of board-feet of manufactured lumber that the tree will provide at the sawmill. So the Forestry Service has its work cut out.

The idea is that the amount of lumber cut, expressed in cubic feet, should not exceed the natural annual growth. Now, when you start talking in cubic footage of lumber in

British Columbia you sound like an astronomer calculating the distance in miles to a pretty far star. The forest lands cover 220,000 square miles, say, four times the size of England, and the annual growth is estimated at two and a half billion cubic feet. So the annual cutting rate is limited to a little over two billion cubic feet and the result is an increasing, instead of a wasting, asset.

That is why I looked down into the Kinoxi Valley with shocked eyes. Normally, in a logging operation, only the mature trees are cut; but here they were taking *everything*. I suppose it was logical. If you are going to flood a valley there is no point in leaving the trees, but this sight offended me. This was a rape of the land, something that had not been since the bad old days before the First World War when the conservation laws came in.

I looked up the valley and did a quick calculation. The new Matterson Lake was going to cover twenty square miles, of which five square miles in the north belonged to Clare Trinavant. That meant that Matterson was cutting a solid fifteen square miles of trees and the Forestry Service was letting him do it because of the dam. That amount of lumber was enough to pay for the dam with a hell of a lot left over. It seemed to me that Matterson was a pretty sharp guy, but he was too damned ruthless for my taste.

I went back to the Land-Rover and drove back down the road and past the dam. Halfway down the escarpment I stopped and again drove off the road but I didn't bother to hide the vehicle this time. I *wanted* to be seen. I rummaged about in my gear and found what I wanted – something to confound the ignorant – and then, in full view of the road I started to act in a suspicious manner. I took my hammer and chipped at rocks, I dug at the ground like a gopher scrabbling a hole, I looked at pebbles through a magnifying-glass and I paced out large areas gazing intently at the dial of an instrument which I held in my hand.

It was nearly an hour before I was noticed. A jeep rocketed up the hill and slammed to a stop and two men got out. As they walked over I slipped off my wrist-watch and palmed it, then stooped to pick up a large rock. Booted feet crunched nearer and I turned. The bigger of the men said, 'What are you doing here?'

'Prospecting,' I said nonchalantly.

'The hell you are! This is private land.'

'I don't think so,' I said.

The other man pointed. 'What's that you got there?'

'This? It's a geiger counter.' I moved it near to the rock I held – and nearer to the luminous dial of my watch – and it buzzed like a demented mosquito. 'Interesting,' I said.

The big man leaned forward. 'What is it?'

'Maybe uranium,' I said. 'But I doubt it. Could be thorium.' I looked at the rock closely, then tossed it away casually. 'That stuff's not payable, but it's an indication. It's an interesting geological structure round here.'

They looked at each other, a little startled; then the big man said, 'That may be, but you're still on private land.'

I said pleasantly, 'You can't stop me prospecting here.'

'Oh no?' he said belligerently.

'Why don't you check with your boss? Might be better that way.'

The smaller man said, 'Yeah, Novak, let's check with Waystrand. I mean, *uranium* – or this other stuff – it sounds important.'

The big man hesitated, then said in a heavy tone, 'Have you got a name, mister?'

'The name's Boyd,' I said. 'Bob Boyd.'

'Okay, Boyd. I'll see the boss. But I still think you're not going to stay round here.'

I watched them go away and smiled, slipping the watch back on my wrist. So Waystrand was some kind of a boss up here. McDougall had said he'd been given a good job at the dam. I had a score to settle with him. I glanced up at the telephone line which followed the road. The big man would tell Waystrand and Waystrand would get on the telephone to Fort Farrell and Howard Matterson's reaction was predictable – he'd blow up.

It wasn't ten minutes before the jeep came back followed by another. I recognized Waystrand – he'd filled out a lot in the last eighteen months; his chest was broader, he looked harder and he wasn't so much the kid still wet behind the ears. But he still wasn't as big as I was, and I reckoned I could take him on if I had to, although I'd have to make it quick before the other two characters could get started. Odds of three to one were not too good.

Waystrand smiled wickedly as he came up. 'So it's you. I wondered about that when I heard the name. Mr Matterson's compliments and will you get the hell out of here.'

'Which Mr Matterson?'

'Howard Matterson.'

'So you're still running and telling tales to him, Jimmy,' I said caustically.

He balled his fists. 'Mr Matterson said I was to get you off this land nice and easy, with no trouble.' He was holding himself in with an effort. 'I owe you something, Boyd; and it wouldn't take much for me to give it to you. Mr Matterson said if you *wouldn't* go quietly I had to see that you went anyway. Now, get off this land and back to Fort Farrell. It's up to you if you go under your own power or if you're carried off.'

I said, 'I have every right to be here.'

Waystrand made a quick sign. 'Okay, boys. Take him.'

'Wait a minute,' I said quickly. 'I've had my say – I'll go.' It would be pointless to get beaten up at this stage, although I would dearly have loved to wipe the contemptuous grin off Waystrand's face.

'You're not so brave, Boyd; not when you're facing a man expecting a fight.'

'I'll take you on any time,' I said. 'When you haven't got a gun.'

He didn't like that, but he did nothing. They watched me pick up my gear and stow it in the Land-Rover and then Waystrand climbed into his jeep and drove slowly down the hill. I followed in the Land-Rover and the other jeep came after me. They were taking no chances of my slipping away.

We got down to the bottom of the escarpment and Waystrand slowed, waving me to a stop. He wheeled round in the jeep and came alongside. 'Wait here, Boyd; and don't try anything funny,' he said, then he shot off and waved down a logging truck that had just come down the hill. He spoke to the driver for a couple of minutes and then came back. 'Okay, big man; on your way – and don't come back, although I'd sure like it if you did.'

'I'll be seeing you, Jimmy,' I said. 'That's for sure.' I slammed in the gear-lever and drove on down the road, following the loaded logging truck which had gone on ahead.

It wasn't very long before I caught up with it. It was going very slowly and I couldn't pass because this was in one of those places where the road builders had made a cutting right down to bedrock and there were steep banks of earth on either side. I couldn't understand why this guy was crawling, but I certainly didn't want to take the chance of passing and being squeezed to a pulp by twenty tons of lumber and metal.

The truck slowed even more and I crawled behind at less than walking pace, fuming at the delay. You put an ordinary nice guy in an automobile and he loses all the common decency he ever had. A guy who'll politely open a door for an old lady will damn' near kill the same old lady by cutting across her bows at sixty miles an hour just to beat a stop light, and he'll think nothing of it. This guy in front probably had his troubles and must have had a good and sound reason for going so slowly. I was in no particular hurry to get back to Fort Farrell but still I sat there and cursed – such is the relationship between a man and his auto.

I glanced into the mirror and was startled. The guy in front certainly had good reasons for going slowly, for coming behind at a hell of a lick was another logging truck, an eighteen-wheeler – twenty or more tons moving at thirty miles an hour. He got so close before he slammed on anchors that I heard the piercing hiss of his air-brakes and he slowed to our crawl with the ugly square front of his truck not a foot from the rear of the Land-Rover.

I was the filling in the nasty sandwich. I could see the driver behind laughing fit to bust and I knew that if I wasn't careful there'd be some red stuff in the sandwich which wouldn't be ketchup. The Land-Rover lurched a little as the heavy fender of the truck rammed into the rear, and there was a crunching noise. I trod delicately on the gas pedal and inched nearer to the truck in front – I couldn't move much nearer or else I'd have a thirty-inch log coming through the windshield. I remembered this cutting from the way in: it was a mile long and right now we were about a quarter way through. The next three-quarters of a mile was going to be tricky.

The truck behind blared its horn and a gap opened up in front as the guy ahead put on speed. I pressed on the gas but not fast enough, because the rear truck rammed me again, harder this time. This was going to be trickier than I thought; it looked as though we were going to do a speed run, and that could be goddam dangerous.

We came to a dip and the speed increased and we zoomed down at forty miles an hour, the truck behind trying to climb up the exhaust pipe of the guy in front and not worrying too much about me, caught in the middle. My hands were sweating and were slippery on the wheel, and I had to do some tricky work with gas pedal, clutch and brake. One mistake on my part – or on theirs – and the Land-Rover would be mashed into scrap-iron and I'd have the engine in my lap.

Three more times I was rammed from behind and I hated to think what was happening to my gear. And once I was nipped, caught between the heavy steel fenders of the two trucks for a fraction of a second. I felt the compression on the chassis and I swear the Land-Rover was momentarily lifted from the ground. There was a log rubbing on the windshield and the glass starred and smashed into a misty opacity and I couldn't see a damned thing ahead.

Fortunately the pressure released and I was running free again with my head stuck out of the side and I saw we were at the end of the cutting. One of the logs on the left side of the front truck seemed to be loaded a little higher than the others, and I judged it was high enough to clear the cab. I had to get out of this squeeze. There was very little room to manoeuvre and those sadistic bastards could hold me there until we got to the sawmill if I couldn't figure a way out.

So I spun the wheel and chanced it and found I was wrong. The log didn't clear the top of the cab – not by a quarter of an inch – and I heard the rending tear of sheet metal. But I couldn't stop then; I fed gas to the engine frantically and tore free to find myself bucketing over the rough ground and heading straight for a big Douglas fir. I hauled on the wheel and swerved again and again, weaving among the trees and driving roughly parallel with the road.

I passed the front truck and saw my chance, so I rammed down hard on the gas pedal and shot ahead of it and fled down the road with that eighteen-wheel monster pounding after me, blaring its horn. I knew better than to stop and fight it out with those guys; they wouldn't stop on the road just because I did and me and the Land-Rover would be a total loss. I had the legs of them and scooted away in front,

passing the turn-off to the sawmill and not stopping until I
was a full mile the other side.

Then I stopped and held up my hands. They were
shaking uncontrollably and, when I moved, my shirt was
clammy against my skin because it was soaked in sweat. I lit
a cigarette and waited until the shakes went away before I
climbed out to survey the damage. The front wasn't too bad,
although a steady drip of water indicated a busted radiator.
The windshield was a total write-off and the top of the cab
looked as though someone had used a blunt can-opener on
it. The rear end was smashed up pretty badly – it looked like
the front end of any normal auto crash. I looked in the back
and saw the shattered wooden case and a clutter of broken
bottles from my field testing kit. There was the acrid stink of
chemicals from the reagents swimming about on the bottom
and I hastily lifted the geiger counter out of the liquid – free
acids don't do delicate instruments any good.

I stepped back and estimated the cost of the damage. Two
bloody noses for two truckers; maybe a broken back for
Jimmy Waystrand; and a brand-new Land-Rover from Mr
Howard Matterson. I was inclined to be a bit lenient on
Howard; I didn't think he'd given any orders to squeeze me
like that. But Jimmy Waystrand certainly had, and he was
going to pay the hard way.

After a while I drove into Fort Farrell, eliciting curious
glances from passers-by in King Street. I pulled into
Summerskill's used car lot and he looked up and said in
alarm, 'Hey, I'm not responsible for that – it happened after
you bought the crate.'

I climbed out. 'I know,' I said soothingly. 'Just get the
thing going again. I think she'll want a new radiator – and
get a rear lamp working somehow.'

He walked round the Land-Rover in a full circle, then
came back and stared at me hard. 'What did you do – get
into a fight with a tank?'

'Something like that,' I agreed.

He waved. 'That rear fender is twisted like a pretzel. How did that happen to a *rear* fender?'

'Maybe it got hot and melted into that shape,' I suggested.

'Cut the wonder. How long will it take?'

'You just want to get the thing moving again? A jury-rig job?'

'That'll do.'

He scratched his head. 'I have an old Land-Rover radiator back of the shed, so you're lucky there. Say a couple of hours.'

'Okay,' I said. 'I'll be back in an hour and give you a hand.' I left him and walked up the street to the Matterson Building. Maybe I just might have the beginnings of a quarrel with Howard.

I breezed into his outer office and said, without breaking stride, 'I'm going to see Matterson.'

'But – but he's busy,' his secretary said agitatedly.

'Sure,' I said, not stopping. 'Howard is a busy, busy man.' I threw open the door of his office and walked inside to find Howard in conference with Donner. 'Hello, Howard,' I said. 'Don't you want to see me?'

'What do you mean by busting in like that?' he demanded. 'Can't you see I'm busy?' He thumbed a switch. 'Miss Kerr, what do you mean by letting people into – '

I reached over and lifted his hand away from the intercom, breaking the connection. 'She didn't let me,' I said softly. 'She couldn't stop me – so don't blame her. Now, I'll ask you a like-minded question. What do you mean by having Waystrand throw me out?'

'That's a silly question,' he snarled. He looked at Donner. 'Tell him.'

Donner cracked his knuckles and said precisely, 'Any geological exploration of Matterson land we'll organize for ourselves. We don't need you to do it for us, Boyd. You'll stay clear in future, I trust.'

'You bet he'll stay clear,' said Matterson.

I said, 'Howard, you've held tree-farm licences for so long that you think you own the goddam land. Give you another few years and you'll think you own the whole province of British Columbia. Your head's getting swelled, Howard.'

'Don't call me Howard,' he snapped. 'Come to the point.'

'All right,' I said. 'I wasn't on Matterson land – I was on Crown land. Anyone with a prospector's licence can fossick on Crown land. Just because you have a licence to grow and cut lumber doesn't mean you can stop me. And if you think you can, I'll slap a court order on you so fast that it'll make your ears spin.'

It took some time to sink in but it finally did and he looked at Donner in a helpless way. I grinned at Donner and mimicked Matterson. 'Tell him.'

Donner said, '*If* you were on Crown land – and that is a matter of question – then perhaps you are right.'

I said, 'There's no perhaps about it; you *know* I'm right.'

Matterson said suddenly, 'I don't think you were on Crown land.'

'Check your maps,' I said helpfully. 'I bet you haven't looked at them for years. You're too accustomed to regarding the whole goddam country as your own.'

Matterson twitched a finger at Donner, who left the room. He looked at me with hard eyes. 'What are you up to, Boyd?'

'Just trying to make a living,' I said easily. 'There's a lot of good prospecting country round here – it's just as good a place to explore as up north, and a lot warmer, too.'

'You might find it too warm,' he said acidly. 'You're not going about things in a friendly way.'

I raised my eyebrows. '*I'm* not! You ought to have been out on the road to Kinoxi this morning. I'd sooner be friendly with a grizzly bear than with some of your truckers. Anyway, I didn't come here to enter a popularity contest.'

'Why did you come here?'

'Maybe you'll find out one day – if you're smart enough, Howard.'

'I told you not to call me Howard,' he said irritatedly.

Donner came in with a map, and I saw it was a copy of the one I had inspected in Tanner's office. Howard spread it on his desk and I said, 'You'll find that the Kinoxi Valley is split between you and Clare Trinavant – she in the north and you in the south with the lion's share. *But* Matterson land stops just short of the escarpment – everything south of that is Crown land. And *that* means that the dam at the top of the escarpment and the powerhouse at the bottom is on Crown land, and I can go fossicking round there any time I like. Any comment?'

Matterson looked up at Donner, who nodded his head slightly. 'It seems that Mr Boyd is correct,' he said.

'You're damn' right I'm correct.' I pointed at Matterson. 'Now there's something else I want to bring up – a matter of a wrecked Land-Rover.'

He glared at me. 'I'm not responsible for the way you drive.'

The way he said it I was certain he knew what had happened. 'All right,' I said. 'I'll be using the Kinoxi road pretty often in the near future. Tell your truckers to keep away from me, or someone will get killed in a road accident – and it won't be me.'

He just showed me his teeth, and said, 'I understand you *were* staying at the Matterson House.' He leaned so heavily on the past tense that the sentence nearly busted in the middle.

'I get the message,' I said. 'Enemies to the death, eh, Howard?' I walked out without saying another word and went down to the Matterson House Hotel.

The desk clerk moved fast but I got in first. 'I understand I've checked out,' I said sourly.

'Er . . . yes, Mr Boyd. I've prepared your bill.'

I paid it, then went up and packed my case and lugged it across the road to Summerskill's car lot. He climbed out from under the Land-Rover and looked at me in a puzzled manner. 'Not ready yet, Mr Boyd.'

'That's all right. I have to get something to eat.'

He scrambled to his feet. 'Hey, Mr Boyd; you know, something funny has happened. I just checked the chassis and it has *bulged*.'

'What do you mean – bulged?'

Summerskill held his hands about a foot apart with curled fingers like a man holding a short length of four-by-two, and brought them together slowly. 'This damn' chassis has been *squoze*.' He wore a baffled look.

'Will that make any difference to its running?'

He shrugged. 'Not much – if you don't expect much.'

'Then leave well alone,' I advised. 'I'll be back as soon as I've had a bite to eat.'

I ate at the Hellenic Café, expecting to see McDougall but he didn't show up. I didn't want to see him at the *Recorder* office so I drifted round town for a while, keeping my eyes open. When after nearly an hour I hadn't seen him, I went back to Summerskill to find that he'd nearly finished the job.

'That'll be forty-five dollars, Mr Boyd,' he said. 'And I'm letting it go cheap.'

I dumped some groceries I had bought into the back of the Land-Rover and took out my wallet, mentally adding it to the account that Matterson was going to pay some day. As I counted out the bills, Summerskill said, 'I wasn't able to do much with the top of the cab. I bashed the metal back into place and put some canvas on top; that'll keep the rain out.'

'Thanks,' I said. 'If I have another accident – and that's not unlikely – you shall have my trade.'

He pulled a sour face. 'You have another accident like that and there'll be nothing left to repair.'

I drove out of town to McDougall's cabin and parked the Land-Rover out of sight after I had unloaded everything. I stripped and changed and heated some water. A little went to make coffee and I washed my shirt and pants in the rest. I stacked the groceries in the pantry and began to get my gear in order, checking to see exactly what was ruined. I was grieving over a busted scintillometer when I heard the noise of a car, and when I ducked my head to look out of the window I saw a battered old Chevvy pulling up outside. McDougall got out.

'I thought I'd find you here,' he said. 'They told me at the hotel you'd checked out.'

'Howard arranged it,' I said.

'I had a telephone call from God not half an hour ago,' said Mac. 'Old Bull is getting stirred up. He wants to know who you are, where you're from, what your intentions are and how long you're going to stay around Fort Farrell.' He smiled. 'He gave me the job of finding out, naturally enough.'

'No comment,' I said.

Mac raised his eyebrows. 'What do you mean?'

'I mean that I'm exercising my God-given right to keep my mouth shut. You tell old Matterson that I refuse to speak to the Press. I want to keep him guessing – I want him to come to me.'

'Good enough,' said Mac. 'But he's lost you. No one knows you're here.'

'We can't keep that a secret for long,' I said. 'Not in a town as small as Fort Farrell.' I smiled. 'So we finally goosed the old boy into moving. I wonder what did it.'

'It could have been anything, from the talk I've heard round town,' said Mac. 'Ben Parker, for instance, thinks you're crazy.'

'Who is Ben Parker?'

'The guy at the bus depot. Clarry Summerskill, on the other hand, holds you in great respect.'

'*What* kind of Summerskill?'

Mac gave me a twisted grin. 'His name is Clarence, and he doesn't like it. He doesn't think it's a suitable moniker for a used car dealer. He once asked me how in hell he could put up a sign saying, 'Honest Clarence', and not get laughed at. Anyway, he told me that any man who could do in three short hours what you did to a Land-Rover must be the toughest guy in Canada. He based that on the fact that you didn't have a scratch on you. What *did* happen, anyway?'

'I'll put some water on for coffee,' I said. 'The Land-Rover's out back. Take a look at it.'

Mac went out to look at the damage and came back wearing a wry face. 'Drop over a cliff?' he asked.

I told him and he grew grave. 'The boys play rough,' he said.

'That's nothing. Just clean fun and games, that's all. It was a private idea of Jimmy Waystrand's; I don't think the Mattersons had anything to do with it. *They* haven't started yet.'

The kettle boiled. 'I'd rather have tea,' said Mac. 'Too much coffee makes me feel nervous and strung up, and we don't want that to happen, do we?' So he made strong black tea which tasted like stewed pennies. He said, 'Why did you go up to the dam, anyway?'

'I wanted to get Howard stirred up,' I said. 'I wanted to get noticed.'

'You did,' Mac said drily.

'How much is that dam costing?' I asked.

Mac pondered. 'Taking everything in – the dam, the powerhouse and the transmission lines – it'll run to six million dollars. Not as big as the Peace River Project, but not small potatoes.'

'I've been doing some figuring,' I said. 'I reckon that Matterson is taking over ten million dollars' worth of lumber out of the Kinoxi Valley. He's taking *everything* out, remember, not the less-than-one-per-cent cut that the Forestry Service usually allows. That leaves him with four million bucks.'

'Nice going,' said Mac.

'It gets better. He doesn't really want that four million dollars – he'd only have to pay tax on it; but the electricity plant does need maintenance and there's depreciation to take into account, so he invests three million dollars and that takes care of it. He makes one million bucks net, and he has free power for the Matterson enterprises for as far into the future as I can see.'

'Not to mention the dough he makes on the power he sells,' said Mac. 'That's pure cream.'

'It's like having a private entrance to Fort Knox,' I said.

Mac grunted. 'This smells of Donner. I've never known such a guy for seeing money where no one else can see it. And it's legal, too.'

I said, 'I think Clare Trinavant is a sentimental fool. She's letting emotion take the place of thinking. The Kinoxi Valley is going to be flooded and there is nothing she can do to stop it.'

'So?'

'So she has five square miles of woodland up there that's going to be wasted, and she's passing up three million dollars just because she has a grudge against the Mattersons. Isn't she aware of that?'

Mac shook his head. 'She's not a businesswoman – takes no interest in it. Her financial affairs are managed by a bank in Vancouver. I doubt if she's given it a thought.'

I said, 'Doesn't the Forestry Service have anything to say about it? It seems silly to waste all that lumber.'

'The Forestry Service has never been known to prosecute anyone for *not* cutting,' he pointed out. 'The problem has never come up before.'

'With three million bucks coming in for sure she could build her own sawmill,' I said forcefully. 'If she doesn't want the Mattersons in on it.'

'Bit late for that, isn't it?' Mac asked.

'That's the pity of it.' I brooded over it. 'She's more like Howard Matterson than she thinks; he is also an emotional type, although a bit more predictable.' I smiled. 'I reckon I can make Howard jump through hoops.'

'Don't think you can treat the old man like that,' said Mac warningly. 'He's tougher and more devious. He'll save up his Sunday punch and sneak it in from an unexpected direction.' He switched the subject. 'What's the next move?'

'More of the same. Old Matterson reacted fast so we must have hit a sore spot. I stir up talk about the Trinavants and I root about up near the dam.'

'Why go near the dam? What's that got to do with it?'

I scratched my head. 'I don't really know; I just have a hunch that there's an answer up there somewhere. We're not really sure that it wasn't my prowling around there that attracted Bull Matterson's interest. Another thing – I'd like to go up to Clare's cabin. How do I get there without crossing Matterson land? That might be a bit unwise now.'

'There's a road in from the back,' said Mac. He didn't ask me why I wanted to go up there, but instead dug out a tattered old map. I studied it and sighed. It was a hell of a long way round and I'd have given my soul for the Matterson Corporation helicopter.

II

The next day I spent in Fort Farrell, spreading the good word and really laying it on thick. Up to then I'd mentioned the name of Trinavant to only two people, but this time I covered a good cross-section of the Fort Farrell population, feeling something like a cross between a private detective and a Gallup pollster. That evening, in the cabin, I totted up the results in approved pollster fashion and sorted out my findings.

One of the things that stood out was the incredible ease with which a man's name could be erased from the public memory. Of the people who had moved into Fort Farrell in the last ten years fully eighty-five per cent of them had never heard of John Trinavant; and the same applied to those young people who had grown to maturity since his death.

The other, older people remembered him with a bit of nudging, and, almost always, with kindness. I came to the conclusion that Shakespeare was dead right: 'The evil that men do lives after them; the good is oft interred with their bones.' Still, the same analogy applies throughout our world. Any murderer can get his name in the newspapers, but if a decent man wishes to announce to the world that he's lived happily with his wife for twenty-five or fifty years he has to pay for it, by God!

There was also a fairly widespread resentment of the Mattersons, tinged somewhat with fear. The Matterson Corporation had got such a grip on the economic life of the community that it could put the squeeze on anybody, in-directly if not directly. Nearly everyone in Fort Farrell had a relative on the Matterson payroll, so there was a strong resistance to answering awkward questions.

Reactions to the name of John Trinavant were surer. Folks seemed amazed at themselves that they had allowed him to be forgotten. *I don't know why, but I haven't thought of old John in years.* I knew why. When the only source of public information in a town closes tight on a subject, when letters to the Editor about a dead man just don't get published, when a powerful man quietly discourages talk, then there is no particular call to remember. The living have their own bustling and multitudinous affairs and the dead slide into oblivion.

There had been talk of a John Trinavant Memorial to face the statue of Lieutenant Farrell in Trinavant Park. *I don't know why, but it never seemed to get off the ground; maybe there wasn't enough money for it – but, sure as hell, John Trinavant pumped enough money into this town. You'd think people would be ashamed of themselves, but they're not – they've just forgotten what he did for Fort Farrell.*

I got tired of hearing the refrain – *I don't know why.* The depressing part of it was that they really didn't know why, they didn't know that Bull Matterson had screwed the lid down tight on the name of Trinavant. He could have given the Hitlers and Stalins a pointer or two on thought control, and more and more I was impressed at the effort which he must have put into this operation, although I still had no idea as to why he had done it.

'Where are the Trinavants buried?' I asked Mac.

'Edmonton,' he said briefly. 'Bull saw to it.'

The Trinavants did not even have a resting-place in the town they had built.

After a day's intensive poking and prying into the Trinavant mystery I decided to give Fort Farrell a miss next day. If two conversations had caused Bull Matterson to react, then that day's work must be giving him connip- tions, and acting on sound psychological principles, I wanted to be hard to find – I wanted to give him time to come really to the boil.

That cut out investigating the site of the dam, so I decided to go up to Clare Trinavant's cabin. Why I wanted to go there I didn't know, but it was as good a place as any to keep out of Matterson's way and maybe I could get in a day of deep thought with some fishing thrown in.

It was a hundred and twenty miles on rutted, jolting roads – a wide swing round the Matterson holdings – and when I reached the cabin I was sore and aching. It was even bigger than I remembered, a long low sprawling structure with a warm red cedar shingle roof. Standing apart from it was another cabin, smaller and simpler, and there was smoke curling from the grey stone chimney. A man emerged carrying a shotgun which he stood leaning against the wall not too far from his hand.

'Mr Waystrand?' I called.

'That's me.'

'I have a letter for you from McDougall of Fort Farrell.'

McDougall had insisted on that because this was Jimmy Waystrand's father, whose allegiance to Clare Trinavant was firm and whose attitude to Bob Boyd was likely to be violent. 'You cut his son and you insulted Clare – or so he thinks,' said Mac. 'You'd better let me straighten him out. I'll give you a letter.'

Waystrand was a man of about fifty with a deeply grooved face as brown as a nut. He read the letter slowly, his lips moving with the words, then gave me a swift glance with hard blue eyes and read it again very carefully to see if he'd got it right first time. Then he said a little hesitantly, 'Old Mac says you're all right.'

I let out my breath slowly. 'I wouldn't know about that – it's not my place to say. But I'd trust his judgment on most things; wouldn't you?'

Waystrand's face crinkled into a reluctant smile. 'I reckon I would. What can I do for you?'

'Not much,' I said. 'A place to pitch a camp – and if you could spare a steelhead from the creek there, I'd be obliged.'

'You're welcome to the trout,' he said. 'But there's no need to camp. There's a bed inside – if you want it. My son's away.' His eyes held mine in an unwinking stare.

'Thanks,' I said. 'That's very kind of you, Mr Waystrand.'

I didn't have to go fishing for my dinner, after all, because Waystrand cooked up a tasty hash and we shared it. He was a slow-moving, taciturn man whose thought processes moved in low gear, but that didn't mean he was stupid – he just took a little longer to reach the right conclusion, that's all. After we had eaten I tried to draw him out. 'Been with Miss Trinavant long?'

He drew on his pipe and expelled a plume of pale blue smoke. 'Quite a time,' he said uninformatively. I sat and said nothing, just waiting for the wheels to go round. He smoked contemplatively for a few minutes, then said, 'I was with the old man.'

'John Trinavant?'

He nodded. 'I started working for John Trinavant when I was a nipper just left school. I've been with the Trinavants ever since.'

'They tell me he was a good man,' I said.

'Just about the best.' He relapsed into contemplation of the glowing coal in the bowl of his pipe.

I said, 'Pity about the accident.'

'Accident?'

'Yes – the auto crash.'

There was another long silence before he took the pipe from his mouth. 'Some folks would call it an accident, I suppose.'

I held my breath. 'But you don't?'

'Mr Trinavant was a good driver,' he said. 'He wouldn't drive too fast on an icy road.'

'It's not certain he was driving. His wife might have been at the wheel – or his son.'

'Not on that car,' said Waystrand positively. 'It was a brand-new Cadillac two weeks old. Mr Trinavant wouldn't let anyone drive that car except himself until the engine got broken in.'

'Then what do you think happened?'

'Lots of funny things going on about that time,' he said obscurely.

'Such as?' I prompted.

He tapped the dottle in his pipe on the heel of his boot. 'You're asking a lot of questions, Boyd; and I don't see why I should answer 'em, except that old Mac said I should. I ain't got too much love for you, Boyd, and I want to find out one thing for sure. Are you going to bring up anything that'll hurt Miss Trinavant?'

I held his eye. 'No, Mr Waystrand. I'm not.'

He stared at me for a moment longer, then waved his arm largely. 'All these woodlands, hundreds of thousands of acres – Bull Matterson got 'em all, 'cept this tract that John left to Miss Trinavant. He got the sawmills, the pulp mills – just about everything that John Trinavant built up. Don't you think the accident came at the right time?'

I felt depressed. All Waystrand had were the same unformulated suspicions that plagued Mac and myself. I said, 'Have you any evidence that it *wasn't* an accident? Anything at all?'

He shook his head heavily. 'Nothing to show.'

'What did Cl . . . Miss Trinavant think about it? I don't mean when it happened, but afterwards.'

'I ain't talked to her about it – it ain't my place – and she's said nothing to me.' He shook the dottle from his pipe into the fire and put the pipe on the mantel. 'I'm going to bed,' he said brusquely.

I stayed up for a while, chasing the thing round in circles, and then went to bed myself, to the sparely furnished room that had been Jimmy Waystrand's. It had a bleak aspect because it was as anonymous as any hotel room; just a bed, a primitive wash-stand, a cupboard and a few bare shelves. It looked as though young Jimmy had cleared out for good, leaving nothing of his youth behind him, and I felt sorry for old Waystrand.

The next day I fished a little and chopped some logs because the log pile looked depleted. Waystrand came out at the sound of the axe and watched me. I had stripped off my shirt because the exercise made me sweat and swinging that axe was hard work. Waystrand regarded me for a while, then said, 'You're a strong man, but you're misusing your strength. That's not the way to use an axe.'

I leaned on the axe and grinned at him. 'Know a better way?'

'Sure; give it to me.' He took the axe and stood poised in front of the log, then swung it down casually. A chip flew and then another – and another. 'See,' he said. 'It's in the turn of the wrists.' He demonstrated in slow motion, then handed back the axe. 'Try it that way.'

I chopped in the way he had shown me, rather inexpertly, and sure enough the work went easier. I said, 'You're experienced with an axe.'

'I used to be a logger for Mr Trinavant – but that was before the accident. I got pinned under a ten-inch log and hurt my back.' He smiled slowly. 'That's why I'm letting you get on with the chopping – it don't do my back no good.'

I chopped for a while, then said, 'Know anything about the value of lumber?'

'Some. I was boss of a section – I picked up something about values.'

'Matterson is clearing out his part of the Kinoxi,' I said. 'He's taking everything – not just the normal Forestry Service allowable cut. What do you think the value per square mile is?'

He pondered for a while and said finally, 'Not much under seven hundred thousand dollars.'

I said, 'Don't you think Miss Trinavant should do something about this end? She'll lose an awful lot of money if those trees are drowned.'

He nodded. 'You know, this land hasn't ever been cut over since John Trinavant died. The trees have been putting on weight in the last twelve years, and there's a lot of mature timber which should have been taken out already. I reckon, if you made a solid cut, this land would run to a million dollars a square mile.'

I whistled. I'd underestimated her loss. Five million bucks was a lot of dough. 'Haven't you talked to her about it?'

'She's not been here to be talked to.' He shrugged rather sheepishly. 'And I'm no great hand with a pen.'

'Maybe I'd better write to her?' I suggested. 'What's her address?'

Waystrand hesitated. 'You write to the bank in Vancouver; they pass it on.' He gave me the address of her bank.

I stayed around until late afternoon, chopping a hell of a lot of logs for Waystrand and cursing young Jimmy with every stroke. That young whelp had no right to leave his old man alone. It was evident that there was no Mrs Waystrand and it wasn't good for a man to be alone, especially one suffering from back trouble.

When I left, Waystrand said, 'If you see my boy, tell him he can come back any time.' He smiled grimly. 'That is, if you can get near enough to talk without him taking a swing at you.'

I didn't tell him that I'd already encountered Jimmy. 'I'll pass on the message when I see him – and I *will* be seeing him.'

'You did right when you straight-armed him that time,' said Waystrand. 'I didn't think so then, but from what Miss Trinavant said afterwards I saw he had it coming.' He put out his hand. 'No hard feelings, Mr Boyd.'

'No hard feelings,' I said, and we shook on it. I put the Land-Rover into gear and bumped down the track, leaving

Waystrand looking after me, a diminishing and rather sad figure.

I made good time on the way back to Fort Farrell but it was dark by the time I was on the narrow track to McDougall's cottage. Halfway along, on a narrow corner, I was obstructed by a car stuck in the mud and only just managed to squeeze through. It was a Lincoln Continental, a big dream-boat the size of a battleship and certainly not the auto for a road like this; the overhangs fore and aft were much too long and it would scrape its fanny on every dip of the road. The trunk top looked big enough to land a helicopter on.

I pushed on to the cabin and saw a light inside. Mac's beat-up Chevvy wasn't around so I wondered who the visitor was. Being of a cautious nature and not knowing what trouble might have stirred up in my absence, I coasted the Land-Rover to a halt very quietly and sneaked across to look through the window before I went in.

A woman was sitting quietly before the fire reading a book. A woman I had never seen before.

SIX

I pushed open the door and she looked up. 'Mr Boyd?'

I regarded her. She looked as out of place in Fort Farrell as a *Vogue* model. She was tall and thin with the emaciated thinness which seems to be fashionable, God knows why. She looked as though she lived on a diet of lettuce with thin brown bread – no butter; to sit down to steak and potatoes would no doubt have killed her by overtaxing an unused digestive system. From head to foot she reflected a world of which the good people of Fort Farrell know little – the jazzed-up, with-it world of the sixties – from the lank straight hair to the mini-skirt and the kinky patent-leather boots. It wasn't a world I particularly liked, but I may be old-fashioned. Anyway, the little-girl style certainly didn't suit this woman, who was probably in her thirties.

'Yes, I'm Boyd.'

She stood up. 'I'm Mrs Atherton,' she said. 'I apologize for just barging in, but everyone does round here, you know.'

I placed her as a Canadian aping a British accent. I said, 'What can I do for you, Mrs Atherton?'

'Oh, it isn't what you can do for me – it's what I can do for you. I heard you were staying here and dropped in to see if I could help. Just being neighbourly, you know.'

She looked as neighbourly as Brigitte Bardot. 'Kind of you to take the trouble,' I said. 'But I doubt if it's necessary. I'm a grown boy, Mrs Atherton.'

She looked up at me. 'I'll say you are,' she said admiringly. 'My, but you are big.'

I noticed she'd helped herself to Mac's Scotch. 'Have *another* drink,' I said ironically.

'Thanks – I believe I will,' she said nonchalantly. 'Will you join me?'

I began to think that to get rid of her was going to be quite a job; there's nothing you can do with an uninsultable woman short of tossing her out on her can, and that's not my style. I said, 'No, I don't think I will.'

'Suit yourself,' she said easily, and poured herself a healthy slug of Mac's jealously conserved *Islay Mist*. 'Are you going to stay in Fort Farrell long, Mr Boyd?'

I sat down. 'Why do you ask?'

'Oh, you don't know how I look forward to seeing a fresh face in this dump. I don't know why I stay here – I really don't.'

I said cautiously, 'Does Mr Atherton work in Fort Farrell?'

She laughed. 'Oh, there's no Mr Atherton – not any more.'

'I'm sorry.'

'No need to be sorry, my dear man; he's not dead – just divorced.' She crossed her legs and gave me a good look at her thigh; those mini-skirts don't hide much, but to me a female knee is an anatomical joint and not a public entertainment, so she was wasting her time. 'Who are you working for?' she asked.

'I'm a freelance,' I said. 'A geologist.'

'Oh dear – a technical man. Well, don't talk to me about it – I'm sure it would be way over my head.'

I began to wonder about the neighbourly bit. Mac's cabin was well off the beaten track and it would be a very good

Samaritan who would drive into the woods outside Fort Farrell to bring comfort and charity, especially if it meant ditching a Lincoln Continental. Mrs Atherton didn't seem to fit the part.

She said, 'What are you looking for – uranium?'

'Could be. Anything that's payable.' I wondered what had put uranium into her mind. Something went 'twang' in my head and a warning bell rang.

'I have been told that the ground has been pretty well picked over round here. You may be wasting your time.' She laughed trillingly and flashed me a brilliant smile. 'But I wouldn't know anything about such technical matters. I only know what I'm told.'

I smiled at her engagingly. 'Well, Mrs Atherton, I prefer to believe my own eyes. I'm not inexperienced, you know.'

She gave me an unbelievably coy look. 'I'll bet you're not.' She downed the second third of her drink. 'Are you interested in history, Mr Boyd?'

I looked at her blankly, unprepared for the switch. 'I haven't thought much about it. What kind of history?'

She swished the Scotch around in her glass. 'One has to do *something* in Fort Farrell or one is sent perfectly crazy,' she said. 'I'm thinking of joining the Fort Farrell Historical Society. Mrs Davenant is President – have you met her?'

'No, I haven't.' For the life of me I couldn't see where this talk was leading, but if Mrs Atherton was interested in history then I was a ring-tailed lemur.

'You wouldn't think it, but I'm really a shy person,' she said. She was dead right – I wouldn't think it. 'I wouldn't want to join the society by myself. I mean – a novice among all those really experienced people. But if someone would join with me to give me some support, that would be different.'

'And you want *me* to join the historical society?'

'They tell me Fort Farrell has a very interesting history. Did you know it was founded by a Lieutenant Farrell way back in . . . oh . . . way back? And he was helped by a man called Trinavant, and the Trinavant family really built up this town.'

'Is that so?' I said drily.

'It's a pity about the Trinavants,' she said casually. 'The whole family was wiped out not very long ago. Isn't it a pity that a family that built a whole town should disappear like that?'

Again there was a 'twang' in my mind and this time the warning bell nearly deafened me. Mrs Atherton was the first person who had broached the subject of the Trinavants of her own free will; all the others had had to be nudged into it. I thought back over what she had said earlier and realized she had tried to warn me off in a not very subtle way, and she had brought up the subject of uranium. I had conned the construction men up at the dam into thinking I was looking for uranium.

I said, 'Surely the *whole* family wasn't wiped out. Isn't there a Miss Clare Trinavant?'

She seemed put out. 'I believe there is,' she said curtly. 'But I hear she's not a *real* Trinavant.'

'Did you know the Trinavants?' I asked.

'Oh, yes,' she said eagerly – too eagerly. 'I knew John Trinavant very well.'

I decided to disappoint her, and stood up. 'I'm sorry, Mrs Atherton. I don't think I'm interested in local history. I'm strictly a technical man and it's not my line.' I smiled. 'It might be different if I were going to put my roots down in Fort Farrell – then I might work up an interest – but I'm a nomad, you know; I keep on the move.'

She looked at me uncertainly. 'Then you're not staying in Fort Farrell long?'

'That depends on what I find,' I said. 'From what you tell me I may not find much. I'm grateful to you for that information, negative though it is.'

She seemed at a loss. 'Then you won't join the historical society?' she said in a small voice. 'You're not interested in Lieutenant Farrell and the Trinavants and . . . er . . . the others who made this place?'

'What possible interest could I have?' I asked heartily.

She stood up. 'Of course. I understand. I should have known better than to ask. Well, Mr Boyd; anything you want you just ask me and I'll try to help you.'

'Where will I contact you?' I asked blandly.

'Oh . . . er . . . the desk clerk at the Matterson House will know where to find me.'

'I'm sure I shall be calling on your help,' I said, and picked up the fur coat which was draped over a chair. I helped her into the coat and caught sight of an envelope on the mantel. It was addressed to me.

I opened it and found a one-line message from McDougall: COME TO THE APARTMENT AS SOON AS YOU GET IN. MAC.

I said, 'You'll need some help in getting your car on the road, Mrs Atherton. I'll get my truck and give you a push.'

She smiled. 'It seems that you are helping me more than I am helping you, Mr Boyd.' She swayed on the teetering high heels of her boots and momentarily pressed against me.

I grinned at her. 'Just being neighbourly, Mrs Atherton; just being neighbourly.'

II

I pulled up in front of the darkened *Recorder* office and saw lights in the upstairs apartment, and got a hell of a surprise when I walked in.

Clare Trinavant was sitting in the big chair facing the door, and the apartment was in a shambles with the contents of cupboards and drawers littering the floor. McDougall turned as I opened the door and stood holding a pile of shirts.

Clare looked at me with no expression. 'Hello, Boyd.'

I smiled at her. 'Welcome home, Trinavant.' I was surprised how glad I was to see her.

'Mac tells me I have an apology to make to you,' she said.

I frowned. 'I don't know what you have to apologize about.'

'I said some pretty hard things about you when you left Fort Farrell. I have just learned they were unjustified; that Howard Matterson and Jimmy Waystrand combined to cook up a bastardly story. I'm sorry about that.'

I shrugged. 'Doesn't matter to me. I'm sorry it happened for your sake.'

She smiled crookedly. 'You mean my reputation? I have no reputation in Fort Farrell. I'm the odd woman who goes abroad and digs up pots and would rather mix with the dirty Arabs than good Christian folk.'

I looked at the mess on the floor. 'What's going on here?'

'I've been canned,' said McDougall matter-of-factly. 'Jimson paid me off this afternoon and told me to get out of the apartment before morning. I'd like the use of the Land-Rover.'

'Sure,' I said. 'I'm sorry about this, Mac.'

'I'm not,' he said. 'You must have stung old Bull where it hurts.'

I looked at Clare. 'What brings you back? I was about to write you.'

A *gamine* grin came to her face. 'Do you remember the story you once told me? About the man who sent a cable to a dozen of his friends: "Fly, all is discovered"?' She nodded towards Mac and dug into the pocket of her tweed skirt. 'A pseudo-Scotsman called Hamish McDougall can also write an intriguing cable.' She unfolded a paper, and read, "IF YOU VALUE YOUR PEACE OF MIND COME BACK QUICKLY". What do you think of that for an attention-getter?'

'It brought you back pretty fast,' I said. 'But it wasn't my idea.'

'I know. Mac told me. I was in London, doing some reading in the British Museum. Mac knew where to get me. I took the first flight out.' She waved her hand. 'Sit down, Bob. We've got some serious talking to do.'

As I pulled up a chair, Mac said, 'I told her about you, son.'

'Everything?'

He nodded. 'She had to know. I reckon she had a right to know. John Trinavant was her nearest kin – and you *were* in the Cadillac when he died.'

I didn't like that very much. I had told Mac the story in confidence and I didn't like the idea of having it spread around. It wasn't the kind of life-story that a lot of people would understand.

Clare watched the expression on my face. 'Don't worry; it will go no further. I've made that very clear to Mac. Now, first of all – what were you going to write me about?'

'About the lumber on your land in the north Kinoxi Valley. Do you know how much it's worth?'

'I hadn't thought about it much,' she admitted. 'I'm not interested in lumber. All I know is that Matterson isn't going to make a cent on it.'

I said, 'I checked with your Mr Waystrand. I'd made an estimate and he confirmed it, or rather, he told me I was way out. If you don't cut those trees you'll lose five million bucks.'

Her eyes widened. 'Five million dollars!' she breathed. 'Why, that's impossible.'

'What's impossible about it?' asked Mac. 'It's a total cut, Clare; every tree. Look, Bob told me a couple of things so I checked on the statistics. A normal Forestry Service controlled cutting operation is mighty selective. Only half of one per cent of the usable lumber is taken and that runs to about five thousand dollars a square mile. The Kinoxi is being stripped to the ground, like they used to do back at the turn of the century. Bob's right.'

Pink spots glowed in her cheeks. 'That penny-pinching sonofabitch,' she said vehemently.

'Who?'

'Donner. He offered me two hundred thousand dollars for the felling rights and I told him to go jump into Matterson Lake as soon as it was deep enough for him to drown in.'

I looked at Mac, who shrugged. 'That's Donner for you,' he agreed.

'Wait a minute,' I said. 'Didn't he raise his price at all?'

She shook her head. 'He didn't have time. I threw him out.'

'Matterson isn't going to let those trees drown if he can help it,' I said. 'Not if he can make money out of them. I bet he'll make another offer before long. But don't take a penny under four million, Clare; he'll make enough profit on that.'

'I don't know what to do,' she said. 'I hate putting money in Matterson's pocket.'

'Don't be sentimental about it,' I said. 'Stick him for as much as you can, and then think of ways of harpooning him once you've got his money. A person who didn't like Matterson could do him a lot of damage with a few million bucks to play around with. You don't have to keep the dough if you consider it tainted.'

She laughed. 'You've got an original mind, Bob.'

I was struck by a thought. 'Do either of you know of a Mrs Atherton?'

Mac's eyebrows crawled up his forehead like two white furry caterpillars until they met his hairline. 'Lucy Atherton? Where in hell did you meet *her*?'

'In your cabin.'

He was struck speechless for a moment and gobbled like a turkey-cock. I looked at Clare, who said, 'Lucy Atherton is Howard's sister. She's a Matterson.'

Comprehension didn't so much dawn as strike like lightning. 'So that's what her game was. She was trying to find out how interested I was in the Trinavants. She didn't get very far.'

I told them what had happened at our meeting, and when I'd finished Mac said, 'Those Mattersons are smart. They knew I wouldn't be at the cabin because I had to get clear here – and they knew you wouldn't know who she was. Old Bull sent her out on a reconnaissance.'

'Tell me more about her.'

'She's in between husbands,' said Mac. 'Atherton was her second – I think – and she divorced him about six months ago. I'm surprised she's around here; she's usually busy on the social round – New York, Miami, Las Vegas. And from what I hear she could be a nympho.'

'She's a man-hungry vixen,' said Clare in a calm, level voice.

I thought about that. When getting the Continental out of the mud I'd had a devil of a job to prevent her raping me. Not that I'm sexless, but she was so goddam thin that a man could cut himself to death on her bones, and anyway I like to make a choice for myself once in a while.

'Now we *know* Bull is getting worried,' said Mac in satisfaction. 'The funny thing is that he doesn't seem to care if we know it. He must have guessed that you'd ask me about the Atherton woman.'

'We'll figure that one out later,' I said. 'It's getting late and we have to get this stuff back to the cabin.'

'You'd better come with us, Clare,' said Mac. 'You can have Bob's bed and the young bucko can sleep out in the woods tonight.'

Clare poked me in the chest with her finger and I knew she was getting pretty smart at interpreting the expression on my face. 'I'll look after my own reputation, Boyd. Did you think I was going to stay at the Matterson House?' she asked cuttingly.

III

I changed gear noisily as I drove up to the cabin and there was a rustle of leaves at the roadside and the sound of something heavy moving away. 'That's funny,' said Mac in perplexity. 'There's been no deer round here before.'

The headlights swung across the front of the cabin and I saw a figure dart away into cover. 'That's no goddam deer,' I said, and jumped clear before the Land-Rover stopped moving. I chased after the man but stopped as I heard a smash of glass from within the cabin and whirled to dive through the doorway. I collided with someone who struck out, but it takes a lot to stop a man my size and I drove him back by sheer weight and momentum.

He gave ground and vanished into the darkness of the cabin and I felt in my pocket for a match. But then I caught the acrid reek of kerosene choking in my throat so thickly that I realized the whole cabin must have been wet with it and that to strike a match would be like lighting up a cigar in a powder-magazine.

There was a movement in the darkness ahead of me and then I heard the crunch of Mac's footsteps coming to the cabin door. 'Stay out of here, Mac,' I yelled.

My eyes were getting accustomed to the interior darkness and I could see the light patch of a window at the back of the cabin. I dropped to one knee in a crouch and looked around slowly. Sure enough, the light patch was momentarily eclipsed as someone moved across it and I had my man placed. He was moving from left to right, trying to get to the door unnoticed. I dived for where I thought his legs were and grabbed him, and he fell on top of me but didn't come to the ground.

Then I felt a sharp pain thumping in my shoulder and had to let go and there was a boot in my face before I could roll over out of the way. By the time I stumbled to the door there was just the sound of running footsteps disappearing in the distance, and I saw Clare bending over a prostrate figure.

It was Mac, and he got groggily to his feet as I walked up. 'Are you all right?'

He held his belly. 'He . . . just rammed . . . me,' he whispered painfully. 'Knocked the wind out of me.'

'Take it easy,' I said.

'We'd better get him into the cabin,' said Clare.

'Stay away from there,' I said harshly. 'It's ready to go off like a bomb. There's a flashlamp in the Land-Rover; will you get it?'

She went away and I walked Mac a few steps to a stump he could sit on. He was wheezing like an old steam engine and I cursed the man who'd done that to him. Clare came back with the lamp and flashed it at me. 'My God!' she exclaimed. 'What happened to your face?'

'It got stepped on. Give me the torch.' I went into the cabin and looked around. The stink of kerosene made me gag and I saw the reason why it should; the place was a mess – all the sheets and blankets had been ripped from the beds, and the mattresses had been knifed open to liberate the stuffing. All this had been piled in the middle of the floor and doused with kerosene. There must have been five gallons because the floor was swimming.

I collected a pressure lantern and some cans from the larder and joined the others. 'We'll have to camp out to-night,' I said. 'The cabin's too dangerous to use until we clean it out. It's lucky I didn't unpack the truck – we still have blankets we can use.'

Mac was better and breathing more easily. He said, 'What's wrong with the cabin?' I told him and he cursed freely until he recollected that Clare was by his elbow. 'Sorry,' he mumbled. 'I got carried away.'

She gave a low laugh. 'I haven't heard cussing like that since Uncle John died. Who do you think did this, Bob?'

'I don't know – I didn't see any faces. But the Mattersons move fast. Mrs Atherton made her report and Matterson acted.'

'We'd better report it to the police,' she said.

Mac snorted. 'A lot of good that will do,' he said disgustedly. 'We didn't see who it was and we have no evidence to connect it with the Mattersons. Anyway, I can't see the cops tackling Bull Matterson – he draws too much water to be bulldozed by Sergeant Gibbons.'

I said, 'You mean that Gibbons has been bought just like everyone else?'

'I mean nothing of the kind,' said Mac. 'Gibbons is a good guy; but he'll need hard evidence before he as much as talks to Matterson – and what evidence have you got? None that Gibbons can use, that's for sure.'

I said, 'Let's make camp and talk about it then. And not too near the cabin, either.'

We camped in a glade a quarter of a mile from the cabin and I lit the lantern and set about making a fire. My left shoulder hurt and when I put my hand to it, it came away sticky with blood. Clare said in alarm, 'What's happened?'

I looked at the blood stupidly. 'My God, I think I've been stabbed!'

IV

I left Clare and Mac to clean out the cabin next morning and drove into Fort Farrell. The wound in my shoulder wasn't too bad; it was a clean cut in the flesh which Clare bound up without too much trouble. It was sore and stiff but it didn't trouble me much once the bleeding was staunched.

Mac said, 'Where are you going?'

'To pay a call,' I said shortly.

'Keep out of trouble – do you hear me?'

'There'll be no trouble for me,' I promised.

The feed-pump was giving trouble, so I left the Land-Rover with Clarry Summerskill, then walked up the street to the police station to find that Sergeant Gibbons was absent from Fort Farrell. There was nothing unusual in that – an RCMP sergeant in the country districts has a big parish and Gibbons's was bigger than most.

The constable listened to what I had to tell him and his brow furrowed when I told him of the stab wound. 'You didn't recognize these men?'

I shook my head. 'It was too dark.'

'Do you – or Mr McDougall – have any enemies?'

I said carefully, 'You might find that these men were employees of Matterson's.'

The constable's face closed up as though a blind was drawn. He said warily, 'You could say that for half the population of Fort Farrell. All right, Mr Boyd; I'll look into it. If you would make a written statement for the record I'd be obliged.'

'I'll send it to you,' I said wearily. I saw I wouldn't get anywhere without hard evidence. 'When is Sergeant Gibbons due back?'

'In a couple of days. I'll see he's informed of this.'

I bet you will, I thought bitterly. This constable would be only too pleased to pass such a hot potato to the sergeant. The sergeant would read my statement, nose around and find nothing and drop the whole thing. Not that one could blame him in the circumstances.

I left the police station and crossed to the Matterson Building. The first person I saw in the foyer was Mrs Atherton. 'Hello there,' she said gaily. 'Where are you going?'

I looked her in the eye. 'I'm going up to rip out your brother's guts.'

She trilled her practised laughter. 'I wouldn't, you know; he's got himself a bodyguard. You wouldn't get near him.' She looked at me appraisingly. 'So the old Scotsman has been talking about me.'

'Nothing to your credit,' I said.

'I really wouldn't go up to see Howard,' she said as I pressed for the elevator. 'It wouldn't do you any good to be bounced from the eighth floor. Besides, the old man wants to see you. That's why I'm here – I've been waiting for you.'

'Bull Matterson wants to see me?'

'That's right. He sent me to get you.'

'If he wants to see me, I'm around town often enough,' I said. 'He can find me when he wants me.'

'Now is that a way to treat an old man?' she asked. 'My father is seventy-seven, Mr Boyd. He doesn't get around much these days.'

I rubbed my chin. 'He doesn't have to, does he? Not when he can get other people to do his running for him. All right, Mrs Atherton. I'll come and see him.'

She smiled sweetly. 'I knew you'd see reason. I have my car just outside.'

We climbed into the Continental and drove out of town to the south. At first, I thought we were heading for Lakeside, the nearest thing to an upper-class suburb Fort Farrell can afford – all the Matterson Corporation executives lived out there – but we by-passed it and headed farther south. Then I realized that Bull Matterson wasn't just an executive and he didn't consider himself as upper class. He was king and he'd built himself a palace appropriate to his station.

On the way Mrs Atherton didn't say much – not after I'd choked her off rudely. I was in no mood for chit-chat from her and made it pretty clear. It didn't seem to worry her. She smoked one cigarette after the other and drove the car with one hand. A woman wearing a mini-skirt and driving a big car leaves little to the imagination, and that didn't worry her either. But she liked to think it worried me because she kept casting sly glances at me out of the corner of her eye.

Matterson's palace was a reproduction French château not much bigger than the Château Frontenac in Quebec, and it gave me an inkling of the type of man he was. It was a type I had thought had died out during the nineteenth century, a robber baron of the Jim Fisk era who would gut a railroad or a corporation and use the money to gut Europe of its treasures. It seemed incredible that such men could still exist in the middle of the twentieth century, but this overgrown castle was proof.

We went into a hall about as big as a medium-sized football field, littered with suits of armour and other bric-à-brac. Or were they fake? I didn't know, but it didn't really make any difference – fake or not, they illuminated Matterson's character. We ignored the huge sweep of staircase and took an elevator which was inconspicuously tucked away in one corner. It wasn't a very big one and Mrs Atherton took the opportunity to make a pass at me during the ride. She pressed hard against me, and said, 'You're not very nice to me, Mr Boyd,' in a reproachful tone.

'I'm not very sociable with rattlesnakes, either,' I observed.

She slapped me, so I slapped her in return. I'm willing to play along with all this bull about the gentle sex as long as they stay gentle, but once they use violence, then all bets are off. They can't expect it both ways, can they? I didn't slap her hard – just enough to make her teeth rattle – but it was unexpected and she stared at me in consternation. In her world she'd been accustomed to slapping men around and they'd taken it like gentlemen, but now one of the poor hypnotized rabbits had stood up and bitten her.

The elevator door slid open silently. She ran out and pointed down the corridor. 'In there, damn you,' she said in a choked voice, and hurried in the opposite direction.

The door opened on to a study lined with books and quiet as a cemetery vault. A lot of good cows had been butchered to provide the bindings on those books and I wondered if they shone with that gentle brown glow because they were well used or because some flunkey brightened them up every day the same time he polished his master's shoes. Tall windows reached from floor to ceiling on the opposite wall and before the windows a big desk was placed; it had a green leather top, tooled in gold.

Behind the desk was a man – Bull Matterson.

I knew he was five years older than McDougall but he looked five years younger, a hale man with a bristling but trim military moustache the same colour as newly fractured cast iron, which matched his hair. He was a big man, broad of shoulder and thick in the trunk, and the muscle was still there, not yet gone to fat. I guessed he still took exercise. The only signs of advanced age were the brown liver spots on the backs of his hands and the rather faded look in his blue eyes.

He waved his hand. 'Sit down, Mr Boyd.' The tone of voice was harsh and direct, a tone to be obeyed.

I looked at the low chair, smiled slightly and remained standing. The old man was up to all the psychological tricks. His head twitched impatiently. 'Sit down, Boyd. That *is* your name, isn't it?'

'That's my name,' I agreed. 'And I'd rather stand. I don't anticipate staying long.'

'As you wish,' he said distantly. 'I've asked you up here for a reason.'

'I hope so,' I said.

A glimmer of a smile broke the iron face. 'It *was* a damn silly thing to say,' he agreed. 'But don't worry; I'm not senile yet. I want to know what you're doing in Fort Farrell.'

'So does everyone else,' I said. 'I don't know what business it is of yours, Mr Matterson.'

'Don't you? A man comes fossicking on my land and you think it's not my business?'

'Crown land,' I corrected.

He waved the distinction aside irritably. 'What are you doing here, Boyd?'

'Just trying to make a living.'

He regarded me thoughtfully. 'You'll get nowhere black-mailing me, young man. Better men than you have tried it and I've broken them.'

I lifted my eyebrows. 'Blackmail! I haven't asked any-thing from you, Mr Matterson, and I don't intend to. Where does the blackmail come in? You might have your secrets to hide, Matterson, but I'm not in the money market where they're concerned.'

'What's your interest in John Trinavant?' he asked bluntly.

'Why should you care?'

He thumped his fist and the solid desk shivered. 'Don't fence with me, you young whippersnapper.'

I leaned over the desk. 'Who, in God's name, do you think you are? And who do you think I am?' He suddenly sat very still. 'I'm not one of the townsfolk of Fort Farrell whom you've whipped into silence. You think I'm going to stand by when you burn out an old man's home?'

His face purpled. 'Are you accusing me of arson, young man?'

'Let's amend it to attempted arson,' I said. 'It didn't work.'

He leaned back. 'Whose house am I supposed to have attempted to burn?'

'Not content with firing McDougall just because you thought he was making friends with the wrong people, you –'

He held up his hand. 'When was this so-called arson attempt made?'

'Last night.'

He flicked a switch. 'Send my daughter to me,' he said brusquely to a hidden microphone. 'Mr Boyd, I assure you that I don't burn down houses. If I did, they'd get burned to the ground; there wouldn't be any half-assed attempts. Now, then: let us get back to the subject. What's your interest in John Trinavant?'

I said, 'Maybe I'm interested in the background of the woman I'm going to marry.' I said it on the spur of the moment, but on second thoughts it didn't seem a half bad idea.

He snorted. 'Oh – a fortune-hunter.'

I grinned at him. 'If I were a fortune-hunter I'd set my sights on your daughter,' I pointed out. 'But it would take a stronger stomach than mine.'

I didn't find out what he would have said to that because just then Lucy Atherton came into the room. Matterson swung round and looked at her. 'An attempt was made to burn out McDougall's place last night,' he said. 'Who did it?'

'How should I know?' she said petulantly.

'Don't lie to me, Lucy,' he said gratingly. 'You've never been good at it.'

She cast a look of dislike at me and shrugged. 'I tell you I don't know.'

'So you don't know,' said Matterson. 'All right: who gave the order – you or Howard? And don't worry about Boyd being here. You tell me the truth, d'you hear?'

'All right, I did,' she burst out. 'I thought it was a good idea at the time. I knew you wanted Boyd out of here.'

Matterson looked at her incredulously. 'And you thought you'd get him out by burning old Mac's cabin? I've fathered an imbecile. Of all the stupid things I ever heard!' He swung out his arm and pointed at me. 'Take a look at this man. He's taken on the job of bucking the Matterson Corporation and already he's been running rings round Howard. Do you think that the burning of a cabin is going to make him just go away?'

She took a deep breath. 'Father, this man hit me.'

I grinned. 'Not before she hit me.'

Matterson ignored me. 'You're not too old for *me* to give you a good lathering, Lucy. Maybe I should have done it sooner. Now get the hell out of here.' He waited until she reached the door. 'And remember – no more tricks. I'll do this my way.'

The door slammed.

I said, 'Your way is legal, of course.'

He stared at me with suffused eyes. 'Everything I do is legal.' He simmered down and took a cheque-book from a drawer. 'I'm sorry about McDougall's cabin – that's not my style. What's the damage?'

I reflected that I was the one who had lectured Clare on sentimentality. Besides, it was Mac's dough, anyway. I said, 'A thousand bucks should cover it,' and added, 'There's also the question of a wrecked Land-Rover that belongs to me.'

He looked up at me under grey eyebrows. 'Don't try to shake me down,' he said acidly. 'What story is this?'

I told him what had happened on the Kinoxi road. 'Howard told Waystrand to bounce me, and Waystrand did it the hard way,' I said.

'I seem to have fathered a family of thugs,' he muttered and scribbled out the cheque, which he tossed across the desk. It was for $3,000.

I said, 'You've given your daughter a warning; what about doing the same for Howard? Any more tricks on his part and he'll lose his beauty – I'll see to that.'

Matterson looked at me appraisingly. 'You could take him at that – it wouldn't be too hard.' There was contempt in his voice for his own son, and for a moment I was on the verge of feeling sorry for him. He picked up the telephone. 'Get me Howard's office at the Matterson Building.'

He put his hand over the mouthpiece. 'I'm not doing this for Howard's sake, Boyd. I'm going to get rid of you, but when I do it'll be legal and there'll be no kickback.'

A squawk came from the telephone. 'Howard? Now get this. Leave Boyd alone. Don't do a damn' thing – I'll handle it. Sure, he'll go up to the dam – he's legally entitled to walk on that land – but what the hell can he do when he gets there? Just leave him alone, d'you hear? And, say, did you have anything to do with that business at McDougall's cabin last night? You don't know – well, ask your fool sister.'

He slammed down the telephone and glared at me. 'Does that satisfy you?'

'Sure,' I said. 'I'm not looking for trouble.'

'You'll get it,' he promised. 'Unless you leave Fort Farrell. With your record it wouldn't be too much trouble to get you tossed in the can.'

I leaned over the desk. 'What record, Mr Matterson?' I asked softly.

'I know who you are,' he said in a voice like gravel. 'Your new face doesn't fool me any, Grant. You have a police record as long as my arm – delinquency, theft, drug-peddling, assault – and if you step out of line just once while you're in Fort Farrell you'll be put away fast. Don't stir anything up here, Grant. Just leave things alone and you'll be safe.'

I took a deep breath. 'You lay it on the line, don't you?'

'That's always been my policy – and I warn a man only once,' he said uncompromisingly.

'So you've bought Sergeant Gibbons.'

'Don't be a fool,' said Matterson. 'I don't have to buy policemen – they're on my side anyway. Gibbons will go by the book and you are recorded on the wrong page.'

I wondered how he knew I had been Grant, and then suddenly I knew who had employed a private investigator to check on me. But he wouldn't have done that unless he had been worried about something; he was still hiding something and that gave me the confidence to say, 'To hell with you, Matterson. I'll go my own way.'

'Then I feel sorry for you,' he said grimly. 'Look, boy: stay out of this. Don't trouble yourself with things that don't concern you.' There was a strange tone in his voice; with any other man one might have thought he was pleading.

I said, 'How do I get back to Fort Farrell? Your daughter brought me up here, but I doubt if she'll be willing to take me back.'

Matterson chuckled coldly. 'The exercise will do you good. It's only five miles.'

I shrugged and walked out on him. I went down the stairs instead of taking the elevator and found the great hall deserted. Going outside the house was like being released from prison and I stood on the front step savouring the fresh air. There were too many tensions in the Matterson household for a man to be comfortable.

Lucy Atherton's Continental was still standing where she had left it, and I saw that the key was still in the ignition lock. I climbed in and drove back to Fort Farrell. The exercise would be even better for her.

V

I parked the Continental outside the Matterson Building, cashed the cheque in the Matterson Bank and walked across to pick up the Land-Rover. Clarry Summerskill said, 'I've fixed the pump, Mr Boyd, but that'll be another fifteen dollars. Look, it'll pay you better to get a new heap – this one is about shot. I've got a jeep just come in which should suit you. I'll take the Land-Rover as a trade-in.'

I grinned. 'How much will you give me on it?'

'Mr Boyd, you've *ruined* it,' he said earnestly. 'All I want it for now are the spare parts, but I'll still give you a good price.'

So we dickered and I ended up by driving back to Mac's cabin in a jeep. Clare and Mac had just about finished cleaning up, although the stink of kerosene still lay heavily on the air inside. I gave Mac a thousand dollars in folding money and he looked at it in surprise. 'What's this?'

'Conscience money,' I said, and told him what had happened.

He nodded. 'Old Bull is a ruthless bastard,' he said. 'But he's never been caught in anything illegal. To tell you the truth, I was a mite surprised at what happened last night.'

Clare said thoughtfully, 'I wonder how he knew you were Grant.'

'He hired a detective to find out – but that's not the point. What I want to know is *why* he thought it necessary to check up on me so many years ago. Another thing that puzzles me is the old man's character.'

'What do you mean?'

I said, 'Look at it this way. He strikes me as being an honest man. He may be as ruthless as Genghis Khan and as tough as hickory, but I think he's straight. Everything he said gave that impression. Now, what could a man like that be hiding?'

'He *did* bring up the question of blackmail,' said Clare tentatively. 'So you want to know what he could be blackmailed for.'

I said, 'What's your impression of him, Mac?'

'Pretty much the same. I said he'd never been *caught* in anything illegal and he never has. You get talk around town that a man couldn't make the dough that he has by legal means, but that's only the talk of a lot of envious failures. Could be that he *is* straight.'

'So what could he have done that makes him talk of blackmail?'

'I've been giving thought to that,' said Mac. 'You'd better sit down, son, because what I've got to tell you might knock you on your back. Clare, put the kettle on; it's about time we had tea, anyway.'

Clare smiled and filled the kettle. Mac waited until she came back. 'This has something to do with you, too,' he said. 'Now I want you both to listen carefully, because this is complicated.'

He seemed to hunt a little, searching for a place to begin, then he said, 'Folks are more different now than they used to be, especially young folks. Time was when you could tell a rich man from a poor man by the way he dressed, but not any more. And that goes in spades for teenagers and college students.

'Now, in that Cadillac which crashed there were four people – John Trinavant, his wife and two young fellows – Frank Trinavant and Robert Boyd Grant, both college students. Frank was the son of a rich man and Robert was a bum – to say the best of him. But you couldn't tell the difference by the way they dressed. You know college kids: they dress in a kind of uniform. Both these boys were dressed in jeans and open-necked shirts and they'd taken off their jackets.'

I said slowly, 'What the hell are you getting at, Mac?'

'Okay, I'll come right out with it,' he said. 'How do you know you are Robert Boyd Grant?'

I opened my mouth to tell him – then shut it again.

He smiled sardonically. 'Just because somebody told you, but not out of your own knowledge.'

Clare said incredulously, 'You think he might be *Frank Trinavant*?'

'He might,' said Mac. 'Look, I've never gone for all this psychiatric crap. Frank was a good boy – and so are you, Bob. I checked on Grant and decided I'd never come across a bigger sonofabitch in my life. It's never made sense to me that you should be Grant. Your psychiatrist, Susskind, explained it all away cleverly by this multiple personality stuff, but I don't give a good goddam for that. I think you're plain Frank Trinavant – still the same guy but you happen to have lost your memory.'

I sat there stunned. After a while my brain got working again in a cranky sort of fashion, and I said, 'Steady on, Mac. Susskind couldn't have made that kind of error.'

'Why couldn't he?' Mac demanded. 'Remember, he was told you were Grant. You've got to realize the way it was. *Matterson* made the identification of the bodies, he tagged the three dead people as Trinavants. Naturally there was no room for error in the case of John Trinavant and his wife, but the dead boy he named as Frank Trinavant.' He snorted. 'I've seen Highway Patrol photographs of that body and how in hell he was sure I'll never know.'

'Surely there must have been some means of identification,' said Clare.

Mac looked at her soberly. 'I don't know if you've seen a really bad auto smash – one followed by a gasoline fire. Bob, here, was burnt beyond recognition – and he lived. The other boy was burnt and killed. The shoes were ripped from their feet and neither of them was wearing a wrist-watch when they were found. The shirts had been pretty near burnt off their backs and they wore identical jeans. They were both husky guys, much about the same size.'

'This is ridiculous,' I said. 'How come I knew so much about geology unless I'd been taking a course like Grant?'

Mac nodded. 'True.' He leaned forward and tapped me on the knee. 'But so was Frank Trinavant. He was majoring in geology too.'

'For God's sake!' I said explosively. 'You'll have me believing in this crazy story. So they were both majoring in geology. Did they know each other?'

'I shouldn't think so,' said Mac. 'Grant went to the University of British Columbia; Trinavant to the University of Alberta. Tell me, Bob, before I go any further: is there anything in all that you know of that would blow this idea to hell? Can you find any sound proof to show that you are Grant and not Frank Trinavant?'

I thought about it until it hurt. Ever since Susskind took me in hand I *knew* I was Grant – but only because I was told so. To make a mean pun, I had taken it for granted. Now it came as a shock to find the matter in question. Yet try as I would, I couldn't think of any real proof to settle it one way or the other.

I shook my head. 'No proof from where I'm standing.'

Mac said gently, 'This leads to an odd situation. If you *are* Frank Trinavant, then you inherit old John's estate which puts Bull Matterson in a hell of a jam. The whole question of the estate goes into the melting-pot again. Maybe he'd still be able to enforce that option agreement in the courts, but the trust fund would revert to you and the financial flapdoodle he's been pulling would come into the open.'

My jaw dropped. 'Wait a minute, Mac. Let's not take this thing too far.'

'I'm just pointing out the logical consequences,' he said. 'If you are Frank Trinavant – and can prove it – you're a pretty rich guy. But you'll be taking the dough from Matterson, and he won't like it. And that's apart from the fact that he'll be branded as a crook and will be lucky to escape jail.'

Clare said, 'No wonder he doesn't want you around.'

I rubbed my chin. 'Mac, you say it all boils down to Matterson's identification of the bodies. Do you think he did it deliberately or was it a mistake? Or was there a mistake at all? I could still be Grant, for all I know and can prove.'

'I think he *wanted* the Trinavants dead,' said Mac flatly. 'I think he took a chance. Remember, the survivor was in a bad way – you weren't expected to live another twelve hours. If Matterson's chance didn't come off – if you survived as Frank Trinavant – then it would have been a mistake on his part, understandable in the circumstances. Hell, maybe he didn't know himself which was which, but he took the chance and it paid off in a way that even he couldn't expect. You survived but without memory – and he'd tagged you as Grant.'

'He talked about blackmail,' I said. 'And from what you've just handed me, he had every justification for believing I would blackmail him – *if I am Grant*. It's just the sort of thing a guy like Grant would do. But would Frank Trinavant blackmail him?'

'No,' said Clare instantly. 'He wasn't the type. Besides, it's not blackmail to demand your own rights.'

'Hell, this thing is biting its own tail,' said Mac disgustedly. 'If you *are* Grant you can't blackmail him – you have no standing. So why is he talking about blackmail?' He stared at me speculatively. 'I think, maybe, he committed one illegal act – a big one – to which you were a witness, and he's scared of it coming to light because it would knock the footing right out from under him.'

'And this illegal act?'

'You know what I mean,' snapped Mac. 'Let's not be mealy-mouthed about it. Let's come right out and say murder.'

* * *

We didn't talk too much about it after that. Mac's final statement was a bit too final, and we couldn't speculate on it without any firm proofs – not out loud, that is. Mac took refuge in chores about the house and refused to say another word, but I noticed he kept a bright eye on me until I got tired of his silent questioning and went out to sit by the stream. Clare took the jeep and went into town on the pretext of buying new blankets and mattresses for Mac.

Mac had handed me the biggest problem I had ever had in my life. I thought back to the days when I was reborn in the Edmonton hospital and searched for any mental clue to my identity – as though I had never done so before. Nothing I found led to any positive result and I found I now had two possible pasts. Of the two I much preferred Trinavant; I had heard enough of John to be proud to be his son. Of course, if I did turn out to be Frank Trinavant, then complications would set in between me and Clare.

I tossed a stone in the stream and idly wondered how close the kinship was between Frank and Clare and could it possibly be a bar to marriage, but I assumed it wouldn't be.

That short and ugly word which had been Mac's final pronouncement had given us pause. We had discussed the possibility in vague terms and it had come to nothing as far as Matterson was concerned. He had his alibi – Mac himself.

I juggled the possibilities and probabilities around, thinking of Grant and Trinavant as two young men whom I might have known in the distant past but without any relationship to me. It was a technique Susskind had taught me to stop me getting too involved in Grant's troubles. I got nowhere, of course, and gave up when Clare came back.

I camped in the woodland glade again that night because Clare had still not gone up to the Kinoxi Valley and the cabin had only two rooms. Again I had the Dream and the hot snow ran in rivers of blood and there was a jangle of sound as though the earth itself was shattering, and I woke up breathless with the cold night air choking in my throat. After a while I built up the fire again and made coffee and drank it, looking towards the cabin where a gleam of light showed where someone was sitting up half the night.

I wondered if it was Clare.

SEVEN

Nothing much happened just after that. I didn't make any move against Bull Matterson and McDougall didn't push me. I think he realized I had to have time to come to terms with the problem he had handed me.

Clare went up to her cabin in the Kinoxi Valley, and before she went I said, 'Maybe you shouldn't have stopped me doing that survey on your land. I might have come across a big strike of manganese or something – enough to have stopped the flooding of the valley.'

She said slowly, 'Suppose you found something now – would it still make a difference?'

'It might – if it were a big enough find. The Government might favour a mining settlement rather than a dam; it would employ more people.'

'Then why don't you come and give the land a check?' She smiled. 'A last-ditch effort.'

'Okay,' I said. 'Give me a few days to get sorted out.'

I went prospecting but nowhere near the dam. In spite of Matterson's assurance of safety, something might have stirred up, say, between me and Jimmy Waystrand – or those truckers, if I came across them – and I wanted no trouble until I had got things clear in my mind. So I fossicked about on the Crown lands to the west, not really looking for anything in particular and with my mind only half on the job.

After two weeks I went back to Fort Farrell, no more decided than I had been when I left. I was dreaming a lot of nights and that wasn't doing me any good, either. The dreams were changing in character and becoming frighteningly real – burnt bodies strewn about an icy landscape, the crackle of flames reddening the snow and a jangling sound that was cruel in its intensity. When I got back to Mac's cabin I was pretty washed-up.

He was concerned about me. 'Sorry to have put this on you, son,' he said. 'Maybe I shouldn't have brought it up.'

'You did right,' I said heavily. 'It's tough on me, Mac, but I can stand it. You know, it comes as quite a shock to discover you have a choice of pasts.'

'I was a fool,' Mac said bluntly. 'Ten minutes' thought and ten cents' worth of understanding and I'd have known better. I've been kicking myself ever since I opened my big mouth.'

'Forget it,' I said.

'But *you* won't, though.' He was silent for a while. 'If you pulled out now and forgot the whole thing I wouldn't think any the worse of you for it, boy. There'd be no recriminations from me – not like last time.'

'I won't do that,' I said. 'Too much has happened. Old Matterson has tried to scare me off, for one thing, and I don't push easy. There are other reasons, too.'

He looked at me with a shrewd eye. 'You haven't finished thinking about this yet. Why don't you give Clare's land the once-over, like you promised. You need more time.'

He wasn't fitted to the role of Cupid, but he meant well and it really wasn't a bad idea, so a couple of days later I left for the North Kinoxi in the jeep. The road hadn't got any better since my last trip, and I was more tired when the big cabin came in sight than if I'd walked all the way.

Waystrand came to meet me with his stiff, slow walk, and I asked, 'Is Miss Trinavant around, Mr Waystrand?'

'Walking in the woods,' he said briefly. 'You staying?'

'For a while,' I said. 'Miss Trinavant wants me to do a survey.' He nodded but said nothing. 'I haven't seen your son yet, so I haven't been able to pass on your message.'

He shrugged heavily. 'Wouldn't make any difference, I suppose. You eaten?'

I shared some food with him and then did some more log-chopping while he looked on with approval at my improved handling of the axe. When I began to sweat I stripped off my shirt, and after a while he said, 'Don't want to be nosy, but was you chawed by a bear?'

I looked down at the cicatrices and shiny skin on my chest. 'More like a Stutz Bearcat,' I said. 'I was in an auto accident.'

'Oh,' was all he vouchsafed, but a puzzled frown came on to his face. Presently he went away and I continued chopping.

Clare came back from the woods towards sunset and appeared glad to see me. She wanted to know if the Mattersons had made any moves, but merely nodded when I said that no move had been made by either side.

We had dinner in the big cabin, during which she asked me about the survey, so after dinner I got out the Government map and indicated what I was going to do and how I was going to go about it. She said, 'Is there much chance of finding anything?'

'Not much, I'm afraid – not from what I saw of the Matterson land in the south. Still, there's always a chance; strikes have been made in the most unlikely places.' I talked about that for quite a while and then drifted into reminiscences of the North-West Territories.

Suddenly Clare said, 'Why don't you go back, Bob? Why don't you leave Fort Farrell? It's not doing you any good.'

'You're the third person who has asked me to quit,' I said. 'Matterson, McDougall and now you.'

'My reasons might be the same as Mac's,' she said. 'But don't couple me with Matterson.'

'I know, Clare,' I said. 'I'm sorry. But I'm not going to quit.'

She knew finality when she heard it and didn't press it any more. Instead, she said, 'Can I come with you when you do the survey?'

'Why not? It's your land,' I said. 'You can keep a close eye on me so I don't skip the hard bits.'

We arranged to leave early, but in fact we didn't get away too soon the following morning. To begin with, I overslept which is something I hardly ever do. For the first time in nearly three weeks I slept soundly without dreaming and awoke refreshed but very late. Clare said she hadn't the heart to wake me and I didn't put up too much of a protest. That was why we were delayed long enough for unexpected, and unwelcome, visitors to drop from the sky.

I was in my room when I heard the helicopter and saw it settle lightly in the open space at the back. Howard Matterson and Donner got out and I saw Clare go forward to meet them. The rotor swished to a stop and the pilot dropped to the ground, so it looked as though Matterson intended to stay for longer than a few minutes.

There seemed to be an argument going on. Howard was jabbering nineteen to the dozen, with Donner putting in his two cents' worth from time to time, while Clare stood with a stony face and answered monosyllabically. Presently Howard waved at the cabin and Clare shrugged. All three of them moved out of sight and I heard them talking in the big main room.

I hesitated, then decided it was none of my business. Clare knew the score about the lumber on her land and I knew she wouldn't let Howard get away with anything. I continued to fill my pack.

I could hear the rumble of Howard's voice, with the lighter, colourless interjections of Donner. Clare appeared to be saying little, and I hoped most of it consisted of 'No.' Presently there was a tap on the door and she came in. 'Won't you join us?' Her lips were compressed and the pink spots on her cheeks were danger signals I had seen before.

I followed her into the main room and Howard scowled and reddened when he saw me. 'What's he doing here?' he demanded.

'What's it to you?' Clare asked. She indicated Donner. 'You've brought your tame accountant. This is *my* adviser.' She turned to me. 'They've doubled their offer,' she said in an acid voice. 'They're offering half a million dollars for the total felling rights on five square miles of my land.'

'Have you put up a counter-offer?' I asked.

'Five million dollars.'

I grinned at her. 'Be reasonable, Clare: the Mattersons wouldn't make a profit out of that. Now, I'm not suggesting you split the difference, but I think that if you subtracted their offer from yours there might be a basis for a sale. Four and a half million bucks.'

'Ridiculous,' said Donner.

I swung on him. 'What's ridiculous about it? You know you're trying to pull a fast one.'

'You keep out of this.' Howard was fuming.

'I'm here by invitation, Howard,' I said. 'Which is more than you are. Sorry to have spoiled your con game, but there it is. You know this land hasn't been cut over for twelve years and you know the amount of mature timber that's ready for the taking. Some of those big trees would go nicely in the mill, wouldn't they? I think it's a reasonable offer, and my advice to you is to take it or leave it.'

'By God, we'll leave it,' he said tightly. 'Come on, Donner.'

I laughed. 'Your father isn't going to like that. He'll have your guts for garters, Howard. I doubt if he ever ruined a deal by being too greedy.'

That stopped him. He glanced at Donner, then said, 'Mind if we have a private conversation?'

'Go ahead,' said Clare. 'There's plenty of room outside.'

They went out, and Clare said, 'I hope you're right.'

'I'm right, but Howard might be obstinate. I think he's a man who sets himself on a course and doesn't deviate. He isn't flexible, and flexibility is very important to a business-man. I'm afraid he might make a fool of himself.'

'What do you mean?'

I said, 'He's so set on making a killing here that it might blind him to a reasonable deal – and I don't think Donner can control him. That might bitch things up. Will you leave the dickering to me?'

She smiled. 'You seem to know what you're doing.'

'Maybe. But the biggest deals I've made so far have been with used car dealers – I may be out of my league here. I never dickered in millions before.'

'Neither have I,' she said. 'But if what I hear about used car dealers is correct, they're as tricky to deal with as any-one else. Try to imagine Howard as Clarry Summerskill.'

'That's an insult to Clarence,' I said.

Howard and Donner came back. Howard said heartily, 'Well, I think we can sort this thing out. I'll disregard the insults I've been offered so far by Boyd and make you a new offer. Clare, I'll double up again and make it a round million dollars – I can't say fairer than that.'

She looked at him coldly. 'Four and a half.'

Donner said in his precise voice, 'You're being too rigid, Miss Trinavant.'

'And you're being too free and easy,' I said. I grinned at Howard. 'I have a proposition. Let's get Tanner, the Forestry Service man, up here to do an independent valuation. I'm sure Clare will abide by his figure if you will.'

I hadn't any fear that Matterson would go for that, and he didn't. His voice sounded like the breaking of ice-floes. 'There's no need to waste time on fooleries. The dam is nearly finished – we close the sluices in two weeks. In less than four months this land will be flooded and we have to get the lumber out before then. That's cutting things very fine and it'll take every man I've got to do it in time – even if we start now.'

'So make a deal now,' I said. 'Come up with a sensible offer.'

He gave me a look of intense dislike. 'Can't we be reasonable, Clare?' he pleaded. 'Can't we talk without this character butting in?'

'I think Bob's doing all right,' she said.

Donner said quickly, 'A million and a half.'

'Four and a half,' said Clare stolidly.

Howard made a noise expressive of disgust, and Donner said, 'We keep coming up, Miss Trinavant, but you make no effort to meet us.'

'That's because I know the value of what I've got.'

I said, 'All right, Donner; we'll come down to meet you. Let's say four and a quarter. What's your counter-offer?'

'For Christ's sake!' said Howard. 'Has he the right to negotiate on your behalf, Clare?'

She looked him in the eye. 'Yes.'

'To hell with that,' he said. 'I'm not dealing with a broken-down geologist who hasn't two cents to rub together.'

'Then the deal's off,' she said, and stood up. 'If you'll excuse us, we have work to do.' I never admired her more than I did then; she was putting all her faith in the negotiating ability of a man she hardly knew. But it sure made me sweat.

Donner cut in quickly, 'Let's not be hasty.' He nudged Howard. 'Something can be worked out here. You asked me for my counter-offer, Boyd. Here it is: two million dollars flat – and not a cent more.'

Donner appeared quite calm but Howard was ready to go off pop. He had come here expecting to get a five-million-dollar property for a mere half-million, and now it was his turn to be squeezed he didn't like it one little bit. But for a moment I wondered if I was making a mistake. My estimate was on my own assessment – which could be wrong because I wasn't a lumberman – and on the word of old Waystrand, a man who did chores around the house.

I felt sweat trickling down my back as I said, 'Nothing doing.'

Howard exploded. 'All right,' he shouted. 'That's an end to it. Let's get the hell out of here, Donner. You've a fool for an adviser, Clare. Boyd couldn't advise a man lost in the desert how to take a drink of water. If you want to take up our final offer, you know where to find me.'

He started to walk out. I glanced at Donner, who obviously didn't want to leave, and I knew I was right, after all. Donner was ready to carry on wheeling and dealing, so therefore he was ready to make another offer; but he'd lost control of Howard as I knew he would. Howard, lost in his rage, wouldn't let him continue, and what I had been afraid of was about to happen.

I said, 'Now is the time to separate the men from the boys. Get old Waystrand in here, Clare.'

She looked at me in surprise, but obediently went outside and I heard her calling for him. Howard also stopped and looked at me uncertainly, fidgeting on one leg; and Donner eyed me speculatively.

Clare came back, and I said, 'I warned you, Howard, that your old man wouldn't like this. If you pass up a good deal in which you can make a damned good profit I don't think he'll let you stay as boss of the Matterson Corporation. What do you say, Donner?'

Donner smiled thinly. 'What would you expect me to say?'

I said to Clare, 'Get pen and paper. Write a formal letter to Bull Matterson offering him the felling rights for four and a quarter million. He'll beat you down to four and still make a cool million bucks profit. And tell him you'd rather deal with a man, not a boy. Waystrand can take the letter to-day.'

Clare went to the writing-desk and sat down. I thought Howard was going to take a swing at me but Donner tugged at his coat and drew him back. They both retreated and Donner whispered urgently. I had a good idea of what he was saying, too. If that letter was ever delivered to old Bull it would be an admission on Howard's part that he'd fallen down on a big job. Already, from what I had seen, the old man held him in contempt and had even given him Donner as a nursemaid. Bull Matterson would never forgive his son for putting a million dollars in jeopardy.

Waystrand came in and Clare looked up. 'I want you to take a letter into Fort Farrell, Matthew.'

The whispering across the room rose to a sibilant crescendo and finally Howard shrugged. Donner said urgently, 'Wait a minute, Miss Trinavant.' He addressed me directly and there was no suggestion that I was not empowered to negotiate. 'Did you mean that, Boyd – that you'd take four million dollars?'

'Miss Trinavant will,' I said.

His lips tightened momentarily. 'All right. I'm empowered to agree.' He took a contract form from his pocket. 'All we need to do is to fill in the amount and get Miss Trinavant's witnessed signature.'

'I don't sign anything before my lawyer checks it,' she said coolly. 'You'll have to wait on that.'

Donner nodded. He didn't expect anything else; he was a legalist himself and that was the way his own mind worked.

'As soon as possible, please.' He pulled out a pen and filled in a blank space in the middle of the contract, then pushed the pen into Howard's hand. Howard hesitated, and Donner said drily, 'Sign – you'd better.'

Howard's lips tightened, then he dashed off his signature. He straightened up and pointed a trembling finger at me. 'Watch it, Boyd – just watch it, that's all. You'll never do this to me again – ever.'

I smiled. 'If it's any consolation, Howard, you never had a chance. We had you whipsawed from the beginning. First, we knew exactly what we had, and, second, I had quite a job talking Clare round into selling; she didn't care if she sold or not, and that's a hell of a bargaining advantage. But you wanted it – you *had* to have it. Your old man would never let you pass it up.'

Donner said, 'You all see that I witness Mr Matterson's signature.' He signed the contract and dropped it on the table. 'I think that's all.'

Howard swung on his heel and left without another word, and Donner followed him. Clare slowly tore into fragments the letter she had written, and looked up at Waystrand. 'You won't have to go into Fort Farrell after all, Matthew.'

Waystrand shuffled his feet and cracked a slow grin. 'Looks like you're being looked after all right, Miss Clare.' He gave me a friendly nod and left.

My legs felt weak so I sat down. Clare said practically, 'You look as though you need a drink.' She went over to the cabinet and brought back a slug of Scotch big enough to kill an elephant. 'Thanks, Bob.'

'I never thought we'd do it,' I said. 'I thought I was going to blow the whole thing. When Howard started to leave . . .' I shook my head.

'You blackmailed him,' she said. 'He's scared to death of his father and you used that to blackmail him.'

'He had it coming – he tried to give you a hell of a raw deal. Old Bull will never know it, though; and he'll be happy with his million bucks.' I looked up at her. 'What are you going to do with your four million?'

She laughed. 'I'll be able to organize my own digs now – I've never been able to afford it before. But first I want to take care of you. I didn't like Howard's crack about a broken-down geologist.'

'Hey!' I said. 'I didn't do that much.'

'You did more than I could have done. I couldn't have faced Howard down like that. I'd hate to play poker with you, Bob Boyd. You certainly deserve a negotiator's fee.'

I hadn't thought about that. Clare said, 'Let's be businesslike about it – you did the job and you get the pay. What about twenty per cent?'

'For God's sake, that's too much.' I saw the glint in her eye. 'Ten per cent.'

'We'll split the difference,' she said. 'Fifteen per cent – and you'll take it.'

I took a mouthful of whisky and nearly choked as I realized I had just made myself $600,000.

II

As I have said, we started off late that morning and didn't get far before we stopped for a bite to eat. The way Clare made a fire, I saw she knew her way around the woods – it was just big enough for its purpose and no bigger, and there was no danger of setting the woods alight. I said, 'How come Waystrand works for you?'

'Matthew? He worked for Uncle John. He was a good logger but he had an accident.'

'He told me about that,' I said.

'He's had a lot of grief,' said Clare. 'His wife died just about the same time; it was cancer, I think. Anyway, he had the boy to bring up, so Uncle John asked him if he'd like to work around the house – the house in Lakeside. He couldn't work as a logger any more, you see.'

I nodded. 'And you took him over, more or less?'

'That's right. He looks after the cabin while I'm away.' She frowned. 'I'm sorry about young Jimmy, though; he's gone wild. He and his father had a dreadful quarrel about something, and Jimmy went to work for the Matterson Corporation.'

I said, 'I think that's what the quarrel was about. The job was a pay-off to Jimmy for blowing the gaff about me to Howard.'

She coloured. 'You mean about that night in the cabin?'

I said, 'I owe Jimmy something for that – and for something else.' I told her of the wild ride down the Kinoxi road sandwiched between the logging trucks.

'You could have been killed!' she said.

'True, but it would have been written off as an accident.' I grinned. 'Old Bull paid up like a gentleman, though. I've got a jeep now.'

I got out the geological maps of the area and explained what I was going to do. She cottoned on fast, and said, 'It's not so different from figuring out where to dig for archaeological remains; it's just that the signs are different.'

I nodded in agreement. 'This area is called the Rocky Mountain Trench. It's a geological fault caused by large-scale continental movement. It doesn't move so as you'd notice, though; it's one of these long-term things. Anyway, in a trench things tend to get churned to the surface and we may find something, even though there was nothing on the Matterson land. I think we'll go right to the head of the valley.'

It wasn't far, not more than ten miles, but we were bushed by the time we got there. I hadn't found anything on the way but I didn't expect to; we had struck in pretty much of a direct line and would do the main exploration going downhill on the way back, zig-zagging from one side of the valley to the other. It's easier that way.

By the time we made camp it was dark. There was no moon and the only light came from the fire which crackled cheerily and shed a pleasant glow. Beyond the fire was a big black nothing away down the valley which I knew was an ocean of trees – Douglas fir, spruce, hemlock, western red cedar – all commercially valuable. I said, 'How much land have you got here?'

'Nearly ten thousand acres,' said Clare. 'Uncle John left it to me.'

'It might pay you to set up your own small sawmill,' I said. 'You have a lot of ripe timber here which needs cutting out.'

'I'd have to haul out the lumber across Matterson land,' she said. 'It's not economical to go the long way round. I'll think about it.'

I let her attend to the cooking while I cut spruce boughs for the beds, one on each side of the fire. She ministered to the fire and the pans deftly with hardly a waste movement, and I could see I couldn't teach her anything about that department. Soon the savoury scent of hash floated up and she called, 'Come and get it.'

As she gave me a plateful of hash she smiled. 'Not as good as the duck you served me.'

'This is fine,' I said. 'Maybe we'll get some fresh meat tomorrow, though.'

We ate and talked quietly, and had coffee. Clare felt in her pack and produced a flask. 'Like a drink?'

I hesitated. I wasn't used to drinking when out in the woods; not out of any high principles, but the amount of liquor you can hump in a pack doesn't go very far, so I never bothered to carry any at all. Still, on a day when a guy can make $600,000 anything can happen, so I said, 'One jigger would go down well.'

It was a nice night. Even in summer you don't get many warm nights in the North-East Interior of British Columbia, but this was one of them – a soft and balmy night with the stars veiled in a haze of cloud. I sipped the whisky, and what with the smell of the wood-smoke and the peaty taste of the Scotch on my tongue I felt relaxed and at ease. Maybe the fact that I had a girl next to me had something to do with it, too; you don't meet many of those in the places I'd been accustomed to camping and when you did they had flat noses, broad cheekbones, blackened teeth and stank of rancid oil – delightful to other Eskimos but no attraction to me.

I undid a button of my shirt to let the air circulate, and stretched my legs. 'I wouldn't have any other life than this,' I said.

'You can do anything you want now,' said Clare.

'Say, that's so, isn't it?' I hadn't thought much about the money; it hadn't yet sunk in that I was pretty rich.

'What are you going to do?' she asked.

I said dreamily, 'I know of a place just north of the Great Slave Lake where a man with a bit of dough – enough to finance a real exploration – would have a chance of striking it rich. It really needs a magnetometer survey and for that you need a plane, or better, a whirlybird – that's where the money comes in.'

'But you *are* rich,' she pointed out. 'Or you will be as soon as the deal goes through. You'll have more than I inherited from Uncle John, and I never thought I was particularly poor.'

I looked at her. 'I said just now I wouldn't want any other life. You have your archaeology – I have my geology. And you know damn' well we don't do those things just to pass the time.'

She smiled. 'I guess you're right.' She peered at me closely. 'That scar – there, on your chest. Is that . . .?'

'The accident? Yes, it is. They don't trouble much with plastic surgery where it doesn't usually show.'

She put her hand out slowly and touched my chest with her fingertips. I said, 'Clare, you *knew* Frank Trinavant. I know I haven't his face, but if I am Frank, then surely to God there must be something of him left in me. Can't you see anything of him?'

Her face was troubled. 'I don't know,' she said hesitatingly. 'It was so long ago and I was so young. I left Canada when I was sixteen and Frank was twenty-two; he treated me as a kid sister and I never really *knew* him.' She shook her head and said again, 'I don't know.'

Her fingertips traced the long length of the scar, and I put my arm round her shoulders and pulled her closer. I said, 'Don't worry about it; it doesn't really matter.'

She smiled and whispered, 'You're so right. It doesn't matter – it doesn't matter at all. I don't care who you are or where you come from. All I know is that you're Bob Boyd.'

Then we were kissing frantically and her arm was about me under my shirt and drawing me closer. There was a hiss and a sudden *wooof* as half a jigger of good Scotch got knocked into the fire, and a great yellow and blue flame soared to the sky.

Later that night I said drowsily, 'You're a hard woman – you made me gather twice as many spruce boughs as we needed.'

She punched me in the ribs and snuggled closer. 'You know what?' she said pensively.

'What?'

'You remember when you slept in the cabin that time – when I warned you about making passes?'

'Mmm – I remember.'

'I *had* to warn you off. If I hadn't I'd have been a gone girl.'

I opened one eye. 'You *would*!'

'Even then,' she said. 'I still feel weak and mushy about it. Do you know you're quite a man, Bob Boyd? Maybe too much for me to handle. You'd better not radiate maleness so much around other women from now on.'

I said, 'Don't be silly.'

'I mean it.'

A few minutes later she said, 'Are you awake?'

'Uh-uh.'

'You won't think I'm silly if I tell you something?'

'Depends what it is.'

There was a silence, then she said, 'You *earned* that nego-tiator's fee, you know – and never forget it. I was glad you earned it for another reason.'

I said sleepily, 'What reason?'

'You're too goddam proud,' she said. 'You might never have done anything about me if you'd thought about it too much. I thought you'd be scared off by my money, but now *you* have money, and it doesn't apply.'

'Nonsense!' I said. 'What's a mere six hundred thousand bucks? I want the lot.' I pulled her closer. 'I want everything you've got.'

She gave a small cry and came to me again. Finally, just as the false dawn hesitated in the sky, she went to sleep, her head on my shoulder and one arm thrown across my chest.

III

The survey that should have taken four days stretched to two weeks. Maybe we were taking the honeymoon before we were married, but, then, so have lots of other folks – it's not the worst crime in the world. All I know is that it was the happiest time of my life.

We talked – my God, how we talked! For two people to really get to know each other takes a hell of a lot of words, in spite of the fact that the most important thing doesn't need words at all. By the time two weeks were up I knew a lot about archaeology I didn't know before and she knew enough geology to know that the survey was a bust.

But neither of us worried about that. Three of the days towards the end were spent near a tiny lake we discovered hidden away in the folds of the hills. We pitched our camp near the edge and swam every morning and afternoon without worrying about costumes, and rubbed each other warm and dry when we came out shivering. At nights, in the hush of the forest, we talked in low tones, mostly about ourselves and about what we were going to do with the rest of our lives. Then we would make love.

But everything ends. One morning she said thoughtfully, 'Matthew must be just about ready to send out a search-party. Do you realize how long we've been gone?'

I grinned. 'Matthew has more sense. I think he's got around to trusting me.' I rubbed my chin. 'Still, we'd better get back, I suppose.'

'Yes,' she said glumly.

We cleaned up the camp and packed our gear in silence. I helped her on with her pack, then said, 'Clare, you know we can't get married right away?'

Her voice was soft with surprise, 'Why ever not?'

I kicked at a stone. 'It wouldn't be fair. If I marry you and stay around here, things are going to bust loose and you might be hurt. If they're going to bust at all I want it to be before we're married.'

She opened her mouth to argue – she was a great arguer – but I stopped her. 'Susskind might be right,' I said. 'If I probe too deeply into my past I might very well go nuts. I wouldn't want that to happen to you.'

She was silent for a while, then she said, 'Supposing I accept that – what do you intend to do?'

'I'm going to break this thing wide open – *before* we're married. I've got something to fight for now, besides myself. If I come through the other side safely, then we'll get married. If not – well, neither of us will have made an irrevocable mistake.'

She said calmly, 'You're the sanest man I know – I'm willing to take a chance on your sanity.'

'Well, I'm not,' I said. 'You don't know what it's like, Clare: not having a past – or having two pasts, for that matter. It eats a man away from the inside. I've got to know, and I've got to take the chance of knowing. Susskind said it might break me in two and I don't want you too much involved.'

'But I am too involved,' she cried. 'Already I am.'

'Not as much as if we were married. Look, if we were married I'd hesitate when it's fatal to hesitate, I wouldn't push hard when pushing might win, I'd not take a chance when it was necessary to take a chance. I'd be thinking of you too damn' much. Give me a month, Clare; just one month.'

Her voice was low. 'All right, a month,' she said. 'Just one month.'

We reached her cabin late at night, weary and out-of-sorts, neither of us having said much to the other during the day. Matthew Waystrand met us, smiled at Clare and gave me a hard look. 'Got the fire lit,' he said gruffly.

I went into my bedroom and shucked off my pack with relief, and when I'd changed into a fresh shirt and pants Clare was already luxuriating in a hot bath. I walked over to Matthew's place and found him smoking before a fire. I said, 'I'm going pretty soon. Look after Miss Trinavant.'

He looked at me glumly. 'Think she needs it more'n usual?'

'She might,' I said, and sat down. 'Did you mail that letter she gave you?' I meant the Matterson contract going to her lawyer in Vancouver.

He nodded. 'Got an answer, too.' He cocked his head. 'She's got it.'

'Good.' I waited for him to say something else and when he didn't I stood up and said, 'I'm going now. I have to get back to Fort Farrell.'

'Wait a minute,' he said. 'I've been thinking about what you said. You wanted to know if anything unusual happened about the time old John was killed. Well, I remember something, but I don't know if you'd call it unusual.'

'What was that?'

'Old Bull bought himself a new car just the week after. It was a Buick.'

'No,' I said. 'I wouldn't call it unusual.'

Waystrand said, 'Funny thing is that it was a replacement for a car he already had – a car he'd had just three months.'

'Now that is funny,' I said softly. 'What was wrong with the old one?'

'Don't know,' said Waystrand laconically. 'But I hardly know what could have gone wrong in three months.'

'What happened to it?'

'Don't know that, either. Just disappeared.'

I thought about it. It would be a devil of a job trying to find out what had happened to a car twelve years earlier, especially a car that had 'just disappeared'. It didn't seem as though there would be much hope in following up such a tenuous lead as that, although who could tell? It might be worth a check in the licensing office. I said, 'Thanks, Matthew – you don't mind me calling you Matthew?'

He frowned. 'You took a long time on that survey of yours. How's Miss Trinavant?'

I grinned. 'Never better – she assured me herself. Why don't you ask her?'

He grunted. 'I don't reckon I will. Yeah, I don't mind you calling me by my given name. That's what it's for, ain't it?'

IV

I left early next morning just after daybreak. I suppose you couldn't have called the few words Clare and I had an argument, but it left a certain amount of tension. She thought I was wrong and she wanted to get married right away, and I thought otherwise, and we had sulked like a couple of kids. Anyway, the tension dissolved in her bed that night; we were getting to be like a regular married couple.

We discussed the Matterson contract which her lawyer had thought not too larcenous, and she signed it and gave it to me. I was to drop it in to Howard's office and get a duplicate signed by him. Just before I left, she said, 'Don't stick your neck out too far, Bob. Old Bull wields a mean axe.'

I reassured her and bumped up the track in the jeep and made Fort Farrell by late morning. McDougall was pottering about his cabin, and looked at me with a knowing eye. 'You look pretty bushy-tailed,' he said. 'Made your fortune yet?'

'Just about,' I said, and told him what had happened with Howard and Donner.

I thought he'd go into convulsions. He gasped and chortled and stamped his foot, and finally burst out with: 'You mean you made six hundred thousand bucks just for insulting Howard Matterson? Where's my coat? I'm going down to the Matterson Building right away.'

I laughed. 'You're dead right.' I gave him the contract. 'See that gets to Howard – but don't part with it until you get a duplicate signed by him. And you'd better check it word for word.'

'You're damned right I will,' said Mac. 'I wouldn't trust that bastard as far as I could throw a moose. What are you going to do?'

'I'm going up to the dam,' I said. 'It seems to worry Howard. What's been happening up there?'

'The dam itself is just about finished; they closed the sluices a couple of days ago and the lake has started to fill up.' He chuckled. 'They've had trouble bringing the generator armatures in; those things are big and heavy and they didn't find them too easy to manage. Got stuck in the mud right outside the powerhouse, so I hear.'

'I'll have a look,' I said. 'Mac, when you're in town I want you to do something. I want you to spread the word that I'm the guy who survived the accident which killed the Trinavants.'

He chuckled. 'I get it – you're putting the pressure on. Okay, I'll spread the word. Everybody in Fort Farrell will know you are Grant by sundown.'

'No,' I said sharply. 'You mention no names. Just say that I'm the guy who survived the accident, nothing more.' He looked at me in bewilderment, so I said, 'Mac, I don't know if I'm Grant and I don't know if I'm Frank Trinavant. Now, Bull Matterson may think I'm Grant, but I want to keep the options open. There may come a time when I have to surprise him.'

'That's tricky,' said Mac admiringly. He eyed me shrewdly. 'So you made up your mind, son.'

'Yes, I made up my mind.'

'Good,' he said heartily. As an apparent afterthought, he said, 'How's Clare?'

'She's fine.'

'You must have given her place a good going-over.'

'I did,' I said smoothly. 'I made absolutely sure there's nothing there worth the digging. Took two whole weeks on the job.'

I could see he was going to pursue the subject a little further so I backed out. 'I'm going up the dam,' I said. 'See you tonight – and do exactly what I said.' I climbed into the jeep and left him to mull it over.

Mac had been right when he said the Matterson Corporation was having trouble with the generators. This was not a big hydro-electric scheme like the Peace River Project at Portage Mountain, but it was big enough to have generators that were mighty hard to handle when transporting them on country roads. They had been shipped up from the States and had got to the railhead quite easily, but from then on they must have been troublesome.

I nearly burst out laughing when I drove past the powerhouse at the bottom of the escarpment. A big logging truck loaded with an armature was bogged down in the mud, surrounded by a sweating, swearing gang shouting fit to bust a gut. Another gang was laying a corduroy road up to the powerhouse – a matter of nearly two hundred yards – and they were up to their knees in an ocean of mud.

I stopped and got out to watch the fun. I didn't envy those construction men one little bit; it was going to be one hell of a job getting that armature to the powerhouse in an intact condition. I looked into the sky and watched the clouds coming in from the west, from the Pacific, and thought it looked like rain. One good downpour and the trouble would be compounded tenfold.

A jeep came up the road and skidded to a halt in the mud and Jimmy Waystrand got out and stamped over. 'What the hell are you doing here?'

I gestured to the stalled truck. 'Just watching the fun.'

His face darkened. 'You're not welcome round here,' he said harshly. 'Beat it!'

'Have you checked with Bull Matterson lately?' I asked mildly. 'Or hasn't Howard passed the word on?'

'Oh, hell!' he said exasperatedly. I could see he was itching to toss me out but he was more afraid of old Bull than he was of me.

I said gently, 'One wrong move from you, Jimmy, and a court order gets slapped on Bull Matterson. That'll cost him money and you can bet your last cent – if you're left with one – that it'll come out of your pay packet. Your best bet is to get on with your job and get that mess cleaned up before it rains again.'

'Rains again!' he said savagely. 'It hasn't rained yet.'

'Oh? Then how come all the mud?'

'How in hell do I know?' he said. 'It just came. It just . . . He stopped and glared at me. 'What the hell am I doing chewing the fat with you?' He turned and went back to his jeep. 'Remember!' he shouted. 'You make no trouble or you get whipped.'

I watched him go, then looked down at the mud interestedly. It looked like ordinary mud. I bent down and took some in my hand and rubbed my fingers together. It felt slimy without any grittiness and was as smooth as soap. It would make a good grade of mud for lubricating an oil drill; maybe Matterson could make a few cents out of bottling and selling it. I tasted it with the tip of my tongue; there was no saltiness, but I didn't expect to find any because the human tongue is not a very reliable guide.

I watched the men slipping and sliding around for a while, then went to the back of the jeep and picked out two empty test-tubes. I picked my way into the middle of the mess, getting thoroughly dirty in the process, and stooped to fill them full of the greyish, slippery goo. Then I went back to the jeep, put the test-tubes away carefully, and drove on up the escarpment.

There was no mud anywhere on the escarpment nor on the road which climbed it. They were still working on the dam, putting in the final touches, but the sluices were closed and the water was building up behind the concrete wall. Already the scene of desolation which I had grieved over was being covered by a clean sheet of water. Perhaps it was a merciful thing to do, to hide the evidence of greed. The new lake spread shallowly into the distance with the occasional spindly tree, too poor for even Bull Matterson to make a profit on, standing forlornly in the flood. Those trees would die as soon as the roots became waterlogged, and they would fall and rot.

I looked back at the activity at the bottom of the escarpment. The men looked like ants I had seen – a crowd of ants trying to drag along the corpse of a big beetle they had found. But they weren't having as much success with the trucks as the ants did with the beetle.

I took one of the test-tubes and looked at it thoughtfully, then put it back in its nest of old newspaper. Ten minutes later I was battling it out on the road back to Fort Farrell.

I badly wanted to use a microscope.

EIGHT

I was still giving myself a headache at the microscope when Mac came back from town. He dumped a box full of groceries on the table which made the slide jiggle. 'What you got there, Bob?'

'Trouble,' I said, without looking up.

'For us?'

'For Matterson,' I said. 'If this is what I think it is, then that dam isn't worth two cents. I could be wrong, though.'

Mac cackled with laughter. 'Hey, that's the best news I've heard in years. What kind of trouble has he got?'

I stood up. 'Take a look and tell me what you see.'

He bent down and peered through the eyepiece. 'Don't see much – just a few bits of rock – leastways, I think it's rock.'

I said, 'That's the stuff that goes to make up clay; it's rock, all right. What else can you tell me about it? Try to describe is as though you were telling a blind man.'

He was silent for a while, then he said, 'Well, this isn't my line. I can't tell you what kind of rock it is, but there are a few big round bits and a lot of smaller flat ones.'

'Would you describe those flat bits as card-shaped?'

'Not so as you'd notice. They're just thin and flat.' He straightened up and rubbed his eyes. 'How big are those things?'

'The big roundish ones are grains of sand – they're pretty big. The little flat ones are about two microns across – they're the clay mineral. In this case I think it's montmorillonite.'

Mac flapped his hand. 'You lost me way back. What's a micron? It's a long time since I went to school and they've changed things pretty much since.'

'A thousandth of a millimetre,' I said.

'And this monty-what-d'you-call-it?'

'Montmorillonite – just a clay mineral. It's quite common.'

He shrugged. 'I don't see anything to get excited about.'

'Few people would,' I said. 'I warned Howard Matterson about this, but the damned fool didn't check. Anyone round here got a drilling-rig, Mac?'

He grinned. 'Think you found an oil well?'

'I want something that'll go through not more than forty feet of soft clay.'

He shook his head. 'Not even that. Anyone who wants to bore for water hires Pete Burke from Fort St John.' He looked at me curiously. 'You seem upset about this.'

I said, 'That dam is going to get smashed up if something isn't done about it fast. At least, I *think* it is.'

'That wouldn't trouble me,' said Mac decisively.

'It might trouble me,' I said. 'No dam – no Matterson Lake, and Clare loses four million dollars because the Forestry Service wouldn't allow the cut.'

Mac stared at me open-mouthed. 'You mean it's going to happen *now*?'

'It might happen to-night. It might not happen for six months. I might be wrong altogether and it might not happen at all.'

He sat down. 'All right, I give up. What can ruin a big chunk of concrete like that overnight?'

'Quick clay,' I said. 'It's pretty deadly stuff. It's killed a lot of people in its time. I haven't time to explain, Mac; I'm going to Fort St John – I want access to a good laboratory.'

I left quickly and, as I started the jeep, I looked across at the cabin and saw Mac scratch his head and bend down to look through the microscope. Then I was moving away from the window fast, the wheels spinning because I was accelerating too fast.

I didn't much like the two hundred miles of night driving, but I made good time and Fort St John hadn't woken up when I arrived; it was dead except for the gas-refining plant on Taylor Flat which never sleeps. I was registered by a drowsy desk clerk at the Hotel Condil and then caught a couple of hours' sleep before breakfast.

Pete Burke was a disappointment. 'Sorry, Mr Boyd; not a chance. I've got three rigs and they're all out. I can't do anything for you for another month – I'm booked up solid.'

That was bad. I said, 'Not even for a bonus – a big one.'

He spread his hands. 'I'm sorry.'

I looked from his office window into his yard. 'There's a rig there,' I said. 'What about that?'

He chuckled. 'Call that a rig! It's a museum piece.'

'Will it go through forty feet of clay and bring back cores?' I asked.

'If that's all you want it to do, it might – with a bit of babying.' He laughed. 'I tell you, that's the first rig I had when I started this business, and it was dropping apart then.'

'You've got a deal,' I said. 'If you throw in some two-inch coring bits.'

'Think you can operate it? I can't spare you a man.'

'I'll manage,' I said, and we got down to the business of figuring out how much it was worth.

I left Burke loading the rig on to the jeep and went in search of a fellow geologist. I found one at the oil company headquarters and bummed the use of a laboratory for a couple of hours. One test-tube full of mud was enough to tell me what I wanted to know: the mineral content was largely montmorillonite as I had suspected, the salt content of the water was under four grams a litre – another bad sign – and half-an-hour's intensive reading of Grim's *Applied Clay Mineralogy* told me to expect the worst.

But inductive reasoning can only go so far and I had to drill to make sure. By early afternoon I was on my way back to Fort Farrell with that drilling rig which looked as if it had been built from an illustration in Agricola's *De Re Metallica*.

II

Next morning, while inhaling the stack of hot-cakes Mac put before me, I said, 'I want an assistant, Mac. Know any husky young guy who isn't scared of the Mattersons?'

'There's me.'

I looked at his scrawny frame. 'I want to haul a drilling-rig up the escarpment by the dam. You couldn't do it, Mac.'

'I guess you're right,' he said dejectedly. 'But can I come along anyway?'

'No harm in that, if you think you're up to it. But I must have another man to help me.'

'What about Clarry Summerskill – he doesn't like Matterson and he's taken a fancy to you?'

I said dubiously, 'Clarry isn't exactly my idea of a husky young guy.'

'He's pretty tough,' said Mac. 'Any guy called Clarence who survives to his age must be tough.'

The idea improved with thinking. I could handle a drilling-rig but the stone-age contraption I'd saddled myself with might be troublesome and it would be handy to have a mechanic around. 'All right,' I said. 'Put it to him. If he agrees, ask him to bring a tool kit – he might have to doctor a diseased engine.'

'He'll come,' said Mac cheerfully. 'His bump of curiosity won't let him keep away.'

By mid-morning we were driving past the powerhouse and heading up the escarpment road. Matterson's construction crew didn't seem to have made any progress in getting that armature towards its resting-place, and there was just as much mud, but more churned up than ever. We didn't stop to watch but headed up the hill, and I stopped about halfway up.

'This is it.' I pointed across the escarpment. 'I want to drill the first hole right in the middle, there.'

Clarry looked up the escarpment at the sheer concrete wall of the dam. 'Pretty big, isn't it? Must have cost every cent of what I heard.' He looked back down the hill. 'Those guys likely to make trouble, Mr Boyd?'

'I don't think so,' I said. 'They've been warned off.' Privately I wasn't too sure; walking around and prospecting was one thing, and operating a drilling-rig was something very different. 'Let's get the gear out.'

The heaviest part was the gasoline engine which drove the monster. Clarry and I manhandled it across the escarpment, staggering and slipping on the slope, and dumped it at the site I had selected, while Mac stayed by the jeep. After that it was pretty easy, though time-consuming, and it was nearly two hours before we were ready to go.

That rig was a perfect bastard, and if Clarry hadn't been along I doubt if I would ever have got it started. The main trouble was the engine, a cranky old two-stroke which refused to start, but Clarry cozened it, and after the first dozen refusals it burst into a noisy clatter. There was so much piston slap that I half expected the connecting-rod to bust clean out of the side of the engine, but it held together by good luck and some magic emanating from Clarry, so I spudded in and the job got under way.

As I expected, the noise brought someone running. A jeep came tearing up the road and halted just behind mine and my two friends of the first encounter came striding across. Novak yelled above the noise of the engine, 'What the hell are you doing?'

I cupped my hand round my ear. 'Can't hear you.'

He came closer. 'What are you doing with this thing?'

'Running a test hole.'

'Turn the damned thing off,' he roared.

I shook my head and waved him away downhill and we walked to a place where polite conversation wasn't so much of a strain on the eardrums. He said forcefully, 'What do you mean – running a test hole?'

'Exactly what I say – making a hole in the ground to see what comes up.'

'You can't do that here.'

'Why not?'

'Because . . . because . . .'

'Because nothing,' I snapped. 'I'm legally entitled to drill on Crown land.'

He was undecided. 'We'll see about that,' he said belligerently, and strode away back to his jeep. I watched him go, then went back to the drill to supervise the lifting of the first core.

Drilling through clay is a snap and we weren't going very deep, anyway. As the cores came up I numbered them in sequence and Mac took them and stowed them away in the jeep. We had finished the first hole before Jimmy Waystrand got round to paying us a visit.

Clarry was regretfully turning off the engine when Mac nudged me. 'Here comes trouble.'

I stood up to meet Waystrand. I could see he was having his own troubles down at the powerhouse by his appearance; he was plastered with mud to mid-thigh, splashed with mud everywhere else, and appeared to be in a short temper. 'Do I have to have trouble with you again?' he demanded.

'Not if you don't want it,' I said. 'I'm not doing anything here to cause you trouble.'

'No?' He pointed to the rig. 'Does Mr Matterson know about that?'

'Not unless someone told him,' I said. 'I didn't ask his permission – I don't have to.'

Waystrand nearly blew his top. 'You're sinking test holes between the Matterson dam and the Matterson power-house, and you don't think you need permission? You must be crazy.'

'It's still Crown land,' I said. 'If Matterson wants to make this his private preserve he'll have to negotiate a treaty with the Government. I can fill this hillside as full of holes as a Swiss cheese, and he can't do anything about it. You might get on the telephone and tell him that. You can also tell him he didn't read my report and he's in big trouble.'

Waystrand laughed. 'He's in trouble?' he said incredulously.

'Sure,' I said. 'So are you, judging by the mud on your pants. It's the same trouble – and you tell Howard exactly that.'

'I'll tell him,' said Waystrand. 'And I can guarantee you won't drill any more holes.' He spat on the ground near my foot and walked away.

Mac said, 'You're pushing it hard, Bob.'

'Maybe,' I said. 'Let's get on with it. I want two more holes today. One on the far side and another back there by the road.'

We hauled the rig across the hillside again and sank another hole to forty feet, and then laboriously hauled it all the way back to a point near the jeep and sank a third hole. Then we were through for the day and packed the rig in the back of the jeep. I wanted to do a lot more boring and normally I would have left the rig on the site but this was not a normal operation and I knew that if I left the rig it would look even more smashed up by morning.

We drove down the hill again and were stopped at the bottom by a car which skidded to a stop blocking the road. Howard Matterson got out and came close. 'Boyd, I've had all I can stand from you,' he said tightly.

I shrugged. 'What have I done now?'

'Jimmy Waystrand says you've been drilling up there. That comes to a stop right now.'

'It might,' I agreed. 'If I've found out what I want to know. I wouldn't have to drill, Howard, if you'd read my report. I told you to watch out for qui– '

'I'm not interested in your goddam report,' he butted in. 'I'm not even interested in your drilling. But what I am interested in is this story I hear about you being the guy who survived the crash in which old Trinavant was killed.'

'Are people saying that?' I said innocently.

'You know goddam well they're saying it. And I want that stopped, too.'

'How can *I* stop it?' I asked. 'I'm not responsible for what folks say to each other. They can say what they like – it doesn't worry me. It seems to worry you, though.' I grinned at him pleasantly. 'Now, I wonder why it should.'

Howard flushed darkly. 'Look, Boyd – or Grant – or whatever else you call yourself – don't try to nose into things that don't concern you. This is the last warning you're going to get. My old man gave you a warning and now it's coming from me, too. I'm not as soft as my old man – he's getting foolish in his old age – and I'm telling you to get to hell out of here before you get pushed.'

I pointed at his car. 'How can I get out with that thing there?'

'Always the wisecracks,' said Howard, but he went back and climbed into his car and opened a clear way. I eased forward and stopped alongside him. 'Howard,' I said. 'I don't push so easily. And another thing – I wouldn't call your father soft. He might get to hear of it and then you'd find out personally how soft he is.'

'I'll give you twenty-four hours,' said Howard, and took off. His exit was spoiled by the mud on the road; his wheels failed to grip and he skidded sideways and the rear of his auto crunched against a rock. I grinned and waved at him and carried on to Fort Farrell.

Clarry Summerskill said thoughtfully, 'I did hear something about that yesterday. Is it right, Mr Boyd?'

'Is what right?'

'That you're this guy, Grant, who was smashed up with John Trinavant?'

I looked at him sideways, and said softly, 'Couldn't I be anyone else besides Grant?'

Summerskill looked puzzled. 'If you were in that crash I don't rightly see who else you could be. What sort of games are you playing, Mr Boyd?'

'Don't think about it too much, Clarry,' advised Mac. 'You might sprain your brain. Boyd knows what he's doing. It's worrying the Mattersons, isn't it? So why should it worry you, too?'

'I don't know that it does,' said Clarry, brightening a little. 'It's just that I don't understand what's going on.'

Mac chuckled. 'Neither does anyone else,' he said. 'Neither does anyone else – but we're getting there slowly.'

Clarry said, 'You want to watch out for Howard Matterson, Mr Boyd – he's got a low boiling-point. When he gets going he can be real wild. Sometimes I think he's a bit nuts.'

I thought so, too, but I said, 'I wouldn't worry too much about that, Clarry, I can handle him.'

When we pulled up in front of Mac's cabin, Clarry said, 'Say, isn't that Miss Trinavant's station wagon?'

'It is,' said Mac. 'And there *she* is.'

Clare waved as she came to meet us. 'I felt restless,' she said. 'I came over to find out what's going on.'

'Glad to have you,' said Mac. He grinned at me. 'You'll have to sleep out in the woods again.'

Clarry said, 'Your auto going all right, Miss Trinavant?'

'Perfectly,' she assured him.

'That's great. Well, Mr Boyd, I'll be getting along home – my wife will be wondering where I am. Will you need me again?'

'I might,' I said. 'Look, Clarry; Howard Matterson saw you with me. Will that make trouble for you? I'm not too popular right now.'

'No trouble as far as I'm concerned – he's been trying to put me out of business for years and he ain't done it yet. You want me, you call on me, Mr Boyd.' He shook his head. 'But I sure wish I knew what was going on.'

Mac said, 'You will, Clarry. As soon as we know ourselves.'

Summerskill went home and Mac shepherded Clare and me into the cabin.

'Bob's being awfully mysterious about something,' he said. 'He's got some crack-brained idea that the dam is going to collapse. If it does, you'll be four million dollars to the bad, Clare.'

She shot me a swift glance. 'Are you serious?'

'I am. I'll be able to tell you more about it when I've looked at the cores I've got in the jeep. Let's unload them, Mac.'

Pretty soon the table was filled with the lengths of two-inch cylindrical core. I arranged them in order and rejected those I didn't want. The cores I selected for inspection had a faint film of moisture on the surface and felt smooth and slick, and a check on the numberings told me that they'd come up from the thirty-foot level. I separated them in three heaps and said to Clare, 'These came from three borings I made today on the escarpment between the dam and the powerhouse.' I stroked one of them and looked at the moisture on my finger. 'If you had as many sticks of dynamite you couldn't have anything more dangerous.'

Mac moved away nervously and I smiled. 'Oh, these are all right here; it's the stuff up at the escarpment I'm worried about. Do you know what "thixotropic" means?'

Clare shook her head and Mac frowned. 'I should know,' he admitted. 'But I'm damned if I do.'

I walked over to a shelf and picked up a squeeze-tube. 'This is the stickum I use on my hair; it's thixotropic gel.' I uncapped the tube and squeezed some of the contents into the palm of my hand. 'Thixotropic means "to change by touch". This stuff is almost solid, but when I rub it in my hands, like this, it liquefies. I brush it on to my hair – so – and each hair gets a coating of the liquid. Then I comb it and, after a while, it reverts to its near solid state, thus keeping the hair in place.'

'Very interesting,' said Mac. 'Thinking of starting a beauty parlour, son?'

I made no comment. Instead I picked up one of the cores. 'This is clay. It was laid down many thousands of years ago by the action of glaciers. The ice ground the rock to powder, and the powder was washed down rivers until it reached either the sea or a lake. I rather think that this was laid down in a fresh-water lake. I'll show you something. Got a sharp knife, Mac?'

He gave me a carving knife and I cut two four-inch lengths from the middle of the same core. One of the lengths I put on the table standing upright. 'I've prepared for this,' I said, 'because people won't believe this unless they see it, and I'll probably have to demonstrate it to Bull Matterson to get it through his thick skull. I have some weights here. How many pounds do you suppose that cylinder of clay can support?'

'I wouldn't know,' said Mac. 'I suppose you *are* getting at something.'

I said, 'The cross-section is a bit over three square inches.' I put a ten-pound weight on the cylinder and quickly added another. 'Twenty pounds.' A five-pound weight went on top of that. 'Twenty-five pounds.' I added more weights, building up a tower supported by the cylinder of clay. 'Those are all the weights I have – twenty-nine pounds. So far we've proved that this clay will support a weight of about fifteen hundred pounds a square foot. Actually, it's much stronger.'

'So what?' said Mac. 'You've proved it's strong. Where has it got you?'

'Is it strong?' I asked softly. 'Give me a jug and a kitchen spoon.'

He grumbled a bit about conjuring tricks, but did what I asked. I winked at Clare and picked up the other clay cylinder. 'Ladies and gentlemen, I assure you there is nothing up my sleeve but my arm.' I put the clay into the jug and stirred vigorously as though I were mixing cake dough. Mac looked at me unimpressed, but Clare was thoughtful.

I said, 'This is the meaning of thixotropic,' and poured the contents of the jug on to the table. A stream of thin mud splashed out and flowed in a widening pool of liquidity. It reached the edge of the table and started to drip on to the floor.

Mac let out a yelp. 'Where did the water come from? You had water already in that jug,' he accused.

'You know I didn't. You gave me the jug yourself.' I pointed at the dark pool. 'How much weight will that support, Mac?'

He looked dumbfounded. Clare stretched out her hand and dipped a finger into the mud. 'But where *did* the water come from, Bob?'

'It was already in the clay.' I pointed at the other cylinder still supporting its tower of weights. 'This stuff is fifty per cent water.'

'I still don't believe it,' said Mac flatly. 'Even though I've seen it.'

'I'll do it again if you like,' I offered.

He flapped his hand. 'Don't bother. Just tell me how this clay can hold water like a sponge.'

'Remember when you looked through the microscope – you saw a lot of little flat chips of rock?' He nodded. 'Those chips are very small, each about five-hundredths of a millimetre, but there are millions of them in a cubic inch. And – this is the point – they're stacked up like a house of cards. Have you ever built up a house of cards, Clare?'

She smiled. 'I've tried, but it's never got very high. Uncle John was an expert at it.'

I said, 'Then you know that a house of cards structure is mostly empty space.' I tapped a core. 'Those spaces are where the water is held.'

Mac still looked a little bewildered, but he said, 'Sounds feasible.'

Clare said quietly, 'There's more, isn't there? You haven't shown us this just as a party trick.'

'No, I haven't,' I said. 'As I said, when this sediment was first laid down it was at the bottom of the sea or a lake. Any salts in the water tend to have an electrolytic action – they act as a kind of glue to stick the whole structure together. If, however, the salts leach out, or if there were very few salts in the first place, as would happen if the deposit were laid down in fresh water, then the glueing effect becomes less. Clare, what is the most characteristic thing about a house of cards?'

'It falls down easily.'

'Right! It's a very unstable structure. I'd like to tell you a couple of stories to illustrate why this stuff is called quick clay. Deposits of quick clay are found wherever there has been much glaciation – mainly in Russia, Scandinavia and Canada. A few years ago, round about the middle fifties, something happened in Nicolet, Quebec. The rug was jerked from under the town. There was a slide which took away a school, a garage, quite a few houses and a bulldozer. The school wound up jammed in a bridge over the river and caught fire. A hole was left six hundred feet long, four hundred feet wide and thirty feet deep.'

I took a deep breath. 'They never found out what triggered that one off. But here's another one. This happened in a place called Surte in Sweden, and Surte is quite a big town. Trouble was it slid into the Gota river. Over a hundred million cubic feet of topsoil went on the rampage and it took with it a railroad, a highway and the homes of three hundred people. *That* one left a hole half a mile long and a third of a mile wide. It was started by someone using a pile-driver on a new building foundation.'

'A pile-driver!' Mac's mouth stayed open.

'It doesn't take much vibration to set quick clay on the move. I told you it was thixotropic, it changes by touch – and it doesn't need much of a touch if the conditions are right. And when it happens the whole of a wide area changes from solid to liquid and the topsoil starts to move – and it moves damn' fast. The Surte disaster took three minutes from start to finish. One house moved four hundred and fifty feet – how would you like to be in a house that took off at nearly twenty miles an hour?'

'I wouldn't,' said Mac grimly.

I said, 'Do you remember what happened to Anchorage?'

'Worst disaster Alaska ever had,' said Mac. 'But that was a proper earthquake.'

'Oh, there *was* an earthquake, but it wasn't that that did the damage to Anchorage. It *did* trigger off a quick clay slide, though. Most of the town happened to be built on quick clay and Anchorage took off for the wide blue yonder, which happened to be in the direction of the Pacific Ocean.'

'I didn't know that,' said Mac.

'There are dozens of other examples,' I said. 'During the war British bombers attacking a chemical factory in Norway set off a slide over an area of fifty thousand square yards. And there was Aberfan in South Wales: that was an artificial situation – the slag heap of a coal mine – but the basic cause was the interaction of clay and water. It killed a schoolful of children.'

Clare said, 'And you think the dam is in danger?'

I gestured at the cores on the table. 'I took three samples from across the escarpment, and they show quick clay right across. I don't know how far it extends up and down, but it's my guess that it's all the way. There's an awful lot of mud appeared down at the bottom. A quick clay slide can travel at twenty miles an hour on a slope of only one degree. The gradient of that escarpment must average fifteen degrees, so that when it goes, it'll go fast. That power plant will be buried under a hundred feet of mud and it'll probably jerk the foundations from under the dam, too. If that happens, then the whole of the new Matterson Lake will follow the mud. I doubt if there'd be much left of the power plant.'

'Or anyone in it,' said Clare quietly.

'Or anyone in it,' I agreed.

Mac hunched his shoulders and stared loweringly at the cores. 'What I don't understand is why it hasn't gone before now. I can remember when they were logging on the escarpment and cutting big trees at that. A full grown Douglas fir hits the ground with a mighty big thump – harder than a pile-driver. The whole slope should have collapsed years ago.'

I said, 'I think the dam is responsible. I think the quick clay layer surfaces somewhere the other side of the dam. Everything was all right until the dam was built, but then they closed the sluices and the water started backing up and covering the quick clay outcropping. Now it's seeping down in the quick clay all under the escarpment.'

Mac nodded. 'That figures.'

'What are you going to do about it?' asked Clare.

'I'll have to tell the Mattersons somehow,' I said. 'I tried to tell Howard this afternoon but he shut me up. In my report I even told him to watch out for quick clay, but I don't think he even read it. You're right, Clare: he's a sloppy businessman.' I stretched. 'But right now I want to find out more about these samples – the water content especially.'

'How will you do that?' asked Mac interestedly.

'Easy. I cut a sample and weigh it, then cook the water out on that stove there, then weigh it again. It's just a sum in subtraction from then on.'

'I'll make supper first,' said Clare. 'Right now you'd better clear up this mess you've made.'

After supper I got down to finding the water content. The shear strength of quick clay depends on the mineral constituents and the amount of water held – it was unfortunate that this particular clay was mainly montmorillonite and deficient in strength. That, combined with a water content of forty per cent, averaged out over three samples, gave it a shear strength of about one ton per square foot.

If I was right and water was seeping into the quick clay strata from the new lake, then conditions would rapidly become worse. Double the water percentage and the shear strength would drop to a mere 500 pounds a square foot, and a heavy-footed construction man could start the whole hillside sliding.

Clare said, 'Is there anything that can be done about it – to save the dam, I mean?'

I sighed. 'I don't know, Clare. They'll have to open the sluices again and get rid of the water in the lake, locate where the clay comes to the surface and then, maybe, they can seal it off. Put a layer of concrete over it, perhaps. But that still leaves the quick clay under the escarpment in a dangerous condition.'

'So what do you do then?' asked Mac.

I grinned. 'Pump some more water into it.' I laughed outright at the expression on his face. 'I mean it, Mac; but we pump in a brine solution with plenty of dissolved salts. That will put in some glue to hold it together and it will cease to be thixotropic.'

'Full of smart answers, aren't you?' said Mac caustically. 'Well, answer this one. How do you propose getting the Matterson Corporation to listen to you in the first place? I can't see you popping into Howard's office tomorrow and getting him to open those sluices. He'd think you were nuts.'

'I could tell him,' said Clare.

Mac snorted in disgust. 'From Howard's point of view, you and Bob have gypped him out of four million bucks that were rightly his. If you tried to get him to close down construction on the dam he'd think you were planning another fast killing. He wouldn't be able to figure how you're going to do it, but he'd be certain you were pulling a fast one.'

I said, 'What about old Bull? He might listen.'

'He might,' said Mac. 'On the other hand, you asked me to spread that story around Fort Farrell and he might have got his dander up about it. I wouldn't bank on him listening to anything you have to say.'

'Oh, hell!' I said. 'Let's sleep on it. Maybe we'll come up with something tomorrow.'

I bedded down in the clearing because Clare had my bed, and I stayed awake thinking of what I had done. Had I achieved anything at all? Fort Farrell had been a murky enough pool when I arrived, but now the waters were stirred up into muddiness and nothing at all could be seen. I was still butting my head against the mystery of the

Trinavants and, so far, nothing had come of my needling the Mattersons.

I began to think about that and came up against something odd. Old Bull had known who I was right from the start and he had got stirred up pretty fast. From that I argued that there was something he had to hide with regard to the Mattersons – and perhaps I was right, because it was he who had clamped down on the name of Trinavant.

Howard, on the other hand, had been stirred up about other things – our argument about Clare, his defeat in the matter of my prospecting on Crown land, another defeat in the matter of the cutting of the lumber on Clare's land. But then I had asked Mac to spread around the story that I was the survivor of the Trinavant auto smash – and Howard had immediately blown his top and given me twenty-four hours to get out of town.

Now, that was very odd! Bull Matterson had known who I was but hadn't told his son – why not? Could it be there was something he didn't want Howard to know?

And Howard – where did he come into all this? Why was he so annoyed when he found who I was? Could he be trying to protect his father?

I heard a twig snap and sat up quickly. A slim shadow was moving through the trees towards me, then Clare said in a warm voice, 'Did you think I was going to let you stay out here alone?'

I chuckled. 'You'll scandalize Mac.'

'He's asleep,' she said, and lay down beside me. 'Besides, it isn't easy to scandalize a newspaperman of his age. He's grown-up, you know.'

III

Next morning, at breakfast, I said, 'I'll have a crack at Howard – try to get him to see sense.'

Mac grunted. 'Do you think you can just walk into the Matterson Building?'

'I'll go up to the escarpment and put a hole in it,' I said. 'That'll bring Howard running to me. Will you ask Clarry if he'll join the party?'

'That'll bring Howard,' Mac agreed.

'You could get into a fight up there,' Clare warned.

'I'll chance that,' I said, and stabbed at a hot-cake viciously. 'It might be just what's needed to bring things into the open. I'm tired of this pussyfooting around. You stay home this time, Mac.'

'You try to keep me away,' Mac growled, and mimicked, 'You can't stop *me* fossicking on Crown land.' He rubbed his eyes. 'Trouble is, I'm a mite tired.'

'Didn't you sleep?'

He kept his eyes studiously on his plate. 'Too much moving around during the night; folks tromping in and out at all hours – could have been Grand Central Station.'

Clare dropped her eyes, and her throat and face flushed deep pink. I smiled amiably. 'Maybe *you* ought to have slept out in the woods – it was right peaceful out there.'

He pushed back his chair. 'I'll go get Clarry.'

I said, 'Tell him there might be trouble, then it's up to him if he comes or not. It's not really his fight.'

'Clarry won't mind a crack at Howard.'

'It's not Howard I'm thinking of,' I said. I had Jimmy Waystrand in mind, and those two bodyguards of his who ran his errands.

But Clarry came and we pushed off up the Kinoxi road. Clare wanted to come too, but I squashed that idea flat. I said, 'When we come back we'll be hungry – and maybe a bit banged up. You have a good dinner waiting, and some bandages and the mercuro-chrome.'

No one stopped us as we drove past the powerhouse and up the escarpment road. We drove nearly to the top before stopping because I wanted to sink a test hole just below the dam. It was essential to find out if the quick clay strata actually ran under the dam.

Clarry and I manhandled the gasoline engine across the escarpment and got the rig set up. No one paid us any attention although we were in plain sight. Down at the bottom of the hill they were still trying to get that generator armature into the power plant and had made a fair amount of progress, using enough logs on the ground to feed Matterson's sawmill for twenty-four hours. I could hear the shouting and cursing as orders were given, but that was drowned out as Clarry started the engine and the drilling began.

I was very careful with the cores as they came up from the thirty-foot level and held one of them out to Mac. 'It's wetter here,' I said.

Mac shifted his boots nervously. 'Are we safe here? It couldn't go now, could it?'

'It could,' I said. 'But I don't think it will – not just yet.' I grinned. 'I'd hate to slide to the bottom, especially with the dam on top of me.'

'You guys talk as though there's going to be an earthquake,' said Clarry.

'Don't sprain your brain,' said Mac. 'I've told you before.' He paused. 'That's exactly what we are talking about.'

'Huh!' Clarry looked about him. 'How can you predict an earthquake?'

'There's one coming now,' I said, and pointed. 'Here comes Howard with storm signals flying.'

He was coming across the hillside with Jimmy Waystrand close behind, and when he got closer I saw he was furious with rage. He shouted, 'I warned you, Boyd; now you'll take the consequences.'

I stood my ground as he came up, keeping a careful eye on Waystrand. I said, 'Howard, you're a damn' fool – you didn't read my report. Look at all that mud down there.'

I don't think he heard a word I said. He stabbed a finger at me. 'You're leaving right now – we don't want you around.'

'We! I suppose you mean you and your father.' This was no good. There was no point in getting into a hassle with him when there were more important things to be discussed. I said, 'Listen, Howard: and, for God's sake, simmer down. You remember I warned you about quick clay?'

He glared at me. 'What's quick clay?'

'Then you didn't read the report – it was all set out in there.'

'To hell with your report – all you keep yammering about is that goddam report. I paid for the damn' thing and whether I read it or not is my affair.'

I said, 'No, it isn't – not by a long chalk. There may be men ki–'

'Will you, for Christ's sake, shut up about it,' he yelled.

Mac said sharply, 'You'd better listen to him, Howard.'

'You keep out of this, you old fool,' commanded Howard. 'And you too, Summerskill. You're both going to regret being mixed up with this man. I'll see you regret it – personally.'

'Howard, lay off McDougall,' I said. 'Or I'll break your back.'

Clarry Summerskill spat expertly and befouled Howard's boot. 'You don't scare me none, Matterson.'

Howard took a step forward and raised his fist. I said quickly, 'Hold it! Your reinforcements are coming, Howard.' I nodded across the hillside to where two men were coming across the rough ground – one a chauffeur in trim uniform supporting the other by the arm.

Bull Matterson had come out of his castle at last.

Clarry's jaw dropped as he stared at the old man and at the big black Bentley parked on the road. 'Well, I'm damned!' he said softly. 'I haven't seen old Bull in years.'

'Maybe he's come out to defend his bull-calf,' said Mac sardonically.

Howard went to help the old man, the very picture of filial devotion, but Bull angrily shook away the offered hand. From the look of him, he was quite spry and able to get on by himself. Mac chuckled. 'Why, the old guy is in better shape than I am.'

I said, 'I have a feeling that this is going to be the moment of truth.'

Mac glanced at me slyly. 'Don't they say that about bull-fighting when the matador poises his sword to kill the bull? You'll have to have a sharp sword to kill this one.'

The old man finally reached us and looked around with a hard eye. To his chauffeur he said curtly, 'Get back to the car.' He cast an eye on the drilling-rig, then swung on Jimmy Waystrand. 'Who are you?'

'Waystrand. I work down on the power plant.'

Matterson lifted his eyebrows. 'Do you? Then get back on your job.'

Waystrand looked uncertainly at Howard, who gave a short nod.

Matterson stared at Clarry. 'I don't think we need you, either,' he said harshly. 'Or you, McDougall.'

I said quietly, 'Go and wait by the jeep, Clarry,' and then stared down the old man. 'McDougall stays.'

'That's up to him,' said Matterson. 'Well, McDougall?'

'I'd like to see a fair fight,' said Mac cheerfully. 'Two against two.' He laughed. 'Bob can take Howard and I reckon you and me are fairly matched for the Old Age Championship.' He felt the top of the gasoline engine to see if it was still hot, then nonchalantly leaned his rump against it.

Matterson swivelled his head. 'Very well. I don't mind a witness for what I'm going to say.' He fixed me with a cold blue eye and I must have been nuts ever to think he had the faded eyes of age. 'I gave you a warning, Grant, and you have chosen to ignore it.'

Howard said, 'Do you really think this guy is Grant – that he was in the crash?'

'Shut up,' said Matterson icily and without turning his head. 'I'll handle this. You've made enough mistakes already – you and your fool sister.' He hadn't taken his eye off me. 'Have you anything to say, Grant?'

'I've got a lot to say – but not about anything that might have happened to John Trinavant and his family. What I want to say is of more immediate impor–'

'I'm not interested in anything else,' Matterson cut in flatly. 'Now put up or shut up. Do you have anything to say? If not, you can get to hell out of here, and I'll see that you do it.'

'Yes,' I said deliberately. 'I might have one or two things to say. But you won't like it.'

'There have been a lot of things in my life I haven't liked,' said Matterson stonily. 'A few more won't make any difference.' He bent forward a little and his chin jutted out. 'But be very careful about any accusations you may make – they may backfire on you.'

I saw Howard moving nervously. 'Christ!' he said, looking at Mac. 'Don't push things.'

'I told you to shut up,' said the old man. 'I won't tell you again. All right, Grant: say your piece, but bear this in mind. My name is Matterson and I own this piece of country. I own it and everyone who lives in it. Those I don't own I can lean on – and they know it.' A grim smile touched his lips. 'I don't usually go about talking this way because it's not good politics – people don't like hearing that kind of truth. But it is the truth and you know it.'

He squared his shoulders. 'Now, do you think anyone is going to take your word against mine? Especially when I bring your record out. The word of a drug-pusher and a drug-addict against mine? Now, say your piece and be damned to you, Grant.'

I looked at him thoughtfully. He evidently believed I had uncovered something and was openly challenging me to reveal it, depending upon Grant's police record to discredit me. It was a hell of a good manoeuvre if I did know something, which I didn't – and if I were Grant.

I said, 'You keep calling me Grant. I wonder why.'

The planes of his iron face altered fractionally. 'What do you mean by that?' he said harshly.

'You ought to know,' I said. 'You identified the bodies.' I smiled grimly. 'What if I'm Frank Trinavant?'

He didn't move but his face went a dirty grey. Then he swayed a little and tried to speak, and an indescribable choking sound burst from his lips. Before anyone could catch him he crashed to the ground like one of his own felled trees.

Howard rushed forward and stooped over him and I looked over his shoulder. The old man was still alive and breathing stertorously. Mac pulled at my sleeve and drew me away. 'Heart-attack,' he said. 'I've seen it before. That's why he never moved from home much.'

In the moment of truth my sword had been sharp enough – perhaps too sharp. But was it the moment of truth? I still didn't know. I still didn't know if I were Grant or Frank Trinavant. I was still a lost soul groping blindly in the past.

NINE

It was touch and go.

Howard and I had a yelling match over Matterson's prostrate body. Howard did most of the yelling – I was trying to cool him off. The chauffeur came across from the Bentley at a dead run, and Mac pulled me away. He jerked his thumb at Howard. 'He'll be too busy with his father to attend to you – but Jimmy Waystrand won't, if he comes up here. Howard will sick his boys on to you like dogs on to a rabbit. We'd better get out of here.'

I hesitated. The old man looked bad and I wanted to stay to see that he was all right; but I saw the force of Mac's argument – this was no place to linger any more. 'Come on,' I said. 'Let's move.'

Clarry Summerskill met us and said, 'What happened – did you hit the old guy?'

'For God's sake!' said Mac disgustedly. 'He had a heart-attack. Get into the jeep.'

'What about the rig?' asked Clarry.

'We leave it,' I said. 'We've done all we can here.' I stared across the hillside at the small group below the dam. 'Maybe we've done too much.'

I drove the jeep down the hill prepared for trouble, but nothing happened as we passed the powerhouse and when we were on the road out I relaxed. Mac said speculatively, 'It knocked the old bastard for six, didn't it? I wonder why?'

'I'm beginning to wonder about Bull Matterson,' I said. 'He doesn't seem too bad to me.'

'After what he said to you?' Mac was outraged.

'Oh, sure; he's tough, and he's not too particular about his methods as long as they work – but I think he's essentially an honest man. If he had deliberately confused the identification in the auto crash he'd have *known* who I was. It wouldn't have come as such a surprise as to give him a heart-attack. He's just had a hell of a shock, Mac.'

'That's true.' He shook his head. 'I don't get it.'

'Neither do I,' said Clarry. 'Will someone tell me what's going on?'

I said, 'You can do something for me, Clarry. Take a trip to the licensing office and check if Bull Matterson registered a new Buick round about the middle of September, 1956. I heard he did.'

'So what?' said Mac.

'So what happened to the old one? Matthew Waystrand told me it was only three months old. You are in the used auto business, Clarry. Is it possible to find out what happened to that car?'

His voice rose. 'After twelve years? I should say it was impossible.' He scratched his head. 'But I'll try.'

We pulled up at Mac's cabin and Clarry went into Fort Farrell in his own car. Mac and I told Clare what had happened and she became gloomy. 'I used to call him Uncle Bull,' she said. Her head came up. 'He wasn't a bad man, you know. It was only when that man Donner came into the business that the Matterson Corporation became really tight-fisted.'

Mac was sceptical. 'Donner isn't the man at the top; he's only a paid hand. It's Bull Matterson who is reaping the profits from the finagling that was done with the Trinavant Trust.'

She smiled wanly. 'I don't think he considered it to be cheating. I think Bull just thought of it as a smart business deal – nothing dishonest.'

'But goddam immoral,' observed Mac.

'I don't think considerations like that ever enter his head,' she said. 'He's just become a machine for making money. Is he really ill, Bob?'

'He didn't look too bright when I saw him last,' I said. 'Mac, what do we do now?'

'What about – the Trinavant business or the dam?' He shrugged. 'I don't think it's up to you this time, Bob. The ball's in Howard's court and he might come after you.'

'We must do something about the dam. Perhaps I can talk to Donner.'

'You'd never get in to see him – Howard will prime him with a suitable story. All you can do is to sit tight and wait for the breaks – or you can leave town.'

I said, 'I wish to God I'd never heard of Fort Farrell.' I looked up. 'Sorry, Clare.'

'Don't be a fool,' said Mac. 'Are you turning soft just because an old man has a heart-attack? Hell, I didn't think he had a heart in the first place. Keep fighting, Bob. Try to give them another slug while they're off balance.'

I said slowly, 'I could get out of town. I could go to Fort St John and try to stir up some interest there. Someone, somewhere, might be intrigued at the idea of a dam collapsing.'

'Might as well go there as anywhere else,' said Mac. 'Because one thing is certain – the Mattersons are mad as hornets right now, and no one in Fort Farrell is going to lift a finger to help you with Howard breathing down his neck. Old Bull was right – the Mattersons own this country and everyone knows it. Nobody will listen to you now, Bob. As for going into Fort St John, you'll have to go through Fort Farrell to do it. My advice to you is to wait until after dark.'

I stared at him. 'Are you crazy? I'm no fugitive.'

His face was serious. 'I've been thinking about that. Now that Bull is out of the way there'll be no one to hold Howard down. Donner can't do it, that's for certain. And Jimmy Waystrand and some of Howard's goons could make an awful mess of you. Remember what happened a couple of years ago to Charley Burns, Clare? A broken leg, a broken arm, four busted ribs and his face kicked in. Those boys play rough – and I'll bet they're looking for you now, so don't go into Fort Farrell just yet.'

Clare stood up. 'There's nothing to stop *me* going into Fort Farrell.'

Mac cocked an eye at her. 'For what?'

'To see Gibbons,' she said. 'It's about time the police were brought into this.'

He shrugged. 'What can Gibbons do? One sergeant of the RCMP can't do a hell of a lot – not in this set-up.'

'I don't care,' she said. 'I'm going to see him.' She marched from the cabin and I heard her car start up. I said to Mac sardonically, 'What was that you were saying a little earlier about giving them another slug while they're off balance?'

'Don't be nippy,' said Mac. 'I spoke a little too fast, that's all. I just hadn't got everything digested.'

'Who was this guy, Burns?'

'Someone who got on the wrong side of Howard. He was beaten up – everyone knows why, but no one could pin anything on Howard. Burns left town and never came back. I'd forgotten about him – and he hadn't got in Howard's hair half as much as you have. I've never seen him so mad as I did this morning.' He got up and looked into the stove. 'I want some tea. I'm just going out to the woodpile.'

He walked out and I just sat there thinking about what to do next. The trouble was that I had still got no further on the Trinavant mystery, and the man who could tell me about it was probably in hospital at that moment. I felt inclined to go into Fort Farrell, walk into the Matterson Building and bust Howard one in the snoot, which might not solve anything but it would do me a lot of good.

The door slammed open and I knew I wouldn't have to go into Fort Farrell. Howard stood on the threshold with a rifle in his hands, and the round hole in the muzzle looked as big as the bottomless pit. 'Now, you sonofabitch,' he said, breathing hard. 'What's this about Frank Trinavant?'

He took two steps forward and the rifle didn't waver. Behind him Lucy Atherton slipped into the cabin and smiled maliciously at me. I started to get out of the chair and he said in a hard voice, 'Sit down, buster; you're not going anywhere.'

I flopped back. 'Why are you interested in Frank Trinavant?' I asked. 'Hasn't he been dead a long time?' It was hard to keep my voice level. Facing a gun has a curious effect on the vocal cords.

'Scared, Boyd?' asked Lucy Atherton.

'Keep quiet,' said Howard. He moistened his lips and came forward slowly and stared at me. 'Are you Frank Trinavant?'

I laughed at him. I had to work at it, but I laughed.

'Damn you, answer me!' he shouted, and his voice cracked. He took a step forward and his face worked convulsively. I kept a wary eye on his right hand and hoped the rifle didn't have too light a trigger. I was hoping that he would come one step closer so I would have a fighting chance of knocking the barrel aside, but he stopped short. 'Now you listen to me,' he said in a trembling voice. 'You're going to answer me and you're going to tell me the truth. Are you Frank Trinavant?'

'What does it matter?' I said. 'I might be Grant – I might be Trinavant. Either way, I was in the car, wasn't I?'

'Yeah, that's right,' he said. 'You were in the car.' He went dangerously calm and studied my face. 'I knew Frank, and I've seen pictures of Grant. You look like neither. You had a lot of surgery, I see. It must have hurt a lot – I hope.'

Lucy Atherton giggled.

'Yeah,' he said. 'You were in the car. It's only if you look real close you can see the scars, Lucy. They're just fine hairlines.'

I said, 'You seem interested, Howard.'

'I wondered about that – you calling me Howard all the time. Frank used to do it. Are you Frank?'

'What's the difference?'

'Sure,' he agreed. 'What's the difference? What did you see in the car? Now you can tell me, or you're going to have to get some more surgery done on that pretty face.'

'You tell me what I saw – and I'll tell you if you're right.'

His face tightened in anger and he made a slight move, but not enough to bring him within range of my hands. It was awkward sitting down; it's not a position from which you can move quickly.

'Let's have no games,' he said harshly. 'Talk!'

A voice from the door said, 'Lay that gun down, Howard, or I'll blow your spine out.'

I flicked my eyes to the door and saw Mac holding a double-barrelled shotgun on Howard. Howard froze and turned slowly, pivoting on his hips. Mac said sharply, 'The gun, Howard – lay it down. I won't tell you again.'

'He's right,' said Lucy quickly. 'He's got a shotgun.'

Howard lowered the rifle and I stood and took it as it slipped from his hands; if it dropped on the floor it might have gone off. I stepped back and looked at Mac, who smiled grimly. 'I put the shotgun into the jeep this morning in case we needed it,' he said. 'Lucky I did. All right, Howard: walk over to that wall. You too, sister Lucy.'

I examined Howard's rifle. The safety-catch was off, and as I worked the action, a round flew out of the breech.

I hadn't been very far from having my head blown off. 'Thanks, Mac,' I said.

'No time for formalities,' he said. 'Howard, sit on the floor with your back to the wall. And you, Lucy. Don't be shy.'

Howard's face was filled with hate. He said, 'You're not going to get far with this kind of thing. My boys will nail you, Boyd.'

'Boyd?' I said. 'I thought it was Grant – or Trinavant. The thing that's eating you, Howard, is that you don't *know*, do you? You're not sure.'

I turned to Mac. 'What do we do now?'

He grinned. 'You go and follow Clare. Make sure she brings Gibbons on the run. We can nail this sonofabitch for armed hold-up. I'll keep him here.'

I looked at Howard dubiously. 'Don't let him jump you.'

'He'd be too scared.' Mac patted the shotgun. 'I've got buckshot in this baby; at this range it would blow him clean in two. Hear that, Howard?'

Matterson said nothing, and Mac added, 'That goes for sister Lucy, too. You just sit there, Mrs Atherton.'

'Okay, Mac,' I said. 'I'll see you within the half-hour.' I picked up Howard's rifle and unloaded it, tossing the bullets into a corner. As I ran for the jeep I threw the rifle into the undergrowth and within a minute I was on my way.

But not for long. There was a corner just before the turn-off to Fort Farrell and, as I spun the wheel and the jeep swung round, I saw a tree felled right across the track. There was hardly time to jam on the brakes and the jeep rammed it head-on. Fortunately I'd slowed for the corner but the impact didn't do the front end of the jeep any good, and I nearly rammed my head through the windshield.

The next thing I knew was that someone was trying to haul me out of the cab. There was a shrill whistle and a shout – 'Here he is!'

Someone's hand was on my shirt, bunching it up and pulling at me. So I bent my head and bit it hard. He yelled and let go, which gave me a moment to collect my wits. I could only see the one man who was coming at me again, so I dived across the cab and out the other side. The front end of a jeep is too restricted for a big guy like me to fight comfortably.

I was still a bit dizzy from the crack on the head but not too dizzy to see the man coming round the rear of the jeep. He came a bit too fast for his own good and ran his kneecap into my boot, which just about ruined him. While he lay on the ground howling in pain I ran for the woods, conscious of the shouts behind and the thud of running boots as at least two men chased me.

I'm not much good for the hundred yards' sprint because I carry too much beef for it, but I can put up a pretty fair turn of speed when necessary. So could the guys behind and for the first five minutes there was nothing in it. But they tended to waste breath on shouting while I kept my big mouth shut, and soon they began to lag behind.

Presently I risked a look over my shoulder. There was no one in sight although I could hear them hollering, so I ducked behind a tree and got my breath back. The shouts came nearer and I heard the crackle of twigs. The first man plunged past and I let him go, stooping to pick up a rock which just fitted into my fist. I heard the second man coming and stepped out from behind the tree right in his path.

He didn't have time to stop – or to do anything at all. His mouth was open in surprise, so I closed it for him, putting all my muscle into a straight jolt to his jaw. It was the rock in my fist that did it, of course; I felt a slight crunch and his feet slid out from under him. He fell on his back and rolled over and he didn't make another move.

I listened for a while. The guy I had let go in front was out of sight but I could still hear him shouting. I also heard other shouts coming from the road, and I estimated there must be a dozen of them, so I took off again at right-angles to my original course, moving as fast as I could without making too much noise.

I didn't do too much thinking at this time, but I realized that these were Matterson's dogs that were set on me with probably Jimmy Waystrand leading the pack. My first job was to give them the slip and that wasn't going to be too easy. These were loggers, used to the woods, and probably they knew more about them than I did. They certainly knew the local country better, so I had to make sure I wasn't herded the way they wanted me to go. A better thing would be to lose them altogether.

The woodland this close to town held a spindly third growth of no commercial value and used mainly for cutting wood for the domestic fires of Fort Farrell. The trouble was that a man could see a long way through it and there was no place to hide, especially if you wore a red woollen shirt like I did. I thought I had got clear without being seen, but a shout went up and I knew I hadn't made it.

I abandoned the quietness bit and put on speed again, running uphill and feeling the strain in my lungs. On top of the rise I looked across the valley and saw the real woodlands with the big trees. Once over there I might have a chance of dodging them, and I went down into that valley lickety-split like a buck rabbit being chased by a fox.

From the shouts behind I reckoned I was keeping my distance, but that was no consolation. Any dozen determined men can run down a loner in the long haul; they can spell and pace each other. But the loner has one advantage – the adrenaline jumped into his system by the knowledge of what will happen to him when he gets caught. I had no illusions about that; a dozen husky loggers don't put out a lot of energy in running cross-country just to play patty-cake at the end of it. If they caught me I'd probably be ruined for life. Once, up in the North-West Territories, I'd seen the results when a man was ganged-up on and booted around; the end-result could hardly be called human.

So I ran for my life because I knew I'd have no life worth living if I lagged. I ignored the muscular pains creeping into my legs, the harsh rasp of air in my throat and the coming stitch in my side. I just settled down for the long, long run across that valley. I didn't look back to see how close they were because that wastes time; not much – maybe fractions of a second every time you turn your head – but fractions of a second add up and could count in the end. I just pumped my legs and kept a watch on the ground ahead of me, choosing the easiest way but not deviating too much from the straight line.

But I kept my ears open and could hear the yells coming from behind, some loud and close and others fainter and farther back. The pack was stringing out with the fittest men to the front. If there had been only two men as before I'd have stopped and fought it out, but there was no chance against a dozen, so I plunged on and lengthened my stride, despite the increasing pain in my side.

The trees were closer now, tall trees reaching to the sky – Douglas fir, red cedar, spruce, hemlock – the big forest that spread north clear to the Yukon. Once lost in there I might have a fighting chance. There were trees big enough to hide a truck behind, let alone a man; there was a confusion of shadow as the sun struck through the leaves and branches creating dappled patterns; there were fallen trees to duck behind and holes to hide in and a thick layer of pine needles on which a man could move quietly if he looked where he was putting his feet. The forest was safety of a sort.

I reached the first big fir and risked a look back. The first man was two hundred yards away and the rest were strung out behind him in a long line. I sprinted for the next tree, changed course and headed for another. Here, at the edge, the trees weren't too crowded and there were large vistas where a man could be seen for quite a long way, but it was a damn' sight better than being caught in the open.

I was moving more slowly now, intent on quietness rather than speed as I dodged from tree to tree, zig-zagging each time and keeping an eye on the way back because I had to make sure I wasn't seen. It was no longer a race – it was a cat-and-mouse game, and I was the mouse.

Now that I was no longer operating on full steam I managed to get my breath back, but my heart still pumped violently until I thought it was going to burst its way through my chest. I managed a grin as I hoped the other guys weren't in better shape and dodged deeper into the forest. Behind, everything had gone quiet and for a moment I thought they had given up, but then I heard a shout from the left and an answering call from the right. They had spread out and had begun to comb the woods.

I pressed on, hoping they had no experienced trackers among them. It was unlikely they would have, but the possibility couldn't be ignored. It was a long time till sunset, nearly four hours to go, and I wondered if Matterson's boys would have enough incentive to go right through with it. I had to find a good hiding-place and let the search flow over me, so I kept my eyes open as I slipped deeper into the dappled green.

Ahead was a rock outcropping of tumbled boulders with plenty of cover in it. I ignored it – they wouldn't pass up a chance like that and they'd search every cranny. Still, that would take time – there's an awful lot of holes where a man *may* be hiding compared to the one he is using, and this was my one hope. I heard a shout from way back and judged they were making poorer time than I, wasting valuable minutes in poking and prying, deviating to look behind that fallen log or into that likely-looking hole where a tree had fallen and torn up its roots.

I didn't want to be driven too far into the forest. I was worried about Mac and how long he could hold Matterson and his sister. Clare had gone to see Gibbons, but there had been no particular urgency at that time and Gibbons might not move his butt fast enough. So I wanted to get back to the cabin somehow, and every yard I was driven into the forest meant another yard to go back.

The firs soared up all round, their massive trunks branchless for a full fifty feet. Yet I found what I was looking for – a young cedar with branches low enough for it to be climbed. I swarmed up into it and crawled out on one of the branches. The spreading boughs would hide me from the ground – I hoped – but as an added precaution I took off that revealing red shirt and wadded it into a bundle. Then I waited.

Nothing happened for over ten minutes, then they came so quietly that I saw the flicker of movement before I heard a sound. A man came into view at the edge of the clearing and looked about him, and I froze into immobility. He was not more than fifty yards away and he was very still as he stared into the woods across the clearing, his head swinging round as he gave the area a real thorough going-over with his eyes. Then he gestured and another man joined him and the two of them walked across the clearing light-footedly.

A man doesn't look up much. The bones of his skull project over his eyes just where his eyebrows are – that's to protect his eyes from the direct sun. And looking up much puts a strain on the neck muscles, too. I guess it's all been designed by nature to protect the delicate eye from glare. Anyway, it so happens that only an experienced searcher will scan the tops of trees – it's something that doesn't occur to the average man and there's a built-in resistance – partly psychological and partly physiological – to see that it doesn't.

These two were no exceptions. They walked across the clearing emulating Fenimore Cooper's heroes and stopped for a moment below the cedar. One of them said, 'I think it's a bust.'

The other cut him short with a chopping motion of his hand. 'Quiet! He could be around here.'

'Not a chance. Hell, he's probably five miles from here by now. Anyway, my feet hurt.'

'More'n your feet'll hurt if Waystrand finds you falling down on the job.'

'Huh, that young punk!'

'Can you whip him? You're welcome to try but I wouldn't put my money on you. Anyway, Matterson wants this guy found, so come on and stop moaning about it.'

They moved away across the clearing but I stayed put. In the distance I heard a shout, but otherwise all was still. I waited a full fifteen minutes before I dropped from the tree and although it was chilly, I had left my shirt up there and out of sight.

I didn't retrace my steps but cut across at an angle in the direction of Mac's cabin. If I could get back there and if Mac still had Howard cooped up he would make a valuable hostage, a passport to safety. I trod carefully, and viewed every open space suspiciously before venturing into it, and I penetrated right to the edge of the forest before I encountered anyone.

In any crowd of men there is always one like this – the man who doesn't pull his weight, the man who goofs off when there's a job to be done. He was sitting with his back to a tree and rolling a cigarette. He had evidently had foot trouble because, although he was wearing his boots, they were unlaced and he must have had them off.

He was a damned nuisance because, although he was goofing off, he was ideally placed at the edge of the forest to survey the scrubland I had to cross to get to Mac's cabin. In fact, if Waystrand had placed him there deliberately he couldn't have chosen a better position.

I retreated noiselessly and looked about for a weapon. This attack had to be sudden and quick; I didn't know how many other guys were within shouting distance and one squawk from him and I'd be on the run again. I selected a length of tree bough and cut the twigs from it with my knife. When I went back he was still there, had got his cigarette lit and was puffing it with enjoyment.

I circled and came up behind the tree very carefully and raised the cudgel as I edged round. He never knew what hit him. The wood caught him on the temple and he didn't even gasp as he fell sideways, the cigarette falling from his lax fingers. I dropped the club and stepped in front of him, automatically stepping on the glowing cigarette as it crisped the pine needles. Hastily I grabbed him under the arms and hauled him to a place where we weren't overlooked.

I had a moment of panic when I thought he was dead, but he groaned and his eyelids fluttered a little before he relapsed into unconsciousness. I had no compunction about hitting a man when he wasn't looking, but I didn't want to kill anybody – not because I didn't feel like it but because a man could get hanged that way. The law is pretty strict about dead bodies and I wanted Gibbons on my side.

He was wearing a dark grey shirt which was just what I wanted, so I stripped it from him and then searched him for good measure. He didn't have much in his pockets – a wallet containing three dollar-bills and some personal papers, a few coins, a box of matches and a pack of tobacco and a jack-knife. I took the matches and the knife and left him the rest, then I put on the shirt, that neutral, pleasantly inconspicuous shirt which was as good as a disguise.

I put him in a place where no one would stumble over him too easily, then walked boldly out of the forest, cutting across the scrubland towards Mac's cabin which couldn't have been more than a mile away according to my calculations. I had gone halfway when someone hailed me.

Fortunately he was a long way off, too far to see my face in the fading light. 'Hey, you! What happened?'

I cupped my hands to my mouth. 'We lost him.'

'Everyone's wanted at McDougall's cabin,' he shouted. 'Matterson wants to talk to you.'

I felt my heart give a sudden bump. What had happened to Mac? I waved, and shouted, 'I'll be there.'

He carried on in the opposite direction, and as he passed, I angled away and kept my face from him. As soon as he was out of sight I broke into a run until I saw lights in the gathering darkness, then I paused, wondering what to do next. I had to find out what had happened to Mac, so I circled the cabin to come at it from the other, unexpected side and as I drew nearer I heard the rumble of the voices of many men.

Someone had brought a pressure-lantern from the cabin and set it up on the stoop, and from where I was lying by the stream I could see there were about twenty men lounging about in front of the cabin. Counting the dozen who had chased me and who were still coming back from the forest, that made a force of at least thirty – maybe more. It looked as though Howard was gathering an army.

I stayed there for a long time, maybe an hour, and tried to figure out what was happening. There was no sign of Mac, nor of Clare and Gibbons. I saw Waystrand come into the group. He looked tired and worn, but then, so did I, and I didn't feel a bit sorry for him. He asked someone an obvious question and was waved to the cabin. I watched him enter and didn't have long to wait for an explanation of the gathering, because almost immediately he came out again followed by Howard.

Howard stood on the stoop and held up his hands and everything became quiet except for the croaking of frogs around me. 'All right,' said Howard loudly. 'You know why you're here. You're going to look for a man – a man called

Boyd. Most of you have seen him around Fort Farrell so you know what he looks like. And you know why we want him, don't you?'

A rumble came from the group of men. Howard said, 'For those of you who came in late – this is it. This man Boyd beat up my father – he hit a man more than twice his age – an old man. My father is seventy-six years old. How old do you reckon Boyd is?'

My blood chilled at the audible reaction from the mob in front of the stoop. 'Now you know why I want him,' yelled Howard. He waved his arm. 'You're all on full pay until he's found, and I'll give a hundred dollars to the man who spots him first.'

A yell went up from the mob and Howard waved his arm violently to get silence. 'What's more,' he shouted, 'I'll give a thousand dollars each to the men who catch him.'

There was pandemonium for a while and Howard let it go on.

I could see the twisted grin on his face in the harsh light of the pressure-lantern. He held up his arms for silence again. 'Now, we've lost him for the moment. He's in the woods out there. He has no food, and my betting is that he's scared. But watch it, because he's armed. I came here to beat the daylights out of him because of what he did to my old man, and he held me up at rifle-point. So watch it.'

Waystrand whispered to him, and Howard said, 'I may be wrong there, boys. Waystrand here says he didn't have a gun when he made for the woods, so that makes your job easier. I'm going to divide you up into teams and you can get going. When you catch him, keep him there and send a message back to me. Understand that – don't try to bring him back into Fort Farrell. This is a slippery guy and I don't want to give him a chance to get away. Keep him on the spot until I get there. Tie him up. If you don't have any rope then break his goddam leg. I won't cry if you rough him up a bit.'

The laughter that broke out was savage. Howard said, 'All right. I want Waystrand, Novak, Simpson and Henderson to head the teams. Come into the cabin, you guys, and I'll lay things out.'

He went back into the cabin followed by Waystrand and three others. I stayed where I was for a couple of minutes, wishing I knew what was being said in the cabin, then I withdrew, slowly and carefully, and went back into the darkness.

If ever I had seen anyone working up a lynching party it had been Howard. The bastard had set a mob thirsting for my blood and I wouldn't be safe anywhere around Fort Farrell – not with a thousand dollars on my head. Those loggers of his were tough boys and he'd filled them up with such a pack of goddam lies that it would be useless for me to try to explain anything.

I was struck by a sudden idea and wormed my way to the place where I had bedded down the previous night, and was deeply thankful that I had slept out and had been sloppy enough not to take my gear back to the cabin. My pack was still lying where I had left it, and I hastily replaced the few items I had taken out. Now I had at least the absolute minimum necessary for a prolonged stay in the woods – everything except food and a weapon.

There came a renewed burst of noise from the direction of the cabin and the sound of several engines starting up. Someone came blundering through the undergrowth and I withdrew away from the cabin, still undecided as to what to do next. In all my life I had never been in as tough a position as this, except when I woke up in hospital to find myself an erased blank. I tightened the pack straps and thought grimly that if a man could survive that experience he could survive this one.

Use your brains, I told myself. *Think of a safe place.*

The only safe place I could think of was the inside of a jail – just as an honoured guest, of course. An RCMP sergeant wouldn't – or shouldn't – let anyone tramp over him and I reckoned I'd be as safe in one of Gibbons's cells as anywhere else until this blew over and I could find someone sane enough to start explaining things to. So I headed for the town, circling around so as not to walk on the road. I wanted to head for Gibbons's place by the least populous route.

I should have known that Howard would have it staked out. The last thing in the world he wanted was for the cops to interfere, and if I got to Gibbons then maybe the jig would be up. Howard would never be able to hide the fact that I didn't hit old Matterson and the truth would inevitably come out, something he couldn't afford to happen. So even though he thought I was somewhere in the woods he had coppered his bet by staking out the police-station just in case I made a run for Gibbons.

Of course I didn't think of that at the time, although I was very careful as I walked the quiet streets of Fort Farrell. It was a linear town, long and thin, built around the one main street, and I had chosen a route which took me past very few houses on the way to the police-station. There was a moon, an unfortunate circumstance, and I tried to keep as much in the shadows as I could. I met nobody on the way and I began to think I would make it. I hoped to God that Gibbons was around.

I was within a hundred yards of the station when I was tackled. I suppose being so near had made me let my guard down. The first thing I knew was a burst of bright light in my eyes as someone shone a flashlight on me – then a cry: 'That's him!'

I ducked and skidded to one side and felt something thump into my pack with a frightening force and the impact threw me off-balance so that I sprawled on the ground. The flashlamp shone around searching, and as it found me I got a boot in my ribs. I rolled frantically away, knowing that if I didn't get up I could be kicked to death. Those loggers' boots are heavy and clinched with steel and a real good kick can smash a man's rib-cage and drive the bone into his lungs.

So I rolled faster and faster although impeded by the pack, trying to escape that damned flashlamp. A voice said hoarsely, 'Get the bastard, Jack!' and a badly aimed boot crashed into the back of my right thigh. I put my hands on the ground and swung round with my legs, flailing them wildly, and tripped up someone who came crashing on top of me.

His head must have hit the ground because he went flaccid and I heaved him off and staggered to my feet just in time to meet a bull-like rush from another man. The guy with the flashlamp was standing well back, damn him, giving me no chance to get away into darkness, but at least it put me and my attackers on equal terms.

I had no odd ideas about fair play – that's a civilized idea and civilization stops when you set thirty men against one. Besides, I had learned my fighting in the North-West Territories, and the Marquess of Queensberry's rules don't hold good north of the 60th Parallel. I swung my boot, sideways on, at the man's kneecap and scraped it forcibly down his shin to end up by stamping with my heel on his foot just above the instep. My left fist went for his guts and my right hand for his chin, palm open so that the heel of my hand forced his head back and my fingertips were in his eyes.

He got in a couple of good body blows while I was doing that but thereafter was fully occupied with his own aches and pains. He howled in anguish as I raked his shin to the bone and his hands came up to protect his eyes. I gave him another thump in the belly and the breath came out of him in a great gasp and he started to crumple. I'm a big guy and pretty strong, so I just picked him up and threw him at my friend with the flashlamp.

He made contact and the flashlamp went out. I heard the glass break as it hit the ground. I didn't stick around to hear

any more because there may have been more of the goons.
I just picked up my feet and headed out of town.

II

By midnight I was well into the forest and pretty well tuck-
ered out. I had been chased from town and nearly caught,
too, and when I doubled back I nearly ran into another
bunch of Matterson's men who must have been pulled in
from the woods. So I gave it up and struck west, that being
the direction I thought they would least expect me to go –
into the wilderness.

I didn't expect to gain anything by going west, but at
least it gave me a breathing-space and time to think out a
plan of action. The moon was high in the sky and I found a
quiet hole among some rocks and shucked off my pack with
relief. I was tired. I had been on the run more or less continuously for ten hours and that tends to take the steam out
of a man. I was hungry, too, but I couldn't do much about
that except tighten up my belt.

I reckoned I was safe for the time being. Matterson
couldn't possibly organize a proper search at night even if
he knew the exact area in which I was hiding, and the only
danger was in someone falling over me by accident. I needed
rest and sleep and I had to have it, because next day was
likely to be even livelier.

I took off my boots and changed my socks. My feet were
going to be my best friends for the foreseeable future and I
didn't want them going bad on me. Then I had a sip of
water from the canteen attached to my pack. I was all right
for water – I had filled the canteen when crossing a stream –
but I still didn't waste it because I didn't know this country
very well and maybe there wouldn't be a stream next time
I wanted one.

I sat back flexing my toes luxuriously and thought of the events of the day. It was the first time I'd been able to put two thoughts together consecutively – all my efforts had been directed to sheer survival.

First, I thought of Clare and wondered what in hell had happened to her. She had gone to see Gibbons pretty early and should have arrived back at Mac's cabin, with or without the cop, long before sunset. Yet I had seen no sign of her during Howard Matterson's lynch-law speech. That left two possibilities – one, that she was in the cabin, which meant she was held under duress; and two, she wasn't in the cabin, in which case I didn't know where the devil she was.

Then there was Mac. Somehow Matterson had come from under Mac's shotgun safely, which meant that something must have happened to Mac. Let's say he was out of the game – and Clare, too – which left me the only one of us free and able to do anything at all. And so far all I had been able to do was to run like an Olympic marathon runner.

I thought of Howard's speech and the specific instructions he had issued and tried to figure out what he meant to do. I was to be held where I was captured until Howard caught up with me. And that added up to a nasty situation, because I couldn't see what he could do with me apart from killing me.

He certainly couldn't kill me openly; I doubted if his men would stand for that. But suppose I was 'accidentally' killed; supposing Howard said that he had killed me in self-defence. There were many ways of arranging something like that. Or I could 'escape' from Howard, never to be seen again. In the deep woods there are places where a body might never be found for a century.

All of which led me to take a fresh look at Howard Matterson. Why would he want me dead? Answer: because it was *he* who had something to do with the crash – not old

Bull. And what could he have to do with the crash? Answer: he had probably arranged it personally – he was probably an outright murderer.

I had checked on where Bull had been when the crash happened, but it had never occurred to me to check on Howard. One doesn't think of a kid of twenty-one as being a murderer when there's someone else at hand with all the motives and qualifications. I had slipped there. Where was Howard when the crash happened? Answer: I didn't know – but I could make a good guess.

After all, he could capture me and take me back to Fort Farrell, and then the whole story would blow up in his face. He *had* to get rid of me and the only way was by another killing.

I shivered slightly. I had led a pretty tough life but I had never been pursued with deadly intention before. This was quite a new experience and likely to be my last. Of course, it was still possible for me to quit. I could head farther west and then south-west to the coast, hitting it at Stewart or Prince Rupert; I could then get lost and never see Fort Farrell again. But I knew I wouldn't do that because of Mac and Clare – especially Clare.

I dug a blanket from my pack and wrapped it round me. I was dead beat and in no fit condition to make important decisions. It would be time enough in daylight to worry about what to do next. I dropped off to sleep with Mac's words echoing in my ears: *Keep fighting; give them another slug while they're off balance.*

It was very good advice whether they were off balance or not. I sleepily made up my mind about two things. The first was that I had to fight on ground of my own choosing, ground that I knew well. The only ground in this area that I knew well was the Kinoxi Valley, and I knew that very well because I had prospected it thoroughly, and I knew I could out-dodge anyone there.

The other vital thing was to make the chasing of Bob Boyd a very unprofitable undertaking. I had to make it unmistakably clear that to harry me in any way wasn't worth anything like a thousand dollars, and the only way these loggers could be taught a lesson like that was by violence. Three of them, perhaps, had already come to this conclusion; one had a busted kneecap, another a busted jaw, and the third a shin laid open to the bone. If stronger measures were necessary for discouragement then I would see they were administered.

I wanted to get Howard in the open from behind his screen of thugs and the only way to do that was to scare them off. It takes a hell of a lot to scare the average logger; it's a dangerous job of work in the first place and they don't scare easily. But it was something I had to do – I had to get them off my back – and I would have to do things so monstrously efficient in their execution that they would think twice about attempting to earn that thousand dollars.

TEN

I was on the move by sunrise next morning and heading north. I reckoned I was twelve miles west of Fort Farrell and so was moving parallel to the road that had been driven up to the Kinoxi Valley, but far enough away from it to be out of the net of Matterson's searchers – I hoped. Hunger was beginning to gnaw at my gut but not so much as to weaken – I could go, maybe, another day and a half before food became a real problem, and I might have to.

I plugged away hour after hour, keeping up a steady pace, travelling faster than I normally did when on the move. I reckon I was keeping up a steady speed of two and a half miles an hour over the ground, which wasn't at all bad across this kind of country. I kept looking back to check the landscape, not so much to see if I was being followed but to make sure I was travelling in a straight line. It's awfully easy to veer and most people do quite unconsciously. That's why, in bad conditions such as fog or thick snow, you find guys getting lost and wandering in circles. I've been told that it's due to differences in the length of your legs and the resulting slight difference in stride. Long ago I'd checked up on my own propensity to veer and figured I tended to swerve about 4° from the straight line and to the right; after I knew that it didn't take much practice to be able to correct it consciously.

But it's always a good idea to check on theory and I like to know what the landscape looks like behind me; such knowledge could be useful if I had to make a run for it. There was, of course, always the possibility of seeing someone else, and I had already figured that in country where the *average* population was one person to three square miles, then anyone I saw was unlikely to pop up accidentally and was therefore to be regarded with suspicion.

I was able to find food of a sort while still on the move. I picked up and pocketed maybe a couple of pounds of mushrooms. I knew they were good eating but I'd never eaten them raw and I wouldn't experiment. I doubted if they'd kill me but I didn't want to be put out of action with possible stomach cramps, so I just kept them by me although my mouth was drooling.

I rested up frequently but not for long each time – about five minutes in the hour. More than that would have tightened my leg muscles and I needed to keep limber. I didn't even stop for long at midday, just enough to change my socks, wash the others in a stream and pin them to the top of my pack to dry out while I was on the move. I filled my water canteen and pressed on north.

Two hours before sunset I began to look round for a place to camp – a nice secluded place – and found one on top of a rise where I had a good view into valleys on both sides. I shucked my pack and spent half an hour just looking, making sure there was no one around, then I undid the pack and produced from the bottom my own personal survival kit.

In the North-West Territories I had been in the wilderness for months at a time, and since rifle ammunition is heavy to carry, I had tended to conserve it and find other ways of getting fresh meat. The little kit which I carried in an old chocolate tin was the result of years of experience and it always lived in the bottom of my pack ready for use.

The jack-rabbits come out and play around just before sunset, so I selected three wire snares, carefully avoiding the fish-hooks in the tin. I once stuck a fish-hook in my finger just at the start of a season and ignored the wound. It festered and I had to come into a trading-post before the season was halfway through with a blood-poisoned finger the size of a banana. That little prick with a hook cost me over a thousand dollars and nearly cost me my right hand so I've been careful of fish-hooks ever since.

I had seen rabbit trails in plenty so I staked out the three snares, then collected some wood for a fire, selecting small dead larch twigs and making sure they were bone dry. I took them back to camp and arranged them so as to make a small fire, but did not put a match to it. It would be time for that after sunset when the smoke would not be noticeable, little though it would be. I found a small birch tree and cut a cylinder of bark with my hunting knife, and arranged it around the fire as a shield, propping it up with small stones so as to allow a bottom draught.

Half an hour after sunset I lit the fire and retreated a hundred yards to see the effect. I could see it because I knew it was there, but it would take a man as good as me or better to find it otherwise. Satisfied about that, I went back, poured some water into a pannikin and set the mushrooms to boil. While they were cooking I went to see if I had any luck with the snares. Two of them were empty but in one I had caught a half-grown doe rabbit. She didn't have more than a couple of mouthfuls of flesh on her but she'd have to satisfy me that night.

After supper I did a circuit of the camp, then came back and risked a cigarette. I reckoned I'd come nearly thirty miles heading due north. If I angled north-west from here I should strike the Kinoxi Valley in about fifteen miles, hitting it about a third of the way up just where Matterson's logging camp was. That could be dangerous but I had to start hitting back. Prowling around the edges of this thing was all very well but it would get me nowhere at all; I had to go smack into the centre and cause some trouble.

After a while I made sure the fire was out and went to sleep.

II

I topped a rise and looked over the Kinoxi Valley at just about two o'clock next afternoon. The new Matterson Lake had spread considerably since I had seen it last, and now covered about one-third of its designed extent, drowning out the wasteland caused by the logging. I was just about level with the northernmost point it had reached. The logged area extended considerably farther and stretched way up the valley, almost, I reckoned, to the Trinavant land. Matterson had just about stripped his land bare.

As the logging had proceeded the camp had been shifted up-valley and I couldn't see it from where I was standing, so I dipped behind the ridge again and headed north, keeping the ridge between me and the valley bottom. Possibly I was now on dangerous ground, but I didn't think so. All my activities so far had been centred on Fort Farrell and on the dam which was to the south at the bottom of the valley.

I put myself in Howard Matterson's place and tried to think his thoughts – a morbid exercise. Boyd had caused trouble in Fort Farrell, so watch it – we nearly caught him there and he might try for it again. Boyd was interested in the dam, he was drilling there – so watch it because he might go back. But Boyd had never shown much interest in the Kinoxi Valley itself, so why should he go there?

I knew what I was going to do there – I was going to raise hell! It was ground I had prospected and I knew all the twists and turns of the streams, all the draws and ravines, all the rises and falls of the land. I was going to stick to the thick forest in the north of the valley, draw in Howard's hunters and then punish them so much that they'd be afraid to push it further. I had to break this deadlock and get Howard in the open.

And I thought the best place to start raising hell was the Matterson logging camp.

I went north for four miles and finally located the camp. It was situated on flat ground in the valley bottom and set right in the middle of the ruined forest. There was too much open ground around it for my liking but that couldn't be helped, and I saw that I could only move about down there at night. So I used the remaining hours of daylight in studying the problem.

There didn't seem to be much doing down there, nor could I hear any sounds of activity from farther up the valley where the loggers should have been felling. It looked as though Howard had pulled most of the men away from the job to look for me and I hoped they were still sitting on their butts around Fort Farrell. There was a plume of smoke rising from what I judged was the cookhouse and my belly rumbled at the thought of food. That was another good reason for going down to the camp.

I watched the camp steadily for the next three hours and didn't see more than six men. It was too far to judge really properly but I guessed these were old-timers, the cooks and bottle-washers employed around the camp who were too old or not fit enough to be of use, either in logging or in chasing Bob Boyd. I didn't see I'd have much trouble there.

I rubbed my chin as I thought of the consequences of Howard's action and the conclusions to be drawn from them. He'd pulled off his loggers at full pay to search for me, and that was wasting him an awful lot of time and money. If he didn't get them back on the job it might be too late to save the trees – unless he'd opened the sluices on the dam to prevent the lake encroaching any farther up the valley. But even then he'd be running into financial trouble; the sawmill must have been geared to this operation and the cutting off of the flow of raw lumber from the valley would have its repercussions there – if he didn't get his loggers back to work pretty soon the sawmill would have to close down.

It seemed to me that Howard wanted me very badly – this was another added brick in the structure of evidence I was building. It wasn't evidence in the legal sense, but it was good enough for me.

Towards dusk I made my preparations. I took the blankets from the pack and strapped them on the outside and, when it was dark enough, I began my descent to the valley floor. I knew of a reasonably easy way and it didn't take long before I was approaching the edge of the camp. There were lights burning in two of the prefabricated huts, but otherwise there was no sign of life beyond the wheezing of a badly played harmonica. I ghosted through the camp, treading easily, and headed for the cookhouse. I didn't see why I shouldn't stock up on supplies at Howard's expense.

The cookhouse had a light burning and the door was ajar. I peered through a window and saw there was no one in sight so I slipped through the doorway and closed the door behind me. A big cooking-pot was steaming on the stove and the smell of hash nearly sent me crazy, but I had no time for luxuries – what I wanted was the stock-room.

I found it at the end of the cookhouse; a small room, shelved all round and filled with canned goods. I began to load cans into my pack, taking great care not to knock them together. I used shirts to separate them in the pack and added a small sack of flour on top. I was about to emerge when someone came into the cookhouse and I closed the door again quickly.

There was only one door from the stock-room and that led into the cookhouse – a natural precaution against the healthy appetites of thieving loggers. For the same reason there was no window, so I had to stay in the stock-room until the cookhouse was vacated or I had to take violent action to get out . . .

I opened the door a crack and saw a man at the stove stirring the pot with a wooden spoon. He tasted, put the spoon back in the pot, and walked to a table to pick up a pack of salt. I saw that he was an elderly man who walked with a limp and knew that violence was out of the question. This man had never done me any harm nor had he set out to hurt me, and I couldn't see myself taking Howard's sins out on him.

He stayed in the cookhouse for an eternity – not more than twenty minutes in reality – and I thought he'd never go. He puttered around in a pestiferous way; he washed a couple of dishes, wrung out a dishrag and set it to dry near the stove, headed towards the stock-room as though he were going to get something, changed his mind in mid-limp just as I thought I'd have to hit him after all, and finally tasted the contents of his pot again, shrugged, and left the cookhouse.

I crept out, checked that all was clear outside, and slid from the cookhouse with my booty. Already an idea had occurred to me. I had decided to raise hell, and raise hell I would. The camp was lit by electricity and I had heard the deep throb of a diesel generator coming from the edge of the camp. It was no trick to find it, guided by the noise it made, and the only difficulty I had was in keeping to the shadows.

The generator chugged away in its own hut. For safety's sake, I explored around before I did anything desperate, and found that the next hut was the saw doctor's shop. In between the two huts was a thousand-gallon tank of diesel oil which, on inspection of the simple tube gauge, proved to be half full. To top it off, there was a felling axe conveniently to hand in the saw shop which, when swung hard against the oil tank, bit through the thin-gauge sheet metal quite easily.

It made quite a noise and I was glad to hear the splash of the oil as it spurted from the jagged hole. I was able to get in another couple of swings before I heard a shout of alarm and by that time I could feel the oil slippery underfoot. I retreated quickly and ignited the paper torch I had prepared and tossed it at the tank, then ran for the darkness.

At first I thought my torch must have gone out, but suddenly there came a great flare and flames shot skyward. I could see the figure of a man hovering uncertainly on the edge of the fire and then I went away, making the best speed I could in spite of my conviction that no one would follow me.

III

By dawn I was comfortably ensconced in the fork of a tree well into the thick forest of the north of the valley. I had eaten well, if coldly, of corned beef and beans and had had a few hours' sleep. The food did me a power of good and I felt ready for anything Matterson could throw at me. As I got myself ready for the day's mayhem I wondered how he would begin.

I soon found out, even before I left that tree. I heard the whirr of slow-moving blades and a helicopter passed overhead not far above treetop level. The downdraught of the rotor blew cold on my face and a few pine needles showered to the ground. The whirlybird departed north but I stayed where I was, and sure enough, it came back a few minutes later but a little to the west.

I dropped out of the tree, brushed myself down, and hoisted the pack. Howard had deduced what I wanted him to deduce and the helicopter reconnaissance was his first move. It was still too early for him to have moved any shock troops into the valley, but it wouldn't be long before they arrived and I speculated how to spend my time.

I could hear the helicopter bumbling down the valley and thought that pretty soon it would be on its way back on a second sweep, so I positioned myself in a good place to see it. It came back flying up the valley dead centre, and I strained my eyes and figured it contained only two men, the pilot and one passenger. I also figured that, if they saw me, they wouldn't come down because the pilot would have to stick with his craft and his passenger wouldn't care to tangle with me alone. That gave me some leeway.

It was a simple enough plan I evolved but it depended on psychology mostly and I wondered if my assessment of Howard's boys was good enough. The only way to find out was to try it and see. It also depended on some primitive technology and I would have to see if the wiles I had learned in the north would work as well on men as on animals.

I went through the forest for half a mile to a game trail I knew of, and there set about the construction of a deadfall. A snare may have been all right for catching a rabbit but you need something bigger for a deer – or a man. There was another thing, too; a deer has no idea of geometry or mechanics and wouldn't understand a deadfall even if you took the trouble to explain. All that was necessary was to avoid man scent and the deer would walk right into it. But a man would recognize a deadfall at first sight, so this one had to be very cleverly constructed.

There was a place where the trail skirted a bank about four feet high and on the other side was a six-foot drop. Anyone going along the trail would of necessity have to pass that point. I manhandled a two-foot boulder to the edge of the bank and checked it with small stones so that it teetered on the edge and would need only a slight touch to send it falling. Then I got out the survival kit and set a snare for a man's foot, using fishing-line run through forked twigs to connect to a single pebble which held the boulder.

The trap took me nearly half an hour to prepare and from time to time I heard the helicopter as it patrolled the other side of the valley. I camouflaged the snare and walked about the deadfall, making sure that it looked innocent to the eye. It was the best I could do, so I walked up the trail about four hundred yards to where it ran through a marshy area. Deliberately I ploughed through the marsh to the dry ground on the other side leaving much evidence of my passage – freshly broken grasses, footprints and gouts of wet mud on the dry land. I went still farther up the trail then struck off to the side and in a wide circle came back to my man-trap.

That was half of the plan. The second half consisted of going down the trail to a clearing through which ran a stream. I dumped my pack by the trail and figured out when the helicopter would be coming over again. I thought it would be coming over that clearing on to the next pass so I sauntered down to the stream and filled my canteen.

I was right, and it came over so unexpectedly it surprised even me. The tall firs muffled the sound until it was roaring overhead. I looked up in surprise and saw the white blob of a face looking down at me. Then I ran for cover as though the devil was at my heels. The 'copter wheeled in the air and made a second pass over the clearing, and then a wider circle and finally it headed down valley going fast. Matterson had found Boyd at last.

I went back to the clearing and regretfully ripped a piece of my shirt and stuck it on a thorn not far up the game trail. I'd see these guys did the right thing even if I had to lead them by the nose. I humped the pack to a convenient place from where I could get a good view of my trap and settled down to wait and used the time to whittle a club with my hunting knife.

By my figuring the helicopter would be back pretty soon. I didn't think it would have to go farther south than the dam, say, ten miles in eight minutes. Give them fifteen minutes to decide the right thing to do, and another eight minutes to get back, and that was a total of about a half-hour. It would come back loaded with men, but it couldn't carry more than four, apart from the pilot. Those it would drop and go back for another load – say, another twenty minutes.

So I had twenty minutes to dispose of four men. Not too long, but enough, I hoped.

It was nearer three-quarters of an hour before I heard it coming back, and by the lower note I knew it had landed in the clearing. Then it rose and began to circle and I wondered how long it was going to do that. If it didn't go away according to my schedule it would wreck everything. It was with relief that I heard it head south again and I kept my eye on the trail to the clearing, hoping that my bait had been taken.

Pretty soon I heard a faint shout which seemed to have a triumphant ring to it – the bait had been swallowed whole. I looked through the screen of leaves and saw them coming up the trail fast. Three of them were armed – two shotguns and one rifle – and I didn't like that much, but I reflected that it wouldn't make any difference because this particular operation depended on surprise.

They came up that trail almost at a run. They were young and fresh and, like a modern army, had been transported to the scene of operations in luxury. If I had to depend on outrunning them I'd be caught in a mile, but that wasn't the intention. I had run the first time because I'd been caught by surprise but now everything had changed. These guys didn't know it but they weren't hunting me – they were victims.

They came along the trail two abreast but were forced into single file where the trail narrowed with the bank on one side and the drop on the other. I held my breath as they came to the trap. The first man avoided the snare and I cursed under my breath; but the second man put his foot right in it and tripped out the pebble. The boulder toppled on to number three catching him in the hip. In his surprise he grabbed hold of the guy in front and they both went over the drop followed by the boulder which weighed the best part of a hundred and fifty pounds.

There was a flurry of shouting and cursing and when all the excitement had died down one man was sitting on the ground looking stupidly at his broken leg and the other was yowling that his hip hurt like hell.

The leader was Novak, the big man I had had words with before. 'Why don't you look where you're putting your big feet?'

'It just fell on me, Novak,' the man with the hurt hip expostulated. 'I didn't do a damn' thing.'

I lay in the bushes not more than twenty feet away and grinned. It had not been a bad estimate that if a big rock pushes a man over a six-foot drop then he's liable to break a bone. The odds had dropped some – it was now three to one.

'I've got a busted leg,' the man on the ground wailed.

Novak climbed down and examined it while I held my breath. If any trace of that snare remained they would know that this was no chance accident. I was lucky – either the fishing-line had broken or Novak didn't see the loop. He stood up and cursed. 'Jesus! We're not here five minutes and there's a man out of action – maybe two. How's your hip?'

'Goddam sore. Maybe I fractured my pelvis.'

Novak did some more grumbling, then said, 'The others will be along soon. You'd better stay here with Banks – splint that leg if you can. Me and Scottie'll get on. Boyd is getting farther away every goddam minute.'

He climbed up on the trail and after a few well-chosen remarks about Banks and his club-footed ancestry, he said, 'Come on, Scottie,' and moved off.

I had to do this fast. I watched them out of sight, then flicked my gaze to Banks. He was bending over the other man and looking at the broken leg and he had his back to me. I broke cover, ran the twenty feet at a crouch and clubbed him before he had time to turn.

He collapsed over the other man, who looked up with frightened eyes. Before he had time to yell I had grabbed a shotgun and was pushing the muzzle in his face. 'One cheep and you'll get worse than a broken leg,' I threatened.

He shut his mouth and his eyes crossed as they tried to focus on that big round iron hole. I said curtly, 'Turn your head.'

'Huh?'

'Turn your head, dammit! I haven't all day.'

Reluctantly he turned his head away. I groped for the club I had dropped and hit him. I was soft, I guess; I didn't relish hitting a man with a broken leg, but I couldn't afford to have him start yelling. Anyway, I didn't hit him hard enough. He sagged a bit and shook his head dizzily and I had to hit him again a bit harder and he flopped out.

I hauled Banks off him and felt a bit dizzy myself. It occurred to me that if I kept thumping people on the skull, sooner or later I'd come across someone with thin bones and I'd kill him. Yet it was a risk I had to run. I had to impress these guys somehow and utter ruthlessness was one way to do it – the only way I could think of.

I took off Banks's belt and hog-tied him quickly, then took off with the shotgun after Novak and Scottie. I don't think more than four minutes had elapsed since they had left. I had to get to the place where the trail crossed the marsh before they did and, because the trail took a wide curve, I had only half the distance to go to get there. I ran like a hare through the trees and arrived breathless and panting just in time to hide behind the tall reeds by the marsh and at the edge of the trail.

I heard them coming, not moving as quickly as they had done at first. I suppose that four men hunting a fugitive have more confidence than two – even if they are armed. Anyway, Novak and Scottie were not coming too fast. Novak was in the lead and caught sight of the trail I had made in the marsh. 'Hey, we're going right,' he shouted. 'Come on, Scottie.'

He plunged past me into the marshy ground, his speed quickening, and Scottie followed a little more slowly, not having seen what all the excitement was about. He never did see, either, because I bounced the butt of the shotgun on the back of his head and he went flat on his face in the mud.

Novak heard him fall and whirled round, but I had already reversed the shotgun and held it on him. 'Drop the rifle, Novak.'

He hesitated. I patted the shotgun. 'I don't know what's in here – birdshot or buckshot – but you're going to find out the hard way if you don't drop that rifle.'

He opened his hands and the rifle fell into the mud. I stepped out of the reeds. 'Okay, come here – real slow.'

He stepped out of the mud on to dry land, his feet making sucking noises. I said, 'Where's Waystrand?'

Novak grinned. 'He's coming – he'll be along.'

'I hope so,' I said, and a puzzled look came over Novak's face. I jerked the gun, indicating the prostrate Scottie. 'Pick him up – and don't put a finger near that shotgun lying there, or I'll blow your head off.'

I stepped off the trail and watched him hoist Scottie on to his back. He was a big man, nearly as big as I am, and Scottie wasn't too much of a load. 'Okay,' I said. 'Back the way you came, Novak.'

I picked up the other shotgun and kept him going at a fast clip down the trail, harrying him unmercifully. By the time we reached the others he was very much out of breath, which was just the way I wanted him. Banks had recovered. He looked up, saw Novak and opened his mouth to yell. Then he saw me and had a shotgun pointing at him and shut his mouth with a snap. The guy with the broken leg was still unconscious.

I said, 'Dump Scottie over the edge.'

Novak turned and gave me a glare but did as I said. He wasn't too careful about it and Scottie would have a right to complain, but I supposed I'd be blamed for everything. I said, 'Now you go over – and do it real slow.'

He lowered himself over the edge and I told him to walk away and keep turned round with his back to me. It was awkward lowering myself but I managed it. Novak tried something, though; as he heard the thump of my heels he whirled round but subsided when he saw I still had him covered.

'All right,' I said. 'Now take off Scottie's belt and tie him – heels to ankles, hog fashion. But, first, take off your own belt and drop it.'

He unbuckled his belt and withdrew it from the loops of his pants and for a moment I thought he was going to throw it at me, but a steadying of the shotgun on his belly made him think otherwise. 'Now drop your pants.'

He swore violently but again did as I said. A guy with his pants around his ankles is in no shape to start a rough-house; it's a very hampering position to be in, as a lot of guys have found out when surprised with other men's wives. But I will say that Novak was a game one – he tried.

He had just finished tying Scottie when he threw himself at my legs in an attempt to bring me down. He ought to have known better because I was trying to get into position to thump him from behind. His jaw ran into the butt of the shotgun just as it was descending on him and that put him out.

I examined Scottie's bonds and, sure enough, Novak had tried to pull a fast one there, too. I made sure of him, then fastened up Novak hurriedly. There wasn't a deal of time left and the helicopter would be coming back any moment. I took a shotgun and splintered the butt against a rock and then filled my pocket with shotgun shells for the other gun. On impulse I searched Novak's pockets and found a blackjack – a small, handy, leather-bound club, lead-weighted and with a wrist loop. I smiled. If I was going to go on skull-bashing I might as well do it with the proper implement.

I put it in my pocket, confiscated a pair of binoculars Scottie carried and grabbed the shotgun. In the distance I could hear the helicopter returning, later than I thought it would.

On impulse I pulled out a scrap of paper and scribbled a message which I left in Novak's open mouth. It read: IF ANY-ONE WANTS THE SAME JUST KEEP ON FOLLOWING ME – BOYD.

Then I took off for the high ground.

No one followed me. I got a reasonably safe distance away, then lay in some bushes and watched the discovery through the glasses. It was too far to hear what was being said, but by the action I could guess at it. The helicopter landed out of sight and presently another four men came up the trail and stumbled across my little quartet. There was a great deal of arm-waving and one guy ran back to stop the helicopter taking off.

Novak was roused and sat up holding his jaw. He didn't seem to be able to speak very well. He spat out the paper in his mouth and someone picked it up and read it. He passed it round the group and I saw one man look over his shoulder nervously; they had made a count of the guns and knew I was now armed.

After a lot of jabber they made a rough stretcher and carried the guy with the broken leg back to the clearing. No one came back, and I didn't blame them. I had disposed of four men in under the half-hour and that must have been unnerving for the others; they didn't relish plunging into the forest with the chance of receiving the same treatment – or worse.

Not that I was in danger of blowing myself up like a bullfrog about what I had done. It had been a combination of skill and luck and was probably unrepeatable. I don't go for this bunk about 'His arm was strong because his cause was just.' In my experience the bad guys of this world usually have the strongest arms – look at Hitler, for instance. But Napoleon did say that the moral is to the physical as three is to one, and he was talking out of hard experience. If you can take the other guys by surprise, get them off balance and split them up, then you can get away with an awful lot.

I put away the glasses and looked at the shotgun, then broke it open to see what would have happened to Novak's belly if I'd pulled the trigger. My blood ran cold when I withdrew the cartridges – these were worse than buckshot. A heavy buckshot load in a 12-gauge carries nine pellets which don't spread too much at short range, but these cartridges held rifled slugs – one to a cartridge.

Some hunting authorities don't allow deer-hunting with rifles, especially in the States, so the arms manufacturers came up with this solution for the shotgunner. You take a slug of soft lead nearly three-quarters of an inch in diameter to fit a 12-gauge barrel and grooved to give it spin in the smooth bore. The damn' thing weighs an ounce and enough powder is packed behind it to give it a muzzle velocity of 1600 feet per second. When a thing like that hits flesh it blows a hole out the other side big enough to put both your fists into. If I had twitched the trigger down at the marsh Novak's belly would have been spattered all over the Kinoxi Valley. No wonder he had dropped his rifle.

I looked at the slug cartridge with distaste and hunted through my booty until I found some small buckshot to reload the shotgun. Fired at not too close a range that would discourage a man without killing him, which was what I wanted. No matter what the other guys did, I had no intention of looking at a noose in a rope one dark morning.

I looked out at the empty landscape, then withdrew to head up valley.

IV

For two days I dodged about the North Kinoxi Valley. Howard Matterson must have talked to his boys, putting some stuffing back into them, because they came looking for me again, but never, I noticed, in teams of less than six. I played tag with them for those two days, always edging over to the east when I could. They never caught sight of me, not even once, because while one man can move quietly, six men moving in a bunch make more than six times the racket. And they took care to move in a bunch. Novak must have told them exactly what happened and they were warned about splitting up.

I made half a dozen deadfalls during those two days but only one was sprung. Still, that resulted in a broken arm for someone, who was taken out by helicopter. Once I heard a barrage of shots from a little ravine I had just left and wondered what was happening. If you get a lot of men wandering about the woods armed with guns some fool is going to pull the trigger at the wrong time, but that's no excuse for the rest of them loosing off. I discovered afterwards that someone had to be taken out with a gunshot wound – someone had shot at him in error, he had shot back and the rest of the boys had let fly. Too bad for him.

The looted food supply was running out and I had to replenish. It was dangerous to go back to the logging camp – Matterson would have it sealed off tight – so I was heading east to Clare's cabin. I knew I could stock up there and I hoped to find Clare. I had to get news to Gibbons about what Howard was doing; he wouldn't look kindly on a manhunt in his territory and he'd move in fast. In any case, I wanted to find out what had happened to Clare.

Twice I made a break to the east, only to find a gang of Matterson's loggers in the way so that I had to fade back and try to circle them. The third time I was lucky and when I got to the cabin I was very tired but not too tired to approach with extreme caution. I had not had much sleep in the last forty-eight hours, mostly restricting myself to catnapping an hour at a time. That's when the loner comes off worst: he's always under pressure while the other guys can take it easy.

It was dusk when I came to the cabin and I lay on the hillside looking down at it for some time. Everything seemed to be quiet and I noted with disappointment that there were no lights in the big cabin, so evidently Clare was absent. Still, it seemed old Waystrand was around because a bright and welcome gleam shone from his place.

I came in to the cabin on a spiral, checking carefully, and was not too stupid to look through the window of Waystrand's cabin to make sure he was alone. He was sitting before the stove, the air about his head blue with pipe-smoke, so I went round to the door and tried to walk in. To my surprise it was locked, something very unusual.

Waystrand's voice rumbled, 'Who's that?'

'Boyd.'

I heard his footsteps on the wooden floor as he came to the door. 'Who did you say?'

'Bob Boyd. Open up, Matthew.'

The door opened a crack after bolts were drawn and a light shone on me. Then he flung the door wide open. 'Come in. Come in, quick.'

I stumbled over the threshold and he slammed the door behind me and shot the bolts. I turned to see him replace a shotgun on the rack on the wall. 'Have they been bothering you, too, Matthew?'

He swung round and I saw his face. He had a shiner – the ripest black eye I've ever seen – and his face was cut about. 'Yeah,' he said heavily. 'I've been bothered. What the hell's going on, Boyd?'

I said, 'Howard Matterson's gone wild and he's after my blood. He's got his boys worked up, too – told them I hammered the daylights out of old Bull.'

'Did you?'

I stared at him. 'What would I want to hit an old man for? Right now I want to massacre Howard, but that's different. Old Bull had a heart-attack – I saw it and McDougall saw it. So did Howard, but he's lying about it.'

Matthew nodded. 'I believe you.'

I said, 'Who gave you the shiner, Matthew?'

He looked down at the floor. 'I had a fight with my own son,' he said. His hands curled up into fists. 'He whipped me – I always thought I could handle him, but he whipped me.'

I said, 'I'll take care of Jimmy, Mr Waystrand. He's second on my list. What happened?'

'He came up here with Howard three days ago,' said Matthew. 'In that 'copter. Wanted to know if you were around. I told him I hadn't seen you, and Howard said that if I did I was to let him know. Then Howard said he wanted to search Miss Trinavant's cabin, and I said he couldn't do that. He said that maybe you were hiding out in there, so I asked him if he was calling me a liar.' Matthew shrugged.

'One thing led to another and my boy hit me – and there was a fight.'

He raised his head. 'He whipped me, Mr Boyd, but they didn't get into the cabin. I came right in here and took that shotgun and told them to get the hell off the place.'

I watched him sink dejectedly into the chair before the stove and felt very sorry for him. 'Did they go without any more trouble?'

He nodded. 'Not much trouble. I thought at one time I'd have to shoot Jimmy. I'd have pulled the trigger, too, and he knew it.' He looked up with grief in his eyes. 'He's gone real bad. I knew it was happening but I never thought the time would come when I'd be ready to shoot my own son.'

'I feel sorry about that,' I said. 'Did Howard cause any ructions?'

'No,' said Matthew with contempt. 'He just stood back and laughed like a hyena while the fight was going on – but he stopped laughing when I pointed the shotgun at his gut.'

That sounded like Howard. I took off my pack and dumped it on the floor. 'Seen anything of Cl– Miss Trinavant?'

'Not seen her for a week,' he said.

I sighed and sat down. Clare hadn't been back to her cabin since this whole thing started and I wondered where she was and what she was doing.

Matthew looked at me in concern. 'You look beat,' he said. 'I've been going on about my own troubles, but you sure got more.'

I said, 'I've been on the run for six days. These woods are crawling with guys hoping for a chance to beat my brains in. If you want to earn a thousand dollars, Matthew, all you have to do is to turn me in to Howard.'

He grunted. 'What would I do with a thousand bucks? You hungry?'

I smiled faintly. 'I couldn't eat more than three moose – my appetite's given out on me.'

'I got a stew that just needs heating up. Won't be more'n fifteen minutes. Why don't you get cleaned up.' He took some keys looped on a string from a box, and tossed them to me. 'Those will open the big cabin. Go get yourself a bath.'

I tossed the keys in my hand. 'You wouldn't let Howard have these.'

'That's different,' he said. 'He ain't a friend of Miss Trinavant.'

I had a hot bath and shaved off a week's growth of beard and then looked and felt more human. When I got back to Matthew's cabin he had a steaming plate of stew waiting for me which I got on the outside of at top speed and then asked for more. He smiled and said, 'Outdoor life agrees with you.'

'Not this kind of life,' I said. I reached over to my coat and took from a pocket one of the rifled slug cartridges which I laid on the table. 'They're loaded for bear, Matthew.'

He picked up the cartridge and, for the first and last time in my experience, he swore profusely, 'Good Christ in heaven!' he said. 'The goddam sons of bitches – I wouldn't use one of those on a deer.' He looked up. 'Old Bull must have died.'

I hadn't thought of that and felt a chill. 'I hope not,' I said sincerely. 'I've been hoping he recovers. He's the only man who can get me out of this hole. He can stand up and tell those loggers that I didn't hammer him – that he had a heart-attack. He can get Howard off my back.'

'Isn't it funny,' said Matthew in a very unfunny and sad voice, 'I've never liked Bull but he and I have a lot in common. Both our boys have gone bad.'

I said nothing to that; there wasn't much I could say. I finished eating and had some coffee and felt a lot better after this first hot meal I'd had in days. Matthew said,

'There's a bed for you all made up. You can sleep well to-night.' He stood up and took down the shotgun. 'I'll have a look around – we don't want your sleep disturbed.'

I turned in to a soft bed and was asleep almost before my head hit the pillow and I slept right through until daybreak and only woke with the sun shining into my eyes. I got up and dressed then went into the main room. There was no sign of Matthew, but there was coffee steaming on the stove and a frypan already laid out with eggs and bacon near by waiting to be fried.

I had a cup of coffee and began to fry up half a dozen eggs. I had just got them ready when I heard someone running outside. I jumped to the window, one hand grabbing the shotgun, and saw Matthew making good time towards the cabin. He crashed open the door and said breathlessly, 'A lot of guys . . . heading for here . . . not more'n ten minutes . . . behind me.'

I took my coat, put it on, and hoisted my pack which felt heavy. 'I put some grub in your pack,' said Matthew. 'Sorry it's all I could do.'

I said quickly, 'You can do something else. Get into Fort Farrell, get hold of Gibbons and tell him what's going on up here. And see if you can find out what's happened to McDougall and Clare. Will you do that?'

'I'll be on my way as soon as I can,' he said. 'But you'd better get out of here. Those boys were coming fast.'

I stepped out of the cabin and made for the trees, slanting my way up the hill to the place from which I had looked down the previous night. When I got there I unslung the glasses and looked down at the cabin.

There were at least six of them that I could see when I sorted out their comings and goings. They were walking in and out of Matthew's cabin as though they owned the place and had broken into Clare's cabin. I presumed they were searching it. I wondered how they had known I was there and concluded that they must have had a watcher staked out, and it was the lights in Clare's cabin when I had a bath that had been the tip-off.

I cursed myself for that piece of stupidity but it was too late for recriminations. When a man gets hungry and tired he begins to slip up like that, to make silly little mistakes he wouldn't make normally. It's by errors like that that a hunted man is usually nailed down, and I thought I'd better watch it in future.

I bit my lips as I focused the glasses on a man delving into the engine of Matthew's pick-up truck. He rooted around under the hood and pulled out a handful of spaghetti – most of the electrical wiring, judging by how much of it there was.

Matthew wouldn't be going to Fort Farrell – or anywhere else – for quite a while.

ELEVEN

The weather turned nasty. Clouds lowered overhead and it rained a lot, and then the clouds came right down to ground level and I walked in a mist. It was good and bad. The poor visibility meant that I couldn't be spotted as easily and the low clouds put that damned helicopter out of action. Twice it had spotted me and put the hounds on my trail, but now it was useless. On the other hand, I was wet all the time and daren't stop to light a fire and dry out. Living constantly in wet clothes, my skin started to whiten and wrinkle and it chafed where rubbed by folds of my shirt and pants. I also developed a bad cold, and a sneeze at the wrong time could be dangerous.

Howard's staffwork had improved. He had me pinned down in a very small area, not more than three square miles, and had cordoned it off tightly. Now he was tightening the noose inexorably. God knows how many men he was using, but there were too many for me to handle. Three times I tried to bust out, using the mist as cover, and three times I failed. The boys weren't afraid to use their shotguns, either, and it was only by chance that I wasn't filled full of holes on my last attempt. As it was, I had heard the whistle of buckshot around me, and one slug grazed me in the thigh. I ducked out of there fast and retreated to a hidey-hole where I slapped a Band-Aid on the wound.

The muscle in my leg was a bit stiff but it didn't slow me down much.

I was wet and cold and miserable, to say nothing of being hungry and tired, and I wondered if I'd come to the end of my tether. It wouldn't have taken much for me to have lain down and slept right on the spot and let them come and find me. But I knew what would happen if I did. I had no particular ambition to go through life crippled even if Howard let it go at that, so I dragged myself wearily to my feet and set off on the move again, prowling through the mist to find a way out of this contracting circle.

I nearly stumbled over the bear. It growled and reared up, towering a good eight feet, waving its forelegs with those cruel claws and showing its teeth. I retreated to a fair distance and considered it thoughtfully.

There's more nonsense talked about the grizzly than any other animal, barring the wolf. Grown men will look you straight in the eye and tell you of the hair-raising experiences they've had with grizzlies; how a grizzly will charge a man on sight, how they can outrun a horse, tear down a tree and create hell generally with no provocation. The truth is that a grizzly is like any other animal and has more sense than to tangle with a man without good reason. True, they're apt to be bad-tempered in the spring when they've just come out of hibernation, but a lot of people are like that when they've just got out of bed.

And they're hungry in the spring, too. The fat has gone from them and their hide hangs loose and they want to be left alone to eat in peace, just like most of us, I guess. And the females have their young in the spring and are touchy about interference, and quite justifiably so in my opinion. Most of the tall tales about grizzlies have been spun around camp fires to impress a tenderfoot or tourist and even more have been poured out of a bottle of rye whiskey.

Now it was high summer – as high as summer gets in British Columbia – and this grizzly was fat and contented. He dropped back on to four legs and continued to do what he had been doing before I interrupted him – grubbing up a juicy root. He kept a wary eye on me, though, and growled once or twice to show he wasn't too scared of me.

I stepped back behind a tree so as not to cause him too much alarm while I figured out what to do about him. I could just go away, of course, but I had a better idea than that because the thought had occurred to me that an 800-pound bear could be a powerful ally if I could recruit him. There are not many men who will face a charging grizzly.

The nearest of Matterson's men were not more than a half-mile from this spot, as I knew to my cost, and were closing in slowly. The natural tendency of the bear would be to move away as they approached. I already knew they made a lot of noise when moving and the bear would soon hear them. The only reason he hadn't heard me was that I'd developed a trick of ghosting along quietly – it's one of the things you learn in a situation like I was in; you learn it or you're dead.

What I had to do was to make the bear ignore his natural inclination. Instead of moving away, he had to move towards the oncoming men, and how in hell could I make him do that? You don't shoo away a grizzly like you do a cow, and I had to come up with an answer fast.

After a moment's thought I took some shotgun shells from my pocket and began to dissect them with my hunting knife, throwing away the slugs but keeping the powder charges. In a little while I had a heap of powder grains wrapped up in a glove to keep them dry. I bent down to dig into the carpet of pine needles with the knife; pine needles have a felting effect when they get matted and shed water like the feathers on a duck, and I didn't have to dig very far to find dry, flammable material.

All the time I kept my eye on brother bear, who was chomping contentedly on his roots while keeping an eye on me. He wasn't going to bother me if I didn't bother him – at least that was the theory I had, although I coppered my bet by choosing an easily climbable tree within sprinting distance. From one of the side pockets of the pack I extracted the folded Government geological map of the area and a notebook I kept in there. I tore up the map into small sheets and ripped pages from the book, crumpling them into spills.

I built a fire on that spot, laying down the paper spills, lacing them liberally with gunpowder and covering the lot with dry pine needles. From the fire I led a short trail of gunpowder for easy ignition, and right in the centre I embedded three shotgun shells.

After listening for a moment and hearing nothing, I circled around the bear about one-sixth of a circle, and built another fire in the same way – and yet another on the other side. He reared and growled when he saw me moving about but subsided when he saw I wasn't coming any closer. Any animal has its 'safe' distance carefully measured out and takes action only if it feels its immediate territory infringed on. The action will then depend on the animal: a deer will run for it – a grizzly will attack.

The fires laid, I waited for Matterson's boys to make the next move, and the bear would give me warning when that was coming since he was between us. I just stood cradling the shotgun in my arms and waited patiently, never taking my eyes off the grizzly.

I didn't hear a thing – but he did. He stirred and turned his head, waving it from side to side like a cobra about to strike. He made snuffling noises, sniffing the wind, and suddenly he growled softly and turned away from me, looking in the other direction. I thanked the years of experience that had taught me how to keep matches dry by filling a full matchbox with melted candle wax so that the matches were embedded in a block of paraffin wax. I ripped three matches free from the block and got them ready to strike.

The bear was backing slowly towards me and away from whatever was coming towards him. He looked back at me uneasily, feeling he was trapped, and whenever a grizzly feels like that the best place to be is somewhere else. I stooped and struck the match and dropped it on the powder trail, which fizzed and flashed into fire. Then I ran like hell to the other fire, shooting into the air as I went.

The bear had lumbered into action as I broke cover and was covering the ground fast heading straight towards me, but the bang of the shotgun gave him pause and he skidded to a halt uncertainly. From behind the bear I heard an excited shout. Someone else had also heard the shot.

The bear turned his head uncertainly and started to move again, but just then one of the shotgun shells in the first fire exploded, just as I ignited the second fire. He didn't like that at all and turned away growling all the time, as I sprinted to the third fire and dropped a match on it.

Bruin didn't know what the hell to do! There was trouble – man trouble – coming up on one side and loud unnerving noises on the other. There were a couple more shouts from the other side of the bear and that almost decided him, but just then all hell broke loose. Two more shells exploded one after the other and half a second later it sounded as though a war had broken out.

The grizzly's nerve broke and he turned and bolted in the opposite direction. I added to the fun by stinging his rump with a charge of buckshot and then began to run, following close in his rear. He charged among the trees like a demon out of hell – nearly half a ton of frightful, ravening ferocity. Actually, he was not so much frightful as frightened, but it's then that the grizzly is at his most dangerous.

I saw three men looking up the slope, aghast at what was coming down on them. I suppose to them it was all teeth and claws and twice as large as life – and another tale would be told in a bar-room if they lived to tell it. They broke and scattered, but one was a little late and the bear gave him a flick in passing. The man screamed as he was slammed into the ground but luckily for him the bear didn't stop his rush to maul him.

I went past at a dead run, my boots skidding on the slippery ground. The bear was moving much faster than I could and was out-distancing me fast. From ahead there was another shout and a couple of shots and I spun round a tree to find a guy waving a shotgun at the departing bear. He turned and saw me coming down at him fast and took a sudden snapshot at me. The hammer of his shotgun fell on an empty chamber and by then I was on to him. I took him in the chest with my shoulder and the impact knocked the feet from under him and he went sprawling, aided by a clout behind the ear I gave him as I went on my way. I had learned something from that bear.

I didn't stop running for fifteen minutes, not until I was sure no one was chasing me. I reckoned they were too busy looking after their casualty – when a bear clouts you in passing there are steel-like claws in his fist. I saw my friend bounding down the hillside and became conscious that the mist was lifting. He slowed up and slowly ambled to a stop, looking behind him. I waved and took another direction because that was one bear I wouldn't like to meet for the next couple of days.

Almost as I had stumbled on the bear I came across the man staring into the haze and wondering what all the noise was about. I had no time for evasive action so I tackled him head on, first ramming the muzzle of the gun into his belly. By the time he had recovered from that I had my hunting knife at his throat.

He eased his head back to an unnatural angle trying to get away from the sharp point and a drool of spittle ran down from one corner of his mouth. I said, 'Don't make a noise – you'll only get hurt.'

He nodded, then stopped as the knife pricked his Adam's apple. I said gently, 'Why are you hunting me?'

He gurgled, but didn't say a thing. I said again, 'Why are you hunting me? I want an answer. A truthful answer.'

It was forced out of him. 'You beat up old Bull Matterson. That was a lousy thing to do.'

'Who said I beat up the old man?'

'Howard was there – he says so. So does Jimmy Waystrand.'

'What does Waystrand know about it? He wasn't there.'

'He reckons he was and Howard doesn't say he wasn't.'

'They're both liars,' I said. 'The old man had a heart-attack. What does he say about it?'

'He don't say nothing. He's sick – real sick.' Hatred looked at me out of the man's eyes.'

'In hospital? Or at home?'

'He's at home, so I heard.' He managed a grin. 'Mister, you've got it coming to you.'

'Old Matterson had a heart-attack,' I said patiently. 'I didn't lay a finger on him. Would a little matter of a thousand dollars have anything to do with me being chased all over these woods?'

He looked at me with contempt. 'That don't matter,' he said. 'We just don't like strangers beating up old men.'

That was probably true. I doubt if these loggers would set out on a manhunt like this on a purely blood-money basis. They weren't bad guys, just fools who'd been whipped up into a frenzy by Howard's lies. The thousand dollars was merely icing on the cake. I said, 'What's your name?'

'Charlie Blunt.'

'Well, Charlie, I wish we could talk this out over a beer, but I regret it's impossible. Look, if I was such a bad guy as Howard makes out I could have knocked out your people like ducks at a shooting-gallery. People have been shooting at me but I haven't shot back. Does that make sense to you?'

A frown wrinkled his face and I could see he was thinking about it. I said, 'Take Novak and those other guys – I could have slit their throats quite easily. Come to that, there's nothing to prevent me from slitting yours right now.'

He tensed and I pricked him with the knife. 'Take it easy, Charlie; I'm not going to. I wouldn't hurt a hair of your head. Do you think that makes sense, either?'

He gulped and shook his head hurriedly. 'Well, think about it,' I said. 'Think about it and talk about it to those other guys back there. Tell them I said old Bull had a heart-attack and that Howard Matterson and Jimmy Waystrand have been feeding them a line. Talking about Jimmy, I don't think much of a guy who'd beat up his own father – do you?'

Blunt's head made a sideways movement. 'Well, he did,' I said. 'All you have to do to prove I'm telling the truth is to ask Matthew Waystrand. His place isn't too far from here – not so far that a man couldn't walk over and get at the truth for once. Talk about that to the other guys, too. Let you and them decide who's telling the truth in this neck of the woods.'

I eased up on the knife. 'I'm going to let you go, Charlie. 'I'm not even going to sap you or tie you up so you won't set the other guys on my trail again. I'm just going to let you go as you are, and if you want to raise a holler that's your privilege. But you can tell the other guys this – tell them I've had a bellyful of running and not hitting back too hard. Tell them I'm getting into a killing mood. Tell them that the next man I see on my trail is a dead man. I think you're very lucky, Charlie, that I picked you to take the message – don't you?'

He lay quiet and didn't say or do anything. I stood up and looked down at him. I said, 'The killing starts with you, Charlie, if you try anything.' I picked up the shotgun and walked away from him without glancing back. I could feel his eyes on my back and it gave me a prickly feeling, not knowing what he was doing. He could be aiming at my back with his gun right at that moment and it took all the will-power I had not to break into a run.

But I had to take a chance on the reasonableness of men some time. I had come to the conclusion that sheer raw violence wouldn't get me out of this jam – that it only produced counter-violence in its turn. I hoped I had put a maggot of doubt in one man's mind, the 'reasonable doubt' that every jury is asked to consider.

I walked on up the hill until I knew I was out of range and the tension eased suddenly. At last I turned and looked back. Way down the hill Blunt was standing, a minuscule figure looking up at me. There was no gun in his hands and he had made no move for or against me. I waved at him and, after a long pause, he waved back. I went on – up and over the hill.

II

The weather cleared up again, and I had broken out of Howard's magic circle. I had no doubt that they would come after me again. To think that a man like Blunt could have any lasting restraint was to fool myself, but at least I had a temporary respite. When, after a whole day, I saw no one and heard no one, I took a chance and killed a deer, hoping there was no one there to hear the shot.

I gralloched it and, being hungry for meat, made a small fire to cook the liver, that being the quickest to cook and most easily digested. Then I quartered the beast and roasted strips of flesh before the fire and stuffed the half-raw pieces into my pack. I didn't stay long in that place but hid the rest of the carcase and moved on, afraid of being cornered. But no one came after me.

I bedded down that night by a stream, something I had never done since this whole chase had started. It was the natural thing to do and I had not done the natural thing ever, out of fear. But I was tired of being unnatural and I didn't care a damn about what happened. I suppose the strain was telling and that I had just about given up. All I wanted was a good night's sleep and I was determined to get it, even though I might be wakened by looking into a gun barrel in the middle of the night.

I cut spruce boughs for my bed, something I hadn't done because the traces could put men on my trail, and even built a fire, not caring whether I was seen or not. I didn't go to the extreme length of stripping before I turned in, but I did spread the blankets, and as I lay there before the fire, full of meat and with the coffee-pot to hand, everything looked cheerful just as most of my camps looked cheerful in better times.

I had made camp early, being wearied to the bone of moving continually, and by dusk I was on the point of falling asleep. Through my drowsiness I heard the throb of an engine and the whir of blades cutting through the air overhead and I jerked myself into wakefulness. It was the goddam helicopter still chasing me – and they must have seen the light of the fire. That blaze would stand out like a beacon in the blackness of the woods.

I think I groaned in despair but I moved my bones stubbornly and got to my feet as the sound died away suddenly in the north. I stretched, and looked round the camp. It was a pity to leave it and go on the run again but it looked as though I had to. Then I thought again. *Why* had I to run? Why shouldn't I stop right here and fight it out?

Still, there was no reason to be taken like a sitting bird, so I figured out a rough plan. It didn't take long to find a log nearly as tall as myself to put under the blankets, and by the time I had finished it looked very like a sleeping man. To add to the illusion I rigged a line to the log so I could move it from a distance to give the appearance of a man stirring in his sleep. I found a convenient place where I could lie down behind a stump and tested it. It would have fooled me if I didn't know the trick.

If anything was to happen that night I would need plenty of light, so I built up the fire again into a good blaze – and I was almost caught by surprise. It was only by a snapping twig in the distance that I realized I had much less time than I thought. I ducked into my hiding-place and checked the shotgun, seeing that it was loaded and I had spare shells. I was quite near the fire so I rubbed some damp earth on the barrel so that it wouldn't gleam in the light and then pushed the gun forward so that it would handle more conveniently.

The suddenness of the impending attack meant one of two things. That the helicopter was scouting just ahead of a main party, or that it had dropped a single load of men – and that meant not more than four. They'd already found out what happened when they did stupid things like that and I wondered if they would try it again.

A twig cracked again in the forest much closer and I tensed, looking from side to side and trying to figure out from which side the attack would come. Just because a twig had cracked to the west didn't mean there wasn't a much smarter guy coming in from the east – or maybe the south. The hair on the nape of my neck prickled; I was to the south and maybe someone was standing right behind me ready to blow my brains out. It hadn't been too smart of me to lie flat on my belly – it's an awkward position to move from, but it was the only way I could stay close in to the camp and still not stick out like a sore thumb.

I was about to take a cautious glance behind me when I saw someone – or something – move out of the corner of my eye, and I froze rigid. The figure came into the firelight and I held my breath as I saw it was Howard Matterson. At last I had drawn the fox.

He came forward as though he were walking on eggshells and stooped over my pack. He wouldn't have any difficulty in identifying it because my name was stencilled on the back. Cautiously I gathered in the slack of my fishing-line and tugged. The log rolled over a little and Howard straightened quickly.

The next thing that happened was that he put the gun he was carrying to his shoulder and the dark night was split by the flash and roar as he put four shotgun shells into the blanket from a distance of less than eight feet as fast as he could operate the action.

I jumped and started sweating. I had all the evidence I needed that Howard wanted me out of the way in the worst way possible. He put his foot to the blanket and kicked it and stubbed his toe on the log. I yelled, 'Howard, you bastard, I've got you covered. Put down tha– '

I didn't get it all out because Howard whirled and let rip again and the blast dazzled my eyes against the darkness of the wood. Someone yelled and gurgled horribly and a body crashed down and rolled forward. I had been right about a smarter guy coming in from behind me. Jimmy Waystrand must have been standing not six feet away from me and Howard had been too goddam quick on the trigger. Young Jimmy had got a bellyful.

I jumped to my feet and took a shot at Howard, but my eyes were still dazzled by the flash of his discharge and I missed. Howard looked at me incredulously and shot blindly in my direction, but he'd forgotten that his automatic shotgun held only five shells and all there was was the dry snap of the hammer.

I must say he moved fast. With one jump he had cleared the fire, going in an unexpected direction, and I heard the splashing as he forded the stream. I took another shot at him into the darkness and must have missed again because I heard him crashing away through the undergrowth on the other side, and gradually the noises became fainter.

I knelt down next to Jimmy. He was as dead as I've seen any man – and I've seen a few. Howard's shotgun must have been loaded with those damned rifled slugs and Jimmy had caught one dead centre in the navel. It had gone clean through and blown the spine out of his back and there was a mess of guts spilled out on the ground.

I rose unsteadily to my feet, walked two paces and vomited. All the good meat I had eaten came up and spilled on the ground just like Jimmy Waystrand's guts. I shivered and shook for five minutes like a man with fever and then got myself under control. I took the shotgun and carefully reloaded with rifled slug shells because Howard deserved only the best. Then I went after him.

It was no trick to follow him. A brief on-and-off glimpse of the flashlamp showed me muddied footprints and broken grasses, but that set me thinking. He still had his gun and had presumably reloaded with another five shells. If the only way I could follow him was with a flashlamp I was about to get my head blown off. It didn't matter how much better I was in the woods on a night as dark as this. If I used a light all he had to do was to hole up, keep quiet and then let go as I conveniently illuminated his target for him. That was sure death.

I stopped short and started thinking again. I hadn't done any real thinking since Howard had pumped four shots into that log – everything had happened so fast. I cranked my brain into low gear and started it working again. There couldn't be anyone else other than Howard or I'd have been nailed back at the camp while I was puking and twitching

over the body of Jimmy Waystrand. The two must have
come from that helicopter which must be within reasonable
walking distance.

I had heard the sound of the helicopter die away to the
north quite suddenly and that must have been where it had
come to earth. There was a place not far to the north where
the soil was thin, a mere skin on the bedrock. No trees grew
there and there was ample space to land that whirlybird.
Howard had plunged away to the west and I reckoned he
wasn't much good in the woods anyway, so there was a
chance I could get to the helicopter first.

I abandoned his trail and moved fast unhampered by the
pack. I had humped that pack continuously over miles of
ground for nearly two weeks and its absence gave me an
airy sense of freedom and lightness. By leaving the pack
I was taking a chance because if I lost it I was done for – I
couldn't hope to survive in the woods without the gear I
had. But I had the reckless feeling that this was the make or
break time: I would either come out on top this night or be
defeated by Howard – and defeat meant a slug in the guts
like Jimmy Waystrand because that was the only way he
could stop me.

I moved fast and quietly, halting every now and then to
listen. I didn't hear Howard but pretty soon I heard the
swish of air driven by rotors and knew that not only was the
helicopter where I thought it was but the pilot was nervous
and ready for a quick take-off. I reckon he'd started his
engine when he heard the shots back at my camp.

Acting on sound principles, I circled round to come on
the helicopter from the opposite direction before coming
out on to the open ground, and when I did come out of
cover it was at the crouch. The noise was enough to make
my approach silent and I came up behind the pilot who
was standing and looking south, waiting for something to
happen.

Something did happen. I pushed the muzzle of the shot-gun in his ribs and he jumped a foot. 'Calm down,' I said. 'This is Boyd. You know who I am?'

'Yeah,' he said nervously.

'That's right,' I said. 'We've met before – nearly two years ago. You took me from the Kinoxi back to Fort Farrell on the last trip. Well, you're going to do it again.' I bored the gun into his ribs with a stronger pressure. 'Now, take six steps forward and don't turn round until I tell you. I think you know better than to try any tricks.'

I watched him walk away and then come to a halt. He could have easily got away from me then because he was just a darker shadow in the darkness of that moonless cloudy night, but he must have been too scared. I think my reputation had spread around. I climbed up into the passen-ger seat and then said, 'Okay, climb up here.'

He clambered up and sat in the pilot's seat rigidly. I said conversationally, 'Now, I can't fly this contraption but you can. You're going to fly it back to Fort Farrell and you're going to do it nice and easy with no tricks.' I pulled out my hunting knife and held it out so the blade glinted in the dim light of the instrument panel. 'You'll have this in your ribs all the way, so if you have any idea of crash-landing this thing just remember that you'll be just as dead as me. You can also take into account that I don't particularly care whether I live or die right now – but you might have differ-ent ideas about that. Got it?'

He nodded. 'Yeah, I've got it. I won't play tricks, Boyd.'

Maliciously I said, 'Mr Boyd to you. Now, get into the air – and make sure you head in the right direction.'

He pulled levers and flicked switches and the engine note deepened and the rotors moved faster. There was a flash from the edge of the clearing and a Perspex panel in the canopy disintegrated. I yelled, 'You'd better make it damned quick before Howard Matterson blows your head off.'

That helicopter suddenly took off like a frightened grasshopper. Howard took another shot and there was a *thunk* from somewhere back of me. The 'copter jinked around in the air and then we were away with the dark tide of firs streaming just below. I felt the pilot take a deep breath and relax in his seat. I felt a bit more relaxed myself as we gained more height and bored steadily south.

Air travel is wonderful. I had walked and run from Fort Farrell and been chased around the Kinoxi Valley for nearly two weeks, and in that wonderful machine we headed straight down the valley and were over the dam in just fifteen minutes with another forty miles – say, half an hour – to go to Fort Farrell. I felt the tension drain out of me but then deliberately tightened up again in case the frightened man next to me should get up his nerve enough to pull a fast one.

Pretty soon I saw the lights of Fort Farrell ahead. I said, 'Bull Matterson should have a landing-strip at the house – does he?'

'Yeah; just next the house.'

'You land there,' I said.

We flew over Fort Farrell and the upper-crust community of Lakeside and suddenly we were over the dark bulk of Matterson's fantastic château and coming down next to it. The helicopter settled and I said, 'Switch off.'

The silence was remarkable when the rotors flopped to a stop. I said, 'Does anyone usually come out to meet you?'

'Not at night.'

That suited me. I said, 'Now, you stay here. If you're not here when I come back then I'll be looking for you one day – and you'll know why, won't you?'

There was a tremble in the pilot's voice. 'I'll stay here, Mr Boyd.' He wasn't much of a man.

I dropped to the ground, put away the knife and hefted the shotgun, then set off towards the house which loomed against the sky. There were a few lights showing, but not many and I reckoned most of the people would be asleep. I didn't know how many servants were needed to keep the place tidy but I thought there wouldn't be many around that time of night.

I intended to go in by the front door since it was the only way I knew and was coming to it when it opened and a light spilled on to the ground in front of the house. I ducked back into what proved to be the house garage, and listened intently to what was going on.

A man said, 'Remember, he must be kept quiet.'

'Yes, doctor,' said a woman.

'If there's any change, ring me at once.' A car door slammed. 'I'll be home all night.' A car engine started and headlights switched on. The car curved round and the headlights momentarily illuminated the interior of the garage, then it was gone down the drive. The front door of the house closed quietly and all was in darkness again.

I waited awhile to let the woman get settled and used the time to explore the garage. By the look of it, in the brief glimpses of my flashlamp, the Mattersons were a ten-car family. There was Mrs Atherton's big Continental, Bull Matterson's Bentley, a couple of run-of-the-mill Pontiacs and a snazzy Aston Martin sports job. I flicked the light farther into the garage towards the back and held it on a Chevvy – it was McDougall's beat-up auto. And standing next to it was Clare's station-wagon!

I swallowed suddenly and wondered where Clare was – and old Mac.

I was wasting time here so I went out of the garage and walked boldly up to the front door and pushed it open. The big hall was dimly lit and I tiptoed up the great curving staircase on my way to the old man's study. I thought I might as well start there – it was the only room I knew in the house.

There was someone inside. The door was ajar and light flooded out into the dimly lit corridor. I peeked inside and saw Lucy Atherton pulling out drawers in Bull Matterson's desk. She tossed papers around with abandon and there was a drift of them on the floor like a bank of snow. She'd be a very suitable person to start with, so I pushed open the door and was across the room before she knew I was there.

I rounded the desk and got her from behind with her neck in the crook of my elbow, choking off her wind. 'No noise,' I said quietly, and dropped the shotgun on the soft carpet. She gurgled when she saw the keen blade of my knife before her eyes. 'Where's the old man?'

I relaxed my grip to give her air enough to speak and she whispered through a bruised throat, 'He's . . . sick.'

I brought the point of the knife closer to her right eye – not more than an inch from the eyeball. 'I won't ask you again.'

'In . . . bedroom.'

'Where's that? Never mind – show me.' I slammed the knife into its sheath and dragged her down with me into a stoop as I picked up the shotgun. I said, 'I'll kill you if you raise a noise, Lucy. I've had enough of your damn' family. Now, where's the room?'

I still kept the choke-hold on her and felt her thin body trembling against mine as I frog-marched her out of the study. Her arm waved wildly at a door, so I said, 'Okay, put your hand on the knob and open it.'

As soon as I saw her turn the knob I kicked the door open and pushed her through. She went down on her knees and sprawled on the thick carpet and I ducked in quickly and closed the door behind and lifted the shotgun in readiness for anything.

Anything proved to be a night nurse in a trim white uniform who looked up with wide eyes. I ignored her and glanced around the room; it was big and gloomy with dark drapes and there was a bed in a pool of shadow. Heaven help me, but it was a four-poster with drapes the same colour as those at the windows but drawn back.

The nurse was trembling but she was plucky. She stood up and demanded, 'Who are you?'

'Where's Bull Matterson?' I asked.

Lucy Atherton was crawling to her feet so I put my boot on her rump and pushed her down again. The nurse trembled even more. 'You can't disturb Mr Matterson; he's a very sick man.' Her voice dropped. 'He's . . . he's *dying.*'

A rasping voice from the darkened bed said, 'Who's dying? I heard that, young woman, and you're talking nonsense.'

The nurse half-turned away from me towards the bed. 'You *must* be quiet, Mr Matterson.' Her head turned and her eyes pleaded with me. *'Please go.'*

Matterson said, 'That you, Boyd?'

'I'm here.'

His voice was sardonic. 'I thought you'd be around. What kept you?' I was about to tell him when he said irritably, 'Why am I kept in darkness? Young lady, switch on a light here.'

'But, Mr Matterson, the doct– '

'Do as I say, damn it. You get me excited and you know what'll happen. Switch on a light.'

The nurse stepped to the bedside and clicked a switch. A bedside lamp lit up the shrunken figure in the big bed. Matterson said, 'Come here, Boyd.'

I hauled Lucy from the floor and pushed her forward. Matterson chuckled. 'Well, well, if it isn't Lucy. Come to see your father at last, have you? Well, what's your story, Boyd? It's a mite late for blackmail.'

I said to the nurse, 'Now, see here: you don't make a move to leave this room – and you keep dead quiet.'

'I'm not going to leave my patient,' she said stiffly.

I smiled at her. 'You'll do.'

'What's all the whispering going on?' inquired Matterson.

I stepped up to the bedside keeping tight hold of Lucy. 'Howard's going hog wild up in the Kinoxi,' I said. 'He's whipped up your loggers into a lynching-party – got them all steamed up with a story of how I beat you up. They've had me on the run for nearly two weeks. And that's not all. Howard's killed a man. He's for the eight o'clock walk.'

Matterson looked at me expressionlessly. He'd aged ten years in two weeks; his cheeks were sunken and the bones of his skull were sharply outlined by the drawn and waxy skin, his lips were bluish and the flesh round his neck had sagged. But there was still a keen intelligence in his eyes. He said tonelessly, 'Who did he kill?'

'A man called Jimmy Waystrand. He didn't intend to kill Waystrand – he thought he was shooting at me.'

'Is that the guy I saw up at the dam?'

'He's the one.' I dropped a shotgun shell on Matterson's chest. 'He was shot with one of these.'

Matterson scrabbled with a dessicated hand and I edged the shell into his fingers. He lifted it before his eyes and said softly, 'Yes, a very efficient way of killing.' The shell dropped from his fingers. 'I knew his father. Matthew's a good man – I haven't seen him in years.' He closed his eyes and I saw a tear squeeze under the eyelid and on to his cheek. 'So Howard's done it again. Aaah, I might have known it would happen.'

'*Again!*' I said urgently. 'Mr Matterson, did Howard kill John Trinavant and his family?'

He opened his eyes and looked up at me. 'Who are you, son? Are you Grant – or are you John Trinavant's boy? I must know.'

I shook my head soberly. 'I don't know, Mr Matterson. I really don't know. I lost my memory in the crash.'

He nodded weakly. 'I thought you'd got it back again.' He paused, and the breath rattled in his throat. 'They were so burned – black flesh and raw meat . . . I didn't know, God help me!' His eyes stared into the vast distances of the past at the horrors of the crash on the Edmonton road. 'I took a chance on the identification – it was for the best,' he said.

Whose best? I thought bitterly, but I let no bitterness come into my voice as I asked evenly, 'Who killed John Trinavant, Mr Matterson?'

Slowly he lifted a wasted hand and pointed a shaking finger at Lucy Atherton. 'She did – she and her hellion brother.'

TWELVE

Lucy Atherton tore her arm from my grasp and ran across the room towards the door. Old Bull, ill though he was, put all his energy into a whipcrack command. *'Lucy!'*

She stopped dead in the middle of the room. Matterson said coldly, 'What load have you got in the gun?'

I said, 'Rifled slugs.'

His voice was even colder. 'You have my permission to put one through her if she takes another step. Hear that, Lucy? I should have done it myself twelve years ago.'

I said, 'I found her in your study going through the desk. I think she was looking for your will.'

'It figures,' said the old man sardonically. 'I sired a brood of devils.' He raised his hand. 'Young woman, plug that telephone in this socket here.'

The nurse started at being addressed directly. All that had been going on was too much for her. I said, 'Do it – and do it fast.' She brought over the telephone and plugged it in by the bedside. As she passed on her way back I asked, 'Have you anything to write with?'

'A pen? Yes, I've got one.'

'You'd better take notes of what's said here. You might have to repeat it in court.'

Matterson fumbled with the telephone and gave up. He said, 'Get Gibbons at the police-station.' He gave me the number and I dialled it, then held the handset to his head. There was a pause before he said, 'Gibbons, this is Matterson . . . my health is none of your damn' concern. Now, listen: get up to my place fast . . . there's been a killing.' His head fell back on to the pillow and I replaced the handset.

I kept the shotgun centred on Lucy's middle. She was white and unnaturally calm, standing there with her arms straight down by her sides. A tic convulsed her right cheek every few seconds. Presently Matterson began to talk in a very low voice and I motioned the nurse nearer so that she could hear what he said. She had a pen and a notebook and scribbled in longhand, but Bull wasn't speaking very fast so she had time to get it all down.

'Howard was envious of Frank,' said the old man softly. 'Young Frank was a good boy and he had everything – brains, strength, popularity – everything Howard lacked. He got good grades in college while Howard ploughed his tests; he got the girls who wouldn't look at Howard, and he looked like being the guy who was going to run the business when old John and I were out of the running, while Howard knew he wouldn't get a look-in. It wasn't that John Trinavant would favour his son against Howard – it was a case of the best man getting the job. And Howard knew that if I got down to making a decision I'd choose Frank Trinavant, too.'

He sighed. 'So Howard killed Frank – and not only Frank. He killed John and his wife, too. He was only twenty-one and he was a triple killer.' He gestured vaguely. 'I don't think it was his idea, I think it was hers. Howard wouldn't have the guts to do a thing like that by himself. I reckon Lucy pushed him into it.' He turned his head and looked at her. 'Howard was a bit like me – not much, but a bit. She took after her mother.' He turned back to me. 'Did you know my wife committed suicide in a lunatic asylum?'

I shook my head, feeling very sorry for him. He was speaking of his son and daughter in the past tense as though they were already dead.

'Yes,' he said heavily. 'I think Lucy is mad – as crazy mad as her mother was towards the end. She saw that Howard had a problem and she solved it for him in her way – the mad way. Young Frank was an obstacle to Howard, so what could be simpler than to get rid of him? The fact that old John and his wife were killed was an incidental occurrence. John wasn't the target – *Frank* was!'

I felt a chill in that big, warm, centrally-heated room – the chill of horror as I looked across at Lucy Atherton who was standing with a blank look on her face as though the matter under discussion did not concern her a whit. It must have been also 'a minor happening of no great consequence' that a hitch-hiker called Grant was also in the car.

Matterson sighed. 'So Lucy talked Howard into it, and that wouldn't be too difficult, I guess. He was always weak and rotten even as a boy. They borrowed my Buick and trailed the Trinavants on the Edmonton road, and ran them off that cliff deliberately and in cold blood. I daresay they took advantage of the fact that John knew the car and knew them.'

My lips were stiff as I asked, 'Who was driving the car?'

'I don't know. Neither of them would ever say. The Buick got knocked around a bit and they couldn't hide that from me. I put two and two together and got Howard cornered and forced it out of him. He crumpled like a wet paper bag.'

He was quiet for a long time, then he said, 'What was I to do? These were my children!' In his voice was a plea for understanding. 'Can a man turn in his own children for murder? So I became their accomplice.' There was now a deep self-contempt in his voice. 'I covered up for them, God help me. I built a wall around them with my money.'

I said gently, 'Was it you who sent the money to the hospital to help Grant?'

'I was pulled two ways – torn down the middle,' he said. 'I didn't want another death on my conscience. Yes, I sent the money – it was the least I could do. And I wanted to keep track of you. I knew you'd lost your memory and I was scared to death you'd get it back. I had a private investigator checking up on you but he lost you somehow. Must have been about the time you changed your name.' His hands groped blindly on the coverlet as he looked into the black past. 'And I was scared you'd start back-tracking in an attempt to find yourself. I had to do something about that and I did what I could. I had to get rid of the name of Trinavant – it's an odd name and sticks in a man's memory. John and his family were the only Trinavants left in Canada – barring Clare – and I knew if you bumped up against that name you'd get curious, so I tried to wipe it out. What put you on to it?'

'Trinavant Park,' I said.

'Ah, yes,' he chuckled. 'I wanted to change that but I couldn't get it past that old bitch, Davenant. She's about the only person in Fort Farrell I couldn't scare hell out of. Independent income,' he explained.

'Anyway, I went on building the company. God knows what for, but it seemed pretty important at the time. I felt lost without John – he was always the brains of the outfit – but then I got hold of Donner and we got going pretty good after that.'

There was no regret for the way he had done it. He was still a tough, ruthless sonofabitch – but an honest sonofabitch by his lights, dim though they were. I heard a sound outside – the sound of a fast-driven car braking hard on the gravel. I looked at the nurse. 'Have you got all that?'

She looked up with misery in her face. 'Yes,' she said flatly. 'And I wish I hadn't.'

'So do I, child,' said Matterson. 'I should have killed the pair of them with my own hands twelve years ago.' His hand came out and plucked at my sleeve. 'You must stop Howard. I know him – he'll go on killing until he's destroyed. He loses his head easily and makes terrible mistakes. He'll kill and kill, thinking he's finding a way out and not knowing he's getting in deeper.'

I said, 'I think we can leave that to Gibbons – he's the professional.' I nodded to the nurse as a faint knocking sound echoed through the house. 'You'd better let him in. I can't leave here with her around.'

I still kept a close watch on Lucy whose face continued to twitch spasmodically. When the nurse had gone I said, 'All right, Lucy: where are they? Where are Clare Trinavant and McDougall?'

A chill had settled on me. I was afraid for them, afraid this crazy woman had killed them. Matterson said bleakly, 'Good Christ! Is there more?'

I ignored him. 'Lucy, where are they?' I could have no pity for her and had no compunction in using any method to get the information from her. I pulled out the hunting knife. 'If you don't tell me, Lucy, I'll carve you up just like I'd carve up a deer – with the difference that you'll feel every cut.'

The old man said nothing but just breathed deeper. Lucy looked at me blankly.

I said, 'All right, Lucy. You've asked for it.' I had to get this over with fast before Gibbons came up. He wouldn't stand for what I was about to do.

Lucy giggled. It was a soft imbecile giggle that shook her whole body, and developed into a maniacal cackle. 'All right,' she yelled at me. 'We put the sexy bitch in the cellar, and the old fool with her. I wanted to kill them both but Howard wouldn't let me, the damn' fool.'

Gibbons heard that. He had opened the door as she began laughing and his face was white. I felt a wave of relief sweep over me and jerked my head at Gibbons. 'The nurse say anything about this?'

'She said a little.' He shook his head. 'I can't believe it.'

'You heard what this one said, though. She's got Clare Trinavant and old McDougall locked in a dungeon of this mausoleum. You'd better put cuffs on her, but watch it – she's homicidal.'

I didn't take the shotgun off her until he had her safely handcuffed and then I tossed it to him. 'The nurse will fill you in on everything,' I said. 'I'm going to find Clare and Mac.' I paused and looked down at the old man. His eyes were closed and he was apparently sleeping peacefully. I looked at the nurse. 'Maybe you'd better tend your patient first. I wouldn't want to lose him now.'

I hurried out and down the staircase. In the hall I found a bewildered-looking man in a dressing-gown. He came over to me at a shuffle, and said in an English accent, 'What's all the fuss? Why are the police here?'

'Who are you?' I asked.

He drew himself up. 'I'm Mr Matterson's butler.'

'Okay, Jeeves; do you have any spare keys for the cellars?'

'I don't know who you are, sir, but – '

'This is police business,' I said impatiently. 'The keys?'

'I have a complete set of all the house keys in my pantry.'

'Go get them – and make it fast.'

I followed him and he took a bunch of keys from a cabinet which contained enough to outfit a locksmith's shop. Then I took him at a run down to the cellars which were of a pattern with the house – too big and mostly unused. I shouted around for a while and at last was rewarded by a faint cry. 'That's it,' I said. 'Open that door.'

He checked a number stencilled on the door and slowly selected a key from the bunch while I dithered with impatience. The door creaked open and then Clare was in my arms. When we unlatched from each other I saw she was filthily dirty, but probably not more than I was. Her face was streaked with dirt and there were runnels down her cheeks where the tears ran. 'Thank God!' I said. 'Thank God you're alive.'

She gave a little cry and turned. 'Mac's bad,' she said. 'They didn't feed us. Howard came down sometimes but we haven't seen him for five days.'

I turned to the butler who was standing with his mouth open. 'Send for a doctor and an ambulance,' I said. 'And move, damn you.'

He trotted off and I went in to see how bad Mac was. It figured, of course. Crazy Lucy wouldn't bother to feed people she already regarded as dead. Clare said, 'We've had no food or water for five days.'

'We'll fix that,' I said, and stooped down to Mac. His breathing was quick and shallow and the pulse was weak. I picked him up in my arms and he seemed to weigh no more than a baby. I carried him upstairs with Clare following and found the butler in the hall. 'A bedroom,' I said. 'And then food for six people – a big pot of coffee and a gallon of water.'

'Water, sir?'

'For Christ's sake, don't repeat what I say. Yes – water.'

We got Mac settled in bed and by that time the butler had aroused the house. I had to caution Clare not to drink water too fast nor to drink too much, and she fell on cold cuts as though she hadn't eaten for five weeks instead of five days. I reflected that I hadn't lived too badly in the Kinoxi Valley, after all.

We left Mac in the care of a doctor and went to find Gibbons who was on the telephone trying to make someone believe the incredible. 'Yes,' he was saying. 'He's loose in the Kinoxi Valley – got a shotgun with rifled slugs. Yes, I said

Howard Matterson. That's right, Bull Matterson's son. Of course I'm sure; I got it from Bull himself.' He looked up at me, then said, 'I've got a guy here who was shot at by Howard.' He sighed and then brightened as though the news had finally sunk in on the other end of the line. 'Look, I'm going up to the Kinoxi myself right now, but it's unlikely that I'll find him – he could be anywhere. I'll need a back-up force – we might have to cordon off a stretch of the woods.'

I smiled a little sadly at Clare. This was where I came in but this time I was on the other end of a manhunt – not the sharp end. Gibbons spoke a few more words into the mouthpiece, then said, 'I'll ring you just before I leave with any more dope I can get.' He put down the telephone. 'This is goddam incredible.'

'You don't have to tell me,' I said tiredly, and sat down. 'Did you really speak to Bull?'

Gibbons nodded and there was a kind of desperate awe in his face. 'He gave me specific instructions,' he said. 'I'm to shoot and kill Howard on sight just as if he were a mad dog.'

'Bull's not too far wrong,' I said. 'You've seen Lucy – she's crazy enough, isn't she?'

Gibbons shuddered slightly, then pulled himself together. 'We don't do things like that, though,' he said firmly. 'I'll bring him in alive.'

'Don't be too much the goddam hero,' I advised. 'He's got a shotgun – a five-shot automatic loaded with 12-gauge rifled slugs. He nearly cut Jimmy Waystrand in two with one shot.' I shrugged. 'But you're the professional. I suppose you know what you're doing.'

Gibbons fingered some sheets of paper. 'Is all this true? All this about them killing the Trinavants years ago?'

'It's a verbatim report of what old Matterson said. I'm witness to that.'

'All right,' he said. 'I have a map here. Show me where you last saw Howard.'

I bent over as he unfolded the map. 'Right there,' I said. 'He took two shots at the helicopter as we were taking off. If you want to get up to the Kinoxi fast that helicopter is just outside the house, and there might even be a pilot, too. If he objects to going back to the Kinoxi tell him I said he was to go.'

Gibbons looked at me closely. 'I got a pretty garbled story from that nurse. I gather you've been on the run from Howard and a bunch of loggers for three weeks.'

'An exaggeration,' I said. 'Less than two weeks.'

'Why the hell didn't you come to me?' Gibbons demanded.

It was then I started to laugh. I laughed until the tears came to my eyes and my sides ached. I laughed myself into hysteria and they had to bring a doctor to calm me down. I was still chuckling when they put me to bed and I fell asleep.

II

I woke up fifteen hours later to find Clare at the bedside. I saw her face in profile and I've never seen anything so lovely. She became aware I was awake and turned. 'Hello, Boyd,' she said.

'Hi, Trinavant.' I stretched luxuriously. 'What time is it?'

'Just past midday.' She looked at me critically. 'You could do with a clean-up. Seen yourself lately?'

I rubbed my jaw. It no longer prickled because the hair had grown too long for that. I said, 'Maybe I'll grow a beard.'

'Just you dare.' She pointed. 'There's a bathroom through there, and I got you a razor.'

'I trust I won't offend your maidenly modesty,' I said as I threw back the sheets. I swung out of bed and walked into the bathroom. The face that stared at me from the big mirror was the face of a stranger – haggard and wild-looking. 'My God!' I said. 'No wonder that pilot was wetting his pants. I bet I could stop cows giving milk.'

'It will come right with the application of soap and water,' she said.

I filled the bath and splashed happily for half an hour, then shaved and dressed. Dressed in my own clothes, too. I said, 'How did these get here?'

'I had them brought from Mac's cabin,' said Clare.

Sudden remembrance hit me. 'How is he?'

'He'll be all right,' she said. 'He's as tough as Bull. *He* seems to be bearing up under the strain, too.'

'I want to get him in court to tell that story,' I said grimly. 'After that I don't care if he drops dead on the spot.'

'Don't be too hard on him, Bob,' said Clare seriously. 'He had a hard decision to make.'

I said no more about it. 'Have you been filled in on all the details of this caper?' I asked.

'Mostly, I guess – except for what you have to tell me. But that can wait, darling. We have plenty of time.' She looked at me straightly. 'Have you decided who you are?'

I shrugged. 'Does it matter? No, Clare; I'm no nearer finding out. I've been thinking about it, though. After the Matterson family a guy like Grant, a drug-pusher, is pretty small potatoes. What's a drug-peddler compared with a couple of multiple murderers? Maybe Grant wasn't such a bad guy, after all. Anyway – as I said – does it matter? As far as I'm concerned I'm just Bob Boyd.'

'Oh, darling, I told you that,' she said. We had a pretty passionate few minutes then, and after coming out of the clinch and wiping off the lipstick, I said, 'I've just thought of a funny thing. I used to have bad dreams – real shockers they were – and I'd wake up sweating and screaming. But you know what? When I was under *real* pressure in the Kinoxi with all those guys after my blood and Howard coming after me with his shotgun I didn't get too much sleep. But when I did sleep I didn't dream at all. I think that's strange.'

She said, 'Perhaps the fact you were in real danger destroyed the imaginary danger of the dream. What's past is past, Bob; a dream can't really hurt you. Let's hope they don't come back.'

I grinned. 'Any nightmares I have from now on are likely to be concerned with that automatic shotgun of Howard's. That really gave me the screaming meemies.'

We went in to see McDougall. He was still under sedation but the doctor said he was going to be all right, and he had a pretty nurse to look after him. He was conscious enough to wink at me, though, and he said drowsily, 'For a minute there, down in that cellar, I thought you were going to let me down, son.'

I didn't see Bull Matterson because his doctor was with him, but I saw the night nurse. I said, 'I'm sorry I busted in on you like that, Miss . . . er . . .'

'Smithson,' she supplied. She smiled. 'That's all right, Mr Boyd.'

'And I'm glad you turned out to be level-headed,' I said. 'A squawking woman rousing the house right then could have queered my pitch.'

'Oh, I wouldn't have made a noise under any circumstances,' said Miss Smithson primly. 'It would have adversely affected Mr Matterson's health.'

I looked straight-facedly at Clare who was disposed to burst into a fit of the giggles and we took our departure of the Matterson residence. As we drove away in Clare's station-wagon I looked into the driving mirror at the over-bloated splendour of that fake castle and heartily wished I'd never see it again.

Clare said pensively, 'Do you know how old Lucy was when she and Howard killed Uncle John, Aunt Anne and Frank?'

'No.'

'She was eighteen years old – just eighteen. How could anybody do anything like that at eighteen?'

I didn't know, so I said nothing and we drove in silence through Fort Farrell and on to the road which led to Mac's cabin. It was only just before the turn-off that I smote the driving wheel, and said, 'My God, I must be nuts! I haven't told anyone about the quick clay. I clean forgot.'

I suppose it wasn't surprising that I had forgotten. I'd had other things on my mind – such as preventing myself getting killed – and Bull Matterson's revelations had also helped to drive it out of my head. I braked to a quick stand-still and prepared to do a U-turn, then had second thoughts. 'I'd better go on up to the dam. The police should have a check-point there to prevent anyone going up into the Kinoxi.'

'Do you think they'll have caught Howard yet?'

'Not a chance,' I said. 'He'll be able to run rings round them. For a while, at least.' I put the car into gear. 'I'll drop you at the cabin.'

'No you won't,' said Clare. 'I'm coming up to the dam.'

I took one look at her and sighed. She had her stubborn expression all set for instant use and I had no time to argue. 'All right,' I said. 'But stay out of trouble.'

We made good time on the Kinoxi road – there were no trucks to hinder progress – but we were stopped by a patrol-man half a mile short of the powerhouse. He flagged us down and walked over to the car. 'This is as far as you go,' he said. 'No one goes beyond this point. We don't want any sightseers.'

'What's happening up there?'

'Nothing that would interest you,' he said patiently. 'Just turn your car round and get going.'

I said, 'My name's Boyd – this is Miss Trinavant. I want to see your boss.'

He stared at me curiously. 'You the Boyd that started all this ruckus?'

'Me!' I said indignantly. 'What about Howard Matterson?'

'I guess it's all right,' he said thoughtfully. 'You'll want to see Captain Crupper – he's up at the dam. If he's not there you wait for him; we don't want anything going wrong in the Kinoxi.'

'Then you haven't caught him yet,' said Clare.

'Not that I know of,' said the patrolman. He stood back and waved us on.

Work was still going on at the powerhouse and I could see a few minuscule figures on top of the sheer concrete wall of the dam. There was still the sea of mud at the bottom of the escarpment, a slick, slimy mess churned up by the wheels of trucks. It had been too much for a couple of trucks which were bogged down to their axles. A team of sweating men had anchored a power-winch on firm ground and was hauling one of them out bodily.

I pulled up next to a big car and found myself looking at Donner, who looked back at me expressionlessly, then got out of the car. I went to meet him with Clare close behind. 'Donner, you're in trouble.' I waved at the powerhouse and up at the dam.

'Trouble!' he said bitterly. 'You think *this* is trouble?' For a reputedly bloodless and nerveless man he was showing a hell of a lot of emotion. 'Those goddam crazy Mattersons,' he burst out. 'They've put me in one hell of a spot.'

I knew what was wrong with him. He was one of those people who make bullets for others to shoot, but he'd never

take responsibility for pulling the trigger himself; a perfect
second-in-command for Bull Matterson but without Bull's
guts. Now he found himself in charge of the Matterson
Empire, if only temporarily, and the strain was telling.
Particularly as the whole thing was about to fall apart.
Nothing could now prevent the whole story coming into the
open, especially the double-dealing with the Trinavant
Trust, and it was easy to see that Donner would be hunting
around for ways to unload the blame on to someone else.

It wouldn't be too hard – Bull Matterson was too sick to
fight back and Howard, the murderer, was a perfect scapegoat.
But it was a trying time for Donner. However, I wasn't interested in his troubles because a bigger danger was impending.

I said, 'This is more trouble than you think. Did you read
my report on the geology of the Kinoxi Valley?'

'That was Howard's baby,' said Donner. 'I'm just the
accountant. I didn't see the report and I wouldn't have
understood it if I had.'

He was already weaselling out from under the chopper;
he could see trouble coming and was disclaiming responsibility. Probably, on the balance of things, he really hadn't
seen the report. Anyway, that didn't matter – what mattered was getting every construction man off the site as
soon as possible.

I pointed up at the escarpment. 'That hillside is in danger
of caving in, Donner. It can go any time. You've got to get
your men out of here.'

He looked at me incredulously. 'Are you crazy? We've
lost enough time already because that dumb bastard
Howard pulled men away to look for you. Every day's delay
is costing us thousands of dollars. We've lost enough time
because of this mud, anyway.'

'Donner, get it through your skull that you're in trouble.
I really mean what I say. That bloody hillside is going to
come down on you.'

He swung his head and stared across at the solid slope of the escarpment, then gave me an odd look. 'What the hell are you talking about? How can a hill cave in?'

'You should have read that report,' I said. 'I found quick clay deposits in the valley. For God's sake, didn't you do a geological survey of the foundations of the dam?'

'That was Howard's business – he looked after the technical side. What's this quick clay?'

'An apparently solid substance that turns liquid if given a sudden shock – and it doesn't need much of a shock. As near as I can check there's a bed of it running right under that dam.' I grinned at him humourlessly. 'Let's look on the bright side. If it goes, then a couple of million tons of topsoil is going to cover your powerhouse – the clay will liquefy and carry the topsoil with it. That's the best that can happen.'

Clare touched my elbow. 'And the worst?'

I nodded towards the dam. 'It might jerk the foundations from under that hunk of concrete. If that happens, then all the water behind the dam will flow right over where we're standing now. How much water is backed up behind there, Donner?'

He didn't answer my question. Instead, he smiled thinly. 'You tell a good story, Boyd. I like it very much, but I don't go for it. You have a good imagination – an earthquake laid on to order shows real creative thought.' He scratched his chin. 'The only thing I can't figure is what you reckon to gain by stopping construction now. I just can't figure your angle.'

I gaped at him. McDougall had been right – this man figured every motive in dollars and cents. I drew a deep breath, and said, 'You stupid, ignorant oaf!' I turned from him in disgust. 'Where's the police captain who's supposed to be here?'

'Here he comes now,' said Donner. 'Coming out of the valley.'

I looked up to the road that clung to the hillside above the dam. A car was coming down, trailing a dust plume behind it. 'Captain Crupper hasn't the power to close down operations,' said Donner. 'I wish I knew what you were figuring, Boyd. Why don't you tell me what you're getting at?'

Clare said hotly, 'Something you wouldn't understand, Donner. He just wants to save your life, although I'm damned if I know why. He also wants to save the lives of all those men, even though they were after his blood not long ago.'

Donner smiled and shrugged. 'Save those speeches for suckers, Miss Trinavant.'

I said, 'Donner, you're in trouble already – but not in real bad trouble because the worst that can happen to you is jail. But I'll tell you something: if anyone gets killed here because you've ignored a warning you'll have a lynch-mob after you and you'll be damned lucky not to be strung up to the nearest tree.'

The police car rolled to a stop quite close and Captain Crupper got out and came over. 'Mr Donner, I asked you to meet me here, but apparently it is now unnecessary.'

Donner said, 'Captain Crupper, this is Mr Boyd and Miss Trinavant.'

Crupper switched hard eyes to me. 'Hm – you stirred up something here, Boyd. I'm sorry it had to happen to you – and to you, Miss Trinavant.' He looked at Donner. 'It appears an investigation of the Matterson Corporation would be in order; running a private manhunt doesn't come under normal business procedures.'

'That was Howard Matterson's affair,' said Donner hastily. 'I knew nothing about it.'

'You won't have to worry about him any more,' said Crupper curtly. 'We've got him.'

'You got on to him fast,' I said. 'I'd have guessed it would take longer.'

With grim humour Crupper said, 'He's not as good in the woods as you, apparently.' His lips tightened. 'It cost us a good man.'

'I'm sorry to hear that.'

He slapped his gloves against his thigh. 'Gibbons was shot in the knee. His leg was amputated this morning.'

So Gibbons had to go and do the heroic bit after all. I said, 'I warned him not to monkey around with Howard. Bull Matterson warned him, too.'

'I know,' said Crupper tiredly. 'But we always try the pacific way first. We can't shoot on sight just on someone's say-so. There are laws in this country, Boyd.'

I hadn't noticed the law around the Kinoxi Valley during the last couple of weeks, but I said nothing about that. 'There's going to be a lot more good men lost if this idiot Donner doesn't pull them off this site.'

Crupper reacted fast. He jerked his head round to look at the powerhouse, then speared me with a cold glance. 'What do you mean by that?'

Donner said silkily, 'Mr Boyd has laid on an instant earthquake. He's been trying to make me believe that hillside is going to collapse.'

'I'm a geologist,' I said deliberately. 'Tell me, Captain: what is the road like up in the Kinoxi? Wet or dry?'

He looked at me as though I had gone mad. 'Pretty dry.'

'I know,' I said. 'You were kicking up quite a cloud of dust coming down the hill. Now tell me, Captain: where the hell do you think all this mud is coming from?' I pointed to the greasy waste around the powerhouse.

Crupper stared at the mud, then looked at me thoughtfully. 'All right. You tell me.'

So I went into it again and finally said, 'Clare, tell the Captain of the demonstration I showed you with the quick clay cores. Don't embroider it – just tell it straight.'

She hesitated. 'Well, Bob had some samples of earth – he'd taken them from up here before Howard ran him off. He took a piece and showed how it could bear a big weight. Then he took another piece and stirred it in a jug. It turned to thin mud. That's about all.'

'Sounds like a conjuring trick,' said the Captain. He sighed. 'Now I have a thing like this dumped on me. Mr Donner, what about pulling your men off pending an expert investigation of the site?'

'Now look here, Crupper,' Donner expostulated. 'We've had enough delay. I'm not going to waste thousands of dollars just on Boyd's word. He's been trying to stop this project all along and I'm not going to let him get away with any more.'

Crupper was troubled. 'There doesn't seem to be anything I can do, Mr Boyd. If I stop work on the dam and nothing is wrong my neck will be on the block.'

'You're damn' right,' said Donner viciously.

Crupper looked at him with dislike. 'However,' he said firmly, 'if I thought it in the public interest I'd stop construction right here and now.'

I said, 'You don't have to take my word for it. Ring the geology faculty at any university. Try to get hold of a soil mechanics specialist if you can, but any competent geologist will be able to confirm it.'

Crupper said with decision, 'Where's your telephone, Mr Donner?'

'Now, wait a minute,' cried Donner. 'You're not going to grind this man's axe for him, are you, Crupper?'

Clare said suddenly, 'Do you know why Bull Matterson had a heart-attack, Donner?'

He shrugged. 'It was something about Boyd being Frank Trinavant. Now, there's a cock-and-bull story!'

'But what if it's true?' she said softly. 'It will mean that Bob Boyd will be bossing the Matterson Corporation in the future. He'll be *your* boss, Donner! I'd think about that if I were you.'

Donner gave her a startled glance, then looked at me. I grinned at Clare and said, 'Check!' She was pulling a bluff but it was good enough to manipulate Donner, so I followed up quickly. 'Do you pull the men off the site or not?'

Donner was bewildered; things were happening too fast for him. 'No!' he said. 'This is impossible. Things don't happen like this.' He was a man who lived too far from nature, manipulating his money counters in drilled formations, unconscious of living in an artificial environment. He could not conceive of a situation he could not control.

Crupper said harshly, 'Put up or shut up. Where's your site boss?'

'Over in the powerhouse,' said Dormer listlessly.

'Let's get over there.' Crupper moved off through the mud.

I said to Clare, 'Take the car and get out of here.'

'I'll go when you go,' she said firmly, and followed me to the powerhouse. There wasn't much I could do about that, short of spanking her, so I let it go. As we went along I sampled the mud, rubbing it between forefinger and thumb. It still had that slick, soapy feeling – the feeling of disaster.

I caught up with Crupper. 'You'd better plan for the worst, Captain. Let's assume the dam goes and the lake busts through here. The flood should follow the course of the Kinoxi River pretty roughly. That area should be evacuated.'

'Thank God this is an underpopulated country,' he said. 'There are only two families likely to be in trouble.' He snapped his fingers. 'And there's a new logging camp just been set up. Where's that goddam telephone?'

Donner came back just as Crupper finished his telephone conversation. Behind him was a big hulk of a man whom I had last seen closely when crashing a gun butt into his jaw.

It was Novak.

He stiffened when he saw me and his hands curled into fists. He shouldered Donner aside and strode over and instinctively I got ready for him, hoping that Crupper could break up the fight quickly. Without taking my eyes off him, I said to Clare, 'Get away from me – fast.'

Novak stood before me with an unsmiling face. 'Boyd, you bastard,' he whispered. His arm came up slowly and I was astonished to see, not a fist but an open hand extended in friendship. 'Sorry about last week,' he said. 'But Howard Matterson had us all steamed up.'

As I took his hand he grinned and rubbed his face. 'You damn' near busted my jaw, you know.'

'I did it without animosity,' I said. 'No hard feelings?'

'No hard feelings.' He laughed. 'But I'd like to take a friendly poke at you some time just to see if I could have licked you.'

'All right,' said Crupper testily, 'This isn't old home week.' He looked at Donner. 'Do you tell him – or must I?'

Donner sagged and looked suddenly much smaller than he really was. He hesitated and said in a low voice, 'Withdraw the men from the site.'

Novak looked at him blankly. 'Huh?'

'You heard him,' said Crupper abruptly. 'Pull out your men.'

'Yeah, I heard him,' said Novak. 'But what the hell?' He tapped Donner on the chest. 'You've been pushing to get this job finished; now you want us to stop. Is that right?'

'That's right,' said Donner sourly.

'Okay!' Novak shrugged. 'Just as long as I get it straight. I don't want any comeback.'

I said, 'Wait a minute; let's do this right. Come with me, Novak.' We went outside and I looked up at the dam. 'How many men have you got here?'

'About sixty.'

'Where are they?'

Novak waved his hand. 'About half are down here at the powerhouse; there are a few up at the dam and maybe a dozen scattered around I don't know where. This is a big site to keep track of everybody. What the hell's going on, anyway?'

I pointed up the escarpment to the dam. 'You see that slope? I don't want anyone walking on it. So those guys up at the dam will have to take to the high ground on either side. See Captain Crupper about getting the boys away from the powerhouse. But remember – no one walks on that slope.'

'I guess you know what you're doing,' he said. 'As long as Donner goes along with it, it's okay by me. Getting the guys off the dam will be easy – we have a phone line up to there.'

'Another thing – have someone open the sluices up there before leaving.' That was merely a gesture – it would take a long time for the new Lake Matterson to empty but whether the slope collapsed or not it would have to be done eventually and the job might as well be started as soon as possible.

Novak went back into the powerhouse but I waited a while – maybe ten minutes – then I saw the small figures of men moving off the dam and away from the danger zone. Satisfied, I went inside to find Crupper organizing the evacuation of the powerhouse. 'Just walk out of here and find high ground,' he was saying. 'Keep off the Fort Farrell road and away from the river – keep off the valley bottom altogether.'

Someone shouted, 'If you're expecting the dam to bust you're crazy.'

'I know it's a good dam,' said Crupper. 'But something's come up and we're just taking precautions. Move, you guys, it's no skin off your nose because you're still on full pay.' He grinned sardonically at Donner, then turned to me. 'That means us, too – everyone gets out of here.'

I was feeling easier. 'Sure. Come on, Clare. This time you are leaving, and so am I.'

Donner said in a high voice, 'So everyone leaves – then what?'

'Then I have a closer look at the situation. I know the dangers and I'll walk on that slope as though on eggs.'

'But what can you *do* about it?'

'It can be stabilized,' I said. 'Others will know more about that than I do. But in my opinion the only way will be to drain the lake and cap the clay outcrop. We can only hope the thing doesn't slip before then.'

Novak said in sudden comprehension, *'Quick clay?'*

'That's right. What do you know about it?'

'I've been a construction man all my life,' he said, 'I'm not all that stupid.'

Someone yelled across the room, 'Novak, we can't find Skinner and Burke.'

'What were they doing?'

'Taking out stumps below the dam.'

Novak bellowed, 'Johnson; where the hell's Johnson?' A burly man detached himself from the crowd and came across. 'Did you send Skinner and Burke to dig stumps below the dam?'

Johnson said, 'That's right. Aren't they around here?'

'Just how were they taking out those stumps?' asked Novak.

'They'd got most of 'em out,' said Johnson. 'But there were three real back-breakers. Skinner has a blasting ticket so I gave him some gelignite.'

Novak went very still and looked at me. 'Christ!' I said. 'They must be stopped.' I could visualize the effect of that sharp jolt on the house-of-cards structure that was quick clay. There would be a sudden collapse, locally at first, but spreading in a chain reaction right across the hillside, just like one domino knocks down the next and the next and so on to the end of the line. Firm clay would be instantaneously transformed into liquid mud and the whole hillside would collapse.

I swung round. 'Clare, get the hell out of here.' She saw the expression on my face and turned away immediately. 'Crupper, get everyone out fast.'

Novak plunged past me, heading for the door. 'I know where they are.' I followed him and we stood staring up at the dam while the powerhouse erupted like an ants' nest stirred with a stick. There was no movement on the escarpment – no movement at all. Just a confusion of shadows as the low sun struck on rocks and trees.

Novak said hoarsely, 'I think they'll be up there – on the right, just under the dam.'

'Come on,' I said, and began to run. It was a long way to the dam and it was uphill and we were pounding up that damned escarpment. I grabbed Novak's arm. 'Take it easy – we might start a slide ourselves.' If the shear strength had fallen according to my estimates it wouldn't take much disturbance to initiate the chain reaction. The shear strength was probably under five hundred pounds a square foot by now – less than the pressure exerted by Novak's boot hitting the ground at a dead run.

We moved gently and as fast as we could up the escarpment and it took us nearly fifteen minutes to do that quartermile. Novak lifted his voice in a shout. 'Skinner! Burke!' The echoes rebounded from the sheer concrete face of the dam which loomed over us.

Someone quite close said, 'Yeah, what do you want?'

I turned. A man was squatting with his back to a boulder and looking up at us curiously. 'Burke!' said Novak explosively. 'Where's Skinner?'

Burke waved. 'Over behind those rocks.'

'What's he doing?'

'We're getting ready to blow that stump – that one, there.'

It was a big stump, the remnant of a tall tree, and I could see the thin detonating wire leading away from it. 'There's going to be no blasting,' said Novak and walked quickly over to the stump.

'Hey!' said Burke in alarm. 'Keep away from there. It's going to blow any second.'

It was one of the bravest things I have seen. Novak calmly leaned over the stump and jerked the wire away, bringing the electrical detonator with it. He tossed it to the ground casually and walked back. 'I said there'll be no blasting,' he said. 'Now, get the hell out of here, Burke.' He pointed up to the road that clung to the hillside above the dam. 'Go that way – not down to the powerhouse.'

Burke shrugged. 'Okay, you're the boss.' He turned and walked off, then paused. 'If you want the blasting stopped you'll have to hurry. Skinner's blowing three stumps all at once. That was only one of them.'

'My God!' I said, and both Novak and I turned towards the jumble of rocks where Skinner was. But it was too late. There was a sharp popping sound in the distance, not very loud, and a nearer *crack* as the detonator Novak had pulled out exploded harmlessly. Two plumes of dust and smoke shot into the air about fifty yards away and hung for a moment before being dissipated by the breeze.

I held my breath and then slowly released it in a sigh. Novak grinned. 'Looks like we got away with it that time,' he said. He put his hand to his forehead then looked at the dampness on his fingers. 'Sure makes a man sweat.'

'We'd better get Skinner off here,' I said. As I said it I heard a faint faraway sound like distant thunder – something more felt inside the head than heard with the ears – and there was an almost imperceptible quiver beneath my feet.

Novak stopped in mid-stride. 'What's that?' He looked about him doubtfully.

The sound – if it was a sound – came again and the quiver of the earth was stronger. 'Look!' I said, and pointed to a tall, spindly tree. The top was shivering like a grass stalk in a strong wind, and as we watched, the whole tree leaned sideways and fell to the earth. 'The slide,' I yelled. 'It's started.'

A figure came into sight across the hillside. 'Skinner!' shouted Novak. 'Get the hell out of there!'

The ground thrummed under my boots and the landscape seemed to change before my eyes. It wasn't anything one could pin down, there was no sudden alteration – just a brief, flickering change. Skinner came running across but he had not come half the distance when the change became catastrophic.

He disappeared. Where he had been was a jumble of moving boulders tossed like corks in a stream as the whole hillside *flowed.* The entire landscape seemed to slip sideways smoothly and there was a deafening noise, the like of which I had never heard before. It was like thunder, it was like the sound of a jet bomber from very close quarters, it was like the drum-roll of tympani in an orchestra magnified a thousand times – and yet it was like none of these. And underneath the clamour was another sound, a glutinous, sucking noise as you might make when pulling a boot out of mud – but this was a giant's boot.

Novak and I stood rooted for a moment helplessly looking at the place where Skinner had vanished. But it was no longer correct to call it a place because a *place* by its nature is a definite locality, a fixed point. Nothing was fixed on this escarpment and the 'place' where Skinner had been ground between the boulders was already a hundred yards downhill and moving away rapidly.

I don't suppose we stood there for more than two or three seconds, although it seemed an eternity. I dragged

myself out of this shocked trance and shouted above the
racket, 'Run for it, Novak. It's spreading this way.'

We turned and plunged across the hillside, heading for
the road which represented safety and life. But the chain
reaction under our feet, flashing through the unstable clay
thirty feet underground, moved faster than we did, and the
seemingly solid ground rocked and slid under us, dipping
and moving like an ocean.

We ran through a scattering of saplings which bent and
swayed in all directions and one fell immediately in front of
us, its roots tearing free from the moving ground. I vaulted
it and ran on but was momentarily held by a half yell, half
grunt from behind. I turned and saw Novak sprawled on the
ground, held down by the branch of another toppled tree.

When I bent to examine him he seemed dazed and only
half-conscious and I struggled violently to release him.
Luckily it was only a sapling but it took all my strength to
shift it. The continuous movement of the ground made me
feel queasy and all the strength seemed to be leeched from
my muscles. It was very hard to think consecutively, too,
because of the tremendous noise – it was like being inside a
monstrous drum beaten on by a giant.

But I got him free and only just in time. A big glacial
boulder moved past, tossing like a cork on a stream, right
over the place where he had been pinned. His eyes were
open but glazed and he had a witless look about him. I
slapped his face hard and a glimmer of intelligence came
back. 'Run,' I shouted. 'Run, goddam you!'

So we ran again, with Novak leaning heavily on my arm,
and I tried to steer a straight course to safety, something
which was damn' near impossible because this was like
crossing a swiftly flowing river and we were being swept
downstream. In front of us a fountain of muddy water suddenly jetted fifteen feet into the air and soaked us. I knew
what that was – the water was being squeezed out of the

quick clay, millions of gallons of it. Already the ground beneath my feet was slippery with mud and we slithered and slid about helplessly as this handicap was added to the violent movements of the earth itself.

But we made it. As we came nearer the edge of the slide the movement became less and I finally let Novak slip to solid ground and sobbed for breath. Not very far away Burke was lying prone, his hands scrabbling into the soil as though to clutch the whole planet to himself. He was screaming at the top of his voice.

From the time the first tree went down to the time I dropped Novak in safety couldn't have been more than one minute – one long minute in which we had run a whole fifty yards. That was no record-breaking time but I don't think a champion sprinter could have bettered it.

I wanted to help Novak and Burke but something, call it professional interest, held my attention on this great catastrophe. The whole of the land was moving downhill at an ever-increasing speed. The front of the slide was just short of the powerhouse and whole trees were being tossed into the air like spillikins and boulders ground and clashed together with a noise like thunder. The front of the flow hit the powerhouse and the walls caved in, and the whole building seemed to fold and disappear under a river of moving earth.

The topsoil flowed away to the south and I thought it was never going to stop. Water, squeezed from the clay, spurted in fountains everywhere, and through the soles of my boots I could feel the vibrations of millions of tons of earth on the move.

But finally it did stop and everything lay quiet except for the occasional rumble here and there as strains were eased and pressures equalized. Not more than two minutes had elapsed since the blasting of the stumps and the slide was fully two thousand feet long and extended five hundred feet from hillside to hillside. Ponds of muddy water lay everywhere. The clay had given up all its water in that awful cataclysm and there would be little danger of a further slide.

I looked down to where the powerhouse had been and saw just a waste of torn earth. The slide had erased the powerhouse and had gone on to cut the Fort Farrell road. The little group of cars that had been parked on the road had vanished, and from the tip of the slide gushed a torrent of muddy water already carving a bed in the soft earth as it rushed to join the Kinoxi River. There was no other movement at all down there and I was painfully aware that Clare might be dead.

Novak got to his feet groggily and jerked his head quickly as though to shake his brains back into position. When he spoke he shouted, 'How the hell . . .?' He looked at me in astonishment and began again more quietly. 'How the hell did we get out of there?' He waved his hand at the slide.

'Sheer luck and strong legs,' I replied.

Burke was still clutching the ground and his screams had not diminished. Novak swung round. 'For God's sake, shut up!' he yelled. 'You've survived.' But Burke took no notice.

A car door slammed on the road above and I looked up to see a policeman staring at the scene as though he couldn't believe his eyes. 'What happened?' he called.

'We used a mite too much gelignite,' shouted Novak sardonically. He walked over to Burke, bent down and clouted him on the side of the head. Burke's screams suddenly stopped but he continued to sob raspingly.

The policeman scrambled down to us. 'Where did you come from?' I asked.

'From up the Kinoxi Valley,' he said. 'I'm taking a prisoner into Fort Farrell.' He clicked his tongue as he gazed down at the blocked road. 'Looks as though I'll have to find another way round.'

'Is that Howard Matterson you have up there?' When he nodded I said, 'Keep tight hold of that bastard. But you'd better go on down there – you might find Captain Crupper, if he's still alive.' I saw another policeman on the road. 'How many are there in your car?'

'Four of us, plus Matterson.'

'You'll be needed in rescue work,' I said. 'You'd better get moving.'

He looked to where Novak was cradling Burke in his arms. 'Will you be all right here?'

I was tempted to go with him to the bottom, but Burke was in no condition to move and Novak couldn't carry him unaided. 'We'll be all right,' I said.

He turned to climb up to the road and at that moment there was a great groan as of intense pain. At first I thought it was Burke but when the sound came again it was much louder and boomed right down the valley.

The dam was groaning under the pressure of water behind it and I knew what that meant. 'Jesus!' I said.

Novak picked up Burke bodily and began to stumble up the hill. The policeman was climbing as if the devil was at his heels, and I ran across to help Novak. 'Don't be a damn' fool,' he panted. 'You can't help.'

It was true; two men couldn't lug Burke up that slope any faster than one, but I hung around Novak in case he slipped. More noises were coming from the great concrete wall of the dam, strange creakings and sudden explosions. I looked over my shoulder and saw something incredible – water under pressure fountaining from *underneath* the dam. It jetted a hundred feet high and spray blew in my face.

'It's going,' I yelled, and looped my arm around a tree, grabbing Novak's leather belt with the other hand.

There was a loud crash and a fissure appeared, zig-zagging down the concrete face from top to bottom. The quick clay had slipped from underneath the dam and the waters of Lake Matterson were blowing the foundations out, leaving nothing to bear the enormous weight.

Another crack appeared on the face of the dam and then the water pressure from behind became too much and the whole massive structure was pushed aside impatiently by a solid wall of water. A great chunk of reinforced concrete was thrown out from the dam; it weighed every ounce of five hundred tons, but it was thrown into the air and toppled in twisting flight until it crashed into the sea of mud below. In the next second it was overwhelmed and covered by the rush of lake water.

And so were we.

We just hadn't been able to go that extra few feet up the hill and the flood swirled in its first crest just above us. I had the sense to see what was coming and to fill my lungs with air before the water hit us so I didn't think I'd drown, but I thought I'd be torn in two as the fast water hit Novak and swung him off his feet.

With one hand grasping his belt I was holding the weight of two big men and I thought my arm would be sprung from its socket. The muscles in the other arm cracked as I desperately hung on to the tree and my lungs were bursting when I finally managed to gulp air.

That first great crest could not last long but while it did it filled the valley from side to side and was a hundred feet deep in that first great lunge to the south. But it dropped rapidly and I was thankful to find the strain taken from me as a policeman grabbed Novak.

He shook his head and gasped. 'I couldn't help it,' he cried desolately. 'I couldn't hold him.'

Burke was gone!

There was a new, although impermanent, river below us which had calmed down to a steady and remorseless multi-million-gallon flow that would ebb, hour by hour, until there would be no more Matterson Lake – just the little stream called the Kinoxi River that had flowed from this valley for the last fifteen thousand years. But it was still a raging torrent, three hundred feet wide and fifty feet deep, when I staggered up and planted my boots firmly on that wonderful solid road.

I leaned on the side of the police car and shuddered violently and then became aware that someone was watching me. In the back of the car, sandwiched between two policemen, was Howard Matterson, and his teeth were drawn back in a wolf-like grin. He looked totally mad.

Someone tapped me on the shoulder. 'Get into the car – we'll take you to the bottom.'

I shook my head. 'If I travel with that man you couldn't stop me killing him.'

The policeman gave me an odd look and shrugged. 'Suit yourself.'

I walked slowly down the road towards the bottom of the hill and desperately wondered if I would find Clare. I was glad to see some survivors; they picked their way slowly down the hillside and walked like somnambulists. I came across Donner; he was smeared with viscid mud from head to foot and was standing looking at the flood water as it streamed past. As I passed him I heard him muttering. Over and over again he was saying, 'Millions of dollars; millions of dollars – all gone! Millions and millions.'

'Bob! Oh, Bob!'

I swung round and the next moment Clare was in my arms, sobbing and laughing at the same time. 'I thought you were dead,' she said. 'Oh, darling, I thought you were dead.'

I managed a grin. 'The Mattersons had a last crack at me but I came through.'

'Hey, Boyd!' It was Crupper, no longer neat and trimly uniformed but looking like a tramp. Any one of his own men would have put him in jail just for looking like he did. He stuck his hand out. 'I never expected to see you again.'

'I thought the same about you,' I said. 'How many were lost?'

'I know of five for certain,' he said gravely. 'We haven't finished checking yet – and God knows what is happening downstream. They didn't have much warning.'

'You can make it seven for certain,' I said. 'Skinner and Burke both bought it. Novak came through.'

'There's a lot needs doing,' said Crupper. 'I'll get on with it.'

I didn't volunteer for anything. I'd had a bellyful of trouble and all I wanted to do was to go away somewhere and be very quiet. Clare took my arm. 'Come,' she said. 'We'll go away from here. If we climb the hill there we might be able to find a way round the flood.'

So we made our way up the hill very slowly, and at the top we rested a while and looked north over the Kinoxi Valley. The waters of Matterson Lake would fall very quickly to reveal the jagged stumps of a raped land. But the trees still stood in the north – the forest in which I had been hunted like an animal. I didn't hate the forest because I reckoned it had saved my life in a way.

I thought I could see the green of the trees in the far distance. Clare and I had lost four million dollars between us because the Forestry Service would never allow a total cut now. Yet we were not displeased. The trees would stay and grow and be cut down in their season, and the deer would browse in their shade – and maybe I would have time to make friends with brother Bruin after having made amends for the scare I gave him.

Clare took my hand and we walked slowly along the crest of the hill. It was a long way home, but we'd make it.

MY OLD MAN'S
TRUMPET

This fictional tale was published in *Argosy*, the short-story magazine, in January 1967. It was introduced by a short biography of the author:

Desmond Bagley is an engineer, has worked in the Rhodesian asbestos mines and Orange Free State goldfields. He now lives in South Africa and cultivates orange trees; he likes good food, quiet conversation, W. H. Auden, and watching the sun go down over a cold gin. He is engaged at present in the study of symbolic logic and the training of an Alsatian bitch.

It all started maybe three weeks ago. I keep a little music shop down in New Orleans. I don't do much business, just enough to keep the wolf from the door, but I couldn't be in any other work. I sell a few records and some sheet music, and condition a few instruments. I've got a good name for instruments; it's the one thing my old man taught me to do well, that and play a horn. I've conditioned instruments for some of the best. Johnny Dodds's clarinet, Fred Robinson's trombone, and once I did Satchmo's trumpet. I got a kick out of that.

Anyway, this day I was in the back room stripping a sugar stick, when I looked through my little spyhole and saw a white boy in the shop. He had my old man's trumpet in his hands and he was stroking it. I keep the trumpet over the glass case on the counter. It's by way of being my lucky piece.

I got up quickly and went into the shop. There wasn't many white folk came into my shop and those that did weren't up to much, and I didn't want one of that kind playing round with my old man's trumpet.

He was standing with his back to me and from the way he was standing I could tell he was pretty miserable. He was tall and rangy and I figured he was from Texas, where they breed them that way. I was going to walk up to him when he half turned and I saw his hands. He sure had a trumpet-player's hands with long fingers and he was cradling that trumpet like it was a new-born baby. His fingers played around with the pistons and his other hand stroked the horn. Back and forward it went, back and forward, stroking that horn.

Then he turned and saw me. His face was thin and he had the bluest eyes I've seen in a man. He smiled and it seemed as if the sun had broke from behind clouds. 'Just admiring this trumpet,' he said.

I said gently, 'Sorry, but it's not for sale.'

He looked at it and sighed. 'It's a good instrument,' he said.

I knew it was a good horn and I knew he must know something about music. 'That was my father's,' I said. 'I wouldn't want to sell that.' I paused. 'I've got a couple in the back room to sell, if you want one.'

He looked at me. 'But not as good as this.'

'No,' I said. 'Not as good as that one.'

His hands tightened round it a little and then relaxed. He put it back on top of the glass case and stepped back, still looking at it. 'That's one of the best I've seen,' he said.

'It's pretty good,' I said. I thought a little. 'Look,' I said, 'I don't let *anybody* play that horn. I play it myself every Saturday night. Me and a few of the boys have a session. Louis Armstrong played that horn, too, when he was in New Orleans. We really went to town that time.' I paused again. 'You can play it if you want to.'

He was still looking at the horn, but he made no move to reach for it. He shook his head regretfully. 'No,' he said in a kind of sad voice, 'I'd better not.' Then he said, 'Thank you,' and was gone out of the shop.

I went to the door and looked up and down the street, but he was nowhere to be seen.

That was the first time I saw him.

In the next few days I saw him pretty often in the street. He must have been rooming nearby, which is pretty unusual for a white boy. He seemed to know his way around, too. He went for the music and knew enough to stay away from the tourist joints. He wanted music, my kind of music, and he knew he wouldn't get it at the high-falutin' places. They have written band parts there.

No, he stuck to the dives where they play for fun, not for a living, and he heard it hot and sweet and from the heart.

I didn't speak to him because I figured he'd come in to the shop. He *had* to come to the shop. Anyone who handled a horn the way he had had to come back; he couldn't stay away.

He *came* in four days later, so silently that he was standing in front of the glass case before I knew he was there. He looked at the horn a space, then looked at me, and said, 'Still not for sale?' He was smiling.

'No, son,' I said, 'still not for sale. I'm sorry.' And I was sorry. He wanted it so bad. But I couldn't sell my old man's trumpet. It wasn't in me.

He reached up and took it down. His fingers wrapped themselves automatically round the pistons.

'You can play it,' I said.

He looked at me with a strange expression. Then he said, 'I'd better not. I'm not allowed to.'

'Oh,' I said. I had him figured. 'You must be like my old man. A doc warned him against it. Lung trouble.'

The white boy said, 'Did he stop playing?'

I shook my head. 'No, he went right ahead. He couldn't not play the horn.' I paused. 'It killed him in the end.'

'I'm sorry,' the white boy said.

I said, 'I don't think he was. He'd rather have been dead than not play. He could have gone on to a clarinet, but he couldn't leave the horn.'

'It's hard,' he said. He put the horn back on to the glass case and walked out of the shop.

So that was it. A horn-player who wasn't allowed to play, but couldn't resist the chance of handling a good instrument. I felt sorry for the kid.

He was in again next day, looking at the horn. I left him alone for a while – I was busy assembling the sugar stick in the back room. After a while I went into the shop. He was standing with the trumpet in his hands, his fingers slowly pumping the pistons and his other hand gently stroking the bell of the horn, back and forward, back and forward. His eyes were closed. It gave me the willies.

I said, 'Look, it's none of my business, son, but why rile yourself? If you ain't allowed to play it, leave it alone.'

He opened his eyes and looked at me with a blank stare. 'It's such a long time since I've played,' he said softly, almost to himself. The way he said it made it seem an awful long time, which was funny because he was only a kid, not more than twenty-three, twenty-four.

Then he seemed to come out of his trance. 'What did you say?' he asked.

I skipped it. 'Can you play the clarinet?' I said.

He seemed doubtful. 'I don't know,' he said, 'I think it would be all right.'

'What did the doctor say?'

He looked at me. 'What?' he said.

'The guy who said you hadn't to blow a trumpet. Did he say anything about a clarinet?'

He smiled thoughtfully. 'No,' he said, 'There wasn't anything said about a clarinet.'

'I've just assembled one in the back room. Like to try it out?'

He smiled. The world lit up. That boy had a nice smile. 'I sure would,' he said.

I went and got the sugar stick. When I got back I saw he had put the trumpet back in its place. I grinned to myself.

I figured that what he wanted was something to take his mind off the horn. A clarinet might do it. I gave it to him.

He took it from me as though he was doubtful of something. Maybe he wondered if he could still play. But it couldn't have been long since he had played. He was only a kid.

His hands set themselves on the keys and he raised it to his lips very slowly. He licked his lips and seemed almost afraid. And then he seemed to stiffen and he blew a riff. It was hot and I knew I had found me a player. I mean a player. A *real* player.

He had played the riff and stopped. He was holding his head on one side as if he was listening for something. Then he went to the door and looked up and down the street.

I said, 'What's the matter?'

He turned, and there was such a look of joy on his face as I've never seen on any man before. Joy seemed to spread all round him and suddenly I was feeling pretty good myself. Then he raised the sugar stick to his lips and started to *play*.

I've heard the clarinet played by some good boys. I've heard Johnny Dodds and Jimmy Strong. But I've never heard it played like this white boy played it. He took it low and he took it high and all the time so sweet. He had the Dixie beat so true that he must have been born in the South. I disremember what he played except that he ended with *Empty Bed Blues*, and I'll remember that for ever. He dragged that blues from his heart and pushed it through the sugar stick and it sounded like all the troubles of the South since before slavery. I was nearly crying when he finished. Me crying!

And then I saw the shop was full.

Folk had come in from the street and were standing round looking at this white boy. They didn't clap or shout when he'd finished, but there was a sort of sigh like a sudden wind on the river in the morning. No one spoke to him.

Some smiled at him as they went out and pretty soon the shop was empty again. I reckon that nobody wanted to break the spell he'd cast on them. They all wanted to keep what he'd given them as long as they could.

And what had he given them? I don't know. I've thought about it long and often and I reckon he'd given the soul back to my own people. Living in a white man's country isn't fun for a negro, and I reckon that when he played my folk's music better than we could, he had shown us that life isn't all kicks, and there's some things we can do together. But I don't know. I'm not clever enough to figure it out.

He was standing with the clarinet in his hands. 'I can play!' he said.

'You can play,' I said flatly; then I woke up. 'My God, you *can* play! With that clarinet you can play in any name band in the States. What the hell are you doing fooling around here?'

He said, half to himself, 'It's not as good as a trumpet.' He said it regretfully.

I said unbelievingly, 'Do you mean you can play the horn better than that clarinet?'

He didn't answer. He was looking at my old man's trumpet on the glass case.

'Look,' I said, 'my name's Williams. Joe Williams. Folks call me Fatso.' I grinned and slapped my belly. 'But that's where the trumpet wind comes from.'

He looked at me. 'My name's – er – call me Jake,' he said, and stuck out his hand.

That night Smiley Jones came to see me. 'Hear you had a shindig at the shop this afternoon,' he said.

'Smiley,' I said, 'I've got hold of a boy who can play the clarinet. I mean *play*.'

'A white boy,' Smiley said. Smiley had some trouble in his life. He had no time for white folk. But this was different.

I said, 'Look, Smiley, I want you and the boys to do me a favour. Tomorrow we have a session. I want the white boy to come.'

'What kind of a white boy is that who'll dig with us shines?' said Smiley. He wasn't asking a question. He didn't want to know. He was just being down on the whites.

'Just hear him, Smiley,' I begged. 'Just you hear him.'

After a lot of arguing, Smiley saw reason or, at least, he agreed that Jake should come with us. But I could see that it was against his nature and he was going to take Jake on his merits, not on my word. Which was a good thing, anyway.

Jake came to the shop next morning. Like all the times he came I never saw him come in. One minute he wasn't there and the next minute he'd be standing in front of the glass case looking at my old man's trumpet.

I said, 'Look, Jake, how'd you like to play in a session?'

His face lit up. 'I sure would,' he said. Then he frowned, 'Think I'm good enough for you boys?' he asked.

I swallowed. 'You'll do,' I said.

He lifted down the trumpet and fingered the pistons. 'Tell me about your old man,' he said. 'I'd like to meet him.'

I stared at him. 'But I told you my old man was dead,' I said.

He was confused. He said, 'I mean I'd have liked to meet him.'

'He died in '34,' I said, 'when I was sixteen. He was a good man, never harmed a soul.' I leaned on the counter. 'He was on the river boats in 1917. A feller who came down from New York said that was the golden age of Dixieland jazz. He said that jazz was made on the river boats. Well, my dad must have helped make it. He was a good horn-player, although he never made a name for himself like some of the others. But he could blow it sweet and true, and hot and true, and hold his own in any jam.'

Jake said, 'How did he die, Fatso?'

I said, 'It was like this. In '28 he was up in St Louis playing in a honky-tonk. He used to get these pains in his chest so he went to the Doc. The Doc asked what he did for a living. My old man said, "Trumpet-player." The Doc said, "That's out."

'It nearly finished my old man. He'd been playing all his life. He couldn't stop now. Trumpet-playing was too great a strain on the lungs and the heart. He could play a clarinet but not a trumpet. But he didn't. He figured that he'd rather play the trumpet. I remember the night. He suddenly got up from his chair and took the trumpet and played solid for three hours. Celebrating his decision. That was in '31.

'I think maybe I was the reason he started playing again. It was the depression. Jobs were scarce, but he could always pick up a few dollars with the horn.

'His chest got worse, but he carried on. It was New Year's Day, '34, that it happened. We were here in New Orleans. New Year's Day is a great day here. Everyone celebrates and there's parties all over the place. A good horn-player can really dig in at New Year. But Pa collapsed just after midnight. Just in '34. He was fifty-six.'

Jake didn't say anything for a while. He just looked at the horn, stroking it with his hand, back and forward, back and forward. Then he said, 'That was tough.'

I said, 'You'd better keep off the horn or maybe you'll end the same way.'

He looked surprised. 'How?'

'You'll die,' I said.

'Oh, that!' he said indifferently.

He put the trumpet back on top of the glass case. 'It would be worse trouble than dying,' he said.

Shortly after that he went, leaving me to figure out what there was in playing a trumpet worse than dying.

That evening we picked up Jake. There were six altogether in my brother's car. Jake, my brother Jim, Smiley, Bill Patley, Little Joe, and me. We used to go up the river quite a piece, maybe fifty or sixty miles, find a quiet place, and get in the groove. It was real nice on those moonlight nights and we always had a few beers to help us along.

We parked the car and I got out the crate of beer and helped Little Joe set up his drums. It was cool on the river after the day and the moon was shining down through a few little clouds.

Smiley opened a beer and had a swallow, then set up his clarinet. I had brought another one for Jake, a real good instrument that a bum had hocked with me. Little Joe set up a rhythm on his trap and Bill joined in softly with his banjo.

I said, 'Let's go,' and swung into *Fireworks* with my old man's trumpet. Jim and Smiley followed in turn on trombone and clarinet. Jake didn't play. He just sat watching and listening with the sugar stick held loosely between his fingers. When we finished he said to Smiley, 'You played that real good.'

Smiley didn't say anything. He just looked at Jake and went and got himself another beer.

I signalled to Little Joe and he swung in on the drums and I followed into *Sugarfoot Strut* good and hot. I finished a riff and waved Jake in. As he played the first notes I heard Smiley give a sharp hiss as though the breath had been driven out of his body.

I looked at him. He was sitting there with the beer forgotten in his hand, and his eyes were wide.

Jake went crazy with that clarinet. The notes rang as clear as a bell over the water beneath the moon. He played it hot and he played it sweet, but mostly hot, and he did things with that sugar stick that I didn't think could be done.

Then he waved Smiley in and they played together. It was really in the groove, one following the other easily and effortlessly. We had something here that players from written music won't never have. I've never heard Smiley play so well, but he couldn't touch Jake.

We all joined in and it was real music. When we finished, Smiley went over to Jake and stuck out his hand. 'You're good,' he said.

Jake took his hand and grinned. 'You're not so bad yourself.'

After that we all had us a beer. We needed it. The boys were excited and everyone was happy. Jake said, 'This is the music.'

I said, 'The best there is.' After a while I said, 'You remember me saying about a feller from New York?'

Jake said, 'Yes.'

'He said something about Dixieland jazz. He said, 'You fellers down here are the cognoscenti of this music.' I didn't know what he meant, so I just said, "I reckon we are." I looked it up in a dictionary after he'd gone.'

Smiley said, 'What did it mean?'

I said, 'It means that we're the fellers in the know about music.'

'Yes,' said Jake, 'I reckon you are.'

That was the first session we had with Jake. We had three sessions altogether.

The second session was like the first, only everyone was happy right from the start. Smiley had seen Jake two or three times during the week. They were real friendly now.

Jake had been in the shop every day. Every day he came in and took down the horn and stroked it, and him and me would talk about music and players. He knew a lot about it, did that boy.

We went to the same place. Going in the car, Little Joe said, 'Say, Jake, don't you work at anything?'

Jake said, 'Sure do, but I'm on a vacation.'

'What do you do?' Smiley said.

Jake didn't answer for a minute, then he said in a soft voice, 'I'm a trumpet-player.'

Nobody spoke, because I'd told them all about Jake and trumpets and not being allowed to play. Everybody shut up because somebody had said the wrong thing.

The week after, Jake came in to the shop every day. He just couldn't keep away from that horn. His attitude was funny. He loved it and seemed afraid of it, all at the same time. I had watched my old man and I knew just what was eating Jake.

Once I caught him just raising the mouthpiece to his lips. He saw me looking at him and grinned sheepishly. 'Just wanted to get the feel of it,' he said.

I took the horn from his hands and put it back on the glass case. I said, 'Now look here, son. Quit worrying about the horn. If you can't play, you can't play, and that's an end to it.' I paused and looked at him. 'Got a girl?'

He shook his head.

I sighed and said, 'Let's go into the back room. I've got a good collection of waxings.'

So we went into the back room and played records. He was taken by one of Louis Armstrong with Lil's Hot Shots. Armstrong on the trumpet, Kid Ory on trombone, Johnny Dodds on clarinet, Lil Hardin Armstrong on piano and Johnny St Cyr on banjo. It was *Georgia Bo Bo*. When it was finished he sighed. 'That Armstrong sure can play,' he said.

I said, 'Jake, isn't there a chance you'll play again?'

He smiled. That wonderful smile. 'Sure, I'll play again. But I don't know when.' The smile went off his face. 'It's so long since I played.'

I said, 'Well, there's a chance. It may not be more than five years. You'll still be young.' He laughed outright. He bent over double, laughing. He couldn't stop laughing.

I didn't get it. I didn't see what I said was funny.

Come Saturday night we all piled into Jim's car and went up-river again. The last session we'd run short of beer, so I'd brought two crates this time. With us six in the car and the beer and the instruments, we were a tight fit. The drums were worst. We always used to kid Little Joe that a little guy like him should have stuck to the piccolo.

But we got there all right and pulled out the drums and the beer, and after I'd helped Joe set up the drums I sat on the river bank watching the water. Little Joe was strumming gently on the trap, and Jake picked up the clarinet and played something so soft and low you couldn't hear it. It was torchy and blue. It had sorrow in it and anger, and a queer kind of longing.

I picked up my old man's trumpet and broke in, switching from minor to major, and loud. He looked at me, his eyes glinting in the moonlight, and suddenly he laughed and, lifting his clarinet, swung it right up to the stars.

It was the same melody, but the mood had changed. Before it was sorrow; now it was joy and triumph. Smiley joined in, and we went to town. I was playing as if I was inspired. I know what Smiley must have felt like when he played with Jake the first time. I couldn't go wrong. The riffs came smoothly and the notes true. I felt my heart lift right up to that old moon.

Then we had finished. 'Zowie,' Smiley said, his chest heaving and the sweat shining on his forehead. 'That's music!'

We broke open the beer and then we played again. What we played I don't know. Jake was improvising as he went along, and we followed him. Yes, we followed him all the way. We played torchy and we played blue. We played it hot and we played it sweet. We played that jazz every way it could be played. The sound of it went echoing over the water and the night wore on and the moon drifted across the sky and still we played on and on.

Then I looked at my watch and it was midnight. I put the horn down and went and opened a beer. It tasted good; cold and good. Then I looked at them. They were drunk, all of them. Not on beer, but on music, on Dixieland jazz.

Then I saw Jake lift up my old man's trumpet. I thought quickly. I had come to like this kid. If he hadn't been white he could have been my own son. I knew he shouldn't play the trumpet and I remembered what had happened to my old man.

I can see Jake now. He lifted that horn to his lips. He was standing with his legs straddled and knees bent and he stooped to the horn. And started to blow.

He blew a note right from the ground floor, right in the bass. I hadn't known that horn could get so low. And he lifted it in a smooth curve of sound right to the moon. Higher and higher. It was the beginning of a riff to end all riffs.

He was standing there, looking at the sky, but with his eyes closed, pouring all his soul into that horn. And it was still going higher and higher.

I jumped over and slapped the horn out of his hands. He let it go and just stood there, looking at the sky with his eyes closed. As if he were looking at something in his own head.

And then the sun rose. In the north. It shone on Jake and got brighter and brighter until it was day. And he was looking at that sky right inside his own head. And it got brighter and brighter, this sun in the north, until you couldn't see. Then I figured what it was. The atom plant, a hundred miles clear up river, had blown itself to hell. The sound came, like thunder, like the anger of God, and the wind and sudden clouds and dust.

I saw the car pitch over into the river and I saw Jake standing there like a man in a trance. Then I didn't see anything more.

I was in hospital quite a time. They brought me my old man's trumpet. It's a bit battered but it'll play. And they tell me that Smiley and Jim, my brother, and Bill Patley and Little Joe are all dead. They found their bodies.

But they didn't find Jake's body.

I reckon he knew he'd done a bad thing. But he had to play the horn. It was such a long time since he played it. I don't think he'll be punished much, for the Lord is an understanding and merciful judge. I guess that by the state of this little old world he'll be called on to play the trumpet again pretty soon.

I sometimes wonder what would have happened if I hadn't knocked the trumpet out of his hands.

I keep my old man's trumpet by my bed and polish it every now and then. Some good boys have played that horn . . . my father and Louis Armstrong.

But the best of them all was Gabriel himself, the Trumpeter of the Lord.